D1472578

"Always a powerful storyteller, Susan Krinard offers another complex, richly textured tale. This is a fully realized world in which werewolves are not just possible but completely plausible. It may also be her most successfully realized romance . . . I was completely absorbed . . . [*Secret of the Wolf*] is a well-written, substantial, and very satisfying read."   —*The Romance Reader*

To Catch a Wolf

"Krinard has created a magical world where the freaks and outcasts exhibit more humanity than the so-called 'normal' people. Her werewolves, tortured souls never resembling their trite Hollywood counterparts, make incredibly sympathetic characters, and this is a truly engrossing story."   —*Booklist* (starred review)

"Superb storytelling . . . compellingly told . . . Krinard uses strong dialogue and a wealth of detail to flesh out her characters and weave together the stories . . . Each character's role in the story is clearly drawn, and each scene richly paves the way for an explosive, satisfying conclusion."   —*Romantic Times* (Top Pick)

"Ms. Krinard brings the reader up close and personal to the life of a werewolf. We feel every nuance of emotion that shudders to life within the protagonists."   —*Rendezvous*

"An enjoyable werewolf historical romance . . . fans will howl for a sequel."   —*Midwest Book Review*

"Susan Krinard delivers another multifaceted and utterly believable story about werewolves . . . an excellent book, told by one of romance's most accomplished storytellers."   —*The Romance Reader*

"Another stunning addition to Ms. Krinard's Wolf series, *To Catch a Wolf* is a deeply complex and riveting story . . . When mixed with background characters, beautiful descriptions of the Colorado landscape, and the intriguing circus atmosphere, [this] is a must-read."
—*Romance Reviews Today*

"Once again, Susan Krinard takes her readers on a journey into the wilderness of the mind and spirit . . . The plot is exciting, taut . . . [*To Catch a Wolf* is] enthralling, uplifting, and certainly a great escape into a paranormal world."
—*A Romance Review*

"Passionate, dramatic, and very romantic, this is one terrific paranormal romance. *To Catch a Wolf* delivers everything a great paranormal romance should. It has a strong sense of atmosphere, not only with respect to its supernatural elements, but with its historical setting. From the winter mountain scenes to everything relating to the circus and its performers, it feels vivid and real and adds a lot to the magic of the story.

"It's a story with genuine suspense as the characters face greater and greater odds, raising the tension for both them and the reader. And most of all, it's a powerful love story between two people who are both outsiders except when they're with each other . . . It's a great read, full of action and drama . . . not to be missed."
—*All About Romance*

"Ms. Krinard weaves a blaze of sexual tension so vivid that even I was dreaming of werewolves one night. When you read the book you will see why . . . I don't want to leave this world of werewolves for a long time to come. *To Catch a Wolf* is so thrilling and imaginative that it almost makes you wish you were a werewolf. Susan Krinard is at the top of her game with this series—mighty fine entertainment in my book."
—*The Belles & Beaux of Romance*

CALL
of the WOLF

Susan Krinard

BERKLEY SENSATION, NEW YORK

THE BERKLEY PUBLISHING GROUP
Published by the Penguin Group
Penguin Group (USA) Inc.
375 Hudson Street, New York, New York 10014, USA
Penguin Group (Canada), 90 Eglinton Avenue East, Suite 700, Toronto, Ontario M4P 2Y3, Canada
(a division of Pearson Penguin Canada Inc.)
Penguin Books Ltd., 80 Strand, London WC2R 0RL, England
Penguin Group Ireland, 25 St. Stephen's Green, Dublin 2, Ireland (a division of Penguin Books Ltd.)
Penguin Group (Australia), 250 Camberwell Road, Camberwell, Victoria 3124, Australia
(a division of Pearson Australia Group Pty. Ltd.)
Penguin Books India Pvt. Ltd., 11 Community Centre, Panchsheel Park, New Delhi—110 017, India
Penguin Group (NZ), Cnr. Airborne and Rosedale Roads, Albany, Auckland 1310, New Zealand
(a division of Pearson New Zealand Ltd.)
Penguin Books (South Africa) (Pty.) Ltd., 24 Sturdee Avenue, Rosebank, Johannesburg 2196,
South Africa

Penguin Books Ltd., Registered Offices: 80 Strand, London WC2R 0RL, England

PRINTING HISTORY
Secret of the Wolf: Berkley edition / October 2001
To Catch a Wolf: Berkley Sensation edition / September 2003
Berkley Sensation trade paperback omnibus edition / May 2006

Library of Congress Cataloging-in-Publication Data

Krinard, Susan.
    [Secret of the wolf]
    Call of the wolf / Susan Krinard.
      p. cm.
    Contents: Secret of the wolf — To catch a wolf.
    ISBN 0-425-20987-3
    1. Werewolves—Fiction. I. Krinard, Susan. Secret of the wolf. II. Title: Secret of the wolf. III. Title.

PS3611.R5445S43 2006
813'.6—dc22

            2005058910

PRINTED IN THE UNITED STATES OF AMERICA

10 9 8 7 6 5 4 3 2 1

CONTENTS

SECRET
of the WOLF

This book is dedicated to every man, woman, and child who has ever suffered the devastating effects of mental illness—those who have faced its challenges and have never given up hope of ultimate victory. It is also dedicated to the courageous men and women who have never ceased to search for cures, and to understand the mysteries of the human heart, mind, and soul.

—Susan Krinard, 2001

Acknowledgments

I wish to thank Fred Larimore for his assistance with information about nineteenth-century Indian Army regiments, officers, and campaigns. His website on this subject is http://pobox.upenn.edu/~fbl/. Any mistakes regarding the British Army are my own.

I am also grateful for the ongoing encouragement, support, and feedback from my friend Eugenia Riley.

Chapter 1

"Stop!"

The vicious drunkard who bent over the cringing boy paused, his fist in midair, as if he had heard the voice of God Himself. Or, at the very least, a policeman with a club.

But if any policeman was to be found in this shabby excuse for a town, he was otherwise engaged. Johanna Schell had no faith in police.

Nor did she have any delusions of divinity. But she trusted in the air of authority she'd cultivated for so many years, and in the strength of her voice.

She crossed the muddy road to the haphazard line of shacks crouched along the docks near the railway station. In the gathering dusk, she could just make out the man's unshaven face, the scar slashing his chin, the filthy clothing. He reeked of cheap liquor. The boy was pitifully thin, bruised, with the hollow, haunted eyes of one who had endured many such beatings. Johanna had seen that look before.

The man squinted at Johanna and produced an expression somewhere between a leer and a smirk. She saw the way he appraised her, judged her, dismissed her with the dubious aid of his diseased brain.

"You talkin' to me?" he demanded, swinging toward her.

"I am." She set down her doctor's bag, took a firmer grip on her valise, and drew up to her full height, almost the equal of his. "You will cease beating that boy, immediately, or I shall summon the authorities."

"The . . . ath-or . . ." He laughed. His young victim shrank in on himself, as if the laughter were only another sign of worse to come. "Who the hell you thin' you are, Miss High-'n'-Mighty Bitch?"

"I am a doctor. I've seen what you're doing to that boy."

"Boy?" He grabbed a handful of the boy's frayed collar and jerked him up. "This boy's m'son. I c'n do whatever I want wi' him. No *ath-or-tee's* gonna stop me. No woman, neither." He spat. "Doctor, huh. How good're you at healin' yerself?"

Johanna ignored his threat. "What has your son done to deserve this?"

The man's dull eyes grew confused. He couldn't answer, of course. There was no reason for the punishment, save for his drunkenness and a natural depravity. But his confusion quickly gave way to resentment. He yanked the boy this way and that, until the lad squeezed his eyes shut and went limp.

"*You* ha' no right to question me!" he snarled. "He's useless! Should throw 'im in the Straits and be done with'm!" He dropped the boy and grinned at Johanna. "You, too. Throw you in the Straits—af'er I have a bit o' fun."

"I doubt that very much," she said. She tested the weight of the valise, grateful for the heavy books that had made carrying it so inconvenient during her visit to San Francisco. She turned to the boy. "Don't be afraid, *mein Junge*. I will help you."

A large, dirty fist thrust itself into the air before Johanna's face. "You better help yerself."

"I generally do," she said. "I've dealt with worse than you."

He stared at her, as if she'd gone quite mad. Most of the denizens of the surrounding neighborhood must run in terror of this bully; he wouldn't be used to defiance. He had surely never faced those cursed by true madness. She had. And though her heart was beating hard and her hands were sweaty inside her gloves, neither madman nor bully would see anything but calm competence in the visage of Dr. Johanna Schell.

Calm competence was usually enough. It reduced hostility in the vast majority of the patients she'd dealt with in her father's private asylum. Even the most unruly of the residents had learned she was no frail girl to be intimidated.

This man was not one of the majority. He stepped close enough that his breath washed over her face in a nauseating cloud. "Looks like I'm gonna have to teach you a lesson . . . *Doctor*," he sneered.

The weight of the books in the valise was much less comforting than it had been a few moments ago. Johanna calculated the best angle of attack. Striking at his face was out of the question. His genitals, however . . .

"Run, boy," she urged the cowering child. "Run for help."

"Run, an' I'll kill you," the man said. "You hear me, boy? Ye're gonna stay and watch." His attention turned to his son just long enough. Johanna swung the valise. It connected. The ruffian grunted in pain and shock. He staggered and flung out his arm, hitting Johanna across the temple. She fell, dazed, as he pulled a knife from the waistband of his trousers and lunged for her.

The knife never reached its goal. Out of the shadows of the nearest alleyway, a dark shape flashed in front of Johanna and seized the bully's wrist. Johanna pushed up onto her elbows, struggling to make sense of what she witnessed.

She couldn't. The shape—the man, whose face remained only a blur—moved too quickly. He flexed the drunkard's arm back at an impossible angle. The knife spun into the dirt.

Now it was the bully who crouched, mewling in fear. The boy had already fled. Johanna's deliverer bestowed as little mercy as the bully had shown his own son. His fist struck like a piston, driving the drunkard onto his back. A second blow followed, and then another.

"You'll kill him!" Johanna shouted, finding her voice. *"Bitte—"*

The avenging angel stopped. Johanna caught a glimpse of gentleman's clothing that had seen better days, a body lean and tall . . . and eyes, their color indistinguishable behind a glare of absolute hatred.

The bully had met his match. This phantom would kill him, without remorse. He reached down to finish the job.

Johanna scrambled to her feet. "Please," she repeated. "Don't kill him, not on my behalf. The boy is safe. Let him go."

She had no way of knowing why the phantom had attacked, if it were for her sake, or the boy's, or some unknown motive of his own. But he paused again, and in that moment Johanna heard the choked sobs of the child she'd thought safely gone. He watched from the corner of a shack, his fist in his mouth, his bruised face white as a beacon.

"For the boy's sake," Johanna said, holding out her hand in supplication. She backed away until she stood beside the boy, reached out to gather him against her side. "Please. *Go.*"

The man straightened. Again she glimpsed his eyes, enough of his face under a stubble of beard to recognize what might have been a kind of coarse handsomeness. Then he hunched over, blending into the shadows. His prey gave one last squeak of terror, a mouse left half-alive by the cat. And the avenger leaped back into the alley from which he'd come.

Johanna took the boy by his shoulders and held him steady. "Are you all right?" she asked, sweeping him with her experienced gaze. Nothing broken. The bruises would mend . . . if his spirit did. "What is your name?"

"Peter," the boy whispered. A tear tracked its way through the dirt on his face, but he straightened under her scrutiny. He looked toward the place where his father lay. "My pa—"

"Peter, I want you to stay right here," she said firmly. "I am a doctor. I'll see to him."

"Is he dead?"

She swallowed, wondering whether it was sadness or relief she heard in his voice. "I don't think he is. But I will not let him hurt you again."

Peter nodded and did as she asked. She returned to the site of the unequal battle and found the bully lying where her rescuer had left him. She knelt to count his pulse and feel for broken bones. The right wrist was fractured, at the very least; he would have swelling in his face and two black eyes in the morning. But he still lived, and she saw no signs of internal bleeding.

She rose and wiped off her skirts, as if she could so easily rid herself of this man's barbarous taint. Odd; she couldn't quite bring herself to apply the same judgment to her phantom, in spite of the harsh punishment he'd dealt out. Hadn't he given the bully a taste of his own medicine?

She shook her head, bemused by her own primitive response. *Her phantom*. He was nothing of the sort—merely another disturbed resident of this fetid dockside warren. He, like the man he'd attacked, undoubtedly had a history of violence dating back to his own childhood. He was likely beyond saving.

But Peter was not. She left his father where he lay, collected the boy, and went in search of a local doctor who could take charge of the case. She had to ask in several disreputable saloons before she got intelligible directions to the home of South Vallejo's physician. He was none too pleased to be called out at dinnertime, but Johanna convinced him that she had the boy's care to consider. Quite naturally, that was a woman's job.

She wasn't above using male prejudices when it suited her purpose.

Peter, it turned out, had no living mother; but an elder, married sister lived in the town of Napa City, a major stop on the Napa Valley Railroad's route north to Silverado Springs. Johanna had no intention of leaving him in his father's "care" another night. She doubted the father would pursue the lad once he was out of reach, and any life would be better than this.

By the time she and Peter reached the Frisby House, a ramshackle two-story frame building that passed for South Vallejo's best hotel, the night was dark and damp with fog. She bought Peter the hotel's plain dinner, which he ate with great appetite, and secured them a small, musty room with two narrow beds. She treated his bruises, checked under his dirty clothes for cuts or abrasions, and did her best to make him wash up with the use of the cracked bowl and pitcher the hotel's housekeeper provided. His youthful reluctance to obey was heartening, if bothersome; his spirit hadn't been broken. There was hope for him yet.

Afterward, he fell into an exhausted sleep. Johanna was left to make the best of her lumpy bed and threadbare blankets, listening to the constant din of frogs in the marshes about the town and remembering, again and again, the burning eyes of the phantom.

Gott in Himmel help any local scoundrel who ran afoul of him without a passerby to interfere. She was not much given to prayer, but she offered up a sincere plea that none of his future victims would be any less deserving than young Peter's father.

And that she, personally, should never see him again.

He knew exactly which room was hers.

As he watched from the ill-lit street across from the Frisby House, he could smell her scent, carried by the cool, wet winds from the Strait and the ocean thirty miles to the west. He'd memorized the smell instantly when he went to work on that cowardly piece of filth among the dockside shacks.

He knew the boy was with her—but now that the whelp was safe, he was of no further interest. The woman was. He could not have said why, for she wasn't the kind of female he sought when sexual hunger came upon him. She wasn't beautiful, though her figure, full of hip and breast, was enough to rouse him.

Maybe it was because she'd stood there, so calm, when the bully attacked her. Remained calm when *he* appeared. He wasn't used to such composure when he was around. He preferred to provoke different emotions.

Maybe he was curious. She was a doctor. A female doctor. Because of her, the bastard would live . . . at least for today. She'd robbed him of his vengeance. She owed him for that.

But it wasn't his way to ponder what could not be explained. He existed by instinct, and emotion, and whim. Now his whim said that he wanted this woman, in a way no weak human soul could understand.

He could go after her, of course. He moved like the fog itself, all but invisible to human senses. He could steal her from that room with no one the wiser. Satisfy himself with her, and be done with it.

No one would stop him, least of all the Other—the one he wouldn't name. To name the Other gave him power. And he wasn't ready to surrender himself.

Someday, he would keep what was his, and damn the Other to darkness and silence forever.

He dug his bare toes into the earth of the street, indifferent to the loss of his shoes. He didn't need them. He shifted from foot to foot, staring at the darkened window.

A bellow of raucous laughter burst from the nearest saloon, distracting him. The smell of liquor and beer drowned out the woman's scent. His mouth felt dry, ready for another drink. *That* took far less effort than climbing into the woman's room. It was the swiftest escape from the memories, the burden the Other had given him.

And in the saloon there were men who would cross him. Ruffians who would see only a lean, oddly dressed tenderfoot with too much money, ripe for the plucking.

He loped to the entrance of the saloon, whose doors spilled light like pale blood into the street, and went in. The room was full of carousers, with a couple of whores for good measure. He sat at the bar, pulled a handful of coins from his pocket, and ordered a whiskey straight. Ten drinks later, even the bartender was staring in amazement. Still it wasn't enough. Not enough to drown the memories.

Someone kicked at his bare foot. He ignored the first blow. The second came harder, accompanied by a loud guffaw.

"Hey, boy. Someone steal yer shoes?"

Still he waited, taking another sip of his whiskey.

"You hear me, you scrawny li'l pissant? I'm talkin' to you." A blunt, dirty hand snatched at the coins. "Where'd ja get all that chickenfeed, eh? You gotta share it with the rest of us. Right, boys?"

He ordered another drink and downed it in one swallow.

"Wha' 'r' you . . . some kind o' freak? Or is that water y'er drinkin'?" The glass was plucked from his hand.

He turned slowly to the man leaning on the nicked wooden bar beside him. Another drunk, of the belligerent variety. A brute, no longer young but massive from hard physical labor, the kind who found a little extra incentive for a quarrel in the contents of a bottle. Just like the one who'd been beating on the boy.

Just what he'd been waiting for.

He smiled with deliberate mockery. "What's it to you, you ugly son of a bitch?"

The drunk let fly after a moment's disbelieving pause. It was pathetically easy to dodge the blow and slip around behind.

He kicked the drunk's feet out from under him. The audience laughed and snickered as the brute went sprawling . . . until the man pulled a pistol from his trousers. His shot went wild and crashed into the stained mirror behind the bar.

Several onlookers jumped the shooter, disarmed him, and tossed him into the street. The bartender cursed over his shattered mirror, and the rest returned to their drinking and whoring.

But the "freak" wasn't satisfied. He stuffed the money back into his pockets and went in pursuit of his prey. He found the drunk on his knees in the street, swearing a blue streak and wiping hands on muddy trousers. Bloodshot eyes lifted to his, narrowed in hate.

"D'you really want to see a freak?" he asked pleasantly. When he had the drunk's full attention, he stripped and Changed. It hurt, the way it always did, but he didn't care. He reveled in the pain. He finished, every muscle and bone screaming in protest, and waited for his prey to realize what he saw.

The drunk's eyes nearly popped from their sockets. He tried to scream. He wet himself and fell into a dead faint.

Laughing with his wolf's grin, he raked his sharp foreclaws along the slack, pockmarked face. Let the drunk remember this encounter, as the previous bully would. Let him scare his fellows with mad tales of men who turned into beasts. No one would believe. They never believed.

He bent back his head and howled. The sound bounced off alley walls and floated on the fog like a banshee's wail. All noise from the saloon stopped; he could almost see the faces turned toward the door, the hasty gulping of whiskey, the furtive gestures made to appease God or the devil.

He belonged to neither. Let them listen and be afraid.

He Changed back, dressed quickly, and turned for the hotel . . . and the woman. But a vast weariness overtook him; curse it though he might, he knew what it portended. The more he fought, the greater the chance the Other would seize control.

He must rest. Find some quiet place where he wouldn't be disturbed, and he might wake still in possession of this body.

With the last of his strength, he began to search for a sleeping place. In the end, he found he could not leave the vicinity of the hotel, where *she* lay. He discovered an abandoned, fire-damaged cottage two blocks away, tore through the boards nailed across the door, and lay down close to a window, where he could still catch the merest whiff of her scent over the smell of burned wood and mouse droppings.

She's mine, he told the Other. *No matter how often you drive me out, I'll come back. I will have her in the end.*

And you will have nothing.

Chapter 2

Though she had made this journey several times since she and her "family" had come to live in California, Johanna never tired of the view she saw from her window as the Napa Valley Railroad made its way north into this little bit of paradise.

Once South Vallejo and the marshy delta were left behind, the valley began in earnest. At first one saw only wide fields of grain and cattle pastures, isolated farms and rolling, nearly bare hills in the distance on either side of the tracks. Majestic, isolated oaks stood sentry singly and in small stands, their branches twisted into fantastic shapes. The native grasses were golden brown, almost the color of caramel. It had taken Johanna several months, that first year, to get used to the arid summers of California. She had come to appreciate their beauty.

At the valley's entrance lay Napa City, the capital and largest town in the county. Its dusty streets boasted the usual assembly of shops, hotels, saloons, and even an opera house. Here the train made an extended stop, and Johanna disembarked to escort Peter to his elder sister's home on the outskirts of town.

He'd been a quiet, solemn companion since they'd left the hotel early this morning. And no wonder: His life had taken an abrupt change in course. Johanna understood the shock of that all too well.

Peter's sister was glad to take him in, though she lived humbly and had the careworn face of most countrywomen. But country folk could also be fiercely loyal to their own. Johanna returned to the train depot satisfied that she'd made the right decision.

It was important that something good had come of last night's confrontation. She hadn't really slept at all in that narrow bed, and it wasn't because of the discomfort. Even now, in the bright midmorning sunshine, she imagined herself back in that foggy alley with the phantom.

Be sensible, she told herself. *You are always sensible.*

She settled back into her seat on the northbound train and turned her attention to the landscape once more. Such openness and abundance refuted the very existence of shadowy avengers. And she was going home.

Home. *Der Haven*, she'd named it . . . the Haven. A simple farm backed up against a wooded hill at the very top of the valley, surrounded by the last of her uncle's vineyards. A place of refuge for the small collection of former patients she and her father had brought with them from Pennsylvania two years ago. They were all that remained of the inmates of Dr. Wilhelm Schell's unorthodox private asylum—the patients with nowhere to go, no one to trust but the physicians who'd cared for them.

Dr. Schell the elder was no longer capable of caring even for himself much of the time. The apoplexy that had struck him down so tragically had curtailed his vigorous movements and the sharp brilliance of his mind. He needed the Haven as much as the others did. It was Johanna's charge to keep the place functioning, its residents content.

And to heal them, if she could. The need to heal was an essential part of her nature, and it made the responsibility worthwhile.

The train left Napa City and passed several small villages, their tiny depots strung along the rail line and its parallel road like knots on a rope: Yountville and Oakville, Rutherford and St. Helena, Bale and Walnut Grove. Gradually the valley narrowed and the hills to either side grew higher, clothed now in brush and trees. The vineyards that were beginning to attract so much interest appeared more frequently, each gnarled grapevine was thick with green leaves and hung with ripening clusters of fruit.

The grapes were very much like people, Johanna thought. Each variety took its own time in ripening, and had to be coaxed along by the vintner. Some were simply more fragile than others.

She blinked at her romantic turn of mind. Quite impractical, such thoughts. But they kept her from thinking about last night, or Peter's ultimate fate, or how well Papa and the others had gotten along without her. If not for the chance to hear an eminent neurologist lecture in San Francisco, she could not have brought herself to leave. But Mrs. Daugherty could be relied upon to look after the Haven for a day or two. Of all the people in the town of Silverado Springs, she was least bothered by the "loonies" who lived with the crazy woman doctor. And she needed the money.

Money. Johanna clasped her hands in her lap. That, too, was never far from her thoughts. When she'd brought her father and the others to California, her uncle's inheritance had been a godsend. Upon his death, Rutger Schell had left his brother the greater portion of his unsold vineyards at the head of the valley, a sizeable house, a fruit orchard, and several acres of wooded hillside. It had seemed sufficient to keep them all comfortable for many years.

But Johanna had miscalculated. Without families paying for the support of patients, without her father's practice, the money went too quickly. First she had sold the outlying vineyards, then the ones closer to the house. Now only the orchard, two acres of vines, and the woods remained. She had little else to sell. They grew much of their own food, but some they had to buy. And there were other necessities.

She smoothed her worn skirts and rejected the self-pity of a sigh. She would simply have to find a solution to the money problem . . . or trust that one would appear in time, as Uncle Rutger's inheritance had come so providentially just after Papa's attack.

Finding the landscape an inadequate distraction, Johanna removed one of the European journals from her valise, unfolded her spectacles, and began to read. Charles Richet's work—quite fascinating, though she could see he was missing the profound healing potential in the new science of hypnosis . . .

A light touch on her shoulder woke her from her trance.

"Silverado Springs, ma'am," the conductor said, tipping his hat. "Last stop."

"Of course. Thank you." Johanna smiled and tucked the book back in her valise. She was the last passenger to leave the train. No one had evinced much interest in a plain, spinsterish woman absorbed in a massive volume, and that suited her very well.

Of course, the people in Silverado Springs itself knew somewhat more of her. Like all small towns, even one prone to the visits of the more worldly health-seeking patients from San Francisco, residents of the Springs made it their business to know the habits of everyone in the vicinity. A woman doctor was certainly a novelty wherever she went.

"That hen medic," was the worst she'd been called—within her hearing. As she descended the steps from the platform and entered Washington Street, the central avenue in Silverado Springs, she could feel the stares of the idlers hanging about Piccini & Son's general store and Taylor's livery stable.

There was scant harm in them. She had encountered much worse in medical school, both in Pennsylvania and in Europe. She had long ago dismissed any doubt that she should not be a physician merely because of her sex . . . let others think what they might. Her father's opinion alone was the one that mattered.

Had mattered.

She adjusted her grip on the valise, passing a family of well-dressed tourists in town to take the waters. Though Silverado Springs was past its prime as a resort, it still had its share of summer visitors, who set up temporary living quarters at the Silverado Springs Hotel. There they could enjoy the warm weather, bathe in mineral springs, and gaze up at the great, bald-topped bulk of Mount St. Helena looming to the east.

She strode north among the neat frame houses of the town's residential section. It was a brisk four-mile walk to Der Haven, one Johanna was well accustomed to. She made her way back to the main, unpaved road, which ended just a little north of Silverado Springs, then continued crosscountry along a wagon path that pointed the way to the small farms clustered where the hills came together to close off the valley.

The Haven was one of the most isolated houses. It was that isolation that made Johanna feel her patients were safe from the prying eyes of the townsfolk.

The very potent sunshine on this particularly warm day in July almost tempted Johanna to remove the pins from her hair and let it fall. No one was liable to see her. But she resisted the impulse and increased her pace.

Surely Papa would be fine. She'd be glad to see him, nonetheless, glad to be back in charge and with everything under her personal guidance. Irene had been on good behavior two days ago; she hadn't made May cry in a week. Lewis, the former Reverend Andersen, was in the midst of one of his low periods, not likely to disrupt the household with his talk of sin and his devotion to excessive cleanliness. Oscar was seldom any trouble. And Harper was . . . Harper, silent and unresponsive as usual. She wasn't about to give up on him.

On any of them.

The toe of her scuffed boot connected with something long and solid lying in the grass. She caught her balance and looked down.

A man lay there, sprawled insensibly on his stomach, most of his body hidden by the tawny grass. It was his shoulder she'd kicked, but he wasn't apt to have felt it. His face was turned away, but she knew he was unconscious.

She knelt beside him and felt for his pulse. It was thready, but regular. The man himself had a lean, tall build and reddish-brown hair. His clothing was that of a gentleman and had seen hard wear; it was dirty and torn. It also stank of alcohol.

Another inebriate. She'd had her fill of that last night. Compressing her lips into a firm line, she carefully rolled the man over.

The first thing that struck her was his handsomeness. His face was the very epitome of an aristocrat's: clean, strong but finely drawn, as if designed by a sculptor bent on depicting the ideal male. His long-fingered hands were tanned from the sun. His lips had a mobile look, even in stillness; his eyelashes were long, his brows slightly darker than his hair, lending strength of character to his features.

Strength he clearly didn't possess, if he'd gotten drunk enough to be lying here. She didn't recognize him from any of the nearby farms or from town.

A stranger. A vagrant. A drunkard somewhat less brutish than the one in Vallejo. Someone who might possibly require her help.

If he'd accept it. And while he remained unconscious, she had no way of transporting him to the Haven. She'd have to get home and harness Daisy to the buggy. If she were very fortunate, he might come to his senses and be gone before she returned.

Just as she was getting to her feet, he opened his eyes.

They were the color of cinnamon, a light reddish-brown to match his hair. They seemed to stare at nothing. His breath caught and shuddered, as if he'd forgotten how to breathe.

"Are you all right?" she asked. "Can you hear me?"

His body jerked, and he lifted his head with obvious effort. She could see his eyes focus on her, the blurred confusion gradually replaced by stunning clarity.

For an instant she thought she knew those eyes. Then the moment of familiarity passed, and he spoke.

"You . . ." he croaked. "You're . . . in danger."

It wasn't in Johanna's nature to laugh in such circumstances. She crouched beside him. "I?"

"Evil," he said. His eyes began to unfocus again. "Evil—you must . . . be careful—"

She touched his forehead. It was damp with sweat, warm but not feverish. If he were experiencing delirium tremens, his symptoms ought to be more extreme. His speech would imply some sort of hallucination . . .

He grabbed her wrist. His grip was paralyzing in its strength. "Listen—" he said. His eyes widened in terror, and abruptly his fingers loosened, freeing her hand and leaving it numb. She shook it several times, concentrating on bringing her own pulse back to a normal speed. Her brief fear was totally without justification; he was in no state to be a danger to anyone.

A quick evaluation of his condition indicated that he was unconscious once again. With a renewed sense of urgency, Johanna made him as comfortable as possible. She had nothing to put over him but the short mantle she'd taken with her to San Francisco. It barely covered his shoulders.

"I will come back for you," she said, knowing he couldn't hear. "It won't be long."

She strode the remaining mile to the Haven in record time. When the whitewashed fence that ran along the perimeter of the orchard came into view, she released the breath she hadn't realized she'd been holding. The branches of the trees, like the grapevines in their neat rows, were hung with ripening fruit, but she had little thought to spare for their bounty.

The Haven was a large, rambling one-story house, constructed of wood and stone with a broad porch bordering three sides. It looked exactly like the refuge she called it, friendly and inviting and lived-in. She half-expected several of the "family" to be waiting on the porch to greet her. But it was Oscar alone who rose from his seat on the stone steps, waving his big hand and grinning from ear to ear.

"Doc Jo!" he said, lumbering toward her. "You're back!"

She noticed at once that the young man's shirt was misbuttoned, and he'd forgotten to wear his braces, so that his trousers fell loosely about his hips. Otherwise he clearly hadn't suffered in her absence.

"Good day, Oscar," she said, taking his outstretched hand. "How is everyone?"

"Good," he said, nodding vigorously. "Only we missed you."

"As I missed you."

"What was the city like? Were there lots and lots of people?"

"A great many, Oscar. But I can't tell you all about it now. First I need your help."

Immediately his guileless face grew wide-eyed and solemn. "I'll help you, Doc. Just tell me what you want me to do."

She patted his arm. "We must go and rescue someone who is ill. I'll need your strength to lift him."

He puffed out his broad chest. "I can do it."

"I know you can. I'm going to harness Daisy to the buggy, and then we'll be on our way. Could you take my valise inside, and tell the others we'll be back shortly?"

Oscar took the valise, lifting it as if it were filled with nothing but air, and trotted back to the house. Johanna crossed the yard to the small pasture just beyond the barn and fetched placid, reliable old Daisy, who tossed her head in greeting and allowed herself to be harnessed without a single mild protest.

If only human beings were so cooperative.

Oscar was waiting for her by the gate, nearly bouncing in his eagerness. He handed her up into the driver's seat and plopped down beside her, jostling the carriage with his weight. Johanna urged Daisy into her fastest pace.

The man was still lying where she'd left him, but his condition was considerably worse. Instead of resting quietly, his lean body was shaking with unmistakable tremors. He'd flung her mantle off into the grass.

Delirium tremens. She had no doubt of it now. He could become very dangerous if he began to hallucinate again. She was profoundly grateful for Oscar's dependable strength.

"This man is very sick," she told him. "We have to take him to the Haven to get well."

Oscar wrinkled his nose. "He stinks!"

"Yes. We'll have to clean him up later." She knelt beside the stranger and took his pulse again. It was racing. He might come out of unconsciousness at any time.

Her hand brushed a bulge beneath his coat, and she felt underneath. A heavy leather pouch hung from a strap over his shoulder. She opened the flap at the top. The purse was bursting with coins, both gold and silver, and a tightly rolled wad of bills. A great deal of money indeed, especially for a man who should have been robbed long since.

She closed his coat. "We'll put him in the back of the buggy," she said to Oscar. "Can you lift him gently, by the shoulders, while I take his feet?"

Oscar did as he was asked, taking great care to be gentle. The inebriate was heavier than his frame would suggest; there must be solid muscle behind it. Johanna had lifted or restrained her share of male patients in her time; she remembered Papa's indulgent pride in her sturdiness. "My Valkyrie," he'd called her.

She ignored the stab of pain at the recollection and helped Oscar maneuver their patient into the back of the buggy, where the rear seat had been removed for the carrying of supplies and patients. This time she'd come prepared. She adjusted blankets beneath and over him, made certain that he was breathing without difficulty, and took the reins again. Oscar twisted in his seat to stare at the man.

"Who is he?" he asked.

"I don't know. We'll find out when he wakes up." If he lived. Many patients didn't survive the delirium. But with a flash of the intuition she'd learned not to dismiss, she guessed that he wasn't one to lie down and die easily.

Remember . . . he's just another patient in need of medical attention— and a drunkard at that. They hadn't accepted inebriates at the old asylum in Pennsylvania. Could the treatment she and her father had developed be used to illuminate the causes of a drunkard's need for alcohol?

She shook her head. Papa had been the one for wild flights of theoretical fancy and unorthodox schemes. Her business now was to keep this man alive.

Careful to avoid the worst ruts in the path, Johanna guided Daisy at a walk back to the house. Most of the Haven's residents were watching for her return, alerted by Oscar's earlier warning.

Irene leaned on the porch railing, patting at her dyed red hair with a beringed hand and posing to display herself to what she considered her best advantage. God knew what she'd think when she saw the new patient.

May, the Haven's youngest at fourteen, hovered at the edge of the porch, ready to flee at a moment's notice. The former reverend, Lewis Andersen, stood like a rigid sentinel, his face set in its worn lines of disapproval and misery. Harper, of course, wasn't there. It took far more than this to awaken him from his inner world.

She and Oscar eased the man from the buggy and carried him to the porch. Lewis stared at the stranger's face and backed away as if he'd seen the devil himself.

"Stinking of damnation," he muttered. His gloved hands sketched out the meaningless, repetitive patterns he adopted when he was upset.

Irene gave a high-pitched giggle and angled for a better view. May peered at the newcomer and took a step closer, as if she felt real interest in him. Then, just as abruptly, she skittered out of sight around the corner of the house.

The spare room was at the very rear of the house, in a portion built of local stone. It was always cool in summer, and isolated from the rest. Johanna and Oscar set their patient down on the bed.

" 'Woe unto them that rise up early in the morning, that they may follow strong drink,' " Lewis said behind them.

"Reverend Andersen, if you would be so kind as to fetch a fresh pitcher of cold water, and a glass," Johanna suggested.

Lewis backed out of the room. He would probably feel the need to wash his hands ten or twenty times before returning with the water, but that would give her a chance to undress her stranger.

"He's very sick," Oscar said solemnly, towering behind her.

"I'm afraid so. I must undress and bathe him and put him to bed, while he is still quiet. He may become excited later on."

"Like Harper does sometimes?"

Oscar hadn't forgotten the last time Harper came out of his cataleptic state in reaction to some waking nightmare, screaming and crying until Johanna could calm him. All the residents had been afraid.

"It is possible," she said. "That's why I want to be ready. Do you think we could borrow some of your clothes for this man when he wakes up?"

Oscar grinned. "I'll go pick some out." He lumbered into the hall, footsteps thundering in the direction of his room.

Left alone, Johanna concentrated on undressing the patient. His shoes were too fancy for extended walking, and she expected to find blisters on his feet. Surprisingly, there were none. The coat had come from a quality tailor, though one might not realize it now.

His liquor-stained shirt was held closed by a few remaining buttons; if he'd had a waistcoat, it was gone. She removed his purse and then the shirt, tucking the pouch and money into the drawer of the night table. No one here would steal it, except perhaps Irene—and she wouldn't think to look.

Stripped to the waist, the stranger confirmed Johanna's guess about a muscular frame beneath the leanness. The pectorals were well developed, as were the deltoids and biceps. His waist was firm and tapered, ridged with muscle. All just as any sculptor could wish. No indication of prolonged illness or injury; not a man who had gone so far in drink that his entire body was ready to fail him. For an inebriate, he appeared to be remarkably healthy.

After a moment's hesitation, she unbuttoned his trousers and tugged them down. He was, after all, just another patient. She had no personal interest in him . . . no matter what some prurient townsfolk might say about a woman doctor concerned with the intimacies of male clients.

She laid his trousers across the back of a chair and briskly discarded his underdrawers. His thighs and legs matched the muscular leanness of his upper body; his hips were well-formed. In fact, every major portion of his anatomy was a masculine ideal.

Johanna licked her lips, grateful the patient was still unconscious.

Leaving him lightly covered, she went into her room, the closest in the hall to this one, and retrieved her basin and a sponge. She drew the chair up beside the bed and gently washed away the sweat from his body.

It was a thing she'd done many, many times, but her hand was just a little unsteady as she guided the sponge from his neck and shoulders down the length of each arm, across his chest, his stomach, each long leg. She turned him gently and bathed his back, glancing once at his muscular buttocks and then away.

She felt tension drain from her body as she finished and replaced the sponge in the basin. He needed a much more thorough bath than this, but she couldn't risk it now. If he had delirium tremens, the chance of hallucinations and agitation was still very real. He would have to be—

He pushed up from the bed before she realized he'd wakened. Fingers clutched at the sheets, and his head tossed deliriously from side to side.

"Where—" He coughed, and his voice cleared. He turned to stare at her. "Who are you?"

"A doctor. Johanna Schell. You're safe here."

He began to shake, violently, his teeth chattering. "Not safe," he said. "No." Fresh sweat covered his forehead and upper lip. His face went white, and Johanna recognized his impending sickness.

Quickly she removed the sponge from the washbowl and offered the bowl to him. He twisted his body and heaved into the receptacle, as if trying to keep her from witnessing his illness. He kept his back turned to her until she gave him a cloth to wipe his face.

"You shouldn't . . . have brought me—" He gasped. He made a warding motion with his hand. "Go 'way."

"I can't do that." She reached for his flailing hand and held it firmly. "What is your name?"

His face went utterly blank. She watched him struggle to find that information, perceiving his panic when he couldn't.

"Don't remember," he said. "Oh, God."

"You are suffering from alcohol withdrawal," she said, keeping her grip on him. "You may experience unpleasant symptoms, but you will not be alone."

The door opened behind her, admitting Lewis with the pitcher of fresh water and a glass on a tray. He set it down on the table by the bed and retreated, holding his hands out from his body as if they had become contaminated. The stranger reared up, staring at Lewis with an almost feral intensity.

"Thank you, Reverend," Johanna said. "Would you be so kind as to close the door behind you?"

He left with alacrity, doubtless to wash his hands another dozen times. Johanna poured out a glass of water and pressed it into her patient's hand, holding it steady with her fingers around his. "You must drink. Your body is badly depleted."

He gazed at her with the driven intensity he'd shown Lewis. *Such remarkable eyes.* She shook herself and lifted the glass toward him. He let her put it to his lips and swallowed the water like a man dying of thirst. She refilled it, and he finished the second as promptly.

"Excellent," she said. "Now you must rest. Rest and proper diet, plenty of water and abstinence from drink are the only cures for your condition. When you are better, we can talk."

"No." He caught her wrist as he had by the wagon road, in that same unbreakable grip. "Can't—" His throat worked, and he spread his fingers around it as if to choke himself. He released her, pushing her away as he did so. He began to run his hands up and down the lengths of his arms, slowly at first and then more and more desperately, as if he were trying to rip something away from his flesh.

"Not me," he said hoarsely. "Not me!"

Here it began, then—the delusions and hallucinations. He might be seeing insects, or snakes, or some other loathsome object. The hallucinations might continue for hours. Calmly she reached down for her doctor's bag and opened it. She carried a very small vial of chloral hydrate, which she used as sparingly as possible. This time she'd probably have no choice.

Her patient was panting now, eyes wide and wild. "Get out," he cried. He clawed at his arms, leaving red streaks. Seriously hurting himself could be the next step.

"Listen to me, my friend. I can make you feel better, sleep until this has passed."

He stopped his frenzied movements. "Help," he whispered.

"Yes." She poured a few drops of the syrup into a small spoon. "If you will take this—"

She thought it might actually work, that he would take the medicine quietly before matters proceeded to a dangerous point. He reached—as much for her as the spoon—his face unyielding. Then he froze, fingers bending into claws. His eyes rolled back in his head.

Johanna flung herself toward the bed just as his seizure began. She half lay across him, holding him down with the weight of her body. He convulsed beneath her. His heart pounded frantically, drawing her own into a sympathetic rhythm. His head slammed back on the pillow, once, again. The rigidity of his body relaxed, every muscle gone limp simultaneously.

The seizure was over. She checked his pulse and his breathing. Not good, but not fatal. Disentangling herself, she retrieved the fallen spoon and poured out new medicine. She pried open his mouth and pushed the spoon between his teeth.

He swallowed normally. She hovered over him for several minutes to make sure it had gone down, and used a clean cloth to mop his wet forehead. With her thumbs she massaged his temples and the space above his eyes, willing him to surrender.

The sharply etched lines between his brows smoothed out under her ministrations. His breathing slowed, steadied. It would be an hour before the chloral hydrate took effect, but in this state sleep might come more quickly.

She permitted herself to draw away at last, dropping into the chair and closing her eyes. She was exhausted, a state she did not enjoy admitting even to herself. Where was Papa's Valkyrie now?

The door swung open with a faint creak. "Doctor Johanna!"

Bridget Daugherty stepped into the room, wiping her hands on her apron. "Well, I'll be! The others didn't even tell me you was home. I was out in the back with the wash—" She glanced at the patient. "You been busy, I see. New guest?"

"For the time being."

Mrs. Daugherty sniffed. "Likkered up. You never took one of them in before."

"The opportunity hadn't arisen," Johanna said crisply. Bridget was a naturally garrulous soul, curious about everything and completely uneducated, but she also felt she owed Johanna a great debt for delivering her eldest daughter's child safe and alive when the other local doctor had proclaimed the case hopeless. She was steady, trustworthy, and tolerant of the odd residents of the Haven. Johanna could ask for no more.

"I found him in the road," she said. "He might have died if I'd left him."

"An' you can't leave any poor soul in need, can you?" Bridget shook her head. "Well, looks like you might need a hand tonight, after supper."

"I would much appreciate it," Johanna said, daring to close her eyes again.

"You're plumb tuckered, Doc," Bridget said. "You ought to rest."

"Not now. He must be watched."

Bridget clucked. "Same old story. Well, at least the wash is done, and I didn't have no trouble from anyone. I'll fix you up a supper tray and feed the rest."

"Thank you, Bridget."

A broad, callused hand settled on her shoulder and squeezed. "There's a letter for you came in yesterday's mail, from that Mrs. Ingram. I put it on your desk." Mrs. Daugherty left the room.

Another letter from May's mother, a full four months after the last. This time it might contain good news, something other than vague hints of her plans to return for her daughter, and the usual questions about May's well-being. But Johanna couldn't count on that.

In any case, the letter could wait. Johanna got to her feet and lifted her new patient's trousers and coat from the back of the chair. They might be washed, mended, and saved, with a little effort. Irene might be persuaded to do it for such a handsome stranger.

She waited out the next hour until it was clear that her patient was sleeping deeply, unlikely to wake for some time. She tucked the sheets and blankets high about his shoulders, smoothing them down over the contours of his upper body.

How beautiful he was, even in sleep.

She stepped sharply away from the bed, barked her shin on the chair, and reached for the doorknob. *Papa.* She must see Papa. He would be waiting, and she'd left him alone so long. Papa would have advice—

No, he wouldn't. Sometimes, when she was very tired, she forgot about the attack and what it had done to him. She expected to walk into his room and feel his arms around her, hear his laugh and his chatter about his latest progress with a patient.

Not today. Not ever again.

But this man might recover. *This* was within her control. She would see that he was up on his feet and well again, whatever it took.

With a final backward glance, she left the room and closed the door behind her.

Chapter 3

He remembered his name.

Quentin. Quentin Forster. Born in Northumberland, England, thirty-two years ago.

And suffering from a throbbing headache, a mouth full of cotton, and eyes that all too slowly focused on the room in which he lay. He blinked against the spill of light from the lace-curtained window. Thank God the sun wasn't shining from that direction.

The window looked out on something green. Peaceful. He braced his arms beneath him and pushed up. Every muscle ached and protested the abuse. The sheets and blankets that had been tucked in at his chin slid down to his waist. He discovered that he was naked.

Instinctively he looked for his clothes. A shirt and trousers, of homely cut and fabric, lay neatly over the back of a chair not far from the bed. They didn't look like his clothes, but it wouldn't be the first time he'd awakened to find his clothing and belongings unfamiliar.

At the other side of the room was a dresser, a washstand with a pitcher, basin and towels, and a three-legged stool painted a bright shade of pink. Something about the color made him want to laugh. It matched his current situation in absurdity.

His bed was wide enough for two, with heavy cast-iron head- and footboards. The mattress was comfortable, the sheets clean. If he'd gotten into this room and this bed under his own power, he had no memory of it.

So where was he? This was not a hotel room. It was too neat and modest: neither a run-down boardinghouse nor an expensive inn that catered to the rich. He'd spent his share of nights in both.

Cautiously he flipped the sheets back and swung his legs over the side of the bed. He endured a brief spell of dizziness, and then tested his weight on his legs. They supported him well enough. Cool air nipped at his skin. He'd been sweating sometime recently; a fever? Or just the aftereffects of another drunken binge?

That was the one thing he was sure of. He'd been drunk. The blank spots in his memory always came after such episodes.

He tottered with all the grace of a babe in leading strings, making his way to the window. It was open the merest crack. He smelled the growing things beyond it even before he looked out. The sweetness of fruit trees. Flowers. Vegetables . . . tomatoes, carrots, peas. Freshly turned earth. The complex mélange of woodland.

Trees and tangled bushes framed the window. A pine- and oak-covered hill rose steeply a few yards beyond. The air was fragrant, with a hint of dampness. He could smell people nearby, but not in the numbers that meant close-packed houses and smoke and waste from thousands of residents, rich and poor and in-between. The only sounds were the singing of birds, a muffled voice, the distant lowing of a cow, the rustle of leaves.

He wasn't still in the City, then. He leaned his forehead against the cool glass, thinking hard. There'd been the saloon in San Francisco . . . gambling, winning . . . making plans to move on, catch the ferry to Oakland across the bay. It didn't really matter where he went, as long as he kept moving.

That was where the latest blank spot in his memory began. And ended here, in this room.

But there was something else. He returned to the bed and grabbed a handful of sheet, lifting it to his nose.

Yes. A woman. He shivered at the memory of her touch, his body's recollection more vague but every bit as real as that of the mind.

A woman. He groaned. Was this some woman's bed he'd shared last night? He couldn't even remember her face, let alone the rest of her. He glanced down at himself. His body wasn't telling him that it had enjoyed a woman recently.

A small mirror hung above the washstand. He looked himself over: He obviously hadn't shaved in a couple of days. Aside from a certain gauntness and the dark half-circles under his eyes, his face was unmarked. No surprise there, and no sign of violence in the vicinity, nothing to indicate that his amnesia hid behavior or incidents he should fear.

But he *was* afraid. This was happening more and more often, his periods of amnesia increasing in length each time. He always swore he wouldn't take another drink . . .

Until it happened again.

As he always did when he awoke this way, he searched the room for other clues. No peculiar objects he didn't remember buying. The shoes beside the bed looked at least a size too large—so, for that matter, did the clothes. In the drawer of the night table lay a heavy pouch of coins and bills: his winnings had been very good indeed, it seemed. And no one had stolen it while he slept.

But something was missing. He emptied the pouch and sifted through the coins.

The ring was gone. His mother's ring, inherited from her own family, the Gévaudans, and given to him upon her death—the last tangible memory of his family. Had he used it as a stake in a game, or drunk it away, or lost it?

He shrugged, shutting off a twinge of pain. His mother had been dead for twenty-four years. She wouldn't know how low he'd sunk.

He reached for the trousers laid over the chair. He was still weak enough that it took rather longer than usual to put them on. The thud of footsteps outside the door found him balancing on one leg like a stork, trouser leg flapping.

The door creaked open slowly. A brown eye pressed up against the crack. Someone—male—was trying very hard not to breathe audibly, making even more noise in the process.

"Come in," Quentin said. His voice felt long-unused. "Come in, if you please."

His secret observer took immediate advantage of the invitation. A sandy-haired giant, near six and a half feet in height, barged into the room. He wore overalls several inches too short and a wide grin, as if he'd never seen anything quite so delightful as a half-dressed man struggling to put his leg into his trousers.

"You're awake!" he said. "Doc Jo will be glad." He pointed at the shirt Quentin hadn't yet tackled. "Them's *my* clothes," he said with an air of pride. "You can borrow them until you're better."

Quentin won his battle with the trousers and sat down. Now he knew the origin of the clothes, in any case. He hadn't thought his taste could suffer such a major lapse. But there'd been the time when he'd woken up in the desert without any clothes at all . . .

"Thank you," he said gravely. He grabbed the shirt, while the overgrown boy watched with fascination. "Boy" seemed the right word for him, in spite of his height and bulk. He couldn't be more than twenty, though he spoke like someone much younger. Simple-minded, perhaps. There were far worse lots in life.

And surely the boy could answer basic questions. "My name is Quentin," he said, buttoning the shirt. "Can you tell me where I am?"

"My name's Oscar," the boy said. "Doc said to go get her when you woke up."

"Doc?"

"Doc Johanna. I helped her bring you here."

So he *hadn't* come of his own volition. And Johanna was a woman's name. A woman doctor. That would explain his memory of a woman's touch.

But this wasn't a hospital. The good doctor's home, perhaps? Had he been so ill?

He stood up and offered his hand. "I'm very pleased to meet you, Oscar. Can you tell me how long I've been here?"

Oscar gazed at the man's hand and suddenly folded his own behind his back in a fit of shyness. "I don't know," he said. "You been very sick. I helped take care of you."

"You and Doc Johanna?" At the boy's nod, he asked, "Where is this place, Oscar?"

"The Haven." He shuffled from foot to foot. "I gotta go get Doc now." He backed away and was out the door with surprising swiftness.

Quentin dropped his hand. The Haven. A very peaceful sort of name, to match the feel of this room. *The Haven.*

To a man like him, it sounded like paradise. But for a man like him, there was no such place.

Aware of a powerful thirst, he went to the washstand and poured himself a glass of cool water from the pitcher. The water was clear, as if it had come from a spring, with a faint tang of minerals. It was the most wonderful thing he'd ever tasted. He was finishing the last of it when the door swung open again.

No giant this time. This one was most definitely female. His practiced gaze took her in with one appreciative sweep, noting the lush curves of a body matched with the height to carry it: a statue, a goddess, an Amazon. He noted and dismissed the black bag in her hand. Her dark, modest dress was almost severe, out of step with the modern fashion of close-fitting cuirass bodices and snug skirts, but it did more to enhance her generous figure than any fancy ball gown might have done.

And as for her face . . .

At first he thought it rather plain. Its shape was oval, with a very slight squareness to the chin, and broad, high cheekbones. Her hair was a common light brown, drawn close in a simple style at the back of her head. Her brows were straight, without the provocative arch that might have lent her greater feminine allure. Her lips were, at the moment, set in a prim line, though they might be full enough when relaxed. Her nose was quite ordinary. And her eyes—her eyes were blue, the brightest thing about her, sharp with intelligence and purpose.

The eyes alone made her attractive. That, and the way she carried herself. Like a queen. Rather like his own twin sister Rowena, in fact . . . except that this doctor was human, and Quentin doubted she carried an ounce of aristocratic blood in that sturdy frame.

She strode into the room and closed the door behind her.

"You should not be out of bed," she said immediately. "Sit down, please."

Quentin obeyed. Her voice—low, a little husky, with just the trace of an accent—demanded instant obedience, and he found himself intrigued. More intrigued by a human being than he'd been in a very long time.

She pulled the chair up beside the bed and laid her palm on his forehead. It was the touch he remembered—that his body remembered. He shivered as if with fever, the tremor radiating south from her hand to his extremities like an electric current. The charge gathered in his groin and lingered there, even when she withdrew her hand. His arousal was immediate and formidable. She might as well have bared her luxurious breasts, within such easy reach of his hands, and offered them up to his exploration.

He swallowed and closed his eyes. His mind was conjuring up these visions because he literally couldn't remember the last time he'd taken a woman to his bed. He was burning up with lust, and he was afraid.

"You aren't warm," Johanna said, as if to herself. She bent to her black bag and removed a gauze packet, unwrapping a glass thermometer. "Please open your mouth—"

If you'll open yours, he thought. Yes; make a joke out of it. That had always saved him before. "Don't you think we ought to be properly introduced before engaging in such intimacies?" he asked with a grin.

She paused as if genuinely surprised, her thermometer suspended in midair.

"My name," he said with a slight bow from the waist, "is Quentin Forster. You must be the famous Doctor Johanna. I understand that I have you to thank for my presence in this very comfortable bed."

She raised one straight eyebrow. "I am Doctor Schell," she said. "I am pleased to see that you remember who you are."

Quentin started. Did she know about his lapses in memory? Had he been here long enough for her to learn so much?

She set down the thermometer and placed her thumb and forefinger above and below his right eye, pulling open his lids. "Very good," she said. "Do you remember how you came to be here?"

He considered lying. No, not with this one. And why bother? He'd be gone soon enough.

"Unfortunately, I do not," he said. "I wish I did, considering the state in which I found myself when I woke up."

She must have understood his intimation, but her expression remained tranquil. It was really quite striking, that face—or would be, if it could be made to smile. Without any good reason at all, Quentin wanted to make her smile.

Maybe then she'd actually see *him*. Remind him that something of the old Quentin was still within him, unsullied—the devil-may-care rogue beloved by the Prince's set in England, the gambler, the jokester who never took anything seriously.

"Your state," she said, "was extremely poor when we brought you here. You're very lucky to be alive, young man."

Young man? He was entering his third decade, and she couldn't be so much as a year older than he was, if that. He laughed. It hurt his chest, but he let it go with abandon.

"Do you find that amusing, Mr. Forster?" she said coolly.

"I'm not an infant, Doctor, and you aren't a grandmother yet, unless I'm very much mistaken." He grabbed her hand and turned it palm up. The hand was lightly callused and strong, but her fingers were tapered and graceful. The fingers of an artist. Fingers that would heal a wound or stroke naked skin with equal skill . . .

"Ah, yes," he intoned with an air of dramatic mystery. "I see that you have a long life ahead of you. You let nothing get in the way of your ambitions. But unexpected adventure awaits. A great challenge. And romance." He drew his finger over the creases in her palm. "A man has come into your life."

She reclaimed her hand without haste. "If that is the best you can do, Mr. Forster, you need additional instruction in fortune-telling."

Was that a twinkle in her blue eyes? Did she have a sense of humor, after all?

"Alas, the gypsies who raised me are far away."

"Then you'd do better to read your own palm, Mr. Forster. You came very near death."

"I doubt it, Doctor. I'm not easy to kill."

Her face grew even more serious, and her voice reminded him of a professor at Oxford who he'd regarded as a personal gadfly. "The effects of inebriety are cumulative," she said. "How long have you been drinking?"

He hid a wince. It wasn't a subject he cared to discuss. "How long have you been a doctor?"

She gazed into his eyes, holding him with sheer will as another werewolf might do. "I do not think you understand, Mr. Forster. You were suffering from acute delirium tremens, a condition that is often fatal. You have been with us for four days, most of which time you have been unconscious or raving. I am frankly amazed to see you capable of rational communication."

Raving. "I suppose I made a nuisance of myself," he said. "What did I rave about?"

"Most of your words were incomprehensible." She cocked her head. "But there was a pattern. When I first found you in a field about a mile from here, you tried to speak to me. You warned me of some evil, that I was in danger."

He shivered. He didn't remember it. He didn't want to. "I'm sorry," he said. "I must have sounded quite mad."

"You have no recollection of this."

He shook his head. "Unfortunately not."

"What is the last thing you do remember?"

"I was staying in San Francisco. I won a bit of money in a game. I was planning to catch the ferry to Oakland."

"You are now near the town of Silverado Springs, in the Napa Valley, some miles north of either San Francisco or Oakland," she said. "Do you often experience these periods of amnesia?"

"Sometimes." What did they say about confession being good for the soul? It certainly seemed to be helping now. "Generally when I have a bit too much to drink." *And half the time I don't even remember the drinking.*

"It seems I owe you a great deal," he said, smiling to charm her away from more questions. "It was kind of you to take me in and look after me. At least I can pay you for your care." He reached for the drawer.

"We can discuss fees later, Mr. Forster."

"Quentin, please."

"Quentin," she said, in that schoolmistress tone. "Make an attempt to grasp that you have been suffering a severe condition for nearly a week, that you have apparently lost any memory of a portion of your life, and that you may not survive another bout. Such a state is not to be taken lightly—"

"Do you take anything lightly, Johanna?"

"Not where a life is concerned. And you are fortunate I do not, or I should have left you in the field."

Beneath her dogged assertiveness he detected the one thing she didn't want him to see—a woman's inevitably soft heart. The sort of heart that had caused her to take in a drunken stranger and care for him with no promise of reward.

And he knew his own strength. If he'd been raving, he might have become dangerous. Dangerous to her and anyone around her.

Perhaps, this time, he'd been lucky.

"Is that why you call this place the Haven?" he asked, gesturing at the room. "You scrape unfortunate sots like me off the floor and minister to them until they're well again?"

"Not as a rule," she said with a twitch of her lips. Humor again—hidden, but there. "You are something of an exception."

He placed his hand over his heart. "I'm honored. But if this is not a Haven for vagabonds such as myself, who does it shelter besides a skilled and lovely lady doctor?"

His compliment seemed to go right over her head. "You have met Oscar," she said. "He is one of the patients here."

"Patients?"

"You might as well know where you are, Mr. Forster, since you are likely to be spending a few more days with us."

"But I'm well, I assure you—"

"I shall be the judge of that." Before he could speak another word, she picked up the thermometer and pushed it into his mouth. His teeth clicked on the glass.

"The Haven," she said, "is what I call our little farm. There are seven of us in residence: myself, my father, Doctor Wilhelm Schell, and five patients. We came to this valley two years ago, when we found it necessary to close our private asylum in Pennsylvania."

"Your—" Quentin tried to speak around the thermometer. Johanna snatched it from his mouth, examined it, and shook her head. "You are a very lucky man, Mr. Forster."

"Quentin," he reminded her. "Yes, I'm exceedingly lucky." He laughed under his breath. "Is this by any chance a madhouse?"

"We do not use that name here. The Haven is different. Our residents are only a few of those we treated in Pennsylvania. Those it seemed best to bring with us." Her voice softened. "They have become very much like family. This is what I want you to understand, Mr.— Quentin. You will be meeting them, and I do not wish you to disrupt our routines out of ignorance." She searched his face. "Does insanity frighten you? Does it disgust you? You will see behavior you may consider peculiar—"

"More peculiar than mine?"

"—and if you cannot treat the residents with the dignity they require, I shall have to make other arrangements for your care."

Yes, there *was* fire in Johanna Schell. It sparked in her eyes when she spoke of her "residents," with all the ferocity of a lioness guarding her cubs. Passion existed in that curvaceous frame . . . not for romance and the usual women's fancies, but to protect those in her care. A woman who took on great responsibility, and relished it.

In that way she was the complete opposite of Quentin himself. Johanna Schell was not like the demimondaines he'd tended to run into during the past several years, nor did she bear any resemblance to the proper and well-bred aristocrats of England. She was something new to him—honest, straightforward, unselfish, with hidden emotions yet to be discovered. He couldn't assign her to a category and dismiss her as unimportant, as he did the other men and women he met briefly in his wanderings. That was what intrigued him most.

Ordinarily, he wouldn't linger long enough to indulge his curiosity. But he found himself admiring this cool, stern, and utterly sensible goddess. Not merely admiring—he was *drawn* to her, and by more than the erotic promise of her touch.

If she'd been *loup-garou*, the explanation would have been simple enough. There was always the possibility of a sudden and unbreakable bond forming between two of werewolf blood. But, even though he lacked his brother's broad mental powers and flawless ability to recognize others of their kind, he knew that Johanna was unmistakably human.

No matter. He couldn't trust himself to remain here longer than strictly necessary. His safety—his sanity—lay in constant motion. And if his worst, half-acknowledged fears were correct . . . if he left turmoil behind each and every time he lost his memory in drink . . .

Guilt was one of the emotions he'd learn to outrun. Sadness was another. And loneliness.

Johanna reminded him that he was lonely. She and her healer's touch.

"I am the last man to judge another's madness," he said at last, meeting her eyes. "You may trust me in that, if in nothing else."

"That sounds like a warning."

"Yes." He smiled crookedly. "But I shan't be the one to prove how unwise it is to bring strange, besotted men home as you would a wee lost puppy."

"I would bet that you are not a puppy, Quentin Forster."

"Ah, do you gamble?"

"Only when I have no other choice." She gathered her skirts and began to rise.

He stopped her, laying his hand on her knee. She had a perfect right to slap him for his forwardness. She went very still. Their gazes locked. He was a gambling man, and he would have wagered all his winnings that she felt his touch the way he felt hers.

Not that any such effect would show on that carefully schooled face.

"What is your opinion. Doctor?" he asked. "Can you help me?"

"If you refer to your dipsomania . . . it is possible, if you wish to change," she said. "If you do not, no one can help you."

"Can I expect a lecture on the evils of drink?"

"There are plenty of reformatory societies for that purpose. I have other techniques."

"I'm fascinated." He let his hand slide just a fraction of an inch. The muscles in her thigh tensed. "Just what are these techniques?"

"They were developed by my father, using the science of hypnosis he learned in Europe, where he was educated as a neurologist. Hypnosis enables a doctor to communicate with that part of the mind that is hidden from a patient's own conscious thoughts. Using this method, a trained physician can help the patient to fight mistaken ideas that create many of his problems." She made a gesture with her hands— controlled, but revealing her enthusiasm as much as her eyes and voice. "In your case, this would be the desire for strong drink. My father's method has proven most effective in a number of cases, where insanity is not too far advanced."

"I've heard of this hypnosis," Quentin said. "It's something like mesmerism—"

"Mesmerism became little more than superstitious nonsense, rejected by men of science. Hypnosis, as we employ it, is far more advanced, yet misconceptions remain. My father—" She stopped.

Quentin noticed that one of her fists had clenched. She caught his glance and relaxed her fingers. "This is hardly the time for a lecture."

"Your father must be an interesting gentleman," Quentin said, watching her face. "I confess that I'm a bit surprised that he sent you to deal with a strange male patient."

The zealous light went out of her eyes. "My father is no longer seeing patients. I received a full medical education in the United States and Europe; you need have no fears about my competence."

"I'm not afraid." He let his lashes drop over his eyes and lowered his voice to a seductive purr. "I shan't mind your company in the least, fair Valkyrie."

She flinched. "Why do you call me that?"

Well, well, well. Something else she was sensitive about, along with her patients, and her father. Had she been mocked for her height and hardy frame in the past? What blind fools men could be.

"Because you remind me of those ancient Teutonic warrior maids," he said. "Girded for battle and prepared to sweep the wounded from the field. I suppose your hair ought to be blonde, but I quite like it just as it is."

She actually blushed. It was the first typically female behavior he'd seen in her.

"That was my father's pet name for me," she whispered. *Was*, as if her father were dead, though she'd said he was here.

"It suits you," he said. "I mean that as a compliment."

She scraped back her chair and stood, shaking off his hand. "If I am to be your physician, Mr. Forster, you had best realize that our relationship must remain strictly professional."

He feigned surprise. "Naturally. If I am to be your patient."

"We shall discuss that possibility at a more appropriate time," she said. "You will stay in bed for the remainder of the day; I shall bring you a healthy breakfast to restore your constitution. And put from your mind any thought of drinking while you remain in this house."

The mere thought of alcohol made Quentin's gorge rise. He crossed his heart. "I promise I'll be good."

That almost imperceptible smile flickered at the corners of her mouth. "I wonder." She turned briskly for the door.

"Doctor—Johanna—"

She stopped, hand on the doorknob.

"Thank you," he said, meaning it. "Thank you for helping me."

"I, too, took the Hippocratic oath," she said. "Rest well, Mr. Forster."

Quentin was very tempted to test her composure by inviting her to join him under the covers, but long training as a gentleman quelled the impulse. Her dignity was not impregnable, but there was no point in wasting all his ammunition at once.

"Until later, then," he said.

He remained seated at the edge of the bed long after she'd left, working out the thoughts and feelings she had provoked in him. They were a mass of uncomfortable contradictions—the very sort of thing he'd avoided by moving on before there was the slightest chance of developing a relationship with anyone, or feeling much of anything at all.

Reflecting deeply on his own emotions was hardly the sort of game at which he was expert. It led him too close to the shadows, like drink. He was more than a little alarmed at the intensity of his reaction to Johanna Schell.

He fell back on the bed, pillowing his head on crossed arms. The ceiling above was a soothing, blank white, luring him toward oblivion. Why not sleep, as the doctor recommended?

But sleep had never been his most reliable mistress—unless he was drunk. His thoughts chased round and round like a wolf after its own tail.

Why did she attract him, unlike so many other women? It wasn't merely her curvaceous body; he'd sampled plenty of those in his time. No; the physical was only a small part of it.

It was her strength—not so much of body as mind and purpose. She carried herself with all the confidence of a man, but no one could mistake her for anything but a woman. She knew who she was and lived in herself without shame or doubt. He couldn't imagine her confounded by any of the fears or petty cares that afflicted so many average lives.

Perhaps she wouldn't be daunted by his demons—those demons he could never quite see, who hovered at the very edges of his consciousness. The ones who reduced him to a pathetic coward, terrified to look too deeply inside himself for fear of what he'd find.

Was Doctor Johanna Schell strong enough to match them? Could her science of hypnosis bring him to the end of his perpetual flight?

That was it. That was the heart of the subject, and of his sudden and half-unwelcome hope. Johanna Schell was like this place, this Haven . . . a sanctuary in the storm his life had become. Her touch not only moved and aroused him, it anchored him, drew him into a quiet place where his demons had no power.

He closed his eyes. God, how he longed for such a place. But to take the risk, to ask for her help and everything that might entail . . .

had he any right? Even if she offered, with all her poise and faith in herself . . . what if that weren't enough?

Better to run. Better to spend one last day to be sure of his recovery, and leave this transient peace behind.

He laughed, as he always did on those rare occasions when his ruminations led him to a state of such maudlin self-pity. Laughter kept the tears at bay, and there was enough of an English gentleman left in him to disdain the ephemeral solace of weeping.

He wasn't that kind of drunk. He wished that he were. He wished that he could reconcile himself to a permanent ending.

But that was another thing a proper English gentleman simply didn't do. Not until there was no other choice.

Quentin covered his face with the soft feather pillow and laughed until no listener would have any doubt at all that he was quite insane.

Chapter 4

Whenever she was troubled, Johanna had always gone to her father.

In their life together, since her mother's death, she had been the sensible one. She'd kept the books and most of the asylum records, saw to her own handful of patients, reminded Papa to eat and helped him dress—each and every task carried out with the same single-minded efficiency.

Wilhelm Schell, for all his brilliance, had been the one with the touch of mischief, the ability to laugh even at the most serious moments. He could be annoyingly impractical. His mind made strange, unfathomable leaps from one concept to another, seemingly without logic. And he was the one who could explain and reassure on those rare occasions when her emotions got themselves in a tangle.

As they were now, due to Mr. Quentin Forster.

Despite all that had changed, Papa's presence still gave her comfort. She went directly from the guest room to her father's room, opening the door a crack to gauge his condition.

He was asleep. If she woke him, he'd only be more confused, and her trivial needs came a distant second to his. She closed the door. The patients had already eaten and were either outside, working in the garden, vineyard, or orchard, or resting in their rooms. She'd have time to make notes on the new patient.

Her office seemed very quiet as she sat down at her desk and took out a notebook. Quentin Forster must have his own set of notes and records of treatments and progress, to join the others neatly stacked in the desk drawer. This record, like May's, would be written entirely in her own hand, without any contribution from her father. The feel of the pen in her hand never failed to calm her thoughts on those rare occasions when they spun too fast for her to discipline.

Her heart gradually slowed from the rapid pace it had set ever since he touched her. Dipping her pen in the inkwell, she made a cool assessment of her new patient, point by logical point.

Quentin Forster. Age, estimated thirty years. Of English descent, probably aristocratic by his accent and general mien. Apparently in good health, in spite of his recent bout of delirium tremens. Clearly he was not the sort who drank constantly, or he could not be in such excellent condition.

In all likelihood he was here in the United States because he was the younger son of some wealthy landowning family, sent to make his fortune conveniently far from England. Such young men were hardly more than parasites, like the idle children of aristocrats everywhere.

Did he drink because he was in exile, or due to some personal weakness in his nature? No need to speculate; she'd learn that soon enough, during one of their first sessions of hypnosis. *If* she decided to take his case.

That was the question. He might very easily disrupt what they had here. Disturb the others.

Disturb her.

His laughing cinnamon eyes flashed in her mind. He was charming and handsome, of that there was no doubt. Intelligent, too. Proficient at reasonable conversation, if one discounted his jesting.

How long had it been since she'd had a truly rational conversation? One that lasted more than a few minutes and didn't leap wildly from subject to subject, or drift off into silence? She'd spoken to a few fellow doctors during the lecture in San Francisco, but they were apt to condescend to her because of her gender, if they paid any attention at all.

Quentin Forster didn't condescend. Except for his one inquiry about her father, he seemed completely unruffled at being attended to by a woman.

If anything, he seemed to relish the prospect.

And that was the challenge he presented. She must keep a professional distance from him, remain unmoved by his teasing and flirtation—something she could do easily enough with other men. Not so easy, perhaps, with him.

You are a woman, she told herself—something Papa had reminded her of on occasion, in the old days. *It is quite logical that you should find a man attractive, sooner or later.* In spite of what some male physicians and social arbiters claimed, she had always believed that women were sexual creatures. Even Johanna Schell.

Simple physical attraction explained much of her sense of discomposure. But why this man? Why now?

She shrugged and closed the notebook. There would be a day or two to decide; she certainly wouldn't turn him out so soon after his initial recovery. She'd make the correct decision . . .

"Well, what's he like?"

Irene came into the office—dramatically, as she always did, floating through the door in her silk dressing gown. Her faded red hair was loose in practiced disarray, and she wore enough face paint to be seen from the farthest rows of a large theater. She planted herself in front of Johanna and struck a provocative pose. "Come, now," she said in theatrical tones. "Don't even think of keeping him all to yourself."

"I suppose you mean the new patient," Johanna said dryly.

"Who else, in this dreadfully boring place?" Irene said with a sniff. "He's the most interesting thing to happen *here* in ages. Such a handsome one, too." Her eyes narrowed. "But you wouldn't notice that, with your withered spinsterish ways. You never notice anything important."

Johanna was used to Irene's narcissism and occasional vindictiveness. One didn't have a conversation with Irene unless it was entirely about Irene. "I noticed," she said. "But I have been somewhat more concerned with the state of his health."

"But he's better now, isn't he?" She stroked her hand—its delicacy marred by bitten fingernails—down her thigh. "You must introduce me to him as soon as possible. I can speed up his recovery."

"I'll introduce him to everyone once he's ready," Johanna said, her voice calm and authoritative. "For now, he needs rest."

"Don't try to fool me, Johanna," Irene said, tossing her head. "You just want to keep him away from *me*. You're afraid that when he sees me, he won't even notice you. Who would?" Her ravaged face took on a faraway look. "When I was on the stage, no man could take his eyes off me. I was the toast of New York and every city I visited. My dressing room was always filled with flowers and suitors on their knees." Her gaze sharpened and focused on Johanna. "It will be so again. Soon I'll have all the money I need to get me back, and then—" She broke off in confusion and hurried on. "But you want to keep me here, a prisoner, because you're jealous." She hissed for emphasis. "You're plain and dull and dried up as an . . . an old prune. You want to make me the same way—"

"I don't want to make you anything, Irene, but happy," Johanna said. Irene's delusion was such that she could not look in a mirror without seeing the promising young actress she'd been at twenty—the girl she'd left behind thirty years ago, sexually exploited and abandoned by a former "protector," lost to the stage and left to make her living through prostitution. She'd been declared mad and eventually found her way into the Schell's private asylum as a charity case. Now she was a part of the "family," if an occasionally difficult one.

Johanna opened another notebook and consulted the week's schedule. "I think we should have another session soon."

Irene primped and preened. "No time for that," she said. "I must go back to rehearsals. I'm to play Juliet, you know, with Edwin Booth himself."

She turned to go, swirling her dressing gown in a clumsy arc that was meant to be elegant. "Send the gentleman to me when he's rested. You'll rue the day if you deprive him of the opportunity to worship at my feet." She laughed girlishly and swept back out of the room.

Cherishing the renewed quiet, Johanna closed her eyes. Irene had relapsed over the past several weeks, convinced that she was in the midst of rehearsals for a play that would never open except in her own mind.

Though it might require many more months, Johanna intended to help Irene become capable of living in the world on her own, even if it was as something of an eccentric. Irene was a gifted seamstress. If she could be made to leave some of her delusions behind, she could put her skills to good use and earn a respectable living. And she could rediscover some measure of happiness in herself.

But that meant facing what she didn't want to face—the fact that she was fifty years old and completely forgotten by her supposed hordes of onetime admirers. If she could only see that there was a different kind of worth that did not depend upon the transience of the flesh . . .

Johanna rose and went back into the hall. She paused to look in on

Harper, who sat in his chair, unmoving and unaware of her fleeting presence. Then she continued on to Papa's room. He was awake now, and had pulled himself up into a half-sitting position, propped up on the layers of pillows at the head of his bed. Thank God he had regained some use of his left arm and leg, though they were still extremely unsteady.

Oscar had helped Johanna build the special bed rails that kept him from tumbling out at night. It looked like a cage—a cage such as his own body and brain had become.

"Papa," she said softly, closing the door behind her. "How are you feeling?"

He peered at her, his left eyelid slightly sagging over once-bright blue eyes. "Johanna?"

"I'm here." She sat on the stool beside the bed and took his left hand. It shook a little, the tendons and veins carved in sharp relief under the fragile, spotted skin. "Did you sleep well?"

"Hmmm," he said. He patted her hand with his right one. "You look tired, *mein Walkürchen*. Working too hard." His words were slurred, but comprehensible. That, too, had improved over time. "What day is it?"

"Wednesday, Papa."

"Good. Good." His bushy white brows drew together. "Where is my schedule, Johanna? I can't remember now if it's my day to see Andersen."

"Don't worry about that, Papa. I'll see to it."

"*Ja*. You always do." He chuckled hoarsely. "Where would I be without my girl . . ." His chin sank onto his chest. Johanna rose to adjust his pillows.

"Are you hungry, Papa? Some nice fresh eggs for breakfast?"

"I don't know." He moved his good hand irritably. "Have you any strudel?"

She smiled, swallowing. He'd always had a terrible sweet tooth. "Not today, Papa. But I can have Mrs. Daugherty bring some from town, perhaps, tomorrow morning."

"Don't bother. I can get it myself—" He struggled to rise, found the bed rails in his way, and tried to move them. The effort exhausted him. "Where are my clothes?"

She fetched the loose, comfortable clothing she'd had made for him, removed the bed rail, and helped him dress. It was a slow process, though not as slow as the bathing, which would wait until this evening. She encouraged him to do as much dressing as he could on his own, but the buttons always defeated him. While his feet were still bare, she them for sores or swelling, then pulled on his stockings and his soft shoes.

Such painstaking care took several hours each day, time taken from the patients, but she could not pass it on to Mrs. Daugherty. Except for the housekeeping and cooking, which took all of Bridget's considerable energy, Johanna could trust no one but herself to do that which must be done at the Haven.

When she was finished with Papa's feet, she worked his left arm gently through a series of exercises, and did the same for his leg. He bore it passively, adrift in his own world.

"Send in my next patient, Johanna," he said. "It's Dieter Roth, isn't it? He's a difficult one, but we're coming along." He patted her arm. "We're coming along."

Dieter Roth was one of their former patients at the asylum, who had been helped enormously by Papa's techniques and gone home before their move to California. But Papa often lost track of time, confusing the past with the present.

"We've a new patient, Papa," she said, fetching a glass of water from the pitcher on the washstand. "He's a dipsomaniac, by all appearances. I haven't treated one like him before."

"There is no reason why inebriety can't be treated as well as any other form of insanity," he said with sudden clarity. "The influences that drive a man to drink are not as simple as some would have us think. I have never believed it is merely a weakness of character."

"Nor do I," Johanna said, her heart lightening. "I haven't taken on a new patient in some time, however. I'm not sure how much he can pay, or if we can afford another charity case."

"We are doctors. We can't turn away those who need our help." The old fire lit his eyes. "And our methods work, Johanna."

"Your methods, Papa," she said, holding the glass to his lips.

"They all laughed at me in Vienna," he said. "But I've proven them wrong—" He choked, and Johanna rubbed his back until he was breathing normally again. His face was very pale.

"I just heard quite an interesting lecture in San Francisco," Johanna said quickly. "The speaker presented some rather controversial theories, not unlike your own. Would you like to hear them?"

But her father wasn't listening. He'd drifted away, lost in some memory that, for him, might be taking place at this very moment.

"Papa?" He didn't respond. She rose and replaced the glass on the washstand, blinking dry eyes.

He couldn't advise her. The decisions were all hers now. She knelt by the bed and rested her head on his lap. He touched her hair, tenderly, as if she were a child again.

"Don't cry, Johanna," he murmured. "Your mother will get well. You'll see."

"Yes, Papa." His hand stroked her head and went still. He had fallen asleep again, as he so often did.

"You're right, Papa," she whispered. "We can't turn away those who need our help. But things . . . are not as they once were." She paused to listen to his steady breathing. Yes, he was asleep, and wouldn't be disturbed by her worry. "We are coming near the end of our funds, Papa. I've sold all the land we can spare; I can't sell the orchard or the last acre of grapevines; they make this place what it is. I don't want the world too close—and it isn't what Uncle Rutger would have wished." She sighed. "I must have Mrs. Daugherty's help with the washing and cooking, and she must be paid a fair wage."

Her father shifted and gave a soft snore.

"We must have medicine, and clothing, the necessities of life—" She smiled wryly to herself. "I can do well enough without luxuries. You know I don't much care for fripperies in any case. I remember when it used to worry you, that I never sought such things. But I would be happy, Papa, if I can continue to carry on in your footsteps."

She raised her head and gazed at his placid face. "*Ach*, Papa. I'll complain no longer. I *will* find a way to continue, you can rest assured of that."

"I hope you'll allow me to help, Dr. Schell."

For just an instant she thought Papa had spoken. But no, the voice was wrong—the timbre a little deeper, the tone lighter, the accent English rather than German.

She spun about to face the door. Quentin Forster stood there, leaning against the doorframe with arms folded and one ankle crossing the other. Except for the faint circles under his eyes, he showed no evidence of his recent ordeal. Oscar's shirt and trousers did not look as oversized on his lanky frame as she'd expected, nor did they detract from his naturally elegant bearing.

Or his handsomeness—though he was in need of a good shave. And a haircut. But the longer hair and the reddish beard starting on his chin only gave his features a more roguish appeal. That slight roughness, combined with his aristocratic air, created a most intriguing combination . . .

She cleared her throat sharply.

"What are you doing out of bed?" she demanded. "I do not remember giving you permission to wander about the house."

He uncrossed his arms and stepped into the room. "You never did arrive with my breakfast."

"I am sorry. I shall see to it shortly."

"I can manage it myself, if you'll point the way to the kitchen." He glanced at her father. "I didn't mean to intrude, but I couldn't help overhearing . . . This is the elder Dr. Schell, I presume?"

Positioning herself to block his view, Johanna stood protectively by Papa's bedside. "Yes. Now, if you will kindly go back to your room—"

With flagrant disobedience he came closer, gazing at her father's face. "I'm very sorry," he said. His expression was serious, as if he truly meant it. "It must have been a terrible loss for you."

Was it possible that he had experienced such losses? Something had driven him to drink. Every one of their patients had suffered; such suffering could lead to madness, or make a mild case of insanity worse.

"He is not dead," she said stiffly.

"But he needs care, and you have the other patients." Quentin looked past the bed to the window, with its view of the small vineyard. "This place has a certain serenity that must benefit your residents a great deal. It would be a pity if you had to sell any more of it."

He'd come just a bit too close—close enough for the small hairs to rise on the back of her neck. She moved nearer to the bed.

"Eavesdropping is not the act of a gentleman, Mr. Forster." She lifted her chin. "How much did you overhear?"

"Enough to know that you could benefit by an influx of capital." He looked about for a chair and, finding none, leaned against the wall. "Earlier, we were discussing the possibility of your treating my . . . propensity for excessive drinking. As it happens, I can pay you well for such treatment. Enough, I believe, to help in your current circumstances."

Johanna's skin grew hot. So he had overheard something she'd meant no one, not even her father, to know. And he spoke with such . . . such presumption, as if he couldn't imagine her refusing his offer.

"We are doctors. We can't turn away those who need our help." Papa had been completely lucid when he spoke those words. He'd lived by them, and she believed in them as much as he did. Even if Forster had been

unable to pay, she would have considered attempting treatment. But she hadn't decided. Now he was forcing her hand.

"If you've any doubts," Quentin Forster said, "the money is in my room. Over one thousand dollars in cash and coin."

So much? She'd never counted it, of course. The sum was considerable from her current perspective.

"I won it quite honestly, in a game of cards." He looked up at her from beneath his auburn lashes, unconsciously—or consciously—seductive.

She turned her back on him and gazed out the window. He had made it extraordinarily difficult for her to say no. The need for money was very real, for the sake of the Haven's residents. With such an incentive, she could think of only one reason to turn him down.

A personal reason. He made her uncomfortable, uncertain. In his presence, she felt a little of her normally unshakable confidence waver. And, at the same time, she was drawn to him, woman to man. He unsettled her, and nothing was nearly so dangerous to a woman of science.

It would not do, not if she was to be his doctor. That would have to be made very clear.

"I could not charge you so much," she said, "nor promise a cure without further consultation."

"You haven't dealt with my particular brand of insanity."

She glanced over her shoulder. "Inebriety is not always equivalent to insanity," she said. "Do you claim another affliction?"

His face closed up, all the easy poise vanished. She'd seen that look before: Panic. Denial. Fear. The sudden realization that he did not wish to uncover the secrets in his own mind and heart—secrets he was not even aware existed.

But no one was forcing him to stay. He was not, like the other residents, incapable of living in the world. He might be at considerable risk to his health—even of death—but if he chose to leave, she could not stop him.

"I have treated many forms of insanity," she said. "Very seldom have we failed to see some improvement. But the rules of conduct here are strict. No alcohol. You must get along with the others. And you must also contribute to the daily work of the farm."

You make it easy on yourself, Johanna, she thought. *He's not the sort to remain steadfast in the face of a challenge. Frighten him enough, and he will leave. He will not be able to unsettle you any longer.*

Repulsed by her own cowardice, she faced him again. "Do you understand, Mr. Forster? I will do my best to help you, but I can make no guarantees. I must retain the right to decide if the treatment is not working. But I will not demand an unreasonable fee—no matter how much I may be in need of funds. I do not ask for charity."

The pinched look on his face cleared, and the tension of his mouth eased into a wry smile. "You wouldn't. But you nearly have me fleeing in terror, Dr. Johanna. I wonder if I'd rather face a herd of charging elephants."

She found herself relaxing as well. "Have you ever faced a herd of elephants, Mr. Forster?"

"Quentin," he corrected. "I've seen my share of elephants. Some were even real." He stood up straight. "Are you afraid of me, Johanna?"

The question was startlingly direct and perfectly sober. He'd sensed her unease. Or perhaps it was another warning . . .

"Aside from the fact that you are a stranger, which in itself calls for caution, I've seen nothing to fear in you."

She didn't think she'd ever seen eyes so compelling. Beneath their veneer of laughter was layer upon layer of ambiguity, a guardedness that might conceal any number of darker emotions, just as he hid his fear.

Finding and healing the source of that fear would be further proof of the Schell technique's validity—possibly even substantiation of her own theory, if the opportunity to test it presented itself in the course of his treatment. She could finally complete the paper she and Papa had begun . . . and the payment she received from Quentin would keep the Haven going for another few months, at least.

"Well?" he asked. "Will you take on my case, Johanna?"

She folded her hands at the level of her waist and nodded briskly, as much to convince herself as to answer him. "We shall begin work as soon as you've been introduced to the others and it's been established that you will—"

"Fit in?" He grinned. "You'd be surprised just how adaptable I am."

Somehow she wasn't in the least surprised. He seemed so at ease, in spite of his obvious problems and the way he'd raved in the throes of his delirium tremens. It was sometimes difficult to remember how very ill he'd been.

He was a mystery, and like all scientists she could not resist such a paradox.

"I would introduce you to my father, but as you see he is sleeping. He will not be very communicative; it is a result of his attack."

"I understand." Quentin came to the side of the bed and looked down at her father. His mobile expression changed again—to one of real compassion. Of knowing.

"I lost my own parents when I was fairly young," he said. "My grandfather raised me, my twin sister, and my elder brother." His mouth twitched. "He was something of a tyrant. Very strict."

Johanna hadn't grown up under such conditions, but she'd seen the damage that could be done to children in such households. "I'm sorry," she said.

He shrugged. "Long ago. And I gave Grandfather as good as I got."

"Were you often in trouble?"

"I'm that transparent, am I?" He chuckled. "Frequently. I was incorrigible, in fact. I doubt that any figure in authority would be tempted to spare the rod in my case."

Had he been beaten, then? "You were not . . . unloved."

"I had my brother and my sister. They could be jolly good companions—but they were a little more conventional. Braden often lectured me to be more upright and dependable." He pulled a face. "Elder brothers, you know."

She didn't; she'd been an only child, and often wondered what it would be like to have siblings. But Quentin didn't speak as though his childhood experiences had contributed to his drinking. That was something she wouldn't be able to determine until she put him under hypnosis.

Yes. She wanted quite urgently to know more about Quentin Forster, childhood and all.

"Well," she said, "the others should be coming in from the garden and vineyard in an hour or so. We generally do outside work in the mornings and early evenings." She examined him critically. "Since you seem steady enough, I'll give you a brief tour of the house, and then introduce you all around."

"I look forward to it," he said. But the twinkle in his cinnamon eyes suggested that he was much less interested in the other patients than he was in her.

That was very likely to change soon enough.

Chapter 5

Whatever possessed you?

Quentin had asked himself that question several times since he'd made the impulsive and reckless decision to remain at the Haven.

The deed was done now. And when he looked at Johanna, with that serious and oddly attractive face that hid so much from the world, he remembered what had driven him to it.

Yes, driven. It certainly hadn't been an act of logic. But then again, so little of what he did could be attributed to anything remotely like common sense.

He'd told himself he should leave. He still could, none the worse for wear, if things became complicated. But he believed that Johanna, alone of all people in the world, had the ability to keep him away from the bottle—and from the consequences that he feared came with it. As long as he didn't drink, he was in control.

At the very least, Johanna would have his money for her good works. She deserved it far more than he did.

He sat on one of the two ancient horsehair armchairs in the room Johanna called the parlor. It was the largest chamber in the house, scattered with mismatched chairs of every size and design, a large central table and several smaller ones, shelves of books, ancient daguerreotypes, an antique mirror that might have survived from better times, and well-worn rugs on the wooden floor. He'd noticed at once that there were no real breakables or fragile items on the shelves or tables—no china figurines, nor decorative plates and delicate china—nothing that a patient of uncertain temperament might smash or use as a weapon. The house, as embodied in this room, was worn, snug, and well lived-in, with nothing of luxury but much of safety.

The house matched Johanna herself. She was not beautiful, and her clothes were plain and much-mended, but no one could doubt her sincerity or her complete acceptance of herself and the world around her.

He'd already toured the roomy kitchen, where he'd been offered a late breakfast of coffee, bread, and eggs, left by the housekeeper, Mrs.

Daugherty. After the meal, Johanna had shown him the smaller room she called her office. The remaining rooms were the patients' chambers, and Johanna respected their privacy. She did, indeed, seem to regard them more as family than men and women afflicted with madness.

"You've met Oscar," Johanna said from her chair opposite his across the parlor. "He is what many call an idiot—his level of intelligence is that of a young child. He is prone to a child's outbursts, but in general he is a gentle soul who asks only to be treated kindly."

"But he cannot be cured of such an affliction, surely," Quentin said.

"No." She leaned forward, her hands clasped at her knees in a posture completely free of feminine self-consciousness. "You see, he was born to a family in which his mother contracted a serious illness during her pregnancy. She died soon after his birth. I know little of his early life, but he was left much on his own as a child, and suffered for it. His father was himself a dying man, and begged my father to take the boy in." She smiled with a touch of sadness. "Oscar has been with us since the age of twelve. The world is not kind to those with his defect."

"As it isn't kind to any who are different," Quentin said. Johanna looked at him with such unexpected warmth that he found his heart beating faster. Good God, was he so much in need of approval, of any meager sign of esteem?

Or was it just Johanna herself?

She blinked, as if she'd caught him staring. Perhaps he had been. "I'm glad you understand," she said, and lapsed into silence.

He was trying to find something intelligent to say—something that might impress her with his wit and breadth of knowledge—when a woman flounced into the room from the hallway.

Never had Quentin seen a more vivid contrast to Johanna, except among the prostitutes who so often became his unsought companions. The woman was near fifty but dressed several decades younger, in flowing clothes that hinted of Bohemian affectation. She wore as much paint as any lady of the evening, but she carried herself like a queen. Once, she might have been pretty. She clearly believed she still was.

Quentin rose. The woman came to stand directly before his chair and assumed a pose. "At last," she said. Her dyed red hair was piled fashionably on top of her head, but a few stray wisps gave her an air of slight dishabille. Her colorless eyes glinted with predatory intent. "Johanna, introduce us at once."

Johanna sighed, so softly that none but Quentin could hear. "Irene—"

"Miss DuBois." The woman sniffed.

"—I would like you to meet Mr. Forster—"

"Quentin," he put in.

Johanna's mouth stiffened. "Quentin, please be acquainted with Miss Irene DuBois, one of our residents." She pronounced the name in the English way, vocalizing the final "e." "Irene, Quentin will be staying with us for a time."

Miss DuBois batted her eyelashes at Quentin. "Delighted, Mr. Forster. I am so glad you have come to see me. I had almost feared that all my admirers had forgotten about me." She extended a beringed hand.

Quentin did the expected and kissed the air above her knuckles. "How could anyone forget you, Miss DuBois?"

"Of course." She laughed, and the sound, much like her face, might once have been beautiful. "I knew at once that you were a man of taste and discretion. You could not have failed to see my performances on the stage on Broadway. I acted at the National Theater, Niblo's Garden, and the Winter Garden; everyone who was anyone came to watch me. When I trod the boards, no other actress was worth seeing."

Careful not to allow the slightest trace of amusement to cross his face, Quentin released her hand. He was beginning to guess what her particular form of madness might be. "The stage lost a great talent when you left it."

"Yes. You see, my doctors told me that I had worked much too hard, out of love for my devotees and my dedication to my art. They insisted that I sit out a season to rest. But I shall be returning very soon, and then the New York stage will be restored to its former glory."

"I'm certain that you shall dazzle your audiences," Quentin said. He glanced beyond her to Johanna, whose expression was unreadable. Did she approve of his playing along? He couldn't tell. "You haven't been here long, I gather?"

"Just for this season," she said. She threw Johanna a disdainful look. "Johanna would like to confine me here forever. This place is so drab without me, and the others simply couldn't get along without a little beauty and culture in their lives. Of course *she* didn't want you to see me. She knew what would happen."

Quentin recognized another cue when he heard it. He felt a profound pity for this woman, who lived in a past that might or might not have been as glorious as she painted it—a past that could never be restored. But he wouldn't be the one to shatter her illusions, even if Johanna's ultimate intent was to do so.

"I doubt very much that the doctor compares herself to you," he said.

Irene fluttered. "I should warn you, Quentin—do not fall in love with me. It is simply too dangerous. I am devoted to my art. But I will receive your homage."

"I shall be glad to give it." He bowed.

"I know it is cruel of me to forsake you," she said, "but I must have my rest." With that, she made her exit stage left.

Johanna was regarding him with a slightly raised eyebrow. "Now you have met Irene," she said.

"And I'm not likely to forget her." He sat down and crossed his legs. "She actually was an actress, wasn't she?"

"Yes. I believe she had a brief career with some modest potential. But she chose to accept the protection of an admirer who promised great things and delivered none of them." She hesitated, obviously thinking better of confiding further in him. "He abandoned her. Eventually, she became as you see her now. She has been with us, here and in the east, for ten years—one of my father's more recalcitrant cases. She does not truly wish to emerge from her delusional world."

"And one must *want* to be healed," Quentin said.

His insight surprised her. It was not what she'd have expected in his sort. "My father believed so."

"Her behavior doesn't trouble you?"

"Because she insults me?" Johanna smiled. "She can't hurt me, Mr. Quentin. I am her doctor. My only concern is for her welfare. And she is by no means the most ill of our residents."

The sound of water rushing from the pump in the kitchen interrupted her words. "Ah. I believe that the Reverend Andersen has come in from the garden. Shall we go see him?"

Quentin followed her into the kitchen, where a thin, raw-boned man with sandy hair bent over the washbasin, furiously pumping water over his hands. As they watched, he picked up a bar of soap and lathered his hands until they were completely submerged in suds, and then rinsed them off again. He repeated the action five more times before Johanna spoke to him.

"Lewis," she said. "May we have a moment of your time?"

He spun about as if startled, hands dripping with soapy water. His gaze twitched from her to Quentin.

"Pardon me," he said. He returned to the basin, reached for the soap, stopped, and rinsed his hands instead. He dried them thoroughly on a towel hung beside the basin and pulled on a pair of white gloves. Only then did he turn his attention to Quentin and Johanna.

"I was working in the garden," he said in a clipped, irritable voice, not meeting their eyes. He lifted his hands and stared at them, as if he could still see specks of dirt invisible to anyone else. Quentin couldn't smell anything on him but the residue of soap, the cloth of the gloves, and well-washed human skin. The man's spotless clothing bore the faint scent of growing things, but no telltale earth. If he had been in the garden, Quentin doubted that he'd touched the ground with anything but the soles of his shoes.

"I am sure the garden is in much better condition for your labors," Johanna said. "Lewis, this is our new resident, Quentin Forster. Quentin, this is the Reverend Lewis Andersen."

"Not now," Andersen muttered. "I must cleanse—" He held his arms out from his sides and looked down the length of his body. "So much sin, filth . . ."

Johanna didn't react to his curious pronouncements. "Would you care to join us for tea in the parlor?"

"The china . . . it is not clean."

"I assure you that it is," Johanna said gently. "Please trust me, Lewis. You have nothing to fear."

He finally looked at her, hunching his bony shoulders. "Very well. A few moments." He started for the door just as Quentin turned to follow Johanna, and their sleeves brushed in passing. Andersen flinched as if he'd been struck.

"Pardon me," Quentin said. Andersen scuttled past him into the parlor and up to the vast stone fireplace at the end of the room, where he stared with horrified fascination into its dark recesses. He shuddered, backed away, and sat down in a chair in the farthest corner. He no longer seemed to notice the presence of anyone else in the room.

"Mr. Andersen has been with us for five years," Johanna said quietly. "Lewis, what do you think of the roses this summer?"

He huddled in his chair, turning his hands back and forth in front of his face. "I have tried and tried to make them perfect, but I fail. I fail."

"If you'll forgive me, Mr. Andersen," Quentin said, "I caught a glimpse of the roses. I've never seen any so beautiful. Your cultivation of them is quite extraordinary."

Andersen stared at Quentin. "You are British." His thin lips stretched in an expression of aversion, and Quentin felt as though he were being judged from the high pulpit of some vast London cathedral.

"You are a sinner," Andersen said abruptly. His eyes bore a hint of fanaticism, but it was more distressed than threatening. "What is your sin?"

The jokes that came so naturally to Quentin's mind seemed very wrong under the circumstances. This man wouldn't understand his levity. "All men sin," he said. "I'm no exception."

"You run from them, but you cannot escape. I know." He locked his fingers together in a grip that must have been painful. "You cannot run from God."

"I doubt very much that God wants to find me," Quentin said, biting his tongue on the impulse to ask the reverend why he'd left his calling. "But I don't pretend to know His mind."

"He will find you. He found me. He found me." He cast a wild look at Johanna and jumped up from his chair. "I must go."

"We'll talk again," Johanna said.

Andersen fled the room with his hands pulled close to his body, careful not to touch any object in his passing.

Quentin blew a breath from puffed cheeks and sank lower in his chair. "If one looks beyond his affliction, he puts me in mind of a vicar I once knew. He wasn't terribly fond of me."

"Lewis has much improved from the early days in Pennsylvania," Johanna said. "When he was brought to our asylum by his family, he was unable to function normally. He spent half of each day washing himself, refusing to touch or be touched. He ate almost nothing. He was no longer able to attend his congregation or give sermons. And he spoke constantly of God's condemnation, of his own sin and worthlessness. He was determined to wash his sin away."

As if that were possible, Quentin thought with a bleak inner laugh. Aloud, he said, "But you've helped him."

"His washing is much less extreme, and on good days he is able to hold rational conversations. His distorted ideas have gradually lessened in their influence. In fact, he curtailed his usual cleansing ritual when we interrupted him—something he would not have done a year ago."

If Andersen had been worse before, Quentin could scarcely imagine his state upon arrival. "What causes him to . . . act as he does?"

"I have come to believe that certain elements of his past experiences caused his mental collapse some years ago. By uncovering them through hypnosis, we have begun to confront them. By confronting them, we cause them to lose their power."

Uncovering the past. A deep chill penetrated his heart. "Another of your father's theories?"

"One of my own." She met his gaze without false modesty. "I am still developing this method of treatment."

He forced the fear aside. "I look forward to observing your technique."

"You shall have your opportunity very soon." She looked in the direction of the hallway. "There are only two others you must meet—May, our youngest, and Harper Lawson. I've seen little of May since you arrived, and she may still be in hiding."

"She's afraid of me?"

"She fears many things. In some ways, she is younger than her age. She came to us two years ago, in a state of hysteria. Her mother left her with us for treatment. Only Oscar and I have been permitted to come close to her. She has greatly improved but, as with the others, progress can be slow."

"What caused her hysteria?"

Once more Johanna hesitated. "I cannot give you details—that must remain confidential between physician and patient. Suffice it to say that her home life was not a happy one."

A leap of intuition, and a subtle change in Johanna's expression, told Quentin what he wished to know. His lip curled over his teeth, almost without his realizing it. "A child who has suffered at the hands of those who should have cared for her," he guessed. "Like Oscar."

Johanna looked down at her folded hands. "This is why my father and I believe so strongly in what we do. To abandon such people to life in an asylum, or as prisoners in their own homes, is unconscionable if there is any way to help."

Under Johanna's dry tones and scholarly speech Quentin heard the ardor that made him so powerfully aware of her. She was devoted to these people, odd as they were. She accepted them. As she might accept *him*.

"You have a very generous spirit," he said with complete sincerity. "The world is fortunate that you chose this profession."

The palest stain of pink touched her high cheekbones. "Some members of the medical community might disagree. Our methods and ideas are controversial among neurologists and asylum directors." She rose and smoothed her skirts. "Come."

He was about to follow her from the room when he heard a muted sound outside the window overlooking the garden. He pushed back the lace curtains just in time to see a girl with short, dark hair tumbled about her face and a book clutched in her arms, dart behind a vine-covered trellis. She held very still, but he could see her brown eyes, wide with alarm.

May. She reminded him very much of a wild creature, not unlike his elder brother Braden's young American wife, Cassidy. But Cassidy hadn't been afraid of anything. This one would bound away like a fawn at the first perception of danger.

Johanna appeared at his shoulder. "You've found her," she said. "May spends most of her time in her room, reading, or in the woods. I don't deny her that freedom. She always remains close to home."

"I have some acquaintance with wild things and places," Quentin said.

"Do you?" Johanna tilted her head to search his eyes. "Perhaps, then, you will understand May."

"I am always in favor of understanding." He lifted his hand, allowing it to graze hers. Unobtrusively she swept her hand behind her skirts and made haste to walk away.

What game are you playing? he asked himself. *What will you do if she begins to respond to your advances?*

He shrugged off the question as he did so many others and trailed after her into the hallway.

She paused outside a closed door. "This is Harper Lawson's room. He seldom leaves it, even for meals." She drew a breath. "Harper was a soldier in the War, fighting with an Indiana regiment. My father had only begun to work with him when he suffered his apoplectic attack. I have since determined that Harper's insanity has its origins in his service, though he was able to live a normal life for some time following the war. I have read other cases in which soldiers such as Harper . . ."

A soldier. Quentin lost the thread of her words, gripped by a sudden wave of dizziness. She'd said the War had made this man insane.

War.

He clutched at the wall, fingers curved into claws. A choking fear rose in his throat. His nostrils flared to the rank smell of smoke, of blood, of sweat and unwashed bodies. The hammering of gunfire reverberated in his ears until he could hear nothing else . . .

Bodies falling. Ambush. Captain Stokes collapsed beside him in midshout, missing part of his face. Blood drenched Quentin's uniform. Young Beringer's legs were shot out from under him. He screamed in a high-pitched wail of pain and terror.

Quentin's vision clouded, narrowed, fixed on the enemy among the rocks above. He could smell the outlaws in their hiding places, carrying out the slaughter from complete safety. There weren't enough men to take them on. This was supposed to have been a simple police action, to capture a minor Pathan bandit who'd been harassing the more amicable Punjabi villagers. Lieutenant Colonel Jeffers couldn't have known that he'd sent them into a trap.

Untouched by the whizzing bullets, Quentin dropped his pistol. He felt nothing. Nothing was the last thing he remembered, until he woke in the hospital tent . . .

•   •   •

"Are you ill?"

He sprang back, heart pounding, before he recognized Johanna's voice. He focused on her grave blue eyes until the trembling had passed.

Blue eyes like still, deep water. Calming. He floated away with them, into a land of peace. *Nirvana*, the Buddhists called it.

"Quentin," she said, drifting somewhere alongside him. "Do you hear me?"

He heard, but he couldn't speak. He didn't know what caused his pulse to beat so high, or why she thought him ill. She had been speaking of Harper, and then . . .

Nothing. Blankness. Moments and words lost to him—then Johanna's voice, her eyes. That was all.

Another one. Another episode of "disappearing," though he hadn't touched a drop of alcohol.

"You were somewhere else just a moment ago," she said. "Do you remember?"

Somewhere else. A place of blood and heat and fear. A narrow defile between jagged cliffs—a trap. Rocky walls closing in; a room of damp stones. Darkness. Hours and hours of darkness, and hunger, and pain. The images bled together in confusion.

And then the orders. Orders that came as hard and deadly as bullets. He threw up his arms, casting the images away. Staggering. Falling.

He found his weight supported against a solid, sweetly curved body.

"You had better sit down," Johanna said. "You have pushed yourself too hard."

Her words pierced the fog in his brain. *Johanna*. She held him. Her arms were strong and sheltering, but soft as a woman's should be. Warm. Comforting.

He gave up all thought and allowed himself the sheer physical pleasure of feeling her body pressed to his. Snug bodice and underclothing couldn't disguise the fullness of breasts that so generously fit the crook of his arm. He rested one hand on her waist, just where it joined the flare of her hips. Her simple dress was a great advantage under the circumstances: no flounces and layers and furbelows to get in the way. Just a bit of cloth and the heat of flesh beneath.

And her scent. Clean, smelling slightly of soap. The scent of woman. A woman who wasn't indifferent to the man she held. Her body was becoming aroused, even if she didn't know it.

He settled his face into the cradle of her upper shoulder, his cheek brushing her neck and jaw. With just a slight tilt of his head, he could kiss the skin above the edge of her collar.

"We shall postpone your introduction to Mr. Lawson," she said, her words muffled in his hair. "I will help you back to bed—"

"Only if you join me in it," he whispered.

"I beg your pardon?"

"I still feel quite . . . dizzy," he said, tightening his hold about her waist.

"We shall take small steps," she said, and began moving him firmly in the direction of his room at the end of the hall. The movement felt very much like an extremely intimate waltz.

"Do you dance, Johanna?" he asked, spreading his hand over the small of her back.

"Seldom, and not with my patients." Her pulse beat erratically, loud enough for Quentin to hear with no effort.

"Such a waste." He stumbled, and his hand slipped lower to cup her buttocks. There was no bustle to impede his progress.

She went stock-still and forcibly pushed him away, turned him about, and marched him with a soldier's tread through the door of his room. Without ceremony or excessive gentleness she let him fall to the bed.

"I had thought," she said, facing him with hands on hips, "that you might join us for dinner tonight. But I think, upon reflection, that you should remain in bed."

Quentin's protest died with the appearance of a rampaging headache. He might as well have been drunk, and earned it. He rolled sideways and stretched out, shielding his eyes from the light.

Johanna's hand settled on his forehead. "You are not feverish," she said. "Good."

Along with the pain in his head had come a very prominent swelling in his nether regions—which Johanna, doctor that she was, could not have failed to observe. Unfortunately, she didn't offer to lay her healing hands on his aching member.

"Do you know what happened to you outside Harper's room?" she asked, dousing his less-than-idle fantasies.

"Nothing," he said. He patted the mattress beside him. "Care to join me? I should like to sample more of your bedside manner."

This time he couldn't even raise a blush in her. "I believe," she said, sitting down in the chair, "that you briefly entered a spontaneous hypnotic state. Quite unusual, but not impossible. It bodes very well for our work together."

Their work. She meant the techniques she wanted to try on him, the cure for his drinking.

"Why did you ask me . . . if I was somewhere else?"

"I thought that you were reliving some episode in your past. As I mentioned before, this can happen in the hypnotic state—"

Reliving the past. His ribs seemed to contract around his heart, pressing down so that he couldn't breath. Was that how it would be, this hypnosis? Going back to the heat and blood and darkness, memories torn from some hidden place he hadn't visited in a decade?

Or worse, deliberately surrendering to the blankness, the nothingness?

"No," he rasped. "I think I . . . I don't think you can help me. I'm sorry, but I must leave." He began to sit up, but her hand stopped him. That capable, gentle hand, fingers spread as if she would capture his heart like some small wounded creature.

"I will not yet ask you what you saw there in the hallway," she said. "I have seen that look on Harper's face. But I can tell you that it is normal to be afraid." Her blue eyes were filled with compassion. "Every man has his reason for drinking. Perhaps your reason is not one you wish to face. But you have the strength and courage to do so."

"No." He laughed hoarsely. "I am a coward."

"No more than any other human being."

The irony of her words stopped his laughter. "And what if you're wrong? What if we start something we can't finish?"

"We will work together to find the answers, Quentin Forster."

Quentin closed his eyes. She'd won. Behind her gentle touch was the force of compulsion, *his* compulsion to remain and seek mending for the wounds even he didn't understand.

His compulsion to stay near her—his healing goddess. His Valkyrie.

For your sake, Johanna, I pray that the answers aren't more dangerous than the questions.

Chapter 6

Johanna loved the early morning, before any of the patients but May had left their rooms—when she had the garden and wood and orchard to herself, and plenty of time to think.

She walked out to the orchard while the dawn air was still lightly touched with mist and the old bantam rooster was completing his ritual welcome to the sun. The neatly pruned apple, peach, and walnut trees in their measured rows, like the vineyard on the other side of the house, contrasted sharply with the wild woods on the hillside beyond.

The vineyard and orchard were unmistakable emblems of man's imposition of order upon nature. Even in the short time Johanna had been in the Valley, she'd seen more fields put to the vine, more houses built for the men and women who worked this rich land. Yet it retained its loveliness.

Such order could be a very good thing, like a physician's aid when complications beset a woman's ordinary process of birth. Or when the mind turned upon itself and must be cured with the help of science.

Johanna leaned against the trunk of a mature apple tree, striving to arrange her thoughts in similar tidy ranks. She'd spent a restless night after yesterday's conversation with Quentin, her mind wholly taken up with the new patient, and not to any useful purpose. It wasn't at all like her to lose sleep just because she encountered the unexpected in her work.

But Quentin had managed to surprise her. His rapid and unprompted transition into an hypnotic state was startling enough, but then to witness what must surely have been a reliving of some great anguish in his past . . .

She pushed away from the tree and began to walk down the center of the row, hands clasped behind her back. It wasn't as if Quentin's capability for such retrogression was unique in Johanna's experience. He clearly hadn't known what he'd revealed during the incident outside Harper's room; amnesia for such episodes was typical. His ravings were those of a man trapped in a situation of great stress and suffering; he had been stricken with the kind of grief and horror she had seen in another of her patients. But Harper was seldom so lucid.

She remembered how Quentin had slipped with equal swiftness

from an embattled state to one quite different, behaving in such a way that she hadn't been able to tell if he were genuinely enervated or playing the rake. His "affectionate" conduct had certainly suggested the latter.

Her cheeks felt warm, in spite of the morning coolness. She was beginning to see that Quentin's ready laughter and flirtatious speech were all part of the way he protected himself, his kind of defense against what was too terrible to bear, like Lewis's washing and Irene's delusions.

But what *had* he borne? Had Quentin Forster been a soldier? His words and expression during the episode implied it. Many former soldiers had turned to drink to blot out memories they couldn't tolerate. She had visited asylums housing men driven insane by the War. Most could not be cured.

Not by conventional methods. Not while so many asylum superintendents and neurologists believed that all madness was hereditary or came from physical lesions in the brain. Papa had never subscribed to that conventional belief. "Insanity," he had said, "is never simple."

Johanna turned at the end of the row and moved to the next, plucking a leaf from a dangling branch. Insanity was never simple, nor was her as-yet-unproven theory. It was still new, tested only by the smallest increments for the safety of her patients. But she'd begun to see results.

The first time she and Papa had witnessed what she called "mental retrogression," she'd been treating Andersen under Papa's supervision. While Andersen was hypnotized, he began to speak, spontaneously and unpredictably, of events that had occurred in his past—events that had clearly contributed to his illness.

Papa had been fascinated, ready to pursue this new avenue with his customary impetuosity. But Andersen had come out of his trance, and they'd had to postpone a second attempt. Papa's attack stopped any further exploration of their discovery.

But Johanna had never forgotten. During the past year she had taken it up again. She began cautiously, meticulously guiding Andersen into a past he was unwilling to speak of outside the hypnotic state. She walked with him through the very ordeals that had twisted his mind into its present illness.

And the treatment was working. Slowly, step by painfully slow step, it was working. Lewis had improved. Her tentative theory came into being, fragile as a new grape in spring.

The mind hid from itself. It was able to conceal its own darkest desires, its greatest fears, those most unpleasant memories it did not want to remember. And when it did so, it inevitably warped the personality out of its proper channels. Until those thoughts and memories were exposed to the light of the conscious mind.

Johanna had become more and more certain that her new method, based upon Papa's work, was the right one to pursue. Why, then, did she question herself when she thought of treating Quentin Forster with that same method? As if by fate, he had appeared on her doorstep—a man who might prove to be the perfect subject: easily hypnotized, suffering from unbearable memories of his past, but clear-minded enough to cooperate. And to wish for healing.

But he was *not* a "subject." He was as real and important to her as any of the others, for all the briefness of their acquaintance.

Johanna unclenched her fingers and let the crushed leaf fall. This idle speculation was unproductive; she'd already made the decision. She'd assured Quentin that she would help him, tried to allay his natural fears. She must not doubt herself if she was to succeed.

She went back to the house, pausing to throw feed to the chickens. That was usually May's job, as was collecting the eggs, but the girl had neglected her duties this morning.

Reminded of the letter in her pocket, Johanna drew it out and opened the envelope. Mrs. Ingram's missives from Europe were infrequent, always sent general delivery and without a return address, but at least the woman made some inquiries after her daughter's welfare, and expressed the intention to come for her eventually. What she did across the ocean she kept to herself, except for her occasional hints about working to make sure that she and May need never live in fear again.

Johanna kept the letters hidden from May. Until Mrs. Ingram actually arrived, there was no point in getting the girl's hopes up. Two years had passed; many more might do so before May's mother saw fit to come for her.

She scanned the first lines of the letter and inadvertently crumpled the edge of the paper. The promises in this one were much more explicit than any before. "Please keep my daughter safe," the last lines said. "I will return for her very soon."

The statement might even be true. But if it were not, Mrs. Ingram need have no fear for May's safety.

She pushed the letter back in her pocket and looked up to find the subject of her musings only a few yards away. May was standing at the border of the garden in her plain, loose-fitting dress, poised on the edge of flight. The object of her riveted attention was Quentin Forster.

He stood as still as she, with the absolute motionlessness of a wild animal. He and May regarded each other minute by minute, as if in silent communication. Then Quentin held out his hand and spoke. Johanna couldn't hear his words, but the tones were low and soothing. He smiled. May flinched, eyes wide, and stared at his hand.

Of course Quentin didn't know any better; she'd failed to properly warn him. May was terrified of strangers, men especially, and Quentin was, in spite of his leanness, an imposing figure. Johanna felt an instinctive need to protect May from any discomfort he might inadvertently cause her. She prepared to go to the girl's rescue.

Then a miracle happened. May reached out to brush Quentin's fingers with hers, withdrew her hand, repeated the gesture. Quentin spoke again, and her piquant, heart-shaped face broke out in a tremulous smile. She answered him, her voice hardly more than a whisper.

The magical moment passed, as it must. May remembered her fear and backed away. Quentin didn't try to hold her. He watched her run off, a faint frown between his brows. Concern. Why should he care about a girl who was a stranger to him?

Why should he not, if he were a decent man? Inebriety, even insanity, did not always destroy what was fundamentally good in a human being.

She strode along the graveled path to join him on the other side of the garden. His engaging smile was back in place by the time she reached him.

"I've finally met your May," he said.

"So I see." She looked him over severely. "You ought to have remained in bed."

"But I had so little incentive. I've always felt that sleeping was a very poor use for a good bed."

This time she managed to control her blush. "A return of your illness will be incentive enough." But he hardly looked as though he needed more time to rest. He'd thrown off his debilitation as if it had never existed. "You have no lingering weakness, no distress?"

"Nothing that a dose of your healing touch wouldn't cure."

"I am surprised, Mr.—Quentin." She must not treat him differently than any of the others. Using first rather than surnames and formal address helped build trust, and she could not abandon the practice simply because it smacked of a greater intimacy when used with this man. "May generally refuses to go anywhere near strangers. She seldom even approaches any of the other patients, except for Oscar. What did you say to her?"

He lowered his voice conspiratorially. "I told her a secret."

What sort of secret? she almost blurted out. Instead, she considered how much she was prepared to trust him with May's well-being.

"I have no objection to you speaking with her . . . *if* you are very careful. It might help her to realize that not all men are—" She stopped herself from revealing too much. "Just remember that she is fragile, and cannot be pushed."

He glanced the way she'd gone. "Poor child. But you are helping her."

"I do what I can," she said coolly. Within the unconstraint and surprising rapport of their conversation lay a trap—that of treating Quentin more like a colleague or sympathetic friend than a patient.

"Breakfast should be ready soon," she said, starting for the house. "Let us go in."

He raised his head to sniff the air. "I thought I smelled cooking." His stomach rumbled audibly.

"I see that you have a healthy appetite," she said dryly. "Mrs. Daugherty arrives early five days a week to cook breakfast, so we shall have something substantial this morning."

Together they went in the back door of the house, passing the patients' rooms. Johanna sent Quentin ahead to the kitchen and looked in on Harper. He sat by the window, staring at the drawn curtains. No change.

If she could succeed in helping Quentin, there might be hope for Harper as well.

The others, with the exception of May, were already gathered about the large oak table in the center of the kitchen. Laid out on the cheerful gingham tablecloth were plates of sliced bread, a crock of fresh butter, a pitcher of milk, and a wedge of cheese.

Irene, at the head of the table, was dressed in a gown Johanna hadn't seen before, smelling of crisp, new fabric and cut along much more fashionable lines than most of the actresses's years old wardrobe. The dress was somewhat vulgar and far more suitable for an evening at the theater than a country breakfast, but Johanna was most interested in its origin. Irene had no income to afford such a gown, nor had she any source for purchasing it.

Unless she had gone into Silverado Springs. Johanna had felt safe in assuming that Irene wouldn't do so, after the first time when she'd crept out to town one night only to be mocked and reviled as a woman both soiled and mad. She had too much pride to risk humiliation again.

Still, it would be wise to speak to her about the dress after breakfast. Irene was not above stealing.

Lewis Andersen, scrupulously honest, wore his habitual unrelieved black and was engaged in carefully refolding his napkin. Oscar eagerly watched Mrs. Daugherty as she put slices of bacon in the frying pan on the great cast-iron stove.

"Good morning, Mrs. Daugherty," Johanna said.

"Mornin', Doc Jo," the older woman said. "Take a seat. I've got bacon today, and fresh milk and butter." She glanced past Johanna to Quentin, never slackening in her preparations. "You must be the new feller. Feelin' better now, I take it?"

Quentin stepped around the table, caught Mrs. Daugherty's broad, chapped hand in his, and kissed it. "Quentin Forster, at your service. And I shall certainly be your most willing slave if that bacon tastes as fine as it smells."

She beamed. "Well, I'll be. A real gen'l'man. Haven't heard your like in some time." She lifted a brow at Johanna. "Can't believe this feller was ever sick."

"I had the best of care," he said, following her glance.

"You can't do better than having Doc Jo to tend you," Mrs. Daugherty said with a vigorous nod. "She wouldn't hear of leavin' your side, not even when she was near fallin' down exhausted. That's the kind of lady she is. She saved my daughter and grandchild. Never will forget."

Johanna longed for a useful task to keep herself occupied, but Mrs. Daugherty had matters well in hand. She'd learned on Mrs. Daugherty's first day at the Haven that the woman found her more of a nuisance than a help in the kitchen. "You keep them hands fer healin'," she'd said. "They ain't no good for cookery."

"Would you sit down, Quentin?" Johanna asked, indicating the chair next to Lewis.

"But I've saved a chair for you, right here," Irene said, ignoring Johanna.

Quentin flashed Johanna an apologetic grin and seated himself next to Irene. She latched on to him immediately, beginning her usual monologue about the theater, how desperate the New York producers were for her return, and how she would fight off her hordes of admirers when she went back. Lewis emerged from absorption with his own sin to stare at her with thin-mouthed condemnation.

"Only the devil waits for you," he said. "Beware, Jezebel—"

Irene sneered. "Pay no attention to *him*. He's crazy."

"Let us try to have a pleasant breakfast," Johanna said. Irene stopped talking with a pout, clinging to Quentin's arm. He made no effort to disentangle himself. Oscar wrenched his gaze from the frying pan to smile shyly at the newcomer.

"Hullo," he said. "I'm glad you're better."

"So am I," Quentin said. He plucked at his shirt. "Thank you for the use of the clothes."

"Do you like them?"

"Very much."

Oscar rewarded him with a gap-toothed grin. "Good." He turned back to Mrs. Daugherty. "Is the bacon done yet?"

"If I ain't careful, you'll eat all of it." She took the pan off the stove and laid the bacon on a serving platter, then took it around the table, beginning with Quentin, who made as if to swoon with joy.

"Wonderful," he said. He waited until the others were served, and offered Irene the plate of bread. Mrs. Daugherty cooked up a dozen eggs while everyone helped themselves to what was on the table.

Johanna seldom had a problem with her appetite, since she firmly believed in the value of hearty eating and good nutrition, but she found herself merely picking at her food. Again and again her gaze turned to Quentin. He was cordial and sympathetic to Irene, but there was a slight remoteness to his speech and manner, as if he were merely indulging her. He seemed to make no judgment of either Lewis or Oscar. Mrs. Daugherty had certainly fallen for his charm.

No grounds, then, to be concerned about his fitting in with the group—at least thus far. The thought made her feel unaccountably breathless. After all, he was hardly likely to remain beyond a few weeks or months. He was not like the other three men, who could not live elsewhere.

As if he'd noticed her preoccupation, he looked directly at her and smiled. "This is the most enjoyable meal I've had in a long time. How grateful I am that you rescued me, Doc Jo."

She winced inwardly at the nickname Mrs. Daugherty had given her. "I'm glad you find the food to your liking."

"More eggs, young man?" Mrs. Daugherty asked, hovering behind his chair with pan and serving spoon in hand. Irene grabbed his arm and glared at the older woman.

Quentin patted his flat stomach. "You've quite filled me up, madam. I think I must reluctantly forgo a third helping. But I have only the highest praise for your culinary expertise."

"Don't he talk fancy," Mrs. Daugherty said, winking at Johanna. "Just 'bout the same as you." She studied Johanna with a speculative eye. "You two could have some pretty edjercated conversations, I s'pose."

Mrs. Daugherty was too perspicacious for Johanna's comfort. She had learned long ago not to mistake a lack of education for a dearth of intelligence.

"Mrs. Daugherty," she said, "would you please prepare trays for Harper and my father? I'd like to deliver their meals."

The older woman shook her head. "Poor feller," she said to Quentin. "Harper's the lad who fought in the War. Never right in the head after that—" She caught herself at Johanna's pointed look and went back to her stove.

Johanna had just about given up on her breakfast when the back door to the kitchen swung open on squeaking hinges, banging against the wall. May rushed in, a sprite in calico, and dashed toward the table. With a darting glance at the others, she stopped by Quentin's chair and laid a bunch of wildflowers across his empty plate. Almost without pause, she snatched a slice of bread from the table and skittered out the door again.

"Well, I'll be," Mrs. Daughtery said. "I never seen her do that before."

Nor had Johanna. Quentin gathered up the flowers and bent his head to appreciate their scent. Irene simmered.

"Why do you let that . . . guttersnipe run wild through the place?" she snapped at Johanna.

"She does no harm," Lewis said, breaking his customary silence for the second time that morning. "Leave her be."

"Oh, is she without sin?" Irene asked with a trilling laugh.

Johanna rose. "Irene, Lewis, I believe it's time for your midmorning chores. If you'd be so kind, Irene, I have a few of Quentin's garments that need repair. Your skill with a needle is unmatched."

"I'll do it . . . for you, Quentin," Irene said, leaning into him. "Ordinarily I don't sully my hands with a seamstress's work."

"I shall be honored," Quentin said.

Lewis, who'd eaten little more than Johanna, scraped back his chair and walked out the back door, tugging repeatedly at the fingers of his gloves.

"I'm gonna see the new calf," Oscar announced.

"Best you all get along," Mrs. Daughtery said, wiping her hands on her stained apron. "I got cleanin' to do. Here's yer trays, Doc Jo."

"Come walk with me in the garden, Quentin," Irene said with a seductive smile. "I have so much more to tell you."

"I regret the necessity of refusing such a flattering invitation, but I believe I must consult with the doctor," Quentin said, slipping free of her hold. "Later, perhaps?"

"I'll leave the clothing in your room, Irene," Johanna said.

The long habit of deferring to Johanna's authority finally sent Irene flouncing off to her room. Oscar marched outside in search of Gertrude's calf. Johanna fetched Harper's tray, but Quentin intercepted her.

"Allow me," he said. "I think it's time I met Mr. Lawson."

"He is unlikely to notice you," she warned. "Harper suffers from severe melancholia and episodes of mania. The former has been much more frequent. He reacts to very few stimuli." After what had happened yesterday with Quentin, she had reason to be cautious. "If you feel ready—"

"I'm fine."

She took leave to doubt it, but this was as good a way as any to see if that episode would be repeated.

"Very well," she said. She led him to Harper's door and opened it. He was where she'd left him, still gazing at drawn curtains as if he could see through them to the world beyond.

"Harper," she said, motioning Quentin to set the tray down on a small table beside Harper's chair, "I've brought your breakfast. I hope you'll try to eat."

Harper's left eyelid twitched. It was acknowledgment of a sort—more than she often received. His thin fingers stretched on the arm of his chair.

"We have a new guest staying with us," she said. "Quentin Forster. He'd very much like to meet you."

Harper turned his head. He looked at the tray, at Johanna, and at last toward Quentin.

"I am pleased to meet you," Quentin said, extending his hand.

Unmoving, Harper gazed at the offered hand while his own fingers continued to twitch. Then, slowly, he lifted his arm from the chair. His hand reached halfway to Quentin's and seemed to lose its purpose. But his gaze rose to meet the stranger's, clearing to lucidity for the first time in many days.

"Sol-jer," he said, his voice rough with disuse.

Quentin glanced at Johanna in surprise. "Yes," he said reluctantly. "Years ago."

Harper shuddered. When the shivers passed he sat still for a long moment, until Johanna was sure any further chance of communication was gone. But he surprised her. He reached clumsily for the spoon on the tray—she never left him any sharp implements, even for eating— and scooped up a helping of egg. Most of it made it to his mouth. He continued to eat, without Johanna's help.

She touched Quentin's arm and led him from the room, amazed and gratified. It appeared that his affinity with May was not a singular occurrence.

"How did you do it?" she asked when the door was closed again. "He has not responded so well in weeks. I have not seen him show such interest in anything since I brought a neighbor's dog to visit—he seems to have a great affection for dogs. But he seldom responds to people." She realized that her hand was still on his arm and let him go, striving to modulate her tone. "He actually acknowledged you, and spoke."

"I'm afraid I can't claim any miraculous technique," Quentin said. "I'm no doctor."

"I wonder how he knew that you were a soldier." She shook her head. "You have a way with people. Quentin—with those who are troubled. It is no small gift."

He half turned away. "Perhaps it's because I am one of them."

She had an almost overwhelming desire to touch him again, to embrace him as . . . yes, as a kindred spirit, like her father had been. More— as a man who desperately needed human companionship and affection.

Was that what she felt for him? Affection?

The truth stole into her heart as if it had been there all along. She *liked* Quentin Forster. She wasn't merely intrigued by him and willing to treat him—not simply attracted to his charm and good looks on a purely physical level.

She liked him, and wanted him to like her.

It had never been vital, in the past, that a patient should like her. Indeed, such expectations were detrimental to treatment; her own feelings were quite unimportant. Quentin's appreciative behavior might not even survive what she had in mind for him. He might hate her in the end, if she made him relive what he wished to forget.

Better that he should hate her than the rest of the world.

"I believe that your insight will help our work together," she said, recovering herself. "I planned to begin this morning, if you feel ready."

He shrugged. "Why not? I am rather curious."

"It's no subject for levity," she said. "The treatment may not always be pleasant."

"Thank you for the warning." He caught her gaze. "And for your honesty, Johanna."

She backed away. "I shall take in my father's breakfast, and make sure the others are settled. Shall we meet in my office in one hour?"

"I'll count the minutes." At first she thought he was going to take her hand and kiss it as he had Mrs. Daugherty's, but he only gave her a shallow bow and turned for his room.

Well, then. It was all proceeding as smoothly as she could hope. Her judgment had proved sound. She had matters—and her own emotions—under firm control.

She took the tray to her father, and readied her mind for the battle ahead.

Chapter 7

If ever Quentin had doubted his cowardice, he was absolutely sure of it now.

He waited for Johanna in her office, perched on the edge of the faded chaise longue that sat across from her desk. He could see a little of the view outside the window opposite; he had a very strong desire to climb through that window.

Instead, he got up and paced a nervous circle about the room, ending at her desk. The polished oak surface was spotless, dust-free, and neatly laid out with a minimum of clutter: a stack of papers or notes, an inkstand and pen, a metronome, a pair of medical books taken from the alphabetized rows in the shelf against the nearest wall . . . and a small vase of wildflowers, similar to those May had brought him at breakfast.

The desk was like the woman herself: orderly, pragmatic, its seeming severity moderated by the homely beauty of a handful of flowers.

Quentin was tempted to upset the perfect balance of the desk: scatter a few papers out of order, or stick a wildflower stem in the inkwell. Just as he had been tempted, more than once, to loosen the tightly bound strands of Johanna's light brown hair.

It wasn't too late to do something just outrageous enough to make her toss him out on his ear, reject him as a patient. He didn't have to go through with this. If Johanna's hypnosis was what she claimed, he wasn't going to be able to hide himself. Not any part or portion.

He sat at Johanna's desk and picked up her pen. The scent of her hands lingered in the glossy wood of the handle. He drew it slowly along his upper lip, thinking through what he'd already debated with himself a hundred times or more.

He *was* crazy, as crazy as any of the other residents of the Haven.

Because he trusted Johanna. He trusted her to help him, she alone of all men or women in the world. He trusted her not only with his uncertain memories, but with the one fact she surely could not accept—she with her logical mind. What would she do with that secret, once she received it into her keeping?

She thought she could cure him of dipsomania. He hadn't told her the rest, the thing he feared, the shadow he never saw except in nightmares and cloudy recollections of conflict and violence. He wasn't even sure it existed except in his imagination.

If it did exist, Johanna would discover it.

The pen snapped between his fingers, driving a splinter into his thumb. He watched a tiny bead of blood well up from the wound. In a few minutes no one would be able to see that the flesh had been broken.

Would he be dead by now, if not for the healing power of his body? Lying in some alley, perhaps, poisoned by alcohol or murdered by cutthroats?

The point was moot. His flesh, his bones, his organs—they all mended in time, barring a fatal stroke to the heart, spine, or brain. Only his mind didn't heal. He understood his mind least of all.

His elder brother, Braden, Earl of Greyburn, had once told him that he'd wasted a good mind in the pursuit of pleasure and frivolity. Braden didn't know about the Punjab, or the shadow that followed Quentin, haunting him from the corner of his vision. The shadow had gone away while he'd lived a fast life in England, unable to match the frantic pace Quentin set. It had returned five years ago, at the Convocation, and ended the life Braden had so disparaged.

I ran out on you, brother—on you and Rowena. I had to. What would you think to see me now?

He glanced at his hand again. The skin was almost smooth where the splinter had pierced it. Yes, his flesh had mended, but what of Johanna's pen? Wasn't it a metaphor for what she was—sound enough in average hands, but so easily broken in the wrong ones . . .

"I see that you are ready to begin."

Johanna stepped into the room, her arms full of books. Quentin jumped up and took them from her, setting them down on the desk.

"I must apologize," he said. "I fear I broke your pen. I'll replace it, of course."

She glanced at the broken pen and then at his face. "It doesn't matter. The pen was of no great value, and I have others." She began to replace the books in their proper slots on the shelf. "Would you please close the door? We shall not be disturbed for the next two hours."

Quentin shut the door and leaned against it. "The other patients?"

"Each has his or her own schedule of chores and rest periods, and we generally have our exercise in the late afternoon, before dinner."

"All very . . . systematic."

She turned to him, propping her arms on the desk. "I find it works best with the mentally afflicted. Order is soothing to the troubled mind."

And to yours, Quentin thought. At the moment, he'd gladly take a little of that soothing himself. He left the safety of the door as if he were walking into the mouth of hell. "How does one go about this hypnosis? Does it involve the laying on of hands?"

"No touching is necessary. It is not mesmerism, with the making of passes over the body."

"A pity." His hands dangled like useless things at his sides, and his mouth was cotton-dry. "What do you want me to do?"

"I have found that a subject is in the most receptive state when fully relaxed," she said, drawing the drapes at the window. The room dimmed to twilight. "Please make yourself comfortable on the chaise longue."

Quentin sat down, hesitated, and swung his legs along the length of the chaise. Johanna pulled her chair from behind her desk and set it a few feet away from the foot of the chaise.

"I will briefly explain what we are about to do." She sat in the chair as straight-backed as the most rigorous arbiter of propriety, hands folded in her lap. "The man who first recognized the science of hypnosis was a Scottish physician by the name of Braid, who wrote that the hypnotic trance, into which I am about to induct you, is the result of a mental state of concentration in which all external distractions are excluded. In this state, the mind is receptive to ideas, even memories, that are ignored or forgotten by the conscious mind. As I explained once before, my father learned that it is possible under these conditions for the physician to introduce corrective thoughts and suggestions the mind would not routinely accept." She drew in a deep breath and clasped her hands. "I shall guide you into that state with the use of specific techniques."

It sounded a trifle too much like the sort of thing Braden had been known to do with the servants at Greyburn, the Forsters' ancestral estate in Northumberland. But that was no "science of hypnosis," not something an ordinary human could manage. A man like Braden could overcome the very will of another, force him to forget rather than remember—a werewolf skill Quentin had lost somewhere along the way.

"Hypnosis also requires a kind of partnership between the doctor and the patient," Johanna said. "There is nothing to fear in it."

"Do you mean that you can't order me to do something against my will?" Quentin asked lightly. "Perform Hamlet's soliloquy while standing on my head?"

She smiled. "That is correct, as far as I have observed. That is why you must wish to be helped. Not all can be hypnotized. But your ability to go into a spontaneous trance, as you did yesterday, is an excellent sign." Her smile faded. "If you trust me. You must trust me, and give yourself into my hands. Can you do that, Quentin?"

Wasn't that what he'd been asking himself all along?

He met her gaze, all levity gone from his voice and his thoughts. "Yes, Johanna. I believe I can."

She blinked, as if taken aback by his sincerity, and he let himself become just a little intoxicated by the remarkable clarity of her eyes. Like a quiet ocean, they were—never troubled by more than the gentlest of waves. How would a man go about awakening their first real storm?

Surely it wasn't his imagination that she looked back at him with the same expectant wonder . . .

"Very well, then," she said. "Have you any further questions?"

"What is your battle strategy, Johanna?"

"I beg your pardon?"

"Your plan to fight my demons of dipsomania."

"It is quite simple. Once I have put you into a hypnotic state, when your mind is open, I shall ask you a few basic questions to determine the depth of your trance. If that is sufficient, I shall ask you more specific questions that have a greater bearing on your condition."

"Such as what drives me to drink. Can't you ask me that without my being in a trance?"

"A part of your mind is in hiding, Quentin," she said slowly. "It protects you from those things you do not want to see . . . or remember."

Quentin gripped the sides of the chaise as if it were a flimsy raft floating in the midst of a sea of hungry sharks. "Perhaps there's a good reason I don't remember."

She gazed at him earnestly, the passion bright in her face. "Can the reason be good if it causes you pain and suffering? If it drives you to risk your life? No." She shook her head. "There is still so much we do not comprehend about the mind, and how the brain and body work together. But I believe that much insanity is created by a kind of . . . separation from one's own true self. If we could only make the self whole again, insanity would be cured. If a man can see himself clearly in the mirror of his own mind, and accept what he sees, he is free."

She spoke with such conviction, such utter certainty. "You'll . . . plunder my memory like an archeologist digging for ancient pot shards," he said with a laugh. "I hope my brain is filled with more than earth and fragments of crockery."

She didn't return his smile. "It contains more than you or I or anyone could ever know. But it may reveal, under hypnosis, what it cannot do when you are fully conscious."

Surely she couldn't perceive the depth of his fear, or hear the drumming of his heart? A woman of her strength would find little to admire in a coward, a man without the courage to overcome his weaknesses—no matter how tolerant she was of the truly mad.

Quentin widened his eyes in an absurd pantomime of terror. "You'll know all my secrets," he whispered. "I shall be overcome with chagrin."

"As your doctor, I would never reveal what I learn to anyone. I shall be honest with you, always." She paused and looked down at her hands. "The choice must be yours. I might simply attempt to convince your mind that you have no need for drink, and go no further. My father was very successful with such techniques . . . in effect suggesting to the open mind that its incorrect assumptions are mistaken, and lead it to change the behavior of the body."

Quentin braced himself against a premature wave of relief. "But?"

"But even if I succeed, the thing that causes you to drink will still be there, untouched." She held his gaze. "Do you understand?"

He thought he understood all too well. He'd have to give up on himself, for Johanna never would. She was that generous, and that remarkable. But he'd recognized that from the beginning.

"If nothing else," he said with false bravado, "I can help you develop your new methods."

Her cheeks reddened. "I am sorry if you think my motives are—"

"No." Impulsively he slid from the chaise and went to her, knelt before her chair and took her hands in his. "I have nothing to lose, Johanna. I'll be your willing subject."

The color in her face remained high, and her hands tensed under his fingers. "Quentin—"

"Shhhh." He kissed first one hand and then the other. "You might as well turn my brain inside out. You've already done it to my heart."

She sucked in her breath. He could hear her heart hammering against her ribs, feel the pulse throb in her wrists, blood and body giving the lie to her mask of composure. "Quentin, you are my patient. We have known each other only a few days. It is not uncommon for patients to think themselves . . . fond of their physicians, particularly when they have come close to death."

There. She'd given him an easy way out. He could laugh it off and beat a prudent retreat, knowing he'd made too reckless a move in the game. A move even he hadn't expected.

Because he hadn't been speaking entirely in jest.

He looked up at her lips, slightly parted as if she'd thought better of further conversation. They were full, naturally rosy without a trace of paint. Had they been kissed before? Had she ever found time in the midst of her doctor's theories to let a man hold her in his arms? In that feminine brain, seething with frightening intelligence and devotion to the study of the mind, had she any conception at all of the pleasures of the flesh?

Once he had known such pleasures intimately and frequently. Women had come gladly to his bed, flattered by his attentions. He'd lived in a world of mutual gratification shared among a well-bred set of rakes, roués, and worldly married women who knew exactly what they were getting and giving away.

Brilliant as she was, Johanna was anything but worldly.

"Please go back to the chaise, Quentin," she said. "We should begin."

The rebuff was clear. She didn't take him seriously. Why should she? He'd become a bitter joke, even to himself. With a sigh he returned to the chaise, resting his head and shoulders on the pillows and wondering if he might not prefer to have various body parts removed without benefit of the new anesthesia.

Johanna rose from her chair and went to the desk. She started the metronome, setting it into a slow, steady *tick-tick*. From a drawer in the desk she produced a candle and matches, which she set down on a small table. She moved the table close to her chair and lit the candle.

"You need not be concerned," she said, resuming her seat. "You will be safe at all times, in this room with me. We may not go beyond the very first stages of trance today, and nothing I do will harm you."

He laughed under his breath. "Fire away, Doctor."

"Relax, as much as you are able. Try to clear your mind of all thoughts and worries. Very good." She lifted her hand. From the end of a chain hung a multifaceted crystal, catching the candlelight as it spun in slow circles. "Do you see this crystal? Look upon it now. Notice its translucence, the quality of light, the gentle motion as it turns round and round."

Quentin looked. There was nothing particularly fascinating about the crystal. He'd much rather gaze at the face above it, glowing with reflected light.

Except she'd made very clear her sentiments regarding his attentions.

"As you watch the crystal," she said, "listen to the rhythm of the metronome. How even and steady it is, like a heartbeat. When you hear it, all your worries and fears leave your mind. You feel at peace."

How could he feel at peace with Johanna so near, her scent drifting across to him? He was like a boy in the schoolroom, fidgeting and impatient to get out into the free, fresh air and away from the useless knowledge they crammed into his head . . .

"You will notice, as you watch the crystal and listen to the beat, that your eyes are growing very heavy. You are sleepy, and yet your mind is clear. Look, Quentin. Look, and listen."

Perversely, he resisted. Johanna was confident of her ability, but she hadn't faced a werewolf subject. What if he chose to fight her? Would she still be so determined to keep at it until she found his "cure"?

"You're resisting, Quentin," she said. "You must let go."

You instruct me to do what you cannot. He set his jaw. *You must work a little harder, Valkyrie.*

"Come, come. This won't do." She gazed into his eyes. "Trust me, Quentin. That is all I ask. Trust me." Her voice softened to a low, soothing drone. "You want my help. I want to help you. Be my ally, Quentin."

Such a cold word, *ally*. It didn't satisfy him, not in the least. But after a few moments he realized that her peculiar magic was working, if not as she expected. It was her voice he listened to, not the metronome—her eyes he watched, not the crystal. He felt himself falling, falling into ocean-deep blue.

"Good," she said. "Very good. You are closing your eyes now. You continue to hear my voice, but your mind is relaxed, open. You are able to answer questions put to you without hesitation. Whatever you experience from now on, it has no power to harm you."

Quentin closed his eyes. Johanna's face remained as a pale shape against the darkness behind his lids. He felt his heartbeat settle into a lazy, comfortable rhythm.

"How do you feel?" she said from a slight distance.

"Fine." And he did. Remarkably well, in fact.

"Excellent. You will notice that your right arm has lost all weight. It is floating up of its own accord."

The sensation of his arm floating in midair felt agreeable and not at all strange. The rest of him felt ready to join the arm.

"What is your full name, Quentin?"

"Quentin . . . Octavius . . . Forster.   The   Honorable.   That means . . . I'm not the earl." He was aware of the oddness of his speech, but it didn't trouble him.

"And who is the earl?"

"My brother, Braden."

"Have you other siblings?"

"My sister, Rowena." He felt a twinge of guilt, but it passed into the same dream state as his other emotions. "I think . . . she's in New York now."

"You have lost touch with her?"

"I . . . haven't written to her in over two years."

"When was the last time you saw her?"

"In England."

"When were you last in England?"

"In 1875. Autumn."

"Why did you leave?"

A darkness intruded upon his tranquillity, drawing him away from Johanna's voice. His arm grew heavy, began to fall.

"You're safe, Quentin," Johanna said. "We will return to that some other time. You may lower your arm now."

He obeyed, feeling the darkness recede again.

"Have you been in America since you left England?"

He nodded. That was an easy question.

"Please tell me what you've been doing since your arrival in this country."

What he'd been doing? He thought back to the first day he'd stepped from the steamer's gangplank onto the dock in New York. He'd gambled in some high-class saloon—winning as he always did, sleeping on a fine bed in a fine hotel, boarding a train heading west the next morning. No plans, no future.

"It isn't . . . very interesting," he said. "Can we talk about something else?"

"As you wish. I once asked you about periods of amnesia following consumption of alcohol. How often have you suffered this?"

"I haven't kept an account."

"What do you do when you wake from such an episode?"

His stomach tightened. "Go. To the next place."

"Why?"

He couldn't make sense of her question. She fell silent, and he allowed himself to drift in pleasant nothingness. This was much better than drinking.

"Think about what happened yesterday, outside of Harper's room," she said.

Yesterday. It came to him, sprung fully formed into his mind. Johanna speaking of soldiers and war. The stench and the blood and the rattling din of guns.

"India—" he began, shivering.

"You're safe, Quentin, calm and at ease. India is far away."

"Far away," he repeated. "I was . . . on the northwest frontier. A subaltern with the Punjab Frontier Force, 51st Sikhs."

"What did you do there?"

"We . . . tried to keep the peace on the borders. Skirmishes with the tribesmen, bandits. Never stopped."

"How many years did you serve in the army?"

"Three. I was nineteen when I got my commission. I requested India."

"What happened in India, Quentin?"

He was nineteen again, eager and itching for action. There hadn't been any major battles in India since the Mutiny, but there were still the hill bandits and the occasional rebellious tribal leader to defy British rule. Quentin had fallen in love with the place, with its scents and colors and exotic ways. It almost didn't matter that nothing seemed to happen except drills and exercises and the occasional punitive foray. He was away from England, from Greyburn and . . .

"You were in a battle," said Johanna.

His first real battle, and his last. It began as a chase, with his captain, a fellow subaltern, and the Indian troops, into the hills after a particularly daring and elusive raider. It ended in slaughter.

He heard his own voice speaking, cool and unmoved, as if it belonged to someone else. As if the things he'd seen had been witnessed by someone else.

"And then?"

"I . . . don't remember." His throat closed up, trying to lock the words inside. That had been the first of the blank times, the beginning of a life of constant motion, desperate escape. "I woke up in hospital at the post, barely hurt. They said most of the men had been saved, the rebels destroyed. They gave me a commendation, but I didn't know what I'd done to earn it. My friends wouldn't tell me. They avoided me, and I didn't know why. *I don't remember.*"

"What do you think happened?"

He shut her out, her and her ugly questions. He drifted back to that agreeable place of nothingness where he simply existed, free of ties and emotion.

"Quentin, are you listening to me?"

"Go away," he muttered.

"We won't talk more about India for now. I would like you to think about something else instead. Remember when you were a child, with Rowena and Braden, before you ever thought of becoming a soldier."

Like a relentless Pied Piper, Johanna seduced him out of hiding. He couldn't help but follow where she led—back to a past that felt less real than a dream.

"Where did you grow up, Quentin?"

His mind went vacant for a moment, and then the words came to him. "Greyburn. My brother's estate in Northumberland. Only it wasn't his then. It was my—my grandfather's."

"And your father?"

"He died when I was a child. So did my mother."

"I'm sorry. That must have been very difficult."

"I was . . . the black sheep." He tried to chuckle. "Always in trouble. The peals Braden rang over my head . . ."

"Your grandfather raised you?"

"He—" His throat closed up again. "He was the earl."

"Did you get along well with your brother and sister?"

"Ro—we were twins. Very close. She could tell . . . what I was feeling, sometimes." He recalled Rowena's fair, piquant face and plunged into a profound sense of loss. "Ah, Rowena—"

"And Braden?"

"He was my elder brother. He did his best, even when he didn't know—"

Seething darkness descended like a curtain over his thoughts, cutting off words, intention, memory.

"Didn't know what, Quentin?"

No. *No.* The answer wouldn't come. He caught at the first safe thing that came into his head.

"There's something you don't know about me," he said. "A secret."

"Can you tell me that secret, Quentin?"

"Of course. I *trust* you." He felt himself float up from the chaise and circle her chair like a disembodied spirit. "Have you ever heard of . . . werewolves?"

"Do you mean a . . . man who becomes a wolf?"

"Yes. Running about on all fours. Howling at the moon." He hummed under his breath. "That's exactly what I am. A werewolf."

Chapter 8

Johanna had thought that she was prepared for just about any sort of revelation. She certainly should have been; as she'd told Quentin, the human mind was an organ of great complexity, capable of almost anything the imagination could devise.

Even of believing its owner to be a creature out of myth and legend. A shape-shifter. A . . . werewolf.

The word she'd heard used for the delusion was lycanthropy, but she'd never encountered it herself, nor read of any contemporary doctor or neurologist who had done so.

Suppressing her reaction, she took stock of Quentin. He was still relaxed, in a deep trance. He'd responded to hypnotism with relative ease—one of those rare men who required virtually no groundwork. He'd already given her much to work with.

But this . . . this she truly hadn't expected.

"Let me make sure I understand," she said. "You are a werewolf."

"Or loup-garou. Some of us . . . prefer the French."

"Us?"

"You don't think I'm the only one, do you?"

"I see." She leaned back in her chair, steepling her fingers under her chin. "Then Braden and your sister are also of these loups-garous?"

"It . . . runs in families."

He spoke with complete confidence, at ease with his "secret" identity. If his belief in lycanthropy lay at the root of his drinking and other fears, he showed no indication of it.

The temptation was very great to pursue this extraordinary turn of events to its natural conclusion. What would he do, if asked to actually become a wolf? She'd read of men and women, under hypnosis, reacting to suggestions that they were something other than human, mimicking the sounds and actions of various animals. Would he do the same, howling and growling, perhaps turning savage?

She couldn't imagine such a thing. But it would be the height of folly to provoke Quentin now. His illness was not merely dipsomania, possibly derived from experiences in the army. His response when she'd asked about his childhood suggested memories he wished to avoid. And now this . . .

"As you say, Quentin," she said, postponing further speculation. "I think we've done enough for one meeting. We shall explore these claims tomorrow, after—"

A shrieking wail came from somewhere beyond the door, rising into a bellow and falling abruptly silent. Johanna shot up from her chair.

"Harper," she whispered. "Quentin, please continue to rest. I'll return shortly."

He didn't answer. She opened the door and strode out into the hallway. Irene, Oscar, and Mrs. Daugherty stood at one end, staring toward Harper's room. Lewis poked his head out from his own room and ducked in again, carefully shutting the door.

"It will be all right," Johanna said. "Mrs. Daugherty, please take Oscar and Irene into the parlor."

With the same care she'd use approaching a wild animal, Johanna opened Harper's door.

He was in his usual place by the window, as if nothing had happened. The only change was that he no longer sat still, but rocked gently, forward and back, with his hands clasped between his knees. She moved closer to study his face. A scream such as she'd heard normally meant he was entering a period of violent mania, as he'd done three times since coming to her and Papa.

If that was the case, handling him would become much more difficult. But he continued to rock, ignoring her. It seemed safe to leave him just long enough to bring Quentin from his trance and send him to luncheon with the others.

Quentin had consumed entirely too many of her thoughts since his arrival. It was almost a relief to have another patient take precedence.

But Quentin wasn't finished with her. When she reentered her office, he was sitting on the edge of the chaise, staring up at the ceiling. He looked toward her, his cinnamon eyes glazed and unfocused, as if still in the trance. Harper's cry hadn't brought him out as she would have expected.

"I like this room," he said dreamily. "It smells good. Like you."

It was definitely time to finish. "Quentin, listen to the sound of my voice. In a few moments I shall be bringing you out of your hypnotic state. Do you want to remember what we have discussed today?"

He swung his feet to the floor and strolled toward her. "I want to remember you." He lifted his hand to brush her face. "Johanna."

His touch was intimate. She felt a physical pang, as if he'd penetrated her flesh.

Her first impression was incorrect. Surely he was awake now. Pretending to be otherwise, though why he should wish—

"I like being with you," he said. "More than any other woman."

"That is enough. Our session is finished, and—"

"You like *me*, Johanna," he said, circling the pad of his thumb around her chin. "More than any other man."

She opened her mouth to deny it and caught her breath. "Go back to the chaise, Quentin." If he were under hypnosis, he would do as she asked, and if he were deceiving her, he'd do the same or be forced to surrender his pretense. "Sit down."

He dropped his hand, began to obey and then stopped, clutching at his head. "You despise me," he said. He started clumsily for the far wall, banged his hip into her desk, and stumbled as if he hadn't seen the obstacle.

Somnambulism. Even he would not take the game so far. And if he were still entranced, he and his mind were at their most vulnerable.

She clenched her fists at her sides. "I do not despise you, Quentin."

He turned about, his gaze moving this way and that as if he couldn't find her. "You said . . . you would help me."

"I will. Have no fear, Quentin. I will."

He smiled, like a glorious sunrise. "Yes." He came to her slowly. His hand found its way to her shoulder, slid around to cup the back of her neck. "My Valkyrie," he said, staring at her mouth. "You're so beautiful."

Mein Gott. He must imagine that he saw someone else.

"Quentin," she said, trying to control the shaking in her voice. "I shall count backward from five to one. As I count, you will become more and more awake, until—"

He leaned so close that his breath caressed her lips. "If I'm asleep, don't wake me." He pulled her into his arms, the motion rife with purpose.

Suddenly she felt small and fragile in a way she hadn't since childhood. Not weak, not disadvantaged, but somehow *protected*.

How could a man like Quentin protect anyone, least of all her? And from what? Her analytical mind, always so ready to examine a problem from all angles, fell strangely mute on the subject.

But it wasn't completely silent. She was still able to make a concise mental roster of her body's reactions to Quentin's embrace.

Heart pounding. Breath short. Skin sensitive to the slightest pressure. Spine thrumming as Quentin's hands stroked her back. Nipples hardening where they met Quentin's chest. And in the vicinity of her reproductive organs . . . an indescribable warmth she hadn't experienced in many, many years.

All the symptoms of physical desire.

There was no doubt of Quentin's.

His lips began the endless descent to meet hers. They made contact. Pressed. Demanded a response.

Her body answered, pushing intellect aside. She opened her mouth and felt Quentin's tongue tease the inner velvet of her lips. An urgent spike of need drove down into her womb. She wrapped her arms around Quentin's waist and let him bend her back as he deepened the kiss, as if she were the veriest, most insubstantial nymph.

A nymph with a bacchante's appetites. And all the while it seemed that Quentin was somnambulating—acting upon the desires his conscious mind kept in check.

She had no such excuse. She kissed him in return, touching her tongue to his, savoring the purely erotic sensations she'd known but once before. Her seat and then her back came to rest on the chaise. Quentin's hand found its way to the aching swell of her breasts, scorched her flesh even through the sturdy, sensible cotton.

"Quentin," she half-protested.

"Johanna," he paused to answer, resuming his kisses on the soft skin under her jaw. "I want you."

His weight came down beside her on the chaise. His erection— quite considerable in size, her dazed mind calculated—pressed into her hip. She generally wore a minimum of petticoats; they hampered her movements and were unhealthily restrictive. What she did wear was hardly a barrier for a determined male.

She was the only barrier. Her will. Her sense of professional ethics. Her reliable common sense, which had somehow fled.

It was definitely time to call it back.

"I will now count backward," she repeated breathlessly. "You will forget all that has happened since we began this hypnotic session. When I reach one, you will wake, alert and refreshed."

He licked the tip of her ear. "Hmmmm."

"Five."

He drew her earlobe into his mouth and suckled it.

"F-four."

His hand settled on the skirts bunched around her calves and began to push up.

"Th . . ." She gulped. "Three."

He searched out the buttons at the top of her high collar.

"Two—"

The first three buttons came undone in swift succession.

"*One.*"

She held her breath. His fingers paused in their relentless work. His lips released her earlobe. He drew back.

The glazed look fell away from his eyes, replaced by complete awareness . . . and confusion. He jumped from the chaise and shook his head like a dog casting water from its coat.

"What happened?" he demanded.

She sat up and unobtrusively rearranged her skirts. "You don't remember?"

"You were about to hypnotize me, weren't you?"

She rose unsteadily from the chaise, leaving the buttons at her collar undone. She was sure she didn't have the fine manual control necessary to do the job.

"I did hypnotize you," she said. "The session went very well."

"I'll be damned—your pardon." He gave her the by-now familiar wry grin. "We're already finished?"

"We are, for today." She had recovered enough to hide her relief. "Have you any idea at all of what took place?"

He frowned. "Was I talking? I seem to remember talking. The subject quite escapes me. I hope I wasn't too much of a bore?"

"Not at all. You were an excellent subject. Limited amnesia is not

rare in such cases." She noted that her words emerged without the qua-
ver she'd feared. If he wondered how he had wakened in such a compromising position, he was too much the gentleman to say so. He
showed no indication of repeating his previous behavior, or any consciousness of his most amazing claims.

"Yes," she said, smoothing her bodice. "The groundwork has been
laid. I understand more clearly how I might help you."

Unease appeared briefly in his eyes. "Just what did I say?"

"I am your doctor. All you said is held in confidence. I shall not
judge you, Quentin."

"Then there was something to judge." He sighed. "I know my life
has hardly been a model of rectitude . . ."

She was on firm ground again. "Sit down, Quentin. There is one
thing I do wish to discuss. You must tell me if the subject distresses you."

He braced himself with his hands on the edge of the chaise. "Go
on. I'm ready."

"Have you ever heard the word . . . *lycanthropy*?"

He burst into a laugh, and kept laughing for a full half-minute.

"Forgive me," he said, wiping tears from his eyes. "What exactly
did I tell you?"

"You told me that you are a loup-garou. A werewolf."

He caught his laugh before it could break free again. "How very
amusing. I appear to be quite imaginative while hypnotized. Do you
think I missed my calling as a writer of Gothic tales for hot-blooded
young ladies?"

Johanna stood and paced to her desk, as if movement alone could
calm her racing thoughts. In her experience, subjects under hypnosis
could not easily lie. Whatever her doubts about his state after Harper's
interruption, she knew he'd been deeply entranced during the first period of questioning. His admission had been real . . . then.

Was this the delusion that led him to drink—one that consumed
his unconscious but did not reach his waking mind? How had such a
thing come about? What had brought so strange a belief into existence?

"What do you know of lycanthropy?" she asked, swinging to face him.

"As much as anyone, I suppose." He shrugged. "Tales of Gypsy
curses and witches donning wolf skins." His eyes twinkled. "Do you
wish to search my person for a wolf skin, Johanna?"

No, he certainly was not aware of what he'd said while hypnotized.
The issue must be explored in future sessions. She felt sure it was important. Most important.

Legends of werewolves were filled with blood and death. Quentin was incapable of violence, but the image of the beast must have great symbolic meaning, the root of everything that troubled him.

"That will not be necessary," she said. "I believe our meeting is over for today, and I wish to consider the results of this session." *Including my own behavior.* "I did not deal directly with your desire for alcohol. Do you feel any need to drink?"

"Not unless it be from your sweet lips."

Was this simply more trifling gallantry, or had he some memory of his recent advances? She was not prepared to face the consequences of confronting him on the subject. Not while she was still so rattled by the experience. And so ashamed.

"Well, then," she said, ignoring his comment. "You may do as you like until luncheon. Harper requires my attention—"

"Is something wrong with him?"

"His illness may have entered a new phase, and I have neglected him." *Because of you.*

"Then I won't keep you."

The moment he was out of the room, Johanna let her rubbery legs give way and sat down, hard. She touched her lips. They still throbbed from Quentin's kisses. Her whole body throbbed. In spite of her thorough knowledge of the biological processes involved, she wouldn't soon be able to dismiss the experience as a mere consequence of her profession.

All the theorizing in the world, all the calm admissions of physical attraction, were no match for the reality.

She had violated the unwritten rules pronouncing that a physician must not become involved with a patient. She could easily have taken control by pushing him away and ending the session—making him understand that such contact between them was entirely inappropriate.

Instead, she'd learned something about herself that was difficult to face, a sign of personal weakness she couldn't afford.

Her disciplined mind had failed her. She'd given in to the desires of her body, as witless as any callow girl.

She rested her head in her hands. How ironic. For Quentin, who must find this sort of thing so easy, the dalliance was forgotten in posthypnotic amnesia. While she, who had abandoned all thought of courtship or love, found herself plunged into the maelstrom all over again.

She picked up her pen with a shaking hand and realized it was the one Quentin had broken. One edge was sharp enough to cut. She swept the pieces to the side of her desk, located another pen in a drawer, and laid out Quentin's casebook.

Initial observations after first hypnotic session:

Patient suffers from delusions of lycanthropy: consequence of former experience in army and childhood?

Prognosis:

Her fingers ached from her fierce grip on the pen. She let it fall. No amount of staring at what she'd written could make Quentin Forster fit neatly between the lines.

Only curing him would bring an end to this . . . this madness. But cure him she must, no matter how long it took.

Only then could she cure herself.

Quentin slipped out of the house on silent feet, bound for the forest on the hill.

He passed through the garden and jumped the low whitewashed fence without meeting any of the other patients. For that he was grateful; his mouth felt as empty of words as a spring gone dry of water. The only thing it was good for now was kissing Johanna.

And *that* had been a mistake.

The land rose abruptly from the Haven's little niche of the Napa Valley. Live oaks and pines marched up the hills and into low mountains, another kind of haven for the wild creatures that made this sylvan paradise their home.

Quentin removed his shoes and stockings a few yards into the woods. He sighed as his feet sank into the soil, made up of the memories of countless autumns and the richly scented dust of pine. He smelled some small animal nearby, a rabbit frozen in fear of a potential hunter. At the base of a massive, red-barked conifer, a larger animal had left its clawed mark.

Life was all around him—life other than human. A life he'd all but left behind. He needed to be reminded of it now.

He started up the steep hillside, drinking in the forest through his feet and with every breath. This country wasn't like Northumberland, with its bare, broad moors and patches of ancient woodland. But it would do. It would more than suffice.

If he could find the courage to Change.

A faint path stretched out before him, worn into the prosperous, sun-dappled earth. Deliberately he left it, breaking into a lope that was as natural to him as superhuman senses. He leaped a small, deep ravine that carried the scent of recent moisture. The steep incline beyond challenged him to a faster pace, and he went up and up until his muscles burned and his clothing was damp with perspiration.

At the top of the hill he paused. The Valley spread out below, a patchwork of vineyards and fields with another range of hills on the opposite side, dominated by the crag-topped Mount St. Helena. Civilization held in the arms of the wilderness.

The image made him groan. His mind was full of similar comparisons, every one having to do with tangled bodies and naked flesh.

His flesh. Johanna's body. A body made for loving. And a mouth . . .

Bloody hell. He still wasn't sure what had made him do it. The decision to kiss Johanna had been spur of the moment, sprung fully grown from a source unbound by reason. He tried to remember his chain of thought beforehand; had he meant it as a joke on the too-serious doctor, a pleasant experiment to test the full extent of his interest in her . . . and hers in him? To see just how far the Valkyrie would melt when she thought she was safe?

That he'd been in a trance for some time he had no doubt. But something had snapped him out of it, and he'd wakened to find Johanna gone. That was when the compulsion struck him, as if he'd temporarily become someone else. Someone who didn't let moral compunction stand in the way of his desires.

The mere recollection of what followed made him ache with wanting. She hadn't pushed him away. She'd responded. God, how she'd responded. And he might have pursued the encounter to its inevitable conclusion if his sense, and hers, hadn't returned just in time.

So he'd grabbed the way out she offered, pretending to be unaware of what he'd done. And she'd acted the same . . . except for the flush in her cheeks, the hesitation in her speech. And the ambrosial scent of a woman aroused.

Quentin pulled his hand through his hair. He'd never been one for celibacy, but getting close to a woman—to anyone—was dangerous the way his life was now. He felt it; he knew it, with all the instincts nature had provided his kind.

He'd gotten himself hopelessly tangled up in Johanna's world. No matter how readily she responded to him, she wouldn't take physical involvement lightly, even if her morals permitted it. She'd buried her own desires so that she could cater, undistracted, to the needs of others. For all her intellect, she was half-blind to the power of her femininity.

And that made her vulnerable.

He knew he could seduce her, awaken the sensual woman under the Valkyrie's armor. He was very good at seduction. She didn't have werewolf senses to give her a fighting chance—only the frank, unwavering gaze that so clearly saw everyone but herself.

But these fantasies that passed through his mind were constructions of air. He still clung to the shredded façade of a gentleman. There could be no passing relationship with Doctor Johanna Schell: Either she remained his doctor, or she became something more. Something no one, human or werewolf, had ever been to him. Could never be, as long as he didn't *remember*.

You got yourself into this, he thought. *You chose to stay and accept her help. You can just as easily get yourself out again.*

By moving on.

He closed his eyes and fought for a sliver of fortitude. He hadn't Changed in many months, at least not that he remembered. Even the thought of Changing awakened vague fears of those blank periods that sent him scurrying from one saloon to another, one town to the next. Always wondering what he might have done. Carrying with him only a foul taste of menace, and violence, and darkness.

He'd told Johanna, under hypnosis, that he was a werewolf. She, logical creature that she was, would safely assume that the outlandish claim was just another symptom of his illness.

She wouldn't believe that he was more than human.

Had he ceased to believe it himself?

Time to find out.

He unbuttoned his borrowed shirt and stripped it off, placing it neatly on a flat rock where it would remain unsoiled. A warm summer breeze caressed his skin, teasing the short hairs on his chest. Already he felt the old sense of blessed freedom that came with the Change.

His trousers were next, folded and laid atop the shirt, and then his drawers. Naked, he stretched until his spine cracked and his hands extended toward the sun as if to borrow its vast energy.

But a different kind of energy filled him, and he imagined Johanna there on the hill. Watching him. Waiting for evidence that he was not entirely mad.

His manhood leapt to life again, stirring with sexual hunger. It was all too easy to picture Johanna naked beside him, under him, her full breasts pushing against his chest, round hips cradling him, strong thighs clasped about his waist as he entered her.

Aching with unrequited lust, he forced physical longing into a more useful channel. He gave himself up to the Change.

It took no more than a few moments for his body to remember its other shape. He melted into an ether of formlessness, floating between two realities, and when his feet touched ground again they were four instead of two.

He shook his coat to test its weight, sucked in a deep lungful of air that was sharper and richer than any human could conceive. A mouse had passed this way an hour ago, leaving tiny droppings. He could hear the distant cry of a hawk in search of the mouse's unfortunate cousin. Wind soughed in the tops of the pines, carrying the scent of a bird's nest and a pair of quarreling squirrels.

Under his paws the earth spoke in a language known only to the beasts. It urged him to run as only his kind could run, able to outpace the swiftest deer and outlast even the ordinary wolves the loups-garous resembled.

There were no wolves left here. They'd long since been killed off by hunters and settlers, driven to more northerly climes. Quentin had the hills and the woods to himself.

He gave in to the call and burst into a dead run from the very place he stood. He plunged among the trees and raced west, higher into the hills. Hardly a branch stirred at his passing. His paws were silent as they struck the ground, curved nails biting deep and releasing. Muscles bunched and lengthened with the perfect efficiency of a machine, and with far more grace. He let his tongue loll between his teeth in a grin of sheer happiness.

This was the way he'd always lived before: for the present, driving away memory in the pursuit of pleasure, whether it came in the form of sex or drink or games of chance . . . or the Change itself. *This* was the only escape that held a trace of honor.

He ran until he reached the crest of the summit dividing one valley from the next. Napa lay behind him, and another cultivated land spread under his gaze from the foot of the range to the silver ocean miles away. Beyond that ocean were other lands, India among them . . .

Suddenly cold, he crouched low and whined in his throat. Fear was back. And it seemed that somewhere inside him a presence reached out, took him by the scruff of the neck, and shook him furiously back and forth, this way and that, until he began to slip out of his skin.

No.

He howled. He jumped to his feet, turned about, and fled as if that same dark presence were a thing he could evade.

Time lost its meaning. He only became sensible of it again when the last stain of sunset bled away behind the western range. He found himself at the foot of the hill beside the Haven's white-washed fence.

Instinct had carried him to the nearest thing to home he possessed.

As a wolf he lacked the ability to laugh, but inwardly he roared. What was the use in contemplating flight—from his lust, from Johanna, from facing the secrets she might expose—if even his lupine self turned against him?

Exhausted, he circled the house to the back door, tail tucked and head low. He wouldn't go to Johanna. He wasn't ready to face her yet.

What he needed was a good stiff drink. If anything resembling one could be had in this place, he'd sniff it out.

The door was open a crack; it was easy for him to nose his way in. No one saw him. He crept down the hall until he reached Harper's room, and stopped at the sound of weeping from within. The door swung in at the tap of his forefoot.

Harper sat in his chair by the window, a tray of half-eaten food on the table beside him. Quentin entered the room, keeping to the shadows along the wall.

Harper didn't notice. Tears streaked his face and pooled in his beard. The rasping noises he made were too soft to be heard by anyone outside the room, unless the listener were more than human. Harper had sanity enough to wish to hide his shame.

Driven by a sense of kinship and pity he didn't fully understand, Quentin padded to Harper's side and touched his nose to the man's dangling fingers. Harper's hand twitched. He shifted in the chair and felt blindly, touching Quentin's muzzle, his forehead, his ears.

"Here, boy," he said, his voice little more than a rattle. "That's a good dog." He stroked Quentin's head with the utmost gentleness.

Quentin stood still, his heart tight in his chest. Hadn't Johanna said something about Harper responding to a dog she'd brought to visit? Harper thought that he was a dog. A natural assumption for a man so detached from the world.

But he'd spoken, to a creature he believed could not judge him. The contact was oddly comforting to them both. Quentin closed his eyes and sighed.

"Don't worry, boy. I'll—" The stroking stopped. Quentin opened his eyes to find Harper gazing down at him, the light from the lamp on the table picking out the gaunt features of his face. His breath came faster, and his hand clenched in the fur of Quentin's mane.

"You," he whispered. "What are you?" The empty, distant look in his eyes sloughed away like a snake's skin, leaving them clear and almost sane.

Quentin could have sworn that those eyes saw him for what he was—saw past the fur and recognized the soul beneath.

He slipped free of Harper's grip and backed away. Harper stared after him, hand poised in midair.

"Don't," he said.

Voices sounded from the hallway. Quentin scrambled out of the room and ran for the back door just ahead of them. He charged straight up the hill without stopping until he reached the place where he'd left his clothes.

Panting hard, he Changed. The air had grown cool, and his bare skin ran with goosebumps as he snatched up his drawers.

Harper *knew*. He wasn't gifted with a werewolf's powers, but there was something about him . . . something that made him different, an outsider among his own kind.

Perhaps they *were* kin, after all.

He started back down the hill, skidding on the matted pine needles.

"Are you running away?"

He spun around at the whispered words. The unexpected intruder resolved into a girl, slight as a doe, the usual book tucked under her arm. May.

"What are you doing out so late?" he demanded. "It isn't safe—"

His words came out more harshly than he'd intended, and she recoiled. He recognized that look. She was expecting to be berated, punished, struck, all because he'd raised his voice to her.

"I'm sorry," he said. "I'm a brute. Forgive me."

Her tightly coiled muscles loosened. "Are you angry with me?"

Damnation. As little as he knew of the child, in spite of the very few insignificant words they'd exchanged, he felt an unaccountably fierce desire to protect her. What had Johanna said? "I have no objection to your speaking with her . . . *if* you are very careful. It might help her to realize that not all men are—"

She hadn't finished the sentence, but he could fill in the rest. He'd seen his share of cruelty in his wanderings. God help anyone who raised a hand to her in his presence.

"Of course I'm not angry," he said, crouching to her level. "I was only worried about you. Worried that you might be running away."

"Not from this place. I like it here. I like—" She bit her lip. "You aren't leaving, are you?"

A few moments past he couldn't have answered that question. Johanna had said that May's mother had left her at the Haven two years ago. Abandoned her, from the look of it. Had this girl known anything but maltreatment and neglect in her former life?

Even his cowardice had its limits. He'd be damned before he added to her pain.

"No, May," he said, "I'm not leaving." He offered his hand. "I seem to have forgotten my shoes. Will you help me find them?"

She smiled—a heartbreaking, elusive thing—and took his hand.

They returned to the house together. A woman stood in the back doorway, lantern held aloft, waiting to guide the errant strays back to safety.

Quentin stopped before her. "You can douse the lamp, my dear doctor," he said, grinning past the lump in his throat. "I'm here to stay."

Chapter 9

Johanna sat up in her bed, throwing off the covers with a jerk. She came to full wakefulness a moment later.

Only a dream. Odd; she so seldom remembered her dreams, and nightmares like this were rarer still. Something about running . . . away from a threat without solid shape, a creature that panted after her, never more than a step or two behind.

A wolf had run at her side. She had felt no fear of the beast, only a sense of companionship and well-being. She remembered arguing with it, about whether to stand and fight, or run; the wolf had won the argument. So they fled, to no avail. At the very last instant, when the thing had almost caught up with them, the wolf whirled about and crouched, a shield between her and their pursuer. And from the mouth of the amorphous shadow came Quentin's baritone, strangely altered: *"I'm here to stay."*

Considering the ridiculous nature of the dream, she ought not to have found it so disturbing.

She pushed her heavy hair away from her face and swung her legs over the side of the bed. For the first time since adolescence she subjected her large, sturdy feet to a critical examination. Vanity was something she'd dispensed with long ago, as being of no use to a female physician in a world of men, and quite pointless in her particular case. She was not beautiful, nor of the dainty sort so many men preferred.

"You pretend to be a man," Rolf had said, all those years past. He had not meant it as a compliment. It was one of the last things Rolf ever said to her before they formally ended their engagement.

He had found her overwhelming, unwomanly. Quentin didn't. The fact that she was comparing the two men troubled her.

She went to the washbasin and bathed her face, neck, and arms with tepid water. A bath would be welcome this evening, if there was time. Mrs. Daugherty was off today, which meant that Johanna would be serving up the meals, conducting Irene and Lewis through their sessions, visiting with May, looking after Papa—he was very much in need of a walk outside in the fresh air—and supervising Oscar in his various activities and chores. She would spend an hour with Harper, hoping to get some further response from him. And then there was Quentin.

She stared at her face in the mirror above the basin. A plain, somewhat ruddy face with high cheekbones, full lips, a slightly snubbed nose—thoroughly Germanic. Serviceable. Honest. All she needed for her work, where trust and compassion mattered far more than beauty.

Quentin had kissed those lips. She touched her mouth. It didn't throb anymore.

Her threadbare cotton nightgown lay against her body like a second skin. She peeled it off and studied her figure with severe objectivity.

Broad shoulders—too broad for the current taste. Full breasts. They might be considered by some to be an asset. Her waist was small enough in proportion, but her hips more than made up for what her waist lacked in inches. Childbearer's hips, in a woman who would almost certainly never bear a child.

Long, strong legs. Arms more like a washerwoman's than a lady's. Large hands.

They seemed small when she was with Quentin.

"Ha," she scoffed, shaking her head. *"Du kannst immer noch ein Dummkopf sein, Johanna."*

She dressed as efficiently as always in austere underdrawers, chemise, a single petticoat, and a mended but perfectly adequate dress several years out of date, meant to be worn with a bustle she didn't own. Homely but sensible shoes. She put up her hair in the regular, utilitarian style, taking no more time on it than she ever did.

Oscar was already at the breakfast table, while Irene lounged at the kitchen door in her wrap, looking out at the bright morning with infinite boredom. Lewis seated himself quietly in his corner. May peeped in the window and dropped from sight.

Quentin made no appearance. Sleeping late, as he was no doubt in the habit of doing.

She realized that she'd been holding her breath, wondering if there would be a lingering awkwardness in facing him. For her own part, she had strengthened her determination to forget yesterday's blunder.

Forget, and forgive herself.

She served up day-old bread, cheese from the pantry, Gertrude's fresh milk, and overcooked eggs, which only Irene complained about. During breakfast, she engaged each of the patients in conversation. Irene and Lewis seemed less inclined to trade their accustomed barbs, but Oscar was his usual irrepressible self, telling of a bird's nest he and May had found in the woods, and the big red dog he'd tried to chase up the hill.

"It was mighty purty," he said. "And big, too. I wanted to pet it."

"Stay away from stray dogs," Lewis said unexpectedly. "They may bite." He paused to divide his second egg into a precise grid of bite-sized pieces.

"Don't you like dogs, Mr. Andersen?" Oscar asked.

"He doesn't like anything." Irene sniffed.

Lewis looked up, his gray eyes bitter with animosity. " 'Judge not lest ye be judged.' "

"That's terribly amusing," Irene said. "Weren't you the kind of preacher who called fire and brimstone down on everyone else in the world?" She leaned on the table, her breasts spilling over the edge of her dressing gown. "I know your kind. People like you are so afraid of their own lusts that they see evil in everyone else."

Johanna looked sharply at Irene, hearing the ring of honesty in her voice. She remembered her resolve to speak to the actress about the new gown—one more thing she'd let slip because of her preoccupation with Quentin.

Lewis shot up from his chair, face pale. "You . . . you—I saw you sneak off into town last night, when you thought no one saw. 'As a jewel of gold in a swine's snout, so is a fair woman which is without discretion.'"

Johanna stood, demanding their attention with her silence. "This is not a place of judgment," she said. "We are here to help one another. Irene, I'll have a word with you after breakfast, in my office."

Irene pressed her lips together and seethed. Oscar, sensitive to arguments, hunched over his plate. Johanna patted his shoulder and reminded him of the game they were to play later that day. He brightened and finished his breakfast.

May didn't repeat yesterday's daring foray into the kitchen, so Johanna left a plate on the doorstep for her. The girl needed more attention than she'd had of late. Johanna planned to lure her into a talk with the promise of a new book she'd brought back from San Francisco, and took a breakfast tray to Harper.

Harper wasn't in his chair. He wasn't even in his room.

Alarmed, Johanna set down the tray and ran into the hall. The back door stood open. She stepped through the doorway and found Harper sitting on the wooden bench in the garden, his hands hanging between his knees.

"Harper," she said.

He turned his head. "Doc," he croaked. "Is that you?"

She closed her eyes and whispered a childhood prayer. "Good morning, Harper. How are you feeling?"

"Tired," he said. "Hungry. Like I've been asleep for a long, long time."

How long had it been since he'd said so many words, with such perfect rationality? It sometimes happened that patients spontaneously emerged from a deep melancholy or cataleptic state, but she hadn't envisioned such a favorable development with Harper.

She masked her excitement and smiled in encouragement. Keep the conversation casual. Let him take the lead.

"I was just about to bring you your breakfast," she said.

"Much obliged." He squinted at her, as if looking into the light. "Where's the dog?"

She felt another surge of hope. His memory must be functioning if he could recall not only her name, but also a brief visit that had occurred months before. "The dog I brought to the Haven in April?"

He shook his head. "Last night. It was last night."

You cannot afford to be overly optimistic, she warned herself. "I'm sorry, Harper. There was no dog here last night."

"It was in my room, right beside me." he said with soft-spoken conviction.

Was he hallucinating? If so, she must tread all the more carefully. "I've left a tray for you in your room," she said. "Would you care to come in?"

"Do you think I could eat out here?" He raised his face to the sky. "The sun's so warm."

"Yes, Harper, of course. I'll return directly."

She left Harper basking in the sunshine and hurried into the house to retrieve the tray. On the way out she noticed that Quentin's door was open, and paused to glance inside. The bed was neatly made, but he wasn't there.

Gott sei Dank. No distractions from that direction . . .

Her relief was short-lived. Harper wasn't alone in the garden. Quentin stood beside the bench, bare-chested, his freshly mended shirt draped over his shoulder. Johanna forgot the tray in her hands.

She gazed mutely at Quentin's back, wide through the shoulders and trim at the waist, and observed with fascination the flex of his muscles as he put on the shirt. Hot prickles stabbed at the base of her spine. Her mouth went dry.

He turned around, feigning surprise. "Johanna. I didn't see you there."

Disregarding the heat in her cheeks, she set the tray down on the bench beside Harper. The former soldier's gaunt face broke into a smile.

"Thank you, ma'am," he said. "It looks delicious."

"You may call me Johanna," she said. "I see you've met Quentin."

"I just got up myself," Quentin offered. "We've been talking."

Johanna looked from Quentin to Harper in concern. They seemed at ease with each other, though she couldn't imagine that Harper had done much of the talking. And while she knew Quentin to be kind, he hadn't her training in dealing with those who'd been seriously ill. He was ill himself.

Yet she had admitted that he had a way with people. Harper had reacted to his presence the first time Quentin visited him in his room. They shared an experience of war and conflict that she did not.

There was so much she had yet to learn, and needed to know, about both men. Would fellow soldiers confide in one another as they wouldn't with a civilian, even their physician?

Her instincts told her that this was an unorthodox but legitimate approach. Harper and Quentin might actually help each other.

It was worth considering, in due course.

"You mustn't tire yourself, Harper," she said. "When you're finished, I'd like you to return to your room and rest. Quentin—" She glanced at him, not permitting her gaze to drift to the open collar of his shirt. "Would you kindly locate May and ask her to come to the parlor? I'm sure she's somewhere about. I have something to give her. You and I shall meet for our next session in my office at three this afternoon."

"I am at your disposal, Doctor," he said, clicking his heels with a British soldier's precision. The gesture was uncharacteristically formal, as if he'd sensed the conflict in her mind and respected it.

"Harper," Quentin said, nodding to the other man. "We'll talk again."

"Yes," Harper said. He watched Quentin stride off toward the woods. Without intending to, Johanna did the same. She recalled Harper's presence only when he gave a low cough.

"A good man," he said.

"Yes." She didn't feel prepared to elaborate on that subject at the moment. She noted with pleasure that Harper had finished his meal; his appetite had returned along with his reason, "If you are still hungry, I can bring you more. Shall we go in?"

Harper struggled to his feet, and Johanna helped him regain his balance.

"Sorry . . . I'm not in better shape, ma'am," he said, flushing.

"You have been confined to your room for many months," she said. "You must be patient in recovering your previous strength." She let him take the next few steps on his own. "How much do you remember?"

He felt his beard, testing its neatly trimmed length. "I remember you, ma'am. The room, and the dog. I can't rightly say that I remember much else."

"That is not surprising. You came to stay with us—my father and me—some time ago. You've been ill, and we hoped to make you better."

"Am I?" He met her gaze with warm hazel eyes, so mild that it was difficult to believe that he'd ever had bouts of manic, even violent behavior.

Even the insane deserved as much honesty as possible. "It is too soon to be sure," she said. "But until this morning, you were not speaking. Now you are. I would like to talk more with you about what has happened, and how you feel."

Depending on how much he did remember, and how stable he seemed, she would gradually introduce the idea of hypnosis and gauge his reaction. In the meantime, she'd spend a few hours each day simply talking, and allowing him to do so.

And if Quentin's company seemed beneficial . . .

Be methodical, Johanna. One step at a time.

Harper was reachable, but far from well. Quentin seemed normal on the surface, but so much was locked away underneath.

There was no telling what might happen in the coming weeks.

Excited, even flustered in a way she considered most singular, she escorted Harper to his room to rest and threw herself into her daily routine. First she met Irene in her office and asked about the woman's new gown. Irene, unsurprisingly, was evasive; after steady questioning, she admitted that she had gone into town to buy the cloth and pattern, and made the gown herself. She pressed her lips together rebelliously when Johanna reminded her that she was not to leave the Haven grounds unescorted. Nothing could induce her to explain how she'd come by the money to purchase the rich fabric for such a garment.

Johanna dismissed Irene and considered the problem. Short of confining the actress to her room, she couldn't be sure that Irene wouldn't visit Silverado Springs again. If she took the woman into town with her more frequently, perhaps Irene's desire to "sneak out" might be lessened.

Satisfied with that temporary solution, Johanna dealt with her father's needs and visited with him for half an hour, pretending that she didn't miss his imperturbable good humor and wise council. Oscar was kept busy with a new puzzle Johanna had ordered, made especially for him by a craftsman in town—one just difficult enough to stretch his mind without causing tears and frustration.

Quentin was as good as his word, and delivered May to the parlor before making himself scarce again. May showed every inclination of wanting to trail after him, but her pallid face lit up when she saw the book Johanna had brought back from San Francisco. Books were the single topic of discussion in which May could become as eloquent as any young girl her age.

Or had been, until Quentin. Johanna suspected she could be encouraged to talk about him with very little effort. She trusted him. Could he be instrumental in helping the girl overcome her remaining fears?

If she continued to think this way, Johanna mused, she'd be forced to acknowledge Quentin as a colleague.

She buried that thought at the bottom of her mind.

Just after luncheon, she conducted a moderately successful meeting with Lewis. If he was not improving as rapidly as he had in the past, at least he was not losing ground. Irene, as usual, was utterly uncooperative and couldn't be drawn into more than the lightest of trances. She was still far from the breakthrough Johanna hoped for.

Quentin appeared at Johanna's office precisely at three o'clock, nonchalant and seemingly at ease about the coming session. Johanna waved him in and closed the door.

"Harper has made quite an improvement, I take it?" he asked.

"Indeed. I have never seen him so lucid, not since he came to us." She gathered the hypnotic paraphernalia and drew up her chair. "Now I will be able to begin working to heal the source of his madness."

Quentin moved toward her. She stood very still and waited, half afraid that he might touch her. He stopped well short of the chair and developed a sudden interest in the view out the window.

"He appears to enjoy your company," she said. "He would benefit from a friend of his own age and gender."

He looked at her. "His recovery means a great deal to you, doesn't it?"

"I have been unable to help him. Now—"

"Now there's a chance." His cinnamon eyes were darker than she remembered, filled with emotions she couldn't interpret. "I hope he knows how lucky he is."

"Science, discipline, and care will heal him, not luck."

"And you," he said softly. "The most essential factor."

She dropped her gaze. "What did you speak of, the two of you?"

"Not much. He briefly mentioned the War. I didn't press him."

"Did he show any signs of distress, or violence?"

"He displayed little feeling at all."

And neither, at this moment, did Quentin. "But he said something that troubled you," she guessed.

"No. No. He reminds me . . . of men I once knew."

And of himself. The hidden self she had yet to discover.

"If you're ready, Quentin," she said, "we will go ahead with the hypnosis."

He took up her suggestion with alacrity and settled on the chaise. She repeated the induction methods of the previous meeting, and Quentin fell into a trance with even less resistance than before.

Nothing else went as hoped. She was unable to coax from him a single new fact or memory about his time in the army, his drinking, his lycanthropy, or his childhood. Either he was not in as deep a trance as she surmised, or he had, since the last meeting, developed much stronger barriers. He might not even be aware he had done so.

At least he didn't resume his amorous advances. He remained detached and as far away as the moon.

She brought him out two hours later. He asked no questions; in fact, he seemed eager to be on his way. Johanna banished her doubts at the disappointing results of the session. She knew her own skill and worth as a doctor. Patience was the remedy for such setbacks—patience, and a firm grasp of a scientist's objectivity. Progress was merely delayed.

What she required was a greater distance from Quentin. He would benefit from the same. The most efficient way to achieve that goal was in the company of others. He should socialize with all the patients, become one of the group.

"I would like you to join us on our walk tonight," she said at the door. "We shall gather in the parlor in a few minutes."

His smile held the same outward amiability as always. "Of course, Doctor. I'll be there."

Just after five o'clock she assembled the patients—all but Harper—together in the parlor for their thrice-weekly evening stroll. Papa was strapped into his special wheelchair, showing some interest in the proceedings, and Oscar was openly eager for the excursion. Lewis wore the black overcoat and gloves he always donned no matter what the weather. Irene was defiantly dressed in a gown and shoes entirely inappropriate for the outing, her way of protesting the exercise, and possibly of showing off to Quentin. May waited outside the door, prepared to trail behind them—at a safe distance, as always.

"Please return to your room and put on more suitable shoes," Johanna told Irene. "You'll hurt your feet, and that is of no benefit to your health—or beauty."

It was an argument that generally worked with the former actress. She flounced back to her room and reappeared wearing low-heeled, button-top shoes that looked ridiculous with the gown.

They set out on the wagon path that led away from the house, south toward the road. Johanna took the lead, pushing her father's chair, followed by Oscar, Quentin, Lewis, Irene, and May.

The day's heat was dissipating at last. Birds darted from one tree to the next, absorbed in their evening songs, and the angled sunlight splashed the fields and trees and scattered farm buildings with liquid gold.

Quentin caught up with her after a quarter of a mile. Johanna took a firmer grip on her father's chair and fixed a neutral smile on her face.

"It's beautiful in this valley," he said, slowing his stride to match her pace. "I don't think I was able to appreciate it when I first arrived."

This was the perfect opportunity to set the tone of their future relationship. "It is lovely. The region where my father grew up, near Mainz, was not dissimilar."

"The Rheinhessen?"

"Yes. You have been there?"

"Once. I did some traveling in Europe now and then. I've even read a bit of German literature: " *'Was vernünftig ist, das ist wirklich; und was virklich ist, das is vernünftig.'* "

Her father looked up at Quentin and laughed. "That will never do, my boy," he said. " *'Was vernünftig ist, das is wirklich; und was virklich ist, das ist vernünftig.'* "

Startled by his participation, Johanna saw that his eyes were clear and focused, his expression animated. Quentin executed a sideways bow.

"I stand corrected, *Herr Doktor*. Do you agree with Hegel's sentiments? 'What is reasonable is real; that which is real is reasonable.' "

"I would not dare argue with the great philosopher," Papa said, shaking his head. "I am but a simple physician."

"That I very much doubt. Hegel also said: 'It is easier to discover a deficiency in individuals, in states, and in Providence, than to see their real import and value.' "

Johanna felt a burst of happiness. The conversation was entirely rational, and Quentin talked to her father as if he were an equal, not an enfeebled old man.

"Ha!" Papa slapped his right hand down on the arm of his wheelchair. "Why did you never introduce me to this young man before, Johanna? He shows great promise." He squinted up at Quentin. "Are you the new doctor? Forgive me, my memory sometimes fails me. I believe you will do very well here. *Ja, sehr gut* . . ." He lapsed into silence, withdrawing into his own thoughts.

"You were expecting another doctor?" Quentin said to Johanna under his breath.

"We had been discussing finding a third doctor to join us at the Schell Asylum in Pennsylvania, in order to expand our practice." She touched her father's head lightly, smoothing his thin gray hair. "It was Papa's dream. He fell ill before we could complete it."

"I'm sorry. We have so little control over our destinies."

He spoke of himself as well as Papa, but she would not permit self-pity. "I do not believe that. There is much we can do to influence what some regard as fate."

"Yes. You'd do battle with the gods themselves, wouldn't you?"

She heard no mockery in his voice, only genuine admiration. It was in his face as well, in his eyes. She brought Papa's wheelchair to a stop and turned away from Quentin to check on the others.

Oscar galloped past on an invisible pony, hooting and kicking up dust. Lewis's coattails flapped like the wings of a great crow. Irene walked as if she were on the stage, each sway of her hips exaggerated. May stopped as soon as Johanna did, maintaining the same precise distance behind, but her gaze sought Quentin with visible longing.

"We will take a short rest," Johanna announced, "and then return to the house." She wheeled her father onto the tawny grass at the edge of the path. They were not far from the place where she'd first discovered Quentin. She wondered if he remembered.

He sat down on the ground beside the wheelchair, plucking a dry stalk and placing it between his teeth. "Our session today wasn't very successful, was it?"

She loosened the strap that held her father safely in the chair. "Progress is not always steady. It is necessary to be patient. At least you've shown no craving for drink."

"I haven't had the opportunity. I suppose I could go into town—"

"Not while you are in my care."

"Warning noted." He patted the ground beside him. "Sit. Even doctors are allowed to rest from time to time, you know."

To decline his invitation would imply that she found his nearness disquieting. She tucked up her skirts and sat down a few feet away. Irene, on the opposite side of the path, was searching fastidiously for a rock to serve as a chair. Oscar ran around and around the field.

"I wish I could be a more promising subject," Quentin said. He tossed the stalk of grass aside. "I fear my presence at the Haven contributes very little."

She opened her mouth on a vehement protest. *That is not true*, she almost said. *You are important . . . important to Harper. To May.*

To—

"You have already agreed to pay," she said quickly.

"And you have yet to take any of my money," he countered. "You said that everyone here does his or her share of the work at the Haven, but you haven't asked me to do anything." His lids drifted half-shut over his eyes. "I'm not really as lazy as I look."

How could any man's voice be so . . . suggestive . . . even when it spoke the most innocuous words? "I shall think of something," she said. "Have you any skill in carpentry? The house needs repairs, as does the barn."

"You'll find I'm also very resourceful." He plucked a wildflower and twirled its stem between his fingers. "Tell me, Johanna—you've spoken of your father's dreams. What of yours?"

She wasn't prepared for the change of topic. "My dreams are the same as my father's. To help and heal those who suffer, using the techniques he developed—"

"I don't mean your goals as a doctor. What do you want as a woman, Johanna?"

The question was much too personal, but she wouldn't let him see how it affected her. "I do not see why the two should be different."

"Most women I've known long for a family. A marriage, children."

"I would hazard a guess that most of the women you knew in England were of your own class."

"You don't think of yourself as being in my class?"

"My father is of the *gebildete Stände*, the educated class, but hardly an aristocrat. My mother was a merchant's daughter."

"But you must confess that you are a woman, Johanna."

I have been told in no uncertain terms that I am not a normal woman at all. "I do not deny my biology."

"Science," he said. "It isn't the answer for everything."

" 'To him who looks upon the world rationally, the world in its turn presents a rational aspect,' " she quoted.

"More Hegel? I have another for you: 'We may affirm absolutely that nothing great in the world has been accomplished without passion.' "

He was playing with her again, and she could not simply dismiss it as she wished to. "My passion is for my work, as was my father's."

"Did he love your mother?"

She pushed to her feet, brushing off her skirt with more vigor than was strictly necessary. "Yes. As I loved her. You may rest assured that I have known love, Mr. Forster."

He stood up behind her, close enough that his breath teased her hair. "I never doubted that you've given love. I only wonder if you have kept enough for yourself."

His words had the unexpected effect of thrusting her into the past—her past. In an instant she was back in the parlor of the house in Philadelphia, and Rolf was the one standing behind her.

Chapter 10

"You must choose, Johanna: lock yourself away in this unwomanly profession or become what you were meant to be." His hands settled on her hips, molded themselves to her breasts. "This body was meant to be loved and bear children. Don't deny what you are—"

She turned to face him. "I cannot abandon what it is in me to be. Of course I wish to marry you, and to have children. But I am good at what I do. I can help others who desperately need it." She met his gaze steadily. "Why must I be the one to choose? Would you give up being a physician for my sake?"

He laughed. "Always so rational. You pretend to be a man. Do you have a heart like a normal woman, or is it a machine within your breast?"

His accusation hurt as little had done since Mama's death. She'd never believed it would come to this—that he, a doctor like herself, who'd once encouraged her in her studies, should betray her now and demand such a sacrifice.

"I wish only to be your equal, Rolf. Your partner—"

He pulled her roughly into his arms and kissed her: a hard, punishing kiss that bruised her mouth. It left her cold and dead inside. This was not the Rolf she knew.

Or had she simply been wrong from the start? Her skill was a threat to him. He did not want her to succeed. If she had used her vaunted intelligence, she should have seen the signs, the symptoms that had led to this moment.

"You will never be my equal, Johanna," Rolf said, pushing away from her, "or any man's, though you pretend to be one. And no other man will want what you are becoming. You'll be lonely the rest of your life, old and barren and dried up inside."

She understood then that he was right. She'd run into many obstacles during her years of study, confronted many men who thought she defied the very role God had intended for all of her sex.

Rolf had changed . . . and so had she.

So be it.

Her face felt stiff, a mask of marble without life. "If you and the world ask me to choose between my heart and my intellect, then I shall do so, Rolf. I will become the very thing you believe me to be. And I will live quite happily without the kind of love you offer."

• • •

"Johanna."

She jerked back to herself. Not Rolf's voice, but Quentin's. His hands rested on her shoulders.

"You were very far away," he said. "Who was he?"

Had she spoken aloud? "I don't know what you mean."

"You were thinking of a man. I can tell."

"It is unimportant." She tried to step free, but his grip tightened.

"Who was he?"

"The subject cannot matter to you, Quentin. You are my patient—"

"Did you love him?"

"Let me go."

He did so, but only after a long hesitation. His unwillingness was palpable.

A shiver of alarm raced down Johanna's spine. Even so small a change in Quentin—the tiniest hint of possessiveness—reminded her that she didn't truly know him.

"I am responsible for helping you," she said. "You are not responsible for me." She raised her voice. "We're returning to the house, everyone."

They answered with various degrees of enthusiasm and trooped back the way they'd come. Quentin had nothing to say, but kept to himself in a kind of brooding silence.

Once back home, Johanna bathed her father, prepared a light dinner for the group, and carried trays to Harper and Papa. Harper continued to exhibit more alertness than he had in the months before, but he was still very quiet. She resolved to set aside several uninterrupted hours tomorrow to spend with him.

After dinner the patients assembled in the parlor. Johanna opened the windows to let in the cooler evening air and made sure everyone was settled. She encouraged the evening gatherings, as she did the walks, so that none of the residents of the Haven lost touch with their own humanity.

Tonight Quentin would join them. Irene was dressed in her gaudiest gown and waiting impatiently for his appearance. Lewis hunched in his corner, whispering to himself. Oscar kept busy with his puzzle. May, much to Johanna's satisfaction, came all the way into the kitchen and hunkered down beside the door, watching for Quentin as attentively as Irene did.

He entered the room, every inch the genuine aristocrat in his brushed and mended suit, supplemented by a waistcoat borrowed from Papa. All eyes were drawn to him, even Johanna's. She couldn't help herself.

Irene sprang to her feet, collected her dignity, and sauntered over to take possession of his arm. "I'm so glad you could come to my little farewell party," she said. "I do apologize for the . . . mixed nature of the guest list."

"You look charming," he said with a slight bow. "As does everyone." He stared at Johanna, and behind his smile was an intensity reminiscent of his odd behavior during the walk.

"Come sit by me," Irene said, tugging him toward the old horsehair sofa. "We have so much to talk about."

Quentin allowed himself to be persuaded, but he continued to gaze at Johanna until he could no longer comfortably do so.

Johanna got up, too restless to continue with her medical journal. Oscar gave her a toothy welcome when she sat on the floor beside him.

"You wanna play, too?" he said, sliding the half-finished puzzle toward her.

"I'm glad you like the puzzle so much," she said. She fit a piece into its slot. He followed with another, pushing his tongue out as he struggled to make the edges match, and clapped his big hands when it slid into place.

Johanna beckoned May to join them, but she only sank down closer to the floor. Nonetheless, the very fact that she was in view was an excellent sign.

Irene alone was incorrigible. As tolerant as Quentin was with her, she couldn't be allowed to monopolize him and ignore the others.

"Irene," Johanna said, "I believe we need a little music. Would you sing for us, please?"

An opportunity to perform was something Irene could not pass up, but she cast Johanna a scornful glance. "Who'll play the piano? You are certainly no hand at it, Johanna—if you can bring yourself to get up off the floor."

"Don't be mean to Doc Jo," Oscar scolded. "It's not nice."

Irene laughed. "What would you know of 'nice,' you—"

Quentin clasped her hand. "Allow me to accompany you, Miss DuBois. My poor abilities may not do justice to your vocal talents, but I hope not to shame you."

She simpered. "You could not do anything badly, my lord."

He shared a conspiratorial look with Johanna. "You do me too much honor, Miss DuBois." He stood up and walked her to the old piano. It bore a fine coat of dust from long disuse. He had just pulled out the bench when Lewis sprang up, produced a handkerchief from his waistcoat pocket, and began to dust the piano with furious diligence. Finished with his work, he sidled past May into the kitchen to wash his hands.

"Thank you, Mr. Andersen," Quentin called after him. He sat

down and ran his fingers gently over the keys. "Only a trifle out of tune," he remarked. "It's a fine old instrument." He leafed through the brown-edged sheet music moldering in a basket beside the piano.

Irene plucked a sheet from his hand. " 'Lily Dale,' " she said. "It's frightfully old, but I shall do what I can." She returned the music to Quentin and assumed a theatrical air, more for his benefit than that of her audience.

"One moment." Quentin turned toward the kitchen door, where May waited so quietly, and held out his hand. "I'll need someone to turn the pages. Will you help me, May?"

The girl ducked her head, on the verge of flight. Then, slowly, she rose and crept into the room, hesitating every few steps like a nervous fawn. She laid her hand in his.

He positioned her on the other side of the piano, away from Irene, who was far from pleased. "I'll let you know when to turn the pages."

But May surprised everyone. "I can read music," she whispered. Even Lewis, returning to the parlor, paused at the rarely heard sound of her voice.

Johanna resumed her seat, puzzled but gratified. May's behavior was truly exceptional, and all due to Quentin. She must actually regard him as a protector, to venture in among the others.

"Well, then," Quentin said. "Shall we begin?"

Anxious to reclaim his attention, Irene hardly waited for him to play the introduction.

> " 'Twas a calm still night, and the moon's pale light,
> Shone soft o'er hill and vale;
> When friends mute with grief stood around the deathbed
> Of my poor lost Lilly Dale.
> Oh! Lilly, sweet Lilly,
> Dear Lilly Dale,
> Now the wild rose blossoms o'er her little green grave,
> 'Neath the trees in the flow'ry vale."

Irene's voice cracked on the high notes, but she was heedless of her own imperfections.

> "Her cheeks, that once glowed with the rose tint of health,
> By the hand of disease had turned pale,
> And the death damp was on the pure white brow

Of my poor lost Lilly Dale.
Oh! Lilly, sweet—"

"Stop!"

She broke off, staring at Lewis. He stood before his chair, fists clenched, face drained of color.

"What's wrong with you?" Irene snapped. "How dare you interrupt my performance. I'll have you thrown out." Her painted lips curled, and her eyes narrowed with crude cunning. "Or does my song remind you of someone, Reverend dear? Is that why you don't like it?"

Lewis didn't move. May pressed back against the nearest wall.

"I think we should try a different song," Johanna said firmly. "Something more cheerful, perhaps."

"As you wish." Irene began to sing again without accompaniment.

"Forth from my dark and dismal cell,
Or from the dark abyss of Hell,
Mad Tom is come to view the world again,
To see if he can cure his distempered brain.
Fears and cares oppress my soul,
Hark how the angry furies howl,
Pluto laughs, and Proserpine is glad,
To see poor angry Tom of Bedlam mad."

Quentin rose from the piano bench. "Miss DuBois—"

She marched into the center of the room and sang directly to Johanna, no longer making any attempt to stay on key.

" 'Will you walk into my parlour?' said a spider to a fly,
' 'Tis the prettiest little parlour that ever you did spy;
You've only got to pop your head within side of the door,
You'll see so many curious things you never saw before!' "

"That is quite enough, Irene," Johanna said. "You may retire to your room."

"Just so you can have him to yourself!" Irene shrieked. "You are the spider, weaving your treacherous webs, but I can weave webs of my own. Soon you won't be able to stop me from doing whatever I want to do. Just wait and see!"

Johanna stepped forward to grasp Irene's wrist. Irene raised her free hand and struck Johanna viciously. Johanna slapped her in return.

The room became a tableau, frozen in time. Johanna regarded her own treacherous hand with horror.

"You bitch," Irene hissed, holding her palm to her reddened cheek. "I'll make you sorry you did that. See if I don't."

Quentin took her arm. "I think you should lie down, Miss DuBois," he said. He was deadly serious, brooking no argument. "I'll escort you—"

"You whore—you harlot!" Lewis shouted. "Leave this house!"

"Be silent!"

Quentin's voice was hardly raised above normal speech, but he might as well have roared. Lewis sat down abruptly. Irene went white. May remained motionless, and Oscar began to wail.

"It's all right, Oscar," Quentin said. "No one is angry with you." Oscar sniffled and rubbed at his eyes. "May, you needn't be afraid. I'll speak to you in a few moments."

May slipped from the room. Quentin steered Irene toward the hall. She didn't resist.

Stunned, Johanna comforted Oscar and got him working on his puzzle again. She went after Quentin and found him emerging from Irene's room, his features devoid of expression. At almost the same instant, Harper stepped into the hallway. His movements were furtive, his posture crouched, as if he expected imminent attack. When he saw Johanna and Quentin, he straightened, though his gaze flicked this way and that, searching for some hidden threat.

"I heard yelling," he whispered. "What's going on?"

"Be at ease, my friend. Just a bit of a row in the parlor." Quentin grinned. "Women on the rampage. Nothing you need worry about."

Harper's shoulders relaxed. "If it's about ladies, I'd better stay out of it."

"Very wise." Quentin glanced at Johanna, who took his hint.

"I'd like to speak with you for a little while before you retire," Johanna said to Harper. "I'll come by within the hour, if that's agreeable."

"Yes," he said. He retreated into his room, and Johanna shut the door. She tested the door to Irene's room and found it barricaded, doubtless with a chair jammed against the inside knob. Well, there was no harm in leaving her alone for a while. It was probably the wisest thing to do.

Composing herself, she turned to Quentin. "What you said to Harper was inappropriate."

"Why? Because I made the comment about women? It wasn't so far from the truth."

She flinched. "I should never have struck Irene. I'm well aware of that. It was inexcusable."

"But understandable." He was as serious as he'd been in the parlor, almost grim.

"No," she said. "I am a doctor."

"And a woman with feelings that can be hurt, like anyone else. Whatever Irene's problems, she went too far."

"You don't understand. I haven't yet been able to reach her, and until I do—"

"She struck you. That cannot be permitted."

"The mistake—the misjudgment—was mine. In any case, you must not interfere."

His eyes lit, turning cinnamon to flame. "I'll always interfere if anyone tries to hurt you."

"*Not* with my patients—"

He took both her hands in a grip both painless and unbreakable. "You watch over your patients with such devotion. Who watches over you?"

"I have never needed anyone to watch over me."

"And what if it was not Irene but someone else who struck you?" he said between his teeth. "A man, capable of doing real harm?"

"None of the men here would hurt me. Certainly not Oscar, or Lewis—"

"How can you be so sure? Do you really think you know everything, Johanna?"

She stared at him, trying to make sense of this change in him. There'd been an inkling of it on the walk, and again in the parlor. He was behaving subtly, but noticeably, out of character.

"I know what I'm doing," she said, in the calm tone she ordinarily used with distraught or manic patients. "Oscar has learned how to control his strength, and as you see he is not aggressive. Lewis reacted as he did because he lost his wife in a tragic manner; Irene's song reminded him of it. I've always taken care with Harper. Are you suggesting I should be concerned about you?"

His pupils constricted in shock, and he let her go. "You think I'd hurt you?"

"If I thought you were a danger to any of us, I'd never have allowed you to stay." She sighed and rubbed her wrists, though she'd hardly felt Quentin's grip—not, at any rate, as pain. "I've seen how well you get along with May, when she would never trust anyone but me. Oscar likes you, and Harper has improved since you came." She turned away, fighting a lump in her throat. "I should be very sorry to see you gone, but I must insist that you not attempt to interfere as you did in the parlor."

Quentin's breath sawed in and out like that of a large, angry beast. The small hairs prickled on the back of Johanna's neck. Her instincts screamed for her to turn around and face him as she would a dangerous animal. A wolf.

Ridiculous. She forced herself to remain where she was until Quentin's silence left her no choice but to speak. He leaned against the wall, his hands braced to either side of his head.

So lonely. Johanna thought. *So sad* . . . "Quentin, I know you mean well—"

In a blur of motion he snapped around, mouth contorted and hands raised as if to strike. She had a single, precisely delineated view of his face. Had she not known who stood before her, she might not have recognized it.

Rage. That was what she saw—rage, and a kind of vicious satisfaction. Quentin's features seemed coarser, more brutish than she could have imagined possible.

Involuntarily she took a step back. Quentin looked like a man ready to kill.

The moment passed instantly, but not before she realized where she'd seen such a thing before. Harper had behaved so from time to time, before he'd entered his long period of cataleptic depression a year ago. He had never hurt anyone, but he'd walked on the edge of violence and might easily have become dangerous. He'd relived his service in the War as though it had never ended, prepared to attack or be attacked, kill or be killed. And after the manic periods passed, he had shown no indication of remembering what he'd said and done.

Quentin had already revisited his own oppressive, half-forgotten memories of war. Was this another manifestation, far less benign than the other?

Sweat pooled on Quentin's brow, as if he had just emerged from a battle. He slumped against the wall with a rueful shake of his head.

"You're right." he said. "I went too far. I'll try to remember my proper place from now on." He smiled to take the sting from his words. Johanna knew at once that he was unaware of his sudden alteration.

"Very well," she said, wanting very much to consult her notes. "If you'll excuse me—"

"Let me prove I'm worthy of your trust," he said, stopping her. "I've been thinking—I know how much care your father requires. He believes I'm a doctor, and he likes me. I'd be glad—honored—to see to his needs, so that you can spend more time with the others."

Time and again Quentin had pushed past the appropriate boundaries of the doctor-patient relationship, and she'd let him do it. With this offer, he reached into a part of her life that she'd kept completely private.

"I told you that my father died when I was very young," he said to her silence. "It would be as much for me as for him."

Did he mean it? And if he did, could she trust him with the only man who'd accepted her, and loved her, without question?

Just now Quentin had revealed a side of his nature utterly foreign to what she knew of him, a new face of his illness. Yet she had always intended that the Haven's residents should help each other, form friendships that would support them in their struggles. Quentin might set a good example. If she had assistance with her father, she'd be able to work more diligently with Irene, May, and Harper. With Quentin himself.

And she was touched. Deeply touched, as much as she'd been troubled a minute before.

"Perhaps you can join me when I visit with him," she said. "After that, we shall see."

"Thank you." He glanced toward Harper's room. "I've another favor to ask. I assume you'll be hypnotizing Harper, now that he's speaking?"

"When he's ready. I shall not rush him."

"I understand," he said. "I request that I be allowed to observe your meetings with him. It might improve my ability to respond when you hypnotize me. I'd like very much to be your model patient."

The mischief was back in his eyes, along with that devil-may-care grin. She found her doubts and concerns banished as if by magic.

"That must be up to Harper," she said. "If he seems competent to make the decision, I shall ask him."

"Fair enough. I promised to speak to May tonight—please give my best wishes to Lewis and Oscar, and apologize for any distress I may have caused." He took a step toward her, stopped. "I will prove myself worthy, Johanna."

He gave her no chance to reply, but swung around and strode out the back door.

· · ·

After she had seen the others to bed, Johanna went to her father's room and sat with him awhile, watching him sleep.

"I believe him, Papa," she said softly. "I trust him." She set her jaw. "I am *not* losing my reason. It is possible to think and feel at the same time, is it not? It's only a matter of finding the proper balance. That is what I must concentrate on. Balance."

Her father murmured something in his sleep that she couldn't make out. She took comfort in it nonetheless. She kissed him on the forehead and left him to his sleep.

Chapter 11

Quentin clucked softly to the old mare, encouraging her on her slow, steady pace toward Silverado Springs. The summer morning was warm, the road not unbearably dusty, and he was remarkably content to be holding the reins of a nearly decrepit equipage as different from his old racing phaetons as Daisy was from the fine-blooded horses he'd once ridden in England.

Oscar perched on the seat at his side, face bright with anticipation. His weight lent a considerable tilt to the buggy, but Quentin was glad for his company.

He'd had much on his mind the past several days. The minor incident in the parlor earlier that week, which he ordinarily would have forgotten, continued to gnaw at his thoughts. It wasn't because Johanna had rightfully reminded him that he had no place in disciplining her patients, or even her vague hint that he might be forced to leave the Haven if he didn't conform to her rules.

No, nothing so simple. The thing that most disturbed him was the brief but very real gap in his memory immediately following her warnings—the familiar sense of losing himself and returning without knowledge of where he'd gone or what he'd done.

It was the second such blank period he'd experienced since awakening in the guest bedchamber. At the Haven, he'd been out of reach of the drink that had always preceded such spells in the past. But this time, as with the first, he hadn't been drinking.

Only an instant, this time. Only a few seconds of disappearing, and then all was normal again. Johanna hadn't shown any alarm. He couldn't have done anything . . . said anything . . . too intolerable.

But he couldn't be sure. And then there'd been the conversation with Johanna on their walk earlier that same day, when he'd been so possessed by jealousy that he'd felt separated from his own mind and body.

A jealousy to which he had no right whatsoever. Johanna had taken that in stride as well, but even she must have her limits.

All he could do was try to make up for his behavior by promising Johanna the full measure of his future support and cooperation.

He'd lived up to that promise, at least. Today he and Oscar were headed into town to pick up much-needed provisions that Mrs. Daugherty hadn't the means to bring with her to the Haven. Among those supplies was lumber to replace the rotten planks in the barn, which Quentin had begun to repair.

He generally had company during his daily chores. May was his second shadow more often than not, satisfied to watch him or, on rare occasions, speak shyly of the book she'd been reading. Oscar was eager to imitate his actions, an unlooked-for responsibility that he tried to treat with the seriousness it deserved. He'd never had to hold himself up as a standard for anyone else's behavior, and it was a daunting task.

As for the others, Lewis responded with guarded civility to his questions about the roses the former minister tended in the garden. Harper was often in Johanna's office or in his room, but Quentin suspected the two of them might eventually become friends.

Only Irene avoided him, and he was glad enough for the reprieve.

Johanna was too busy to spare much time for him outside of their so-far fruitless hypnotic sessions, but he was constantly aware of her—of her scent drifting out a window, the low, familiar sound of her voice, the firm tread of her step. His heart skipped the proverbial beat every time she came near. He hid his little vulnerabilities from her quite well.

And, gradually, she seemed to dismiss any remaining concerns she might have held about him. She permitted him to spend additional time with her father, providing meticulous instruction on Dr. Schell's care. He needed bathing, help with eating, exercise of his wasted limbs, trips into the garden, and company most of all.

Quentin had seen Johanna's doubt—doubt that he could seriously wish to take on such burdensome and tedious care for a stranger. Doubt even about his motives. But after the first two days, she had trusted

Quentin with her father's morning bath and meal. She'd spent that time with the patients, Harper and May in particular, and thanked Quentin at the end of the day with real warmth and gratitude.

Johanna's gratitude. How ironic that it should mean so much to him. But looking after the elder Dr. Schell wasn't some scheme born of his inconvenient desire for one of her rare smiles. It felt almost like caring for his own father—a man he hardly remembered, dead when he was a boy. He caught glimpses, in talking to the old man, in watching him and Johanna together, of what it would have been like to grow up with such paternal love and support.

Dr. Schell's brilliance, spirit, and compassion lived on in his daughter. And Wilhelm Schell bore no resemblance to the ruling figure in Quentin's childhood.

Tiberius Forster, the late Earl of Greyburn.

Quentin's mind slid away from the image like a raindrop on the skin of a perfect grape. Tiberius Forster was long dead. That was another life, another world.

"We're not moving!"

He came back to himself at Oscar's plaintive observation. Daisy had stopped to graze on the golden grasses at the side of the lane, taking advantage of Quentin's inattention.

Quentin shook his head. "She's a wily one, isn't she? Would you like to take the reins, Oscar?"

"You bet!" He reached for the lines eagerly, and Quentin carefully placed them in the boy's hands, covering the much larger fingers with his own.

"C'mon, Daisy!" Oscar crowed, and soon they were on their way again.

Quentin had seen Silverado Springs from a distance but had never entered the town. It was as Johanna had described it to him: neat, peaceful, respectable, and well-provisioned enough for the flocks of moneyed resort-goers who came to the hot and mineral springs to bathe and improve their health. Aside from the springs and the attached hotels and amusements, it was much like a thousand other such towns that Quentin had visited, in California and elsewhere.

Retrieving the reins from Oscar, Quentin followed Johanna's directions to the general store on the main street. It would have been impossible to miss. The usual idlers lounged, smoked, or talked on the wooden porch, looking for something to alleviate their perpetual boredom. Quentin was mindful of their stares as he tied Daisy to the hitching post.

Johanna had warned him to expect a certain amount of wariness from the local populace. He couldn't help but laugh to himself; these good people might have more reason to be wary if they knew what he really was.

Oscar was oblivious to anything but the prospect of tasting the licorice Quentin had promised him. He bounded up the stairs, nearly upsetting one of the lounger's chairs.

"Damned idiot," the man muttered to one of his fellows, aiming a chewed wad of tobacco through a hole in the planks of the porch. "Shouldn't let him run loose."

Quentin paused on his way up the stairs to glance at the man, an ill-shaven lout whose belly protruded from between his suspenders. "Did he do you any harm?" he asked.

"Damn near knocked me out've my chair," the man said. "Who're you?" He snickered. "Another one of them loonies? You sure don't look like it."

"You'd be surprised," Quentin said. "My name is Quentin Forster. Young Oscar there is my friend."

The man debated how best to reply and decided to err on the side of caution. "You some hired man of the doc's?"

"I am boarding at the Haven," he said.

Another man, at the end of the row, made a low sound. "I'll bet," he whispered to his nearest companion. "Wonder how many male 'boarders' the lady doctor takes on there? Wouldn't I like to find out. She sure ain't picky . . ."

Quentin's vision dimmed, and the blood pounded in his ears. He sucked in his breath. "I shall pretend I didn't hear that remark," he said.

Clearly the speaker hadn't intended it to be heard. He took a hasty swallow from his bottle.

Before he could be tempted to take more definitive action, Quentin followed Oscar into the store. The boy had his nose pressed to the glass of the candy counter, practically ready to devour the glass in order to reach the treats within. The counter creaked ominously under Oscar's weight.

The gray-haired storekeeper seemed relieved when Quentin paid for the licorice and Oscar scampered outside to enjoy it. Quentin looked at the door, wondering if he ought to leave the boy alone with the insolent loafers.

"Don't mind them," the storekeeper said, heaving a sack of flour onto the counter. "They're all bark and no bite."

"They seem to dislike Dr. Schell," Quentin said. "Why?"

"She doesn't come into town much, so no one's gotten to learn much about her. A bit of a mystery, so to speak. People around here only know that she has lunatics at her place who would usually be in the State Asylum. Worry they might scare off the tourists, or that her patients might run mad and hurt someone." He shrugged. "And there's some who just plain don't trust a woman doctor. But she's always paid her bills, and I've found her right pleasant, if the quiet sort. I've never heard any harm of her or the people up at old Schell's place." He regarded Quentin curiously. "You can't be one of her patients."

"Because I'm too normal?" Quentin smiled and shook his head. "We all have our oddities, Mr. Piccini. Some of us are simply better at hiding them than others."

"Can't argue with that." The storekeeper filled a wooden crate with the smaller items on Mrs. Daugherty's list, set it beside the sacks of flour and sugar, and wiped his hands on his apron. "I'll go ahead and take this out, and you can square up with me afterward."

"That would be most—" Quentin stopped in the act of lifting the sack of flour to his shoulder and cocked an ear toward the door. "Excuse me just a moment."

He stepped outside to find the loiterers crowded at the porch railing, watching a scene that bore all the earmarks of a disaster.

Oscar stood in the middle of the street, turning in a bewildered circle, while a pack of boys yelled taunts at him from every side. The gang, its members ranging in age from perhaps fourteen to twenty and too well-dressed to be vagrants, had already done some damage. Oscar's licorice lay trampled in the dirt at his feet.

It couldn't be the first time he'd been mocked for his childlike slowness, but the Haven sheltered and protected him from such abuse. His eyes swam with tears. He would have made two of any of the boys, but he was heavily outnumbered. He didn't know how to defend himself against such an assault.

"Come on, you big dummy!" one of the pack bellowed. "Can't you fight at all? Or is your brain the size of a walnut?" The others joined in his raucous laughter.

Quentin dropped the sack of flour and started down the stairs. The men on the porch made no move to interfere. If they had planned to incite the bullies in their game, they thought better of it now and remained silent.

One of the bullies feinted toward Oscar, shouting and whistling, while another played at bear-baiting with a stick. Oscar flailed with one big hand and knocked the stick away. A boy, watching for his chance, maneuvered behind him and landed a punch to Oscar's backside.

With a howl, Oscar spun around, lashing out at his attacker. By simple good fortune, his fist connected with the boy's face. Blood spurted, and an explosion of dust shot into the air as the bully landed on his bottom. Oscar staggered back, not understanding what he'd done. The boy screamed in pain and rolled on the ground, clutching his broken nose.

All at once the rest of the boys flung themselves on Oscar, wolves pulling down a great bull elk. But no wolf would behave as cruelly as these humans did. Dust rose in choking waves; the smell of blood from the bully's nose filled Quentin's nostrils. He waded into the melee and thrust the boys aside with measured swipes of his arms, making a deliberate effort to leash his strength. The ringleader had pummeled Oscar to his knees, his blows striking past Oscar's upraised arms.

It was Oscar's blood that spilled now. The odor was maddening. Quentin lifted the bully by his collar, dangling him in midair like a pup held by the scruff of its neck in its mother's jaws. The boy's contorted face was the last thing he saw clearly.

Rage. Searing, mindless rage filled him. It turned his vision red and his reason to utter chaos. Shouts came to him distantly—adult cries of alarm and warning and threat. He ignored them like the squawks of so many cowardly birds.

Vultures, waiting for the carcass. Scavengers ready to attack anything too weak to resist.

They'd hurt Oscar. Hurt him . . .

"Quen'in?" Someone tugged on his arm. His gaze focused on Oscar's tear-streaked, upturned face. "I'm scared. I want to go home!"

Something in that woebegone voice reached him as nothing else could. He opened his hand and let the bully boy fall. Like a terrified rodent, the boy scuttled away.

What is happening to me?

His mind cleared, and he realized that he hadn't lost himself. He *remembered*: the rage, the desire to hurt. He hadn't gone anywhere near the saloon.

Sick fear gathered in the pit of his belly. He took Oscar by the arm and pulled him toward the buggy. Motion surged at the edges of his sight, townspeople curious and angry and ready to blame Oscar for what their own children had done. Blame Quentin as well.

Oscar scrambled up into the seat, unable to hide his terror. "Come on!" he sobbed. "Quen'in—"

"Loonies!" a man yelled. "Go on back to the madhouse!"

Quentin climbed in and took the reins. He saw with a start that the buggy's boot already held the sacks and crate from the store. The storekeeper edged up to the buggy, one eye on the growing crowd.

"I saw how it happened," the storekeeper whispered. "I've loaded up your supplies. I know the Doc's good for it. You'd better leave now."

"Thank you," Quentin said. "I'll remember your kindness."

"Don't judge us all by these few," Piccini said. His fleshy face grew sad. "My sister was never right after she had her last baby. Folks are too quick to cast out those who are different. But you might want to warn the Doc not to let that woman—Irene—come into town for a while, until things settle down."

Quentin nodded, withholding his hand for fear that he might bring the crowd's wrath down on a decent man. He slapped the reins across Daisy's flanks and turned the buggy for home.

"Don't judge us all by these few," the storekeeper had said. Quentin knew too much of men to believe they were all alike. But how was he to judge himself? He'd brought trouble on Johanna by trying to help her. How much more harshly would Silverado Springs regard her now?

And as for Irene . . . if she'd been visiting the town so frequently as to be noticed, Johanna must know.

He and Oscar were a solemn pair as they unharnessed Daisy and put the buggy away. In the privacy of the barn. Quentin looked over Oscar's injuries and found no worse than a few bruises and a small cut that would heal on its own. Oscar had done the greater damage without even trying.

Quentin shuddered. If Oscar hadn't stopped *him* . . .

Johanna would have to know of this, but not right away. Put it off as long as possible. "I think you should go and play, Oscar," Quentin said gently. "Forget about what happened in town. It wasn't your fault."

Oscar sat down on a bale of hay, head in his hands. "I was stupid."

"No. You're not—"

"I *am* stupid. I am!" He lumbered to his feet and charged out of the barn. Quentin let him go. He had much to learn about children—or those who thought like children—and Oscar was not without pride.

The house was quiet when Quentin carried the provisions inside. Lewis was reading in his parlor corner. He looked up, searched Quentin's face, and seemed about to speak. Quentin slipped past him, through the hall, and out the back door. The peace of the woods beckoned.

He Changed, assuming his wolf form with relief. He shook the taint of anger from his red coat and ran up into the hills. After a span of time that his human side estimated as half an hour, he returned to the edge of the Haven's clearing and Changed back. He was just buttoning his shirt when he realized he was being watched.

The scent was that of dry, cool skin, leached of nearly all its natural odor, and an overabundance of soap. Lewis Andersen. Quentin turned his head to watch for the betrayal of movement. Leaves rustled, and a black-clad figure fled with a snapping of twigs and branches, noisily skirting the edge of the clearing until he was out of view.

Lewis Andersen. Quentin grimaced and finished dressing. He should have taken more care, but all he'd thought to do was Change and leave his human problems behind for a short, precious time.

Had Lewis seen him Change? He wasn't the kind to report such knowledge to the world at large, but given his state of mind, Quentin very much feared such a bizarre sight would only worsen his condition. He'd surely see a shapechanger as a creature of the devil—if he weren't convinced of his own madness.

Can you possibly make matters worse? he asked himself. He was very much afraid he knew the answer.

He walked back to the house, too preoccupied to sense Johanna until she met him on the garden path.

"Quentin! I'm glad you're back." She smiled—actually smiled at him, oblivious to what he'd done. His heart lodged in his throat.

"The goods are in the kitchen," he said. "Oscar is somewhere about." He summoned up his courage. "Johanna, you and I must talk—"

"Yes, we will attempt another session this afternoon. But I wished to tell you that Harper has agreed to let you observe my work with him, and we are about to begin."

The timing could not have been worse. He was in no state to concentrate on Johanna's techniques, not when he had so much to explain.

She saw his reluctance and misinterpreted it. "I know that our meetings have not been as productive as we hoped, but I believe you may benefit from this. Harper is another excellent hypnotic subject. All our work thus far has been most promising. This is the first time I will ask him to talk of the War itself." She touched Quentin's arm lightly; the hairs stood up all over his body. "He trusts you. Quentin, and that is why he wishes to have you present."

"I wouldn't desert a comrade in arms," Quentin said with a humorless smile. "Lead on."

The chaise longue with which Quentin had become so familiar was now occupied by Harper, who looked fully relaxed, his hands folded across his chest and his eyes closed. Quentin knew that emotion seethed under Harper's skin; no human being could suffer as he had and mend so quickly.

Johanna insisted that the acceptance of one's past held the mind's true cure. Quentin's stomach knotted with dread more intense than any he'd experienced when he was Johanna's subject. God help him, he didn't want to visit Harper's past, see into Harper's soul.

But it was too late to back out now. He took a second chair behind Johanna and concentrated on her routines as she darkened the room and led Harper into a trance. Her voice was rich and persuasive, tender as a mother's.

The muscles in the former soldier's face went slack. His breathing slowed, hands rising and falling with the steady motion of his chest.

"Harper," Johanna said. "Do you hear me?"

"Yes." Harper's voice was deeper than usual, slightly slurred but intelligible.

"Good. You will now remember all the things we discussed and practiced in our previous meetings. You know there is nothing to fear."

"Yes."

"As we agreed, I am now going to ask you to remember the days when you served with the Twenty-second Indiana Regiment. As you talk of this time, you will feel no distress, nor fear, no pain unless that is what you wish. You will be able to separate yourself from all you experience if you find it too difficult. Do you understand?"

"Yes."

"Then I would like you to think back to the time when you first volunteered to serve. How you felt when you joined, and why you made the decision to do so."

Harper was silent for several moments. "I didn't want to go, you know," he murmured. "I never was much of one for fighting. Everyone in town knew that. My friends—they were all ready to join up as soon as the first shot was fired. No one said anything to me, but they looked.

I always felt them looking. And all I wanted was just to stay home and blacksmith like my pa." He sighed. "It was a good life, working with horses. I didn't think I'd like shooting people."

"That was quite natural," Johanna said. "Please go on, Harper."

"I was seventeen when I decided that I had to serve."

"What made you decide?"

"Jimmy Beebe came over to talk to me the day before. The regiment was forming up. He was all fired up to go and get him some Rebs. He gave me his pouch of tobacco and promised he'd share it with me, even-Steven, if I came along. That's when I knew."

"Knew what, Harper?"

"That if I didn't go along, he was going to die."

Johanna had no doubt that she'd heard him correctly.

She paused to consider her next question, listening to Quentin's muted breathing behind her.

She was glad to have him there, someone who understood what she was doing and could lend a measure of support. Not that she required such support. But she'd missed his company over the past few days, while she'd been so fully occupied with the other patients.

Yes; she could admit it, if only to herself. She'd *missed* Quentin. His conversation, his grin, his friendship. Oh, they saw each other at meals and during the walks and parlor gatherings, but only in passing. Not even long enough for Quentin to disquiet her with one of his vaguely salacious comments.

She'd recognized the need for distance between them, and had gotten what she wanted. Only it wasn't what she wanted after all.

What she wanted, and what was right, were two different things.

For Quentin had surprised her once again. He was very good with her father, as he was with May and Oscar. He accepted each of them for what he or she was, expecting no more. He asked nothing for himself, and if not for his complete lack of progress in their sessions, she could not have been more pleased. Pleased . . . and very much aware of her growing admiration for him.

At least the work that kept her away from Quentin also prevented any more uncomfortable scenes between them. But she couldn't forget those that had already occurred: the kiss; Quentin's strange possessiveness on their walk; his fierce, almost violent desire to protect her after the altercation with Irene in the parlor.

The consequences of those moments had not disappeared. They

had simply gone dormant, as if waiting for some new spark to bring them back to the forefront of her mind. And emotions.

Emotions she couldn't afford to dwell on now, no matter how much her heartbeat accelerated at his mere proximity. This was another test of her discipline, and she would not fail it.

She coughed behind her hand. "Harper, you said you thought your friend was going to die."

"I *knew* he was going to die," the soldier said hoarsely. "I saw it in the pouch. It came on me suddenlike. I saw him lying dead on the ground, with the tobacco spilling out, all bloody. And some other boys I knew—they were there, too. All dead."

Though his voice remained calm, Johanna knew he maintained his self-command by the merest thread. "Remember," she said, "none of these memories can harm you now. You are safe. Would you describe this knowledge of your friend's death as a sort of vision?"

"Yes."

"Had you had such visions before?"

"Yes." Harper's throat worked. "Lots of times, but never like this. Small things. I could tell where a horse had been traveling when I shoed him. I knew who Katle Young was going to marry when I held the ring her mother gave her."

Johanna resisted the impulse to glance back at Quentin to gauge his reaction. "So you could see the past and predict the future."

"Not always. Never as strong as when I saw Jimmy die. So I signed up with the Twenty-second and went south with the boys."

"Did you think you could protect them?"

"I don't know. I just knew I had to go."

"And what was it like, Harper?"

His voice dropped to a whisper. "It was hell. At first, my friends all were full of pepper and ready to fight. But then we saw how it would be. The endless marching through the mud and freezing nights, no supplies, shoes wearing out. Never enough food. And the battles. The noise." He lifted his hands to his ears and squeezed his eyes tight. "It never stopped. Jimmy tried to run away. They would've shot him as a deserter. I stopped him. And then I knew he was still going to die."

All at once Johanna understood. "It didn't only happen with Jimmy, did it?" she asked gently.

"No." Tears spilled over onto his cheeks. "All I had to do was touch my friends' guns—or their blankets, or their tin cups—and I saw what would happen to them. I kept trying to stop it. I couldn't." He clenched his fists. "They kept dying. Blown apart. Legs gone. Faces. Oh, God—"

"You blame yourself for what happened."

"I was the one who couldn't be killed. The bullets and shells never hit me. I hardly got wounded. And I was the one who should have died. *I* was—"

"Listen to me, Harper," she interrupted. "You've done very well, but we have accomplished enough for today. Now you'll allow the past to fade, let go of the pain, and prepare to return to the present."

"But I-I deserved—"

"To die," Quentin said behind her. "I deserved to die."

She pivoted in astonishment. Quentin's face was blank, his eyes staring. He gave no indication of being aware of his baffling declaration.

Astonishing. Johanna momentarily lost her train of thought, shaken by the conviction in Quentin's voice. So deeply did he identify with Harper that he'd fallen into a trance himself, and what came so spontaneously from his unconscious mind was more distressing than she could have predicted.

But this wasn't Harper's pain he was experiencing. It was his own.

He needed her. He needed her *now*.

Johanna rose from her chair and moved quickly to Harper's side. "Harper, you did not deserve to die. You did what you could to help your friends. You served with honor and loyalty. In time, you will come to understand why your memories bring so much guilt and unhappiness, and realize that you need no longer carry these burdens."

"I won't do it," Quentin shouted. "You can't make me!"

Johanna flinched. Quentin's anguish reverberated through her body, but she could not comfort him yet. She grimly concentrated on finishing the task at hand. "Harper, I will count backward from five to one. You will awaken, peaceful and refreshed, and rest until you feel ready to rise. What you remember of the War cannot hurt you, and you will begin to believe that healing is possible. Because it is possible."

"Yes," Harper murmured.

Johanna brought him out, watching carefully to make sure that he was conscious and at peace.

She turned back to the man behind her. "Quentin—" She paused at the tortured expression on his face. "Quentin, it will be all right—"

"No!" he cried. "I don't care what you do, I won't—" He tumbled from the chair and crouched on the ground, arms flung around his head. "I won't kill them!"

Chapter 12

Gott in Himmel.

Johanna sank to her knees beside him, reaching out as if to hold him, letting her arms fall to her sides again. She could not, at such a crucial juncture, forget herself, no matter how much she wished to console him. He needed her to be strong.

"Quentin, it's Johanna. You hear my voice."

He pulled his head closer to his chest and whimpered, a lost, despairing sound.

She locked her arms rigidly in place. "You do hear me, Quentin."

"Yes," he gasped. "Don't let him—"

"No one will hurt you. I will not let them." She hugged herself. "To whom were you speaking?"

"I can't—"

"He is not here now. Tell me his name."

"Grandfather." He looked up, face wet with tears. "My grandfather."

His grandfather. "*He was something of a tyrant,*" Quentin had said. "*I gave as good as I got.*"

Maybe he hadn't.

"Where are you now, Quentin?" she asked.

"In the cellar. At Greyburn."

She shivered with foreboding. "How old are you?"

"I'm . . . eleven. Almost twelve."

He was reliving his childhood—the hidden childhood she'd never gotten him to reveal in more than bits and pieces. For just a moment his glazed eyes shone with pride. "I can Change now."

"Change?"

"Into a wolf, of course. That's because I'm a man." The fear returned, wild with defiance. "That's why he wants me to—to—"

"I'm here with you, Quentin. You can talk to me. What did he want you to do?"

He chewed his lip so hard that she feared he'd tear through the skin. "The kittens. He brought the kittens from the barn." He hugged himself. "He says I have to learn. He says I should like it—"

She didn't have to ask him again what his grandfather had wanted him to do. He'd already told her. "*I won't kill them.*"

What sort of monster would ask his grandchild to kill kittens on command?

"You don't have to like it, Quentin."

"If I don't do what he says—I *won't*—he locks me up in here. Sometimes I don't know how long. I get hungry. Not very cold—" He sniffed and wiped at his nose. "We don't get cold easy. But then Grandfather brings the ropes—" He broke off and crawled to lean against the wall, curling into himself.

It was enough. She wouldn't force him to experience more of this . . . this torture. For that was what it must be. The questions could wait for another time.

"It's all right, Quentin," she said. "You're going to be all right now."

"Don't tell Braden." He stared at her almost as if he really saw her. "Don't tell him. He'll do something and Grandfather will hurt him. Rowena doesn't know. I make sure she doesn't find out. Promise you won't tell!"

"I promise." She swallowed hard. "Take my hand."

He did so with such immediate trust that she felt dizzy.

"We're going to leave here, now," she said. "Can you do what I say?"

His eyes—those rich cinnamon eyes overlaid with pain—gazed right into hers. "Yes."

"Then I want you to remember another place, another time. The Napa Valley, and the Haven, and the room where I am talking to you. You've been here before."

"I . . . can't."

"You will. It's a restful place, where the sun shines and the air smells like green things. Here you cannot be hurt."

"There is no such place."

"At the Haven there are people who care for you."

His face was utterly open, all hope and gratitude. "Do you . . . care for me?" he whispered.

It had been possible until that moment to maintain some semblance of detachment. With that simple, guileless question, objectivity shattered along with her heart. She pulled him into her arms.

"Yes," she said. "I care for you, Quentin."

His mute sobs shook her body. He fought them, as any boy might fight such humiliating weakness, and yet he clung to her. His mind had journeyed back to his childhood, but his arms were still those of a man, strong and apt to wring the breath from her lungs.

She stroked damp hair away from his forehead and murmured in what she imagined must be a maternal fashion, but she felt anything but maternal. His cheek rested on her breast. His breath burned through the fabric of her bodice. Soon he'd wake, and no longer be a child. What then?

As if he heard her thoughts, he stiffened and pulled himself up. The child in his eyes still reached for her, but she could see it—him—fading away, subsumed by another presence. Quentin, coming out of the trance at last.

But he didn't let her go. "You care for me?" he said, his voice nearly a snarl. "Liar."

Her heart stopped. "Quentin—"

"Don't call me that!" He shook her, just enough so that she felt clearly how much he could hurt her if he chose. "You think you can *help* him?"

"I don't perceive your meaning," she said. She couldn't show any hesitation now, or uncertainty. "Please explain."

They were knee to knee, chest to chest. Each of his harsh breaths rocked her forward and back. "*He* explains. I don't have to." He jerked her against him. She turned her head just before his lips touched hers.

"Never again," he rasped. "It will never happen again. Do you hear me?"

"Yes. I hear you."

"He tries to shut me out, but I won't be buried." His fingers framed her face. "He won't take what he wants. But I will."

He was going to kiss her. Not gently, not lovingly, but with the merciless drive to dominate.

"No, Quentin," she said, planting her hands between them. "It's time for you to come back. I will count backward from five to one—"

"No." He pushed her away. "*No.*" Leaping to his feet, he flung himself against the wall like a caged animal, raking at it with curved fingers. His nails bit deeply enough to tear the wallpaper.

"That's enough, my friend." A tall, lean shape passed between Johanna and the madman Quentin had become.

"The enemy is gone," Harper said. "The War is over."

Quentin swung about, teeth bared. He looked just as he had that night in the hall, more bestial than human, his features shifting into something almost unrecognizable. His eyes narrowed to slits, spewing hatred at the world.

This was the wolf he claimed to be, the dangerous lycanthrope Johanna had assumed was a product of Quentin's wounded mind. This was the transformation he spoke of, and she didn't for an instant believe that he controlled it.

She got to her feet and stood shoulder to shoulder with Harper.

"It's safe to return, Quentin," she said. "You're safe. Come back to us."

Whether it was because of her words, Harper's tranquil presence, or something within Quentin himself, he began at last to respond. The savage light left his eyes. His body went boneless, sliding along the wall to the ground.

Harper knelt beside him. "Are you all right, brother?"

Quentin squeezed his eyes shut and opened them again. "What?" He braced his hands on the floor. "Did I fall?"

"You could say that," Harper said. He glanced at Johanna with a faint frown.

She shook her head in warning. "How are you feeling, Quentin?"

"Dizzy." He pushed at the wall to regain his feet. His face was expressionless. "Something happened . . . like before, didn't it?"

Her memory made the leap to their first session, when he'd kissed her and promptly forgotten.

"I'm not sure," she said. "When I was working with Harper, you entered a spontaneous trance."

"Again?" He smiled raggedly at Harper. "Sorry about the interruption, old chap. I hope I didn't spoil it." He pressed his forehead with the heels of his hands. "I appear to be just a little too susceptible to the good doctor's expert technique."

"You are extraordinarily sensitive to hypnotic induction," Johanna said. "I had thought, given our last few sessions—"

"That I was safe?" He laughed. "My old friends in England would be amused to hear that I'm sensitive to much of anything." He looked from her to Harper and back again. "The way you're both staring at me, I suppose I must have stood on my head and recited Shakespeare. Or did I sing 'God Save the Queen' horribly off-key?"

His jokes failed to conceal the real fear in his eyes. He suspected something of what had happened. His gaze found the torn wallpaper, and his expression froze.

"I must have been very badly off-key." He yawned behind his hand. "It's all quite exhausting, really. I'm ready for a nap—if you'll both excuse me."

Johanna's stomach twisted with the realization that she was afraid. Not of Quentin, but *for* him. She'd seen him transform from hurting, vulnerable child to an angry, violent man. Neither was a part of the Quentin she knew. Both were somehow connected to terrible childhood pain—and either might be the means of destroying him.

The Quentin she knew would more likely harm himself than any other creature.

"I would like you to go straight to your room and rest," she told him. "Will you remain there until I come for you?"

"You'll be lucky if you can get me to wake up," he said. "Don't hold luncheon for me."

He gave her and Harper a choppy salute and left the room.

Harper let out a long breath and sat down on the edge of the chaise. "Was I like that when I was hypnotized?"

"No." She moved behind her desk, trying to regain a sense of calm. "Thank you for your assistance."

"What did happen, with him?"

"I cannot tell you, Harper. Not for the time being." She shuffled a pile of papers. "How do you feel?"

He cocked his head. "Better. Except that I don't really remember much of what we talked about."

"That's quite normal. You will begin to remember things as you are ready to do so. We'll continue to work toward that end."

He was silent long enough that she was forced to look up from her papers and meet his gaze.

"It's funny, isn't it," he said, "how we're all hiding, one way or another."

She searched for a response that wouldn't betray her. "It's the nature of the mind to hide from itself. But it is possible to come out of hiding, and find life again."

"You'd know best, Doc. You'd know best." He stopped at the door. "You'll let me know if you need help?"

With Quentin, he meant. With the unpredictable savage they had both confronted.

"Yes," she said. "Thank you, Harper."

Once he'd returned to his own room, she gave up all pretense of examining her notes and let the disordered tide of her thoughts wash through her.

She should be glad. Today Quentin had made definite progress—exceptional, in fact. She was now convinced that the delusions he suffered must arise out of his childhood.

But the complications of his condition only grew more formidable with every new discovery. She'd underestimated the extent of his illness. He'd illustrated his claims of lycanthropy by becoming someone—something—who possessed the ruthless ferocity of a wild beast, a barbarous taste for tyranny.

Yet there'd been the child: innocent, abused, begging for help. And the man she'd come to know, who so willingly gave of himself.

Where was the real Quentin?

Which one was the man she had sworn to cure?

An unfamiliar thread of panic lurked inside her—the very real fear that she wouldn't be able to handle his case. She had been too careless. What if he should turn truly violent and threaten the others?

What if she were forced to remand his care to someone else, at a facility where he could be restrained . . .

Sickness filled her throat. Yes, she might betray him—to people who knew nothing of the work she and her father had done, who'd put his sanity in even greater jeopardy with their ignorance and primitive treatments.

She would not trust any traditional asylum with Quentin Forster. He mattered too much. As all her patients mattered. Until she had no other option, she would continue to treat him as best she knew how.

That best must be better than she'd ever done before. The time would come when she'd have to be honest with Quentin about the dangers of his condition. As soon as she had enough information to devise a theory, and explain . . .

"I must speak with you, Miss Schell."

Lewis walked into the room, moving very much like a man with an important secret he was half-afraid to reveal, but determined nevertheless to do his duty. His chin jerked up and down several times as he came to a halt before her desk.

"I must speak with you, Miss Schell," he said again.

"What is it, Lewis?" she asked. "You seem concerned."

He shuffled from foot to foot. Johanna noted the sweat beading his brow, and the fact that the long hair he kept so meticulously combed over his balding head hung loose and unkempt.

"I am concerned—most concerned," he said quickly. "I tell you this only to protect us all from evil." He would not meet her eyes. "You must believe me."

"Please, sit down—" she began, but he shook his head.

"That man—Quentin Forster—I saw him in the woods this morning."

She came fully alert. "Did you?"

"Yes. I saw him—" He swallowed. "He was . . . unclothed."

Johanna bit back a wild laugh. Lewis's sense of righteousness would find such a thing appalling, though that begged the question of why Quentin would be . . .

Unclothed. She shivered. "Mr. Forster was in the woods, not wearing his clothing?"

"It's worse. Much worse." He closed his eyes. "He . . . undressed, and then I saw him . . . I saw him . . ."

"You may confide in me, Lewis."

He gulped. "I saw him change . . . into a wolf."

Mein Gott. At last Johanna remembered to breathe. "You saw Quentin turn into a wolf?"

"Yes. I'm not insane. I saw it with my own eyes." He clutched at the lapels of his coat. "Evil. He must be evil. The devil's work—"

Johanna stood, pressing her hands flat against the desk to quell her unsteadiness. How was it possible that Lewis had been pulled into Quentin's unconscious delusion of lycanthropy, when he could have no knowledge of it? When Quentin himself spoke of it only under hypnosis?

"Quentin is not evil, Lewis," she said. "I do not disbelieve you, but perhaps there is some other explanation for what you saw."

"No. I know what it was."

"A dog—"

"*No!*" He lifted his chin and met her gaze. "I know I have not always been well. But this was no hallucination. We are all in terrible danger."

Johanna found herself bereft of answers. Lewis was not one to fabricate tales, like Irene. Had Quentin indeed been running naked in the woods? Had he gone down on all fours and howled and behaved in such a way to persuade Lewis that he had turned into a wolf? If so, she had seriously failed in her work on behalf of both men.

A werewolf would be an unmistakable symbol of the demonic to one such as Lewis. Sin—his own and the world's—was one of his great obsessions. One she'd hoped was diminishing.

As she'd hoped the worst of Quentin's illness had been revealed.

"If there is evil, we will deal with it," she said, summoning all her calm. "You must trust me, Lewis. Wickedness has no power over us if we keep our minds clear."

His bony, austere face was filled with the desire to believe her. "I had to tell you. To warn you. We can still cast him out."

"Give me a little time to observe and determine the safest course. I am not without resources. Do you think you can go to your room and rest, now that you've shared this with me?"

He wrung his gloved hands. "You will call me if you need my help? I know of the greatest iniquities—" She saw the start of tears in his eyes. "Do not trust him, Miss Schell."

"I promise to take no chances." She walked ahead of him and opened the door. He went meekly enough to his room, though his gaze darted about the hall until he was safely behind the door.

Alone, Johanna loosened the tight rein on her emotions. She paced the length of her office and back again several times, consulting her father's pocket watch at the final turn. Bridget should have been here hours ago; it was already after lunch. The patients must be fed.

And she'd have to call for Quentin again, no matter how much he'd so recently suffered.

The kitchen door swung open, its creaking audible across the house. Mrs. Daugherty, at last. Johanna went to meet her.

"Sorry I'm late," Mrs. Daugherty said. "M' grandson had the colic and my daughter needed a bit of help." She squinted at Johanna. "You seem a might peaked. That Irene been givin' you trouble?"

"No, not at all." Irene, in fact, had been exceptionally furtive over the past few days. "Thank you for your concern. Can you prepare luncheon? I am behind today."

"'Course. Just send 'em all out and I'll take care of 'em." She began to roll up her sleeves and paused, pursing her lips. "Before I forget, I have a message for you." She rummaged in her skirt pocket. "Here you are."

Johanna took the slightly damp envelope from Mrs. Daugherty's blunt fingers. "A message? From whom?"

"Young feller in town—a doctor, like you." She winked. "A right handsome one, at that."

A doctor? Johanna turned the envelope over. Her name was written out in an elegant hand, but the sender remained anonymous. "Did he give his name?"

"I can't rightly recall. It was some foreign name, at that. Something with a 'B.' But he was quite the gentleman. Said he'd heard of you and wanted to . . . 'consult with you.' Yes, that was the word." She grinned. "I'd best get to work while you go read your letter."

A doctor. A foreign doctor, who wished to consult with her. She hadn't realized that anyone outside the valley knew of her work; she hadn't had time to write papers or attend more than a handful of lectures, let alone speak at length with her peers—if any of them would regard her as such. Few would likely remember her father after three years and a move across the country, in spite of his controversial papers and reputation as an eccentric.

Her mind crowded with speculation, Johanna hurried back to her office and opened the envelope. The stationery was lightly scented, but the writing was indubitably masculine, it was addressed to Doctor Johanna Schell.

"Dear Dr. Schell." it began. *"I hope that you will grant me the honor and privilege of introducing myself to you: Feodor Bolkonsky, doctor of Neurology from the University of Berlin. I have recently had the great pleasure of becoming acquainted with the theories of your father, Dr. Wilhelm Schell, and your own work in the field of treatment of the insane. I am currently residing in the Silverado Springs Hotel, and would be most grateful if—"*

Johanna finished the letter at breakneck speed and then read it through more slowly.

Dr. Feodor Bolkonsky. She'd never heard of him, but that was no surprise. Her life here had been meaningful but insular, set far apart from those theorists and physicians and asylum superintendents whose work was garnering recognition in the rest of the country and abroad.

This Dr. Bolkonsky knew of *her*. He knew she was a woman, and obviously didn't care. He was not only familiar with the Schells' practice, but had made the effort to find and read her father's scarce papers and was aware that she was carrying on in the wake of Wilhelm Schell's disability.

He wanted her to come into Silverado Springs to dine with him and review the hypnotic treatment that he himself had begun to explore, comparing his experiences with her own. And he asked as humbly as any student.

Only minutes ago she'd been mourning the lack of physicians who shared her ideas and passion for real cures of insanity. And here, as if sent by fate, was a man who might not only understand, but could conceivably provide her with advice in treating Quentin. Perhaps he, himself, was capable of taking on Quentin's care should she find her situation too . . .

Overwhelming, Johanna? When before have you turned coward, simply because a case became difficult?

And when, she answered herself, *was it ever so personal?*

She carefully refolded the letter and tucked it back in its envelope. She took a number of deep, rhythmic breaths to calm the too-rapid pace of her heartbeat. The prospect of losing Quentin to another doctor was a matter of professional necessity, not of personal needs. It might very well be in his best interest.

If it were possible at all.

"Sufficient to the day," Johanna thought. And today she must continue to present a tranquil and competent face to the rest of the patients. She went to the dining room to join the others for luncheon.

Half the Haven's residents were sitting down to lunch in their usual places. Neither Quentin nor Lewis was present. Harper had taken Lewis's chair, his hair neatly combed and his beard trimmed.

Irene's eyes gleamed with satisfaction, as if she harbored glorious secrets she delighted in concealing. Her attitude was markedly changed from her brooding conduct earlier in the week. May stood in the kitchen doorway, looking for Quentin. When she didn't see him, she grabbed a sandwich from a plate on the table and ran outside.

Johanna drew Mrs. Daugherty aside. "Do you think it might be possible for you to come back tomorrow and bring another girl from town? I have an appointment in the Springs and may be gone half the day and into the evening."

Mrs. Daugherty cocked her head. "Well, I do know of a girl or two who could use the work, if I can convince 'em not to be scairt. How much could you pay?"

Bless the woman for her bluntness. "If the girl is satisfactory and is willing to help you see to the patients, I'll abide with whatever you think is fair."

"Just the way you did when I first came here," Mrs. Daugherty said. "It's a good thing I'm an honest woman!"

"We couldn't get along without you. Do you think that you could go back into town this afternoon and let me know by dinnertime if you've found someone?"

"Don't see why not. If I have help, I can do all the washing tomorrow."

"Excellent."

"It's that doctor, ain't it?" Mrs. Daugherty asked. "The one who sent you the letter. Meeting him, are you?"

"He's asked to consult with me. I don't often get the opportunity."

"'Course." The older woman bustled back to the stove. "I'll get things settled up here and head back to town."

Too restless to eat, Johanna took a tray in to her father and found him clean, contented, and alert. He had a broad grin for her, and ate with real gusto.

"I've been neglecting you, Papa," she said, helping him cut a piece of cold roast beef into small pieces. "I am sorry."

He tasted a bite and rolled his eyes. "*Sehr gut.*" After a moment he looked at her. "Don't worry, *meine Walkürchen.* The young man has been very good company."

Quentin. "He's been spending much time with you?"

"A fine lad. Knows how to tell a good joke."

"You like him very much, Papa."

"Don't you?"

That old, piercing gaze caught her unaware. "Of course I do. But he is a—" She'd almost said patient, and remembered that her father had thought him a doctor.

"We made a good choice, bringing him in," Papa said. "He has a healer's touch."

A healer's touch. Her father had always been a keen judge of character. Was he still? There could be no doubt that Quentin had done him only good, as he had May.

But then there was Lewis. And Irene, who was now avoiding him. And today's disconcerting revelations.

She put her father to bed and went to seek Quentin. He was already waiting for her in the hall.

"We must talk," he said.

Her mind's eye filled with a tantalizing vision of Quentin standing naked in the woods, then shifted to the image of his face, snarling and brutal. Suddenly she didn't want to be alone with him in her office, or anywhere inside four walls.

"Yes," she said. "Shall we go to the vineyard?"

It was a place of tidily spaced rows of vines pruned into tortured shrubs, each standing alone, well-disciplined troops of obstinate old men laden with burdens of new grapes.

The kind of place where he and Johanna could be together yet totally apart.

Quentin paused to run his fingers over the plump, nearly ripe fruit on the nearest vine, pretending to be fascinated by them. All the while his senses were focused on the woman a few feet away.

Of the little he recalled from his latest memory lapse, one thing stood clear in his mind: Johanna's arms. Johanna's touch. Johanna, holding him, comforting him. Johanna's voice whispering, "I care for you, Quentin."

What had he done to provoke those words, that tenderness? And what had happened afterward to bring the wariness into her eyes, while Harper watched vigilantly beside her?

He crushed a grape between his fingers and let the pulp fall. "What did I do, Johanna?" he asked. "You told me that I entered another spontaneous trance, but I know very well that's not all." He sought her eyes. "Tell me the truth."

She paused in her own examination of an immature bunch of grapes and looked up. She was too restrained, too emotionless. Hiding something from him.

Something he wasn't going to like.

"As you know," she said, "our past few meetings have not been very successful. I haven't been able to fully hypnotize you, as I did at first. But this time—" Her body tensed as if to take a step toward him, but she reached for the nearest vine instead. "You underwent a sort of transformation. It was as if you were indeed a child again. A child who had suffered much."

He laughed, torn by mingled relief and dread. "Ah, the agonies of youth. I must have disgusted you."

"*Stop.*" She didn't touch him, but the sheer force of her determination silenced him. "You make light of it, but things happened in your childhood that must have affected you deeply. You told me about your grandfather—"

Her voice faded. Between one moment and the next, his mind went blank. Pictures, like photographs frozen in time, came to him one by one. Greyburn. Playing on the vast lawn with Rowena and Braden. The Great Hall hung with its swords and shields and immense wooden doors carved with images of wolves and men. His mother in bed, slowly dying. The room with the armor, where Grandfather dealt out punishment. And the cellar . . .

A swell of dizziness sent him grabbing a handful of leaves as if their frailty could support him. They tore from the vine and fluttered to the ground.

Johanna caught him in her arms. She held him until he could stand again, and let him go.

"I am sorry," she said. "I know this will not be easy for you, Quentin. But I believe what happened today is significant. You must not give up."

He clasped his hands behind his back to disguise their trembling. He wanted to give up. If not for the memory of Johanna's arms about him, protecting, caring . . . loving . . .

"Was that all I did? Behave like a child?" He clenched his teeth. "Did I become . . . aggressive?"

The minute alterations in her scent and her stance gave her away, though she hardly moved. "Have you reason to believe that you might?" she said, her voice unnaturally quiet.

She was sidestepping his questions with more of her own. How could he explain? How, when he didn't understand it himself? "There may have been times when I didn't behave quite properly."

"Times you don't remember, because of the gaps in your memory? Yes, you told me about them in our first session, but I assumed—" She broke off and looked away, her expression bleak. "Have you experienced such gaps since you came to the Haven?"

He went cold. "Yes."

"But you have not been drinking."

He shook his head.

"Do you remember *any* occasion when you became aggressive, here or in the past?"

Until this morning, he could have answered "yes" with perfect honesty. Until this morning, he'd had only the sense of wrongness following his many binges. He'd see wariness in the eyes of strangers, sometimes fear, even hatred. That was when he knew it was time to move on.

But this morning, in town, he had remembered: the anger, the wildness, the desire to hurt those who had bullied Oscar.

"You must be honest with me, Quentin." Her face had gone a little pale under its ruddiness.

"I've tried to be," he said, choking on the half-truth. His nails bit into his palms. "Did I attempt to hurt you, or Harper?"

"No." She wasn't lying, but she withheld something from him, and she wouldn't meet his eyes. The only solace he could find was in her nearness; she still trusted him enough to put herself within his easy reach. He was torn between the desire to weep and to catch her up in his arms and kiss her until she was breathless.

"I would never hurt you," he whispered. "Not you or anyone at the Haven. But there is something you must know." He gazed off across the rows of vines, and beyond to the fields and wooded hills. "Something happened this morning, when I went into town with Oscar."

He told her, slowly, of the incident in Silverado Springs, Oscar's predicament, and what he had done. She listened as dispassionately as if he were reciting a list of the provisions he'd brought back from town.

"You were trying to protect Oscar," she said after a long, charged silence. "You didn't hurt the boy."

"No."

"Then it seems to me that your reaction was not unwarranted." She spoke as if by rote, all passion quenched. "Oscar could not defend himself. It is in our desire to succor the weak and helpless that we rise above the beasts."

Was she creating excuses for him, or had he failed to make her understand? *You do a disservice to the beasts, Johanna. It is men who are the savages.*

"I fear," he said, "that I didn't improve the Haven's reputation in Silverado Springs."

"That does not concern me. It will take time to make people realize that insanity or mental deficiency is neither a shame nor a sin." She blinked several times, returning from a place inside herself, and finally looked at him.

"When you first came to us," she said, "I thought the drinking was the cause of your illness. I was wrong." She searched his eyes, piercing straight to the heart. "It's the shadows that haunt you. The shadows of your past. The ones that came to life in your childhood, and followed you into India. And led you finally to us."

Quentin felt as if she'd sifted his mind like one of the true loup-garou blood. She knew him better than he knew himself. But when had he ever really known himself?

She drew in a breath. "You do want help, Quentin. No matter what difficulties we may face."

God help him. "Yes."

"Even if it means—" She paused, and again he was left with the certainty that she had stopped herself from speaking frankly. But not because she was afraid of him. He hadn't yet driven her to that.

Did she fear *for* him?

"There is one more thing I must ask you now," she said.

He braced himself. "Ask."

"Lewis came to me today. He claimed to have seen you change into a wolf."

Quentin couldn't quite stifle a bitter laugh at the absurdity of it. "Oh, lord."

She simply stared at him. "Were you running in the woods unclothed, as Lewis claims?"

How could he answer? "I was in the woods. I did a bit of running."

"And did you feel the desire to become a wolf, Quentin?"

The quandary was most ironic: to let Johanna believe him even more insane than he was, or tell her the unvarnished truth.

If any human could be trusted, with the facts of his nature, she could. But such knowledge would place more burdens upon her—the burden of belief in the face of all she knew, the burden of secrecy . . . and the burden of acceptance. If she *could* accept.

It was too great a risk. Their relationship hung in the balance.

And what relationship is that?

"A wolf, at least, very seldom doubts his own sanity," he said at last.

Her face revealed her thoughts as distinctly as chalk on a slate. "Is this all you have to tell me?"

"I wish I were not such a disappointment to you, Johanna."

Rare temper sparked in her eyes. "You did not mention any of this to Lewis?"

"No. I was trying for a little solitude."

She clearly had more to say, but held her tongue. "Lewis was very upset. It will be best for you to stay away from him. And if you feel any urge toward—"

"Running naked in the woods?"

"—any desire to turn into a wolf, you will come straight to me."

"I understand. The next time I feel the need to divest myself of my clothing, I will most certainly go straight to you."

Her fair skin caught fire. "We'll continue this conversation later. I shall be going into town for part of the day tomorrow, and have arrangements to make."

He caught her arm as she turned to go. "I have a question for you, Johanna."

She tilted her face to his, and his body tightened with desire.

"When I was in my trance . . . did I kiss you?"

The flush spread from her neckline to her forehead. It was all he needed to know. He bent just enough to fit his mouth to hers, and kissed her again. Lightly, a mere brush of the lips was all he dared to attempt. The shock that coursed through him was as powerful as anything he'd felt while buried deep in the aroused body of a woman in the throes of her passion.

Any woman but Johanna.

She didn't strike him, or stumble away. Her eyes lost their bright hue, leaving her cheeks with the only color in her face. Her lips parted and closed again without uttering a sound. If not for the heightened richness of her scent and the audible speeding of her heart, she might have seemed unmoved.

When he let her go she simply turned and walked back toward the house, her skirts trailing unheeded in the fecund earth.

Chapter 13

The thick limb of the old, blasted oak split in two at the first blow of Quentin's axe. It was only one of many such branches he planned to reduce to firewood this morning; no telling how long the pieces of the felled tree had lain at the side of the house, awaiting someone able and willing to make them useful.

Winter was far away, but Quentin had a clear choice of vigorous physical labor or going in search of a bottle.

He swung the axe again. The morning was hot, and his bare skin ran with sweat. May and Oscar had watched for a while, well out of the way of flying chips of wood, and then had gone off to the woods. Lewis was avoiding him, as expected, along with Irene. Mrs. Daugherty and a hired girl from town were busy with washing. And Johanna . . .

Johanna was gone to town. On business, she said. Something about meeting another doctor. Quentin felt her absence like a physical ache.

His entire body ached with wanting her.

A chunk of wood the size of a man's thigh flew a good several yards and landed with a thud. Quentin let the axe slide from his grip and wiped his hands on his trousers.

Careful. He might find chopping up a tree satisfying given the scarcity of more pleasurable exercise, but not at the risk of doing real damage to the landscape or its denizens. He retrieved the axe, clamped his teeth together, and lifted it for another attack. He drove the head so deep in the wood that it stuck. He snorted in disgust.

"The tree's already dead, friend."

Quentin left the axe where it was and turned on his heel. Either Harper had approached with the silence of a loup-garou, or Quentin had gone deaf to the world. He thought the latter much more likely.

Harper raised his hands. "Sorry. Shouldn't have snuck up on you like that."

"No harm done," Quentin said, concealing his surprise. It wasn't that he and Harper hadn't talked, but this was the first time the man had sought him out.

And Harper was beginning to carry the look of a healthy man— healthy in body and spirit. His eyes were no longer sunk so deeply in his face; the etched lines between his brows and at the sides of his mouth had flattened. There was even a hint of greater fullness under his cheekbones, a little more flesh over his ribs.

That was how much good a few hypnotic treatments with Johanna had done him.

But it was the expression in Harper's eyes that had changed the most. They hadn't entirely lost their haunted look, but they were clear and sane. No more retreating into a world of his own. He was of *this* world now, and planned to remain in it.

He had more backbone than Quentin did.

Company was not what Quentin had in mind, but now that Harper was here he felt the tension drain from his muscles. Any distraction from thoughts of Johanna was welcome.

He sat down on the largest branch and stretched his legs. Harper joined him, turning his face up to the sun.

The quiet between them was comfortable, almost comforting. Quentin hadn't expected it. Harper had witnessed his spontaneous trance yesterday, and all that it entailed. It wasn't his business to with-hold judgment, as Johanna did, and yet he seemed perfectly at ease.

Perhaps nothing so bad had happened after all. But if Johanna had failed to tell Quentin the whole truth about yesterday's incident, Harper might be persuaded to fill in the blanks.

"Thank you," he said. "For what you did yesterday."

Harper shrugged. "Just helping a comrade in need."

"Even though we didn't fight for the same country, or in the same war?"

The other man's gaze had an uncanny directness. "You sure about that?"

He was equally direct in his speech. Quentin bit back the impulse to ask him what he meant.

"I seem to remember," Quentin said, "you saying something about the enemy being gone, and the war over. I gather that I needed the reminder."

Harper didn't answer straight away. He stretched out his own legs— long enough to match Quentin's—and cracked his knuckles. Each movement he made was that of a man who felt joy in the simplest actions.

A simple man, Harper. Except that he claimed to see visions.

"You needed to be reminded, then," Harper said at last.

"Because the enemy isn't gone," Quentin said. "The war isn't over." He smiled bitterly. "Are you here about yesterday, Harper? Do you have something to tell me?" His mind raced with dire possibilities, matching the tempo of his heartbeat. "Did I do something to frighten Johanna?"

"Doc?" Harper chuckled, as if he found the notion of Johanna afraid inconceivable. "No. Not in the way you mean."

Quentin released his breath. "What did I do, Harper?"

"Reckon she'll talk about that in her own time." Harper searched his pockets for something that wasn't there. "I don't remember very much of what I said. Must have talked about what happened during the War. Don't want to think of that yet. Not just yet." He shivered. "Doc says it'll come back to me when I'm ready. I reckon it's the same with you."

So Harper wouldn't discuss it as Quentin had hoped, not without further prompting. Still, his casual manner laid to rest Quentin's most immediate fears.

"Do you remember anything about the past few years, while you've been with the Schells?" he asked.

"Not much. Didn't want to come out. Not until . . ." He shot Quentin a keen look. "Why're you here, Mr. Forster?"

"We hardly need stand on formality." He offered his hand. "Quentin."

"You know my name." Harper gripped his hand with strong, thin fingers. "I don't remember when you first showed up, either."

Quentin rested his palms on the rough, peeling bark of the oak. "I . . . stumbled across the Haven two weeks ago."

"Seems longer."

"It *feels* longer." As if he'd known the people of the Haven forever. Wanted Johanna forever.

Harper closed his eyes. "My family sent me to the docs years ago. Guess I was too hard for them to care for, after I went back to Indiana. I know I was crazy. I owe whatever I've got now to Doc Schell."

Quentin shifted on the branch. He didn't want Harper's personal confidences. The man bared his heart for all the world to see.

As he'd bared *his* to Johanna.

"She is a remarkable woman," Quentin said stiffly.

"Is that what you think?" Harper nudged at the dirt with the toe of his boot. "I reckoned you had a slightly different opinion."

Quentin jumped up and paced away. "I don't understand you."

"You understand." Harper leaned back, clasping his hands behind his head. "You're pining after that woman, and she feels the same. It's just that neither one of you'll admit it."

Quentin clenched his fists. Was it that obvious, then? Or was Harper the only one sane, experienced, and observant enough to notice?

"One of your visions, Harper?" Quentin snapped without thinking.

"Guess I must have talked about that when I was hypnotized," Harper said. "Seeing things, and all. Don't blame you for doubting." He scratched his beard. "It's something I can't help. Every time I touch a thing that people have touched—well, it happens. It's just that for a long time I wasn't letting anything through."

Had Quentin been an ordinary man, he might have scoffed at Harper's words. Who, after all, believed in visions spawned from merely touching an object?

Who believed in werewolves?

"I reckon you need proof," Harper said.

"You have nothing to prove to me."

"No. It's always our own selves we have to prove to." Harper stood up and reached for the handle of the axe that stood almost perpendicular to the stout oak branch in which it was embedded.

"You've been working with this axe," he said. He tugged at the handle, but it wouldn't be moved. "You didn't work long, but you put a lot into it. Enough for me to see."

The short hairs stood up on the back of Quentin's neck. "See what, Harper?"

"A little of you." He frowned. "Isn't easy to explain. Sometimes . . . I can feel something about a person from a thing they just touched. If they only used it a brief while, it doesn't linger. If it's a thing people have had for a long time, that's what makes the difference. Sometimes I see what a body's been doing, or where he's been in the past. Or I see what's going to happen to him." His prominent Adam's apple bobbed. "Right now, I can see what you intended to do—chop this tree to bits because you wanted to stop thinking about other things."

"Very good," Quentin said with heavy sarcasm.

"You think you can stop wanting the lady if you tucker yourself out. But you aren't going to finish what you started."

"Perhaps because I'm sitting here instead of working."

"I'm just telling you what I see. And what I don't see."

"Is that why you're here, then? To predict my future?"

Harper clasped his fingers together until his knuckles stood out from the flesh. "I wasn't able to help my friends when I saw what was coming for them. Maybe this time . . ." He sought Quentin's gaze, his own earnest and grave. "I see that you have many trials ahead. Someone is following you—someone you know. He'll hurt you if he can. You may find what you seek, but your fate depends on the decisions you make."

Quentin laughed. "Isn't that true of every man's fate?"

"No." Harper looked up at the bulk of Mount St. Helena rising to the east. "Or if it is, I can't always see it."

"That's fortunate, or you'd be very unpopular among your fellow men."

Pain flashed in Harper's eyes. "I found that out early on. That's why I never talked too much. People don't want to know. I didn't want to know, either."

Quentin felt something disagreeably like shame. Who was he to mock this man? Harper had his own tribulations, and he thought he was trying to help. He exposed himself out of a sense of friendship. He thought Quentin was worth the effort.

True friends had been a rare commodity in Quentin's life, through no one's fault but his own. He'd either driven them away or run from them, every one. Quentin Forster, the ever-popular, who made people laugh or gasp or shake their heads, but never left them bored.

And he always left.

"I'm sorry," he said. "Some secrets are best left unshared."

"And some have to be." Harper looked back at him. "You've been running a long time, my friend. Pretty soon you'll have to stop running and face what's after you. There's no other way."

"You received all this from an axe handle?"

"No." Harper dangled his hands between his knees. "No."

Quentin took the handle of the axe in both hands and jerked it free. "Thank you for your advice. Now, if you don't mind, I think I'll continue my work—"

Harper stood up. "You've come to the right place. Quentin. This is where you make a stand, and fight."

Quentin swung around, and Harper stepped away from his bared teeth. "Will Johanna come to harm by helping me? Will she?"

"Is that what you're most afraid of, or is it the way you feel about her?"

"*Will she?*"

"I don't see everything. I just know that you and the doc—" He sighed and shook his head. "I've told you all I can."

"You said someone was following me, someone I know. Who?"

Harper took another step back. "I have to rest now." His voice grew muffled, detached. "I'm tired."

"Harper—" Quentin reached out, but Harper was already walking back toward the house, stooped and weary. Quentin let him go.

"Your fate depends on the decisions you make," Harper had said. But it wasn't just Quentin's own fate at stake. Harper had told him little about himself he didn't already know. And as for the business about someone stalking him . . .

He thought about the many times he'd lost track of hours and events, and his frequent sense of wrongness following those times. Had he committed some reprehensible act that had won him enemies? If so, why hadn't he sensed pursuit? Loups-garous had too many advantages over humans, at the very least in the keenness of their senses. And he hadn't met another werewolf in all his journeying across America.

But he *was* running. Harper was right about that. The soldier had recognized a man running from himself.

The very thing that made him want to run from the Haven was the same element that kept him here, chained to this place by fragile dreams and desperate hunger.

Johanna.

"You're pining after that woman, and she feels the same. It's just that neither one of you'll admit it."

Hope had an insidious way of popping up in the most unexpected places. Deadly hope, that intensified desire to fever pitch.

Desire obliterated every other need, even the need for escape. The very idea of lying with Johanna was more than he could bear. It raised within him the rapacious predator that wasn't appeased with stolen kisses in vineyards, or a gentleman's restraint. It urged him, over and over, to let go. Take what he wanted.

Take Johanna.

She wants you.

He swore foully and slammed the axe into the branch.

Half of the branch spun into the air and flew like a cannonball to the edge of the woods. He could prove at least one of Harper's predictions false.

He raised the axe and brought it down on the branch with all his strength.

Johanna was already to the edge of Silverado Springs before she realized she'd driven the entire distance with no notion of how she'd made the trip.

She gave thanks to patient, reliable Daisy, who'd followed the path to town on her own. At the moment, the horse seemed to possess more intelligence than her owner.

The same scene kept repeating itself again and again in her mind, just as it had done all last night and this morning.

"When I was in my trance, did I kiss you, Johanna?"

She touched her lips. The kiss in the vineyard was nothing compared to the one he'd given her during his first hypnotic session, yet it had been all she could do to preserve her mask of indifference and walk away as if she remained unmoved.

Was he finally remembering that first kiss? Did he remember her uninhibited response?

She could only pray he did not. At least she'd given him no encouragement. And they would both have more vital concerns to explore in their next session.

If there was a next session.

She sat up straighter in the buggy's seat and patted the top of her hair. All pins were in place, and she wore her best dress—the only one really suitable for meeting a fellow physician. For the next few hours, she hoped to be thinking and speaking of nothing but professional matters.

Silverado Springs's main street was sleepy at this time of day, when luncheon was past and anyone who had no need to be working outside sought shelter from the heat. Even the usual loafers at the general store were absent. But as Johanna drove Daisy to the Silverado Springs Hotel, she passed a handful of townsfolk who looked at her askance and walked quickly away.

Quentin had warned her. He'd warned her about many things, if she'd had the common sense to listen.

She arrived at the hotel and gave Daisy into the keeping of the stable boy, providing the lad with enough coins to see to her comfort. There was no mirror to check her appearance, so she satisfied herself with a few more minor adjustments to her coiffure and brushing off the narrow skirt of her dress.

The Silverado Springs Hotel was no longer the fashionable place it had been a decade ago, but it did enough business to maintain the gardens, grounds, and mineral baths that were its claim to fame. The lobby was empty save for a tourist couple discussing possible local excursions with the concierge.

Johanna scanned the lobby a second time and sat down to wait in one of the slightly worn chairs. She was early, and it wouldn't do to seem overeager. This Dr. Bolkonsky might prove to be a disappointment, after all.

She picked up a magazine and was idly perusing an advertisement for women's hats when she smelled the strong and woody scent of expensive cologne.

Her gaze moved up from the man's highly polished black boots with white spats, snug gray trousers, single-breasted blue coat over a gray silk waistcoat, immaculate shirt and cravat to the face above his starched stand collar. There she stopped, catching her breath.

He was beautiful. No other word would suit. And though her head had never been easily turned by masculine beauty—at least not until two weeks ago—she found herself hardly able to believe this man was real.

Golden hair spilled in waves to his shoulders, framing a face made to inspire angels to flights of song. His features were strong enough to be completely male, but delicately carved, refined with the aesthetic appeal of a true intellectual. His eyebrows were several shades darker than his hair, lending his expression greater definition; his nose held an aristocratic arch. The sensitive mouth curved up in a charming smile.

Charming, beautiful, perfect. Too perfect, she decided. A man without flaw must inevitably grow tiresome. Quentin's face—attractive but humanly imperfect—hovered in the back of her mind.

"Dr. Schell, I presume?" the man asked, banishing Quentin's image. He tipped his top hat and clicked his heels. "I am Dr. Feodor Bolkonsky, at your service. *Sehr erfreut, Sie kennenzulernen, Frau Doktor.*"

"You speak German!" Johanna rose, offering her hand. He took it in a firm clasp that did not condescend to her gender. *"Sagten Sie nicht, Sie hätten in Deutschland studiert, Herr Doktor?"*

"Ja, in der Tat." He switched back to English, still smiling. "I have made it my business to learn everything possible about your work, and your father's. I have been looking forward to our meeting with great anticipation."

"As have I." She returned his smile, feeling foolish for no good reason. "There is so much I have been unable to discuss with others of like mind."

He extended his arm. "I think you will find me very much of a mind with you and your father, Dr. Schell. It was because of my interest in hypnosis that I first encountered the elder Dr. Schell's work, and realized that much I had been considering had already been taken up by you. I hope you do not mind my familiarity; I feel as if I know you."

"I am not one to stand upon formality," she answered. "To the contrary, it is excessive dedication to useless convention that all too often stands in the way of true progress."

"Ah! A woman after my own heart. I can already see that we think alike." He briefly rested his hand on her fingers. "We both believe that what some consider irregular methods are often the only ones that bring results."

He led her to a small private room off the main dining salon, where he offered her a seat and ordered refreshments. "It is some hours until dinner, but I thought we might occupy them with no difficulty." He took the seat beside her. "I hope you brought some of your case notes and observations, Dr. Schell. I've heard something of the Haven since I arrived in town."

"I'm sure you didn't judge us on the rumors circulating here," she said, concealing her unexpected anxiety. "Many people have an unreasoning fear of madness, when so few of the insane pose any danger whatsoever."

"As you say. I am sure what you do here is the work of a pioneer who deserves far more recognition than she has received."

Johanna blushed as she hadn't done with anyone but Quentin. "You give me too much credit, *Herr Doktor*—"

"You will call me Feodor. No formalities, *verstehen sie?*"

"Yes." She sat forward in her chair. "I am not pursuing this work with an interest in fame. It was my father's hope that we might develop new techniques to ease the burden of insanity. I believe we have made real progress, and I am more than happy to share what we've discovered. If you have worked with hypnosis, I have no doubt that there is much I can learn from you . . . particularly if you have recently been in Europe. We are so out of touch, here."

"I hope to remedy that situation," he said. "I've brought texts from Germany and France, as well as some of my own notes." His smile warmed. "I feel sure this will not be our only meeting."

Johanna resisted the urge to clear her throat nervously. It was much too soon to bring up Quentin's case, but Feodor Bolkonsky seemed a most extraordinary man. He might very well be what she'd been hoping for.

"Will you be staying long?" she asked.

"I am currently residing in San Francisco, which is why it was possible for me to seek you out. To my great good fortune."

"I was recently in San Francisco for a lecture," she said, flattered by his compliment. "I don't recall seeing you there—"

"Sadly, I was out of town at the time." He lifted a brown leather satchel resting against the side of his chair and set it on the small table between them. He opened the satchel and pulled out a pair of new books. "I hope you'll accept these as a token of my esteem, Dr. Schell."

She touched the covers reverently. Both were texts by well-regarded neurologists in Europe whose works she had been unable to obtain in America. "Thank you . . . Feodor. You must call me Johanna."

"I will, with pleasure."

They spent a few more minutes in small talk, on subjects ranging from the comparative weather in San Francisco and the Napa Valley to the latest play Feodor had seen in the city. But then the real discussion began. Johanna swiftly lost track of time as they exchanged opinions on such fascinating topics as Wundt's *Principles of Physiological Psychology* and Charcot's theories on hysteria.

Feodor's knowledge of hypnosis was more thorough than that of any other doctor Johanna had met, even in the East. He agreed with her belief that insanity was not merely the result of lesions of the brain, but often stemmed from purely emotional causes. He shared her hope that hypnosis might prove an invaluable method to cure many types of madness, and possibly a number of physical illnesses as well. She couldn't wait to hear his thoughts on her theory that taking patients into their pasts, in search of inciting causes of insanity, was highly beneficial.

They hadn't yet reached the subject of specific cases when Feodor pulled out his watch and made a sound of surprise. "How quickly the hours have flown. I see it's time for dinner. I've arranged a private meal for us here. It will allow us to continue our talk."

"That sounds excellent." When he turned away to summon a

waiter, she touched her cheek, wondering if it looked as warm as it felt. Her mouth was dry from the long conversation.

"A little wine before dinner?" Feodor asked. A waiter had already cleared and set the table, and was presenting a bottle of wine in a silver cooler.

"Please," Johanna said. The waiter poured, and Feodor tasted his wine with a connoisseur's deliberation.

"It will do." He signaled the waiter to pour for Johanna. In spite of her desire to be cautious, thirst made her take a much larger sip of the wine than was prudent.

"Bring water, as well," Feodor ordered the waiter, who hurried off. He leaned back in his chair and watched Johanna. She set down her glass, still strangely flustered at being the focus of his attention.

"I hope," she said, "that after our meal I may have an opportunity to consult with you about a particular patient. The situation is rather delicate—"

"You may, of course, rely on my complete discretion. I will be most interested to hear the details." He sipped his wine. "You said that you have four patients, I believe?"

"Five, now—I have a new case as of two weeks ago. And one of the original four is really not a patient in the strictest sense of the word. He, like the others, had few choices about where to go."

"But you and your father took all of them in."

"We have benefited as much as they have."

Feodor leaned toward her. "You are too modest, Johanna. These people are not merely medical subjects to you."

She couldn't argue with him in that. She wondered how well she would do in any argument with such a man.

And yet she wasn't disturbed at the idea of having met her equal, a male doctor who neither condescended to her nor betrayed resentment at her accomplishments.

He captured her gaze, drawing her out as surely as the summer sun brought the Valley's grapes to ripeness. "Who is your most intriguing patient, Johanna?"

"Quentin Forster," she answered, without thinking. She'd meant to discuss her cases in general terms before revealing names, and then only if she felt comfortable in doing so.

"Is he your newest one?" he asked.

Now that the subject was broached, her feelings were decidedly mixed. She was inclined to trust Bolkonsky, and he definitely had the necessary skills and approach to treat someone like Quentin. But to speak candidly about Quentin was going to be more difficult than she had imagined.

"Yes," she said. "A case of dipsomania, complicated by . . . delusions of lycanthropy."

"Fascinating." Feodor stroked his lower lip. "Was he brought to you by family members?"

"No. He found us."

"And have you had success in treating his condition?"

"I am . . . presently considering my options."

"Tell me about him," Bolkonsky said. "Perhaps you can benefit by a second opinion."

She took another quick sip of wine. "I was not being accurate when I said that Quentin was my most intriguing patient. Irene DuBois is also a considerable challenge—"

"Irene DuBois? The actress? I saw her once on Broadway. Very . . . interesting."

Surprised, Johanna glanced at his face and caught a faint shift in expression, as if he'd blurted out something he hadn't intended to say.

"My apologies for interrupting," he said, recovering smoothly. "You were speaking of Quentin Forster—?"

"Actually, my greatest progress has been with a former soldier in the War, who has suffered intermittent mania and long periods of catalepsy and melancholy. Let me tell you a bit about him, instead."

Feodor listened, but she could have sworn that a flash of displeasure darkened his ice-blue eyes. That, she decided, must be the work of her overly sensitized imagination.

Soon enough dinner arrived to rescue her, and they ate in relative silence. The food was delicious, exquisitely prepared, and nothing like Mrs. Daugherty's plain but nutritious cooking. Johanna enjoyed it less than she'd expected. She deliberately avoided finishing her wine, even when Feodor offered more.

But after-dinner conversation returned to easier channels. She rose to leave, several hours later, in good charity with Feodor Bolkonsky and somewhat bemused by her earlier disquiet.

"Thank you so much for the dinner, and the excellent company," she said.

"You will come back tomorrow?" Feodor asked as he escorted her to the stable, where they waited for the stable boy to harness Daisy. "I realize that you have your own business to attend to, but I should very much like to continue our discussion of this intriguing patient of yours."

"Harper?"

"Quentin Forster. A lycanthrope is something I've never encountered before. And it's precisely the kind of case I feel is best suited to my particular skills."

How could she continue to demur, when Bolkonsky was so eager to help? She couldn't have been given a more advantageous opportunity.

"I look forward to it." She gave the well-fed horse a pat on the withers and accepted Feodor's help into the buggy. "Is two o'clock satisfactory?"

He took her hand and kissed the air above it. "More than satisfactory."

"Until tomorrow, then. *Auf Wiedersehen.*"

"*Auf Wiedersehen,* my dear doctor."

Johanna hurried Daisy into a trot, following the path by the last light of day. Something like elation hummed through her body and filled her mind with a hundred new ideas. How much she'd missed, living here in the country! But surely there were few like Dr. Bolkonsky, who could understand and match the flow of her thoughts so perfectly.

Mrs. Daugherty was waiting up for her, concern evident in the set of her mouth. "Thought you'd never get back," she said. "My girl's gone home."

"I'm sorry. I shouldn't have stayed away so long." She had a powerful urge to hug Mrs. Daugherty, which would doubtless startle the old woman into believing she had run mad herself.

"I take it yer meetin' went well?"

"Very well, thank you." She caught the smells of leftover dinner in the kitchen. "Everyone has retired?"

"Far as I know. Since you weren't here, they all went to bed early. I checked up on your pa, but young Quentin has been takin' right good care of him."

"Yes." Her heart did a somersault at the thought of seeing him again. She felt so much hope.

And a very strong need for a long, hot soak. "I know it's late, Bridget, but could you help me prepare a bath?"

"I always keep water heatin' on the stove." The older woman squinted at Johanna and slowly smiled. "Well, well. You're in the mood for luxuriatin', I can see that. He is a handsome sort, your doctor."

Johanna pretended not to hear the innuendo. "If you're sure you don't mind—"

"Not at all. You just go to your room and I'll take care of the rest."

Tripping lightly down the hall, Johanna paused to listen, hearing only the quiet of a settled household. Papa was asleep. She went to her room and threw open the windows to the evening breeze.

Her bathtub, separate from the hip bath used by the others in the pantry off the kitchen, was set in a corner of her room behind a screen. It was a small, personal indulgence she wasn't able to use nearly often enough.

She hummed under her breath as she undressed. Mrs. Daugherty came in with a bucket of steaming water and emptied it into the tub, then brought in two more buckets of cool water to mix in. It made for a very shallow and lukewarm bath, but Johanna wasn't about to complain. She stepped behind the screen and shed the rest of her clothing.

"Will you take my dress for cleaning and brushing, Mrs. Daugherty? I may need it again soon."

"I will indeed."

"Also, can you bring your girl tomorrow? I may have another appointment in town."

The older woman chuckled. "Will you, now. Well, I s'pose my daughter can spare me an extra day or two this week. Good night. Doc Jo."

"And you." She waited until Mrs. Daugherty had closed the door, and sank into the tub. If only she had that wine now . . .

"Johanna."

She sat bolt upright in the tub, sending water splashing over the edge. *Quentin.*

Chapter 14

She was quite naked.

Quentin knew that, had known before he walked through the door. The scent of her skin had carried into the hallway, a perfume of bare flesh tinged with the minerals in the water and a trace of perspiration that carried the unmistakable signature of arousal.

Not blatantly sexual, perhaps. But arousal just the same. And it had drawn Quentin to her with the force of a deadly compulsion.

He stopped at the sound of her indrawn breath. He'd given her warning. She was safe behind the screen. But he wasn't safe. He wasn't safe at all.

All day long he'd chopped at the fallen tree, trying to sweat her out of his system. It hadn't worked. Harper's words rang in his head with each blow of the axe, and he'd paced and listened and smelled the air for the first hint of her return to the Haven.

Now she was here, and he couldn't wait any longer.

"Quentin?" Her usually steady voice carried a quiver. "This is not a good time. I will speak with you in the morning—"

"You were gone all day." His words sounded harsh even to his own ears.

"Please leave," she said. He heard the splashing of water, imagined her covering her full breasts with her arms in an instinctively protective gesture. He wet his lips.

"I won't hurt you." An absurd statement. Of course he wouldn't hurt her, wouldn't rush around the screen and scoop her from the water and lay her on the bed and ravish her . . .

"I would appreciate some privacy," she said.

So would I. With you. He struggled to rein in his unruly imagination. His mind was spinning wanton images of him and Johanna cavorting in her bed, of her uninhibited cries as he entered and rode her, of her skin flushed with passion.

He could see far more than just her face if he stepped around the screen. He wildly considered going back out to the yard, amid the stacks of new made firewood, and resuming his attack on the fallen oak he had yet to defeat.

It wouldn't help. Nothing helped.

"Mrs. Daugherty told me you went to meet a doctor," he said. *A male doctor.*

"That is not your concern," she said sharply. Johanna was seldom angry.

Her indignation did nothing to quell his own helpless arousal. Nor did the heavy scent of a man's expensive cologne on her clothing, in the room—and underlying it, too faint to identify, the smell of a strange male.

He moved to her bed, where she'd laid out her undergarments. They smelled only of *her*. The chemise was of material too coarse to be of the best quality, but he stroked it against his face as if it were made of the finest silk. He inhaled her.

"What are you doing?" she demanded. "This is not appropriate behavior. Leave at once."

She spoke as if to a child. Or a madman. He laughed hoarsely. "What are you afraid of, Johanna? I just came in to say good-night."

Do what she asks, he told himself. *Leave.*

Why should you? another part answered. *Harper said she wants you. Make her admit it.*

He sat down on the edge of Johanna's bed, trapped between two conflicting forces. His mind was the battleground. He couldn't get a grip on his thoughts, let alone make them obey his will.

"Quentin?"

He didn't trust himself to answer. The ugly, lustful propensity within him ruled his voice. Another Quentin spoke in his mind, a second self, mocking his restraint—twisting in his brain until the agony made him reach for a bottle that wasn't there.

"I know you're still here, Quentin," Johanna said. Her voice had calmed, becoming that of the impersonal physician once more. Quentin nearly hated her for that self-possession.

He was consumed by darker compulsions.

Obsessed.

"I am getting out now," she said.

He could almost see her rising naked from the water. Lifting one long leg and then the other, water streaming over her soft, fair skin. Breasts glistening, each erect nipple crowned by clinging drops. Belly slightly rounded, full hips made to cradle a man's body, strong thighs with a secret thatch of brown curls between.

Quentin thrust his fingers into the bedcover, grabbing fistfuls of quilted cloth.

Johanna walked out from behind the screen. She didn't cower or try to cover herself, though she must have seen at once that he hadn't averted his gaze. She stood tall and defiant, her arms at her sides, only the rapid rise and fall of her breasts revealing her emotion.

"Is this what you wished to see?" she asked. "Look, then."

Oblivious to shame, Quentin complied. He devoured her with his eyes. Her face was flushed, as he'd imagined it; her hair fell in wanton disarray about her shoulders, an errant lock trailing over one full breast.

Her breasts were magnificent. Firm, lush, begging to be suckled.

Her shoulders were broad enough to support them in perfect proportion. Her waist narrowed beneath them, flaring out into generous hips.
She held her legs close together, but he glimpsed the blush of her sex
behind the screen of curls.

And he smelled her. That body, such fertile ground for a man's
seed, revealed her true desires, the ones she dared not show with her
fearless blue gaze.

Arousal. Moisture that gathered and spilled over to ease a man's
passage, perfume surely even a human male could scent.

His own body was more than ready. He ached. He throbbed. Sati-
ation was only moments away. He could seize her now and she would
hardly resist. On the floor, against the wall: lying beneath him or on her
knees, again and again until he'd had enough . . .

He rose. He fumbled for the buttons of his trousers. She watched
and didn't move, silently pleading with him to take her. Take her.

One step. Another. He dragged his gaze from her body to her face.
Her eyes.

Johanna's eyes. Waiting for him to betray her trust.

No.

His feet sealed to the floor. His muscles spasmed. He managed to
make them function at last, moving him back. Away from Johanna, one
inch at a time, toward the door.

Howling. He heard howling, from somewhere in the center of his
being. The rage of a thwarted monster. If Johanna spoke, he couldn't
hear her. By touch alone he found the doorknob and turned it. The
howling pursued him all the way back to his room.

Johanna's legs buckled.

She dropped to her knees on the floor, giving her trembling muscles a chance to recover. Never in her life had she felt so weak, or so
confused.

Not afraid. That was the remarkable thing. She'd seen as soon as
she stepped out from behind the screen what Quentin intended.

But Quentin would never commit rape. That certainty helped her
to stand still and wait for Quentin to realize it himself.

Not before she had been driven nearly to the very edge of her faith
and reason. Not before she'd realized that some part of her almost
wished he had followed through with the impulses that ruled him.

Gott in Himmel. Self-disgust tightened her throat. She pushed herself to her feet and went to the door. The hallway was quiet and dark.

Her door had a lock, like all the rooms in the house, but she hadn't felt the need to use it since taking up residence here.

If she turned the key now, would it be to protect herself from Quentin, or impose an artificial defense against her own emotions? She left the door unlocked and stumbled to the bed, feeling for her dressing gown. She had to concentrate to get the sleeves over her arms and the sash tied about her waist. By the time that simple task was finished, her sense was restored.

Sense, but not equilibrium. That would take a little more effort.

She sat on the edge of the bed, where Quentin had been. The spot was still warm from his body, but she didn't flinch away. This had to be faced, and squarely.

What had happened? She could only guess what had set off Quentin's bizarre behavior—and her own equally aberrant response to it.

Revealing herself to Quentin had been the height of folly. Had she actually believed it might help him?

She backed away from the painful thought of her own lapse and tried to consider the causes for Quentin's conduct.

She'd been gone all day, true. She didn't know what might have happened during her absence, except that Mrs. Daugherty had nothing to report.

Quentin had acted as though intoxicated, but she hadn't smelled alcohol. Something had gone very wrong.

The wrongness was the same she'd seen yesterday in their last session, and in the parlor. In his eyes lurked a shadow Quentin, a man-beast filled with lust, irrational hunger, even a kind of cruelty. A creature who wanted her, making no attempt to hide it. And Quentin wanted her just as much.

That was the truth she had avoided, danced around, regarded with the sham of a scientist's detachment. Just as she had failed to admit that Quentin might be far more afflicted than he appeared. The part of his mind that controlled the darkest human instincts had briefly lost some interior battle, here in this room, a battle in which she was the prize.

Hypnosis released the shadow Quentin. So, she suspected, did drink. Neither had been used tonight. What had triggered it? Could it possibly be the kiss in the vineyard, and jealousy the ordinary Quentin couldn't admit?

The only way to be sure was to hypnotize him again. And she couldn't trust herself to do it. She'd come too close to forsaking everything she believed in.

She wanted him.

There. It was said, admitted fully, if only in her mind. She wanted to know what it would be like to lie in his arms, feel his kisses all over her body, experience the joining of flesh she had only read about. She wanted to explore the lean, honed muscles she had only glimpsed before, see those red-gold eyes alight with the pleasure she gave him, and know ecstasy in return.

Quentin would give her ecstasy. She had no doubt that he was a superb and experienced lover, as accomplished in that skill as he was articulate and charming. And even if the Quentin she wanted had been temporarily absent, replaced by someone feral and dangerous, her feelings had not vanished. She saw now that they were a permanent part of her being. She understood that she had stepped out from behind the screen, knowing he was waiting, *because* of them.

Mere modesty did not keep her from his bed. Society's conventions did not trouble her. A woman was physically capable of enjoying the act of love, and should be free to do so. She understood fully what was involved in the practice of sexual intercourse, in theory at least.

As long as she remained Quentin's doctor, that theory would never be tested. But if Bolkonsky were able to treat him . . .

Good God. Had she been fooling herself? She had assumed that sending Quentin to another doctor was best for him, because she had begun to lose both control and objectivity in his particular case. He was unable to regard her as a doctor, and she hadn't been successful in maintaining the necessary distance and authority. Better to send him away than fail him.

Oh, yes, she found him attractive, fascinating, impossible to ignore. She had reacted too strongly to his kisses. She was never so aware of being a woman as in his presence.

But she had not envisioned a lasting relationship between them, not even in her dreams. Now she saw the selfishness of her motives.

If Bolkonsky took Quentin's case, he wouldn't be her patient. He'd be able to get well, without distractions. And then . . .

Then he could come back to her, man to woman, and all would happen naturally as it was meant to. She'd have Quentin for herself.

Unless, when he was cured, he didn't want her. Unless his interest was a patient's preoccupation with his doctor, the desires of a man separated from the rest of humanity, bound to vanish when he was restored to health and sanity.

She laughed. *How you build castles of air, Johanna. Be careful, lest they send you smashing back to the earth.*

• • •

He waited for her in the hotel lobby as he bad yesterday, a little more serious and less inclined to light conversation than he'd previously been.

That suited Johanna very well. They had much ground to cover, not least of all the issue of Quentin's future care.

She refused to dwell on last night's dreams, or how she'd awakened drenched in perspiration and aching with unsated needs. Quentin Forster was at the center of those dreams: red, seething, burning. Feodor Bolkonsky was cool, collected, the consummate professional, and just being in his presence reminded her that she was first and foremost a doctor.

She'd momentarily considered discussing Bolkonsky with Quentin that morning, but Quentin was nowhere to be found. Harper mentioned seeing him heading for the woods, and he hadn't returned for luncheon.

Was he feeling chagrined about last night? Did he remember it at all? She was almost glad not to have to face him again so soon. Today's meeting with Bolkonsky would surely give her a much-needed sounding board.

"I am very glad to see you again, Feodor," she said when she and Bolkonsky were seated in the private room. "I have an important subject to discuss with you." She readied herself. "Yesterday I mentioned the case of Quentin Forster, and you seemed particularly—"

He held up a gloved hand. "I beg forgiveness for interrupting you, but there is an urgent matter I must bring up before we continue."

"Urgent?" She saw now that she had overestimated his tranquillity. His fair skin was flushed, and his lips were pressed tightly together. She determined that he was angry, though not with her. Someone—or something—else had upset him before her arrival.

"Of course," she said. "Please go on."

"You must understand, Johanna. I had not planned for it to be this way, or to introduce the topic in such unseemly haste, so soon after we met. I have no choice." He cleared his throat. "It concerns another patient of yours, one May Ingram."

May had been so far from Johanna's mind that at first she was certain she'd misunderstood. "May? You know of her?"

"Yes. You see. I have been retained by May's father, Chester Ingram, to consult with you about returning her to his care."

With one brief sentence, Feodor set Johanna's thoughts in complete disorder. May's *father*.

Caught between fear and anger, she got up from her chair and paced to the window. She'd hoped never to be put in this position, though she had always known it was a possibility, ever since that night two years ago when a frantic Mrs. Ingram had brought May to the Haven.

Rain. A mother and young girl on the doorstep, soaking wet, carrying a pair of small traveling bags as if they were on a weekend visit to friends in the country.

"You are Dr. Johanna Schell?" the woman had asked. "I need your help."

Johanna had let them in. In short bursts of speech, the woman—young, well-dressed, and with a haggard, careworn face, told Johanna why she'd come. Not very coherently, not in great detail, but enough to make clear the extremity of her errand.

May had confirmed the truth of her mother's words when she'd suffered an hysterical fit right there in the parlor, and Johanna made her decision. With it had come certain promises and assumptions. May's mother vanished into the night, and didn't return.

Now May's father had appeared out of the blue, a man whose role in her flight had only been hinted at in Mrs. Ingram's hushed narrative. Those hints had been enough, more than enough at the time . . .

"Johanna?" Feodor stood at her elbow, frowning in concern. "I have upset you."

"You have surprised me." She made her way back to the chair and sat down, willing her heartbeat to slow. "I did not expect such deception from you, Doctor. This is the real reason you sought me out, is it not?"

Feodor sighed. "I would have wished to find you in any case, Johanna, for the work you and your father have done. This simply provided an additional excuse. I was quite surprised to learn that the girl Mr. Ingram searched for was a patient of yours."

At the moment, Johanna had scant interest in sorting out his motives. "Perhaps you had better start from the beginning."

"Of course." He sat down and regarded her earnestly. "I had only recently come to San Francisco, with the intention of remaining a few months, when I met Mr. Ingram at a social occasion. You must have heard of him: He is a prominent banker in the city."

Yes, she knew that much. Mr. Chester Ingram was a powerful man of great influence, no doubt. "Go on," she said.

"While we were talking, I told Mr. Ingram of my theories involving hypnosis. Mr. Ingram expressed regret that I had not been on hand to look after his wife two years ago, when she ran off with their daughter and disappeared. It seemed that Mrs. Ingram, having become mentally unstable, had labored under the delusion that her life was in danger, though she'd had everything a woman could desire."

Everything of material goods, he meant. "Was her condition diagnosed as insanity?"

"You must know as well as anyone," Bolkonsky said gravely. "Did you not meet her yourself?"

"Yes." There was no point in denying it now. "I did not find her to be insane, merely frightened."

"Ah." Bolkonsky was a little less cool than before, which hardly rectified his less-than-honorable behavior. Johanna did not trust his cordiality. "Mr. Ingram deeply missed his wife and daughter, and since May was subject to hysterical fits, he was most worried that she would not be suitably cared for. During most of the past two years he had believed both of them unrecoverable. He but recently discovered that May might still be in the area, and was having the possibility investigated.

"A few days later, he informed me that his daughter was a patient at a small private clinic in the Napa Valley, one administrated by the daughter of Dr. Wilhelm Schell. Naturally, I told him what I knew of your family's spotless reputation. He asked me if I might approach you about releasing his daughter into his care, so as to minimize the girl's discomfort. It is his desire that I should continue any treatment that may be necessary in light of what she has suffered."

At least Bolkonsky was aware that some trauma might have been involved. He surely underestimated it.

"I see," she said. "I believe I understand." Coldness seeped into her stomach. "It is true that Mrs. Ingram came to me two years ago, in an extreme state of distress, and begged me to look after her daughter, who was indeed suffering from hysteria. She said she was running from great danger, and could not care for May under the circumstances. I took the girl in. Mrs. Ingram asked me to promise not to reveal May's location, or her true name, until such time as she returned."

"But she did not come back."

"No." Johanna wasn't giving Bolkonsky a whit more information than she had to, and that included news of Mrs. Ingram's recent letter hinting at an expeditious return from Europe.

Bolkonsky shook his head. "It is a measure of your good heart and devotion to our profession that you have maintained the child at your own expense. Now that is no longer necessary. I know that you must have accepted Mrs. Ingram's mad tales, or you would have contacted May's father long ago."

Mad tales. Her intuition had long since told her otherwise.

"She was May's mother. I had no reason to disbelieve her, and I fully expected her to come back within a few months."

"Of course." Bolkonsky smiled. "You could only offer help to those in need, and maintain your doctor's confidentiality. But now you can hear the truth. I have spoken at great length with May's father. His wife was profoundly disturbed, from a family with a history of madness. Mr. Ingram had her under a doctor's care, but he was unsuccessful in curing her madness. Due to the lapses of an inattentive servant, she escaped with May before dawn one morning."

And made her way, evidently, to the Napa Valley. "I have seen many patients with such delusions," Johanna said.

"And sometimes it is difficult to tell where delusion ends and reality begins. But May has been without a parent for two years. There is a certain fear that she might inherit her mother's madness, due to her tendency toward hysteria—"

"May is not mad." Johanna gathered her feet under her and thought better of it. *Be calm. Do not let him see your anger. He must believe you his ally, not his enemy.* "She has not suffered an hysterical episode for a year."

"If she is cured of hysteria, Mr. Ingram and I have you to thank."

"Perhaps. But she still suffers from extreme shyness and a fear of the outside world, particularly men. You propose to take her from the Haven at a very critical time."

Bolkonsky nodded with obvious sympathy. "I would prefer to leave her in your care and make the transition very slowly, but Mr. Ingram is eager to be reunited with the daughter he'd thought lost. I anticipated the awkwardness of this, and asked that we continue in consultation with you, and with all due caution, so as not to upset May unduly. Mr. Ingram has agreed."

Johanna bit the inside of her lip. In spite of Bolkonsky's mild words, she had no doubt that he meant what he said. A parent had legal rights to his child that she, as a doctor, did not.

Johanna had never known how Mrs. Ingram had heard of the Haven, then so newly founded in the Valley, or why she'd given a strange doctor so much trust. But Johanna had been determined not to betray that trust.

If even half of what Johanna suspected were true, she dared not allow May to go back to her father.

There was the chance, however slight, that she was wrong, and Mrs. Ingram was truly unstable. Johanna hadn't had time to assess the woman's condition properly. She'd taken action based upon her own experience of similar cases over the years—upon that, and May's hysterical state.

She had no facts, only supposition. Bolkonsky believed Mr. Ingram—or so he said. Only yesterday she'd judged the foreign doctor of sound mind and good heart, but her opinion of him had sunk considerably in twenty-four hours. Her previous trust was out of the question.

That was grounds enough to proceed with extreme caution.

"I am glad to hear that Mr. Ingram recognizes the necessity of moving slowly, for May's sake," she said. "She has come to regard the Haven as her home. She will not do well if she is forced to leave abruptly."

"Quite understandable." Feodor had returned to his former elegant poise, leaving Johanna no doubt as to his confidence. "Between the two of us, I'm certain that we can achieve this in the best way possible." He reached for Johanna's hands. "Together, Johanna. You and I will work together to help May and reunite her with her loving father. I shall consider it a privilege."

Johanna withdrew her hand before he could make contact. "I think that it might be best if you come to the Haven to visit May before we proceed further. I feel certain that when you see her, you will—"

"That will not be advisable. As you said, the Haven has been her home for two years. Neutral ground would be better. I suggest that you bring May to me here at the hotel. I have large and comfortable rooms that can serve for any examination or necessary treatment."

Johanna gazed at him through narrowed eyes. He was prevaricating. May would be better off being evaluated at the Haven, but Johanna sensed that Bolkonsky did not wish to visit her home for reasons of his own. Still, this was not the time to raise objections. She must save her ammunition, and buy time.

"I will need to prepare her for coming into town. In a week—"

"I'm afraid her father will not be content to wait so long. He is exerting a certain pressure upon me to act promptly. It must be tomorrow."

Such coercion explained Bolkonsky's earlier signs of anger. No doubt he disliked being pressured by a client; he was a man who expected to get his own way. How foolish she'd been to be dazzled by him.

And this was the end of her hopes about finding Quentin a good, fully impartial doctor to continue his treatment. Transferring him to Bolkonsky was now out of the question.

"Tomorrow is too soon," she said. "I must insist—"

"I'm sorry, Johanna. You'll see the wisdom of this, I feel sure. I fear that if we do not do as he asks, Mr. Ingram may involve the law . . . and neither one of us wishes that."

Johanna recognized a threat when she heard one. "There is one thing I will not allow, and that is May being hurt. If at any time I feel that she is harmed by this, I will stop it."

Bolkonsky withdrew a step. "You do realize that her father has complete authority over his own child."

"I meant what I said."

"*You* could not do otherwise." He tossed back his golden hair in an arrogant gesture. "I continue to admire your professional devotion."

This Feodor Bolkonsky was fully capable of mockery. "May and I will meet with you, as you requested," she said, "but I shall expect to see Mr. Ingram privately for an examination of my own. Then I shall determine if and when she is fit to meet her father."

"Agreed. Shall I expect you and Miss Ingram here tomorrow at one o'clock?"

May's voluntary appearance was a preferable alternative to her seizure from the Haven by force. "We'll be here."

"Then I shall bid you adieu, so that you will have the time you need with Miss Ingram. I am sorry that our other business has been delayed, but I hope we shall have future opportunities to discuss your other patients." He tipped his hat, clicked his heels, and strode from the room.

He was annoyed, the polished Dr. Bolkonksy, that she had dared to argue with him. But he expected to prevail. Why should he not, in dealing with a woman?

He did not know her. And she was well aware that her most dangerous opponent was May's father, not this foppish physician who so excelled in manipulation and deception.

Daisy seemed to sense Johanna's worry as they drove back to the Haven. Half-formed plans were already hatching in Johanna's mind, ranging from the deliberate to the desperate. Finding solid proof of Ingram's alleged improprieties with his daughter and facing the influential businessman in a court of law was certainly one of the more desperate, if it came to that.

But deliberation won. The best scheme was to delay Bolkonsky and Ingram until firm arrangements could be made—arrangements for May's safety. Let Bolkonsky and Ingram believe she was cooperating. Resistance too soon would arouse their suspicions.

If there was even a grain of truth in Bolkonsky's claims of Mrs. Ingram's madness, Johanna much preferred to err on the side of caution. May could always be returned—if, against all Johanna's instincts, Ingram proved to be worthy of his daughter.

May was almost old enough to live on her own, but her mind was still that of a frightened girl. She was not ready for the world. She would do best residing with someone she could learn to trust, if she had to leave the Haven. Someone who could hide her as long as necessary.

May's precarious situation would consume all Johanna's time and effort from now until this matter of Mr. Ingram was satisfactorily resolved. The other patients would have to wait. And Quentin . . .

She had no choice but to put his treatment aside until she found another suitable doctor. That might take weeks, or months—every day a test of her will. She could only hope that his condition didn't worsen.

She unharnessed Daisy, gave her a measure of grain, and started toward the house. May was not in the garden or, as far as she could see, in the orchard or vineyard. In the full heat of the day, the patients were apt to be resting in their rooms.

Like a coward, she hoped Quentin remained in his. She wasn't to be so lucky. Quentin and May were together in the parlor, the girl reading to him in her light, hesitant voice. Mrs. Daugherty knitted on the sofa. All three looked up as Johanna entered.

Quentin blanched. He must remember at least some of what had happened last night. How much did he remember? . . . That was the question. But he collected himself, spoke softly to May, and rose from his chair.

"Good afternoon, Johanna," he said.

"Good afternoon."

"Back so soon?" Mrs. Daugherty asked. "Didn't expect you 'til evenin'."

"My plans have changed." She smiled at May. "May, I'd like to talk to you, in my office."

May glanced at Quentin, who nodded. "We can finish the book later," he said. "I do want to know what becomes of Avis."

"You won't read ahead?" May asked.

Quentin crossed his heart. "I promise."

May set the book down and went to Johanna. Quentin took the opportunity to slip from the room.

Relieved, Johanna took May into the office and shut the door. "You have had a good day?" she asked as the girl perched at the edge of the chaise longue.

"We spent the afternoon reading." May's tremulous smile lit up her face. "Quentin said I have a lovely voice."

"You enjoy Quentin's company, don't you?"

"Oh, yes. He is wonderful."

Wonderful. That was not the sort of word May was in the habit of using, when she spoke at all. And though she had been the most relaxed in Johanna's company, something in her was always held in reserve. Even after she had overcome the more blatant symptoms of hysteria, she remained fearful and bereft of real trust for the world.

Today, May was happy. Genuinely happy, as she hadn't been since her mother's departure. Oh, there'd been moments of contentment and pleasure, but May had seldom reflected the joy of her name.

Johanna had seen enough of human character to postulate that May's happiness was due to more than Quentin's kindness and gentle attention. The girl was just old enough to fall in love. Quentin was agreeable and handsome. What could be more natural?

In other young girls, nothing at all. In May, it was a miracle.

Quentin, of course, would never take advantage of such tender emotions. He behaved toward her like an affectionate elder brother; he did May much good by teaching her that not all men were to be feared.

Those lessons were soon to be put to the test.

"Why don't you lie back and be comfortable," she instructed the girl. May did as she was told, her thoughts clearly on something— someone—else.

"May, this may be a difficult question, but I want you to answer it as best you can." She breathed in deeply. "Do you remember your father?"

The answer was very long in coming. So long, in fact, that Johanna finally realized May hadn't heard her. She repeated the question, and still May was silent.

"Tell me about Quentin," Johanna said.

May began to speak with enthusiasm, smiling up at the ceiling. Her hearing was not impaired, nor was her understanding. She simply did not want to hear or think or speak of her father.

She never had. But that was not the sort of proof that would hold up in court. May had not yet reached the age of consent.

Johanna let May's monologue run its course, attempted without success to return to the subject of May's father, and then set her loose.

May virtually skipped from the room. Doubtless she was going in search of Quentin.

She was free to seek him out.

After a half-hour of notations in her records, Johanna went to her father's room and sat with him a while. He slept peacefully on clean linens, hair combed and beard trimmed with loving attention. Quentin's work.

In the hour before dinner, she went out to her favorite place in the orchard to think. She caught a glimpse of something moving in the wood on the hill—a flash of motion and color, red amid the green. A while later Quentin emerged from the wood. He carried his head and shoulders set low, a man bearing a burden he wanted no one else to see.

She almost called out to him. In the end, her will—and her fear—were stronger than desire.

Chapter 15

The next afternoon, braced for the ordeal to come, Johanna took May into town.

She had finally given May half the truth about their reasons for going; she said that she wanted May to meet a doctor friend of hers, making sure that May understood that this "friend" was a man. She refused to be any less honest with her young patient. Had May reacted with a return to hysteria, or run off into the woods, Johanna would have postponed the meeting indefinitely and proceeded with the next move.

But May wasn't unduly disturbed. She didn't freeze in terror at the prospect of leaving the Haven or meeting a stranger. It was a vivid mark of her improvement that she went willingly, even with a touch of enthusiasm when Johanna promised to look for new books at the general store.

May had wanted Quentin to accompany them. But Quentin's presence would be a wild card in a very tenuous situation.

So she and May went alone, the girl outfitted in her second-best dress, Johanna in her most sober gown. She found herself driving more slowly than usual, preparing herself for any eventuality and the absolute necessity of deceiving Bolkonsky, just as he'd deluded her.

All too soon they were in Silverado Springs. May seemed not to notice the sometimes hostile stares of the townspeople; she simply hunched in her seat beside Johanna. At the hotel, she took hold of Johanna's hand and clutched it so emphatically that her delicate bones seemed in danger of breaking.

"Don't leave me," she begged. "Don't leave me alone."

"I'll be here with you," Johanna said. She gave the girl a quick hug. "It will be all right." *No matter what I must do to make it so.*

A clerk in the lobby informed Johanna that Dr. Bolkonsky awaited their arrival in his suite of rooms, and offered to lead the way. Bolkonsky opened the door to her knock.

His blue gaze immediately fell on May. "Ah, Miss Ingram. I'm so glad you could come today."

May shrank behind Johanna. "I want to go home," she whispered.

Johanna and Bolkonsky exchanged a guarded look. "Of course you do," he said gently. "And you will, soon enough. In the meantime, ladies, won't you come in and take refreshments with me?" He smiled at May. "I have some delicious biscuits and jam and cakes."

May's wary expression matched Johanna's own feelings. She led May into the sitting room, unobtrusively keeping herself between the girl and Bolkonsky.

Bolkonsky's suite was undoubtedly the hotel's finest accommodation, its furnishings rich and only a little out of date. Bolkonsky's practice must be very successful indeed, if he were not heir to some fortune that allowed him to spend money so freely. Johanna realized that she'd never inquired about his family or background beyond his education. Now she wished she knew a great deal more about him.

"Please, sit down," he said, offering the women chairs near the window. He personally served the refreshments, but the biscuit May selected remained uneaten in her hand.

"Well, May," he said. "As I said, I'm glad you and Johanna could come to see me today. She has told me much about you."

May stared at him—openly, not with the brief, darting looks she ordinarily employed with strangers. "Why?" she asked.

Bolkonsky glanced at Johanna in surprise. It *was* unlike May to be so direct. Johanna was no less startled, but also proud of the girl's courage. This meeting might be endured without disaster.

"Johanna surely told you that I am a doctor, as she is," Bolkonsky said.

"I know you've been staying at the Haven, and that you are familiar with Dr. Schell's methods. I had hoped you might talk with me, and perhaps allow me to hypnotize you. It would be a very great help to me, you see."

May crumbled her biscuit between her fingers. She looked at Johanna with pleading in her eyes.

"I would rather not," she said. "Johanna . . ."

"I know I am still a stranger to you," Bolkonsky said, "but I hope to remedy that situation." He picked up a book from a side table. "I understand that you enjoy reading. I've brought a book for you—"

"I don't want it." May bolted from her chair and moved behind Johanna's. "I don't like him," she whispered in Johanna's ear. "If Quentin were here—"

"Ah. Quentin," Bolkonsky said. "Is he a friend of yours?"

"Yes." May's face hardened into a mask of defiance. "*You* aren't my friend."

This went far beyond remarkable behavior for a girl who feared nearly everyone and everything. Johanna hid a triumphant smile. This would not be such a one-sided battle after all.

"Is there a place where I might have a word with May?" she asked Bolkonsky.

"Certainly. Just through the door behind you." He smiled again at May. "Take your time."

Johanna took May's hand and led her into the bedchamber Bolkonsky indicated. She closed the connecting door between the rooms.

"May, I must ask you a question. Please answer honestly. Why do you dislike Dr. Bolkonsky so much?"

May stood rigidly against the wall, her fingers curled into fists. "Do we have to talk to him? I'd like to go home now."

Johanna rested her hand on May's dark head. "I know you would. Think of this as a sort of play, with you and me as the actors."

"Like Irene?"

"Perhaps not exactly like Irene. But I like Dr. Bolkonsky no more than you do." She smiled encouragement. "I need your help to make the doctor think that we are both happy to be here. I wouldn't ask you without good reason."

"He knows Quentin, doesn't he?"

The odd certainty in her voice took Johanna aback. "Only in the way he knows of you, as a resident of the Haven. Why?"

She began to shake. "I'm afraid."

It wasn't an answer, but Johanna could see that May had reached the end of her endurance. Damn Bolkonsky—and her own failure to find some alternative to bringing May to town.

"I'll speak to the doctor and tell him you are not well." She cupped May's cheek in her palm. "You remain here until I come for you."

For the first time May smiled. "Thank you, Johanna."

"You're welcome." She left Johanna in the room and opened the door to the sitting room.

Bolkonsky was no longer alone. Another man stood beside him, head bent toward the doctor in hushed conversation.

Johanna stopped, misgiving blooming into alarm. The man was tall, large-boned, and well, if loudly, dressed; his features were heavier than May's, the eyes a muddy gray rather than dark brown. But Johanna knew who he must be.

"Dr. Schell," Bolkonsky said, stepping in front of his coconspirator. "I . . . something unexpected has happened. May I introduce Mr. Chester Ingram, May's father. Mr. Ingram, Dr. Johanna Schell."

Barely inclining her head to the intruder, Johanna fixed Bolkonsky with a cold stare. "I thought we had agreed—"

"Yes. But Mr. Ingram has expressed a reluctance to wait to meet his daughter again. It is understandable, after all . . ."

Understandable—or planned all along? Johanna turned her gaze on Ingram. "Mr. Ingram, May has been under my care for the past two years, as you know. She is subject to hysterical fits if exposed to upsetting conditions." She fortified herself for the unaccustomed lies. "I brought her today with the expectation that she would have the necessary time to adjust to the prospect of returning to your care. I was to speak with Dr. Bolkonsky, and arrange a later meeting between you and your daughter."

Ingram pushed past Bolkonsky. He carried himself with the air of a man who was used to command, and did not like being so addressed by a woman.

"So Dr. Bolkonsky told me . . . Miss . . . Dr. Schell," he said. "But I have been wrongfully separated from my daughter, whom I love, for two long years." His eyes narrowed in calculating assessment. "I know that my wife brought May to you with crazy stories born of her own madness. I don't blame you for believing her; she is very persuasive. But now it's time for May to come home, for us to be a family again. I will brook no needless delays."

"Needless?" Johanna fought to control her anger, and the instant hostility she felt for this man. Hostility, and fear—for May's sake. This was a man from whom a woman might flee in fear for her health. Or her life.

"You do want what is best for your daughter, Mr. Ingram?" She stepped closer to him, looking up into his face. "I have worked long with May to overcome her fears—the fears she has shown ever since she came to me. If you wish her to become hysterical again, then by all means proceed as you have been."

Ingram glanced at Bolkonsky in outraged amazement. "*This* is the doctor you told me was to be trusted? She—" He broke off, staring toward the door to the bedchamber. May stood on the threshold, utterly still. Her face had lost all color.

"May," her father said hoarsely. He opened his arms. "May, my darling—"

With a choking gasp, May bent backward at the waist, her spine forming a sharp curve. Johanna barely made it to her in time to catch her before she fell. The girl convulsed, her teeth clicking together.

Johanna yanked a curtain cord from the window, eased May to the ground, and pushed the cord into her mouth to prevent her from biting her tongue.

Bolkonsky dropped to his knees beside her and helped hold May down. In a few moments it was over. May's face was bathed in sweat; her body was limp. She kept her eyes tightly closed.

"*Gott in Himmel,*" Johanna whispered. One bout of hysteria, and all the progress of the past year was lost. She had been so sure that May was over the fits for good.

Arrogance on her own part. Sheer arrogance, hubris, stupidity . . .

May's father came toward them and crouched as if to take May in his arms. Bolkonsky forestalled him and carried May into the bedchamber himself. Johanna sat beside May, shielding her from any further male intrusion.

"Move away at once. Let me be alone with her," Johanna said, adjusting the pillows under May's head. "She has not had such a fit in over a year; you will have to explain to Mr. Ingram the severity of her relapse. We expected too much of her, too soon."

"I must concur with your analysis," Bolkonsky said.

Johanna didn't allow him to see her surprise at his sudden cooperation. "Then make Mr. Ingram understand that he cannot take May with him until she has fully adjusted to the prospect, however much time that may require. Unless he wishes her to become even more ill." She twisted to meet Bolkonsky's gaze. "Surely you see that she fears her father. Do you still believe she belongs with him?"

The Russian doctor stroked his chin. "This is a setback, Johanna, but we can still find a satisfactory conclusion. I will see what I can do."

"And ask him to leave these rooms so that I can take May back to the buggy. I will not have her suffer again today."

Bolkonsky answered with a bow and retreated. The door remained opened a crack behind him.

"What the hell is going on?" Ingram demanded. "What's happened to my daughter? I thought you said this woman cured her."

"I have no cause to doubt—" Bolkonsky began.

"She's useless, a charlatan. I won't have May in her care one minute longer—"

The door closed, shutting off his words. May remained still and mute.

"All will be well," Johanna murmured, stroking damp hair away from the girl's face. "We'll be home very soon."

May opened her eyes. "Where am I?"

"Don't worry about that now. Just rest."

"I'm not tired." She reached for Johanna's hand. "Are we going now?"

Given what May had just experienced, that was a regular speech. She hardly seemed aware of what had set off her fit, or why she'd been afraid. Johanna cast up a wordless prayer of gratitude.

"Soon," Johanna assured her. Bolkonsky entered the room, hovering in the doorway. Johanna joined him out of May's hearing.

"He's gone," Bolkonsky said. "I'll keep you informed as to his decision regarding his daughter."

"*Sehr gut*. I think it best if we postpone any more meetings for at least a week. Mr. Ingram should return to San Francisco for the time being."

Bolkonsky didn't reply. His cool stare swept over May. "She seems recovered enough. I will send you a message at the Haven."

Nodding her agreement, Johanna helped May up from the bed and walked her slowly back to the stable. May showed no further reaction to what had happened, nor made any reference to Bolkonsky or her father. It was as if they had already ceased to exist for her.

And they would soon enough. The time for mere planning was past.

Oscar galloped out to meet them when they arrived at the Haven, and immediately took charge of Daisy. Johanna saw May to her room and made sure she was calm and comfortable, then visited her father and Harper. She made an appointment to talk with Irene and Lewis before dinner, and then took Mrs. Daugherty aside where they could not be overheard.

It was not a great leap of faith to trust the older woman with vital secrets, and Mrs. Daugherty was canny enough to have understood something of May's reasons for being at the Haven. She listened to Johanna's brief explanations with a furrowed brow and an increasingly dark expression.

"You were right to come to me," she said. "I know just what to do. I've a cousin over in Sacramento—she's got girls near May's age, and she'd take her in if I asked. Warm-hearted woman who never turned down a body in need."

"Like you," Johanna said, clasping Bridget's hands. "I have reason to believe that May's mother could return for her soon. If we can keep her safe until then—"

"How fast d' we have to get her away?"

"I think I've bought us a week. Time enough for a letter to reach your cousin."

"Then let me get to writin' it, an' I'll get it out in tomorrow's post."

Grateful and relieved, Johanna wandered about the house aimlessly for half an hour and finally found herself standing in front of Quentin's door.

Her feet had carried her there without her brain's participation. She knew why. Her mind was bursting with a thousand concerns she wanted to share with someone who would understand, her worries for May chief among them. She went to Quentin instinctively, as once she'd gone to her father.

He wasn't her father. How could she even consider it, after the events of two nights ago? If she couldn't treat him as a patient, far less could she confide in him as a peer. To do so would put them both in jeopardy.

Nor dared she tell him what had happened at the hotel, given his closeness to May. It was a grave shortcoming that she felt the need to confess her fears to him.

To what purpose? So that he might put his arms around her and tell her it would be all right, as she'd so glibly told May?

So that he might kiss her?

She shivered and rested her forehead against the wood of the door.

Johanna stood just outside.

Quentin could smell her, hear her breathing, sense her agitation through the flimsy barrier of wood. It was the first and only time she'd sought him out since he'd gone to her room the night before; he'd made himself scarce, and she'd been busy with May.

Visiting with that new male doctor in town.

The hair rose on the back of his neck, and he smoothed it down with one hand.

Jealousy. Wasn't that what had sent him to invade Johanna's most private sanctum? Johanna had returned from town that day with a spring in her step and eyes alight with pleasure. Quentin had watched her, reluctant to go too near because of the potency of his feelings. Afraid to trust himself around her.

Jealousy. Oh, he'd denied it vehemently to himself. He knew nothing of this Bolkonsky beyond his name and what little Mrs. Daugherty had told him. He was no physician to share Johanna's professional life and interests. He had no claim on her—none that extended beyond his imagination. But he had entered her room, uninvited, as no gentleman would do. That was where the memories became confused.

Just like before, as if some outside force had snatched control of his mind and body, he could recall only scraps of conversation—enough to know that he'd behaved badly. Enough to send him slinking from her room in shame, and avoid her thereafter.

What he remembered with painful intensity was arousal—overwhelming, single-minded lust—and the sight of Johanna's naked body.

All it took was that one memory, and he felt as he had then. He spread his hand against the door as if he could touch her flesh. Mold it between his hands. Kiss it in a thousand ways and a thousand places.

He groaned. At least he knew he hadn't attempted to ravish her, or he'd have been ejected from the house. Scant consolation.

No consolation at all.

It didn't help that he suspected the situation with Johanna, May, and the mysterious Dr. Bolkonsky had not turned out as Johanna hoped. Her manner had been considerably more sober yesterday, after her second meeting with the doctor. And today . . .

Today she'd taken May to town with her, an extraordinary occurrence in itself. She certainly hadn't confided in him, but he'd seen her face upon her return, when she was too preoccupied to notice his presence.

And May had come directly to him.

He'd tried to speak with May, to learn why she'd gone with Johanna and what had transpired, but she hadn't responded to his careful questions.

Quentin had never made a habit of studying human nature, but his werewolf blood made it relatively easy to know what humans were feeling. Johanna was no better than May at hiding her emotions. She was distracted and worried.

He had added to that burden.

What was he to Johanna Schell? A source of confusion, of apprehension, perhaps even of fear. He might be her patient, but he was not her lover, or her keeper.

He might become her obedient hound, awaiting his chance to roll on his back in abject apology. A woman might tell a dog what she wouldn't share with a wolf.

Should he hear that anyone or anything had hurt her or May, hound would become wolf in an instant.

And do what? he asked himself, laughing derisively at his own conceit. *This wolf's fangs have been pulled.*

"Quentin? Are you there?"

He leaned into the door, resting his forehead against the wood.

"I'm here."

"We'll be having dinner soon, and a gathering in the parlor afterward. I hope you'll join us."

It would be the first such gathering since things had gone so wrong a week ago. Johanna was striving for a sense of normality.

"I'll be there," he said. *And I'll behave myself—at least enough to learn what is troubling you and May.*

Her footsteps moved away from the door. So, she was dodging the chance to speak to him alone.

Wise, from her perspective. But two people could be alone even in a crowd, and he'd find a way.

Dinner was a tense, quiet affair. Even Mrs. Daugherty said little. Afterward, in the parlor, Lewis made exaggerated efforts to stay far away from Quentin. Irene claimed the entire sofa; she smiled like the idiomatic cat who'd eaten the canary. Harper took a chair by the empty hearth, his gaze shifting from Johanna to Quentin and back again. Wilhelm Schell nodded to himself from his wheelchair and Oscar played with his puzzle, while May sat cross-legged on the carpet at Quentin's feet. Johanna ensconced herself at the head of the room, separate from everyone else—especially Quentin.

She needn't have worried, when the two of them were accompanied by six potential chaperons.

Chaperons with no power to prevent a loup-garou from doing whatever he wished . . .

No. He forced out the savage, alien thoughts and concentrated on his objective. He had to get Johanna to himself, but not for the reasons his vivid imagination suggested. Casually, he picked up his chair and carried it close to Johanna's. May scrambled to follow him. From the sofa, Irene snickered.

Johanna concealed any hint of discomfort. "Quentin," she said, loudly enough for the others to hear. "How was your day?"

Such banalities were just another shield between them. "Better, I think, than yours," he said under his breath.

She pretended not to hear him. "You have such a handsome voice, Quentin. I thought you might read to us this evening, from one of May's books." She smiled down at the girl. "Would you like to choose one, May?"

"By all means," Quentin said, grasping the opportunity. "May, didn't you tell me the other day that you'd found an abandoned bird's nest? I'd very much like to see it, if you'll bring it along when you fetch your book."

The girl hesitated, sliding a glance at Johanna. "I'll get it," she said, and scurried into the hall.

Johanna sat very stiff and tall in her chair. Quentin smiled vaguely about the room for the benefit of the other patients, as if he had nothing at all on his mind.

"About the other night—" he began.

"There is something I must tell you—" Johanna said.

They stopped at the same moment and stared at each other.

"Ladies first, by all means," Quentin said.

"No. Please continue."

He lowered his voice to a hoarse whisper. "Johanna, I owe you a profound apology. I came into your room uninvited. I behaved like a cad. I am sorry."

She breathed in and out several times. "Do you remember what you said and did?"

"I remember . . . enough." He tried to capture her eyes. "I wasn't myself, Johanna. Will you accept my apologies?"

"Of course, Quentin. As a doctor, I understand such things. Let us speak no more of it."

His lip curled. There was his answer. It always came back to that, didn't it? Her professional detachment was her shield—maiden's armor, to protect her from unwanted intimacy or the chance of transgressing the patterns and accommodations of her life. She could still look at him and act as though he hadn't seen her naked body, never come close to—

He tried to stop the thoughts as they spilled, unchecked, from the dark reaches of his mind, but they were stronger than he was. "Shall we speak of Dr. Bolkonsky instead?"

She flinched, hardly more than a twitch of an eyebrow.

"You took May into town today," he said, "to see this Bolkonsky."

"Yes, I did."

"And something went wrong."

Johanna drew her legs under the chair. "May is not used to leaving the Haven."

"It was more than that. I saw both of you when you came back. She was terrified, and you were gravely upset."

"This is a personal matter."

"Personal? For you, or for May?" He leaned closer to her, and she angled away. "If it concerns May's well-being, it concerns me as well."

She straightened and met his gaze. "I appreciate your friendship for May, but she is my patient, not yours. And soon—" She broke off and visibly braced herself. "Given the complications that have attended my attempts to treat you, it seems best for everyone if I locate another doctor who can take over your case."

He felt not so much shock as anger—righteous, cleansing anger. He clenched his fists in his lap. "You mean you want to get rid of me."

Her eyes widened. "No. Quentin. It's for your own good."

"For *your* good, because you're afraid."

Her expression grew remote. "I wish only for you to receive the best of care. I may not be able to provide it . . . as I'd hoped." She swallowed. "You will not be leaving right away. There are few doctors to whom I'd entrust any of my patients, and the search will require diligence. In the meantime—"

"In the meantime, we'll go on like this, avoiding each other, avoiding the truth. Neither doctor and patient, nor friends, nor lovers."

She paled. "I would hope that we are friends, Quentin."

Her distress drained the unwonted anger from his body. What was he doing to her? It couldn't have been easy to admit that she no longer felt qualified to act as his doctor, even though he was the one to blame. How could he expect her to acknowledge anything else?

"Johanna—"

May chose that moment to return to the parlor, bearing the bird's nest in her cupped hands and a book tucked under her arm. She laid the nest at Quentin's feet. A porcelain fragment of a blue robin's egg rested at its center.

Quentin smiled for May's sake. "A treasure indeed," he said, lightly touching the nest. "Surprisingly sturdy, for all that it's made of twigs." He glanced at Johanna. "Very much like the human mind."

"And should it tear, it can be mended," she said with her usual composure. "If the desire is strong enough."

"Not so the egg inside." He tapped the broken shell with his fingertip. "No mending it once it breaks."

"Then we must take that much greater care to protect it. May, did you bring your book?"

With a little sigh of compliance, May began leafing through the book to find her favorite passage.

Irene, feeling neglected, arose from her royal seat and sauntered over to join Lewis. He ignored her, and so she turned her attentions to Harper. Quentin heard the murmur of their conversation, during which Irene strove in vain to attract Harper's interest. He responded with neutral courtesy, which offended Irene's sense of self-importance. She whirled about and set her sights on more familiar prey.

"I hear you have a new lover, Johanna."

Johanna blinked at the sudden attack. "I beg your pardon?"

"That handsome new doctor in town, Bolkonsky." Irene's smile was poisonous. "I don't know why you ever thought he would have an interest in *you*."

May dropped her book on the carpet and stared at Irene. Quentin touched her shoulder. She was trembling.

"Why don't we go for a walk, May," he suggested. "You can show me where you found the nest."

The girl refused to budge. Johanna rose to take Irene's arm and steer her away from the others. Despite the low pitch of her voice, Quentin heard every word she spoke.

"How do you know about Dr. Bolkonsky, Irene?"

"You think I'm stupid, don't you? Just because I've been forced to live out here in this rural backwater with a house full of loonies and old maids—" She shook off Johanna's hand with a sneer. "Well, I do know about Feodor Bolkonsky. I know a lot more than you would ever guess. I still have admirers who have no intention of leaving me here to rot, and I—" She caught her painted lower lip between her teeth. "You might as well give up, Johanna." She pointed her chin toward Quentin. "Take *him* if you want. I don't."

She flounced back to the sofa, leaving Johanna to stare after her. Quentin wasn't in the least surprised that Irene DuBois had her own devious ways of tapping into the local gossip, even if the town considered her one of the "loonies" herself. She certainly wouldn't balk at prying into Johanna's personal and professional affairs.

She might even have already done what Quentin planned to do tonight. He hoped that Johanna didn't draw the same conclusion.

"Trust a woman like Irene to know the names of every eligible male within a hundred-mile radius," he joked when Johanna rejoined him. "I believe that I should pity the man."

"I do not." She sat down again, her expression shut to him. There'd be no further chance for conversation tonight.

Quentin did as he was asked and read May's passage from *The Story of Avis*. The others made a pretense of listening, but he doubted they truly heard. When the gathering broke up an hour later, Harper made as if to speak to Quentin, only to fall silent. Quentin didn't encourage him. All his attention was centered on Johanna and May, the doctor and the innocent. They needed him, and, come the end of the world, he wasn't about to let them down.

Just after the stroke of midnight, when everyone was tucked safely in his or her bed, Quentin slipped into Johanna's office. He knew exactly what he was looking for, and where to find it.

If he felt like a thief in the night, that was exactly what he was. Johanna kept her notes in the desk drawer, unlocked. She obviously hadn't expected any of her patients to go rifling through them. Not Irene, who might have already done so. Certainly not Quentin.

The recent entries about her meetings with Bolkonsky, and the visit with May, were tucked into the front of her notebook. Quentin sat down at her desk and read by the sliver of moonlight that shone through the office window. He sifted the lines of careful handwriting until he found the pertinent section.

The earlier notations rang with the confident satisfaction she'd shown after the first encounter with Bolkonsky. What she said of the man bordered on infatuation. Quentin's hair bristled, and he had to force his mouth to close over his teeth, which had a tendency to bare at every mention of Bolkonsky's name.

Fool, he told himself. *Concentrate*.

Concentration paid off. Yes, she thought very highly of the doctor at first. Enough to be flattered by his attention, to write glowingly of his knowledge of hypnosis and his study of her father's work. She even wrote of her hopes that Bolkonsky might become Quentin's new doctor.

But the next meeting's entry was different. *May's father*, he read, and stopped.

May's father. A Mr. Chester Ingram, a wealthy San Francisco magnate, a man Johanna had never mentioned. Bolkonsky had come to Silverado Springs to recover Ingram's daughter, lost to him two years ago. And he'd deceived Johanna in order to gain her trust before revealing his true motive for summoning her.

That was why she'd taken May into town.

Quentin set down the page and stared out the window. Johanna must have known of May's father, but she had deliberately not contacted him. She'd kept the child here, apart from Ingram, and was distressed at his appearance. Quentin remembered what she'd told him before he met May for the first time: "Her mother left her with us for treatment. I suspect her home life was not a happy one."

No reference to the mother here. Only a description of May's visit to town, where something had gone terribly wrong.

An hysterical fit. Terror. All because May's father had come into the room against Johanna's wishes and recommendations.

The terse sentences Johanna had written here hinted at so much more than they revealed. The one point made abundantly clear was that Johanna did not want to release May to her father . . . and had no intention of doing so.

Quentin swallowed the sourness in his throat and replaced the notes in their original order, then began a second search that took him to the bookshelves against the wall, and the boxes of older records.

The ink was faded on the original entries, made the night May came to the Haven. Quentin read them through without stopping, every line, until he understood the cause for Johanna's apprehension.

No proof, of course. Only speculation, the pleas of a frantic mother, the implications behind a young girl's bizarre behavior. Behavior that had changed when she was left alone to heal.

Only to be reawakened when she met her father face-to-face.

The sound of crumpling paper drew Quentin's unfocused stare to his hands. He'd crushed the sheets into balls in his fist. Releasing a shaky breath, he smoothed the paper flat on the desk.

No matter. Johanna would know someone had been rummaging about in her private papers, and it wouldn't take her long to determine the culprit.

Quentin reassembled the notes and restored them to their place in the box. The tight sickness in his chest was abating, replaced by the cold, metallic sting of compulsion. He left the room, and the house, in a body most would have mistakenly called human.

No one stirred on the grounds of the Silverado Springs Hotel. The staff had retired, the guests were asleep, and the night clerk was completely inattentive to werewolves on the prowl. Quentin easily slipped past him and found the register that listed Mr. Ingram's room.

He didn't know why he was here. He had ceased to think clearly from the moment he put Johanna's notes away. The fog in his mind had become so familiar that he hardly questioned it.

Tonight it drove him to the doors of the hotel's best suite. But the occupants behind these doors were not sleeping. He could hear the creaking of furniture, the whispers, the guttural laughter.

A man and a girl. He'd heard such whispers before.

His urge to kick down the door subsided as quickly as it came. He retraced his steps to the lobby and out into the night, circling the hotel until he located the suite's windows, open to the cool air.

Why should a man like Ingram bother to take precautions against intruders? What had he to fear? Quentin vaulted over the windowsill, avoiding the clutch of heavy draperies. He found himself in a darkened parlor only a room away from the voices—louder now, the man's whispering more insistent, the girl's strained.

He crept to the connecting doorway and looked through.

The girl could not have been more than fourteen, her maid's skirts bunched up around her thighs as she sat on Ingram's knee. She could have passed for much younger. She squirmed and leaned away from him as he nuzzled her cheek.

"Don't pretend you're innocent," he said, running his hand over her stocking. "I know you want it."

"Please, sir," she said. "I have to get home."

He chuckled. "Don't you want the sweet I promised you? It's right here in my pocket—"

Quentin's legs gave way. He caught himself against the wall, doubling over with dry heaves. The nausea and rage within him were such that he knew with sudden clarity what would happen if he walked through that door.

He flung back his head and howled.

Ingram's startled oath was muffled by the girl's scream of terror. Quentin crouched beside the window, waiting just long enough to hear the suite's outer doors slam and the girl's running footsteps down the hallway. Then he turned and leaped back through the window, his thoughts intent on one thing only.

Drink. Inebriety. Intoxication. The complete and total annihilation of all thought and feeling in the tender care of a bottle of whiskey. Even at this hour the Springs Saloon would still be open for business.

Chapter 16

"He hasn't come back, has he?"

Johanna turned at the sly insinuation in Irene's voice, letting the curtain fall from her hand. The rutted lane that led to the Haven's gate was as empty in late afternoon as it had been since early morning. Quentin was still missing, nowhere to be found in the house or the orchard or vineyard, not even in the woods where May had sought him when he'd failed to appear for lunch.

"It's so touching to see you worry over him," Irene cooed. "Just like the faithful wife."

The words struck more surely than any other insult Irene could concoct. Johanna stepped away from the kitchen window and met Irene's arch stare. "He is my patient, as you are. In fact, I have been neglecting you, Irene. I apologize."

"Don't apologize. I haven't had to listen to your boring speeches." She sat down at the kitchen table, draping her body over the chair in a languorous pose. "But it doesn't really matter, after all. I won't be stuck in this place much longer."

Johanna had heard this many times before, but for the past week Irene had been uncommonly quiet, even retiring—at least until last night.

Now she wanted to talk, and Johanna knew that she ought to take advantage of the opportunity. The other patients had all been seen today; merely waiting around for Quentin was a waste of valuable time.

Yet she was haunted by the fear that his absence was permanent. She'd told him of her plan to find another doctor for him, abruptly and without adequate explanation, chill as an alpine winter. Why should he stay, if she gave him no reason to do so?

She diverted her attention to the situation at hand. "Would you care to join me in my office and discuss it?" she asked Irene. "I'd very much like to try another hypnotic session, if you are willing."

"How predictable you are." Irene yawned. "Predictable, and stupid. You're so busy prying into people's heads that you don't even know what's happening right under your nose."

Johanna knotted her hands behind her back. "Would you care to enlighten me?"

"Why should I? You've always been so cruel to me." The older woman's eyes sparked with pleasure in her perceived power. "You've enjoyed torturing me. Well, now the shoe is on the other foot."

"I'm afraid I don't understand what you mean."

"Always that superior tone, as if you don't feel anything." Her voice began to shake. "Oh, yes, the great doctor. Just like God. So smart, so sure. Everything is so clear and easy for you. You look at people as if they were specimens in jars, and you can arrange them any way you like."

"Irene—"

"I'm sick of you and your hypocrisy! You're a whore underneath your starched collars. I know that you want Quentin Forster. But he won't have you, will he?"

White-hot anger bolted through Johanna. Irene shouldn't be affecting her this way.

"Go ahead, hit me again," Irene hissed. "I know you want to."

Johanna unclenched her fist and spread her hand on the table. "No, Irene. I realize that you're suffering. If you'll only allow me to—"

"You can't help me." The storm passed, leaving Irene panting and strangely rational. "But sometime soon you're going to find out what it's like to be helpless while other people take everything away from you, and there won't be anything you can do about it." She swept to the door. "As for Quentin," she threw back over her shoulder. "I saw him head for town late last night—after he was in your office going through your papers."

Johanna absorbed Irene's words. Quentin going through her papers? She wasn't shocked at the idea that Irene had done so, and had considered locking her office after the woman's outburst last night. But Quentin—

What had he said? *"If it concerns May's well-being, it concerns me as well."*

If he'd gotten into Johanna's notes about May, he would have read of her suspicions. And if he'd gone into town . . .

She nearly knocked over her chair in her haste to get up. She hurried to her room, changed her clothes and shoes, looked in on her father, and went out to the barn. No time to harness Daisy to the buggy.

May and Oscar were half-heartedly mucking out the cow's stall as she plucked the old sidesaddle off its stand. Oscar put down the shovel to help her. May watched, her gaze darting about and her expression pinched.

"Where's Quen'in?" Oscar asked. "May and I can't find him."

"That's what I hope to learn," Johanna said. She checked the girth strap and patted Daisy's withers.

"Are you going to town?" Oscar asked. "Can I come?"

"Not this time, Oscar." She smiled at May. "I'm going alone. I'd like you both to remain here, in case Quentin comes back while I'm gone."

May's shoulders sagged with relief, and Johanna realized that she'd feared being forced to return to Silverado Springs.

Not while I'm here, Johanna thought.

Or as long as Quentin was capable of interfering.

"Quen'in didn't read to us today," Oscar complained. He sensed Johanna's worry even though he didn't know the reason for it.

Johanna positioned an old crate she used as a mounting block and swung up into the saddle. "May, you're an excellent reader. Can't you read to Oscar this evening? I would consider it a favor."

May took a step toward her. "When will you be back?"

"No later than sunset. Can I rely on you to look after Oscar?"

May hesitated, glanced at Oscar, and nodded firmly.

"*Sher gut.*" Johanna guided Daisy out of the barn, May and Oscar trailing after. She waved good-bye and set off at a trot for town.

Silverado Springs buzzed like a jostled hornet's nest. A far larger than ordinary number of idlers stood on the street and porches, men and women who'd left their posts at store counters and desks to gossip over some new and exciting occurrence. Heads turned, as usual, when she rode in, but the stares lingered, and the hum of conversation stilled in her wake.

She didn't have to look far for someone to enlighten her. Bolkonsky stood under the awning of Mrs. Sapp's dressmaking shop, deep in conversation with a man in an officious-looking suit. He glanced up, caught sight of her, and waved acknowledgment. Johanna dismounted and tied Daisy to the nearest hitching post.

Bolkonsky finished his conversation and came to meet her. His smooth, handsome face bore the marks of recent strain.

"How are you, Johanna?" he asked. "Well, I hope?"

She saw no purpose in polite chitchat. "What is going on here?"

"We had best find a more private place to talk."

She folded her arms across her chest. "What has happened?"

"I'd thought you might have heard. Mr. Ingram was attacked and injured last night in the hotel."

"Attacked?" Her heart jumped. "By whom?"

"No one is sure—yet." He took her elbow and led her away from the prying eyes and ears of the locals. "Ingram didn't see his face. One maid at the hotel said . . . but that can wait."

Johanna remembered to breathe. "How badly is he injured?"

"He suffered a broken arm and a large collection of bruises. It could have been much worse, according to his report. But he was able to defend himself, and his attacker fled."

"A robbery?"

"Nothing was taken."

"I assume the authorities have been called in," she said. "Why was he attacked, if not in the course of a theft?"

"That is the question." Bolkonsky pursed his lips. "That is what the entire town is discussing. Apparently this has never happened before in Silverado Springs; it has deeply upset the residents. Since Ingram is a stranger here, no one can determine a motive for such an attack. And some of the speculation—" He stopped her and looked deep into her eyes. "It involves you, or more specifically, your patients."

Johanna forgot to breathe again. "What do you mean?"

"Some say—you know how these ignorant, small-town folk can be— that one of your patients might have come to town and attacked Ingram."

"That is ridiculous." She stepped back and turned in a small, agitated circle. "None of the Haven's residents would have done such a thing. When has any one of them ever come here and caused trouble?"

"Johanna," Bolkonsky said softly, "I agree with you. I know as well as you do the misconceptions held about the insane. But I have been listening to the gossip. Quentin Forster and one of your other patients caused a minor disturbance here several days ago. A matter of fisticuffs with local children."

Of course. Johanna hadn't forgotten. She'd known all along how that one incident could feed the fire of any prejudices the local folk already harbored.

"Oscar wouldn't hurt anyone," she said. "He was the one attacked. He merely defended himself."

"But he is certainly big enough to do damage if he wished, according to what I've heard. It's much easier for the ignorant to place the blame on outsiders than look among themselves for a culprit. And then there is Quentin—"

Quentin. The crux of the business. Quentin, who'd been missing all day. Who'd been worried for May. Who might have learned of May's father, and her acute misgivings about him.

"When did this attack occur?" she asked.

"Last night, well after midnight. A few drunks from the saloon claimed to have observed someone running away from the hotel, but no one clearly saw him, except a maid who was able to describe his general height and build."

Johanna didn't ask for the description. She felt cold all the way to her bones.

Why? Why should she jump to the same conclusions held by these unenlightened townsfolk? Quentin had exhibited occasional lapses into a darker state, a side of himself that hinted of undispelled pain and anger. He claimed, under hypnosis, to be a lycanthrope. He'd suffered periods of amnesia related to his drinking. He'd even admitted to concern for his own occasionally erratic behavior.

But he was not dangerously insane. He'd never acted overtly violent in any way—not with her, or the others. Surely reading of Johanna's suspicions about Ingram wouldn't be enough to send him tearing into town to attack a stranger.

But if that possibility were as ludicrous as it seemed, why was she trembling?

"What is it. Johanna?"

She shook herself from her bleak thoughts and met Bolkonsky's gaze. "If feelings against my patients are running so high, I must return to the Haven."

"Johanna—are any of your patients unaccounted for?"

"No." The lie came far too easily, but she felt free of guilt for the transgression. "I must be getting back."

"Why did you come to town, Johanna?" he asked, too insistently. "We still have the situation with May to resolve. You understand that in light of what has happened, Mr. Ingram is most anxious to leave Silverado Springs as soon as he is able to."

"We agreed upon a week at least. Dr. Bolkonsky."

"Did we?" His upper lip twitched. "I can make no guarantees, Dr. Schell."

His renewed formality came as a warning. She nodded and turned to collect Daisy. The pointed stares of the townsfolk made unpleasant sense, now. She could only pray that the residents of Silverado Springs were mistaken in their conjectures.

Once home again, she gave Daisy into a curious Oscar's care and began another circuit of the Haven's grounds, on foot, starting with the vineyard and ending at the orchard.

That was where she found him.

The half-conscious man slumped against a young apple tree was not the one she'd known for the past two weeks. He bore more resemblance to the stranger she'd rescued on the lane to the Haven, clothes dirty and abraded, face unshaven, hair matted and tangled. He raised his head from his chest to look at her through bloodshot eyes.

"Johanna," he croaked.

He had been drinking. She smelled it on him, but she would have known even without the stench. It was amazing that he could be in such poor condition after only a single day of imbibing.

Unless his state had to do with other, less benign activities.

"Quentin," she said, shaping each word distinctly. "Where have you been?"

He tried to get up and fell back, head rolling against the tree trunk. "At . . . the saloon." He coughed out a laugh. "Can't you tell?"

"Is that all?"

"I . . . don't remember."

Such a simple, terrible phrase. "Tell me what you do remember."

On the second try his efforts to stand were more successful. He propped himself against the tree, swaying.

"I went into town," he mumbled.

"Did you go through the papers in my office?"

"I wanted to find out about May."

"And you did."

He took a step toward her and paused to catch his balance. "I found out about her father."

Lecturing him on the impropriety of viewing private documents was the furthest thing from Johanna's mind. "And you went into town to do what, Quentin?"

"To . . . see him."

"Did you see him?"

"I think—" He clutched at his head. *"Don't Please."*

He wasn't talking to her, she was certain of it. "What did you do when you saw him, Quentin?"

With uncharacteristic awkwardness he spun on his foot and staggered back to the tree, hugging it with both arms. "I went and got drunk."

"Something happened in town last night, Quentin, while you were gone."

His profile was stark and pale, cheek pressed to rough bark. "God."

Johanna came to a decision. She couldn't leave him like this, or allow both of them to remain unaware of what he'd done and unprepared for the consequences. Patient or not, she must continue to treat him to the best of her ability until this crisis was past.

"I would like to hypnotize you, Quentin—now. Can you walk with me to my office?"

He pushed away and started for the house, not waiting for her. She caught up and took a firm grip on his arm. May saw them first, and came running. Her face fell when she got a good look at Quentin.

"Quentin isn't feeling well," Johanna said, guiding him past the girl. "He needs to rest."

"Yes," May whispered. Oscar joined her, but neither made a move to follow them into the house.

Quentin fell back onto the chaise as if the short walk from the orchard had exhausted him. She made a more thorough inspection of his body for wounds or evidence of struggle, but found none. If he had been the one to attack Ingram, the other man hadn't left a mark on him when he'd defended himself.

If Quentin had attacked. If . . .

His half-dazed state made him even more susceptible to hypnosis than usual, and he went into a deep trance the moment she finished her induction.

"I would like you to do the best you can to answer my questions, Quentin. Reach into your memory, with no fear of what you may find."

His closed lids fluttered, but he made no answer.

"Let us start from the beginning. You went into town."

"Yes." His voice was flat, unemotional.

"To see May's father."

"Yes."

"Why?"

"I was worried about May. I read in your notes that he might have hurt her before she came here."

Johanna damned her own meticulous nature that demanded the recording of each thought and observation related to every patient within her care. No matter how based upon conjecture or guesswork. She doubly damned her carelessness in not locking those notes away.

"Did you think that May was in danger from her father?" she asked.

"I had to find out."

"And did you?"

Silence. She must approach the subject more cautiously.

"How did you find him?"

"You said where he was. I went to the hotel and found his rooms."

"When was this, Quentin?"

"After midnight."

That jibed with what Irene had said. "Was he there?"

Quentin's jaw tightened. "Yes."

"What did you observe when you found him?"

"He was . . . with a young girl."

Johanna became aware that her hands were fastened upon the arms of her chair. She stretched her fingers one by one.

"What was he doing, Quentin?"

"Forcing his attentions upon her."

She shut down her own feelings. "In what way?"

No answer.

"What did you feel, when you saw this?"

No answer.

"Why was it so important to you to protect May, Quentin?"

He turned his head sharply on the chaise's pillow, but still said nothing.

Obviously the ordinary method of questioning wasn't going to work, and she didn't have the leisure to experiment over days or weeks. Time for an entirely new, and potentially dangerous, tack.

"Quentin," she said slowly, "you once told me that you could change into a wolf."

He seemed to stop breathing.

"I'd like to see you do that now. Change for me, Quentin."

She had no idea what would happen, or even if he'd try to obey. She waited, knowing what she might have unleashed but prepared to face whatever might come.

Quentin opened his eyes. He looked across the ceiling, rose on his elbows, and lowered his gaze to hers.

"You called, Doctor Schell?" he said, smiling around bared teeth. "I've been waiting for you."

Oh, yes, he had changed. It was in the slight thickening of his features: the cruelty in them, the harshness, the narrow satisfaction in his eyes. They had lost every trace of warmth, their color like nothing so much as that of dried blood.

Complete antipathy. Utter loathing. Pure hate.

She knew this Quentin. She had encountered him before without even realizing it.

"Cat got your tongue?" he mocked. He swung his legs over the chaise. "I like you better this way, Johanna. Speechless."

"Quentin?"

"He's gone. You wanted him to change, didn't you?" He stood up, looming over her with curled fingers. "Well, he's changed. Now *I'm* here."

The moment had come.

Fenris tested the feel of his body, slipping into it as easily as if he put on a coat. He'd worn it not so long ago, and had almost tasted Johanna's lips. He'd nearly gained control last night, and that evening when Johanna had so wantonly displayed herself. But Quentin had held on, pushing him back each time.

Now *he* was in command. Never had he felt so liberated: in full daylight, his mind clear, and in the presence of one who could see him for what he was. No drunken haze inherited from Quentin's weakness. No waiting until the precise combination of emotion and drink and circumstance gave him the strength to escape.

The unwitting, luscious, naive Johanna Schell had let him out of his cage.

He looked her up and down, giving free rein to his lust. Quentin's lust as well, if that milksop would ever admit it. But Quentin was far away, helpless, as *he* was helpless during so much of their bitterly shared existence.

Quentin wouldn't be alive if not for him. But Quentin was afraid of living.

He wasn't.

"Surprised to see me?" he asked, walking slowly toward Johanna. "You shouldn't be. We've met before."

She held her ground, bracing one hand against the back of her chair. "Who are you?"

At least she wasn't so stupid as to believe he wasn't real. Not that her mind mattered to him in the slightest. Her body was what he wanted. He stripped her to nakedness with a thought, and in another had her panting beneath him, begging for mercy. Turning thought to action would take but a few minutes more.

"Who are you?" she repeated, more firmly. Her jaw was set, her gaze steady in an excellent approximation of courage. He laughed.

"Fenris," he said. He reached out and casually snapped off the uppermost button of her collar with a flick of a finger.

"Fenris," she echoed. "The monster Wolf, offspring of Loki and enemy of the gods, who remains chained in Asgard until Ragnarok."

"Not always," he said, licking his lips and watching her face as she realized his intentions. "Not today." He ran his finger down the center of her bodice, pressing between her breasts.

Her deep breath defied him. "Where is Quentin?"

"I told you." He grasped her elbow and jerked her toward him. "He's gone."

"Where?"

He tilted her head back, yanking the pins from her hair. "Where he can't stop me."

"You share his body."

"He squanders it." He tore off the second and third buttons of her bodice. "I use it. As I'll use yours."

Her pupils narrowed to pinpricks, swallowed in a sea of blue. "I understand," she said. "All the strange things Quentin has done, the behavior that made no sense—it was you."

"Stop wasting our time," he growled.

"When will . . ." She gave an almost inaudible gasp as he squeezed her breast in his hand. "When will he return?"

"When I'm finished. If I let him." He ground his erection between her thighs. "No more talk. Take off your dress."

She was stronger than he'd realized. Her resistance was a solid thing of bone and muscle, preventing him from relieving her of her bodice.

The resistance was what excited him. Making her admit she wanted him to take her was more exciting still.

"Release me," she demanded.

"Lying to yourself, Doctor?" He bent his head and grazed her neck with his teeth, nipping just firmly enough to make her feel it. "You can't wait to find out what it's like to have me pounding my way inside you."

"You have no access to my thoughts . . . Fenris. What you propose is simply rape, nothing more."

The sheer coolness of her accusation filled him with rage. He twisted one of her arms behind her so that she couldn't move without pain. "It's Quentin, isn't it? You've been lusting after him like a bitch in heat. You think you can have him and get rid of me. It isn't going to work. Once I take you, he'll be that much weaker."

"Quentin's honor is more potent than your violence."

"Is it?" He laughed. "The honor that made him go to your room with only one thing in mind?"

"That wasn't Quentin."

"It was both of us. But I'm getting stronger all the time. And when I'm done, Quentin'll never show his face again. First I'll take his woman, and then the rest of his miserable life." He jerked her arm, forcing her to cry out. "Open your legs for me, woman."

"I will not." She stared straight into his eyes. "Do you know everything Quentin knows?"

He laughed in contempt. "More. Much more." He licked the underside of her jaw. "You pretend to be a tight little virgin, but I saw your body when you were with him, your tits all hard and your juices flowing. I smelled your lust. I smell it now."

"Does *he* know about you?"

She was distracting him with all her questions. "Shut up." He pushed her to the chaise and turned her so that she would fall on her back.

"You do intend to rape me, then," she said. "Now I know you are not Quentin."

"Quentin!" He flung her down and fell on top of her, holding himself just above with his braced arms. "Did he ever kiss you like this?"

He seized her mouth, hard, thrusting his tongue deep inside. She lay quiet under him, unresponsive. A howl of fury built up in his throat.

"Quentin would never kiss me like that," she said, when she could speak again. "He is a gentleman. I do not know what you are." Intermittent shivers rushed through her body, as if she were only half able to control them. "You have the strength to do what you like with me, but I doubt that you will find it entirely pleasant."

He raised his fist to hit her, saw the glint of fear under the stalwart façade, and let his hand fall. For all her brave display of fortitude, she was weaker than he was. Weaker, and not to be abused. That was the rule.

Quentin. Quentin did this to him. *Quentin's* rules still bound him. If he tried to break them, he would lose.

"Damn you," he snarled. "I will make you beg for it."

She touched him then, deliberately, spreading her fingers across his chest in a gesture that both invited and repelled.

"I have a better idea," she said with that excruciating, deceptive calm. "I'll strike a bargain with you. You want me—but not unwilling."

Oh, yes, he wanted her—now, as he'd wanted her from the very beginning, willing or unwilling.

"I'll give myself to you freely," she said, "if you answer my questions."

Questions, always questions. He leaned so close that her breath filled his mouth like wine. "Why should I bargain?"

"Because—" She paused, some calculation moving behind her eyes. "Because if you rape me, you'll be no better than May's father abusing that girl at the hotel."

The impact of her words sent his soul spinning like a top. For a moment he lost possession of his body, felt it slipping away from him.

Quentin was trying to take it back.

"No," he cried. *"Not yet."* He leaped away from Johanna and flung himself at the nearest wall, pounding his body against it until the pain convinced him that it remained in his power.

His body. *His.*

"Fenris?"

She stood by the chaise, unruffled, not even bothering to close the gap in her bodice.

Arrogant bitch. "A bargain," he said, hating and wanting so much that his bruised body screamed with the unrequited need to hurt in turn.

"You will answer?" she asked.

"Five minutes," he said. "And then—" He smiled and pointed at the chaise in a way she could not possibly misunderstand.

Chapter 17

Johanna let herself sag against the chaise, just enough to be sure that her body would not fail her, not enough for Fenris to sense her vulnerability.

Or her fear.

His thoughts were transparent on his altered face. She had prayed that hers remained hidden, and it seemed as if her prayers were answered. She held the advantage. Reason must always win out over savagery.

She had no doubt that Fenris was capable of savagery. That was what made the situation so remarkable, why fascination warred with fear and kept her mind racing.

For Fenris *was* Quentin. Not Quentin as she knew him, but another manifestation of his personality, ordinarily hidden from the world. She'd caught glimpses of him before, but now she had no further doubts.

And with his appearance came hope for the answers she had sought.

She had heard of such phenomena, read of them in books, rare though they were: incidences of two personalities sharing a single body, alternating ownership of it. In France there'd been the case of a woman named Felida. Two completely dissimilar women had existed in separate lives, total opposites in nature and ambitions. One, the original Felida, had been dull and gentle: the other, which her physician called her "second state," was flirtatious and wild. When one held ownership of the body, the other disappeared. And only the second personality knew of the other's existence or remembered the other's experiences. For Felida, whole periods of time—hours, weeks, eventually months—simply vanished.

Never before had Johanna the occasion to witness this bizarre syndrome for herself. It explained so much, yet her knowledge was pathetically deficient. If she could only speak to Fenris as she did Quentin, win his trust, she might find the way to heal Quentin's complex illness.

The key lay in this personality she confronted, in his mysterious origins—and in how much he differed from the gentle man she knew.

In at least one way he resembled Quentin. Her mention of May's father had been an act of desperation, based upon speculation and instinct. What Quentin hated, Fenris might also hate.

As what Quentin desired, Fenris also desired, without the inhibitions. And yet Fenris had been prepared to make a bargain.

"Four minutes," Fenris said.

She focused on him again, seeking Quentin behind that sneering mask. He was there, no matter how deeply buried he seemed.

"You were in town last night," she said, speaking as she would to any patient.

He wasn't fooled: his sharp white incisors flashed a predatory glint. "Yes."

"You attacked May's father, did you not?"

"Yes—once I got rid of Quentin." His lips contorted in disdain. "Is that the best you can do?"

"Why did you attack him?"

"I don't need a reason." He stretched, cracking the joints in his spine. "I enjoyed it."

He was lying. He had a reason. He, or Quentin.

"You said before that you know much more than Quentin does. What did you mean?"

"Can't you guess, Johanna?" Her name on his lips became almost an obscenity, laced with the threat of sexual perversions beyond naming.

"Quentin doesn't realize you exist," she said. "But you know everything he does, feels, thinks."

"Another brilliant deduction." Idly, he touched himself, outlining the heavy fullness of his erection. "He pretends I don't exist, to save himself. Stupid fool. If I weren't here, he would have died long ago. I keep him alive only for my own sake."

"You keep him alive?"

"He's a weakling and a coward."

"But you are not." She locked her gaze on his face and refused to look elsewhere. "You . . . do things he wouldn't. You are willing to fight, even harm others, as he would not."

He clapped his hands. "Bravo, Doctor."

Once more she mentally catalogued all she'd read about the condition sometimes known as "splitting of the personality," or "double consciousness." "You and Quentin share the same body," she said. "You cannot control it at the same time. But Quentin is the one who holds it most often. Is that not correct?"

Baleful light flickered in his eyes. "Until now."

"When you control your body, Quentin goes away. He can't affect what you do. He isn't even aware of your existence." More pieces of the puzzle fell into place. "But if he doesn't know about you, he can't consciously let you out. When do you take possession, Fenris? What makes it possible?"

He took a step forward. "You're nearly out of time, Johanna."

"Answer my question."

"I come when he's afraid to act, when he meets what he can't face. When he tries to escape into drink and can't hold his liquor."

"When he gets angry," she guessed, "so angry that he feels he may do violence."

"When he can't protect himself." His fingers curled like claws. "Then *I* come."

"And what makes him so angry and afraid, Fenris?"

The ruthless mockery in Fenris's eyes subsided, replaced for an instant with confusion.

She was close, so close. A few more questions answered and her supposition would be confirmed.

"When were you born, Fenris?" she asked.

He looked through her to some distant time and place.

"What is your first memory?"

His expression darkened, became so rigid that it looked as though it might crack with a single twitch.

"The cellar," he said hoarsely.

"The cellar, where?"

"Greyburn."

Just as she had suspected. She subdued her excitement.

"How old were you?"

"Eight."

"Why did you come then, Fenris?"

"He called me."

"Quentin? Quentin called you?"

"To make sure he wouldn't die."

Her throat closed in on itself. "Why would he die?"

Fenris closed his eyes. "It hurt too much. He wanted to kill—"

"What hurt, Fenris?"

He shook his head wildly. Johanna recalled that one session with Quentin . . . his childlike cries, speaking to someone from his past: *If I don't do what he says—I won't—he locks me up in here . . . then Grandfather brings the ropes—*

"You were beaten," she said, her voice thick to her own ears. "Who hurt you, Fenris?"

"You know. *He* told you."

"His—your grandfather."

She hadn't thought it possible that Fenris's face could grow more malevolent, but it did so now. Hate beyond hate. The promise of punishment beyond the fires of hell itself.

"Yes," he whispered.

"He wanted you to hurt something, and you wouldn't."

"Quentin wouldn't."

"But you did?"

"I took the punishment." Fenris's lips drew away from his teeth. "And I fought back."

She almost found it in her heart to pity the grandfather who had created such a monster. Had Fenris taken revenge?

"Quentin knew about you then, when he called you for help," she said. "Did he forget? What made him forget, Fenris?"

"He forgot everything." Fenris backed up and slammed his arms against the wall. "*I* remember. *I* suffered it all for him."

And you hate him for it. Fenris was hatred—Quentin's hatred and pain and terror. The memories he couldn't face.

"I'm sorry, Fenris," she said. "I'm sorry you had to suffer so much."

His gaze became terrifyingly lucid. "Sorry?" He threw back his head and laughed. "You think you can help him, don't you?"

"Help him—and you."

"I don't need help." He pushed free of the wall and advanced on her. "When the time is right, Quentin will disappear. Only I'll be here." His feet made no sound on the floor. "Get used to it, Johanna. You're mine."

The backs of her thighs bumped against the chaise. Fenris's evil intent, his unfettered lust, poured over her like a dirty fog. Her flesh crawled with it.

Quentin's body would lie against hers; Quentin's hands would touch her, his weight move upon her. But Quentin would not be there.

Fenris had said she wanted Quentin. She did. Only Quentin. And he alone could save her now.

"Quentin," she said, searching his face. "I know you're there. It's time to wake up."

"It won't do you any good," Fenris said. "He's cowering in his little corner, and he won't return until it's too late."

"Quentin was the one who created you, and he can banish you as well." She lifted her chin and gave Fenris stare for stare. "It's not your time, or your place. Go."

Fenris flinched, as if her command had actually affected him. He shook himself and took another step toward her. One more and he'd be on top of her.

"Quentin," Johanna repeated. She reached out and pressed her palm to Fenris's cheek. "You have nothing to fear. Come back to me."

The unshaven skin under her hand twitched and jumped. Fenris opened his mouth on a scream.

"You lied," he roared. "I'll make you—"

He didn't complete his threat. It faded to a whisper, and the ferocious glint in his eyes went out like a snuffed candle. The transformation she'd witnessed so recently began to reverse itself as he surrendered his body to its original and rightful owner.

Quentin's eyes fixed on her in bewilderment, as warm as they had ever been. "What did you say?"

She knew instantly that he remembered nothing of Fenris's appearance, or what had been said since his other self had seized his body. He had spoken of "shadows" that haunted him, but those shadows had no name or personality he could grasp with his conscious mind. For him, it must seem as if he'd simply lost track of the conversation.

Fenris hadn't lied. Quentin was unaware that he lived a double life. He didn't know that he had attacked May's father.

Johanna's first impulse was to tell him everything. He deserved to know, and curing such a profound illness could not begin until he confronted the dark half of himself. She understood with a deep, unwavering insight that any cure must come from the deliberate reunion of Quentin's divided selves.

But how was such a thing to be accomplished? She had no experience to draw on, nothing but a few scattered cases to use as precedents. Fenris had been "born" in a time of great suffering, created by Quentin's own mind to bear the unbearable. She guessed that he had also emerged during the battle in India, the "massacre" that Quentin didn't consciously remember. And any number of times since.

Even so, she could not believe that Fenris was a killer. He must remain alive because he still served a purpose—a purpose that Quentin could not acknowledge.

If she told Quentin of Fenris now, she might be taking a terrible risk. He knew something had happened with May's father, but Fenris hid the true facts from his conscious mind. In his own way, Fenris was protecting Quentin from a more deadly madness—one that could destroy both of them.

Only by exposing Quentin's hidden rage, and the suffering in his past, could she eliminate the menace of Fenris's insidious presence. Only with Fenris's cooperation could she cure Quentin without shattering his sanity forever.

"What was your last question, Johanna?" Quentin said with a ragged smile. "I'm afraid I don't remember."

"It doesn't matter." She let her hand fall. "Our session is over, for now."

"Did you find out what you wanted?"

"Enough, for the time being."

He dropped his head into his hands, as if the dim light in the room hurt his eyes. "Did I . . . do anything? In town?"

"No, Quentin. *You* did not."

"You aren't lying to me."

She felt slightly ill. "No."

"And May—she's safe? You won't let anything happen to her."

"I promise you, Quentin. She will be safe."

"Then I think . . . I'll go and rest." He walked unsteadily to the door and turned. "I thought I might finally be over it—the drinking, and what comes after. I was wrong." He stared at the floor between his feet. "You were right, Johanna. There's nothing you can do to help me."

Her visceral protest stuck in her throat. He walked out of the room as if he didn't expect one.

She went to her desk, sat down, and attempted to take notes. Her hand only managed to make uneven ink blots on the paper.

Notes were unnecessary. She was all too sensible of her current predicament: two equally urgent cases, May's and Quentin's strangely—and dangerously—interconnected. Fenris had attacked Ingram. He might reappear at any time if provoked—if May should be threatened again. And there was no telling how far he might go.

Why did Fenris, and Quentin, react so strongly to May's situation? Quentin had said that Ingram was "forcing his attentions" upon a young maid at the hotel. Fenris knew all that Quentin experienced. He had acted upon Quentin's desires. In his mind, May and the maid were one and the same.

Quentin would have understood the difference, but Fenris didn't care. He was a force immune to reason and negotiation, to all the civilizing elements that made Quentin who he was.

As long as Fenris continued to exist, Quentin must be watched, and kept close to the Haven. There were times she could not be with him—at night, and when she saw the other patients. That meant she had to believe that Fenris would remain dormant as long as Quentin was not provoked.

Restraining him by physical means was out of the question. And so, now, was sending him to another doctor. The responsibility was entirely hers. And if she could no longer call him her patient . . .

He remained her friend. She would lay down her life for him. She would save him, if it was the last thing she accomplished as a doctor.

Or a woman.

Resolutely she set aside her pen, gathered her notes, and hid them in a new place behind several heavy medical volumes on her bookshelf.

She resumed her routine until dinnertime, visiting her father and the other patients and joining them at the table in the usual manner. Quentin remained in his room.

She tossed and turned that night. When she slept at last, vivid dreams swept her away on a tide of ever-changing images, both nightmarish and sublime. She found herself in Quentin's arms, turning her face up to his tender kisses, feeling his hands on her body. Between one moment and the next, in the manner of dreams, she was naked in his bed.

He stretched his length over her, murmuring endearments as he stroked her belly, her most intimate places. Her own voice emerged as a low moan of anticipation and need. She was about to be initiated into the mystery she knew only as theory: the supreme pleasure of sexual ecstasy, the joining of a man and woman in the act of love . . .

He kissed her. She cried out in pain, tasting blood on her lips.

Fenris held her; Fenris pushed her thighs apart and laughed in his victory. She fought him, raking his face and his chest with her nails, but he was immune to hurt. He pressed down, overpowering her, smothering her, possessing her.

"Quentin!"

The cry yanked her from the dream and halfway out of the bed. For a terrifying instant she couldn't move. Her nightgown was twisted around her body and wedged between her legs; the sheets lay spilled on the floor.

Hunched up against the pillows, she concentrated on catching her breath. Her skin was clammy to the touch, her heart leaping from beat to beat like a panicked doe.

Still halfway caught in the snares of her own mind, she crawled from the bed and felt her way to the door.

Quentin. She must see him, make sure of . . . what? That he wasn't the cruel and ruthless creature who laughed as he subjugated all her strength and confidence, and stripped her of herself? Or was it to prove she wasn't afraid?

She bumped into the walls of the hallway and flailed for the knob of Quentin's door.

Her clumsy movements would surely have awakened the heaviest sleeper. But as she reached Quentin's bedside she found him insensible, locked in a fathomless sleep.

In sleep, he was at peace. Fenris had no part of that face, those lips softly curved in some pleasant dream. She knelt beside the bed and gazed at him until the last remnants of her nightmare shredded and drifted away into the summer night.

This was Quentin. This was the man who had made such a vital place in the life of the Haven. The man who had held her in the dream, claimed her long before Fenris broke free to taunt and bully.

But no man claimed her. She belonged only to herself. She couldn't be taken.

She could *give.*

She leaned over the bed and kissed his brow, meaning it to end there. His skin was warm and slightly damp, tasting of male. One taste was somehow not enough. She kissed the outer corner of his eyelid, and then the high arch of his cheekbone. He sighed through slightly parted lips. She caught the last trace of his breath with her own mouth.

The dream wasn't over. She felt his arms come up around her, gently, neither constraining nor demanding.

"Johanna?" he murmured.

She tensed to flee, suddenly aware of where she was and what she did. The darkness was no hiding place. Quentin was awake. He held her. Not like Fenris, with the desire to seize and devour, but as if he had the most uncertain clasp on a miracle and might crush it with a twitch of his finger.

The decision was hers to make. She wasn't even sure how she'd come to this moment.

But she *did* know: She'd come to it step by slow, plodding step, just as she treated her patients in small, alternating increments of gratifying progress and frustrating reversal.

The dream was only an excuse. Hadn't it all been leading to this, from the hour she'd saved him by the lane? Hadn't she admitted her attraction at the beginning, no matter how much she fought it?

Quentin faced a terrible challenge. She'd vowed to see him through it, regardless of the cost. Fenris wished to drive her away from this man, who knew but half of himself.

She wouldn't be driven. But she must choose, now for all time: to remain apart from him, clutching at the last scraps of objectivity, or to forsake her principles and surrender to her heart.

Logic dictated the obvious answer. Logic, which had no more power to force her hand than did fear. But once she abandoned it, she couldn't turn back.

"Am I dreaming?" Quentin asked. "Are you here, Johanna?"

Muscle by muscle she allowed her body to melt against him. "I'm here."

He stroked the palm of his hand up her cheek and across her hairline, smoothing the stray wisps that had come loose from her braids. "Why?"

Answer him. Answer with the truth . . .

"I dreamed," she said. "Dreamed of you."

"What did you dream?"

"That . . . I was with you. Here, in your room."

"With me." His hand, stilled in its motion, moved again to cup the back of her head. But he drew her no closer. "As you are now?"

"Yes."

"I've also dreamed, Johanna," he said, stroking the pad of his thumb along the bridge of her nose. "But dreams do not always match reality."

As if she, of all women, were not fully cognizant of such facts. "Sometimes dreams reflect reality very well indeed."

"Or give us warnings." He let her go. Her skin felt suddenly cold in the absence of his touch. "Johanna, I think you'd better leave."

"You want me to go?" she said. "After all the—" She stopped herself, moved back to sit on the edge of the bed and began again. "You have, in the past, led me to believe that you are attracted to me. Was I mistaken?"

He sat up, and the sheets slid down to pool in his lap. She bit down hard on her lower lip.

"Why the change, Johanna?" he countered. "Why come to me now? You've been avoiding me." He smiled in self-mockery. "With good cause, I've behaved . . . less than admirably. Yesterday was just more proof that I'm not to be trusted."

"Yesterday you said that I couldn't help you—"

"You said it yourself, Johanna. I told you that you were right."

"I was *wrong*." She glared at him, trying to make him understand.

"I thought that I was no longer to be your patient."

"No. Not my patient."

"Then what, Johanna?"

That was the question, and now she had no choice but to answer. *Answer him.*

"Let me . . . let me show you," she whispered.

He turned his head. "Again, why now? Is it pity?"

She reared back. "Pity? Can you say such a thing, when—" She pressed her lips together. "I do not waste my time on pity."

"No." He met her gaze, and his eyes softened. "You're a curious woman, Johanna."

"It is a hazard of my occupation," she said. The nightgown was still damp with perspiration, and she realized that she was shivering. "Either you want me, Quentin, or you do not. I would appreciate an expeditious decision."

He laughed aloud. "Oh, Johanna, Johanna. Even now you can't stop playing the doctor."

"I don't play at anything," she said. "If that is your answer—"

His hand came to rest on her knee, burning through the muslin of her nightgown. "My answer, Johanna . . . is that I've always wanted you. From the very beginning."

A gush of heat rushed to the core of her body. "Then we need not talk any longer." She placed her hand carefully on his chest. It was bare, sleek with soft hair, and strongly muscled. The heat pooled between her thighs. "I am not afraid."

He seized her wrist. "Do you know what you're asking?"

"Is it so great a sacrifice on your part?"

"Not on mine." He eased his grip and ran his fingers up and down her arm. The sensation was delicious, but she tried not to let herself become distracted.

"You are concerned for my honor," she said. For all his joking and flirtation, he was no despoiler of women.

He was not. Fenris was another matter.

"I've known many women," he said. "I know what society demands."

"Of your aristocratic females, perhaps," she said. "But I am not a member of your society, nor am I attempting to make my way into an advantageous marriage."

He worked his fingers between hers. "You don't wish to be married?"

"We have had this conversation before, have we not? I have found that my work and marriage are not compatible."

"I'm sorry," he said.

"Do not pity *me*, Quentin. Do you think less of me, for making this offer?"

"No." He squeezed her hand. "You could never be less than honorable."

Her eyes began to prickle with incipient tears. "Then there is no obstacle—"

"What of your professional reputation?" His voice hardened. "I did not tell you before, but when I went into town with Oscar, comments were made regarding your possible relationship with male patients."

"I know. As they've undoubtedly been made in the past. I am not the first woman doctor to face such prejudices. But if they already suspect or prefer to believe that I am a loose woman of dubious morals, what we do now will make no difference."

"You must have plans for the future—"

"Yes. And I will continue with those plans. I am perfectly capable of discretion. What I do as a physician is entirely apart from what I choose as a person. A woman."

The bed shook with his silent laughter. "And to think I once asked you what you wanted as a woman, and doubted you'd ever allow yourself to find out."

"You have also made assumptions, Quentin," she said. "I thank you—for your gallantry, and your desire to protect me. But I do not need your protection, nor that of any man. I can make my own decisions and weigh the consequences."

He was quiet for a long time. "You know that our relationship can never be the same if we go forward."

"I know." And she did. It was long past time for regrets. Neither one of them had much to lose by proceeding to the next logical step.

And she knew, in the center of her being where scientific discipline held no sway, that a more intimate connection between them would only strengthen her ability to help him. She'd always relied on intuition in her approach to treating the insane. She saw with complete clarity, for the first time in her life, that emotion was the very basis of that intuition. Her feelings for Quentin were an inextricable part of her.

Feelings she wasn't yet prepared to name.

But there was a final reason why the hour had come to let fall the barriers she'd constructed to keep them apart.

"You think you can have him and get rid of me," Fenris had said. *"Once I take you, he'll be that much weaker."*

If that were possible, the reverse must also be true. She had the chance to circumvent Fenris's plans here and now. He might return at any moment, but if Quentin was first, Fenris was disarmed. The act of love would be for mutual pleasure, not domination. And Fenris would lose some of his power.

Over her, and over his other self.

"I am as fully committed to seeking your cure as I ever was," she said slowly. "But we will do it together."

"Together." He held out his arms. She moved into them, feeling as though she'd been rescued from the midst of an icy desert. "This method of rational discussion is a strange, dry way to go about love-making. It's a technique I never thought to try."

"With all your other lovers?"

"Ah, yes." He rested his forehead in the hollow of her shoulder. "There is so much you don't know about me, Johanna."

"No two people can hope to know one another completely."

"I'm still a drunkard, and I don't know what I'm capable of when . . . I lose control. If you give yourself to me, you do more than risk your reputation."

It was the plainest warning he could give. He wasn't aware of Fenris, and still he was afraid for her—but he didn't reckon on the greatest danger she faced.

Losing her heart. Facing life alone when he left her, as surely he must—as Rolf had left her, and her father.

That, too, was her decision: to take the risk, knowing full well that the future was an unknown quantity. She'd already turned her back on a woman's traditional fate.

She wouldn't force Quentin to bear the burden of unreasonable expectations. She went into this with her eyes wide open. What happened beyond tonight was in the lap of the gods. And if she got with child . . .

She would cope with that eventuality if and when it came, as she'd always done.

Words were insufficient to persuade Quentin of her sincerity. The time for hesitation was past.

Deliberately she pressed her weight against him, bearing back down among the pillows. She laced her hands behind his neck, amid the wavy strands of his auburn hair, and kissed him on the mouth.

At last, he believed her.

Chapter 18

Now Quentin was sure that there was more to sleep than nightmares.

Johanna had come to him. She was in his bed, practically begging to be loved. And he hadn't the strength to deny her, even when he knew he should.

Even when he knew how unworthy he was.

Why now? What had changed? She'd never really answered that

question. If he'd thought it was pity that drove her, after seeing him in such a pathetic state, fallen from his high resolves, his memory a blank . . .

But it wasn't pity. He sensed that she'd withheld the full truth about what had happened while he was drunk in town, but she wouldn't come to him if he'd committed any acts of violence. She was far too sane to commit her body to a lunatic.

Not Johanna. If she gave herself, it was with full comprehension, and of her own desire. She was as bold as any lady of the evening— unashamed, yet endearingly innocent at the same time; self-assured, yet betraying just a trace of feminine insecurity. Those very contrasts were what made her unique in all his wide experience.

He had known, from their first conversation, that loving her would be the premier experience of his lifetime. She'd give everything she had, for she knew no other way. And she'd chosen him to be her teacher in the arts of love.

But she was inexperienced, naive for all her intelligence. She needed guidance and a gentle hand.

She needed a lover who would take her so far, and no further.

Oh, it would be so easy to surrender to his own baser instincts and relieve her of the virginity she had so little use for. She was convinced that she'd accepted the potential repercussions of her actions. But he knew better. And he wouldn't let her destroy her life and career for a night's pleasure.

Not his pleasure, at any rate. All he'd done was to cause her trouble. Tonight, he'd bring her joy. And she wouldn't have to sacrifice anything but an hour's governance of her body.

As for her heart . . .

Wasn't it what he'd wanted, to break down that shell of cool restraint? But he'd never really believed it would come to this. He'd been so careful to avoid closeness with other human beings for the last several years. Was it because he thought Johanna was safe from his wiles that he'd dared so much with her, risked such intimacies?

If so, his scheme had backfired. Now he felt the heavy weight of responsibility. He might be weak, a coward and a scoundrel, but he had enough honor to keep her away from the crumbling brink of complete disaster. To regard tonight as a one-time miracle, not the beginning of a future that could never be.

As for tomorrow . . . it would take care of itself, one way or another. He believed in Johanna's good sense. And in his own instinct for survival.

She bent to kiss him again, and this time he met her halfway. He spread his hands across her back and kissed her as he'd always wanted to, without reserve or second thoughts: deeply, thoroughly, teasing her lips apart with his tongue and seeking inward. Her panting breath swept into his mouth.

Already he could feel her nipples like firm little buttons pressing his chest. She smelled exquisitely of woman, perspiration, and the unmistakable scent of desire. Her thighs straddled his, round and firm. Instead of shying away from the thrust of his manhood, patently outlined through the sheets that barely covered him, she rubbed herself against it.

He groaned. "Johanna," he said, "unless you want this to end very quickly, you'd better stop."

"Am I doing something wrong?" She sat up, her gaze sweeping from his face to his loins. Her hand found him, unerringly, and stroked, tugging the sheet below his hip-bones. "This is the source of pleasure, is it not?"

"Yes," he said through his teeth. "Bloody hell—excuse me, Johanna." He caught her hand and lifted it away from him. "You're just too good at it."

She smiled. "Am I? I have been a student of human nature for a long time. And I know my anatomy—"

"It isn't all anatomy." He grabbed the edge of the sheet and pulled it higher as he sat up, afraid that if he didn't keep himself covered he'd find his way inside her. Before she could see his movement as a rejection, he cupped her hands between his.

"Do you know where the center of your pleasure is, Johanna?"

The darkness wasn't enough to hide the flush in her cheeks from eyes like his. "I believe so."

"Have you ever touched it yourself?"

The blush cascaded down her neck to the collar of her nightgown. "I . . . have never been one of those who holds that such activity is a form of abuse that can lead to blindness and insanity. But I have not . . ." She swallowed. "Not purposely."

He tried not to imagine how she might have done so accidentally. "Then you'll have to allow me to show you."

"Right now?" Her voice squeaked several notes higher.

"In a few moments." He slid his hand up her arm to her shoulder. "Relax, Johanna. This is supposed to be enjoyable."

"I know." She made a visible effort to loosen her muscles. "What is next, then?"

"This is also not a textbook lesson," he said, working his hand under the open collar of her nightgown. "There are no rules."

"No. Of course not." She held very still while he undid a few buttons and brushed his fingers down from her collarbone to the deep cleft between her breasts.

He'd thought of this countless times, holding her naked breasts in his hands. She was bountiful, richly endowed, any man's dream of abundance. She had no idea how desirable she was.

Slowly he covered her breast with his hand. She gasped. Her firm nipple rubbed against his palm. He curved his fingers around it, squeezing with utmost gentleness. She closed her eyes.

"It feels—"

"Tell me how it feels, Johanna."

"I can't." She breathed in and out rapidly. "I hadn't realized that my . . . that they could be so—"

"Sensitive? You have no idea, my Valkyrie." He pulled her forward, ignoring the warmth of her rump on his groin, and lifted her breast through the vee of her neckline. Cradling it between his hands, he lowered his head.

Her amazed cry was all he could have wished for. He curled his tongue around her nipple, wetting it thoroughly, and then began to suckle. She arched up against him. When he'd had his way with one breast, he gave equal attention to the other. By then Johanna was hardly breathing at all.

"Oh," she whispered.

"This is what they were made for, Johanna," he said, pressing his face between her breasts. "To be pleasured and to give pleasure."

If she meant to protest his dismissal of their biological function, she hadn't enough presence of mind to do so.

"You . . . enjoy—"

"Indubitably." To prove it, he caressed her again.

"Quentin?"

"Yes . . ."

"I have read about the experience of orgasm—" She kept her eyes firmly closed, as if to protect herself from embarrassment. "But I do not know what it's like. Can you explain it to me?"

He pulled back and muffled a laugh. "It's not something one can explain . . . especially from a man to a woman."

"Is it possible to achieve without actual intercourse?"

"Why?"

"Because I think . . . I think . . ." She opened her mouth and shuddered, rising up on her knees and falling back again. The impact on his erection was astonishing. Stars danced in front of his eyes.

"No," she said. "No, I . . . must have been mistaken. For a moment, I thought—"

Filled with an inexpressible tenderness, Quentin drew her close. "You'll know, Johanna," he said. He caught her face between his hands and kissed the tip of her nose. "And we aren't nearly finished yet."

Johanna was finally compelled to confess her ignorance.

She hadn't had the slightest notion, for all her reading and observation, how wonderful sex could be. And Quentin had just begun.

It wasn't only the physical sensations, which of themselves were startling and indescribable. It was also the closeness—physical and emotional—that was so much more than the proximity of bodies.

She was eager to continue, but she contained herself. She was no wild wanton to lose every last vestige of common sense, forget where she was and why. She wanted to fully absorb every experience.

In case it never happened again.

"What is next?" she asked in a voice she hoped didn't betray her enthusiasm.

"I'll show you." He set his hands at her waist and lifted her easily, placing her on the bed beside him. He rolled over to cover her with his body.

Johanna tensed. His position reminded her too much of Fenris, and the feeling of helplessness she so despised. But Quentin made no move to constrain her. He leaned on one elbow and drew his fingers through her hair with his other hand, working the braids loose.

"Trust me, Johanna," he said.

"I do." She allowed him to separate the strands of her hair and spread it out across the pillow.

"Beautiful," he said.

"A very ordinary brown," she corrected.

"Let me be the judge of that." He kissed her, lightly at first, and then with greater passion. Her arms moved of their own accord to pull him down. He demonstrated the amazing variations possible in a simple kiss, from agile use of the tongue to subtle movements of strong, masculine lips.

And then he showed her all the other places on her body that could also be kissed.

He began with the other parts of her face: brow, cheeks, chin, jawline. He suckled the lobe of her ear, provoking waves of delicious shivers. She hadn't suspected how incredibly sensitive the flesh of her neck and its junction with her shoulder could be, especially when he grazed it with his teeth and salved it with his tongue afterward.

Inch by meticulous inch he worked his way down her body. She almost cried out in anticipation as he reached her breasts and repeated his previous caresses. His mouth closed over her nipple, sucking and tugging in a way that sent lances of sensation shooting directly into her womb.

She felt . . . beautiful. Her breasts were beautiful, the slight roundness of her stomach, the full breadth of her hips. Each part he worshipped in turn. He kissed the gentle projection of her ribs and ran his tongue in teasing circles around her navel. All the while she felt him drawing closer to the place that begged for his attentions. Her breath rang hoarse and loud in her own ears.

He paused, giving her brief deliverance from the high pitch of excitement. Yet she didn't want him to stop.

"Please," she murmured.

"You aren't afraid?" he asked again. His voice was just as unsteady as hers. "I can slow down, if you like."

"No," she answered, half in a daze. "No."

"It was a very foolish question." He took her hips between his hands and kissed his way down her body again.

The first touch of his tongue to her femininity was a considerable shock. She felt as if she'd been struck by lightning, every volt of it focused on this one part of her body. She thought she might die in the next few seconds.

She didn't die. Quentin was an expert. He pushed his tongue into the soft, moist flesh, stroking and exploring. She clutched handfuls of sheet in her fists, wondering how she could bear it. How any woman could. And to think that some male physicians actually believed that females could or should not know this . . . this ecstasy.

A moan escaped her. Quentin's caresses became more urgent, as if he were propelling her toward the climax he'd promised she would recognize. Surely she was already there. But the feeling of sheer pleasure became one of rising, rising toward some immeasurable height, a Valhalla that only the blessed could know.

Quentin led her there, drew her to the edge, and then let her go.

She exploded, tumbled, spun to the bottom in a rush of light and joy. Quentin was waiting for her. She felt herself pulse against his mouth while he reveled in her delight.

Every limb weighted with gratified exhaustion, Johanna rested her head on the pillow and let the overwhelming sensations fade. At last she knew what it was to reach the ultimate physical completion. The feelings Quentin had aroused in her when he'd touched her breasts were nothing compared to this. She couldn't help giggling a little at her own naïveté.

"I don't believe I've ever heard you giggle before," Quentin said, rolling onto his back beside her. "You found it acceptable?"

"Acceptable? You can ask that when—" She paused, noting the gleam of bedevilment in his eye. The hopeless rogue. She reached for his hand. "More than acceptable."

"I am glad." He propped himself up on his elbow to gaze at her. "You have a certain natural talent yourself."

"But I've done nothing. It has been quite—one-sided, has it not?" Quentin licked his lips. "I found it very pleasant, I assure you."

"But you have not—we have not finished." Even as she spoke, she felt a renewed ache between her thighs—the ache of emptiness, of a powerful need to be filled in a way only Quentin could do.

"Not everything must be done at once," he said. "We aren't on a schedule, are we?"

He was putting her off, she was sure of it. In spite of his initial acquiescence, he hadn't let go of his qualms. He held back from the ultimate expression of the desire she knew he felt. The bold stance of his admirable, rather awesome male part had not diminished in the slightest.

She sat up and slid her hand down his belly. "Maybe not," she said. "But now it is my turn."

"You needn't—" He gulped back his words as she reached the base of his manhood and stroked up with one finger. He was so hard, so silky, and so very fascinating.

"I have seen this before, of course," she said in her best professional voice, "but never one so, so . . . superior."

"Thank you," he said. "I think."

"And never in this state, I must confess." She wrapped her hand around him and drew it up and down experimentally. His body jerked. "How long can you maintain it, I wonder?"

"Not . . . very much longer," he rasped. "Johanna—"

"I'm not being too rough?" She smiled serenely and reversed the direction of her caress.

He groaned in answer. After a few moments of experimentation she found just the right rhythm. He gave up any effort to speak and closed his eyes.

She loved the feeling of pleasuring him as he had done for her.

Still it was not enough. Her innate, driving curiosity remained unassuaged.

One thing remained to be tried. She adjusted her position so that she could bend over him without losing her balance.

Quentin's eyes shot open. He muttered an oath, his whole body going rigid as she proceeded with her explorations. His fingers caught in her hair. His breathing grew more and more uneven. At what she perceived to be the last possible instant, he pushed her away and swung his feet over the side of the bed, shuddering.

"I wasn't finished," she protested. "Come back here—"

"No." He turned about in one motion and bore her back onto the bed. "Not this time."

Her heart began to pound at half again its normal speed. This was it, then. He lay over her, braced on his arms, the sleek and now-familiar shape of his manhood pressed into her belly. Her insides had become liquid with wanting him; her body couldn't be more eager to accept him.

He would enter, and thrust, and move within her. She knew what it would be like. She could imagine it so well that the excitement sparked all over again, threatening to burst out of control before he so much as breached her maidenhead.

"Quentin," she whispered. "I am ready. Now, *mein Herz.*"

He repositioned himself, nudging her legs apart. He slid into place like a key ready to enter a well-oiled lock. Just the smallest movement, the merest thrust . . .

And he withdrew, clumsy with unfulfilled desire. Johanna bit her lips to keep from crying out in frustration.

"Not today, Johanna," he said, turning his head from her.

"Why?" Tears collected in her throat—rare, unwelcome visitors. "Why?"

"It isn't your fault, Johanna. Never think that." He looked at her, all humor fled from his face. "I can't, Johanna. It isn't for lack of wanting you." He tried, and failed, to smile. "I've never wanted a woman so much in my life. But the time isn't right. You know it as well as I do. Too much is at stake, too much uncertain."

"But I explained to you—"

"I know. I wanted to share what I could with you, Johanna. While I still had the chance. But if there's ever to be—more between us, things have to be different. Don't you see?"

She folded her arms across her breasts, bereft, somehow ashamed.

Though her body wailed protest and her emotions seethed with anger
and sorrow, her intellect understood him completely.

One night wouldn't be enough. Not for her. Once they joined,
she'd want him for all time. But such promises could not be made,
such castles built, while Fenris stood by and waited to usurp
Quentin's place.

She pulled the tousled sheets up to her shoulders and drew them
tight. "I see," she said.

"Don't hate me, Johanna." He knelt before her, pleading with his
eyes—this aristocrat, this fine and handsome madman who had loved
her so magnificently. "I couldn't bear it if you hated me."

"Hate you?" *Mein Gott.* Hate him . . . how could she hate the man
she loved?

A shot of ice water mingled with the blood in her veins.

Love.

She smoothed her face to serenity and took his hand. "I could never
hate you, Quentin. Not for any reason."

He lifted her hand to his lips and kissed it lingeringly. "My dear
Valkyrie."

Her heart stopped and started again, heavy and sluggish. She
turned her hand to cup his cheek.

"Thank you," she said. "Thank you for tonight."

Mute, he kissed her palm and rose from the bed. He flipped back
the sheets and gathered her up in his arms, lifting her against his chest.
In a few long, silent steps he carried her from his room to hers, and laid
her down in her own cool bed.

"Sleep, Johanna," he said. He kissed her forehead and then her lips,
almost chastely. "Sleep well."

She slept so well that she woke sometime after sunrise, her body
singing with remembered ecstasy after a night of glorious dreams.

Dreams that completed what she and Quentin had not.

She moved about the room only half awake, trying to hold on to
the fantasies. And the memories. She saw herself in the mirror and
wondered at this vision, this goddess she saw before her. She touched
her breasts and remembered how Quentin had caressed and suckled
them. She pressed her hand to her belly and imagined it filled with
Quentin's child.

That was not to be. Not so long as things remained as they were.
And she must take great pains to be sure that the other patients didn't

realize how her relationship with Quentin had changed. But now she knew what she wanted above all things in the world.

Once she'd told herself that the only way to be free of her attraction to Quentin was to cure him. Curing him was still the only route to happiness for them both. They had gone beyond the safe association of doctor and patient, but she had a greater advantage than any she'd possessed in the past. She knew the full depth of Quentin's illness, and had faced his inner nemesis without submitting to it. She had a strong theory about how Fenris had come to exist.

And she had love on her side.

Love. It was much too new an idea to embrace fully. She must grow used to it by stages, little by little, until it became one with her heart. Love, and all its attendant expectations.

She smiled foolishly at her reflection in the mirror and began to dress.

With the perfectly valid excuse of keeping an eye on him, she paused at Quentin's door on the way to the kitchen. His belongings were in place and the bed was neatly made, but he had already stepped out. To the woods, undoubtedly, alone or with May. Once she'd started the morning routine, she'd make certain of his whereabouts and ask him to remain on Haven grounds.

Furthermore, she must prepare May for her escape to Sacramento without alerting Quentin to the specifics of her plans for the girl. With luck, Bridget would hear back from her cousin soon, and she'd accompany May to a place where Bolkonsky and Ingram wouldn't find her. Much must be accomplished in the coming days.

Mrs. Daugherty was at work in the kitchen, making breakfast. When she saw Johanna she stopped her work and bustled forward with an envelope in her hand.

"Doc Jo!" she said, a little out of breath. "I have somethin' for you. Just an hour ago, that Dr. Bolkonsky met me on the road and asked me to deliver this." She scowled. "He said it was urgent."

That made it urgent for Johanna as well. She tore open the envelope. The letter was yet another request for her to meet him—not in town, but at a point halfway between the Haven and Silverado Springs. Once again he declined to visit the Haven, expecting her to come to him.

Nevertheless, she couldn't afford to ignore him. Keeping him satisfied was her best way of holding him off until May was gone.

She made her rounds to visit her father and the other patients, seeing to their immediate needs, and then asked Oscar to help her saddle Daisy.

"Have you seen Quentin this morning?" she asked as she took the reins.

"Nope. Not this mornin'." Oscar rubbed Daisy's nose. "May went out to look for him."

They weren't together, then. But Johanna refused to be concerned. May wouldn't venture far from the Haven, given her experience in Silverado Springs. And after last night, Johanna suspected that Quentin had as much to think about as she did.

"Oscar, you know the places where May likes to go. Would you find her and bring her home straightaway?"

"I will, Doc Jo."

"Thank you." She clucked to Daisy and set out for Bolkonsky's rendezvous.

He was waiting for her as promised, mounted on one of the best horses from the town livery. His animal's restless pawing reflected the anxious expression on Bolkonsky's deceptively handsome face.

"Johanna. I'm glad you came."

She drew Daisy up beside him. "You said it was urgent."

"Yes." His voice held a note of strain, and he kept looking back over his shoulder toward town as if he expected followers. "Something new has happened in Silverado Springs that I felt you should know about directly. Before someone else arrives to inform you."

Foreboding stiffened Johanna's shoulders. "Go on."

"Another man has been attacked," he said. "Last night, well after midnight. His body was discovered just outside of Silverado Springs. I am told the man was a local mine owner of some wealth, known chiefly for his cruel treatment of his Chinese workers. He was not well liked, so I hear—but someone resented him enough to kill him."

"He's dead?"

"Torn apart, I hear, though I have not seen the body."

A metallic taste coated her mouth. "And they suspect that one of my patients is responsible."

"Yes." He gave her a grave and sympathetic look. "I thought it best to warn you, so that you are prepared. After the previous attack on Ingram . . . the crowd was in an ugly mood this morning, and I fear—" He sighed. "I fear they may take matters into their own hands."

"Without proof?"

"What proof does a mob need? And there is more . . . two men from town claim to have identified a man lurking near the place when the mine owner was found. He bears, from the description, a striking resemblance to your Quentin Forster."

With as much stern discipline as she'd ever employed, Johanna prevented herself from showing any reaction. "I see."

"You do know where he is?"

"Naturally. It's all an unfortunate mistake. I thank you for your warning." She turned Daisy away, but Bolkonsky caught at her reins.

"My dear Johanna, I understand your dismay, but you can see now why it is necessary for me to take May with dispatch. She may be in danger from this—this madman, whoever he may be."

"But we agreed—"

"I'm sorry, Johanna. I'll be coming within the next few hours to fetch her. I would appreciate it if you'd have the girl's belongings packed and ready." He patted her arm. "I would prefer this to be as pleasant as possible, for all of us—without involving any outside authorities."

Bolkonsky had made just such a threat before. The last thing she wanted now was the local law sniffing about the Haven.

"Very well," she said. "I will do my best."

She sawed at Daisy's reins a little too violently, and the mare tossed up her head with a snort. She murmured an apology and kicked the horse into a gallop for home, not bothering with farewells. Let Bolkonsky look to himself.

As she must look to May and Quentin. All at once everything was falling apart, the reins of control slipping through her fingers. She had no notes or textbooks to consult, no protocols to fall back on.

Quentin—Fenris—was all but accused of being a killer. If, indeed, Bolkonsky was telling the truth. He was not a man to be trusted on any count, but she had to assume the worst. And May was in immediate danger.

So short a time ago she'd been filled with hope and happiness, imagining a future built upon love as well as science.

That future, and all she'd ever believed in, was crumbling before her eyes.

Chapter 19

Quentin turned over in his bed, breathing in the scent of Johanna's body. Her perfume saturated the sheets, filling him with fresh desire and the urge to roll about and rub the scent into his skin like the wolf he could so easily become.

Last night, after the loving, he'd run as a wolf—swift, sure, and silent. There was no other way to express the joy, the fullness of his heart. And the frustration of self-denial.

He'd done the right thing. He knew that, Johanna was still a virgin, free to give herself to another man without regret.

Or free to choose him, if by some miraculous turn of events fate granted him one more chance.

He got up and walked to the window, stretching in the shafts of morning sunlight until his bones cracked. Another chance. Was it possible?

Only if he wanted Johanna, a life with her, enough to change: not from man to wolf, but from drunk to sober, from ne'er-do-well to competent adult, from coward to hero.

He laughed at himself and pressed his forehead to the sun-warmed glass. The heroism was all Johanna's, if she could deliver him from his demons. But she couldn't do it alone. He must give up every trace of resistance and let her into his innermost heart, where she could drag his fears into the light. Where he must confront them unflinchingly, even those—especially those—he had never seen except as shadows.

How he hated choices. Easier to run. Easier until you found yourself bound by stronger chains than any in that dark, stinking cellar . . .

No. That dungeon was far away, Johanna was here, and now. Soon he'd see her, and all they'd shared would become his only reality. Soon he'd be a whole man again, able to love.

He mouthed the word and choked on helpless laughter. Quentin Forster, in love—with a distinctly unglamorous, too-serious woman well past her first youth.

An absurdity. Just like the rest of his life. Why should he be surprised?

Whistling with nonsensical happiness, he washed and dressed with extra care. This late in the morning, Johanna would be busy with the others, but Mrs. Daugherty was bound to have some leftovers from breakfast. He'd bide his time, visit Wilhelm and talk to Harper. He was surprised that May hadn't come looking for him, but somewhat relieved, May was too young to be aware of what had passed between him and Johanna.

Or was she? His good humor dimmed. May. What was to be done about her?

Trapped in indecision, he walked out the door and found Lewis Andersen waiting in the hallway.

The former minister shrank back as Quentin appeared, holding his gloved hands high like a shield between them.

"Did you do it?" he whispered. "Did you kill that man?"

"What?" His guts knotted. "What did you say?"

"Thou . . . thou cursed creature of Satan. Did you kill him?"

Quentin backed into the wall and felt blindly for its support. "Kill who?"

"The owner of the Red Star quicksilver mine—Ronald Ketchum. The actress told us about it. He was found dead, torn apart." He sucked his breath through his teeth. "You did it, didn't you? You are evil." His hands trembled. "You will not kill again. I will stop you."

Even in the midst of his horror, Quentin admired Andersen's courage. The man was hardly the heroic sort, yet he stood face-to-face with what he believed to be a monster. A killer. He had more grit than anyone knew.

"If this is true," Quentin said past the constriction in his throat, "you won't have to stop me." He took a step forward.

Andersen held his ground. He began to sing in a high-pitched, wavering voice—a hymn, "Soldiers of Christ Arise," that Quentin remembered hearing in his childhood.

"I won't hurt you," he said, taking another step. "I must find Doctor Schell."

"*Stop.*" Andersen produced a gun from inside his coat and pointed it at Quentin's chest. Where he had acquired such a weapon, or how he knew enough to use it, was a subject for wild speculation.

Quentin raised his hands. "Shoot, if you must," he said, floating within a bizarre calm. "I won't prevent it."

"But *I* will."

Johanna came up behind Andersen. She set her hand on his shoulder. "Give me the gun, Lewis."

"But he is a killer, spawn of the devil, I must—"

"You don't want to hurt anyone, Lewis. Even if what you say is true, he is entitled to representation before the law, is he not?"

Her calm, reasonable voice worked its usual magic on Andersen. The muzzle of the gun tilted down. Johanna pried it from Andersen's fingers and held the weapon as gingerly as if it were a poisonous snake.

"You would not listen before," Andersen said, never taking his gaze from Quentin. "You must listen now. He will come after you next."

"What makes you believe that, Lewis?"

His thin face puckered. "I *know*."

"I have never given you cause to distrust my judgment, have I?"

"No."

"Then trust me now. Quentin will not hurt me. He won't hurt any of us." She looked into Quentin's eyes. "Whatever he may be, Quentin is not evil. No more than you or I."

"You will . . . keep the gun?"

"Yes. I must speak to Quentin now, but I shall not fail to protect myself. You would help me best if you'd gather the others and bring them into the parlor. Please fetch Mrs. Daugherty as well, and ask her to bring my father out of his room. It's very important that everyone stay indoors today."

Andersen bobbed his head. "Yes. Yes, I understand." He cast Quentin a glance composed of equal parts fear and loathing and scuttled backward down the hall, watching them both until he passed out of view.

Johanna released a long breath and stared at the gun in her hand.

"You won't need that against me, Johanna," Quentin said lightly. Better to joke than to run wailing in despair.

He hadn't known quite what to expect of their first meeting after last night's loving. Awkwardness, yes, and perhaps a little shyness on her part. A new familiarity between them. Possibly even her resolve that it should never happen again. Anything but this.

His latest, brief flirtation with hope had already come to an end. Andersen had seen to that—Andersen and his accusations.

Accusations Johanna confirmed with the bleak, drawn expression on her face.

It was still a beautiful face, though the hair hung bedraggled about her shoulders and her forehead was moist with perspiration. He'd have to be dead not to appreciate it, however desperate his circumstances. Her face, her lips, her form from crown to toe were imprinted upon his hands and his lips and his heart.

He didn't dare embrace her, though his mind and soul and body demanded the solace of her arms. He didn't dare move at all.

"Andersen was telling the truth," he said. "Someone was killed last night."

"So I have heard."

"And you think . . . that I had something to do with it."

Anguish darkened her eyes to pewter. "When you left me—" Her voice faltered just for an instant. "Afterward, where did you go?"

"To the woods. And then back here."

"Do you remember every moment?"

Did he? Could he be certain he hadn't forgotten the forgetting itself? He remembered falling into bed, exhausted from his run, and then sinking into what he presumed was a deep, uninterrupted sleep . . .

"I didn't drink," he said, frantically sifting his mind for plausible alibis. "I knew nothing of this Mr. Ketchum before Andersen told me."

"He was known to mistreat his Chinese workers. As—" Her throat worked. "—as May's father might have mistreated her."

His lungs stopped working. "You said something happened in town . . . the night I got drunk. You never told me what it was."

"May's father was attacked and wounded."

"Oh, God." He fell back against the wall and clutched at his head. Trouble always followed in his footsteps, wherever he went, whispering of violence, of fear and hatred and suspicion. It had found him again, in this last and final sanctuary.

But in all those times past, the whispers had never been of murder.

He forced himself to look at her instead of cringing like a whipped dog. "Did I kill this man?" he asked, letting blessed numbness seep into his body.

She shook her head, too fiercely. It savaged his heart to see her so torn, so vulnerable. She was the very pillar of solid strength to everyone here, including himself.

He'd undermined that fortitude ever since he came to the Haven, hour by hour and day by day. Last night had shattered the remaining foundations of her life, and left her with nothing to be sure of.

"Johanna," he said. "Did someone see me do this thing?" He straightened, staring past her. "I'll go into town at once and give myself up—"

"No." She raised her chin. "We know nothing yet. No facts, only rumor. But there is something I must tell you, something I recently discovered. I wish that circumstances permitted me to explain more gradually. I fear it may be difficult for—" Tears filled her eyes. "I am sorry, Quentin."

She led him into her office, still clutching the gun in a death grip, and closed the door.

Then she told him.

He didn't react at all.

Johanna watched for signs of horror, denial, incredulity. None came. He listened to her account of Fenris's emergence, unmoving, as if she were describing a rather uninteresting acquaintance.

That was abnormal in itself, almost frightening. She carefully edited her description of Fenris's advances upon her, but she doubted very much that he'd failed to guess what she omitted.

When she was finished, he gazed blankly at the wall and said nothing. Minutes ticked by. Precious minutes that she dared not waste, for May's sake as well as his.

Bolkonsky might arrive in a matter of hours. Oscar had not returned from his search for May, and if he did not come soon she'd go looking herself. Her original plan for the girl's escape was no longer viable; Bridget would simply have to spirit May out of the area while Johanna concocted a story that Bolkonsky and Ingram were bound to find wildly implausible. But she didn't dare risk facing them down with May still present.

Watching Quentin's face, Johanna mourned inside. She grieved for him, for May, for the man who had been killed, whatever his crimes in life. She grieved for what had been so briefly captured last night. She longed to touch Quentin, kiss him, and knew how impossible it was. Her organs had turned to water, filling her body like a reservoir apt to spill over into a flood of tears once she opened the gates.

That she must not do. Her brain must become as sharp as a scalpel, her heart as hard as marble.

"You never suspected this," she said at last.

"No." He turned his head toward her, but his eyes wouldn't focus. "Not this. I felt a shadow ... the shadow I ran from. And it was always—" He laughed. "It was me all along."

She quenched the desire to comfort him with soothing words and promises she couldn't keep. "Not you, Quentin. A part of you, born at a time when you desperately needed help and found none."

"Fenris," he whispered. "It even has its own name. *He.*" He rose from the chaise and walked across the room, slow and halting as an old man. "All these times I've lost my memory—after the drinking—he's come out. That's what you're saying. He lives in my body with me. He takes over and does things—terrible things."

"So Fenris claims—and Bolkonsky. But there is no proof, Quentin."

"Except that two people have been attacked since I came to the Haven." He finally met her gaze. "And I don't remember. But someone saw me, didn't they, Johanna?"

"No one witnessed the attack on May's father. Fenris admitted it himself."

He closed his eyes. "Why? Why did he do it?"

"He wouldn't say. But I think . . ." She prepared herself to hurt Quentin again. "Your concern for May became something different for Fenris. You share a mind and a body. He felt what you feel, knew what you knew, but he was not constrained by the bonds of civilized behavior, or by the reason that tells us right from wrong."

"You mean that he did what I wanted to do, but couldn't."

"There is so much I don't know and can only theorize. I'm sorry."

"Your theories are more than reasonable." He sat down again, as if he couldn't remain still. "I never stayed long in any one place, because after a few days or weeks I always sensed something wrong. Sometimes it was just a hunch, a bad feeling in my gut. Rumors, the stares of people around me that told me that I wasn't welcome. Sometimes I heard stories. And once in a while, the law came after me." His voice became a monotone, devoid of emotion. "I didn't let myself think that my drinking did serious damage to anyone but myself." He smiled a chilling smile. "But you think that's what lets Fenris out."

"It's possible, but—"

"Just as it's possible that I killed this businessman last night."

"I do not believe . . . You said that you had no memory lapse—"

"I was asleep. Do you remember every moment when you're asleep, Johanna?" He raised his hands, crooked his fingers, stared at them as if they belonged to someone else. "Don't try to make it easy for me. I'm not a child. If a man died, it might very well have been by these hands." He pressed his temples. "You said that I created Fenris. *I* am responsible."

"No." She was losing mastery of this conversation, and she must get it back. "Quentin—I am convinced that we can reach Fenris. He is the hidden part of yourself. Somehow, you and I must find a way to communicate with him. Bring him into the light, and confront him."

"And until then?" He slammed his fist into the wall. "I can't stop what I feel. I can't even sense his existence. How can I prevent him from taking over and . . . attacking someone again? How many times have I hurt people in the past, and not known it?"

The tears built painfully behind her eyelids. "We *will* find a way. But now you must listen to me. Regardless of what actually happened, certain witnesses are claiming to have seen you in the vicinity of Ketchum's body. That was enough to rouse the town."

"You mean a mob." His gaze grew keen and alert. "A mob is coming to the Haven to get me."

"That is why we must take immediate precautions, for you and—"

"You knew about Fenris last night, and you still came to me. Why, Johanna?" His eyes glittered with unshed tears. "Why would you give yourself to a monster?"

"Because I—I . . ." How would it help, to tell him she loved him? Another burden for him to carry, another load of guilt and self-loathing, because in his own mind he didn't deserve to be loved.

"You were afraid of Fenris," he said with devastating insight. "Coming to me was a way to challenge your fear." He smiled, without bitterness or mockery. "I hope it helped you. I'd like to believe it did. I'd like to think we shared something other than sorrow, before I go."

"*Quentin.*"

"Don't deceive yourself. I must give myself to these people, to the law, before they come and destroy what little peace I've left you."

"That is out of the question. They may—"

"Hang me? I have heard that such things happen in this country. With justification, in my case."

"You have an illness. You are not a criminal."

"How can you be sure, Johanna? And what do you propose to do to keep me 'safe'? Bind me in chains so that Fenris can't escape again? Lock me in a padded room and push my food through the bars? Oh, no." He shuddered violently. "I'll take the rope, and gladly. It will end this farce I've made of my life."

"I will not lock you away." Tears ran down her face. She couldn't stop them. "You must go into hiding until things settle down. And it's not only you who is in danger. Because of what's happened, Bolkonsky has threatened to come for May this very day."

Quentin's body twitched, as if he'd experienced a sudden shock. "May. You have a plan to save her."

"I will not give her up to her father. Oscar has been looking for her, but I must have her ready to leave within the hour. You must go as well."

"I'll find her."

She swung on him. "*Go*. Do not make things more difficult—"

"Johanna." He spoke so gently, as if in the midst of sweet loving. "No one is better suited to bringing her back than I am." He smiled with tender sadness. "I have something to show you, something I should have shared long ago."

As she watched, uncomprehending, he began to remove his clothing. She couldn't avert her eyes. In her office, in full daylight, he was a thousand times more beautiful than he'd been in his dark bedchamber.

Her body woke despite the urgency of the situation, responding to the potent promise of his masculinity. *Lewis was right*, she thought dazedly. *Naked in the woods* . . .

The last of his clothing fell to the floor, and the outlines of his form seemed to shift and shimmer. Mist, the very color of his eyes, appeared from nowhere to gather about him like a magic cloak. It swallowed him up entirely.

Quentin vanished. All she saw at first, as the mist cleared, was a flash of sharp white teeth and russet fur. Then she realized what had taken Quentin's place.

A wolf. A wolf whose pelt was the shade of Quentin's hair, thick and sleek. A wolf with great triangular ears and a plume of a tail, immense paws, and slitted golden-red eyes.

He grinned at her. Quentin's grin.

She clutched at the back of her chair. His gaze was no beast's. Those were Quentin's eyes.

The wolf *was* Quentin.

His lycanthropy was real. His unconscious mind had told the truth. Lewis *had* seen him change into a wolf.

One less symptom of insanity to worry about. Or one more. Now he was three: wolf, Quentin, Fenris.

She laughed, muffling the sound behind her hand. The wolf—Quentin—no creature of fear but a beast as magnificent as the man—flowed toward her like liquid copper and nudged her other hand. His nose was warm and dry.

"The joke is on me," she said, wondering if she was making any sense. "Did you think this would make matters simpler?"

He lay down at her feet and rested his jaw on her foot. It was a gesture of love and trust she could not mistake. He was tame as a dog, utterly loyal, adoring her with his lupine eyes and the rasp of his tongue across her fingers.

Consigning one more secret to her keeping.

She plunged her hand into the thick guard hairs about his great neck and felt him tremble. "Quentin—if you still understand me— I . . . don't know what to say."

He slipped away. The mist enveloped him again. She was unable to observe the actual change, try though she might; the scientist was never long absent from her nature. He stepped, naked, from the dispersing cloud, retrieved his clothes, and dressed in silence.

"You need say nothing," he said. "I didn't believe that showing you this would make matters simpler. But it should make clear why I cannot remain."

"Because—" She tried to assemble words into proper sentences, drawing them into a line like a child's scattered alphabet blocks. They remained hopelessly disordered.

"Because I am not human," he completed for her. He sighed, and she felt his absolute weariness. "There are others like me throughout the world. We are stronger and faster than men, with senses a thousand times more keen. We are infinitely more dangerous if we choose to be."

"The nature of the wolf—"

"Is not what men have made it. We are neither cursed nor the children of Satan. The vicious cruelty men attribute to wolves is the product of fear and ignorance. There has been evil among the loups-garous—I have seen it myself—but no more than is found among men."

Question after question crowded Johanna's mind. How many cases of insanity might have been attributed to this very real ability? How did these loups-garous fit into the evolution of life and the human race, creatures Darwin had not even imagined? How had they remained hidden so long?

Not one of those questions was important.

"You are not a killer, Quentin," she said. She held out her hand. He brushed her fingertips with his own, fleeting as the mist that marked his transformation. "You are a wonder."

"If I have killed"—he worked his hands open and closed—"the fault is in me, not my kind. I am an aberration. But my abilities make me deadly. I can't trust my own body, and neither can you. If I don't stop myself, no one can."

"Then how can mere human law contain you?" she cried. "If you give yourself up to the authorities, what makes you believe that Fenris won't do anything to get you free again?"

"That's why he exists, isn't it?" He lifted his head. "Tell me, Johanna. Where can I go? Does the place exist where Fenris can do no harm?"

"Yes. But only if we make that place together."

"There is another option."

"I will not let you take it."

He laughed hoarsely. "I've never managed suicide thus far. Success is by no means assured."

"Fenris would stop you. *He* wants to survive."

"And there is only one who can match him, Johanna, whatever sort of creature he is." He thumped his chest with his fist. "He is *me*."

"Yet you haven't even met him." She strode forward until she stood nearly eye to eye with him. "You can't possibly fight what you can't see and don't remember. Without my help—"

"Have you ever cured a man with this disease, Johanna? Have you ever treated a werewolf? No," he said, forestalling her answer. "May needs you now. I won't put either of you in further danger."

She opened her mouth for another protest, and he silenced her with his lips. He kissed her as if it were the last time, hard enough to leave his impression seared into her skin. She held him as if by sheer physical strength she could prevent him from going.

But she was only human. He set her back and kept her apart from him. His endearing, crooked smile made a brief appearance and was just as quickly gone. "I'll find May and bring her back to you. If you need help after I'm gone, ask Harper. He's a capable man, and a real purpose is what he needs to be whole."

Johanna found nothing to say, not a single reasonable argument. Her legs began to tremble. Quentin guided her to her chair and sat her down in it.

"Good-bye, Johanna," he said. His breath hitched, as if he would say something more. "Good-bye."

Her vision blurred. She blinked, and Quentin was gone.

Gone for good.

Chapter 20

"No." Johanna tried to stand, faltered, sat down again. "*Quentin.*"

Someone banged on the office door. Oscar barged in, frightened and upset.

"Doc Jo?" he said. "I couldn't find May. I'm sorry." He pushed his hands deep in his pockets. "Mrs. Daugherty said to come get you. There's something going on in the yard. Lots of people. They look mad."

Gott in Himmel. The mob of townsfolk Bolkonsky had warned her about. Were they already here?

Her question was answered soon enough. A shout from outside came from the direction of the front gate, and it was not a cry of greeting. Necessity gave her the will to move. She hurried to the window and looked out. Possibly twenty men, and a few women, were gathered just beyond the gate. They swayed back and forth as one, like some huge, restive, hungry beast.

She knew what had to be done. Quentin would find May and keep her from harm; Johanna's trust in him remained unshaken. It would be up to her to keep the mob at bay.

"Is everyone else in the parlor?" she asked Oscar.

"Yes. Mr. Andersen got us. He said to wait for you."

"Good. I want you all to stay there, and not move. Do you understand?"

"Are those people going to hurt us?"

Who'd told him that? she wondered. Andersen? Or had Oscar seen enough ugliness in his life to recognize it in the folk of Silverado Springs?

"Let's go to the parlor." She took his hand and led him down the hall to where the others waited. Andersen was pacing up and down the length of the room, rubbing his hands. Harper, beside her father in his wheelchair, gazed toward the kitchen, where Mrs. Daugherty waited nervously in the doorway. Irene, her expression half obscured by her garish face paint, perched on the edge of the sofa.

"What's going on?" Mrs. Daugherty demanded.

It seemed impossible that Mrs. Daugherty, with her ready ear for gossip, knew nothing of last night's incident, or of the townspeople bent on their version of justice. Yet she'd offered no warning. Johanna went to her side and spoke in a whisper. "You did not hear about what happened to the mine owner?"

"I haven't been in town since yesterday mornin'. I stayed with Mrs. Bergstrom last night, way up along the Foss stage route. She's alone now, and ailin', and I—" She pressed her lips together. "Why're them people here, Doc Jo?"

"There is no time to explain. I need you to help keep everyone calm and quiet." She addressed the others. "There is no cause for alarm. I would like you all to remain here, together, until I return. I am going to speak to the people outside."

"I know why they're here," Irene said shrilly. "They've come to get Quentin. He murdered that man in town."

Johanna was no longer surprised by the things Irene knew. It was her own failure that she hadn't paid more attention to the older woman and monitored her activities.

One of many failures that were coming back to haunt her.

"I don't believe it!" Mrs. Daugherty said.

"*They* do," Harper said, pointing his chin toward the kitchen door. Everyone glanced at him in surprise. He, along with Johanna's father, was the only one who showed no outward sign of concern. "Is Quentin all right?"

"Yes." She looked at him more carefully, remembering Quentin's advice. "Harper, please give Mrs. Daugherty any assistance she needs."

"I reckon you're the one who'll need help," he said, getting to his feet. "I'll come with you."

"As you wish. The rest of you stay inside." She strode for the door and stepped out, Harper at her heels.

The people stirred when they saw her, setting off a ripple of low, hostile voices. She recognized several respectable townsfolk she'd spoken to or dealt with at one time or another, including the blacksmith and the butcher, but most of them were idlers who commonly hung about in the street, drinking and gossiping.

She thought of the gun she'd left on the desk in her office. Foolish; she should have hidden it, or at least brought it along.

And would you use it, Johanna?

"Gentlemen," Johanna said. "How may I help you?"

They obviously hadn't expected such a moderate response to their fearsome presence. The blacksmith looked about uneasily. Others shuffled their feet.

One of the men, a burly giant with a scar across his chin, stepped in front of the rest. She didn't know him, but it was clear that he relished his role as ringleader.

"You know why we're here!" he shouted. "You got all them loonies holed up in this place, and one of 'em killed Ketchum!"

Raised voices supported his accusation. Fists, some wielding farm tools, waved in the air.

"And you are Mr.—" She inclined her head in invitation.

"Mungo," he said with a belligerent sneer.

"I just heard of Mr. Ketchum's unfortunate death," she said. "I'm sorry that you have felt the need to visit the Haven under such circumstances."

Mungo scowled. "Don't try to protect 'im! We know who did it."

Johanna didn't allow her voice to waver in the least. "If you believe one of my patients committed this act, why have you not summoned the constable? I would certainly be glad to cooperate with the proper authorities."

"Don't think you can put us off with your high-and-mighty airs, woman," he taunted. "We al'ays knew something like this would happen, with crazies living near us. This man Forster caused trouble in town b'fore, an' Quigley saw 'im right near where Ketchum was kil't!"

"Nevertheless, until you bring a representative of the law. I will not permit you to bother my patients."

Harper stepped up to her side. "You heard the lady. Go on home, before you regret what you're doing."

"Loony!" Mungo spat at his feet. "We know all about you. We know about every crazy in this place. We c'n run you out and no one'll stop us. If you don't bring Forster to us, we'll go in and get 'im!"

He started toward Johanna. Men followed in straggling twos and threes. Harper moved ahead of Johanna, readying for attack.

A streak of russet plunged between Harper and Mungo, striking the ringleader on the legs so that he staggered and fell. Johanna got a single good look at the wolf—bristling, fangs bared, eyes blazing with demonic fury—before it fell on the leaders of the mob.

Muttered imprecations became screams. Men ran every which way, seeking escape as hell snapped at their heels. Mungo found himself gazing up into the open maw of a beast long thought to be extinct in

California—except that no such creature had ever existed except in the darkest imaginings of men more clever than he. He shrieked and covered his face with his arms.

Johanna didn't dare cry out for fear of giving Quentin away. Harper dashed in front of her, seized Mungo's arm, and yanked him to his feet. The man didn't linger. He stumbled over his own legs in his haste to follow the others.

The wolf chased them as far as the gate, turned about once to look at Johanna, and leaped the fence with breathtaking grace. In a heartbeat he had vanished.

Harper returned to her side. "Lord have mercy," he whispered. "It's real, then."

She stared at him, wondering how long this state of perpetual confusion would last. "What is real, Harper?"

"You don't have to worry, Doc. I know I'm not crazy, and neither are you."

She had no energy left to pose sensible questions and interpret ambiguous answers. "You know?"

"I thought I'd seen all the wonders and terrors this world has to offer." He laughed under his breath. "A dog came by to see me, before I came out of myself. Least I thought it was a dog. He spoke to me—not like people, but the way other things do, sometimes. Later I had the same feeling around Quentin. Then the Reverend started muttering about men changing into wolves . . . I just sort of put things together."

Quentin was not the only remarkable man at the Haven. "And you accept this?"

"Don't rightly have much choice, do I?" He scratched his chin and looked down the lane beyond the gate, where the dust was just beginning to settle. "I don't reckon the folks from town will be back anytime soon. They'll have other things to gossip about for a while."

"No doubt. But after today, we can't make any assumptions." This entire conversation felt like a dream within a dream. She remembered what Quentin had said of Harper, urging her to rely on him. She badly needed his stolid dispassion. "How much do you know of what's been happening in town?"

"I keep my ear to the ground. Irene gossips."

And how did Irene know so much? That question must also wait until later. "There are many things I have been unable to tell you and the others. Are you aware that May's father has come to the Springs to take her from the Haven, with the help of a man named Bolkonsky, and that

I have opposed this reunion for the sake of May's health and happiness?"

"I've watched May these past few days." He motioned to the place where the mob had stood. "It has something to do with all this?"

"May's father was assaulted in his hotel shortly before Ketchum was killed." She swallowed. "Quentin has been very protective of May."

He didn't ask if she believed Quentin had done the assaulting. "Why would Quentin go after this Ketchum?"

Explaining Fenris and her tenuous theories about him was not an option. "Matters have gone terribly awry, Harper. I ask for your trust . . . and I may need your help, if you feel able."

"Yes," he said simply. "Quentin's leaving the Haven, isn't he?"

She held back tears by sheer force of will. "He went to look for May. He must have found her, if he was able to—" She gestured wordlessly at the trampled earth. "May will be leaving as well, as soon as we can make her ready. Let us go inside."

Mrs. Daugherty stood sentinel by the kitchen door, clutching a cast-iron pan to ward off potential invaders.

"What happened?" she demanded. "First that man was makin' threats, and then I see him an' his friends a'runnin' like the devil hisself was after 'em."

Thank God Mrs. Daugherty hadn't seen the wolf. "They thought better of their behavior. Has May come back?"

"I saw her in the parlor with the others just a moment ago, but they been mighty quiet since. Haven't seen Quentin." She followed Johanna into the parlor. "I thought someone should stand guard—"

She broke off. The parlor was empty except for Johanna's father, who was dozing in his chair. Johanna's heart clenched in panic.

"I didn't hear anyone leave!" Mrs. Daugherty protested.

"Please look through the house, Mrs. Daugherty," Johanna said. "Harper and I will search outside."

She rushed down the hall to the rear door, knowing that the others weren't in their rooms. Harper found Lewis at the edge of the garden, sitting in the dirt. Blood matted the thinning hair at the back of his head.

"Someone hit me," he said in faint outrage, accepting Harper's support. Johanna knelt beside him to examine the wound, which was rapidly developing into a goose's egg. He was lucky to have received such a glancing blow.

"I told them all to stay inside," Lewis said. "That . . . Quentin Forster brought May into the parlor and left again, but the girl had hardly been here a minute when that pernicious female, DuBois—she whispered to May and led her out the back door." He wiped at his soiled trousers and stared at the earth stains on his hands as if he would weep. "I tried to stop them. I followed them, and then someone struck me—"

"We'll find them, Lewis."

"But the wolf-beast—the mob—"

"They're gone. But I must find May." She took a clean handkerchief from her pocket and pressed it over Lewis's wound. "Hold this firmly in place. Harper will take you in, and I'll see to your injury as soon as I can."

She nodded to Harper, who supported Lewis to his feet. For once, Lewis did not reject the touch.

Someone had struck Lewis with the obvious intent of rendering him unconscious, or at least incapable of action. Irene had lured May outside, in spite of being told to remain in the parlor, after Quentin had delivered the girl safely home and gone out to confront the mob.

The confusion of the past few minutes would be an ideal diversion for one who wished to approach the Haven from the opposite direction unobserved. One who wished to remove a certain patient without interference.

Bolkonsky.

Dummkopf, Johanna swore at herself. "May! May, do you hear me?" She ran through the garden and turned toward the wood. She almost missed the book that lay face-down on the path to the orchard.

May's book, Elizabeth Stuart Phelps' *The Story of Avis.* She bent to pick it up and saw the footprints beside it, lightly engraved in the shade-moistened earth. Two sets of footprints, a girl's and a woman's.

Johanna followed their course like a hound dog with its nose to the trail. Just within the orchard itself a third set of prints, unmistakably male, joined the first two. They traveled together for a few yards more, and then the girl's disappeared.

That was where she found Irene.

The woman stood in the shade of an apple tree, holding a battered carpetbag against her chest. Her attention was entirely focused on the lane just beyond the orchard fence. May was not with her.

"Irene," Johanna said.

Irene's head snapped around. Her eyes widened in an expression of naked fear.

"Where is May?" Johanna demanded. "Where is she, Irene?"

"She's not here!" Irene stepped away from the tree, holding the carpetbag in front of her. "Go away. Leave me alone!"

"I know you took her out of the parlor," Johanna said, making no effort to quell her anger. "Was it you who hit Andersen?" She grabbed Irene's arm. "Where is May?"

"Gone!" Irene stretched her lips in a grotesque smile. "Gone to be with her father, and you're too late!"

"Was it Bolkonsky? You know him, don't you? He told you to bring May to him while the mob from town came after Quentin, didn't he?" She gave Irene a shake. "Tell me the truth!"

"Yes, I know Feodor!" She laughed. "You always thought I stayed locked up here like the others, because you never paid attention to me. You've always thought I was stupid, didn't you? But I knew everything that went on in town. I went at night. I watched, and I listened, and those country bumpkins never knew that the great Irene DuBois was among them."

Johanna let Irene go, stunned at her own blindness. The clues had all been there, had she chosen to see them—Lewis's complaint about Irene's visits to town, her new gown, her more frequent references to leaving the Haven, her unusual confidence. Johanna had never guessed that Irene was so superb an actress. All the woman's dramatic posturing had merely seemed evidence of her unyielding delusions . . .

"I knew when the handsome Doctor Bolkonsky came to town," Irene said. "I had my eye on him from the beginning. He was different, the kind of man I've been waiting for. I knew when you went to see him, and that he'd never be interested in *you*."

"Oh, Irene," Johanna whispered.

"He's been in love with me ever since he saw me on Broadway. He told me all about poor little May and what you were doing to keep her away from her father—the same way you tried to keep me from my true destiny. He needed someone to tell him what was going on here, and report to him. I agreed to help him get May away from you, and he promised to take me to San Francisco and set me up on the stage, where I belong." She tossed her head. "We just had to wait for the right time. You made it so easy—you, and Quentin!"

"It was Bolkonsky who sent the mob here, wasn't it? *He* stirred them up, and only pretended to warn me—"

"As I said, you made it easy for us. The people in town were already upset when they found Ketchum's body, especially after the attack on May's father. They were looking for someone to blame. Feodor told them that he was afraid your new patient, Quentin, had something to do with it. He was worried that you had lost control over your loonies. People listened to him—he's a doctor, after all!" She laughed. "The rest took care of itself. All I had to do was get May to come with me while you were busy. Quentin brought her back just in time, but she wanted to follow him when he left. I told her I could take her to him. Feodor's man was waiting for us outside."

The third set of footprints. "Bolkonsky wasn't here?"

"He's coming to get me." Irene's eyes glazed over with visions of her glorious future. "All the city will be at my feet, just like Feodor. You can't stop me now!"

Johanna followed her expectant gaze to the lane. Not for an instant did Johanna believe that Bolkonsky intended to take Irene away. A man such as he would have no personal interest in a haggard, aging actress. He'd merely used Irene as men had used her before, to serve his own ends.

Nothing about Bolkonsky was as it seemed. He'd deceived Johanna time and again—put the residents of the Haven at risk—as a ploy to return May to her father. He'd given her the news about the attack on Ingram, and planted the blame for Mr. Ketchum's death on Quentin.

Had Quentin been seen near Ketchum's body, or was that another of Bolkonsky's fabrications? Why was Bolkonsky so dedicated to Ingram's cause? Was it money, or something else she couldn't begin to imagine?

Putting such speculation from her mind, Johanna followed the male footprints as they crossed the orchard and continued on toward the wood.

"You won't find her," Irene shouted after her. "You've lost Quentin, too. You've failed, Johanna!"

Her triumphant words nipped at Johanna's heels, stinging with every step. Irene assumed she'd give up. Would Bolkonsky, and May's father, assume the same? Ingram had his business in San Francisco. He'd take May there, secure in his power.

Yet Bolkonsky had carefully avoided bringing in the authorities at any time in their dealings, preferring the use of subterfuge to steal May from the Haven. There must be a reason. Perhaps May's father had wanted certain secrets out of the public eye.

Secrets Johanna might attempt to expose, at the risk of her own professional destruction. But hadn't she already compromised her vocation, possibly beyond mending?

She passed out of the orchard and into the wild groves of oak and madrona. Her eyes caught a sudden change in the earth, and she stopped.

The ground was trampled here, marked by some struggle, and the man's footprints formed a mad pattern intermingled with the spoor of a wolf.

This was where Quentin had gone, after chasing the mob away. He'd followed May's captor, and caught up with him.

But where were they?

Johanna knelt to study the tracks. May's footprints had also reappeared, as if her captor had set her down after carrying her for some distance. Johanna found a final set of prints, almost lost amid the others.

Those of a barefoot man, about Quentin's size.

Leaves rattled a few feet away. Johanna scooted about to face the sound. A man's blunt-fingered hand reached out from a cluster of bushes, to the accompaniment of a hoarse groan.

Johanna pushed aside branches. The man was a stranger, a big, nasty-looking character with a scarred face and shoes that matched the prints of May's kidnapper. Aside from a few scratches, he seemed unharmed, though he was just recovering consciousness. Johanna had no pity to spare for him.

"Where is May?" she demanded.

"Wolf," he muttered. His eyes opened, bloodshot and terrified. "Devil!"

She grabbed his shoulders. "Who took May?"

"Th' devil man!" He covered his eyes like a child hiding from a nightmare. "He'll kill me."

"Only if I do not." She tightened her grip. "Bolkonsky hired you to take May from the Haven, didn't he?"

"He'll . . . *kill* me."

Did he mean Bolkonsky or Quentin?

"You were to deliver May to Bolkonsky, weren't you?" she asked. "Where were you to meet him?"

"*Let me.*"

She looked up to find Harper behind her, his ordinarily mild eyes glittering with a dangerous light. He crouched over the man, long fingers working.

"You answer the lady now, or I'll go get my friend the wolf and let him play with you," Harper said in a cold, flat voice. "Where were you taking the girl?"

The kidnapper's eyes went wide as saucers. "The . . . the old Miller ruin by Ritchey Creek." He snatched at Johanna's hands. "Please, don't let the demon get me!" He fell to whimpering gibberish about wolf-devils and repenting his sins. "If I tell you who really killed Ketchum, can I be saved?"

"Tell us," Johanna demanded.

"It was on Bolkonsky's orders. I didn't do it, I swear! I only lured him where . . ." He gulped. "We was supposed to tell everyone that your man killed him. I'll testify that it wasn't him, I swear I will!"

Johanna pried his fingers from her wrists and gave silent thanks. Whatever Fenris might have done in the past, he hadn't taken the mine owner's life.

She drew Harper aside. "Everything is all right back at the house?"

"As right as it can be. Mrs. Daugherty is staying with the others."

"Did you see Irene?"

"She was crying, over by the orchard."

Had she begun to realize that Bolkonsky would not be coming? "She has been meeting Bolkonsky without my knowledge. Since I opposed returning May to her father, Bolkonsky planned this clandestine abduction. Irene brought May out of the house while we were occupied with the mob, so that this man could take her. He didn't succeed, but May is still missing."

Harper met her gaze with perfect comprehension. "Quentin was here. You think he took her?"

"I don't know." She clasped her hands over her roiling stomach. "It is a possibility."

"He would have taken her to protect her from this Bolkonsky."

Quentin would have. But Quentin would also contact Johanna to let her know that May was safe. How long would it take Bolkonsky or May's father to seek the help of the law?

Brush crackled and twigs snapped. May's would-be kidnapper had stumbled to his feet and was making a clumsy attempt at escape. Harper started toward him, but Johanna held him back.

"Let him go. He's too frightened to be a further threat, and we haven't time to deal with him now."

Harper frowned after the man until he was out of sight, then glanced at the ground at Johanna's feet. "Is that May's book?"

She bent to pick up the book she'd set down when she examined the footprints. The pages were creased and soiled. "She must have taken it with her when Irene lured her outside."

"May I have it?"

She handed it to Harper. He stroked the dirt-stained cover with reverent fingers, and she remembered his claims of reading men's pasts and futures in everyday objects.

If he thought that he could use some inborn magical power to help her locate May, she was not prepared to discourage him. Desperate circumstances called for desperate measures. And until this very morning, she had not believed in the existence of genuine lycanthropes.

Nor had she believed that she could falter in all her fine aspirations, all her high standards, all her confidence in logic and reason and her own well-trained abilities.

But she had.

"I must talk to Mrs. Daugherty," she said, trying to fill the terrifying void in her heart with words and plans. "She can go into town and listen for news. I'll ride to the place where Bolkonsky was to collect May. There is a chance he is still waiting. I may learn something of value."

"You shouldn't go alone." Harper shortened his stride to match hers as they walked briskly back toward the house. Irene had disappeared from the orchard.

"There is no time for argument," Johanna said. "It is much to ask, but if you can take care of my father and Oscar I will be deeply obliged to you. I will show you what my father requires. Lewis should be no trouble. As for Irene—"

"I'll keep an eye on her," he said. "When I find her, I'll put her in her room and keep her there."

"Thank you." She paused just beyond the back door to clasp his hand. "You are a good man, Harper."

"Without you and Quentin, I wouldn't be a man at all." He squeezed her hand and let it fall. "Tell me what I need to do."

Within an hour she had laid out the bare bones of the situation to a fretful Mrs. Daugherty, including an account of the bizarre appearance of a wolf, and asked her to take the buggy into town to glean any news or gossip about Dr. Bolkonsky, May's father, or the aftermath of the siege on the Haven. Whatever the people of Silverado Springs might think of Johanna and the Haven's residents, they wouldn't hold Mrs. Daugherty accountable.

While Harper went in search of Irene, Johanna told Oscar that May had gone away for a little while, and that he mustn't worry. Lewis was in his room, but responded to her brief explanation with peculiar blankness.

She hadn't time to do more with him. She took Lewis's gun from her office, kissed her father on the forehead, and asked for Oscar's help in saddling Daisy.

The mare carried her at a willing canter to the meeting place Bolkonsky's henchman had described, but it was deserted. If Bolkonsky had been waiting, he'd either given up or been told of his plan's failure.

With any luck—more than she deserved—he knew no more of May's whereabouts than Johanna did.

Avoiding the roads that would take her close to Silverado Springs, Johanna returned to the Haven. Harper came running to meet her.

"I think you'd better come with me right away," he said grimly.

She dismounted and followed him to the vineyard. The tableau that greeted her froze her in her tracks.

Irene was on her knees in the dirt, weeping hysterically. Lewis stood over her, holding a kitchen knife between his shaking hands. His head jerked up at Johanna's approach.

"Stay away!" he warned. He pointed the knife at Irene.

Johanna held up her hands. "Lewis. Put the knife down."

"Evil!" Lewis shouted. "All is evil. Don't you see? First the devil wolf, and now this Jezebel, who has betrayed us all."

"No!" Irene shrieked. "Please—"

It was possible, in spite of the day's many disasters, for things to get worse. Johanna recognized that Lewis had reached the limits of his tolerance. He was on the verge of submitting to total madness, and there was nothing she could do to help him.

"You cannot hurt her, Lewis," she said urgently. "No more than you could hurt Quentin."

"I failed!" Lewis cried. "The beast is loose, because of me! I must rid the world of this whore of Babylon, who let them take the child—yes, I heard everything!" The knife began to dip, and he snapped it toward the sky. "She is like all the daughters of Eve, in league with Satan. Just like, like—"

"Irene is not the enemy," Johanna said. "Another man has taken May. We must find a way to get her back. That is all that matters."

"No! Evil must be wiped out, lest it swallow us all." He swung the knife in a wild arc. "I failed before—failed—but this time—"

" 'Let he who is without sin,' " Johanna quoted, " 'cast the first stone.' Are you without sin, Reverend?"

Lewis gasped, mouth working. "Without sin?" He fell to his knees. "She betrayed me. My Hetty. She lay with another man, and I sent her away. I sent her out to die." Water ran from his eyes and nose. " 'Thou hypocrite, first cast out the beam out of thine own eye!' " He pressed the point of the knife against his own chest.

Harper bolted toward him. Johanna dashed to Irene and dragged her away. With a cry, Lewis allowed Harper to wrench the knife from his hand. He fell prone upon the earth, his arms clasped over his head.

Johanna half-carried Irene back to the house and returned to the vineyard. Harper knelt beside Lewis, whose sobs had hushed to ordinary weeping. The madness was gone from his face.

"He'll be all right," Harper said. "I'll take care of him."

Johanna knew when she had run out of choices. "I will ask Mrs. Daugherty to take charge of Irene, but it will be up to you to keep Lewis quiet and hold things together while I am gone."

"To find May?"

"We will wait for Mrs. Daugherty's news," she said, "and then I shall decide what to do. But I need you here, Harper. I'll leave the gun with you, but I must go alone."

Harper touched the handle of the knife. "Me and Bridget will do what needs to be done."

Johanna had no doubt that he meant what he said. Fighting exhaustion, she tended Irene and went back to the kitchen to await Bridget's return. Everything within her screamed to ride out again, in any and all directions. She knew the utter futility of such a plan.

Three long hours later the buggy drew up in the yard and Mrs. Daugherty climbed out. Johanna met her at the front steps.

"I came back as quick as I could," she panted. "The town's abuzz with talk of the wolf. People who weren't here think the rest of 'em's crazy. No wolf's been seen in these parts in years." She shook her head, unable to believe it herself. "Some are saying the wolf must have kilt Ketchum, and they're gathering men to hunt it down."

No worse than Johanna had expected. "And Bolkonsky?"

"Well, it appears he and Ingram lit out of town this morning, just before the mob came. No one's seen 'em since."

So Bolkonsky must have left straight after "warning" Johanna about the mob. But he apparently hadn't summoned the authorities to search for May, which bought her a little time.

Time for what? She was no closer to being able to locate Quentin than she'd been before. And she had assumed that *Quentin* had May.

There was another explanation for those bare footprints intermingled with May's. Fenris. He arose from Quentin's mind when Quentin was threatened. What better time than after the mob's attack to seize Quentin's body?

And if he had, what did he want with May? Were Quentin's protective instincts enough to arouse like instincts from Fenris's dark, twisted heart? Or had he some unfathomable, fell purpose of his own?

Johanna sat down in a kitchen chair and bent her head low between her knees. This sickness and dread and terror were only the beginning of her punishment.

She had transgressed. She had sinned far worse than Lewis, with all his warnings of Biblical wrath, could imagine. Her deadly sin had been her arrogant presumption that she understood the human mind and its frailties, that she could cure illnesses that daunted far better doctors than she. She had ridden high and serene on the crest of her own wisdom, her own faith in the infallibility of science.

Above all, she had forgotten the sacred trust of every physician. She had allowed herself to fall in love, to become personally involved, with a patient. The very weakness she had deplored in other females had entrapped her. Had she remained pure, true to her calling, she would have kept a closer eye on Irene and Lewis, protected May, dealt effectively with Fenris, and found Quentin's cure. In her blind passion, she'd thrown all that away.

Love had not healed, but destroyed.

"You need rest, Doc Jo," Mrs. Daugherty said. "I'll see that everyone gets fed. You take care of yourself."

Hadn't she done too much of that already? The others, even Harper, were counting on her to remain strong. She had no right to indulge in hysterics or personal grief.

But she did need rest; she'd be useless without it. A little more patience might turn up the one piece of information she needed to make the next crucial decision.

After that, common sense be damned. She would find May and Quentin—or Fenris—if she had to search every inch of this Valley, and beyond.

"Thank you, Mrs. Daugherty," she said. She made her rounds like an automaton, went to her room, and fell facedown on the bed. And she wept. She wept until the pillowcase and the pillow beneath were soaked, so silently that no one came to inquire. Afterwards she washed her face, visited her father, and returned to her room to pace the floor through the long, excruciating night.

Just after dawn an unfamiliar young man came to the front door. Johanna rushed out to meet him, indifferent to her ravaged appearance.

It was obvious that he, too, had been up all night. "You the lady they call Doc Johanna?" he asked, scratching his dirty hair.

"I am. Have you something for me?"

"Sure have." He pulled out a sweat-stained, coarsely folded sheet of paper. "A man at the Bale depot gave me this an' told me to deliver it to you soon as I could get here. Paid me well—not the kind of man you cross." He shuddered. "Took me long enough to find this place."

Johanna snatched the paper from his hand. The words had been scrawled almost illegibly on a sheet of lady's stationery.

"You know that I have May," the words said. *"If you want her back, come to the corner of Jackson and Kearny in San Francisco tomorrow night. A man will be waiting to bring you to me."*

It was signed with a single letter: *F.*

Chapter 21

The place stank. That was the first thing he always noticed when he woke to another foggy San Francisco dusk.

All of the Barbary Coast reeked: of human sweat, rotting fish, stale saltwater, alcohol, cheap perfume, and broken dreams.

It was the closest place to home Fenris had ever found.

And so he ignored the offensive stench and established his territory here, in this boarded-up whorehouse in Devil's Acre, jammed between Jackson's bordello and a saloon where more than one unwary sailor had been known to suffer the loss of everything he owned—even his life.

He stretched out on the stained mattress and looked across the room with its peeling wallpaper and moth-eaten furniture. His wolf's eyes needed no light to see the girl huddled on the decrepit sofa he'd made for her bed. A blanket—relatively clean, for he'd stolen it from one of the better whorehouses—swathed her fragile form from chin to toe. Stray light caught the motion of her pupils as she stared back at him.

What did she think she saw?

Quentin had become the wolf to save Johanna from the mob. Quentin had followed May's kidnapper, set her free, and driven the man to his knees in fear.

But it was Fenris who took human shape again: Fenris who put the terror of damnation into the half-wit he'd chosen, on a whim, not to kill; Fenris who seized May and carried her off without any sort of plan, realizing only miles later what he had.

The means to bring Johanna to him.

Quentin would have taken May to protect her against those who'd harm her. Fenris had no such noble motives. But when he looked at the girl, as he did now, he did not wish her ill.

He almost pitied her. The mawkishness of it sickened him.

He arched his back to work stiff muscles and got up, reaching for his trousers. May watched him, unmoving. Afraid, with good cause. She'd seen him change from wolf to man; few humans witnessed such a transformation and remained unaltered.

Yet in all the time since he had caught her up outside the Haven and carried her away to the south—while he had stolen clothing and coins from unsuspecting farmers and bought tickets at the Bale depot for the next train to San Francisco—not once had she screamed or fainted or fallen into hysterics. She understood what he required of her. She became his meek companion, a mute little sister who wasn't quite right in the head. Fenris discouraged the curiosity and sympathy of strangers.

He'd rifled a lady's baggage at the depot and stole the materials to write his letter to Johanna. He'd paid a boy to deliver it to the Haven, promising retribution if the note didn't reach its destination by morning. The boy took his meaning, just as May did.

He and May reached San Francisco by nightfall. Fenris could have found his way across the city blindfolded; he knew every gambling den and house of ill repute from Murderer's Corner to Deadman's Alley. He and Quentin had shared San Francisco, but here Fenris truly reigned. Especially at night.

May had clung to him, the lesser of two evils, as he led her to his old haunts on the Barbary Coast. His derelict house remained as he'd left it, for no intruder had dared trespass in his absence. The citizens of the Coast knew *him* too well.

And he, Fenris, was still in control. Quentin hadn't the strength to return. He'd been defeated by the knowledge that he'd lost Johanna—and that he was not alone in his own body. He reached out blindly as he sought a link to his other self, a means of recognition and communication. Fenris pushed him back with hardly an effort.

Eventually Quentin would give up. Johanna wouldn't, so long as she believed that she could reach him. Fenris would teach her the futility of that false hope.

Two days had passed since she'd have received his letter—time enough to arrange for her absence from the Haven. He expected her this very evening.

Then he'd have to decide what to do with May.

He finished buttoning his trousers, reached for the chipped plate on the table beside the boarded window, and tore off a chunk of the sourdough bread he'd stolen from the baker's that morning. May's hungry stare was like the annoying buzz of an insect.

"You want this?" he said, holding up the loaf. "Take it." He tossed it toward the couch. She scrambled up to catch it, too late, and it landed on the grimy floor. She sat on the edge of the sofa, the blanket still wrapped around her, and looked at the bread as if it were a million miles out of reach. He waited for her to burst into tears.

She didn't. She raised her head and gazed at him, her pale face set in resignation.

"You aren't Quentin, are you?" she said.

Ironic that she should ask that question first, when she must have wondered *what* he was.

"No," he said mockingly. "I'm not Quentin."

Her brow furrowed. "I don't understand."

"You don't have to." He picked up the bread, brushed it off with his fingers, and thrust it into her hands. "Eat."

"I'm not hungry."

"You're a liar."

She shrank back a little, as if she expected a beating for her defiance. He was tempted to give her what she asked for, but his muscles refused to lift his arm.

Quentin. *Damn* Quentin.

"Eat or starve. I don't care." He turned his back on her and went for the half-empty bottle of whiskey balanced atop a broken armoire.

"Who are you?"

Her rash persistence surprised him, given her ordeal. He took a swig from the bottle.

"Fenris," he said.

"Fenris." She wet her lips. "You're not . . . a regular person."

He laughed at the absurdity of her understatement. "You're right." He leered at her, showing all his teeth. "I'm a monster. Just like Quentin."

"Quentin isn't—" Her protest subsided into a long, fluttering breath. "You and Quentin . . . are the same, aren't you?"

She wasn't completely stupid. "Don't go crying after him. You won't find him here."

She absorbed that in silence. "But he's not really gone, is he?"

"Shut up."

"Quentin is my friend. He always tried to help me."

He slammed the bottle down on the armoire. "I told you to shut up."

"*You* helped me," she whispered. "You saved me from that man, the one who wanted to take me back to my father."

Pain exploded in his head. "*I'm . . . not . . . Quentin.*" He strode toward her, hard and fast, bent on meting out swift punishment. She leaned back against the sofa, not so much as raising her arms to protect herself.

But in her eyes was the tiniest glint of spirit. It brought him up short.

"Will you hurt me, like my father?" she asked.

His headache worked to split his brain down the middle. "I'm not your father," he snarled.

"No," she said. "*He* pretended to love me."

He'd never heard such a voice, such aching acceptance and sorrow. The girl Quentin knew hadn't spoken of her past, not to him nor to Johanna. That girl had always been afraid.

Like the boy. The boy in the cellar, who'd cried out for help and found it.

Fenris clenched his teeth and fell to his knees beside the sofa. Something inside drove him to ask what he didn't want to know, didn't want to feel.

"What did he do to you?"

She closed her eyes. "He . . . he came to me when I was sleeping. He touched me."

Fingernails scraped against the bare floorboards, and Fenris realized they were his own.

"I don't want to go back," she said. "Please, don't make me go back."

He jumped to his feet. "You're not going anywhere."

"You don't have to take care of me. Quentin—"

"Quentin is a coward and a fool." He seized her chin in his hand, deliberately relaxed his fingers so that he would not damage her skin and bones. "He couldn't even take care of himself."

Her eyes filled with tears. "Someone hurt him? His . . . his father?"

Grandfather. Please no more . . .

Fenris roared. He saw Quentin—himself—May—bound and helpless while one who should have loved and protected gave torment instead.

Killing rage replaced all semblance of thought. Tiberius Forster was dead, but Chester Ingram was not. The man called Bolkonsky was not.

The girl had become a wraith to him, like a half-forgotten dream. He started toward the door.

"Quentin?"

He stopped.

"Quentin, please come back."

Quentin heard. Quentin stirred in his prison, struggling to respond. He groped in darkness for his voice and his being. A shaft of light burst from an opening door.

Fenris flung his weight against that door, but not before Quentin saw him.

"You," Quentin said. "You're real."

The moment in which they faced each other was infinitesimal, but it was enough for Quentin to understand. Understanding was a new and powerful weapon, but he didn't yet know how to use it. He was paralyzed by horror.

Fenris heard the girl's tread behind him. "Quentin—"

"I'm here," he whispered in Quentin's voice.

Fenris howled. He slammed the door inside his mind and sealed it with a hundred massive locks forged by his furious will.

He couldn't kill Quentin, no more than he could kill a man already dead, or the girl shivering within her enshrouding blanket.

But Quentin couldn't stop him from eliminating Ingram, because it was what they both wanted. It was the work for which Fenris had been born.

He turned to the girl, seeing her face as if through a sheer veil of bloodred silk.

"Wait here," he said with an icy smile. "I'm going to visit your father."

Johanna arrived at the San Francisco Ferry House on the evening's last boat and disembarked with the small group of passengers from Oakland. The others scattered to their various destinations, hailing hackney coaches or meeting friends, many chattering happily as if they looked forward to an enjoyable visit.

The sun was just setting, and already the night was damp and cold, lacking the Napa Valley's summer warmth. San Francisco's weather perfectly matched the chill in Johanna's heart. The coldness had settled in with the delivery of Fenris's letter, and hadn't left her since.

She'd done what needed doing in spite of her fears, arranging for Mrs. Daugherty and Harper to handle the running of the Haven and the most basic care of the other patients and her father. She hoped she would not be gone long enough to put a strain on Mrs. Daugherty's generosity, or compromise Harper's dramatic improvement. At least she had Mrs. Daugherty's assurance that the townspeople had lost their interest in revisiting the Haven . . . for the time being.

It hadn't been easy to lie to the patients, especially to Harper. Harper guessed that Quentin had taken May, but he didn't know that Fenris existed. She'd told him that she was going to meet Quentin in San Francisco and arrange for May's safe disposition. Mrs. Daugherty and the patients had been given a much simpler story. None of them knew the complexity of May's situation with her father.

But Harper wasn't satisfied. He'd held May's book, his brow creased in worry, and told Johanna that Quentin and May were in serious danger.

She could hardly refute him, and she respected him too much to offer comforting platitudes.

She pulled Fenris's note from her coat pocket and read the scrawled address once more. She wasn't familiar enough with San Francisco to recognize the location, but someone at her hotel would be sure to know. She suspected that the place was in a very bad part of town.

She had no doubt that Fenris was waiting for her.

Squaring her shoulders, she flagged down the nearest hired hack and gave the driver the address of a modest but respectable hotel on Market Street, where she'd stayed for the lecture nearly three weeks ago. Once there, she strode to the desk with her single bag and waited impatiently behind another woman who was completing her registration.

After an interminable period, the woman turned from the desk and bumped into Johanna.

"I beg your pardon," the woman said, echoing Johanna's apology. They broke off simultaneously, and the woman peered into her face. Johanna felt a jolt of startled recognition.

"Dr. Schell?" the woman said. "Dr. Johanna Schell? It is you, is it not?"

Johanna took an involuntary step backward. "Mrs. . . . Mrs. Ingram?"

"Yes. Oh, it is you!" She beamed, and Johanna thought back to the last night she'd seen this unfortunate woman, haggard and terrified for herself and her daughter. "What an amazing coincidence to meet you here, of all places! And I was just making the arrangements to come to the Valley to see you."

She extended her gloved hand, and Johanna took it, praying that her trembling was not too obvious.

Mrs. Ingram. May's mother, who had disappeared for a full two years—communicating only through the occasional letter—who had trusted Johanna with her daughter's well-being when she could trust no one else. Her most recent letter had promised her return in the very near future, and she'd been as good as her word.

She had greatly changed. Her cheeks glowed with health and confidence; her eyes sparkled with genuine happiness. The happiness of a mother about to be reunited with a beloved child.

"I understand your hesitation in greeting me," Mrs. Ingram said, becoming serious. "I must have seemed a terrible mother to you, leaving my child as I did. My letters were hardly adequate, but I had reason for hiding my whereabouts."

Johanna found her voice. "Mrs. Ingram—I knew, when I accepted May, that you faced great difficulties."

"And I knew you would care for my girl and make her well." She squeezed Johanna's hand. "I knew the moment we met. But everything has changed. It has taken me two years, but I have the means of making certain that my husband can never threaten us again. I can pay you for all your good work, and May and I can live together in peace."

"I am . . . glad to hear it," Johanna said.

"I'm sure you have a great many questions, and I shall be happy to answer them soon. Are you in town on business? Perhaps you will allow me to accompany you back to the Haven." She smiled self-consciously. "It will be easier for her to meet me again if you are with me. I'm sure she's grown to love you, and I've been gone so long. Perhaps she blames me for leaving her."

Johanna swallowed. "Mrs. Ingram—"

"Forgive my chatter. My life has changed so, and it doesn't quite seem real as yet." She glanced toward the clerk behind the desk. "I must be keeping you. Please tell me—how is May? I can't wait to see her."

"May—May has improved, Mrs. Ingram. She has made friends at the Haven, and reads constantly. She's becoming a young woman."

Little truths to cover the big ones that could not be spoken, truths no better than lies. Lies would not protect Johanna, or undo her many mistakes. They would only spare this woman more suffering.

Mrs. Ingram closed her eyes. "I knew it. I have felt all these months that everything will be right at last. Thank you, Dr. Schell."

Johanna cleared her throat. "It seems that we are staying in the same hotel."

"As you see. I had planned to go to Silverado Springs tomorrow—"

"Might you delay a day or two? I have certain business to attend here in the city before I return. I have very good and reliable assistants at the Haven, but I agree that it would be best if we see May together."

Mrs. Ingram made a valiant try at hiding her disappointment. "Yes. I see. Of course I will wait on your convenience. A few more days can hardly make a difference." Her smile returned. "As it happens, it will allow me to put a few final details of my own plans in place."

"Very good." Johanna thought of Mr. Ingram, and wondered what resources this revitalized woman had found to give her such spirit to face him again. She hoped it was enough to thoroughly emasculate him.

But none of that mattered until she had May safely back.

"I'm very glad that things have turned out so well for you," she said, despising herself.

"Of course." Mrs. Ingram clasped her hand again. "Thank you. Thank you so much."

Johanna averted her gaze and waited until the other woman had gone up to her room. Only then did she register, leave her bag in her room, and hail a conveyance that would take her to Fenris's rendezvous.

"The Barbary Coast?" the hackney driver said, shaking his head. "Bad place for a decent woman at any time of day. At night—"

"It is where I must go," she said. "Please take me there quickly."

"As you say, ma'am. On your own head be it." He clucked his tongue, helped her into the coach, and climbed up to the driver's seat. "Don't say I didn't warn you."

Johanna sank back into the seat and closed her eyes. The warning came too late.

All he could see was fog.

Quentin woke into his body with a sense of disorientation and icy metal against his fingers. He unclenched his fists from the ironwork bars forming a high, decorative fence that marked the boundaries of a landscaped garden. The garden of a large, handsome Second Empire house, with a slated mansard roof and lights burning in a pair of gabled windows on the second floor.

His vision cleared further, and he saw that the fog was not so thick as he'd imagined. It swirled between buildings much like this one, the dwellings of rich and prosperous folk perched atop a hill overlooking the city.

The city of San Francisco. Nob Hill, in fact; he recognized the neighborhood, though it was one he'd seldom frequented during his previous residence. He had no idea how he had come to be here—in the city, or at this particular place. He didn't know whose house this was, or why he'd been bent on trespass.

The last memory he could summon to mind was one of Changing from wolf to man in the woods near the Haven, May gazing at him in shock while her erstwhile kidnapper scuttled away. He remembered surrendering to instinct. Raw emotion. Despair. Anger.

He'd left the door open—

To Fenris.

He slumped to the ground at the foot of the ironwork fence and squeezed his eyes shut. How much time had passed? Hours, or days? What had this body done while it lay in another's control?

He opened his eyes and stared at his hands. They looked the same. There was no blood on them. His clothing was unfamiliar, not what he would have chosen. But when he'd Changed, he hadn't been wearing anything.

Fenris had dressed this body to suit himself. And come to San Francisco.

But Quentin had control again, for no reason that he could fathom. If anger and irrational emotion gave Fenris the edge, what had made him flee? Why had he brought Quentin to this place? To what had Fenris come?

And why?

Quentin pushed his palms against his temples. *Think.* His own intention had been to leave Johanna and the others and seek out some distant, isolated place where he could wrestle with his own demons—with Fenris—free of the fear of harming innocents. He'd delayed his departure long enough to scare off the mob and rescue May. He'd known that Bolkonsky or Ingram must be responsible for her abduction, but he hadn't thought beyond seeing her returned safely to Johanna.

Fenris had taken his mind before he faced an impossible decision. But what Fenris wanted was more a mystery to him than it had been to Johanna.

Johanna. She'd begged him not to go, to trust her to help him. Cure him. He couldn't think of her without an agony of desire and sorrow and love.

Fenris didn't love Johanna . . .

But he'd wanted her.

Yes. Quentin slammed his head against the iron bars. That was what Fenris was after—he felt it in his gut like the dregs of a nightmare. Johanna had come to *his* bed because of Fenris.

Because Fenris had threatened her, and she wanted to give Quentin willingly what Fenris desired to take by force.

If Fenris was everything Quentin was afraid to be, he would have remained at the Haven and seized what he wanted. He wouldn't have considered the consequences.

Unless something had restrained him, redirected his desires. Some-*one*. If that person had been Johanna, surely she would have brought Quentin back. She had the skill, the courage, and the stubbornness.

No. The last he'd seen of Johanna was when she faced down the mob. He was sure that Fenris hadn't been near her since.

But who else could hold Fenris in check . . . except his other self?

Hope made Quentin catch his breath. Could he have been fighting without knowing it? Fenris had every advantage, with access to Quentin's memories, while Quentin remained in darkness. Until Johanna had told him, he hadn't known that Fenris existed. Now the implacable shadow had a name. A name was something to fight.

"Somehow," Johanna had said, "you and I must find a way to communicate with him. Bring him into the light, and confront him."

But this was not a matter of communication and confrontation. It was war. The battle was solely Quentin's—Quentin the coward, the ne'er-do-well, who had mustered up an inner core of strength to resist.

And he had to make use of it while he could. He had to learn what Fenris was doing in San Francisco, and then find a way to stop him. Expel him for good. Take back his life.

Win Johanna's love.

She'd never said she loved him. This was his great chance to prove himself worthy of her—worthy of the life he might create when Fenris was gone. Salvation. A new beginning.

Failure had only one consequence: oblivion. Death. That was the final act Quentin Forster would commit should Fenris win the battle.

Do you hear me? he called into the depths of his mind. *I'm not running anymore, Fenris-the-shadow.*

An answer came—not in a voice, but as a memory. A memory of emotion, a red haze of rage, the scents of rot and hopelessness, the view of a face.

May's face. Quentin strove to grasp the memory and pull it closer. Like a weighted chain, it slipped from his hold.

But not before the memory gave up one last clue: an alley, a sign, a familiar streetcorner. The Barbary Coast. *That* was a part of the city Quentin knew, a den of iniquity that Fenris had shared with him all those times he'd wakened with no memory of his recent past.

That was where Fenris laired. And May was with him.

May. What did Fenris want with her?

Quentin pulled himself to his feet and swallowed the bile in his throat. *Run*, he commanded himself. *Save her.*

A vicious presence stirred, reaching, tearing, laughing. *You are Fenris. Save her from yourself*.

He stood very still, emptying his thoughts until his body and mind went chill and heavy. The presence fled. It could not survive—Fenris could not survive—where fear and anger were absent. Even love must be severed until Fenris was gone.

Love he'd already lost.

In cold-blooded dispassion, he turned and began to walk toward hell.

Chapter 22

Johanna could almost imagine the stink of sulfur and brimstone.

The man who greeted her on the street corner where the hackney driver had left her was as seedy a character as any she'd met, wearing a patch over one eye and a sour, gap-toothed smile.

"You the doc?" he asked, scratching his flea-infested rags.

"Yes. Are you the man who is to take me to . . . Were you sent here for me?"

"Aye. I'm to take you to *him*. He's put the word out that no one in the Acre's to bother you." He leered at her brazenly. "Good thing. You wouldn't last a minute."

Johanna was not inclined to argue. Did Fenris have so much power here?

"C'mon," the man said. He set off down the ill-lit street, passing dance halls and opium dens, groggeries and deadfalls by the dozens. Shadows scurried and staggered from building to building: cutthroats, drunks, prostitutes, and thieves of every description. Some of them stopped to stare, a few graced her with catcalls, but none approached.

This was Fenris's kingdom.

She thrust her hand into her coat pocket and felt for the gun. Using it would literally be a matter of last resort, if May had to be protected. And even then she wasn't sure she could kill.

The person she'd be killing was the man she loved.

Her guide turned down an alley and Johanna followed, alert to every movement. The place to which One-eye brought her was a boarded-up house with cracked and staring eyes for windows. Even rats must avoid the place. There was just enough moonlight, filtered through fog, for Johanna to make out the door.

She turned to speak to One-eye, but he'd already slipped away. His services were no longer required, and she suspected that he had no desire to meet his master face-to-face.

The steps leading up to the door were fragile with rot, and Johanna moved carefully. To walk in unannounced would not be wise. Fenris was unstable, unpredictable. He might turn on May if angered.

Gott in Himmel, if he hurt her—

She knocked. The door creaked open. A single brown eye peered through the crack.

"Johanna?" May whispered.

"May!"

May pulled the door inward and rushed over the threshold into Johanna's arms. "You're here! You came to find me."

Peering past May into the lightless room, Johanna couldn't see anyone else inside. She smoothed back May's unkempt hair.

"Are you all right, *mein Liebling?*"

"Yes." A shiver worked its way through her thin body. "I'm all right."

"Let me look at you." She held May's shoulders and examined her. There were no signs of damage except a bit of dirt and a general dishevelment. Fenris hadn't hurt her—and he'd left her alone.

To remain standing on the doorstep, in plain sight, was the height of folly, but Johanna didn't wish to be trapped within should Fenris return. She led May just inside the door and half closed it.

"Where is he?" she asked, deliberately using the unspecified pronoun. She didn't know how much May had observed of Quentin's dual nature, or how well she had dealt with it. "He went out," May said. "To find my father."

So Fenris's absence was not unmitigated good fortune. "Did he say why?" Johanna asked.

"I think he wants to hurt him."

Himmel! What unspeakable ordeals had May been through since Fenris had taken her? She'd seen the man she'd thought of as a friend, a protector, become something grotesque and evil. How could she do other than retreat into fits of hysteria or catalepsy?

But she met Johanna's gaze steadily, her body straight and still. Trusting. Waiting. Expecting Johanna to make everything better again.

She didn't understand that her physician had discovered the depths of her own weakness and folly.

"We must leave, immediately," Johanna said. "Is there anything you need to take from this place?"

May didn't move. "What about my father?"

It was not uncommon for the children of abusive parents to maintain an attachment, even love, for those who had mistreated them. But May hadn't wanted anything to do with her father. Did she want to protect Ingram, or was she hoping he'd be removed permanently from her life? More likely, she was simply confused, torn by conflicting needs and desires. Who could blame her?

Johanna could see May to a safe place and go to the police. It was a certain death warrant for those men who went after him, for Fenris was more than human. He'd kill without compunction. "I'll get you to safety," she told May, "and then I'll do what I can."

May buried her face in Johanna's bodice. "Please don't leave me alone."

"Oh, she won't leave you, Miss Ingram," said a familiar, masculine baritone. "At least not yet."

Johanna turned, pushing May behind her. She knew that voice, though his face was in shadow.

Bolkonsky.

He walked through the door and kicked it shut with one well-shod foot. In the semidarkness, his pale hair flowed like tarnished silver to his shoulders. The gun in his hand had the same dull sheen.

"I wish we had met under less unfortunate circumstances, Johanna," he said, tipping his hat with his free hand. "How was your trip to San Francisco?"

Johanna reached into her pocket. Bolkonsky cocked his gun. "Please hold your hands away from your sides," he said. "I'd rather not be forced to shoot you."

She obeyed, stunned at the hatred she felt. "You will not take her. I will not let you."

"So you've said many times, in one fashion or another," he said.

"When my man didn't arrive with the girl at the appointed time, I knew something had gone wrong. Eventually I learned why."

"You went to a great deal of trouble to take May from the Haven," Johanna said coldly. "Did her father hope to spirit her away with none the wiser? Did you both think I'd give up so easily?"

"Your stubbornness is almost admirable. But it doesn't matter now."

Johanna eyed the door behind him. What she needed was a diversion, one that would allow her to grab her gun.

"Why doesn't it matter?" she asked, shuffling a step forward. "You cannot expect me to remain silent. I can make things very uncomfortable for May's father. Ingram may be powerful, but, as you said, I am extremely stubborn."

"You're hardly in a position to threaten," he said pleasantly.

"I do not fear for my reputation, professional or otherwise, if sacrificing it means saving May. And if you intend to use that"—she nodded toward his gun and moved another step—"you'll hardly draw attention away from your patron, or yourself."

"You're right. And if it were my intention to take May to her father, I might even be concerned. But that was never my true object, Johanna."

She checked her subtle forward motion. "What?"

"My dear girl, have I managed to surprise you? How delightful." He smiled. "The focus of all my efforts—my seeking of your acquaintance and that of May's father, my pursuit of the girl, everything I've done since we met—has been another of your patients. Can you guess which one?"

The face of each of the Haven's residents flashed through her mind in the space of a second. It could be any one of them, except possibly Oscar—each had his or her own past secrets even she didn't know.

But, without so much as a single iota of corroborative evidence, her intuition told her the answer.

"Quentin," she whispered.

"Excellent. You're a bright woman, for a human."

The hair rose on the back of her neck. "Who are you?"

"Quentin knows me. We're old friends."

Behind him, the door groaned. Bolkonsky leaped about, graceful as a dancer. Johanna reached into her pocket and pulled out the gun. Bolkonsky thrust out one arm without even looking at her, knocking the gun from her hand. Then he hit her in the chest, and all the air poured from her lungs. She fell to her knees, gasping, just as Bolkonsky yanked the door open to reveal the man on the other side.

"Quentin!" May cried.

Johanna peered through the black spots that crowded her vision. Quentin stood in the doorway, hands at his sides, staring at Bolkonsky. Quentin, not Fenris. The difference was plain to her heart, if not her eyes. She had no voice to call out a warning.

"Quentin," Bolkonsky said. "It's been a long time."

"Stefan Boroskov," Quentin said, dull surprise in his voice. His gaze found Johanna, and May just behind her. "Let them go."

"I think not." Bolkonsky—Boroskov—retrieved Johanna's gun, tucked it under his coat, and gestured with his own weapon. "Come in, old friend. We have so much to talk about."

Quentin had expected disaster, but hardly of this magnitude. He could ill afford the luxury of astonishment.

He walked into a room half-familiar in its rank decay, and came to a stop between Johanna and Boroskov. His thoughts were reluctant to focus, but this was the time above all when he must remain master of his mind.

That brittle clarity was all he had with which to face one of his family's oldest enemies.

Stefan Boroskov, who he'd last seen in England five years ago. Boroskov, with Johanna and May Quentin knew how May had come to be here—Fenris had brought her. Johanna had surely followed in search of one or both of them. But Boroskov . . .

"Now that we're all together," the Russian said, "I think we should have formal introductions. If you please, Quentin?"

He ignored Boroskov and spoke to Johanna. "This was your Bolkonsky, wasn't he?"

"Yes." She tried to convey some message with her eyes that he couldn't interpret. "That is what he called himself."

"And I never suspected." He turned back to his enemy. "How did you contrive that, Boroskov? You stayed away from the Haven, but I should have smelled you."

"You didn't notice the scent of cologne about Johanna's person?" he asked. "I've found that it masks subtler odors wonderfully well."

"You have execrable taste in cologne."

"Ah. I'm wounded to the quick." Boroskov touched his heart. "Yes, to Johanna I was Feodor Bolkonsky, fellow practitioner to the insane and mentally afflicted, spokesman for little May Ingram's bereaved father."

"Who is he?" Johanna demanded, her gaze fixed on Boroskov. She moved to Quentin's side, her shoulder brushing his. The contact sent his pulse spiralling. "Why has he done this, Quentin? What does he want with you?"

Of course. Boroskov had tried to kidnap May, but the girl wasn't what he wanted. His failure had been temporary. His real prey had come to him.

"Such a curious human," Boroskov commented. "Perhaps you ought to explain, Quentin, before she grows faint with confusion."

Quentin laughed, the movement hurting his chest. "Johanna? You don't know her, Boroskov."

"But I do. Please, the introductions."

Quentin bowed with heavy irony. "Johanna, may I present Stefan Boroskov," he said, deliberately omitting the Russian's title. "His family and mine have been acquainted for many generations. He is . . . like me."

Johanna understood. "A loup-garou," she said. She reached behind her to touch May's arm.

"Ah, she knows!" Boroskov said. "My informant at the Haven did not."

"Your informant?" Johanna put in.

"Irene DuBois. She gave me information about you and the Haven even before I first contacted you, my dear doctor. We loups-garous have certain . . . talents. I would have learned all I needed to know even had Irene not been so easy to manipulate. Because of her eagerness to cooperate, and her considerable acting talents. I was able to conveniently arrange my various distractions." He clucked at Johanna. "You didn't keep your records and notes locked away. Not at all wise."

"That explains—" Johanna began. Her expression hardened. "You promised to take Irene away in exchange for her help in kidnapping May."

"Among other things. But those are mere details. Of course Irene didn't know of Quentin's nature, nor my own. Yet you and May do. Who else among your patients has guessed, I wonder?"

"None," Quentin lied. By now at least two others did, but he wasn't about to jeopardize them by suggesting otherwise. Boroskov despised humans, and would not tolerate a perceived threat of any kind. "Did you think I'd go about advertising it?"

"Who knows what a drunkard might do in his cups? Did you ever cure him of that, Johanna? But I digress. You were about to elucidate our relationship, Quentin, when I so rudely interrupted."

Quentin grasped at the change of subject. "Of course." He turned to Johanna. "The Forsters and the Boroskovs have been . . . at odds for many years. Five years ago, Stefan and his brother attempted to kill my brother, Braden, the earl of Greyburn, in a treacherous fight, hoping to capture the leadership of the loups-garous. The Boroskovs lost, and Braden sent them home with their tails between their legs. He chose not to kill them, though it was his right to do so." He smiled, showing his teeth. "Apparently it was a mistake."

Boroskov shook his head. "I don't know how much you've told her before, Quentin, but I fear you haven't made matters any less confusing for our doctor. You see, my dear girl, he has not defined the political complexities of our society, to which few humans are privy. He has also neglected to mention the reason behind his family's hatred for mine."

"Milena," Quentin said. "His sister and Braden's former wife, who betrayed and blinded him before she herself died."

As he expected, Boroskov's face contorted in anger. "Was *murdered*. Alas, that I don't have time to explain the truth, Johanna."

"Your society," Johanna said to Quentin, as if Boroskov hadn't spoken. "Are there so many of you?"

"We're scattered, but there are still a few hundred families working to preserve our race," Quentin said. "Within human society, we live as humans. Away from it, we have our own rules, our own way of life. It is not always an ideal existence."

"For good reason," Boroskov said. "We are superior, and yet we live like whipped curs, hiding in our dens. And that is why, decades ago, your grandfather and my father developed the great Cause of attaining dominance over humanity."

Quentin's muscles seized up. *Grandfather.* The presence seething below the surface of his thoughts took strength from his instinctive reaction. "That may have been your Cause," he said with an effort, "but it was never my brother's. He wished only to save our kind from extinction."

"Your brother turned from the path set by those stronger and wiser than he," Boroskov said. "He perverted the Cause into something paltry and wretched."

"He defeated *you*."

"Temporarily, yes. But his lack of ruthlessness is one of his weaknesses, and the reason why I am here now."

"Why are you here, Boroskov? What do you want with me, and Johanna?"

Boroskov tilted his gun toward the floor. "You may well wonder. In these past few years of following your progress, you've never shown any sign of remembering."

"Following me?"

"Oh, not personally. Not until the past six months. I had trusted human servants, aware of our secrets, tracking your movements and sending back their observations. You were so caught up in your own miseries that you were oblivious to their presence."

Quentin recalled a hundred times when he had ignored the sense of being watched. It was a pathetic werewolf indeed who could not detect a human follower. But he had little self-respect to lose.

"You are about to ask why I had you followed," Boroskov prompted.

"The question had occurred to me." Quentin glanced at Johanna and subtly pushed her behind him. May was quiet as a mouse. "You said I showed no signs of remembering. Remembering what?"

"That is part of my story. Patience." He waved Johanna and May toward the dilapidated sofa. "Sit down, dear doctor, and take the child with you."

Johanna looked to Quentin. He nodded, and she led May to the couch. She did not sit.

"Your brother, Braden, inherited the Cause without understanding its true purpose," Boroskov said. "We shall never know how much your grandfather, the previous earl, told him. Perhaps he died before he could reveal all his plans." He shook his head. "The arranged marriages between our scattered families, to restore our blood to its former strength and numbers, was only a small part of his Cause. In time, your grandfather and my father intended that our people should take their rightful places as rulers of the world."

Quentin laughed until his belly knotted in pain, and laughed harder still at Boroskov's expression. "World conquest? When most of us can't even meet every five years without squabbling like infants?"

"Because Braden cannot rule as a leader must. But the former earl and my father made a pact, to develop a means of ensuring that the true Cause would not be subverted. And that is where you come in, Quentin."

"Of course," Quentin said, catching his breath. "You want to use me to take revenge on Braden, or force him to step down. Surely you can't believe I would cooperate."

"I am disappointed in you, my boy," Boroskov said. "Nothing nearly so obvious." He met Quentin's eyes in a direct stare, werewolf to werewolf. "You were to play a very special role in our future plans. And from my observations, you may be what we had hoped for."

"Me?" Quentin's throat was too raw for laughing, but he managed a rasping chuckle. "I was never good for much of anything—certainly

not for your Cause. I got away before Braden could pin me to some female of his choosing." He wiped at his eyes. "Did you want me to take
Braden's place?"

"Hardly. That role is mine. But you will be at my right hand."

"You have a very strange sense of humor, Boroskov."

"I am not laughing." He adjusted the fit of his glove, dangling his
gun from one finger. "I told you that your grandfather and my father
made a separate, secret pact. They knew that our goal of conquest
would not be an easy one, or swift. It would take many generations to
achieve. And over those generations, we would require soldiers who
would be trained and willing to commit whatever acts we might deem
necessary in pursuit of our goals."

"Soldiers," Quentin repeated.

"Soldiers stronger and faster than any human. And ruthless, disciplined from childhood to obey their leaders without question."

"Murderers, you mean," Quentin said, struck with a sudden chill.
"Assassins."

"Quite. When the time came, such specially trained detachments
would be sent into the field to remove select human leaders, businessmen whose assets would become our own—any who might conceivably
stand in our way. But first we had to learn how to create such a special
'army.' Your grandfather, and my father, chose one each of their offspring upon whom to experiment."

Quentin couldn't respond. He saw the cellar, smelled the sweat of
his own fear and blood. Grandfather . . .

"They chose their subjects as young children, to allow for the
greatest tractability of character. There was a risk that the subjects
might be damaged in the attempt, so your grandfather chose you as the
most expendable."

Quentin's teeth ground together with an audible crack.

"Your instruction was begun when you were a boy," Boroskov said.
"You were to be broken to your grandfather's will by any means necessary, become indifferent to murder and absolutely obedient.

"You see, my brother—you were meant to be a killer."

Johanna felt for the seat behind her and fell into it. May gave a soft
whimper.

Quentin was a statue, staring at Boroskov as if the Russian had be-
spelled him with his evil.

"You do remember something of those days, don't you?" Boroskov asked, almost gently. "I see it in your eyes. Your grandfather's methods were harsh, no doubt, but necessary. I have none of his notes on his procedures, but I can guess what he did."

"The cellar," Quentin whispered, as if he didn't realize he spoke. Johanna rose to go to him, but Boroskov pointed his gun in her direction.

"No. Your usefulness is past, my dear doctor. No more coddling. He is mine, now."

"You are wrong," she said. "He belongs to himself."

"Cling to your illusions if you must," he said. "You, too, know of his sufferings, do you not? You have discovered many of his secrets. But you cannot imagine what it is like to be one of us. I will be—I am— closer to Quentin than any other living being. For I was my father's selection as one of the new army."

Johanna met his gaze and understood. If Quentin's form of madness had been born in the tortures he'd endured in his grandfather's cellar, then Boroskov's came from the same source.

"Yes, my father trained me," he said. "I did not break. I grew stronger. I saw what had to be done. But somewhere, somehow, Quentin's instruction faltered. He broke free of his grandfather's influence in his adolescence, and for a time we believed he was a loss to us."

Johanna took another step toward Quentin, disregarding Boroskov's threat. "You are not a failure, Quentin."

"No, he is not. When he ran from England, from the skirmish his brother won over me, I knew he had begun to recall those things he'd tried to forget. The training he'd rejected. His deep and binding brotherhood to me."

"No," Quentin croaked.

"Why deny it? You feel the truth already. Yes, you escaped your grandfather. When you came of age, you joined the Army and went to India. Even then I was watching you, and waiting. I was not disappointed. It was there that your grandfather's careful work began to bear fruit." He smiled sympathetically. "Do you remember the time when you single-handedly rescued your men from ambush by the tribesmen? You killed eight of the enemy, they said. They called you a hero, but they were afraid. You were something they had never seen before—a berserker, who did not leave the field until every foe was dead."

"God," Quentin said, his face stark with horror.

"The necessary instincts were coming to the fore—to kill your enemies without mercy. But you were undirected. You did not yet have a cause that bound you. You returned to England, and led a meaningless life of pleasure and forgetfulness. But that came to an end when I arrived at Greyburn to challenge Braden."

"I was a coward."

"No. You felt drawn to me, to what we shared. You had begun to sense what you were, felt the stirring of your blood at the sight of violence. So you ran. But you could not run from your destiny. It followed you here, to America. My men reported the many times your training rose unbidden, to put the humans in their place."

"I killed," Quentin said hollowly, making it a question.

"No. But you created enough havoc to prove that you had what we required. Each time you moved on, losing yourself in drink, as if you could escape what you knew you were destined to be. Each time, the warrior within you could not be restrained. All it needed was discipline, and a master to temper your violence. I will be the one to complete what your grandfather began."

Slowly Quentin's expression relaxed, and he looked at Johanna with full comprehension. It was as if everything he had wrestled with became clear in an instant. Just as it had for Johanna. Her heart ached for him.

"Why did you involve Johanna and May?" he asked.

"When I first followed you to San Francisco, I was prepared to seek you out. But you proved surprisingly elusive, until I was able to track you to the Napa Valley. There, I learned of Doctor Schell's new patient, and obtained informants who could give me the information I needed—most notably Irene DuBois. From her, I learned of Johanna's other patients, including May.

"It soon became clear to me that you had indeed located a haven, a place where you might find the help you sought, the support that would make it easier for you to resist. I had to pry you loose. Miss Ingram's situation presented the ideal opportunity to disrupt your life at the Haven, and pull Johanna's attention from you. I had Irene look through Dr. Schell's notes, and she told me that May was essentially in hiding from her father, a wealthy businessman in San Francisco."

"You forced Irene to obey you?" Johanna demanded.

"He could do it, Johanna," Quentin said, his voice betraying no trace of emotion. "Our kind have mental abilities humans do not. He could make her do as he chose, and erase her memory of the events."

"Indeed, but force was hardly necessary," Boroskov said. "I merely turned her thoughts from certain subjects, and encouraged her in others."

Johanna filed that astonishing fact aside for further examination, one more among a hundred others. "So you used May to get at Quentin," she addressed Boroskov.

"I approached May's father in San Francisco and told him that I knew of his daughter's whereabouts, if he wished her back. He did. He trusted me as a learned doctor, who could restore his daughter to him without inconvenient fuss or awkwardness."

"It didn't quite work out that way," Quentin said.

"No, but it doesn't matter. I achieved what I intended. I diverted Johanna from her work with you, kept both of you off balance and worried about May while I perfected my plans. Irene DuBois was most useful in reporting on your actions, with very little persuasion from me—she was quick enough to believe me smitten. She also had scant love for either of you." He sighed. "But you, apparently, had become quite enamored of each other—an annoyance at first, but it proved to be a factor in my favor." He cocked a brow. "Did you really believe, Quentin, that Johanna could save you?"

"I always believed in her."

"But that wasn't enough, was it?" He turned to Johanna. "When it was obvious that you would not let May go, and Quentin was no further along in being detached from you and the Haven, I arranged for the death of the mine owner, and saw it blamed on Quentin. A simple thing to manipulate the ignorant humans in Silverado Springs."

"I didn't kill . . ." Quentin began.

"No. You may take credit for Ingram's beating, but not Ketchum's death. While the mob came to the Haven, I had one of my men abduct May. I knew, from Irene's reports, that you would inevitably follow to rescue her, and once you were out of Johanna's sphere of influence it would be easy enough to trap you. Though my man failed, you are here. You took May, and I followed." He addressed Johanna. "A pity you had to involve yourself further. I rather liked you, dear doctor."

"You won't hurt her," Quentin said. "Not her, or May, or anyone else." The change in him was subtle, but Johanna recognized it. He seemed to grow, gathering his strength, preparing for bedlam.

He was being threatened. Those he cared for were in peril. Inside him, Fenris was awakening. Fenris, who *was* the very thing his own grandfather had tried to create. Fenris, who might be a match for Stefan Boroskov.

"If you cooperate, I'll have no need," Boroskov said. "I do not worry that the doctor will expose us. No one will believe her—they will merely think her infected with her patients' madness. And May is merely a child."

"If I do as you tell me, you'll let them go," Quentin said.

Boroskov shrugged.

"And if I don't cooperate, you'll kill them."

"Johanna, perhaps. The girl I may simply return to her father."

Quentin lunged at the Russian. "You scum—"

"Yes." Boroskov's eyes lit. "Yes. Let it go, Quentin. Remember who you were meant to be." He held out his hand.

"Come, my brother. Take what I offer. You have no place in the human world, or in that of your brother. You are not the weakling you've believed yourself to be. You are one of the true, new blood of the werewolf race, the hope of our people. Your future is in my hands. *Our* future."

Johanna watched in horror as Quentin took Boroskov's hand.

Chapter 23

He'd forgotten who he was.

He hung, suspended, between two wills, two souls. One cried out for release, for a peace he had never known; the other screamed in triumph, sensing final liberation from all the chains that had bound him.

Only one anchor offered itself. He clutched the extended hand.

It anchored him to the present as memories crashed about him like a storm. The first time Grandfather had taken him to the cellar, a few months after Mother's death, and explained what he was to become. The years of beatings, starvation, promises of dire punishment he'd kept hidden from Braden and Rowena—yes, even from his twin, who thought she knew everything about him. How he'd fooled them, laughing his way through hell.

Sometime, in those years, Fenris had been born: to take the punishment, to endure the pain—and, in the end, to turn against his tormenter.

Alien, terrifying images spun in an endless loop through his mind. Grandfather's face, grim and merciless, leaning over to administer his brand of "discipline" . . . his expression dissolving into astonishment. And fear.

Victory. Grandfather never took him to the cellar again. The beatings didn't stop, not entirely. But the terror did. Eventually Grandfather died, and he'd thought himself free. The memories faded. His other self had little reason for existence, and went into dormancy. Whatever he had once known, or guessed, of Fenris was buried under layer upon layer of protective armor.

But he remained haunted still. He looked for escape in every sort of harmless debauchery available to a young man of good family who possessed a generous income. He gained a reputation as a rake and gamester, ever amiable and full of high spirits.

Those spirits had led him to join the Queen's Army as a subaltern on the northwestern frontier of India. He'd sought adventure, and found violence instead. And his other self, so long asleep, woke to kill when he could not. Details of the battle he hadn't remembered formed an explosion of bloodred, smoke gray, and smothering black behind his eyelids.

He'd awakened in the hospital and, after his swift recovery, was prompted to resign his commission. Boroskov was right; he'd been a hero who'd saved his troops, but what he had done was too terrible for his comrades and officers to accept. He'd never known why, until now.

Fenris was responsible.

So home he came, to take up the threads of his civilian life, running occasional errands for his brother the earl and otherwise losing himself in the pursuit of pleasure. Everyone knew that the honorable Quentin Forster hated any sort of conflict.

Then the year of the Convocation had arrived—that grand meeting of the world's werewolf families on Braden's Greyburn estates in the far north of England. Boroskov had disrupted the proceedings with his challenge to Braden. And when Braden won the fight, Quentin ran. Ran all the way to America, and had never stopped running.

Because Fenris could no longer be forced back in his dark corner. Because the memory lapses had already begun, and the implacable urges, half recalled, could no longer be borne.

America offered no sanctuary. The Other was always with him. But he blocked the awareness that would have led him to recognize what he was becoming.

"You know, don't you?" Boroskov said. "You see that I speak the truth."

Quentin heard the voice as if he were under water, on the verge of drowning. It was seductive, commanding, and the coward within wanted nothing more than to give himself up to its master.

He disregarded the coward's whimpers and sought the one who would fight, no matter what the odds.

Fenris. Fenris, who was Boroskov's ideal killer, except that he would never obey any master. Who would turn on the one who tried to control him?

Fenris would save them both.

But something snapped inside. It was as if the restoration of Quentin's memories sapped Fenris's strength—as if their absence alone had been the foundation of Fenris's very existence. He stirred, roared, writhed in impotent fury.

And vanished.

"Quentin!"

Johanna. He pushed his way toward the lightless surface high above him, let go of Boroskov's hand, and grasped the other that plunged so fearlessly into the seething waters.

He opened his eyes and looked into hers. She smiled, warm and brave.

"How touching," Boroskov said.

Quentin realized that he'd made a crucial mistake. One glance at Boroskov's face told him that the Russian knew he'd won his internal struggle.

Quentin's only secret advantage, however dangerous, was Fenris. And Fenris was gone.

"I thought, for a moment, that you had come to your senses," Boroskov said. "But I see you will need further persuasion."

"Boroskov," Johanna said. "You said that you had been intended by your father to become one of these assassins, like Quentin."

He glanced at her through half-lidded eyes. "What of it?"

"You were tortured, as he was."

Quentin followed her line of thinking and despaired at her hopeful ignorance. Stefan Boroskov was not one to be reasoned with, drawn from past suffering to recognize the source of his own evil.

Boroskov laughed. "Ah, Johanna. Let me guess . . . you wish to persuade me that I, too, can be relieved of my sorrowful burdens. What will you do, place me under hypnosis and assure me that I can be cured of my madness?"

"You didn't choose who you were to be, did you, Stefan?" she said, her gaze locked on his. "Your father chose for you. He betrayed his own son."

"And he paid for this so-called betrayal," Boroskov said. "I killed him when I came of age, and took his title and all he owned. But he taught me much, and his goals were worthy. They are now mine."

"And so you have become what he was."

"I have become more than he ever was. And I will succeed where he did not."

Johanna shook her head. "No, Stefan. There can be no peace in such a victory. If you'd only let me help you—"

"Enough!" He swept out his hand, and Quentin barely had time to intercept the blow. It sent him stumbling, but he caught his balance and placed himself between Boroskov and Johanna.

"Never touch her again," he said.

"That is your choice." Boroskov smiled at Johanna. "My dear doctor, you have proven yourself a failure in rehabilitating your patient, and I suspect you know it. But you can save him yet." He negligently twirled his pistol. "I have the power to force Quentin to bend to my will. It is one of the superior skills the greatest among loups-garous possess, and I'll use it if I must. But I would prefer his cooperation, to spare myself a waste of time and resources.

"Convince him, Johanna. Convince him to do as I command, and you will be allowed to leave with the girl. I have no further interest in your affairs. But if you do not succeed—" He shrugged. "I don't think I need elaborate." He pushed past Quentin and seized May's arm before either Quentin or Johanna could react.

"Now," he said, gesturing toward a doorway at the rear of the room, "if you will kindly go through that door." He aimed the gun at Johanna until Quentin obeyed, and she followed, casting anxious glances at May.

The door led into a black hallway and to more closed doors, one of which Boroskov kicked open with his foot. The room was as lightless and dank as the rest of the house, its sole furnishing a soiled mattress scattered with a heap of blankets.

"I'll leave you two alone now, to make your tender farewells. You have two hours. The girl will come with me—in the off chance that you get the notion to take an unscheduled trip."

Quentin growled, stricken with the savage fury that should have summoned his other self. Fenris remained silent. "If you hurt her," he rasped, "so much as a hair on her head, you'd better kill me."

"As I said," Boroskov replied, dragging May toward the door, "that is entirely up to you." He bowed to Johanna and walked out. A lock clicked into place, and Boroskov's footsteps, accompanied by May's stumbling counterpoint, receded down the hall. A minute later Quentin heard hoofbeats, the jingle of harness, and the clatter of a carriage driving away.

Johanna went to the door and rested her hands against the scored wood and peeling paint. She had no hope of breaking the lock. Quentin might have the strength, but what good would come of that? Boroskov had them trapped as surely as if he'd barred them in a cage.

And there was nothing she could do about it.

Nothing.

"Where is he taking May?" she whispered.

"To his henchmen, no doubt, for safekeeping," Quentin said. His voice emerged from the darkness, somewhere in the vicinity of the mattress. "He won't harm her. He has no reason to."

She struck her forehead against the door once, and then again. Quentin was at her side before she could strike again.

"Johanna."

She turned. Quentin looked at her, such transparent compassion on his face that her body bowed under the weight of her emotions.

Shame. Fear. Anger. At herself most of all. Johanna Schell, the great and innovative doctor who would show the world how the insane could be healed. It had all become one vast joke.

Worst was the hopelessness that stripped her of even the desire to continue fighting.

"Well," she said, her voice cracking. "What now? I have not a single suggestion to make to you. Shall we draw lots to see who shall live and who shall die?"

He remained where he was, as if he feared to approach her. As one might fear to approach a lunatic. "Don't blame yourself," he said in a raw whisper. "You're not responsible."

"Am I not?"

"I brought all this down on your head, Johanna, and on May's. *I.* My own selfishness—"

"And my insufferable arrogance. Now we shall spend the time Boroskov has left us discussing which one of us is more contemptible." She walked to the mattress and sat down. "Perhaps that is his plan: divide and conquer. Not that I should ever be the least threat to him—"

"You heard him, Johanna. He'll use you as a way to get to me."

"And May as the means of forcing both of us to do his bidding."

She rested her head in her hands and began to rock. "I am sorry. So sorry. So sorry—"

"*Stop it.*" Quentin knelt before her and took her hands, pulling them away from her face. "Don't leave me now, Johanna."

Was he afraid that she was descending into madness? She wished it were possible. Possible to let go, dismiss reality, and resign every responsibility for her life. She felt like collapsing into Quentin's arms and wailing like a child, begging for him to make it all better.

Even May hadn't done that. May had kept her head and her courage, and look what she had received as a reward.

She, Johanna Schell, was supposed to be the strong one. No longer. All her illusions were cracked apart like the last of her mother's china figurines, destroyed by an angry patient. Like a mind that had borne too much.

"I never thought I'd see the day when you felt sorry for yourself." Quentin forced her chin up. "*Look* at me, Johanna."

She had no choice. He compelled her with his eyes, with his voice, with his will. Above all, with his heart.

His gentle, generous heart, warped into a monster by pain. Fenris was nowhere visible in his gaze, in spite of all that provoked him. Where had he gone?

"Johanna," he said, stroking her chin with his thumb. "I brought you and May into this. I was selfish—selfish in wanting the peace your Haven offered, though I knew my mere presence was a menace to everything I valued. I refused to consider the dangers once I had . . . grown to care for you. And I never dreamed that Boroskov was part of the danger. If I could only go back—"

"I was arrogant," she interrupted harshly. "I thought I had perfect mastery over the situation with May. I was so sure I could cure you, even share your bed without making a single compromise." Tears dripped onto her sleeves. She thought they must be hers. "I thought I had all the answers—and this is where they've led us both."

He rested his forehead against hers. "We are pitiful creatures, are we not?"

She looked for mockery in his eyes and found none. His smile was heartwrenchingly calm.

"You've . . . given me a chance at something I didn't have for most of my life, Johanna. Faith in myself and in my ability to rise above what I'd become. Hope."

And what worth has it now? she wanted to rail at him. *What worth has anything?*

"We can't fight him," he said. "He's too strong. He has skills I do not. And I . . . I can't kill." He kissed her lips with a feather-touch. "I won't allow you or May to pay for my debilities. When Boroskov returns, I will tell him that I'll go with him—after I've watched him release you and May."

She shook her head wildly.

"I assure you that I won't let him use me."

"You mean that you'll die before you become his assassin."

"Yes. You know it's right, Johanna. I can't be unleashed on the world, as unstable as I am." He skimmed his knuckles across her cheek. "If I can stop Boroskov for good—any sacrifice is worth it. He's my kind. It's up to me. And if I succeed . . . I'll have redeemed myself."

"And escaped one more time," she lashed out. "Never having had to face life squarely. An easy end to all your suffering."

"You said you didn't have the answers." His voice grew distant, as if he were withdrawing into himself. "This is mine. You must be the one to go on living, so that you can help people as you were meant to."

"I can help no one."

"You can. I know you, Johanna. You're too strong to give up. Not even for me." He began to rise. "I'm sorry."

She grabbed his hands to stop him. "I am not strong!" she cried. "I want to do what I wish, only what *I* wish. The world can go to hell. I want to be happy—" She wrapped her arms around Quentin's neck and kissed him hard on the mouth.

The room disappeared. The stale scent of the mattress, the cold dampness of the floor and the walls, vanished.

Happiness was not hers to own. Perhaps even hope was beyond her reach. But she could snatch what small joys were to be had in this terrible place.

And when she left, she'd take a part of Quentin with her.

The part he had held back the first time.

Now she'd have all of him.

She tugged at the bottom of Quentin's rough shirt, barely glancing up to see his response. The pupils of his eyes had grown very large, engulfing the color.

"Johanna—"

"No talking. No words." She kissed him again. He responded ardently, recognizing, as she did, how little time they had left. He would not deny her.

She lay back upon the blankets, and he knelt over her. He stroked his hand from the top of her bodice to her skirts, cupping his fingers against her womanhood. Her body reacted instantly. He found the hem by touch alone, watching her face, and drew her skirts up around her thighs.

Hard and fast was how it must be. Johanna's breath grew short. She gripped Quentin's hands and met his questioning gaze.

"Yes, Quentin," she said. "Yes."

"I've wanted you, but not like this," he murmured. "I wanted to love you the way you deserve to be loved."

"I don't know what I deserve," she said. "But if you ever cared for me, give me something to take away."

In answer he brushed his fingers up the length of her stocking, seeking bare flesh. Her unadorned, knee-length drawers posed no barrier to him. He opened them and touched her moist skin.

She arched up into his caresses. The memory of the last time flooded into her mind, joining with the present. She feared that her body's completion might come too fast, before she could feel Quentin moving inside her.

"Don't . . . wait," she begged.

He whispered unintelligible endearments and joined her on the mattress. He parted her legs with his hands, raising her skirts to her waist.

Too slow. She didn't want his tenderness now, only to be possessed, claimed by him forever. She seized the front of his shirt to bring him closer and all but tore at the buttons of his trousers. He was hard under her fingertips. She set him free and held him between her hands.

"Do you wish to make us both suffer?" she demanded fiercely. "Do you?"

He closed his eyes with a groan and flung himself down upon her. The drumming of his heartbeat pierced her bodice, the flesh and bone beneath to mingle with her own heart's frantic pace. His skin was burning where it touched her, the cloth of his trousers deliciously rough on her flesh. His hips found their natural cradle between her thighs, and just as she rose to meet him she felt the clean, swift thrust of his entry.

Nothing had prepared her for this. There was an instant of discomfort, and then a sweet ache more beautiful than anything they'd done before. He moved, withdrew, then thrust again. Fire filled her womb. She throbbed in time to his motions, each pulse drawing him deeper.

He kissed her lips and her chin and her cheeks, murmuring her name like a nonsensical rhyme. She clenched her legs about his waist. Abruptly, with stunning ease, he lifted her from the mattress and carried her, still impaled, to the nearest wall. He held her there, his strong hands cupping her buttocks, and thrust again and again, making her feel what it was to be in another's power and willingly submit.

It was that surrender that finally pushed her over the brink. Her body and her mind ceased all resistance. She gasped and pressed her head back against the wall as the waves of pleasure came. Still he did not finish, not until the pulsing had stopped and she went boneless in his arms. Then, with one last great thrust, he found his own completion.

He kissed her and let her slide to the floor. When her legs trembled in reaction, he swept her up and carried her back to the blankets, drawing her into his lap. She felt raw and fragile and lost in bliss.

Bliss that couldn't last. It had no more substance than the fog outside these walls, no more solidity than sand on the ocean shore.

Like sand, it slipped through her fingers and was gone. But it left in its wake the hard, bright knowledge of what must be done.

She was afraid. Fear had been an abstract concept before this moment, no matter how much she'd thought herself capable of it. Never before had so much been at stake.

If she failed in this, it would mean Quentin's sanity, if not his life. It might mean letting loose a creature prone to violence few men could envision, and relinquishing Quentin's chance to fetter Boroskov.

She didn't know if she could do what her plan demanded. Her deficiencies had become all too clear, and all too deadly. She must be far more daring, more cool-headed, and more skillful than her best image of herself, let alone the flawed woman she'd turned out to be.

Her mouth went dry, and her heart beat so loudly that Quentin must have heard. He shifted her about and held her face steady between his hands.

"What is it?" he asked. "Did I hurt you, Johanna?"

"No." She swallowed. "There is something I must tell you, Quentin." The slightly dazed look left his eyes. His mouth tightened. "Tell me."

"I love you."

He laughed in startlement, and saw Johanna's face. She was serious. More than serious; she was giving him the most precious gift she had.

Johanna—his grave, beloved Johanna, gazed at him as if he were someone worthy of love. As if they sat in a rose-scented bower, and he were the gentleman he was born to be, she the brave and true lady her soul and spirit made her.

"Johanna," he said, choking back ridiculous tears. "God."

"I know it's hardly a suitable time to make such a declaration." She wriggled from his hold and stood, shaking her skirts down around her ankles as if she dismissed what had just passed between them. "In light of what we've just done . . ."

"Do you know what we've done?" he asked. "I've been with other women, yes. But none of them—not one of them—" How could he tell her that he could take her a hundred times more and not get his fill of her? She made him feel formidable, sure of himself, the man he might have been.

Might have been, but was not. Johanna carried that Quentin away with her and sent the familiar craven Quentin back in his place. The man who was so very good at running.

The man who couldn't speak the words she wanted to hear.

Her back was turned to him, head high, spine erect. The pliable, passionate woman slipped from her body like a ghost. What remained was not Doctor Johanna Schell but some brittle reproduction held together by filaments of habit and sheer pluck, a doppelgänger who spoke with Johanna's voice in a parody of her competent manner.

"Forgive me," she said. "It was foolish of me to speak as I did, but I was not sure I'd get another chance."

"Johanna," he whispered.

"We need not dwell on it any longer. In fact, we must put it behind us now if we are to save ourselves." Her shoulders rose and fell. "I have an idea, Quentin. A dangerous idea, and so much of it depends upon you. I do not know if I am capable of what is necessary."

He stood up, took a few steps toward her, stopped at the stiffening of her body. She took another deep breath. "You've said that you wish to go with Boroskov and find a way to overcome him. But I believe there is a chance to defeat him, here and now, by confronting him with what he would never expect to see."

Dire premonition turned guilt and grief to icy lumps in his chest. "Fenris."

"Fenris." She turned to face him, her expression blank. "Boroskov knows nothing of him, though your other self is the embodiment of what his father, and your grandfather, desired to create."

"Something evil, murderous—"

"But Fenris is a *part* of you, Quentin. He has your werewolf abilities, as well as the very traits of character that make him an equal to Boroskov in ruthlessness and lust for power. Don't you see?"

"I see. I see very clearly."

"Then . . . we have no choice but to enlist Fenris's help in defeating Boroskov."

The last remnants of the ephemeral well-being that had come with their loving drained from Quentin's body. "Yes," he said. "Get Fenris to fight in my place, because he is the last thing our enemy will be expecting. The only problem with your otherwise excellent idea is that I've already tried it. I can't make him come."

"You've tried to summon Fenris?" She frowned. "But you've never truly met him, only sensed his presence—"

"Just before I found you and May and Boroskov, I woke up in another part of town with no memory of how I'd arrived in San Francisco. It hasn't been long since Fenris was here. But now—he is *gone.*"

Her eyes darkened. "How can this be?"

"Oh, I'm not free of him. He still perverts our joint existence as he wishes it to be. I'd rip him out of my soul if I could."

"That is what you cannot do." She held his gaze unblinkingly. "I know little of this, Quentin. It is beyond my meager experience. But I think that you must find a way to accept him as part of yourself."

"Part of myself? Should I let him use and discard you, and destroy everything in his path? Is that what you want me to be, Johanna?"

Her jaw clenched. "No. But you can't simply erase him. He won't let you. You and Fenris are two halves of what was meant to be a single whole. Neither one of you is . . . complete without the other. And now he has the means, perhaps the only means, of saving us all."

Her theory made a bizarre kind of sense. He felt the merciless logic of it, though his insides turned to ice. Fenris, the lost piece of the puzzle, the final answer.

"Even if you're right," he said, "why should he help us? What has he to gain?"

"It is true that he's said that he intends to displace you, Quentin—just as you want to erase him. That is part of the risk. The greater part. But you will not be alone." He caught a glimpse of her heart in her eyes. "We shall contact him through hypnosis. I will be with you. But *you* must be willing to let him out, under our control. Yours and mine, together. You must truly face him for the first time in your life."

He sat down, too numb to remain on his feet. "You think that I can influence such a monster?"

"Fenris has no friends, no brothers. If you convince him that he is more than your brother—if you embrace him rather than reject him . . ."

Quentin smiled through his terror. "Embrace?"

"His needs are yours, Quentin. He must be acknowledged, for he was your creation, and he suffered on your behalf."

"My creation, born of my cowardice."

"You were a child. You were not to blame. But now you know Fenris exists, and why."

And only Fenris could kill Boroskov.

Quentin slammed his fist into the wall, feeling it give under the blow. "He'll be our hired assassin," he said hoarsely. "But the blood will still be on these." He raised his hands and rotated them slowly. "I'll become what he is."

He waited for another facile answer, but none came. Her eyes welled up with the tears she must have been fighting all along. She crumpled in on herself. The counterfeit Johanna Schell became a vulnerable young woman who questioned everything she'd ever believed worthy and strong and true in her own nature.

It struck him with the full force of revelation that this was her greatest fear, that she lacked the skill to do what she proposed; not that he didn't return her feelings or rejected her love, but that she would ultimately fail them both.

He turned his face to the wall, unable to hide his emotions. He ached to hold her close and assure her that it would be all right. To tell her that he loved her.

But he couldn't. And with that realization came a second revelation, too overwhelming to deny.

Words of love and empty platitudes were not what Johanna needed from him now. What she required most was the strength, the fortitude, the self-reliance that was so much a part of her being. She needed to remember that she was a doctor of great skill and bravery.

By admitting her love to him, by loving him, she had relinquished the very qualities she most needed to win the coming war. If he denied her this chance she'd never regain the spirit and assurance to continue with her work. She would be ruined in every way that mattered.

To do what she asked, he must hold fast all the way to his soul. No running, no slipping away. The surrender he must make was to his deepest self and the memories that had created him.

He had to do it for her. For Johanna.

He stood up and strode toward her, stopping mere inches away.

"Very well," he said roughly, "Let us proceed."

"No." She bowed her head. "I was wrong to suggest it. I recognize that I am no longer fit—"

"Fit?" He took her by the shoulders and made her look at him. "You think that you are fatally flawed, don't you, Johanna? You've made too many mistakes. You've misjudged. You don't trust yourself, and you don't expect anyone else to trust you, either. You have your theories, but you have no confidence in them. You're just going to . . . give up."

Her body trembled violently. "You don't understand. If I'm wrong—"

"Have you suddenly lost all the skills you had when I first came to the Haven?"

She stared at him. "No, I—"

"You still know how to hypnotize me, I presume."

"Yes."

"That's how you'll call out Fenris, so that I can face him."

"Yes, but—"

"We don't have much time. You'd better get started."

She pulled free, jerking up her chin with a touch of the old spirit. "I cannot be within your mind, Quentin. I can only begin the process. In the end, you must fight three battles—with Fenris, with Boroskov, and with yourself. You must ally with Fenris to win over Boroskov, become the guiding intellect behind Fenris's hatred. Without you, there can be no victory."

"Without you, we haven't a chance in hell." He grinned. "But damned if I don't love a challenge."

Chapter 24

Johanna's heart broke into a thousand pieces and slowly, bit by bit, re-assembled itself. It bathed in the healing warmth of Quentin's grin, took strength from the enormity of his faith in her, grew until it stretched the walls of her ribs and expanded beyond the mere physical boundaries of flesh.

The gift of his trust held her heart safe, like a magical coffer made of precious gold and priceless stones hidden in a cave on the highest mountaintop. She'd asked that he be strong, and he was—strong in the face of fear she knew as well as she did her own. His great courage lay in his willingness to confront his fear, and challenge her to do the same.

She'd been sure, for so long, that love was a luxury she could ill afford. When she let down her guard, it had happened just as she predicted: Once she opened the gates to emotion, she could not close them again. Out spilled the fear, the doubts, the indecisiveness, the despair, weaknesses that stripped away the unassailable façade of Dr. Johanna Schell. The rational moorings upon which she'd built her life snapped and sent her crashing down into bedlam.

That Dr. Schell had been extinguished, and the new creature born out of the ferment was blind and deaf and nameless, searching desperately for identity in the midst of chaos, prepared to grasp at any anchor. She was close to becoming the very thing she most despised: dependent and helpless.

Looking into Quentin's eyes, she recognized the truth. His only hope was to acknowledge and unite both halves of himself. She was no different.

She must summon her doctor's skills to give Quentin the chance he needed, but she could no longer rely on the old definitions of competence. Rationality was not enough. If she rejected her emotions, her fear, her love, she would be fighting with only half a weapon. Dr. Johanna Schell had not disappeared; she had merely evolved.

Love *was* her anchor. Love for this man, who'd turned her life upside down, who'd begun to heal a physician who hadn't learned how to heal herself.

Overcome with gratitude, Johanna stretched up to kiss him. He stepped just out of reach and averted his face before her lips touched his.

It hurt. She couldn't guess which of her many shortcomings, or his regrets, made him withdraw. But what might have been a devastating blow was a minor bruise she could and must bear. Love remained steady and sound, unaffected by anything Quentin Forster, Fenris, or Boroskov could do or say.

"Please sit down, Quentin," she said evenly. "If you are ready, we will begin."

Aware that Boroskov might return at any moment, Johanna ushered Quentin into a trance as quickly as she dared and, with a whispered prayer, called Fenris out of the darkness.

It was like shouting into a chasm miles deep. Minutes ticked by. Johanna tried every trick she knew, and still Fenris didn't answer.

Quentin had warned her that Fenris was gone. She didn't believe it. He was waiting, holed up like a hibernating bear, dangerous to wake and biding his time for his own incomprehensible purpose.

Then she remembered what Fenris wanted more than anything in the world except permanent mastery of Quentin's body. She had asked Quentin to try to accept Fenris as a part of himself. How could he do so if she refused to accept Fenris the same way?

Accept him, even submit to his lust. Another risk she had to take.

"Fenris," she said. "I know you hear me. I am waiting for you. I need you. I need *you*, Fenris."

Quentin jerked.

"Come to me," she coaxed, her voice filled with promises. "Help me."

The muscles in Quentin's face suddenly shifted, swiftly completing the subtle but distinct change to the coarser features of his other self. His eyes snapped open and focused on her.

Her comparison of Fenris to a hibernating bear was apt indeed. He lunged up from the mattress and stalked toward her, every line of his body shouting violent intent.

"You want *my* help?" he snarled. "I still have some use to you, now that he's had you?"

She could only guess what it had been like for Fenris to experience Quentin's life as an observer, watching and unable to interfere as she lay with Quentin at the Haven, seizing control only to lose it again before he could complete his goal.

"Yes, Fenris," she said, refusing to flinch. "You know of Boroskov—"

He grabbed her by the arms, almost lifting her from her feet. "I know everything. You gave yourself to the weakling. But I brought you here, didn't I?" His fingers bit into her sleeves. "Now you're in trouble because of *him*. But when I save your pretty little neck, you plan to get rid of me, don't you?" He gave her a shake. "Don't you?"

Of course. He hadn't been so far "gone" that he'd failed to hear her discussion with Quentin. The only defense she had left was to make him understand.

"Haven't you always defended Quentin from his enemies, and yours?" she asked, ignoring the pain. "You and Quentin share a fate, just as you share a body. You can't escape what happens to him."

"You're calling me a coward?"

"Quentin said you were gone, even when he tried to find you. You ran from Boroskov, didn't you? You buried yourself deep, because you know that what Boroskov wants is worse than anything Quentin could do. Worse than anything you could be."

He let her drop. "Boroskov is like me," he said. "Why shouldn't I ally myself with him?"

"Because you won't be anyone's slave. Because you know he'll eventually destroy you. Because he embraces the evils that you endured for Quentin's sake."

"Words. Boroskov wants power. I want the same thing."

"No. You want the pain to stop."

"And when it stops, I'll be gone. There won't be anything left." He bared his teeth, but the gesture was ruined by the quivering of his mouth. "Quentin will have you. I'll have nothing."

Fenris the monster was gone indeed. Now she heard the voice of the boy he had been, callow and immature, desperate to find some meaning in his hellish existence.

Begging to be loved.

It wasn't cold reason Fenris needed, but intimacy. Not animal lust, but true caring. Like Quentin. Like herself.

She had to love Fenris as she loved Quentin in order to set him free.

She closed the space between them and lifted her hand to his cheek. "When I see you, Fenris, I don't see Boroskov. I see Quentin. I see what both of you share. I see the man I love."

He stared at her. "You're lying."

In answer she did as she had done with Quentin not so long ago. She drew his face down to hers, and kissed him.

The kiss was given, not taken. And it was devastating. Fenris froze in shock. Johanna pressed against him, and he felt the heat of his rage drawn from his body through the gentle parting of her lips.

Without the rage, he didn't know who he was. Johanna had summoned him forth against his will, against every instinct of self-preservation he had learned in childhood.

Something was happening inside him, an unfamiliar transformation he couldn't comprehend. It frightened him. He didn't let Johanna see his fear, but lifted her high and kissed her in return, hard enough to remind her who was master.

Even in that he lied to himself.

He put her down and looked around the room. Boroskov was coming, he could sense it. But he had Johanna. He could still win.

"I'll save you," he told her. He threw his weight against the door,
and the rotten wood cracked. Another blow tore it from its hinges. He
seized Johanna's upper arm and pulled her out into the hallway.
"Boroskov won't find us again."

Her weight dragged against his arm. "We can't leave, Fenris. You
know we can't, for May's sake."

He spun about and snarled at her defiance. He could force her. He
was so much stronger than she was. But she was strong in a different
way, and he'd never seen it until now.

"You know everything Quentin knows," she said, making no attempt to free herself from his grasp. "He has been running all his life,
and you've helped him by hiding his own darkness away where he's never
been forced to face it. Now he must recognize you, Fenris, and you must
help him make a stand against Boroskov. For the sake of you both."

"Not for me—"

"Yes, Fenris. For you." She turned her hand to cup his arm in a tender touch. "Quentin needs you, but not in the way he once did. He
needs you to be whole, as you need him. Your division was never meant
to be. It's time for the rejoining. Time to begin living again."

He didn't want to hear her. "You love *me*," he insisted.

" 'Yes. As I love Quentin. But I can't choose, Fenris. Not if you are
both dead. Neither one of you is strong enough to defeat Boroskov
alone. You and Quentin must confront him as one, or he will win."

"*Quentin* will win."

"Trust me, Fenris. Look into my eyes, and know that you can
trust me."

"*No.*" He yanked away from her, but she caught him and held
him fast.

"Let Quentin out, Fenris," she said, her cheek pressed to his chest.
"Let him share your body, just for a moment, and I'll show you that
there's nothing to fear."

He closed his eyes, feeling Quentin within him. Quentin was
aware, already sharing Fenris's consciousness. But he could not come
out unless Fenris let him.

Fenris knew how to take control from Quentin, but not how to release the Other without losing himself.

"Let me help you," Johanna said. She took his hand and began to
speak low, like a mother to her child. He hardly heard the words. But in

his mind a door swung open, and his rival, the weakling, the one he'd always despised, walked through.

They stared at each other, reflections in a distorted mirror. Quentin was smooth and handsome and refined, everything Fenris was not. He flinched and crouched as if he might flee at a whisper.

"You're afraid," Fenris said contemptuously. "You're always afraid."

"Yes," Quentin said. He held up his hand. It was trembling. "But you're afraid, too."

"I'm stronger than you are! I'll win. *I'll* take Johanna."

"Maybe you could. But you won't win her heart, Fenris."

"She loves me!"

"She has a great heart. And she loves what we can become. Together." He smiled raggedly. "I could have met you long ago, Fenris, but I was a coward. Johanna taught me to be brave. She has shown me that you are a necessary part of me, as I am necessary to you."

"I don't need you."

"You can go on living half a life, Fenris. You might even take my half away from me. But Grandfather will have won. Grandfather and Boroskov. They created you as much as I. More than I. They made you into a killer. You were helpless, just as I was. But you aren't helpless any longer."

Helpless. Fenris choked on a howl.

"Make your own choice, Fenris," Quentin said. "Let us defy Grandfather and all his schemes. Let us do battle . . . together." He held out his hand. "You are my strength, the part of me that survives and goes on fighting. Without you, I can't defend the woman we both love."

"*I don't . . . need you!*"

"You don't know how to love, Fenris, or how to stop hurting people. I'm the side of you that can live in the world and search for a little happiness." He breathed in and out, his face very pale. "You *are* me."

A sound like thunder crashed between them. The air in the no-place where they stood filled with the scent of the Enemy.

Boroskov.

Reality rushed in like a great ocean wave, slapping Quentin back to consciousness. Fenris disappeared from his inner sight, and he found himself standing in the center of the main room, his hand extended.

Empty.

Johanna wore a look of dazed startlement, her gaze moving quickly from him to the door. Boroskov was coming. Quentin could smell him, as Fenris had done, but there was no time to prepare. Shoes drummed hollowly on the outer porch, accompanied by the clanking of metal.

"Fenris?" Johanna whispered.

He shook his head, and then Boroskov stepped inside. He bore in his hands a pair of manacles and a length of chain.

"I trust you have come to the right decision," he said, closing the door behind him.

"Where is May?" Quentin demanded.

"Are you ready to submit to me?"

Quentin stared straight ahead. "Yes. Let them go."

Johanna made a wordless sound of distress. Her scheme hadn't succeeded. Fenris had refused the joining Quentin proposed, and Quentin knew why.

He hadn't wanted it enough. His words might have been steady, even sincere, but his heart and his mind were screaming denial: *Don't let the monster in.* How could Fenris not recognize his imposture?

"You must realize that I can't simply accept your word," Boroskov said. He lifted the manacles. "You will wear these until we are securely on the next ship bound for Russia. The girl is in the hands of my associates, and will be released in twenty-four hours. Doctor Schell may leave now, with the understanding that May pays with her life if she visits the authorities."

Quentin stared at the chains, his tongue thick in his mouth. "Why should I trust you?"

"Because the alternative is immediate death for those you profess to love. Oh, I know you can break these chains as easily as I, but you won't do so. And when we are back in Russia, it will be my pleasure to complete the instruction your grandfather abandoned."

"No," Johanna said.

"Hold out your hands," Boroskov commanded.

"Let Johanna go first," Quentin said.

Boroskov jerked his head toward the door. "Go."

Johanna didn't move.

"*Go!*" Quentin shouted. His head seemed to split apart. "Get out!"

"You have five seconds," Boroskov said.

Johanna grabbed Quentin's rigid arm. "Fenris! Will you let yourself be put in chains all over again? Will you submit to Boroskov's torture? Who will save *you*, Fenris, when the pain begins?"

Quentin tried to shake her off, but the agony in his head redoubled. The smell of Johanna's skin intoxicated him like a drug.

"I love you," she said.

Boroskov pushed her aside. Chains rattled. The absurdly smooth kid of Boroskov's glove touched his wrist, followed by the rough chill of metal.

Senses dimmed. All he could see was red, within and without, and he knew he wasn't alone inside his skin.

Fenris had arrived. Like a hot wind, he swept everything before him. He controlled, but he allowed Quentin to share what he knew and saw. The two of them no longer faced each other in some zone of truce created in his mind, but looked out from the same eyes.

They met Boroskov's gaze and smiled.

Boroskov stepped back, as if he sensed the change. His nostrils flared. He snatched at Johanna, but she scrambled out of his way.

The temporary confusion was enough for Quentin and Fenris. They struck fast and hard, snapping Boroskov's head back with the force of their blow. Before he could recover, they leaped onto him, pinning him to the stained floor.

Boroskov gaped. "Quentin?"

"I'll win this time, Boroskov," Fenris said, holding Quentin mute. "Do you submit?"

"Who are you?"

Fenris prepared to roar out his name. Quentin, feeling his identity slipping away, resisted with all the desperation of his most ancient terrors. His revolt froze the body he and Fenris shared. Boroskov kicked up with his legs like a bucking horse and threw them off. They stumbled and fell.

Who are you?

Quentin—Fenris—Quentin. The time of decision had come at last. Two wills locked in implacable combat, forsaking their brief and tenuous alliance. Only one would survive.

Distantly, through the din of their clashing thoughts, they heard Johanna's exclamation of alarm and warning. They smelled the new intruders just before they burst into the room: Harper in the lead, bearing a wooden beam like a club; Oscar right behind him, fists raised; and then Irene and Lewis Andersen. The Haven's residents crowded through the door, and Boroskov lunged out of their path.

"Harper!" Johanna cried.

The former soldier advanced on Boroskov, beam at the ready. "You all right, Doc?"

Irene forced her way past the wall of Oscar's bulk and stood before Boroskov, her face bare of paint and her body drawn up high.

"You," she hissed. "You betrayed me. You deserted me—"

"Get back!" Johanna shouted.

Boroskov sent Irene flying across the room with one blow. Lewis Andersen ran to tend her crumpled form. Harper lifted the beam, and Oscar came to stand beside him.

"You bastard," Harper said. "You aren't going to hurt anyone else."

Boroskov laughed. "Rescued just in the nick of time," he said. "Your mad humans, dear Johanna, have more fortitude and resourcefulness than I would have suspected." He snatched the beam from Harper's hands as if it were a twig. "A few more deaths on your conscience will make little difference, will they, Quentin?"

Unable to act, to move, even to breathe, Quentin saw the end of everything he had come to love. He was incapable of speech, but it didn't matter. Fenris would hear him.

If only one of them could have this body for the years to come, it must be the one who could save the others. If Quentin—if all he knew as himself—must die, so be it.

His fear vanished.

"My life is yours, Fenris," he said. *"Take it. Stop Boroskov."*

His heart—Fenris's heart—jarred to a stop and then started up again at double the pace.

Free.

Quentin felt what Fenris felt as he charged at Boroskov, ripped the beam from his grasp, carried him with the weight of his body up against the wall.

"You . . . won't . . . win," Fenris panted, his hand grinding into the Russian's throat. But he did not strike to kill.

Give me your strength, he asked Quentin. And Quentin gave it, all he had, even to the last shred of his identity.

Fenris took it. And this time, miracle of miracles, the sharing was complete. Together they knew the fierce joy of a new power filling muscles and organs, flesh and bones, mind and spirit—a sense of completion they had blindly sought all their lives. They knew courage blended with hope, strength matched with restraint, anger channeled by discipline and resolve.

Fenris stared into Boroskov's eyes and summoned up the mental gifts of the werewolf breed, the gifts Quentin had never been able to find within himself. He drove into Boroskov's mind.

Boroskov met him, will for will. But Fenris stepped aside with animal cunning, let Boroskov's mental counterattack slide past, and plunged deep into the Russian's memories.

All the memories. Pain. Torment. Darkness. Punishment for disobedience, pleasure for cooperation. Day after day, night after night. Father's face. Grandfather's. Masks of sinister purpose and merciless brutality.

Kill. Kill. Kill.

Chapter 25

Boroskov screamed. Quentin felt the jolt of sudden abandonment as Fenris left his body.

His body.

He fell against Boroskov like a puppet with cut strings. The Russian continued to scream, clawing at the wall behind him. With sheer stubborn determination, Quentin worked his numb hands to life and pinned Boroskov's arms to his sides. He sensed Johanna very near, the others watching in astonishment. He didn't let them distract him. He held onto Boroskov until the Russian's flailing stopped. His screams faded to whimpers, and then nothing.

The silence was so intense that Quentin could hear the sounds of people moving in the streets outside, drawn by the commotion. Cautiously he released Boroskov. The Russian slumped to the ground, blank-eyed. Spittle ran from the corner of his mouth.

"Quentin?" Johanna said.

"I'm here."

Johanna knelt beside Quentin and touched Boroskov's throat. "He's alive," she said, "but unconscious."

"Yes. And I don't think he'll be waking soon." Quentin closed his eyes and breathed out slowly. "Is everyone all right?"

"Yes," she said. "I've already checked on Irene—she'll be badly bruised, but nothing is broken. She was very fortunate." The straight line of her lips promised a long list of questions for the Haven's heedless residents when this was finished. "We must find out what Boroskov did with May. She could still be in danger."

"We'll find her," he said with absolute conviction. Real confidence, not the false bravado that had sustained him for so long. He reached for her hand and squeezed it gently. Boroskov couldn't have taken her far."

"And Fenris?" she asked, for his ears alone.

"He came when we needed him," he said. "You were right. He was the one who finally defeated Boroskov."

"Was he?" Her eyes, so beautiful even now, demanded more from him, a deeper truth.

Such truths were no longer to be feared. Quentin searched his heart and found all the fear shrivelled up and bereft of power. Just as the memories, freed from Fenris's mind, could no longer distort his life, though it might take him years to fully reconcile himself to him.

"*We* defeated him," he amended. "Fenris and I. But only after I realized that I had to make my surrender complete. I had to trust him with everything I am. As I trust you."

"You accepted him at last," she said, stroking his hand. "You let him out. And yet he did not kill Boroskov."

"No." Quentin smiled—no bitterness or mockery, only a sense of peace, almost too new to seem real. "He used powers I lost long ago, if I ever had them. He met Boroskov on his own ground—on the ground we shared, all three of us. And then he—" He paused, trying to put the impossible into words. "He joined with Boroskov, and gave me back myself."

"He . . . joined—"

He touched his temple. "Fenris is gone, but he's not. What he was is still in me—the parts I needed, just as you said. The parts that make me a whole man again. But the rest—it's Boroskov's, now."

He could see she didn't understand. He didn't truly understand it himself. Fenris had willingly flung his being into Boroskov's mind, and the two had become one.

Fenris had not killed Boroskov. He'd left him hopelessly mad.

"Perhaps one day I can explain," he said. "Suffice it to say that Boroskov will not be a threat to anyone, human or otherwise. Fenris will stop him."

Johanna shivered, her scientific curiosity left without answers, and she looked at the Russian. "I judge him to be in a cataleptic state. We cannot leave him here."

"It will be necessary to confine him to some place where he can be cared for—and watched, in the rare event that I am mistaken."

"An asylum," she said, sadness in her eyes.

"But not the Haven."

She glanced away. "I could not care for him, in any case. I am not sure if I am qualified to see patients again."

He cupped her chin in his hand and turned her toward him. "Johanna—don't you know that I—we—couldn't have done this without you? I never would have found the courage to recognize the darker part of myself, or the memories that created it, if you had not shown me the way. You made it possible."

"You give me far too much credit," she said with a faint, self-deprecating smile. "I have learned that we doctors do not cure our patients. We merely help them, just a little, to cure themselves—if we are very lucky."

"You're wrong, Doc."

Harper came to crouch beside them, looking from Johanna and Quentin to Boroskov and back again. "None of us would be where we are now, if not for you."

Johanna's eyes sharpened. "How *did* you come to be here, Harper? What possessed you to put yourself and the others in danger by following me?" She looked beyond him to the remaining three patients. Oscar was perched on a broken chair, kicking his legs and looking quite unperturbed by the recent action. Amazingly enough, Lewis Andersen sat beside Irene, half supporting her. He was brushing himself off with a once-pristine white handkerchief, glancing about the filthy room with visible distaste. Irene gave a loud sniff, and he belatedly passed the kerchief to the actress, who blew her nose into it. His narrow upper lip curled, but he did not draw away from her. Something had changed with Lewis during Quentin's absence.

"It's a long story," Harper said, addressing Johanna's frown with a wry nod. "You remember when I told you that I get visions from things belonging to people, things they've touched. I took May's book right after she was kidnapped. I had lots of things of yours, Doc, and I had this—" He pulled a woman's ring from his pocket and pressed it into Quentin's hand. "I saw Irene with it, not long after I came out of my long sleep. I don't know how she got it. She dropped it and ran away, guiltylike, when she saw me, and I picked it up. Knew it was yours right away." He shrugged in embarrassment. "Sorry I kept it so long. I had a feeling I'd need it."

"I'd wondered what had become of it," Quentin said. "I'd thought it was gone forever." He kissed the ring and slipped it onto his little finger. "Thank you, Harper."

"You're welcome." He glanced at Johanna. "I couldn't just let you come out here alone, Doc, knowing what'd happened. So right after you left, I started concentrating on these things. And I could see where May was. I could see you, and Quentin, only he didn't feel right." He cocked his head at Quentin.

"Another long story," Quentin said. "You were saying?"

"Well, I got enough of a sense of where to look that I talked to Mrs. Daugherty and asked her if she could hire some help to see to the others while I was gone. But Miss DuBois overheard, and she asked me if I knew where Bolkonsky was." He glanced at Boroskov. "She was in a right taking. Didn't do any good to tell her no. She insisted on coming along, said she'd follow if I didn't let her. And then Andersen found out, and he said he wasn't going to let either one of us go without him— though he did a right lot of scrubbing and praying before we left."

Johanna rubbed at her eyes. "*Mein Gott.*"

"Then, well . . . Oscar wouldn't be left behind, either. He's strong, so I thought he might come in handy. Lewis donated some money he'd saved, and we took the train and the ferry to San Francisco. Then I just followed what the visions told me."

Quentin exchanged glances with Johanna. Both of them knew that Harper and the others had only the vaguest idea of the danger they'd rushed into. But even leaving the safety of the Haven had been a great act of valor for people who had feared and distrusted the world, or themselves. An act of valor, and of selfless loyalty.

"You should not have done it," Johanna said thickly. "But I thank you for your concern." She brushed at her cheeks. "Mrs. Daugherty is still at the Haven with my father?"

"Of course," Harper said. "She warned me that if we didn't all come back in a few days, she'd get the law involved."

"That is not necessary." Johanna rose. "We will go home as quickly as we can, as soon as we find May—"

"I can help," Harper said. "I still have her book in my pack. She'll be all right."

Johanna shook her head, her eyes suspiciously bright. She gave Quentin an intensely private glance, acknowledging that their conversation was not over. "Lewis?"

The former reverend gave up his attempt to clean his blackened gloves and rose from the couch. "Doctor?"

"We must find May, and I will need Quentin's and Harper's help. Will you look after Irene and Oscar if we take you to a hotel where they can rest?"

Andersen stood very straight. "'The Lord is my strength, in whom I will trust.' I can, Doctor Schell. Simply tell me where to go."

"Thank you." She smiled at Irene and Oscar. Irene sniffled, but her habitual hostility was as absent from her face as the garish paint. Oscar sang a nursery song under his breath.

"Are we going home now?" he asked.

"Very soon." She drew close to Quentin again, and his constant physical and mental awareness of her rose to a higher pitch. He felt a little of Fenris's irrational desire to drag her off to a dark corner and ravish her, but also the patience to wait. Their time would come.

"I'm afraid you will have to use the manacles on Boroskov," she whispered. "If we leave him here until May is safe, will he escape?"

"No."

He could see that she was still adjusting to his new self-assurance, but she didn't question him. "Very well. I'll take the others outside, and wait for you. Then we shall escort Lewis, Oscar, and Irene to my hotel and go in search of May."

Quentin hid a smile of love and admiration. His dear, headstrong Johanna. She couldn't help but take command. She might have suffered a few doubts in the course of this day's work, but she'd rally in the end. She was too strong to do otherwise.

Just as she'd made him strong with her love.

"I'll be right with you," he said. As she turned to gather the patients, he caught her and pulled her into his arms. In full view of their gawking audience, he kissed her soundly.

"For Fenris," he said. "And for me."

Quentin held nothing back.

Every one of his inhuman senses worked in perfect harmony, as they hadn't done in years. It was almost ridiculously easy to follow Boroskov's trail to the place where May was hidden. He had no need of Harper's psychic abilities.

If not for the girl, he would have left Johanna and Harper behind. But they needed to be a part of this, and so he let them follow.

The old warehouse, at the edge of the Barbary Coast, was guarded by a small army of Boroskov's henchmen, who looked ready to put up a nasty fight. The Russian wouldn't have left so many if he had been as confident as he pretended. But even in this he'd miscalculated.

Quentin felt no reluctance to face them, no fear of what he might do once unleashed. Nor was he inclined to explain to them their master's incapacitated condition. He knew a more efficient way of gaining their surrender. His anger, and his strength, were under his complete command.

He didn't bother to Change. He pushed Harper and Johanna behind him, expecting their obedience, and stalked his prey with bared teeth and a hard, predatory stare.

Boroskov's men couldn't have known what he was, but they recognized danger. Like the mob from the Springs, they shifted and muttered among themselves, brandishing knives and pistols as if those alone could hinder a werewolf.

They had no hope of stopping the reborn Quentin Forster.

The assortment of thugs, footpads, and ruffians kept up their bluff until he was within spitting distance, and then the first of them broke and ran. One fired his pistol; Quentin effortlessly dodged the bullet. Another three split off from the group and dashed around the nearest corner.

Of those who remained, two might have been quite a challenge for an ordinary man. Quentin dispatched one of them with a handy facer before the fellow knew what was coming. The second lunged with a wicked, long-bladed knife, and was rewarded with a dislocated shoulder. The pitiful remnants of Boroskov's army thought better of their erstwhile loyalty and took to their heels.

May was loosely tied up in a small office inside the warehouse. If she'd had a personal guard, he'd heard the commotion outside and made himself scarce.

The girl stared at Quentin in astonishment, struggling against her bonds.

"You came!" she cried, gamely fighting back tears. "I knew you would. I knew—" She paused. "Quentin? It is you?"

Quentin snapped the ropes with a flick of his fingers and lifted her into his arms. Johanna and Harper rushed to his side.

"It's me, little one." He kissed her forehead and passed her into Johanna's arms. "You're safe. We're all safe."

Johanna hugged May and met Quentin's gaze over the girl's head. Her eyes blazed with pride and affection.

"Yes," she said. "We are whole again." She set May back and wiped the girl's tears with her thumb. "And there is more, *liebchen*. Your mother has come home."

The first promise of dawn lay upon the eastern horizon when they arrived at Johanna's hotel. The three they'd left behind were waiting in the lobby: Lewis and Irene in a matching pair of armchairs by the window, Oscar sprawled and snoring across one of the hard settees. A jubilant greeting followed, but it was not to be the happiest.

Johanna went to fetch Mrs. Ingram herself. Quentin never learned what passed between them, but May's mother came flying down the stairs in her dressing gown, and a moment later mother and daughter embraced in a flurry of endearments and joyful sobs.

Quentin couldn't steal so much as a second alone with Johanna. But he watched her—he never tired of doing so—and saw her mingled sadness and pleasure in the family reunion. His heart swelled with the same mixed emotions. She had much to be proud of, and much to let go. He swore to make up for every one of her losses.

"Reckon that's the prettiest sight I ever did see," Harper said, coming to stand beside him.

"Yes," Quentin answered. "I reckon it is." But his eyes were only for the sturdy, practical woman who gravely received Mrs. Ingram's breathless thanks.

Harper smiled. "You have a lot of catching up to do, brother."

"And a lot of living," Quentin agreed. "For both of us."

"In that case," Harper said, "I reckon we'd better get started."

The gate to the Haven stood open, as if in welcome. On every side the vineyard, woods, and orchards held steadfast in spite of the travails of men.

Mrs. Daugherty came out onto the porch, shading her eyes and looking ready to let loose with a terrific scold. Oscar ran ahead of everyone and charged up the stairs, bursting with news for the housekeeper.

Johanna stopped at the gate and let the tears come. Quentin put his arm around her and nuzzled her hair.

"Glad to be home?" he asked.

"No," she said, wondering if this tendency to weep at the drop of a hat was a temporary affliction. She sincerely hoped so. "I'd much rather be back in San Francisco, battling monsters."

He chuckled and kissed her temple. "I wonder."

Mrs. Ingram cleared her throat and came forward to join them.

May clung to her arm, as she'd done ever since mother and daughter had been reunited in San Francisco. The girl was radiant, as if her recent experiences had shocked her out of the remnants of the old troubles. Johanna could not envision her suffering from hysteria ever again—as long as she was given a chance to grow up well outside her father's pernicious shadow. Mrs. Ingram intended to do just that.

May wasn't the only one to benefit from adversity. Lewis Andersen seemed to have experienced an epiphany during his confrontation with Irene in the vineyard. Although he remained fastidious and vigilant, he had actually removed his gloves during the ferry and train ride home. He had been seen to smile, with nary a word of sins or sinners. Instead, his quotes from the Bible were those of hope and inspiration.

Though he continued to regard Quentin with nervous suspicion, he didn't seem inclined to expose Quentin's secret to the world. Gradually he was allowing himself to touch and be touched—especially with Irene, who was sober and quiet and changed in ways Johanna expected to find most remarkable.

What precisely had changed Irene remained to be explored, but Johanna suspected that she, too, had been forced to see herself clearly for the first time in many years. Johanna hoped to make Irene's transition to reality as painless as possible. She and Lewis might be sufficiently recovered to leave the Haven in a matter of months.

As for Quentin . . .

She glanced up at him shyly, amazed all over again at the strength of her passion. She tried very hard not to let him see it. She'd accepted his support on the journey home, needing it more than she had any other man's, glad enough to let herself be a little dependent for a few brief hours.

But she did not deceive herself. The Quentin who stood with her now was not the one who had left the Haven a mere few days ago. Oh, the alterations were subtle enough: They lay in his unflinching carriage, the challenge in his eyes, the assurance in his walk—the way he spoke, as if a real future existed, and the way he gathered everyone he cared for under the cloak of his protection. He was no longer afraid.

His past might still haunt him for a time, the memories Fenris had restored to him. He had become neither perfect nor incapable of guilt and regret. But now he would be able to deal with that past and accept it, just as he'd accepted Fenris.

Did he still need her? Was it too much to ask, that he should wish to remain with someone who reminded him so much of the obstacles he'd overcome?

Quentin had his own life to seek, a family waiting to embrace him, a nonhuman heritage to explore. She would not keep him from the future he chose.

But within her heart was a kernel of hope. They had shared so much. If only they could share the rest of their lives . . .

"It has been a long time," Mrs. Ingram said. "Isn't it strange, how things have come full circle, and yet that circle has led us to a better place." She smiled at her daughter. "A wonderful place."

"Indeed," Johanna said. "It has been a long two days. Shall we go inside?"

Mrs. Daugherty hurried down the steps, Oscar trailing along beside her like an overgrown pup. "I was so worried, wonderin' what you was all up to in the city!" She clucked her tongue. "You all look fit enough, but I hope you never do it again!"

"Believe me," Quentin said, grabbing her work-roughened hand for a kiss, "I hope the same."

"Oh, you." She blushed and gave him a mock frown. "Doc Jo, your papa's fine. He asked for you, and I said you'd be back soon."

"Thank you," Johanna said. "Thank you, Bridget. I don't know what I would have done without your loyalty."

"Go on." She turned back to Quentin. "There's a feller here to see you—been here since morning. I told him I didn't rightly know when any of you'd be back, but he said he had to wait." She smiled knowingly. "Said he'd come all the way from New Mexico Territory, tracking you down for your sister."

"Rowena?" Quentin said, his face reflecting startled joy.

"That's the name. He's waitin' in the parlor. Just about eaten us out of house and home, too. So the rest of you better come on in and get your supper!"

"Yes," Johanna said, stepping aside. "Go in. Mrs. Ingram, please make yourself at home. I'll join you directly."

The others dutifully followed Oscar and Mrs. Daugherty up the stairs, leaving Quentin and Johanna alone.

"Rowena," Quentin said. "I can't believe it. Rowena found me here?"

"Your sister? I thought your family was in England."

"She came to America shortly before I did, for reasons I'll explain when I can. We kept in touch for a while, but then I—" He bowed his head. "She's probably been sick with worry."

"Then you must talk to this man immediately." She pressed his hands. "And I must go to my father."

"Yes." He hardly seemed to see her, his thoughts centered on those he had known long before Johanna. "Yes."

She went up the stairs ahead of him, her heart bursting with happiness for Quentin and a sorrow she couldn't acknowledge.

Her father sat in his wheelchair in the parlor, gazing at the wall with a slight smile on his face. He blinked and turned his head to look at her as she entered the room.

"Johanna," he said. "It's good to see you."

"And you, Papa." She knelt before him and took his hands. "I missed you."

"That's my Valkyrie," he said vaguely, touching her hair. "How is the new doctor working out?"

He meant Quentin, of course. He probably hadn't even noticed that so many of the Haven's residents had been gone. Johanna was grateful for that small favor.

"He may not be able to remain, Papa," she said gently, playing along with his assumptions. "He's been called to see to his own affairs in another part of the country."

"A pity. I liked him very much. A personable, intelligent young man."

So much like the old Wilhelm Schell. She rested her head on his knees. "Yes, Papa. I . . . liked him very much, also."

"You are sure that you cannot persuade him to remain? Our work is so very important here."

Yes, it was. For all her doubts about her own competence, her desire to surrender the responsibility forever, she knew Papa was right. She couldn't take the easy way and give up everything she and her father had worked to establish. To do so would betray what she and Quentin had found, in themselves and each other.

But she didn't wish to go on alone as she'd done for so long, independent and free of personal ties. She knew what it was to love. Quentin was the lost half of herself. She needed him as he'd needed Fenris.

She had to tell him. Outright, with none of the usual protections against hurt and disappointment. She must find exactly the right moment, and pray she didn't trip over her own tongue.

As for the Haven, she had also given that careful consideration on the trip back to the Valley. Though Quentin would eventually be cleared of guilt in the matter of Ketchum's death, suspicion about the Haven's residents would not so easily be dispelled. Now that May was leaving, Harper was cured, and Irene and Lewis had made such progress, it would be much less difficult to start again elsewhere, perhaps in another state. Begin another Haven, to help whoever needed sanctuary in a complex and sometimes frightening world.

A world Johanna would never view again with the same eyes. Or the same heart.

She spoke to her father of this and that, the trivialities that so often filled his once-brilliant mind. She took comfort in such things, as he did. She brought him his tray, helped him eat the dinner Mrs. Daugherty had prepared, and took him to his room to rest.

Then she went to face Quentin.

May was just leaving the parlor when Johanna found him there. She saw on his face that he'd been making his farewells to the girl; sadness and pride mingled in his cinnamon eyes.

He glanced toward the kitchen, where May had gone to join her mother. "May will be leaving us soon," he said. "Her mother tells me that she has assembled certain damaging information about Mr. Ingram's personal and business practices that will make him very unlikely to interfere with her decision to take May to Europe. It's something of a miracle, how things have changed for both of them."

"Indeed." Johanna sat on the chair nearest the fireplace and folded her hands in her lap. "It is far more than I could have hoped."

"But things have changed for all of us, haven't they?" He sat down on the sofa opposite her. "I sometimes wonder if I'm dreaming. And then I look at you, and realize there is such a thing as heaven on earth."

She shivered as if with fever. *Now. Tell him now.* But she was as tongue-tied as she'd feared, driven mute by his tender words. All that would come to her was a single stuttered question.

"What . . . what had the messenger to say of your sister? Is she well?"

"Better than well." He leaned back, watching her with a secret smile. "The little vixen has married—an American, no less—and I didn't even know it! Another long and complicated story, which she promises to tell me in detail when we meet again. But she's never sounded happier. I confess that she almost doesn't sound like herself at all. And she tells me that my brother's family in England is well, his two young children growing like weeds. They're all on excellent terms now . . ." His smile faded. "We've been too long apart. She said she's had men searching for me for over two years, since I stopped writing. I owe my family a great many explanations."

"There is . . . nothing to stop you from tendering them in person," Johanna said, managing a smile of her own. "Your sister found you at the right time."

"Yes. I'm myself again—more myself than I've ever been."

"Then you should not delay going to her."

He gazed at her with that long, unblinking, predator's stare that Fenris had bestowed upon him. "Do you want me to go, Johanna?"

No! Not without me . . . She swallowed the cry. *No need to become hysterical, Johanna. Calm, calm and prudence.*

"I want you to be happy," she said. "You have so much to reclaim, Quentin. All the things you left behind, in England—your family, your heritage—"

"My old ways as a rake and ne'er-do-well?" he said. "Oh, yes. The second son, returning home to become a burden on his family."

"You would not be a burden on anyone," she said, her throat growing thick with passion.

"Except upon you."

She surged to her feet. "You were never a burden. You were my patient, and then my friend. My dear friend."

"Only a friend, Johanna?" He rose with deliberation. "As I recall, you told me that you loved me."

This was the moment. *Speak.* Her mouth was so dry that she could hardly swallow.

"You promised me, Johanna, that you'd see me through to a cure. Are you going to abandon me now?"

"You are no longer my patient. You have not been, since we—" She caught her breath, her face unbearably hot. "In any case, you have made remarkable progress, crossed the most difficult threshold."

"But I'm not cured, you know. I have all of Fenris's memories, as well as my own. Ugly memories." He wasn't joking any longer. "I must learn how to forgive myself. I don't know if I can do it alone."

She refused to let him belittle his own extraordinary accomplishments. "You are strong, Quentin, or you would not have survived."

"Not that strong," he said, walking toward her. "Not strong enough to leave you." He knelt at her feet. "You see, I love you, Johanna."

He loves me. He . . . *loves* . . . *me.* Her entire body vibrated like a metronome, and her mind went utterly blank.

"Patients often think that they love their doctors. It is a common—"

He sealed her lips with his finger. "But you just said I'm not your patient, Johanna. Can't you make up your mind?" He sighed and shook his head. "Let me help you."

Giving her no time to prepare, he leaned forward and kissed her. Deeply, passionately, with everything he was and could become, with Fenris's ferocity and Quentin's gentleness.

"I have a proposition for you, dear doctor," he said, when he let her up for air. "Be my wife."

"Quentin—I want you to know that I . . . I—"

"You might as well take pity on me." He smiled, the old smile laced with both wickedness and a new resolve. "I've been waiting to love you in a proper bed ever since that night in the Barbary Coast."

Rampant desire made it impossible to concentrate. "I have been trying to tell you, but I am not very good—" She wet her lips and croaked out a laugh. "Quentin, I need you. I do not wish to go on without you by my side. I love you."

He gave a crow of triumph and kissed her again. She laced her arms around his neck and hugged him as if he might vanish if she dared let loose. Was she dreaming?

"You know—" She gulped and started again. "I am merely human. How will your family accept—"

"My family cares about me, and they'll love you for the remarkable woman you are." He bared his teeth. "I assure you that they will."

"But you must want to return to England."

"America is my home now. My old life is over."

"You . . . understand that I am a doctor." She laughed again, nervous and jubilant. "I am not much of a cook. Nor a housekeeper—"

He took her face in his hands. "My Valkyrie. I would never ask you to give up your great gifts for healing the mind." He kissed her hands, one by one. "I know very well that you can get along without me. But together—" He swung her off her feet and twirled her in a dizzy circle. "Beware to anyone who stands in our way!"

They kissed, and danced about the parlor like a pair of dervishes, until Johanna's hair came loose and they both looked as though they'd just left the bedroom. Johanna didn't even bother to straighten her frock.

This was not madness. She loved, and was loved by, a man who expected, even demanded that she embrace her gifts, just as he embraced his. He'd never regard her as anything but an equal. A friend, a helpmate, a lover.

She knew she'd have cause to doubt herself again. So would Quentin. But they would no longer be alone in fighting their battles. She need not be strong and sensible and responsible every moment of every day; Quentin could be those things for her.

As she would be for him.

"At least one matter is relatively straightforward," she said, summoning up the breath to speak. "I have already considered that it would be best for the Haven's residents to relocate to a place far from Silverado Springs, where we can start afresh. You said that your sister lives in New Mexico. We should be able to sell my uncle's remaining land for a good price. Surely there is land to be bought and room to build in the Territory. I will have to talk to the others, but—"

"Does that mental machinery of yours ever cease its work?" he teased, kissing her on the nose. "Of course, my Valkyrie. I've passed through the Territory, once or twice. It's a wild country, but there is still room for men and women to grow. We'll find our place there."

"You won't mind sharing our lives with my patients?"

"Not at all. As long as we have a little time to ourselves." He gave her a delightful sample of what he had in mind for their private times. Johanna found her thoughts turning with increasing persistence to her bed down the hall.

But she still had obligations. "I must say good-bye to May and Mrs. Ingram. And there's your messenger—"

"Not quite yet. You didn't answer my question." He dropped to one knee again, and took her hand between his. "Will you marry me, Johanna?"

She felt the smile on her face growing and growing until it became a ridiculous grin. "It seems a perfectly rational thing to do."

He jumped up, caught her about the waist and whirled her around and around with such a caterwauling that Mrs. Daugherty, Irene, Harper, Lewis, Oscar, May, and Mrs. Ingram came to watch in amazement.

Johanna only laughed. If she'd gone a little mad, it was a price she was willing to pay.

Author's Notes

Secret of the Wolf is a work of fiction. As an author, I love to explore intriguing story ideas that may or may not necessarily reflect my own personal beliefs or those of current specialists in a given field.

In *Secret of the Wolf*, Johanna Schell is an early "psychiatrist" who used the relatively new science of hypnosis to help her patients. The modern concept of the trance state was made popular by Franz Anton Mesmer in the last quarter of the eighteenth century. Mesmer advocated the concept of "animal magnetism." The Marquis de Puysegur was the first to describe the three central features of hypnosis. But it was James Braid who, in 1843, coined the word "hypnosis," and he wrote many papers on the subject as well as using forms of hypnotism in his medical practice. In 1845, James Esdaile performed his first operation under hypnosis, or "hypnoanesthesia." However, as the nineteenth century progressed, hypnotism fell out of favor and most physicians considered its therapeutic use a stumbling block to acceptance by the medical community.

In the mid-nineteenth century, a French country physician, Ambroise-Auguste Liebault, began using the method to treat various illnesses in his rural patients. He wrote a book that was largely ignored, and it was not until a colleague, Hyppolyte Bernheim, paid him a visit in 1882 and adopted his methods that hypnosis was revived as a respectable therapeutic tool.

Johanna is ahead of her time in this respect, since she and her father continued to develop medical applications of hypnosis during a period when it was out of fashion.

Today, hypnosis is used to treat many kinds of disorders and remains a somewhat controversial type of therapy. More controversial, however, is the concept of "suppressed memory" and "Multiple Personality Disorder." There are wildly divergent views on both subjects.

Some psychiatrists, psychologists, and specialists are advocates of the concept of "suppressed or recovered memory," in which a person—

usually a child—will "hide" a traumatic experience from the conscious mind. The theory is that such hidden memories may be uncovered through hypnosis and other forms of treatment. In *Secret of the Wolf*, Quentin possesses such memories. Some mental-health specialists believe that the act of uncovering these memories will help effect a cure. Others strongly believe that "recovered memories" are often implanted by the therapist, or are simply an amalgam of wishes, beliefs, and actual memories.

Some advocates of the suppressed memory theory believe that traumatic childhood experiences can result in Multiple Personality Disorder, or MPD, which is now called Dissociative Identity Disorder (DSM-IV). The brain "separates" itself into at least two personalities with different functions, which allow the child to deal with the unbearable. Others claim that the additional personalities do not really exist at all, but are the products of the therapy itself.

The concept of MPD/DID was born in the seventeenth century, when Paracelsus recorded the case of a woman who claimed that another personality stole her money. In 1812, Benjamin Rush described several cases that fit the modern definition of MPD/DID. The case of Mary Reynolds, in 1817, was described by Silas Weir Mitchell as one of "double consciousness." Later in the nineteenth century, a number of physicians and psychologists, including Eugene Azam, reported cases of two or more personalities sharing the same body. Interestingly enough, the early cases were nearly always a matter of only two personalities; it was not until the twentieth century that cases of true multiples were uncovered.

Post-traumatic Stress Disorder, a recently named phenomenon, is displayed by the character of Harper in *Secret of the Wolf*. In the nineteenth century, the condition was variously known as "soldier's heart," "railway spine," traumatic neurosis, nervous shock, and various forms of neurasthenia and hysteria. During WWI, it was called "shell shock." Today, entire fields of study are devoted to PTSD, its causes, symptoms, and cures. As with the other conditions mentioned above, there is considerable debate about the specific parameters of PTSD.

I neither advocate nor refute these theories in *Secret of the Wolf*. They are used in a fictional sense to tell a story.

Because these subjects are so controversial and many-sided, I offer a selection of sources for further information. A full spectrum of opinion on these subjects is represented in the following.

Disclaimer: *Susan Krinard does not in any way advocate or recommend these websites and/or books as representing her personal beliefs, the current state of mental health research, or the "truth or falsehood" of hypnotherapy, suppressed/false memories, or MPD. Susan Krinard does not advocate the services of any practitioner or organization mentioned, or linked to, the following websites, nor is she responsible for website content. Viewers should visit at their own risk.*

Websites

History of Psychiatry and Mental Health Treatment

http://psy.utmb.edu/research/psyepi/course/1concept/history/
    history.htm
http://www.psychnet-uk.com/training_ethics/history_of_psych.htm
http://www.geocities.com/Athens/Delphi/6061/en_linha.htm

Hypnosis/History of Hypnosis

http://ks.essortment.com/hypnosishistory_rcdg.htm
http://www.infinityinst.com/articles/ixnartic.html
http://www.hypnotherapy.freeserve.co.uk/History%20of%20
    Hypnosis.htm

Hypnotherapy

http://www.alternativemedicinechannel.com/hypnotherapy/
http://home.earthlink.net/~johnsonsaga/hypnotherapy2.html

Suppressed/Recovered Memory and False Memory Syndrome

http://www.brown.edu/Departments/Taubman_Center/
    Recovmenm/Archive.html
http://www.skeptic.com/02.3.hochman-fms.html
http://www.mhsource.com/pt/p991137.html
http://www.vuw.ac.nz/psyc/fitzMemory/contents.html

MPD/DID

http://www.dissociation.com/index/Definition/
http://www.religioustolerance.org/mpd_did.htm
http://www.psycom.net/mchugh.html
http://www.csicop.org/si/9805/witch.html
http://www.usc.edu/dept/law-lib/law-center/usclaw94/saksart.html
http://www.ac.wwu.edu/~n9140024/CampbellPM.htmi
http://www.golden.net/~soul/didpro.html

Partial Bibliography

Berrios, German and Porter, Roy, eds. *A History of Clinical Psychiatry: The Origin and History of Psychiatric Disorders.* New York: New York University Press, 1995.

Bliss, Eugene L. *Multiple Personality, Allied Disorders and Hypnosis.* Oxford: Oxford University Press, 1986.

Brown, Peter. *The Hypnotic Brain: Hypnotherapy and Social Communication.* New Haven, Conn.: Yale University Press, 1991.

Dean, Eric T., Jr. *Shook Over Hell: Post-Traumatic Stress, Vietnam, and the Civil War.* Cambridge: Harvard University Press, 1997.

Ellenberger, Henri F. *The Discovery of the Unsconscious.* New York: Basic Books, Inc., 1970.

Gauld, Alan. *A History of Hypnotisim.* Cambridge: Cambridge University Press, 1992.

Grob, Gerald N. *The Mad Among Us: A History of the Care of America's Mentally Ill.* Cambridge: Harvard University Press, 1994.

Hacking, Ian. *Rewriting the Soul: Multiple Personality and the Science of Memory.* Princeton, N.J.: Princeton Paperbacks, 1995.

Jackson, Stanley W. *Care of the Psyche: A History of Psychological Healing.* New Haven, Conn.: Yale University Press, 1999.

Morrison, James. *DSM-IV Made Easy.* New York: The Guildford Press, 1995.

Reid, William and Balis, George. *The Treatment of Psychiatric Disorders, Third Edition.* New York: Brunnner/Mazel, 1997.

Sargant, William. *Battle for the Mind: A Physiology of Conversion and Brain-Washing.* Cambridge: Malor Books, 1997.

Scull, Andrew, ed. *Madhouses, Mad-Doctors, and Madmen: The Social History of Psychiatry in the Victorian Era.* Philadelphia: The University of Pennsylvania Press, 1981.

Shay, Jonathan. *Achilles in Vietnam: Combat Trauma and the Undoing of Character.* New York: Simon & Schuster, 1994.

Shorter, Edward. *A History of Psychiatry: From the Era of the Asylum to the Age of Prozac.* New York: John Wiley & Sons. Inc., 1997.

Stone, Michael H. *Healing the Mind: A History of Psychiatry from Antiquity to the Present.* New York: W. W. Norton & Company, Inc., 1997.

To Catch a Wolf

Prologue

Free.

Morgan paused just outside the gates of the Territorial Penitentiary, staring through the bars at the cold, hard faces of the men who had kept him caged for the last five years. He knew that their blank expressions hid relief—relief that the one prisoner they couldn't break was leaving their jurisdiction.

They'd stopped trying to beat him after the first year, because he gave them no reason other than their dislike of his silence. They left him almost entirely alone after the second year, and so did the other convicts. Even though he never attempted escape, they kept him in his cell all but an hour each day, and let him out only under heavy guard with half a dozen rifles trained at his head.

He'd learned how to keep his sanity when the scents of wood and river came to him through the barred window. He'd learned to exist in a place where everything he had been died a slow and lingering death.

It was easier than the one his father had suffered.

With no possessions but memory and the clothes upon his back, he turned away from the high stone walls. The road led east, to the town of Cañon City with its houses and shops and saloons. To the west rose the peaks of the Sangre de Cristos, and to the north Pike's Peak and Colorado Springs. The border with New Mexico Territory lay a hundred miles to the south, as the crow flies.

The road that had led him to Colorado in search of his father had begun in the west, in California. But his mother and sister were no longer waiting in the little mountain cabin. Four years after his trial and incarceration in various jails and then here at the Territorial Penitentiary, he had received the one letter of his nine-year term.

His uncle Jonas had been brief. Edith Holt was dead, and his sister Cassidy had gone with Jonas to his ranch in New Mexico. There she would have a decent upbringing away from the unsavory influence of her kin.

Cassidy had been six when Morgan left. She would be a woman now, familiar with courting and kissing and all the things Morgan had missed. She might even have started a family of her own. She'd have no place in her life for an ex-convict.

Better that Cassidy should forget he ever existed. He had no family. He was alone. And he would remain alone.

There were many ways to be alone in Colorado. Not every valley was a booming mining town, nor was every hill swarming with eager prospectors. There were places where wolves still avoided the hunters' guns and traps.

That was where Morgan would go. North, and west, into the high mountains, the deep valleys. There he would forget he had ever been a man.

His feet, so used to measuring the dimensions of his cell, were slow to remember what it was to stride. Autumn dust rose in little puffs about his dilapidated shoes. He stepped out of the shapeless leather and kicked the shoes away.

He walked a hundred paces down the road and turned north where only animal trails marked the path. No one called after him, neither a curse nor a farewell. He dismissed the humans from his mind.

Time as men measured it had long since lost its meaning. He walked for many days, drinking from trickling streams and springs and rivers, eating what he sensed was fit and safe. Where men made their stink of waste and metal, he passed by unseen. The season they called Indian summer lingered well into the mountains. Golden leaves rustled under his feet. Then snow fell, and he shook off the cold as he had done in the years of captivity.

At last there came a day when he heard the wolves howl.

The scent of men did not reach here. The air stung his nostrils with the promise of winter, and turned to fog with each breath.

He looked up at the unbarred sky and howled. The wolves answered. They came, silent to any who walked on two legs. When they ringed him in, hackles raised and teeth bared, he stripped off the remains of his ragged clothing and walked among them without fear. As they shrank back, he Changed.

The wolves recognized him, though they had surely never seen his like before. They crouched low in obeisance. The mated pair who led the pack whined anxiously, and he told them in a language they understood that he would not usurp their sovereignty as long as he shared the fate of the pack.

So they welcomed him. He made himself known to each wolf in turn, his black-furred shoulders rising above those of the others, twice the height of the smallest beast. Then he sent them away, and became a man for the last time.

He gathered his discarded clothing and laid them in a neat pile upon the virgin ground. With his hands he dug a deep hole, placed the shirt and trousers inside, and smoothed the dirt over the remnants of his humanity.

A snowflake kissed Morgan's shoulder. Another joined it, and its kinfolk danced and spun out of the sky to offer a final benediction. He ran his fingers over his face, feeling the gauntness and the sharp planes, the scar where a fellow inmate had stabbed him through the cheek and left only the slightest mark. There would be no such mark on the wolf. And the weight in his chest, so long ignored, would shrivel and be forgotten.

With a shrug of his shoulders, he Changed. Snowflakes caught in his fur. The richness of the forest poured over him and embraced him.

Howls rose from the nearest slope. He answered and broke into a lope, covering the broken ground effortlessly. The years sloughed away one by one, like human skin and bone, until his heart lay naked to the world. It froze into a lump of ice, untouched and untouchable.

Now he was truly free.

Chapter 1

DENVER, COLORADO, JUNE 1880

One by one the members of the Ladies' Aid Society rose from their chairs and sofas in the Munroes' grand parlor and took leave of their hostess. Narrow silk and brocade skirts rustled, confining legs that seldom found practical use save to convey their owners from mansion to carriage and from carriage to shop.

Athena Sophia Munroe did not rise to see her guests to the door. She extended her gloved hand and accepted the offered farewells like a queen upon a throne. A queen as luxuriously confined as the most favored consort in a pasha's harem.

She smiled and found a compliment for each lady in turn, listening to their chatter as Brinkley led them into the hall.

Cecily Hockensmith lingered, waving her fan indolently against the hot, dry air.

"What is to be done about this awful heat?" she exclaimed. "Everyone advised us to go to the mountains for the summer, but Papa did not wish to miss any business opportunities." She made a moue of distaste. "Business, always business. Is it not frightfully dull?"

"The men do not seem to find it so," Athena said. She thought of Niall, hard at work in some stifling office while she sat at her ease at home. "It is true that many families do leave the city in the summer. That is why our attendance today was less than it would be at other times. In the autumn, we will have our full complement again."

Miss Hockensmith closed her eyes and sighed. "We always went to Newport during the summers in New York. Ah, those fresh ocean breezes. How pleasant it was."

Athena nodded with polite sympathy. "It must seem very different in Denver, with the ocean so far away."

"Have you ever visited the sea, my dear?"

"I am afraid not. I was to attend school in the east, but—"

"You must go one day, Miss Munroe. You cannot miss it."

Athena imagined herself by the waves, breathing in the salt air and letting the water bathe her feet. The picture was so enticing that it hurt.

"I would like to take the orphans to the ocean," she said quickly. "They would appreciate it more than anyone."

"Ah, yes, the dear orphans." Miss Hockensmith grew serious, meeting Athena's gaze with an air of troubled concern. "I hope you won't mind a bit of sisterly advice. I have been observing you ever since our arrival, Miss Munroe. I confess that I have never seen anyone work as tirelessly as you on behalf of the masses. Why, even our greatest philanthropists in New York did not become so . . . personally involved in such work."

Athena straightened in her chair. "You compliment me too highly, Miss Hockensmith. I do little enough, and I have the assistance of many others. It seems to me that it is our duty, as the more fortunate, to do what we can to aid the less."

Miss Hockensmith raised a plucked brow. "Naturally. But the or-

phanage, the fallen women, the unemployed men in Globeville and Swansea—are you quite sure that you have not taken on too much, my dear?" Her dark eyes sparkled with compassion. "I fear that you will exhaust yourself with the Winter Ball, among so many other ventures. You know that I would be more than happy to assist you. I had much experience with organizing affairs of this sort in New York. And I do so wish to help the dear little orphans."

Athena looked up at Cecily, at her height and presence and midnight-black hair above a pale, lovely face. The lady was used to being ruler in her own kingdom, and who could blame her? She had sacrificed a great deal to come to Denver with her father.

"Of course," Athena said. "Your advice and experience will be most welcome. I shall need everyone's help to make the second Winter Ball a success equal to last year's."

"It is a shame that we had not yet come to town then," Cecily said, "but I am sure you made an excellent job of it. Certainly your ballroom is one of the finest I have seen in Denver . . . for a modest gathering. How you must enjoy dancing in it."

Athena made a slight adjustment to her perfectly arranged skirts as if some part of her might have been exposed by an inadvertent motion. She was grateful for Cecily's oblivious comment; far better these occasional pricks than the slash of pity.

Denver society no longer had reason to pity her. Had she not proven herself capable of contributing as much as anyone in her work for those less fortunate? Was her formal parlor not one of the most stylish and tasteful in Denver? Did not the wives and daughters of her brother's colleagues trust her judgment on everything from the latest Paris fashions to the hiring of servants?

I am no different than any of them. No different.

"But oh, how thoughtless of me," Cecily said. "Pray do not think—" With a show of confusion, Cecily created a minor hurricane with her fan. "It was not my intention to remind you—"

"Please, Miss Hockensmith. Do not distress yourself. I assure you that I am not in the least offended by the subject of dancing." She laughed lightly. "It is a ball, after all! And you are a most elegant dancer."

Cecily Hockensmith had perfected the fine art of the blush. "You flatter me, Miss Munroe. It is only natural that a woman should dance well when provided with a superlative partner."

Athena knew to whom Miss Hockensmith referred. Athena made it

a point to take note of every ripple in the generally calm waters that made up Denver's elite social circle. The stylish lady from New York—as yet unmarried—had paid particular notice to Niall from the first. It was no wonder. Niall Munroe was a handsome man of dignified bearing and considerable assets.

But Niall had not reciprocated the interest, though he had courteously danced with Cecily at Mrs. William Byers's anniversary ball. Nor was he a particularly fine dancer. Business had prevented him from mastering such niceties.

Inwardly, Athena sighed. What was she to do with Niall? Could Miss Hockensmith be the right woman for him?

The mere thought was uncomfortable. But why? There was much to admire in Miss Hockensmith, and her father might become Niall's new business partner. *You will be seeing much of her now that they have settled in Denver. Perhaps we will become great friends. How wonderful it would be if I could help Niall and Miss Hockensmith find happiness. . . .*

Cheered at the notion, Athena pushed aside her faint unease and pressed Cecily's hand. "I doubt that you shall find a shortage of partners at the Winter Ball."

"Thank you, Miss Munroe. But please consider my offer of help. I should not wish you to tire yourself. Your brother did mention that you work much too hard."

Niall again. "Do you not have a brother, Miss Hockensmith? You know how they are. I think they must secretly believe that no sister ever grows up to be a woman."

"And a woman such as yourself would not wish to remain dependent. I admire your courage." Cecily closed her fan. "Nevertheless, do call upon me at any time, Miss Munroe."

"Athena, please. We are such a small circle in Denver."

"And formality is best reserved for those outside it." Athena had the brief, uncharitable thought that Cecily must have practiced her perfect smile before a mirror. "I am certain we shall become bosom friends, dear Athena."

"Then I look forward to seeing you at our next meeting."

With a graceful turn, Cecily swept to the door. Athena admired the way she moved so that her form-fitting skirts maintained a column almost undisturbed by the motion of her legs.

As if she had no need of legs at all.

Athena wheeled her chair to the window and drew back the curtains. All of the carriages had gone, even Cecily's. Not one of the ladies

would consider walking home, though most lived within a few blocks of the fashionable quarter along Fourteenth Street.

Would they choose to walk tonight if they might never walk again? *You are morbid this evening,* she chided herself. *Niall will soon be home.*

And Niall deserved peace and tranquility after a long day of business. Athena deftly maneuvered her wheelchair to the kitchen to consult Monsieur Savard about the evening's dinner. She rearranged the roses displayed on a low rosewood table in the marble and oak-paneled entry hall, and spoke with the housekeeper regarding the new chambermaid and the hiring of a laundress to replace the woman who had returned to her native France.

When all was completed to her satisfaction, she took up her usual place at her secretary in the private sitting room and began to sort through the various letters, invitations, and responses to her charitable campaigns. She basked in each small victory and refused to regard the minor failures. Where the orphans were concerned—or the unmarried mothers, or the poor men up by the smelters, looking for work—she could be remarkably persistent. She had something to fight for.

Something that was beyond herself and her petty problems.

In the hall outside the front door opened, and Athena heard the boom of her brother's voice, followed by the cultured tenor of Brinkley's. Niall strode into the room, a typical look of preoccupation on his handsome face. He paused just inside the door and noticed Athena with vague surprise, as if he did not find her waiting in precisely the same place every evening.

"Good evening, Niall," she said. "How was your day?"

"Very good, thank you. And yours?"

It was the comforting ritual they always followed, though seldom had either one something truly noteworthy to report. Niall ran their father's business and handled Athena's inheritance, providing her with a very liberal allowance; she, in turn, kept the house and played hostess when his business associates gathered for dinner or a sociable meeting.

But there were times, like this evening, when Athena felt a treacherous yearning for something more. If only Niall would take some real interest in her activities. . . .

"It went quite well," she said. "The Aid Society met to discuss the Winter Ball—"

"That's months away," he said, pouring his usual whiskey at the sideboard.

"Yes. But the Munroe successes have always come from excellent planning. I only follow your and Papa's examples." She smiled to take the challenge from her words. "I regard my work as worthy of such care."

Niall downed his drink. "I'm not so sure that the beneficiaries of your charity are worthy of your efforts—or the money you spend on them." He poured another drink and frowned at the inoffensive glass. "You are much too generous."

Athena retained her smile. Niall had always been blunt, and this was hardly a new argument. "We agreed long ago that you would make the money, and I would see that some portion of it went to help the less fortunate, according to my own judgment."

"A judgment based upon emotion and sentimentality."

Athena wheeled closer to him and touched his sleeve. "What is it, Niall? Is something troubling you?"

He set the second drink down untouched and looked directly at her. "One of those 'fallen women' you attempted to reform was caught trying to steal the wallet of a very influential financier from Chicago."

"One of my girls? How do you know?"

"When she was caught, she blurted out your name. She seemed to think that you would intercede for her." He swept up the glass and downed the contents quickly. "It was not a pleasant circumstance to hear my sister's name on the lips of a whore."

Athena stared at her interlaced fingers. "You witnessed this yourself?"

Niall paced to her desk and shuffled the stack of papers and bills. "I was consulting with the gentleman regarding a business venture of some importance when she accosted him on the street. It is fortunate that he caught her. She is now in jail where she belongs."

Niall had always been the hardheaded, ambitious one in the family, Athena the heart and conscience. He was more annoyed with his sister than with the poor young woman who had been driven to such an act. Annoyed because Athena's work had inadvertently disrupted his business. Because she had failed.

"It is entirely my fault," she said meekly. "I will pay the girl's fine, and—"

"I forbid it. Some people can't be helped, Athena. They only become more entrenched in their laziness and dependence."

She looked up to meet Niall's gaze. The flinty gray of his eyes had softened, and she saw the pity and guilt in his face. Not for those he spoke of, but for her.

"Have you ever tried to help," she asked, "simply for the sake of it? With no hope of profit or gain?"

"Have you?" His mouth was a rigid line, almost cruel. "Hasn't your work paid dividends in the admiration and respect of your ladies? Hasn't it won you a place for yourself where no one can feel sorry for you?"

Athena clutched the iron-rimmed wheels of her chair and jerked it backward as if he had struck at her. "I am sorry that I have disappointed you."

He shook his head and made a slashing gesture with the side of his hand. "No. No. But it is completely unnecessary to exhaust yourself by becoming indispensable to every philanthropic cause in Denver. The Munroes already have the city's—the nation's—respect and admiration. We never had to fight for it. No one stands above us in influence or capital. As long as you are my sister, your position is assured."

Even though I cannot dance, or make a grand tour of Europe, or even enjoy a social luncheon at the Windsor. "Of course you are right, Niall," she said, regaining her composure. "I appreciate all you have done for me."

"Athena . . ." He grimaced. "I'm poor company tonight. Perhaps you should dine alone."

"No, please. I understand the pressures you face. Let us speak no more of this. M. Savard has prepared your favorite meal, and you would not wish to disappoint him."

He sighed. "Very well." It was impossible for her to take his arm, so he positioned himself behind her chair and pushed her to the dining room. He placed her at one end of the table and assumed his seat at the opposite end. Each setting was elegantly arranged, with a cloisonné vase of fresh flowers at the center of the vast oak table, low enough so as not to obstruct the view down its impressive length.

Brinkley appeared to direct the parlormaid and footman in serving the first course. For a time they ate in silence while Athena searched for some innocuous subject to draw Niall close again.

"I saw Miss Hockensmith today," she began. "She is quite taken with you, I believe. She will be expecting your attentions at the Winter Ball."

"Will she?" He never lifted his eyes from his plate.

How little he truly knew of women, for all his vast experience of the world. How lonely he must be with only those dry businessmen as companions, and how oblivious to his own loneliness. His sister was simply not enough.

Until recently, she had not considered the damaging effects of that loneliness. At the ripe age of twenty-six, she had seen more and more of her peers married and managing households of their own. She remembered a time when even she had held such aspirations.

Selfish aspirations, with no thought of others. It was Niall she must worry about now. She knew his real reason for avoiding the bonds of matrimony.

It was she. Athena Munroe, bound to him with the implacable chains of guilt. All he might have dreamed as a boy, all the old wildness, had been abandoned for her care, her happiness.

But how could she be content when she knew that he was not, even if his ultimate happiness meant that she must be alone? Was that not a small sacrifice to make after all those *he* had made?

As long as she had her work . . .

"Miss Hockensmith is rather lovely, you know," she said. "Quite willing to help in the work of the Society, and with the orphans. I seem to remember that you had been considering her father for some sort of partnership."

He peered at her over the top of the flowers. "Do you wish to become my business adviser, Athena, or are you simply matchmaking?"

His attempt at humor warmed her. "It would not hurt you to show occasional courtesies to my friends."

He muttered something too low for her to hear, which was not an easy feat. Her ears still functioned perfectly well, and better than those of anyone she had met in her lifetime.

"I beg your pardon?"

"Nothing." He nodded to Brinkley, who had brought the dessert. He stabbed at the pudding as if it were a tough slice of beef. At last he set his spoon down and looked at Athena. The back of her neck prickled as if at the gathering of a prairie thunderstorm.

"This makes the fifth summer that you have not gone to the ranch," he said. "I don't like it, Athena. The heat and dust is unhealthy for you. You need fresh air and quiet, and by remaining in Denver you are certainly not getting it. I will not have you becoming ill because of your own stubbornness."

Athena sampled her pudding, barely tasting it. "I am in good health, Niall. There is no danger—"

"You think me unobservant, but I have seen the changes in you. You've convinced yourself that you can solve all of Denver's problems single-handedly, without taking any rest for yourself."

"Rest? Look at me." She swept her hand down the length of her body. "I have plenty of rest. It is the people I try to help who have no rest, struggling as they do every day simply to survive."

"Our own father struggled when he first came to Denver, and no one gave him charity. He would have turned it away."

"Not everyone in this world is alike, Niall. You know that as well as anyone."

They stared at each other. There were two subjects they almost never brought up between them: Athena's accident, and the nature she had inherited from her mother. Athena deliberately avoided thinking about either; the first could not be undone, and the second she had left behind forever.

She had not known her mother. Perhaps that was why she felt so deeply for the orphans, who had lost much more.

"I have kept my promise to you," Athena said, the words sliding past the lump in her throat. "You promised not to interfere in my chosen occupation."

He scowled, rising from his chair. "I did not promise to let you do whatever you pleased, no matter what the cost. Your insistence upon visiting the tent city and the warehouse district is foolhardy in the extreme."

Her skin went cold. How had Niall learned of that? She had been so careful to go incognito, cloaked and hooded and accompanied by a brawny former soldier she had employed after her orphanage administrator had urged her to take some protection. Had it not been for her immobility, she needn't have feared any man, even in the worst part of the city.

Do not think of what might have been. Do not.

"You have paid employees to send on such tasks," Niall continued. "No one, least of all the members of your Society, expects you to dirty your hands or endanger your person. You are no common shopgirl, Athena. Your fine Miss Hockensmith could not approve of such impropriety."

In her heart Athena knew he was right, but she had chosen to take the risk, knowing that the other ladies would not expect a cripple to be capable of such adventures.

They were the only adventures permitted her, now. Among the orphans, or the inebriates, or the poor folk in their threadbare tents along the South Platte, she could not possibly be an object of pity. It was she who held the advantages, she who gave. No one reminded her, however inadvertently, of what she had lost.

And they *needed* her.

"They are people, Niall," she said earnestly. "It is not enough to have someone deliver the food and see that they have fresh water and clothing and coal enough to get through the winter. They must be encouraged, led to see that there is a better life to strive for. Without real examples, how can they learn?"

"Let someone else do the teaching. Someone who is . . . unencumbered."

She pushed away from the table and spun her chair about. "Am I not an encumbrance upon you, Niall? Your worry for me is distracting you from your important work, and wouldn't it be so much easier if I would sit quietly and knit stockings until you find some use for me?"

Her outburst hung in the air like a choking haze. Athena touched her throat, amazed and chagrined. Had that self-pitying, selfish tirade come from her, or had some harpy assumed her shape and voice? What had possessed her?

Have you any use at all, Athena Munroe?

Niall walked the length of the table and stopped before her, grave and strangely quiet. "Yes, Athena. It is what I would prefer—to see you safe and content. But I know that is not possible."

"But I am . . . I am content! Don't you see—"

"I am sorry. You leave me no choice. Either you agree to cease these clandestine visits to the slums, and reduce your commitments to a reasonable number, or I must take steps to see that you are removed to a place where you can reconsider your priorities."

Icy terror swept through her. "The Winter Ball—you cannot expect me to give that up, or abandon the orphans. Papa's money made it possible. I am only doing what he wished."

"It is your choice, Athena. I could see to it that you are relieved of all your self-imposed duties—and I shall, if I believe it will save you from yourself."

"If only you thought of something besides making money—"

"The money you are so glad to have?"

Tears burned behind her eyes. "Where did you get your hard heart, Niall? It was not from Papa. Your mother—"

"Leave our mother out of this."

"She was never my mother. She did not wish to be."

Niall's fair skin reddened. "She acknowledged you as hers, when she might have—"

"I know what she might have done," Athena said quietly. "I know." She wheeled about and started toward the door. "If you will forgive me, Niall, I am tired. I will go up to my room now."

"Athena—"

"Good-night."

She heard the bang of Niall's fist on the table as she entered the hall. Brinkley appeared, ever bland and efficient, to help her to her room. He steered her into the Otis hydraulic safety elevator at the end of the hall and closed the gate.

After two years Athena was used to the curious motion of the device, which Niall had insisted was the perfect solution for the problem of stairs. And now, of course, the grand Windsor hotel had an elevator of its own. Niall's foresight matched their father's in every way.

So did his devotion to her. A devotion that imprisoned him as surely as her chair did Athena.

At the second floor, Brinkley met her to roll back the gate and step aside. He had been too long with the family to ask if she wished to be taken to her room. Fran would be waiting in the small chamber adjacent to hers, and all Athena wished to do now was retire.

How had things gone so wrong? How had she managed to quarrel with her brother, when they so seldom lifted their voices to each other? She could never beat Niall in an argument, and she did not make the mistake of doubting his threats.

Fran helped her undress and get into bed, and she lay staring up at the ceiling for a long while. She had wanted Niall's happiness; she needed to continue her work without hindrance. Somehow she must distract Niall from his focus on her, and at the same time prove that she was fully capable of caring for herself.

If you were truly independent . . .

But how? Niall still controlled her inheritance, according to the terms of Papa's will. She could not demand her portion unless Niall agreed. And he saw her as what she was—a cripple.

She tried to move her legs. They remained lumps under the blankets, only the toes capable of wiggling. She had given up on walking long ago.

There must be some other way of convincing Niall that she was a sensible, mature, strong woman in mind and spirit if not in body. Some way to relieve him of his guilt once and for all.

She drifted into a twilight world between sleep and waking, and it seemed that she was running—running on four legs instead of two. Four whole, healthy, powerful legs. And she was not alone.

In dreams, she could pretend.

Chapter 2

SOUTHERN COLORADO, JUNE 1880

Voices.

They drew him toward flickering light and the smell of human habitation, though he had left that world behind in a time beyond memory. He could not have said, even had he been capable of speech, why he fled the hunters into the arms of other men instead of to the deep wilderness.

Madness. Yet the pain drove him, and the knowledge that he was near death. The voices were very close.

Firelight seared his eyes. He plunged into the circle made by the many human dwellings and staggered to a stop. The baying of hounds resounded from the forest's edge.

Raised voices, cries of alarm, shouting like the howls of wolves. He braced himself for more pain, ready to expend the last of his strength if they came with ropes to bind him.

None did. Tall shapes darted in and out of his blurred sight. Human scent washed over him. His legs buckled, and he fell to his side. Each breath brought searing agony. Little by little, the light and the remnant of his senses faded. Then came the darkness.

Peace.

He returned to himself slowly, and the voices were still there. They flooded his mind like tainted water: human words, human thoughts, human images.

But now he understood what he heard. And he, himself, was human.

"Jesus, Mary, and Joseph! Did you see that?"

"Remarkable," said the second, deeper voice. "Quite astonishing."

A murmur of agreement and disbelief followed. "Since we all witnessed it," said a third voice, marked by a gentle drawl, "we must con-clude that it was not a delusion."

"Delusions don't bleed," the first voice said. "Whatever he is, he's been shot."

"He may be dangerous," came a fourth. "Do not touch him, Caitlin."

"Can't you see that he is too badly hurt to be a danger to anyone?"

He opened his eyes and tried to bring the world into focus. His senses were dulled, hearing and smell filtered through awkward human organs. The body he now wore refused to respond to his commands.

Memory came, and understanding. Between his lower ribs lodged the hunter's bullet, the same that had caught him as he fled the human's dogs. It would not have been a fatal injury had he remained a wolf.

But he had not. Somehow, in some way beyond his will, he had Changed. The wolf had run to men, and the man within him had be-trayed the wolf. And now he lay in his own blood, firelight dancing over naked skin, suspended halfway between life and death.

He could not make out the faces around him, but he smelled them clearly: woven cloth, leather, sweat, and horseflesh. A dozen men and women whose voices came more swiftly now, like midsummer rain.

"He appears to be regaining consciousness."

"He will bleed to death if we don't help him."

"Help him? We know nothing about him."

"It's possible that whoever shot him had good reason."

"Maybe he can't talk at all!"

He struggled to remember how to move his mouth and tongue to form words, how to speak the name he had worn in that past life.

Morgan. Morgan Holt, who accepted help from no one. No debt, no obligation, and no charity. Yet he had come here. He was completely in their power.

With a fierce act of will, he shut away the distractions of thought and memory. He summoned up his dwindling strength and called upon the wolf within.

Nothing. Nothing but pain, and night. Blood whistled behind his ears. His heart stuttered, stopped, sprang to sluggish life again.

One of his would be rescuers came near, and he tried to pull away. Calloused skin brushed his. He was too weak to shudder in disgust. He floated, disembodied, in a limbo where only the voices were solid.

"Come, children," the first voice said. "Help me move him to my tent."

"We hardly have enough food left to keep ourselves alive, let alone an outsider."

"An outsider? Just look at him! He's like us!"

"Caitlin and Harry are correct. We cannot leave him to die, and I believe I hear sounds of pursuit."

"You know as well as anyone how the townies are, and how they treat those who are different."

A face, round, male, and bewhiskered, took solid form from the fog. "Can you hear me, young man? We wish to help you. My name is Harry, Harry French. You find yourself among the troupers of French's Fantastic Family Circus. Never fear, you are quite safe here—"

"He *will* die if you keep talking, Harry."

Another face drew near: younger, more delicate, framed by a mass of red hair. "He won't die. He came here for a reason, I know it. To help us, as we help him."

"One of your 'feelings,' Firefly?" said the gentle drawl.

"Something made him come to us. We've needed a miracle. Maybe this is it."

"If he survives and is willing to aid us."

"I agree with Caitlin," the old man said. "He is the good luck we have waited for, and we must save him. Tor!"

Heavy footfalls approached. Broad hands seized Morgan, and he was lifted in arms bulging with muscle and tight as a vise. A great void opened up around him as he lost contact with the earth. From the depths of his throat came a single, pathetic snarl.

"Do not worry, Tor. You won't bite, will you, young man? No, indeed. Caitlin, come with me. The rest of you had better watch for those dogs and whoever is with them."

"They won't make it past us, Harry."

That voice was the last for a very long time. When he woke again, he lay on a cot under several blankets, surrounded by the scents of animals and humans. He tried to sort through the smells, connecting each to its name: canvas, straw, rope, oil, metal, mildew, old cooking. His limbs were weighted; his chest ached with every breath.

But he was alive.

Dim sunlight found its way through the canvas stretched overhead. The small space was crowded with crates, some of which served as platforms for other unidentifiable objects. The cot was the only furniture in the tent, save for a folding chair and small table.

Outside the canvas walls, Morgan could hear the noise of a busy camp. Dogs barked, horses whinnied, and men's voices made a continuous drone.

They had brought him here. They had saved his life. A string of curses came back to him in all their crude inventiveness, but his throat was too dry to speak.

He tensed his muscles. One by one his fingers obeyed his commands. He was not a prisoner. He could tear through those walls of canvas as if they were tissue, once he regained his strength. He felt the healing of his wound, flesh knitting hour by hour.

He concentrated on shifting his legs. A wall of gray pain dropped behind his eyes. He fell back among the blankets, breathing harshly through his teeth.

A wave of human scent blew into the tent, riding on dust-laden air.

"Ah, you're awake! Very good, very good. It did seem touch and go for a—No, no, you mustn't try to move just yet!"

The voice was the first he had heard, the one that belonged to the old man with the whiskers. Harry French. Morgan blinked the haze from his eyes. The bulky silhouette resolved into a stout, gray-haired gentleman in a patched black coat, bright red waistcoat stretched over a prominent belly, and trousers in gray and black checks. A white, upward-curving moustache was the crowning glory of an otherwise homely face, wrinkled with age and burned by the sun.

The ability to laugh had deserted Morgan long before he had chosen the wolf's way. But something in that comical face and broad grin woke a peculiar sensation within him, and his belly moved in a painful heave. He coughed.

"Oh, dear, oh, dear," Harry French's hands sketched a pattern of distress. "You must be dry as a bone. Water—yes, that's what you need, and perhaps a bit of whiskey for good measure. I believe we still have a bottle or two left." He turned as if to leave and then spun about in midstep. "Foolish, foolish. We have not been properly introduced, though perhaps you remember my name?"

His innocent enthusiasm reminded Morgan of a wolf pup still wet behind the ears. "Harry . . . French," he said hoarsely.

Harry clapped his hands. "You did understand! Wonderful. Delightful. Perhaps you also recall where you are?"

Circus. Words were coming thick and fast now, but it took Morgan a moment to assemble the images. He had seen a circus, once, when he was fifteen and without a penny in the world. The wagons and tents had been set up on an empty lot on the outskirts of a prosperous

Nevada mining town. He'd sneaked into the main tent and hid behind the risers to watch the show, until a member of the crew had caught him and booted him off the lot.

That boy had not remained a child much longer.

"How . . ." He cleared his throat, remembering how to move his lips and tongue. "How long?"

"How long have you been with us?" Harry French nibbled the edge of his moustache. "Six days, I believe. Yes, six. You've made quite a remarkable recovery. A bit more rest, that's all you need." He beamed and rocked back on his heels. "We are your friends. No need to tell us anything you don't wish. You can rest assured that we won't give your secret away—no, no. We understand."

Your secret. Morgan stiffened and slowly relaxed again. His anonymous rescuers could not know anything of his past, but they had seen him Change and hadn't the sense to be afraid.

"We're all a little odd here, you see," French said, as if he had guessed Morgan's thoughts. "Oh, we're nothing at all like the big railroad outfits, with the poor creatures in cages and great star performers. I like to think of us as a family, a family of very special people. Those who have no other place to go—they find their way to me, sooner or later, just as you have."

He drew a pocketwatch from his vest, glanced at the face, and stuffed it back in. "Dear, oh, dear. I had promised to speak to Strauss about the food stores. Strauss is our chief cook. We are running low on victuals, and I fear my accounting skills have never been—" He broke off with an apologetic sigh. "You must think me quite addled. We have not been as prosperous of late as we might wish. A series of misfortunes—bad luck, as it were. That is why we are camped here in the wilderness and cannot offer you a decent hotel bed. I do so worry about my children, and what will become of us—but I am confident our luck has changed. Yes, indeed. You will meet the others soon." He glanced at his watch again. "You will excuse me, dear boy? I'll send someone with food and drink straightaway."

Before Morgan could frame a belated response, French was out of the tent. His words resounded in Morgan's sensitive ears for several minutes after he left.

But what he had said aroused more feelings Morgan had abandoned as a wolf: worry, consternation, and fear. Not the sensible respect for nature's fickleness or the hunter's gun, but a dread far more nebulous.

"He won't die. He came here for a reason, I know it. To help us, as we help him. . . . We've needed a miracle. . . . He is the good luck we have waited for . . ."

Premonitions of a fate worse than mere death seized Morgan with renewed urgency. He braced himself on his arms and pushed up again, relieved to find that his body functioned in spite of the pain. He could escape. It was not too late.

There was only one way to learn if he was healed enough. He closed his eyes and willed the Change.

Deep inside his body, the core of his being began to shift. He felt it, not as pain, but a natural transition. It was as if each atom became fluid and reshaped itself like clay in the hands of a master potter.

But the Change did not complete. It met the barrier of his injury and paused, forcing his body to make a decision based upon a single law: survival.

Survival meant preserving strength instead of draining it for the Change. Morgan opened his eyes and found himself unrecognizable, neither wolf nor human. A monster.

Instinct made the decision for him. He returned to human shape. Dizziness and nausea held him immobile for a few seconds, but he pressed beyond his body's exhaustion and clambered to his feet. Sheer determination propelled him toward the sliver of dimming light that marked the tent's entrance.

Sunset lent the camp a certain softness that almost disguised the atmosphere of shabbiness and adversity. Tents and colorfully painted wagons, marked with hard use and frequent repair, lay scattered at the edge of a wide valley filled with sagebrush and saltbush. A herd of sway-backed horses clumped together in a makeshift corral.

Everywhere there was a certain frantic activity, as if the members of Harry French's Family Circus did not dare to stop moving. People hurried to and fro, wrapped in much-mended coats and blankets. A man juggled several bright red balls without seeming to touch them. An impossibly slender woman balanced on a wire almost too fine to be visible to normal eyes. Dogs ran about yapping and jumping through hoops.

The one quiet place was centered at a fire beside an open tent furnished with rows of rickety wooden tables and benches. There a fat man cooked a dismally small section of meat on a spit, attended by a mob of barefoot children who watched with the grim concentration of hunger.

Morgan knew poverty when he saw it. He had suffered hunger many times in his life, and had traveled with no more possessions than the clothing on his back. His great advantage had been the wolf, which had allowed him to hunt and to survive under conditions that would have killed an ordinary man.

These folk were not so fortunate. It did not take much imagination to see that they had suffered the "bad luck" Harry French had mentioned, though Morgan knew little of circuses and what made them prosper or fail.

He did understand that no man helped another without expecting something in return. Harry French's "children" hoped for something from him, something he could not give them. He might outrun guilt, as he'd outrun so much else. If he left, now, without facing those who had saved him. . . .

"You're not going so soon?"

He looked down at the familiar voice and met a pair of blue eyes in a pixie's face, topped by a blaze of wildly curling red hair. Here was the second of his rescuers—his captors—the one who had claimed some undisclosed purpose for him. She seemed hardly more than a child, flat-chested and narrow-hipped. The tights, knee-length skirt, and snug bodice she wore only emphasized her boyish shape.

She was the first woman he had seen in a decade, and he felt nothing. Neither his heart nor his body stirred. He realized with a shock that this girl reminded him of his sister Cassidy, so dimly remembered. Only Cassidy's hair had been black, like his.

The girl whistled through her teeth. "You heal quickly, don't you?" She clasped her hands behind her back and circled him, clucking under her breath. "Do you always walk around stark naked? I liked you better as a wolf."

"Then get out of my way, and you won't see me again."

She placed her hands on her hips. "Well, at least you can speak."

Morgan bared his teeth. *Too late*, his mind wailed. *Too late*. "Who are you?"

"I'm Caitlin—Caitlin Hughes. Do you have a name?"

"Morgan. Holt."

"Well, Holt, do you know where you are?"

"The old man told me."

"That old man is Harry, who agreed to take you in, and don't you say anything bad about him, or you'll answer to the rest of us." She glared at him. "I doubt that it occurred to him that you would just up and leave without a word, after we saved your life."

The hairs rose on the back of Morgan's neck. "I did not ask you to help me."

"You came to us, didn't you?" She gestured about her eloquently. "We haven't much to spare, nothing at all for outsiders, but we accepted you. Who else would have done that? You owe us more than running away like a whipped cur."

Obligation. Morgan stared across the grounds and at the freedom beyond, so rapidly slipping from his grasp. "You think . . . there is a reason that I came," he said, pitching his voice in mockery.

"I know there is."

"There is no reason for anything that happens."

"You really believe that, don't you?" She shook her head. "Whatever you are, wherever you came from, I think there is some honor in you, or you would already be gone. That's why you are going to help us."

He met her gaze, and she took one step back. "You play a dangerous game."

"You don't frighten me. I've seen too much."

She was a little afraid, but she hid it well. He felt the first stirrings of grudging respect, as he had felt fear of bonds that had nothing to do with prison walls.

"I have nothing to give you," he said harshly.

"But you do. You have something very valuable. We make our living by showing people things they've never seen before. And you are something very few people have seen."

"You want me to . . . go on display?" The idea was so absurd that it erased both doubt and fear. He turned to go.

Her hand caught at him. His first impulse was to remove it by the swiftest means possible, regardless of the damage to her. He held himself rigid instead, and growled.

"I can't let you go. Not until you promise to meet the people who helped you."

Morgan recognized the trap, and that he must pay a price to escape it. He gave the girl a terse nod. The language of her body told him that she had not been sure he would agree and knew full well that she could not stop him. She ducked into the tent and reemerged with his blanket.

"Put this on," she said, "and come with me."

He took the blanket and draped it over his shoulders. Caitlin marched across the camp toward the nearest tent. People called out greetings in the twilight, voices warm with friendship. Morgan hunched into his blanket and deafened himself to Caitlin's cheery responses. They were not his friends, and neither was she.

They reached a tent as shabby and patched as the others, and Caitlin lifted the flap. "Go on inside," she said.

He hesitated. Three distinct and familiar human scents permeated the air. This was yet another trap, another way to hold him.

"Don't worry," Caitlin said. "You could break Ulysses in two if you wanted, and Florizel is harmless. As for Tamar—" She shrugged.

Morgan tried to lay back ears that remained stubbornly fixed in place and entered the tent.

Two men sat at a pair of folding chairs on either side of a small table, intent on a game of cards. One of them was of average size, but his skin was pale as the moon, and his hair the same ghostly hue.

The other was the height of a child, legs dangling well above the ground. He was dressed impeccably in proportioned trousers, vest, and coat, all made of what Morgan guessed to be expensive cloth. His boots shone with recent polishing. His features were handsome, his thick yellow hair the sort that any dandy might envy. But nature had shaped his body into a parody of a normal man's.

Behind them stood a woman of overwhelming sensuality, lushly curved and with skin that shimmered as if imbedded with a hundred tiny gemstones. Her thick black hair fell almost to her waist. A pair of snakes wound about her shoulders and upper arms, tongues darting.

The serpent woman stared at Morgan with dark, glittering eyes. At the table, the albino threw down his hand of cards with a breath of disgust.

"Don't even attempt to deny it, Wakefield. You let me win again."

The little man lifted his brows. "You need not play if you find it unpleasant," he said in a smooth Southern drawl. "I do apologize if I have offended."

The albino snorted and looked toward Morgan. Wakefield followed his glance.

"Ah," he said. "I see that our patient has recovered." He slid down from his chair. Caitlin went to his side, her slight form towering above him.

"Ulysses, this is Morgan Holt. Morgan Holt, this is Ulysses Marcus Aurelius Wakefield."

The dwarf executed a surprisingly graceful bow. "I am at your service, sir."

Caitlin shook her head. "Your Southern courtesy is wasted on this one, Professor."

"Indeed. And you, of course, have not in any way provoked him, Firefly."

Caitlin snorted. She glanced at the dark woman. "This is Tamar, the snake charmer. And Florizel"—she indicated the pale man with a nod—"is our chief Joey. That's 'clown' in towny talk."

Florizel regarded Morgan with mournful wariness. "This is your Wolf-Man?" he said. "This is our final hope, our savior?"

"Florizel, you talk too much," Caitlin said.

"I do not believe that this is the time for familial squabbles," Ulysses said. He looked up at Morgan with the same fearlessness as Caitlin's, but his came from a deeper, quieter place. He was as removed from passion as Morgan sought to be.

"It is unfortunate that we were unable to consult your wishes, Mr. Holt," he said, "but you were insensible at the time. Caitlin is prone to strong feelings—premonitions, if you will—that move her to rash action. She often fails to apply logic when it would be most useful. She sees your particular talent as a possible solution to our quandary—which you may have observed."

"She wants me to work for you," Morgan said. "To be one of your . . . freaks."

"To be one of us," Ulysses corrected. "You were alone and on the verge of death when you arrived. Have you somewhere else to go?"

"I prefer to be alone." Even as he spoke, Morgan did not understand why he had admitted that much to a stranger. He lifted his lip. "I am alone."

"It is a rare man who truly prefers solitude," Ulysses said. "As for Caitlin's hopes—many of the troupers have no home other than this. It is their family. Harry took in the first outcast ten years ago, and he has never turned away anyone in need. But our troupe has faced one misfortune after another in recent months—theft of our capital, the illness of our horses, and grave mishaps of weather. We have insufficient resources to feed ourselves and nothing saved for winter quarters. We are now in a precarious position that may require us to disband if we wish to survive. You, with your unique gift, appear to have arrived at a most propitious moment."

Morgan thought of his adopted pack, all dead, and what it had been like to be part of a greater whole. Yet he had always been separate, even then. Always.

"I can't save you," he said. "Let me go."

Ulysses studied Morgan for a long stretch of silence. "You are what they call a hard man, Morgan Holt, one who has lived apart from civilization for some time. You are accustomed to caring for yourself. You are exceptionally skilled in survival. You do not care for the entanglements of emotion, and that is why you resent any debt placed upon you. Yet you still suffer the pull of obligation. Why?"

Morgan felt as if he were being taken apart piece by piece like the inner workings of a clock. "You are smart, little man," he said softly. "But you don't know everything."

"I believe you are a man of honor, Mr. Holt, though the world may not recognize that quality." His broad brow creased. "You have faced some great trial that has tested your faith in mankind and driven you into the wilderness. But now you find yourself among those who might begin to understand."

Words. Accurate words, razor sharp, that wove themselves into a wire made for a single purpose. The noose was tightening inch by inch. Morgan backed away, prepared to toss the blanket and run. Caitlin held out her hand as if to stay him again, and for once she appeared as vulnerable as any other girl of her age.

Morgan took another step and struck a warm, firm surface. Hands caught at him to steady him. He spun about to face Harry French, who held a bottle of whiskey in one broad, chapped hand. The old man blinked in surprise.

"You should not be on your feet," he said. He looked beyond Morgan to the others. "Caitlin, why did you let him get up? You are pale, my boy, much too pale."

"Mr. Holt is leaving us, Harry," Caitlin said.

Harry's face fell, and it was as if the sun had gone behind a cloud. "Oh, I see. I see."

The disappointment on this old man's face pierced Morgan's dormant heart more surely than any of Caitlin's reproaches or Ulysses's recital of disaster. For a moment he saw his father's face, and the dying of dreams. The end of all hope.

"Well, well," Harry said, trying to smile, "we must at least share a drink before you depart. I did, as you see, manage to find one bottle."

"The only one left," Caitlin said. "Don't waste it, Harry."

"We place no price on kindness, Caitlin." He set the bottle down on the small table and drew a pair of glasses from his coat. "Let us drink to your recovery, Mr. Holt—and to your continuing good health." He poured and offered Morgan the first glass.

Morgan stared down at it. Had he been able to stomach the stuff, he could not have swallowed it down past the lump in his throat. "I don't drink."

"Ah. Very admirable." Harry lifted his own glass, gazed at it wistfully, and set it back down. "There is no escaping our troubles in the bottle, no, indeed."

Morgan turned his face away. Harry patted his shoulder.

"Think nothing of it, my boy. We asked too much of a stranger. But you must not go until morning, after you have had a good meal—"

Morgan shook him off and strode out of the tent. He walked blindly across the lot, shivering though he did not feel the evening chill. He stopped at the edge of the camp, let the blanket fall, and willed the Change. His body protested, but it obeyed. He began to run to the hills.

The low woodland of pinon, juniper, and oak closed in about him, and the voices of the circus folk became the distant cries of birds. Thick fur rippled and flowed about his body. Small game fled before him. His broad paws devoured the miles. The sky lit his path with a thousand stars. The clean air sang to him. Human voices, human thoughts were left in the dust of his passing. Far, far to the north, the wolves called him to the old life of forgetfulness.

He had made it over the first range of pine-clad hills and into the adjoining valley before the tether snapped him to a stop. He raged and fought it, but it pulled him southward, back across the mountains step by reluctant step.

He had never taken charity, nor become dependent upon anyone. He was whole, but only because *they* had made him so. His body was free, but not his heart. Not so long as the debt remained unpaid.

Obligation was not belonging. It did not mean friendship, or love, or any of the worthless words men used so freely. It did not bind him forever.

He would make his pact, serve out his time, and leave without regret.

Sunset was driving shadows down into the valley when he reached the woods above the camp. He sensed the wrongness at once, and the alien scents of strangers. Cries came faintly from the cluster of wagons and tents. Morgan set off at a fast run down the hillside.

The handful of men who were causing the trouble might have been rowdies from the nearest town, grubstakers who had lost their claims, or even desperados from over the New Mexico border. They, like wolves, would attack where they saw weakness, but they took joy in the tormenting.

One brawny fellow staggered under Caitlin's insignificant weight while she pummeled his head and shoulders; Harry was wringing his hands and shouting warnings from the sidelines, and the oversized trouper, Tor, had two of the other townies by their collars. The fourth invader held Ulysses Wakefield suspended in his arms.

"Sir," Ulysses said with impeccable dignity, "You are mistaken if you believe that we have anything worth stealing. I have no wish for violence."

"Violence!" the ruffian spat. "Why, you li'l speck—"

Morgan plunged among them and seized Ulysses's tormenter around the ankle. Teeth pierced wool and flesh. The man yelped and dropped the dwarf. Ulysses curled into a tumble and jumped to his feet, brushing off his clothing. His eyes met Morgan's. He nodded, slowly, unsmiling.

Morgan wheeled about on his hind feet and went for Caitlin's opponent.

"Wolf!" the first man cried. "It's a wolf!" Like the coward he was, he took off as fast as his limp would allow. Caitlin leaped from her adversary's back, and he dashed after his fellow. Tor's two captives picked themselves off the ground and followed suit. Morgan let them go.

"That should teach them," Caitlin said, slapping the dust from her hands. She eyed Morgan. "About time you showed up."

From all parts of the camp, the other troupers gathered close against the night. Children ran from the tents, whooping at the excitement as their parents scolded them. Morgan stood at the center of the loose circle, as alien as he had ever been, and Changed.

There were a few gasps, and murmurs, and one exclamation. No one fled. Harry, Caitlin, and Ulysses drew near, with Tamar close behind. Moonlight silvered the skin of the snake charmer, unearthly in her beauty, whose creatures coiled and rustled about her shoulders.

"So it is true," she said, looking at Caitlin. "He is what you claimed."

"And he can save us, Tamar. He is one of us."

"He is one of us," Ulysses repeated gravely.

"Welcome," Harry said, clapping Morgan on his bare shoulder. "Welcome and thanks, my boy. Your return was most timely indeed." He rubbed his hands and beamed at them all. "My dears, I think it is best if we move on straightaway. If one band of ruffians has discovered us, others may as well. We have much to prepare now that our new friend has joined us, new towns to conquer." His eyes lit up like a child's. "The Wolf-Man," he said. "We have much to do!"

Tamar slipped closer to Morgan. The patches of scaly skin on her bare arms winked and glistened. "Will you share my wagon tonight, Wolf-Man?"

Caitlin snorted. The twined snakes on Tamar's shoulders reared up.

Ulysses stepped between them. "Mr. Holt can, I believe, decide for himself."

"I'll walk," Morgan said. He met Harry's gaze. "I owe you a debt. I will repay it."

"I know you will, dear boy. Your generosity—"

"I am neither generous nor honorable. I don't want your thanks. I don't want anything from any of you."

"Someday," Caitlin said, "you'll need someone, Morgan Holt. I hope I'm there when it happens."

She marched away toward the tents, and the others followed. Morgan remained where they had left him, listening to the snap of canvas, the stamps and snorts of the horses, and the soft calls of the troupers and crew as they broke camp. He made himself blind to the stars that had been his only roof for so many years, deaf to the summons of the wilderness and the deep terror in his heart.

Someday you'll need someone.

Never. Never again.

Chapter 3

COLORADO SPRINGS, OCTOBER 1880

"Is it real?"

"It can't be. These circus people know every trick there is. Born thieves and swindlers, all of 'em."

The two farmers stood a few feet away from the bars of the cage, just near enough to feel daring. The older one, a frayed bit of straw between his teeth, gave a knowing nod.

"Purest fakery, all of it, take my word." He spat into the trampled straw at his feet.

"Maybe you're right," the younger hayseed said, "but it sure looks real to me." He grinned slyly. "You want to go in there and find out?"

"They won't let no one in there."

"Then just put your hand up to the bar. See what it does."

The milling crowd between the two men shouted mocking encouragement. "Go on!" a store clerk urged. "Stick your hand in and see what happens!"

The farmer glared. "I ain't here for your amusement—" He jumped back with a cry as Morgan lunged at the bars, baring his teeth for effect. The farmer's companion fell onto his knees and crawled away among the feet of the observers. Within seconds, the crowd was abuzz with delight and terror, pressed as far toward the rear of the tent as they could go.

"B'God, it *is* real!"

"Don't you dare swear, Cal!" a woman cried. "It's a minion of the Devil himself!"

"Aw, it's just a man in a fur suit . . ."

Morgan stalked the length of the cage and back again, curling clawed fingers in menacing fashion, and retreated to his corner. Some foolhardy soul poked a stick through the bars; he snapped it in two with a casual swipe of a hand. A lady shrieked and pretended to swoon. He had seen it all a hundred times.

One of the sideshow talkers arrived to herd the townies to the next attraction and on to the big tent for the show. Once again The Terrifying Wolf-Man was a spectacular success.

Morgan released his hold on the Change and let himself become human again. He had grown used to the discomfort that accompanied the unnatural half-shaping, but it was only after the performance that he felt the ache deep in his bones and muscles.

Stiff and sore, he let himself out of the cage and shrugged into his dressing gown. He splashed his face with water as if he could wash away the stares of the humans, the constant smell of their bodies crammed into the small tent day after day. Always the same ritual, the same contempt, the same resolution.

Tomorrow. Tomorrow I'll go. I've done enough.

He laughed and pushed wet hair away from his face. He'd let it grow until it reached his shoulders, heavy and wild like a wolf's pelt. He meant it to remind him of who he was, and who he was not.

He stripped off the dressing gown and pulled on a shirt and

trousers. Nearly five months he had been with the circus. Five months, and Harry had said just yesterday that the troupe had enough money saved to set up in winter quarters without the risk of disbanding.

Thanks to the Wolf-Man, whose fearsome reputation had preceded the circus in every town, village, and fly-speck camp they'd visited. It didn't matter that French's Fantastic Family Circus was still a modest wagon show, sunable to compete in grandeur with the great Barnum or Forepaugh. Each farmer or rancher, merchant, or whore—young and old, male and female, simple or smart—had to see for himself if the creature was real, or as fake as the farmer had claimed. Some came back two or three times. None of them ever learned the truth.

They didn't want to. And Morgan endured their ignorant speculation and taunted them with his poses and snarls. He had learned to be amused at the blindness of men.

The troupers were equally blind. They had accepted him completely, welcoming him as if he had always lived among them, but he had done for them all he was capable of doing.

Tomorrow, I go.

He rinsed the sour taste from his mouth and walked out into the night. Beyond the lanterns that marked the perimeter of the circus grounds lay a swathe of darkness, and beyond that the lights and bustle of Colorado Springs. The cries and applause of the audience in the big top drowned out the murmur of crickets and the soughing of the wind in the cottonwoods along the creek. Every night he stood and listened, poised to run from everything he despised.

I could leave now, he thought. But he remained where he was, turning his face to the north where men held sway. He had not gone into town since the troupe's arrival three days ago; he never slept in the cheap hotel rooms shared by the troupe's top performers when they could find such accommodations.

But it was not Colorado Springs that drew his attention northward instead of west into the mountains. Instinct, the only part of himself he dared trust, whispered in a lost and unlamented tongue.

You are not alone, it said.

He shivered violently, as if the words were raindrops to be shaken from his coat. He had been alone since he'd left home at fourteen. In all his years of searching for Aaron Holt, there had never been another like him or his mother or sister.

You cannot hide forever.

He snarled and turned south, toward the big top. For once safety lay in the crowd, where the voices of his past did not reach. He strode past loitering townies along the midway and entered the pad room where the troupers dressed and prepared for their entrance. The smell of human bodies assaulted him once more. The crowd roared approval as the clowns completed their performance.

"Is it tonight, then?"

Morgan looked down at Ulysses, who still wore his scholar's robes and mortarboard. The "Little Professor" was, according to the sideshow talker, both the smallest and most brilliant man on earth. He could answer any question, and sometimes made remarkably accurate judgments of character. Morgan knew that only too well.

Morgan showed his teeth in a half-smile. "Reading my mind, Professor?"

"Not at all. Simple logic and observation." He flipped back the sleeves of his robes. "Our finances appear to be in good order. You have achieved what you set out to do. Your debt to us is paid, is it not?"

Us. It was always us, the troupers against the world, and Morgan just outside the circle. He wanted it that way.

"Harry would be most disappointed if you failed to bid him farewell." Ulysses removed the oversized cap with its gold tassel and held it between his manicured hands. "Caitlin, as well."

By unspoken consent, they both moved to the back door, the trouper's entrance, to get a better view of the big top's interior. Caitlin was just beginning her act, balanced gracefully atop the bare back of one of her well-trained gray geldings as it cantered around the ring. With each circling, Caitlin somersaulted over banners held by her assistants, landing perfectly each time. Her bare feet, blessed with remarkably flexible toes, never lost their grip. Red hair bounced above a laughing face.

"Caitlin cannot understand your desire for solitude," Ulysses said. "She, more than any of us, has kept the troupe together. But you have no ties to bind you here. You do not seek a home among others like yourself."

"There are no others like me."

Ulysses raised his brows. "While it is true that I have never observed a second member of your species, I theorize that you do have kin somewhere—family—who share your gifts."

It was not the first time that Ulysses had tried to pry into Morgan's past. If anyone had the right to ask, he did. The two of them shared living quarters, and Ulysses's dispassionate nature suited Morgan's desire for privacy.

Morgan grudgingly admired the little man's detachment from the scourge of emotion. But Ulysses had one besetting flaw, and that was his curiosity. On more than one occasion, that persistent quest for knowledge had pierced Morgan's careful guard.

"I have no family," he said. "Do not feel sorry for me, Professor. I don't need what you and the others want."

"But you have changed," Ulysses said. "Whether or not you wish to admit it, you are different from the man who came to us months ago. Harry and Caitlin saw it in you from the beginning."

"Saw what? That I could be tamed like a dog to a leash? Men will sooner kill each other than give up any part of what they are."

"Men will fight for what they believe in. What do you believe, my friend?"

"That a man who trusts anyone but himself is a fool."

"Perhaps. But to be a fool is better than to be without hope."

"The way you cling to the hope that your family will take you back?"

Such small cruelties were usually enough to stop anyone fool enough to demand amiable fellowship from Morgan Holt. Ulysses was made of stronger stuff.

"Touché," he said. "Pope said that fools rush in where angels fear to tread, and neither of us is an angel." He turned to go, just as the applause of the crowd marked the end of Caitlin's act.

Cursing himself, Morgan stepped in front of the little man. "Damn you," he said softly. "You should leave me alone, Professor."

Ulysses gave him one of his rare and wistful smiles. "Even wise men can be fools in friendship. Alas, notwithstanding my family's disappointment in me, they raised me to be a gentleman."

"And I am not. I belong with the wolves. Not here."

"We all, at one time or another, doubt where we belong. If you will excuse me—"

"I am—" Morgan still had not learned how to apologize without the words sticking in his throat. "I was too harsh."

Ulysses bowed. "It is no matter. And now I have letters to write."

"Your family?"

"A gentleman's duty, I fear."

"Even though they never answer."

"They are family," Ulysses said. "One will do much for family that one will not for a stranger."

The old pain could sometimes catch Morgan unaware, as it did now. "I prefer to remain a stranger."

"Sometimes that choice is made for you, regardless of your inclinations. But if you choose to leave us tonight, do not forget us."

This time Morgan let him go. He had never yet won a debate with Ulysses Marcus Aurelius Wakefield.

"He has feelings also, you know."

Caitlin walked up beside him, dabbing at her face with a cloth. Her bare arms, neck, and face were moist with perspiration, and tendrils of her hair clung to her cheek. The barking of Vico's trick dogs in the ring signaled the beginning of the next act.

Morgan watched the canines' antics with faint contempt, remembering how Vico had tried to convince him to play tame wolf among the curs. "The Professor can take care of himself."

"Is that why you always stick to him like a burr whenever we go among the townies?"

"The Professor is right. Your imagination does run away with you."

"You are a terrible liar. You'd rather die than admit you care for anyone, or anything."

"And why should he admit that to you?" As silent as her serpents, Tamar appeared beside them. "You try to change him into something he is not." The snake charmer's heavy-lidded eyes swept over Morgan. "It is not a mistake I make."

Morgan took a careful step back. Tamar had a unique power of her own—to fascinate nearly every man who came within her grasp. She was tall, lithe, and beautiful, despite the coldness of her eyes. The lilt of her exotic accent worked like venom mixed in honeyed wine. No towny knew that the luxurious wig of raven-black tresses concealed a head as smooth as snakeskin. Most of her suitors would not have cared. They were smitten.

But all of them, towny or trouper, she ignored . . . save Morgan. He avoided her, and so she pursued all the more relentlessly.

She slid close to him, running her supple hand the length of his arm. "You are weary, my friend. Leave these who do not understand. Come to my tent, and I will soothe your brow with scented oils and sing ancient songs of love."

Only a dead man could fail to be aware of the sexuality Tamar exuded with every whispered word, every motion. The circus folk were no Puritans, but he ignored the few invitations he received. To take a trouper as a lover, even casually, meant stronger ties with the circus. He preferred the anonymity of women who sold their services for a price.

Even so, he was tempted. His body was hungry for the release it had been denied so long. Sex was touching without true intimacy, pleasure without commitment—not as it was among the wolves. Tamar might be satisfied to know she had conquered him, if only for a night.

A slow smile curved Tamar's lips. Her hands left his arm and wandered lower. He flinched. She laughed under her breath.

"My poor, poor wolf. You are sick. Tamar can ease your pain." She cupped him boldly. "No one understands you as I do. Come, my fine stallion. We will ride fast and far."

Caitlin made a rude noise, jerking Morgan from his daze. "The man who wrote about the subtlety of serpents cannot have been thinking of you, Tamar."

"And no man would want you," she hissed. "You stink of horses. You are shaped like a stick. Morgan would not have you if you begged him."

"Morgan is my friend." Caitlin cast Morgan an apologetic look. "I don't seduce my friends."

"I do not think you are a woman at all. Why don't you find another girl to play with?"

"That is hardly an insult worthy of you, Tamar. Where's the poison in your tongue?"

Morgan growled. Two pairs of feminine eyes fixed on him, and Tamar shut her mouth. Caitlin folded her arms across her chest and started to speak.

"Be quiet," he said. "If you want to fight, wait until I am gone."

"Gone?" Caitlin repeated.

"I'm leaving tonight."

Tamar clutched his arm. He shook off her grasp and met Caitlin's stricken gaze. "The Professor said I should tell you before I go."

"How very kind of you. How gentlemanly."

"I never claimed to be either. I have repaid the debt—"

"And now you go on your merry way without a thought for what you're leaving behind."

"I made no promises."

"Good riddance, then."

"You are strong, Firefly. The strong survive."

"If you don't say good-bye to Harry, I will hunt you down and kill you myself."

"I would be a fool to risk your anger."

"You would never make a good clown, Morgan Holt," she said, tears thick in her throat. "Go on. *Go.*" She ran back into the big top as the band struck up the finale.

He obeyed before she could change her mind. Tamar had already slipped out of the pad room, for which he was profoundly grateful. But he hadn't come away unscathed. The unfamiliar, bitter taste of regret burned on his tongue.

This was sadness. Guilt. He had let himself grow too close to Caitlin—and to Ulysses, and Harry. There was still one final ordeal ahead.

He waited by himself at the edge of the lot until the stream of townies emerging from the big top heralded the end of the show. Laughter and excited chatter dwindled and faded, only a few children lingering to catch a final glimpse of the freaks by moonlight. The rest drifted past the ticket wagon, down the midway and toward the town lights.

The performers came next—Florizel and the clowns, Vico with his dogs, Caitlin and her assistants leading the horses to their pickets, Regina the bird-boned rope-walker, Tor the strong man, and all the others. They left the tent singly or in small groups, each to his or her own wagon or tent. The roustabouts and crew would work through the night to tear down the big top and prepare the troupe for departure before dawn.

But even the rest would not sleep. It was a time for celebration, because at last the troupe could afford to take up winter quarters and rest until spring without fear of disbanding or starvation. The "freaks" of French's Fantastic Family Circus would keep their beloved home and sanctuary for another year.

And Morgan would abandon it as he had every other home he had ever known.

The last, solitary figure to leave the big top moved with the deliberation of a man who suffered the aches of old age and believed no one was watching. Morgan skirted the edge of the lot and paused just outside of Harry's tent until he heard the sound of pouring liquid and a satisfied sigh.

Bloodshot brown eyes looked up as Morgan entered. Harry set down his glass, and his snowy moustache lifted in a grin.

"My dear boy," he said. "Pull up a stool. I believe that we can call our final performance in Colorado Springs yet another triumph, don't you agree?" He lifted his bottle. "Perhaps tonight? No, no, of course not." He took another swallow and smacked his lips. "All the more for me!"

Morgan ducked his head. In many ways this was the most difficult, this farewell. Caitlin was not naive, in spite of her small size and pixie's face. Ulysses was too pragmatic to believe that Morgan would stay. But Harry . . . Harry French was still a child, unaffected by the punishing hand of experience.

"It's all thanks to you, of course," Harry continued. "We have already found a lovely spot for winter quarters, in Texas. Far better than the old one in Ohio. We will all have plenty of rest and time to improve our acts." He chuckled. "No point in confining ourselves to the smallest towns. All we need do is take care to avoid direct competition with the big outfits. We may not be large, but we have the finest attractions in the west!"

"Harry—"

"Yes? Did you say something, my boy?"

Morgan steeled himself. "I am leaving, Harry."

Harry grew very quiet. He set down his glass. "Well, well. We knew this day would come, didn't we? Though I had hoped—"

"I am . . . grateful for what you did," Morgan said. His voice sounded rough and harsh, and he made an effort to soften it. "You know that gratitude does not . . . come easy to me."

"Ah, yes. Yes, I know." He gave a small laugh that blew out his whiskers. "That makes it so much more important when you give it."

"Don't, Harry. I am not worth . . . this—"

"Feeling?" Harry didn't raise his eyes. "Feelings are difficult for you. I know that, too. You are a man of few words, and yet . . ." He looked up, tears in his eyes. "I do not believe you are a man of no sentiment. Otherwise you would not have come to make your farewells."

"You see what you wish to see."

"My eyes are old and weak, but some things one sees with the heart. In some ways, for all your abilities, you are blind, my son."

"Do not call me that."

Harry flinched from his snarl but remained where he was. "Forgive an old fool, Morgan. I have made it a policy never to seek into the pasts of my people, and I have broken that rule with you. I only wish . . . that I might convince you that you are a better man than you think."

Morgan's temples had begun to throb. The hair on the back of his neck stood up at the premonition of disaster. "I came to say good-bye, and to . . . thank you." He backed toward the tent's entrance and stood awkwardly for a final second, despising his hesitation, and strode from the tent.

He got no farther than the foot of the hills. He had not Changed. His heart weighed him down, cold and smothering like a heavy snowfall. He would have welcomed a strong snow now. It would disperse the scents of those he left behind, and draw a veil between the world and the wordless silence of the wild.

The solitude. The loneliness. A howl built in the back of his throat, the only sound of grief he could make.

But the snow did not answer his summons. The sense of wrongness he had felt in Harry's tent had grown. An evil scent wafted up from the prairie, the acrid smell of smoke.

He turned to face the east. A roiling cloud rose from the circus lot far below. Something very large was burning.

He ran more swiftly than any human, bare feet finding purchase on loose pebbles and sharp rock. The smoke curled inside his lungs and stung his skin. Soon the light of a towering fire obscured the moon and stars. By the time he reached the lot he had to force his way through the crowd of onlookers drawn by the spectacle of a large and destructive blaze.

Flames devoured what was left of the big top, and several other tents and wagons were burning as well. Troupers stood about in forlorn knots, helpless, as the local volunteer fire department struggled to extinguish the conflagration.

But the damage had been done. The prop wagons had been among those destroyed, along with a number of tents and most of Harry's office wagon—the one that held the troupe's wages and savings.

Sifting subtler scents from the overwhelming stench of smoldering ash, Morgan found his way to Harry.

The old man was not alone. Caitlin and Ulysses stood with him. Firelight picked out the grief on each upturned face. All the progress the troupe had made since Morgan's coming had been undone in an hour.

"Harry," he said.

The old man turned, his eyes wells of misery. "Morgan?"

"You've come back?" Caitlin asked. Her face broke into a broad grin. "You couldn't abandon us, not now. Not ever." She flung herself at him and embraced him tightly. Morgan endured the touch in stoic silence.

Harry's eyes met his over Caitlin's head. "You are a good man, Morgan Holt."

Caitlin stepped back and wiped at her face with her coatsleeve. "What do we do next, Harry?"

He looked at the billows of smoke that rose from the dying fire. "We continue, as we always have. We find a way to go on, even if we must perform through the winter."

"We go on," Caitlin agreed. "And we stay together."

Ulysses moved to Morgan's side. "I hope that Caitlin does not suffer a grave disappointment," he said softly. "It is much worse than Harry admits."

"I know."

"You are remaining with us?"

"I will stay. I have no choice, do I?"

"I sometimes wonder," Ulysses said, "if Caitlin is not right, and there is a reason for such events—one beyond our understanding."

"Then whoever makes such reasons has no love for me—or you."

" 'The heart has its reasons which reason knows not of.' "

"You are a fraud, Professor," Morgan said. "You still listen to your heart."

"And you do not?"

Morgan turned on his heel and walked away.

Chapter 4

The fire had drawn Niall, though he might have missed it had he not left his hotel for a late-night stroll. Colorado Springs was not so great a town to ignore a good-sized conflagration, especially when it was burning up a visiting circus.

So Niall followed the crowds to the outskirts of town, where most of the blaze had already been extinguished. He had not seen the circus perform, preoccupied as he had been with the business he had recently completed in New Mexico, but he recognized disaster when he saw it. He watched with detached curiosity as the circus people ran to and fro, gesticulating and crying out as some new loss was discovered.

He could almost pity them. His father had suffered such setbacks in his early years of business in Denver, but he had persevered and overcome them. He had been daring and ruthless as well as shrewd, as one had to be in these times. Niall had carried on in his footsteps. The Munroe fortune had doubled in the seven years since Niall had taken control.

But he had started with an advantage. These people, vagrants and mountebanks, lived on the edge of ruin. He doubted any of them would accept a decent, steady job in place of the life they lived.

Once he had considered the wandering life himself. Once he'd had no thought of the future beyond the next five minutes. Athena had paid for his folly. Now he spent every day trying to make it right. And failing.

He pushed his hands into the pockets of his greatcoat and remembered his last conversation with Athena. *"Where did you get your hard heart, Niall?"*

She simply could not understand. How could she, sheltered as she was? And he intended to keep her that way. She had no conception of the dangers of the world, the cruelties it held for a young woman foolish enough to believe she could change it.

Niall sighed and looked at the stars, visible now that the smoke had begun to clear. When was the last time he had glanced up to notice the constellations, or walked for the sake of walking? He took for granted what Athena was unable to do, because of him.

Well, now he had an opportunity to prove Athena wrong about the nature of his heart, if he chose to take it.

He dropped his gaze and followed a lone figure as it crossed the lot with a purposeful stride. One of the performers. A woman—by no means curvaceous, almost childlike—but graceful nonetheless. In fact, the way she moved was arresting, and he found himself staring after her when she disappeared into one of the undamaged tents.

It wasn't until he was almost there that he realized he had been walking toward that very tent. He stopped, considering retreat. This was not his world, or his business.

But his sudden impulse to help demanded that he find someone to accept his generosity. He pulled his wallet from his pocket and examined the contents. A hundred dollars would be more than adequate.

A head poked through the tent flap. It was crowned by an untidy cap of curly red hair, and the face beneath was attached to the young woman he had followed.

She stared at him, nonplussed. He tipped his hat.

"Forgive me," he said, "but have I the pleasure of addressing one of the performers of this establishment?"

The girl burst into laughter. "You talk like Ulysses. Who are you?"

It was his turn to be taken aback. That she could laugh at such a time amazed him, but her bluntness was astounding.

"I beg your pardon," he said. "My name is Niall Munroe. I could not help but notice the damage you have suffered as the result of the fire—"

"Did you?" She stepped fully from the tent, and he got his first good look at her. His initial impression had been correct: she was slight, boyishly slim in an oversized coat, and elfin in size and bearing, but her eyes were bright and her smile dazzling. "And why should you care, Niall Munroe?"

Indeed. He thought once more of walking away, but her eyes held him rooted to the spot. "I had thought to offer my assistance," he said stiffly, "but if you have no use for it, Miss—"

"Hughes. Caitlin Hughes. And I still wonder why a towny should care what happens to people like us."

Towny. She spoke the word like an epithet. He drew himself up to his considerably greater height. "In Denver, it is customary for the fortunate to assist those who are less so. When I noted the degree of your misfortune, I hardly thought that you would be likely to reject any offer of help."

"Oh." She widened her eyes. "I understand. You are a very rich man from the big city, and you wish to give us charity."

He slammed his hat back on his head. "I see I have offended you, so I will be on my way—"

"No. Wait." She bit her full lower lip and sighed. "I'm—we are not very used to townies offering help. Most of the time, they—" She broke off. "You'll have to speak to Harry."

"Harry?"

"He is the manager and owner. I'm sure he'd be very happy to see you, Mr. Munroe."

He had the absurd desire to ask her to call him Niall. "I would be obliged, Miss Hughes."

She flushed, raising freckles on her pale skin. He wondered again how he could possibly find such a ragamuffin attractive.

Caitlin looked up the long, slim length of the gentleman and cursed herself for an idiot. She knew as well as anyone that the troupe was in dire straits, even if she pretended otherwise for Harry's sake. If some towny wanted to offer help, who was she to say no? Even if all of the alarm bells in her head were going off at once.

Yet, she had to admit, this fellow was no ordinary towny. He was dressed like someone with a great deal of money. He carried himself like a prince. He was handsome, in a cold sort of way. And he looked at her with a strange intensity she couldn't ignore.

Morgan had that intensity. But when *he* looked at her, she saw only a friend. She felt no prickling in her belly, nor heat in her cheeks.

"I'll tell him that you have come," she said, retreating quickly into the tent.

"Back so soon?" Harry said, looking up from the chaos of ledgers and papers he had salvaged from the office wagon. His face was drawn and haggard. "What is it, Firefly?"

"There is a man outside—a towny—who . . . well, as peculiar as it seems, he wishes to help us."

"Indeed?" Harry pursued his lips. "That is peculiar. Well, send him in, by all means!"

Caitlin nodded and went outside to Niall Munroe. He was fidgeting, something she hadn't expected to see in such a dignified gentleman. It made him seem more human, somehow.

"Harry—Mr. French—will see you now," she said.

"Thank you." He nodded and stepped into the tent.

Caitlin waited outside, pacing back and forth. The scent of burnt canvas and wood was choking, but the tingling in her nerves only heightened her hope. Could Niall Munroe's appearance be yet another miracle? Several months ago, she'd been certain that Morgan had been meant to come when he did. Now her intuition was telling her the same thing of the gentleman stranger.

Your intuition, or something much more physical?

She shook her head in self-disgust, but waited out the long hour while Munroe consulted with Harry. Munroe emerged at last, settled his hat on his head, and buttoned his coat against the night's chill. He did not seem surprised to find her still there.

"Good-night, Miss Hughes," he said. "We shall meet again."

She flushed at his bow and looked elsewhere until he was some distance across the lot and headed toward town. Harry appeared a moment later.

"You will not believe this, my dear, but we are saved yet again!"

"Saved?" she murmured.

"That gentleman, Mr. Munroe, has offered us an engagement in Denver, a private performance for his family's orphanage. The Munroes are very important people in Colorado—I have heard of them myself. They are extremely wealthy and influential. Mr. Munroe's sister is quite a central figure in Denver society and does much good work. He wishes to contribute to her charities in a most novel way. He has agreed to replace our tents, provide us with a lot on land he owns, and pay us very well indeed. So well, in fact, that it will more than make up for this night's losses."

"So much?" Caitlin could no longer see Munroe's form, yet she continued to search against all reason. "It is so late in the season—"

"One last performance, and then we may have enough to winter over as we had planned. How can we turn down such an opportunity?"

We can't. Of course we can't. Yet Caitlin felt a wild see-sawing of dread and anticipation, as if she were attempting a new and very dangerous stunt.

"When are we to leave?" she asked.

"As soon as we can be ready. I shall call the troupers together at dawn and share the good news." He clasped his hands. "Ah, it has turned out to be a much better night than events would suggest! Who knows where such patronage might lead?"

Indeed. Harry always found the good in everything, but she felt the same sense of anticipation.

Of one thing she was certain. Their lives were about to change—hers, Morgan's, everyone's. She couldn't begin to guess where those changes were leading, but Fate had intervened with a vengeance.

After tonight, nothing would be the same again.

The tall, familiar figure strode up the drive, and Athena rolled away from the parlor windows to face the door. Niall had come home.

He had been gone a very long four months. Strange that in spite of their last argument, she had missed him terribly. Not even the constant social and philanthropic commitments had been completely successful in easing her loneliness.

When did it begin? she asked herself, listening for the door and Brinkley's greeting. *When did I become . . . dissatisfied?*

She could not pinpoint the precise day or date, but the feeling of emptiness had been growing, and it troubled her. She had spent wasted hours looking out the window at her friends and neighbors walking and riding in the crisp autumn air, and remembering what it had been like to kick at piles of leaves and dash across the park on a high-spirited horse.

But her friends and fellow Society members had been as attentive as always in their visits, just as generous in their contributions. The orphans and poor folk still responded to her visits with solemn gratitude. There was no good reason for her disaffection.

Surely it was the change of seasons that made her feel so restless. Now that Niall was back, those troublesome emotions would dissipate. His opposition to much of her work might even fire a renewed determination. Yes, that was what she needed—fresh inspiration, something to fight for.

The front door opened. Brinkley's voice welcomed his employer home, and Niall's footsteps echoed in the vestibule.

Athena sat up straight and had her best smile ready for him when he walked into the parlor. She held out her hands.

"Niall, welcome home! It is so wonderful to have you back."

He bent to take her hands and kissed them. "Athena. You are looking well—and lovely, as ever."

Athena searched his face. He, too, was looking well; his ordinarily sober gray eyes were almost sparkling, as if with some hidden mischief. They reminded her of the old days, when Niall had been . . . when it had been so much easier for him to laugh. So much easier for both of them.

"Sit down, and tell me all about your business," she said, signaling for the parlormaid to bring tea, coffee, and biscuits. "Was it very successful?"

Niall smiled and sat in his armchair facing the fireplace. "You have never taken any interest in my business."

"Perhaps it is time I did."

"And perhaps it is past time that I take an interest in yours."

She grew alert. "I am . . . sorry about our argument before you left—"

"No. You were quite right. I have been too harsh, without understanding."

Her heart swelled with hope. "That is kind of you, Niall. Nothing would please me more than if you wished to help."

"Then I trust you will be pleased with what I have brought you today."

Athena did not allow herself to show vulgar excitement. Niall often brought her gifts upon his return from business trips, but never with such pleasure.

"I do not see a package," she said, leaning as if to look behind him. "I cannot imagine what you can have brought from the mines in the south!"

"Oh, it will not fit in any sort of box," he said with mock solemnity. "Indeed, you will have to come outside to see it."

Alarm stopped the air in her lungs. "Here at the house?"

"It would not even fit on the grounds. You must come out with me, in the carriage, if you want your present."

She looked down at her lap and the carefully arranged folds of her gown. "You know . . . that is not easy for me, Niall."

"You go out to the orphanage and among the poor."

"Yes, but that is different—"

"Because they have no right to pity you?"

She flinched at his too-acute observation. For a moment he looked uncomfortable. "I realize that you do not enjoy going into the city, or even on social calls," he said. "But I think you will wish to make an exception in this case."

She met his gaze. There was a hint of a challenge in it, and that was shock enough to win her full attention. He was so apt to want to protect her, and now he urged her to go out. There was something special about this, indeed.

"Very well," she said slowly. "If you will take refreshment while I prepare—"

"Nonsense. You are fine as you are." He rang for Brinkley. "Please call Miss Munroe's maid, and tell Romero that we will be needing the rockaway."

Fran appeared to settle Athena's wrap about her shoulders and pushed her chair down the hall. Only moments ago Athena had been wishing for some new source of inspiration, and her wish seemed to have run away with her.

Fran, Romero, and Niall bundled her into the carriage and covered her legs with another wrap. She forced herself to look out the window as they set off, catching glimpses of several women she knew walking arm in arm, a new mansion going up on Welton, the streetcar on its way to the business district. Everything about Denver was moving, too busy to slow down for an instant.

She expected Niall to stop the carriage at any time, but they rattled on out of the better part of town, past more modest dwellings with livestock kept in dusty yards, and on to an area near the outskirts of the city. The Munroes owned several empty lots there, and Niall had often said that he expected the investment to pay off when the city expanded and required the land for new construction.

Curious despite herself, Athena looked for anything unusual. The carriage made a turn down a dirt track, and there, spread across a field of autumn grasses, was her surprise.

A circus. She recognized the tents, the colorful wagons, the peculiar folk moving about with their animals and bright costumes. Niall smiled, pleased at her confusion.

"You wonder why I bring you to a circus?" he asked. "Before I left, you chided me about my failure to help those in need. You will be pleased to know that I have listened. I have not only assisted these people in their time of need, but I have engaged them to perform for your orphanage at my expense."

Athena stared at him and realized her mouth was agape. "Niall . . . I am . . . I could never have imagined—"

He signaled Romero to stop at the edge of the lot. "I wanted you to see this for yourself, and meet those I've hired to entertain your children."

"Oh, Niall. The children will be so delighted, I know it."

He reached across the seats to press her hand. "So long as it delights you, Athena. Shall we?"

He and Romero helped her down, and her chair was taken from its special rack in the boot. Athena was too busy absorbing the view to notice the bumpy, uncomfortable ride over the rough ground as Niall pushed her chair toward the tents.

A fat, jolly-looking man with white whiskers came to meet them as they approached the largest tent, the one she supposed must house the main performances. He was eccentrically dressed, but quite normal in contrast to a few of the people she had glimpsed at work or practice on the lot.

"My dear, dear Mr. Munroe!" the stout man said effusively. He pumped Niall's hand and looked down at Athena. "And this must be your lovely sister!"

"Athena," Niall said, "may I present Mr. Harry French, the manager and owner of French's Fantastic Family Circus. Mr. French, Miss Athena Munroe."

"Delighted, delighted beyond words." French beamed at her. "May I say how very charmed I am to make your acquaintance?"

Athena liked Harry French instantly. She returned his smile and pressed his hand.

"I am glad to meet you, Mr. French. My brother tells me that you have come to Denver to entertain the children of our orphanage. I know they will consider it the experience of a lifetime."

Harry blushed, his skin contrasting even more vividly with the white of his moustache. "We shall do our best, indeed we shall. Your brother has done us a great favor. You see, we had suffered a number of misfortunes, and he offered a solution to our difficulties. He is most generous. Oh, yes, most generous."

Niall looked away. "I hope that you will not find it inconvenient to show my sister something of your establishment, Mr. French," he said gruffly.

"My pleasure. Oh, yes. We are still setting up, but I am sure—ah, there are a few of my troupers, if you would care to follow—"

He set off at a waddling trot. Niall sighed and steered Athena after him.

"Do you think this is the right circumstance for introductions?"

Athena asked. "Perhaps it would be better to invite them to our home instead."

"You astonish me, Athena," Niall said. "One doesn't invite such people to one's home."

She could not argue. From all she had heard, circus folk were deemed little better than vagrants, dirty and ignorant. They were not the sort of people she usually dealt with—neither needy and dependent, nor wealthy and cultured.

But surely it was a matter of finding the right way to speak to them. The troupers Harry French had mentioned were standing in a group looking at the large tent, talking amongst themselves. Athena noticed the new look of the canvas, without so much as a scuff or tear. Many of the other tents had a worn appearance, as did the wagons.

"Miss Munroe," Harry said, waving her and Niall forward, "I am pleased to present to you my troupers, whom I feel I may boast are among the finest in our nation." He rocked back on his heels and swept out his arm in a grand gesture. "Caitlin Hughes, our graceful Lady Principal or equestrienne: Ulysses Marcus Aurelius Wakefield, also known as the Little Professor, genius and prognosticator; Tamar the Queen of the Snakes, and Morgan, our—"

"Very pleased to meet you, Miss Munroe." The girl French had introduced as Caitlin stepped forward, began to hold out her hand, and dropped it awkwardly. She was pretty in an unusual, impish way, very small in her circus costume of tights and short skirt. She glanced at Niall. "Harry told us that we'll be performing for the orphans you care for. It is very kind of you and Mr. Munroe to help children who don't have a home."

Athena smiled. The girl could not be very well educated, and certainly was not refined, but Athena warmed to her as quickly as she had to Harry French. "Good afternoon, Miss Hughes. I know that I will look forward to your performance."

Caitlin blushed as red as her hair and stepped back. The small man beside her bowed to Athena.

"Ulysses Wakefield, your most obedient servant," he said with a soft Southern drawl. "I trust that you will find our humble company worthy of your highest expectations."

How strange it was to look upon another person who carried a physical burden so much greater than her own. Here was a gentleman, by his clothing, manner, and speech, yet though she was seated he could meet her gaze while standing straight on his own two, short legs. His face was handsome, and he carried himself as if he were of average height. But he, like Athena, must often face a world that could not understand.

She offered her hand. "I know I shall not be disappointed, Mr. Wakefield," she said. He kissed the air above her knuckles, leaving her feeling unaccountably flattered. She looked up at the third person and lost any sense of comfort.

Tamar was tall, voluptuous, and beautiful, but her black eyes were devoid of warmth. Her lips remained flat and unwelcoming. A darting, reptilian head thrust out from under her dark wrap.

"Miss Munroe," she said, her voice low and heavily accented. "I hope you do not find it inconvenient to come here."

"No. Not at all, thank you." Athena kept her hands folded in her lap and held Tamar's gaze, resolved not to let her unease show. It was clear she would receive no friendlier greeting from the Queen of the Snakes. But an even more disturbing sensation centered on her temple, seeming to emanate from the direction of the man Harry had not quite finished introducing.

She turned her head. Her eyes met those of the last man. She could have sworn that even her legs felt the impact of that golden gaze.

"Oh, yes," Harry said, bumbling up beside them. "How remiss of me. Miss Munroe, please meet Morgan Holt."

Chapter 5

So strong was the sense that they had met that Athena almost asked him where he had been and how he had fared over the years.

She caught herself before she made an embarrassing mistake. They had not met before. He was a stranger, though her heart insisted otherwise. A stranger who compelled her to stare in defiance of all good manners and propriety.

Morgan Holt was tall, though not quite so tall as Niall. He was broad through the shoulders and lean through the hip in the way of a natural athlete. While the others wore coats and wraps against the autumn wind, he was dressed in an open-necked cotton shirt and simple trousers, and his feet were bare.

But his face made such oddities insignificant. Oh, he was handsome enough—not in the conventional way preferred by the women in Denver society, but undeniably attractive. "Rugged" was the word that came to mind. He was clean-shaven, making no concession to the fashion for long side-whiskers and moustaches. His black hair fell to his shoulders, like an Indian's, and his brows were dark slashes above piercing golden eyes. Yet something in his face, in his expression, held a fascination for her that went far beyond looks.

Secrets. His face was full of secrets, a calm surface over hidden currents that bubbled and boiled. Utter fearlessness. Fierce independence. All the things she wished she possessed.

Morgan was a man who would never beg for a place in the world. Never have to prove anything. No one would pity him.

He blinked like a cat in the sun. She came to herself abruptly and realized that he was giving her the same methodical examination to which she had subjected him. His eyes grew hooded as they tracked from her face to her lower body and the chair with its special wheels. And then he met her gaze, and she saw what she had dreaded . . . and expected.

When men looked at her, they did not see a woman. They saw a cripple, a girl never permitted to grow up, a creature to be protected and pampered but never loved. Not as a man loved a woman, as her father had loved her mother.

Most of the time she was able to ignore masculine discomfort with her affliction. Most of the time she didn't allow herself to think of Niall's business partners, or her friends' brothers, as men at all. That entire part of her being remained safely locked away.

Until a man like this one came along. And suddenly, painfully, she was aware of his potent maleness and her own shortcomings as a woman.

"Miss Munroe," he said.

She started, hardly expecting him to speak. "I am pleased to make your acquaintance, Mr. Holt," she said, grasping at the rote phrase. "What is your area of expertise in the circus?" She smiled cautiously. "Are you the lion tamer, perhaps?"

He made a sound in his throat that she guessed was a laugh. "There are no lions here. No animals in cages, except for one. You could say that I tame him, as much as he can be tamed."

His voice was baritone, a little rough, without the accents of refinement that Mr. Wakefield's held, or the hint of a more advanced education that marked Harry French's speech. It had its own particular music, like the sighing of wind in mountain pines.

"And what sort of beast is it, Mr. Holt?" she asked.

"One you have never seen before."

"Rare and deadly, I suppose?"

"Yes." He stared at her face as if he could discern her thoughts through sheer determination. "What do you do, Miss Munroe? What is your . . . expertise? Or do you have one?"

He was mocking her. She prided herself on reading voice and expressions, and there was no doubt that Morgan Holt meant to provoke.

She glanced around to see if Niall was listening, but he was deep in conversation with Mr. French and Caitlin Hughes. Ulysses had gone, and only Tamar watched from a distance, her snakes coiling about her upper arm.

"You refer, perhaps, to this?" she said, gesturing at her lower body. "Do you judge that one in my situation is unable to do anything of worth? I assure you that neither my mind nor my heart are paralyzed, Mr. Holt."

As soon as the words left her mouth she wondered where they had come from, and why she had revealed so much to a hostile stranger. He did not know her, nor she him, yet already she felt as if they were at odds, engaged in a battle for which she did not understand the cause.

And that was ridiculous. If anything, he was an employee, part of a world separated from hers by class, money, and inclination.

"I am sorry," she said coolly. "I misunderstood your question."

"Harry says your family are important people in Colorado," he said. "Your brother hired the troupe knowing Harry had to accept his offer, whether he wanted to or not." He scraped a hollow in the earth with his foot. "When you have money, anything is possible, isn't it?"

Now she understood his antagonism. He did not feel contempt for her disability, merely for her wealth. He resented what he and his people lacked, and what they owed Niall. Perhaps his own background was one of poverty.

That was no excuse for his discourtesy. "I think I see," she said. "You have decided that having money renders a person incapable of virtue or honest work. It is wealth that you object to, even when it provides you with employment. I am truly sorry that your life has been so difficult, Mr. Holt."

Ah. *That* penetrated his armor. "Very kind of you, Miss Munroe," he said with a curl of his lip. "I guess when you spend your life helping your inferiors, you don't notice what your own life is missing."

She did not allow him to see her flinch. Who in heaven's name did he think he was? He did not know her, or anything about her. She held on to her temper, bewildered by her growing anger. She had almost forgotten what real anger was. It distressed her far more than anything Morgan Holt had said.

"I can see that my activities would not interest you," she murmured. "I do not tame dangerous beasts, merely persuade reluctant ones."

"What would you call me?" he asked softly. "Dangerous, or reluctant?"

His questions made no sense except as another pointless provocation. That he could be dangerous she had little doubt . . . though not to her. How could he be? He was only a man—proud, rude, and difficult, but still a man. She could escape his company whenever she wished. And as for reluctant . . .

"You seem to like riddles, Mr. Holt," she said, "but I prefer to save such amusements for my friends."

They stared at each other. Athena felt increasingly uncomfortable, and the new, phantom tingling in her legs grew more pronounced. No, not in her legs . . . somewhat above and between them. Her mouth went dry. She thought about calling out to Niall and asking him to take her home, but her throat issued only a whisper.

This was quite ridiculous. Mr. Holt was a challenge, but she had faced such challenges before, from ruthless businessmen and distrustful poor alike. She felt sure that she could win, if not Morgan's liking, at least his respect. It seemed important that she do so, as long as she did not concede too much. It was necessary if she was to help him.

Help him? What had put such a thought into her head? He was neither destitute nor ill, merely ill-mannered.

"I did not mean to be discourteous," she said. "We simply do not understand one another. We are—"

"Too different." A strange expression passed over his face. Had she not known better, she might have thought it wistfulness. Loneliness. But then he laughed, shattering the illusion. "If I ever came to your world, Miss Munroe, you would have to keep me on a leash."

She knew better than to back down. There must be something truly wrong with him—a great bitterness, or some subtle disorder of the mind. And yet, even as she considered it, she knew the explanation was too simple. There was much more to Morgan Holt than met the eye.

His eyes. What was it about his eyes?

The uneasy silence came to a halt with a sudden commotion at the edge of the lot. A string of handsome carriages drew up behind Niall's, and Athena recognized them immediately. She sighed with mingled relief and apprehension. She didn't know who had told her friends about the circus, but she was glad enough of the distraction.

"If you will excuse me, Mr. Holt." She wheeled her chair about, intending to make her own way, but she found herself being propelled forward by strong, sure hands. She knew the touch was not Niall's. In spite of Morgan Holt's surliness, he pushed her chair with skill, avoiding stones and potholes as deftly as if he had been doing it all his life.

Perhaps it was a form of apology. She could scarcely object when her friends were already coming to greet her. Cecily Hockensmith was in the lead, followed by several of the younger and more adventuresome ladies in Athena's circle. They advanced in a flock, exclaiming and staring at the astonishing sights and smells.

"My dear Athena!" Cecily said, holding out her hands. "We heard about this wonderful new scheme of your brother's, and just had to come and see for ourselves. How clever of him, to hire a circus just for the dear orphans. How very original!"

Suzanne Gottschalk, blond and beautiful, lifted her handkerchief to her nose. "How very . . . fragrant it is."

Millicent Osborn trilled a laugh. "Of course, silly. Have you never seen a circus before?" She nodded at Athena. "Do not pay any attention to Suzanne. We are all so impressed, are we not?"

"Indeed," Grace Renshaw said, sliding her spectacles up her nose. "Yet another feather in your charitable cap, so to speak. I do not know what the unfortunate of our city would do without you and Mr. Munroe."

Athena hid her pleasure and greeted them all with a smile. "You praise me far too highly. It was indeed my brother's idea, and quite unexpected. I have just arrived myself."

"Then we are not too late for a tour," Millicent said. "It must be terribly exotic. And, of course, we shall want to contribute to the performance—you must allow us to help!" She looked up over Athena's head. "Perhaps this . . . gentleman?"

Athena was keenly aware of Morgan behind her, of his earthy scent and masculine bulk. And the obvious fact that he was not a gentleman. He was more than likely prepared to insult her friends as he had tried to insult her. She could only pray that he did not.

"Ladies," she said, "may I present Mr. Morgan Holt, one of the performers of French's Fantastic Family Circus."

The ladies fell silent, gazing at Holt. Athena wondered if they were having the same reaction she had, or if they merely found him an uncouth curiosity. Most of her friends did not share her habit of going into the slums to distribute food and clothing. To them, he would not seem much different from the "lower elements" their fathers and brothers warned them about.

"I declare," Suzanne exclaimed. Millicent giggled, and Grace shushed her.

The back of Athena's neck continued to prickle. "I am sure that Mr. French will be pleased to show us the grounds, but Mr. Holt may have other engagements."

"What a pity," Cecily said with frosty emphasis. "We do not wish to keep you, Mr. Holt."

A gentleman would have taken Cecily's dismissal with good grace and beat a dignified retreat, but Morgan Holt did not move. Instead, it was Cecily who took a step back, bumping into Suzanne and causing a minor disturbance.

"I have no other . . . engagements," Holt said, faint mockery in his tone. "Should I show you the wolves first, Miss Munroe?"

Morgan stood still and let himself be stared at, as contemptuous as a raven surrounded by chattering sparrows. No, not sparrows, but extravagantly plumed parrots who had ventured from their cages for an afternoon.

The leader of the flock accepted their homage in regal majesty, prim and proper in her wheeled chair and only slightly less gaudy than the others. And he wondered, not for the first time, why he remained with her.

Their meeting had been less than cordial. Even had he not known her identity, he would have pegged her as the kind of woman—lady—who had existed only on the fringes of his life: an engraving in a tattered magazine; a beribboned mannequin on the arm of some overstuffed peacock parading down the dusty main street of a nameless town; a face from the box seats during a performance.

What else should she be? He knew what kind of people she and her brother were. His father had envied and aped them all his life. How many promises Aaron Holt had made, to his wife and children, always beginning and ending the same: "You'll lack for nothing once I make my strike," or "When I'm rich, in just another year or two . . ."

Athena Munroe came from a world Morgan touched only by rare chance, as alien to him as tea cakes to a timber wolf. The fabric of her gown alone might have seen a poor family through an entire winter. The pearls about her slender neck and in her ears were tasteful and even more costly. She wouldn't have looked at him twice if he hadn't spoken first.

And yet, within the space of a few minutes, he had said more to her than he generally did to his fellow troupers in a day.

And he was afraid.

He knew the reason, though it made no sense. When he had first seen Athena Munroe, when he had looked into her bright hazel eyes, he felt for an instant that he'd found the source of the voice. The voice, the call from the north, the one he had ignored and dismissed that last night in Colorado Springs.

The feeling persisted even when he realized the folly of such thoughts. It certainly was not her beauty that held him rooted to the spot, staring like a boy with his first woman.

Athena Munroe's face was pleasant and even of feature, with slightly full lips and high cheekbones. Her skin was clear, her jaw stubbornly firm. Her hair was an unremarkable brown. What figure he could see was slender. But her eyes . . .

Her eyes held unexpected depths. They shifted in color with every small motion, from brown to green and back again. They gazed at Morgan with a perplexing combination of vulnerability and defiance, and he had sensed that she was afraid—not of him, but of his pity.

She was a cripple. He could not imagine a fate more awful than to be trapped as she was, unable to run. That was the other, unlooked-for quality he'd seen in her eyes—the abiding sadness of permanent, devastating loss.

Loss he understood. Pity came, and with it the kind of emotion he despised. He had provoked and taunted her, hoping to shatter his unwilling sympathy, to chase her away or incite some pompous remark that would bolster his dislike of her kind.

But she had answered him with spirit, even attempted an apology, and he felt the stirrings of reluctant admiration at her courage. He had remained by her side to help her when he should have walked away. That had been a mistake.

She was not like him. She was a lady—spoiled, protected, used to having her way—and now that he saw her among her own people, he knew that his sympathy had been misplaced.

"Wolves, Mr. Holt?" she asked lightly, not bothering to turn toward him. "I thought you had said that there were no wild beasts in your circus."

He wheeled her chair around. "No beasts, Miss Munroe—only men who act like them."

"Of course. I have already seen an example. Would you not prefer to return to your friends?"

She, like the cold, black-haired beauty among the parrots, was trying to dismiss him. He smiled, showing his teeth. "I am all you have at the moment, Miss Munroe."

"Perhaps we ought to come at another time," the black-haired woman said.

"No," Athena replied. "If Mr. Holt is willing to guide us, then let us go ahead, by all means." She nodded to Morgan. "If you please."

So she turned her disadvantage around and kept her dignity, putting him in his place again. No, *she* didn't need his pity. He planted himself behind the chair and pushed her in the direction of the big tent, pursued by the clacking beaks of Athena's parrots.

He was debating how best to shock the silly creatures into flight when Athena's brother strode up to join them. He tipped his hat to the ladies, who simpered in return, and smiled down at his sister.

"Well? Are you pleased, my dear? I did warn you that these people are not what you are accustomed to, but—"

"It is lovely, Niall. Thank you." She half turned her head, as if she were trying to catch a glimpse of Morgan's face. "Have you met Mr. Holt? I believe he . . . handles the animals."

Niall glanced at Morgan with indifference, and then focused with a hard stare. It was obvious that he had not noticed who pushed Athena's chair. Morgan's instincts came fully awake, as they did in the presence of an enemy.

"We have not met," Niall said. "Mr. Holt, I will escort the ladies."

"Mr. Holt was about to take us on a tour—" Athena began.

"Mr. French has arranged one for a more appropriate time," Niall said. His gaze remained fixed on Morgan. "All of you ladies will be welcome, of course."

The black-haired woman pressed close to Munroe. "I was just telling Athena how very generous it is of you to provide such grand entertainment for the children."

"I fear that I cannot take credit, Miss Hockensmith. This was entirely Athena's idea."

"Niall—" Athena began.

"Please do not deny it," Miss Hockensmith said, covering Athena's hand on the chair arm. "You do so much, my dear. We can but admire your dedication."

Morgan studied the woman. His immediate dislike for her was almost as intense as it was for Niall. She hung on Munroe as if she claimed him for her mate, but his scent revealed no trace of interest.

Athena gently withdrew her hand. "You are too kind, as always."

"Not at all. But surely you tire yourself, dear Athena. We should all go back, as your brother has advised."

Morgan tightened his grip on the chair handles, recognizing what he was seeing. Athena was the lead female of her pack, and Hockensmith coveted her place. Among wolves such competition could lead to injury, even death. But these creatures were more likely to squabble and peck than rend and tear. He watched Athena to see how she would respond.

But he was denied the chance to find out, for Harry and Caitlin reappeared, Tamar a few yards behind. Caitlin stopped several feet away from the society ladies. She looked at Niall Munroe, and he looked back. The scent of attraction was unmistakable.

Munroe and Caitlin? As likely a pairing as himself and Munroe's sister. But he was not the only one to have noticed that mutual stare. Miss Hockensmith's dark eyes were narrowly centered on Caitlin. She all but snarled.

Harry bustled up to Athena's chair, a trio of rolled posters in his hands. "Ah, Mr. Munroe, Miss Munroe . . . ladies! I had thought them all burned in the fire, but I have managed to salvage several of our papers. You may find them amusing." He handed one to Niall, one to Athena, and the third to Miss Hockensmith. "We would normally have many more printed in advance when we are to play in a town, but since this is a performance for your children, Miss Munroe, that will not be necessary."

Niall Munroe tucked his poster under his arm without unrolling it, and Miss Hockensmith did likewise. Athena glanced at it and smiled up at Harry.

"I'm sure the children will enjoy seeing this. Thank you, Mr. French."

He nodded and glanced at Morgan. "Ah, Morgan, my lad. Perhaps Mr. Munroe has told you that we plan a tour and rehearsal for Miss Munroe and her friends in a few days' time. We wish to be at our best, do we not?"

Morgan understood the hint, if not Harry's reason for giving it. He stepped away from Athena's chair. Unexpectedly, Athena pivoted to face him and smiled as she had at Harry.

He forgot whatever had been in his mind. Speech failed him.

"Thank you, Mr. Holt, for offering to escort us," she said, extending her hand. "We shall meet again."

He took her hand without conscious thought. It was small and warm in his, and her glove did not lessen the firmness of her grip. Why should a pampered rich girl be so strong?

"Would you like to see my little pet, Miss Munroe?" Tamar pushed between them, stretching one of her snakes toward Athena's face. The serpent probed the air, tongue flickering. Athena flinched and held very still.

"Tamar," Harry said, "I do not think that Miss Munroe—"

"Oh, do not worry. He is quite harmless." Tamar stroked the scaled head tenderly. "Harmless to *my* friends."

"*Tamar.*" Morgan grabbed her arm. "Take it away and leave her alone."

She let herself be pulled aside. "Of course, my darling wolf." She smiled at Athena. "I am certain that we will become better acquainted. I have many other little companions eager to meet you."

Niall took a step toward Tamar, looked at Morgan, and clenched his jaw. "Mr. French, I trust that you will make sure that no dangerous animals are allowed to run loose on these grounds." At Harry's hasty reassurance, he assumed his position behind his sister's chair. "Come, Athena. I'll take you back to the carriage. Miss Hockensmith, ladies."

He tipped his hat with one final, telltale glance at Caitlin and set off at a rapid stride before Athena could speak again. Most of her adoring flock went with them, and Tamar stalked away toward the tents.

Miss Hockensmith lingered. She dismissed Morgan with a glance and subjected Caitlin to a long, slow examination.

"Are you one of the performers, dear?" she asked. "What a very daring costume. If you go into the city, I do hope you will wear something less . . . provocative."

Caitlin glanced down at her tights and skirt. "I—"

Morgan saw with astonishment that Caitlin's sharp tongue had gone as mute as his own. He turned on Miss Hockensmith. "Caitlin has a reason for what she wears. You dress like that"—he indicated the woman's elaborate gown with a jerk of his chin—"to make males sniff after you."

She stared at Morgan, her lips parted in utter shock. "How dare you."

"He dares . . . quite a bit," Caitlin said, finding her voice. "I would not annoy him."

No insult quite fitting enough came to Miss Hockensmith. "I . . . I see that Mr. Munroe has been taken in by . . . by . . . I shall have to tell him—"

Morgan growled. Not a small growl from deep in the throat, but the kind he would use on a lesser wolf who came too near a challenge. Miss Hockensmith paled and took several hasty steps back, almost tripping on her ridiculously confining skirts. Without another word she spun around and hastened after the others.

Caitlin let out an explosive sigh. "That was not a good idea, Morgan."

"They are all alike, Firefly. Do not trust them."

"I don't think you follow your own advice."

"What?"

"I saw the way you looked at Athena Munroe."

For the second time in a handful of minutes she astounded him. "And how was that?"

"The way I've never seen you look at a woman before."

"You had better cut your hair, Firefly. It's getting in your eyes."

She shook her head. "You have a good poker face, Morgan, but you're a terrible liar. What was it about her? Her pretty voice? Her fine manners?" Caitlin's expression was uncommonly serious. "You have better taste than I thought. I liked her."

"And you never liked outsiders," he said harshly. "Until today."

"Niall Munroe is a gentleman. This is his doing, after all. He didn't have to be so generous."

"What is it about him, Firefly? His fine suit? The fancy way he talks? Most females would consider him handsome."

"The way his sister looked at you, she must think you're pretty handsome yourself."

The hair behind his ears bristled. "*I* am no gentleman."

"And I am no lady. Still—" She shrugged. "My feelings have been wrong before. Maybe they are this time."

He didn't ask her what particular "feelings" she referred to. If she chose to moon after the cold-blooded Niall Munroe, it was her privilege— so long as she did not expect others to have such feelings. Him least of all.

Caitlin yawned with exaggerated indifference. "Well, I am off to bed. It will be dawn soon. You should rest too—even wolves need sleep." She set off for her tent, and after a moment he headed for the one he shared with Ulysses.

The little man was lying on his cot, arms pillowing his head. He opened his eyes when Morgan walked in.

"Something is disturbing you," he observed. "I noted it when we met the Munroes."

"Everyone is interested in my feelings tonight," Morgan growled.

Ulysses rose on his elbows. "It is only that you so seldom reveal your inner thoughts, and it is rare that I am able to observe them."

"I should be honored that you find them entertaining."

"Nothing of the sort." Ulysses swung his short legs over the edge of the cot. "I am naturally concerned about the well-being of my fellow performers, especially when one of them has sacrificed much to remain among us."

Morgan poured water from a pitcher and drank several glasses in succession. "There is nothing wrong with me. I have no interest in this Athena Munroe."

"Ah."

"Sometimes, Wakefield, your brains get in the way of your sense."

"Perhaps. But your own objectivity is frequently in question, my friend."

"When have you seen me with a woman?"

"Never. But you are not like other men—except, I venture, in one essential manner. Neither man nor wolf is without certain instincts for the preservation of his kind."

"Including you?"

"It would be most inadvisable for me to father children," Ulysses said gravely. "But you have a gift worth preserving."

"I have met Miss Munroe once, and already you and Caitlin have decided that I want her." He laughed. "As if she would have me, crippled though she is. I am not human. Worry about Caitlin, not me."

Ulysses was silent for a time. "I feel that it is incumbent upon me to warn you that you talk in your sleep."

Morgan turned sharply to face him. "What?"

"You have spoken of things . . . deeply painful. I know you would not wish to share them with outsiders, but I am your friend, Morgan. I will listen, should you—"

"What did I say?"

Ulysses held his gaze without fear. "You spoke of your father. And of prison bars."

Morgan slammed his glass on the sawhorse that served as a table. "I am a convict. Does that change your friendship, Professor?"

"No. It only convinces me that you must speak of these things to someone if you are to put them behind you."

"As you've put your past behind you?" Morgan laughed. "I—"

The tent flap opened and Tamar eased inside. She glanced at Ulysses and ignored him, making straight for Morgan.

"I waited for you," she said.

Morgan eyed her coldly. "I was not aware we planned to meet."

"But you do not wish to spend this night alone."

"You make yourself foolish, Tamar," Ulysses said, the words clipped like a Yankee's.

"I do not care for your opinion, little man."

"Morgan wants no part of you."

"Oh, does the mannequin speak for you now, my wolf?"

She sat on the cot beside Morgan and breathed in his ear. "Is he your master? Or are you in love already with the little girl in the chair?"

Morgan stiffened. "If you want tender sentiments, look somewhere else."

"Ah, but I find love as tedious as you do. We have much in common, you and I. We share only what we wish to share, no more." Her long tongue curled about his earlobe. "Come. Come away, and let me show you."

Morgan's body had begun to throb in a way he had ignored one too many times. This was pain he didn't have to endure, especially when the cure was so free of consequences. He and Tamar could use each other without illusions or expectations.

Ulysses and Caitlin thought he was attracted to Athena Munroe. There was one way of making them see how wrong they were—and purging his own senses of Athena's unsettling effect.

He got up, pulling Tamar with him. "Very well," he said. "We'll give each other what we want. But don't expect a lover. I am in no mood for gentleness."

The pupils of her eyes were large with desire and excitement. "I do not want it." She darted forward and kissed him, pushing her tongue into his mouth. He responded with equal violence, despising himself. As she led him from the tent, she cast a final, triumphant glance at Ulysses.

Morgan did not look back.

Chapter 6

The streets of Denver's business district were everything Morgan hated. He stalked up Sixteenth Street, keeping his eyes fixed on his course, head down against the occasional stares and doing his best to ignore the cacophonous noise and overripe smells of horses, dung, spoiled food, smoke, unwashed human flesh, and the scent of many humans crowded together.

He would rather not have come here at all. The Munroes' boundless generosity had provided the circus's principal performers with lodgings at Denver's finest hotel, the Windsor. Morgan might have been included among those so favored, but he would sooner hang than stay in the city. Visiting it was bad enough.

So he remained on the lot with the roustabouts, crew, and lesser performers, watching the circus come to life again. At the end of the first few days in Denver, French's Fantastic Family Circus was back in trim, busy with practice and preparation for the orphans' performance to be held at the end of the week. Everyone had enough to eat, and new costumes were being constructed by the seamstress to replace those that had worn out or burned in the fire.

Harry supervised the improvements and restorations with even more joviality than before. Caitlin had groomed her horses to a satin sheen of renewed health, Florizel and his cohorts were perfecting a new clown act of which he was inordinately proud, and the jugglers, aerialists, acrobats, and dog trainers went about their tasks with cheerful absorption. Hope wafted in the air like a seductive perfume.

Morgan kept to himself. He did not visit Tamar again. His one night with her had been more than enough to purge him of any desire to share her bed a second time. She was easy to put from his thoughts.

The same could not be said of Athena Munroe. They hadn't met again, yet her eyes and her scent came back to him both waking and sleeping. There was no reason in it, and no sense. On the day that Miss Munroe and her society friends were to have their promised tour of the circus, he made an immediate decision to visit Ulysses at the Windsor and remain there. The only way to rid his thoughts of Athena Munroe was to avoid her as much as possible until the troupe left Denver.

It could not be soon enough for him. He walked in the street just off the plank sidewalks, preferring the feel of gravel to dead wood, and constant clouds of dust to human contact. He wore shoes, so as not to attract too much attention—that was one of his few concessions to civilization. And he would not embarrass Ulysses.

He slipped between carriages, drays, and wagons bearing every kind of freight. Water tank wagons sprayed the dirt in a vain effort to keep down the dust, and dirty water ran down the ditches on either side of the street. Fetid odors from the river and smelters hung in the still air. Bands of idle boys stood about and mocked passersby, though they left Morgan strictly alone.

He winced at the continual din of sawing and hammering as new construction went up throughout the district. The tall brick and iron buildings on either side of the street seemed to draw inward a little more with each step he took, as if they intended to crush him. He passed numerous Chinese laundries squeezed between saloons and mercantiles, the Mint with its disintegrating bricks, and the vast Tabor block at the corner of Larimer.

The Windsor Hotel rose a full five stories at the busy intersection of Eighteenth and Larimer, ponderous in heavy gray stone. Morgan stared up at it, all the hairs on his body standing at attention. Men and women, most well-dressed and prosperous, went blithely in and out the door as if the sheer weight of the construction might not topple over upon them at any moment.

"Are you drunk?" someone shouted. "Get out of the way!"

He sprang to the side just as a heavily laden wagon bore down on the place he had been standing. His ears ached with the noise. He could run away from it—either back to the lot or into the hotel.

He stepped up onto the sidewalk and braved the doors. A pair of befrilled matrons, busy with their conversation, bumped into him coming out. They paused to gawk at him and then hurried on their way.

The lobby opened up around him, a glittering cavern of gilded ornamentation, wrought iron, and polished brass. Chairs and sofas with velvet cushions were arranged in groupings with potted plants. Laughter and conversation echoed. Morgan caught the smell of freshly cooked food from another entrance, which he guessed must lead to the Windsor's dining room.

He kept close to the edge of the vast space and worked his way to the desk where young male clerks waited on guests with their bags and bundles. Morgan stood to the side while the nearest clerk finished with the elderly couple at the desk, summoned a uniformed bellboy, and noticed Morgan.

"May I help you?" he asked, assessing Morgan with a practiced eye.

"Ulysses Wakefield," Morgan said. "His room."

The clerk consulted a ledger and nodded. "Yes, he is a guest with us. Mr. Wakefield is expecting you?"

"Tell me where he is, and I'll find him."

"I will send a boy to let him know you are here, Mr.—"

"Holt."

"Very good, Mr. Holt." He rang a bell. "Just a moment."

Morgan leaned against the counter, his ears pricking at every sound. Drifts of choking perfume streamed after fashionably gowned women like invisible trains. The artificial fragrances that human females used so freely almost succeeded in covering up their natural scents. Yet one such scent came to him, newly familiar, and he surveyed the room to find its source.

He picked her out from among yet another cluster of prattling females—one of the parrots who had come after Athena Munroe to see the circus. He quickly identified two more of the remaining three ladies as among those who had been with Athena on the lot. Only the black-haired one was missing.

Morgan stepped away from the registration desk to get a closer look. Athena was not among the women, but he heard the name "Munroe" rise above the general conversation.

"Sir?"

Ignoring the clerk's query, Morgan made a sudden decision and started after Athena's friends. No one noted his passage. He followed the women as far as the entrance to the dining room, where an officious-looking man directed them to a large table nearby. Morgan paused to study the room.

It was a much fancier place than any hash house or saloon Morgan had been in before his imprisonment, and there were many women as well as men eating and drinking at the white-linened tables. They sipped their wine and ate their steaks without a care in the world.

The attendant gave Morgan a dubious look, as if he would have liked to direct Morgan to some less high-toned establishment. "Luncheon for one, sir?"

A small, unoccupied table stood fairly close to the ladies'. "Bring a steak to that table," he said. "Rare. And plain water." He showed his teeth. "Don't worry. I can pay for it."

The man opened and closed his mouth. "Very good, sir."

Morgan didn't wait to be shown to his place. He sat down on the upholstered chair, sifting through the interwoven conversations.

"Oh, but really, dear, you did not miss much. We were invited to view a rehearsal today, but I declined."

"And I. Once was quite enough."

The two voices belonged to Athena's friends. Morgan cocked his head without turning it.

"Was this Athena's idea?" a third woman asked.

"So her brother says. And isn't it just like her, bringing an entire circus to Denver for her orphans?"

"Really—it is too ridiculous. She cannot resist trying to surpass what anyone else does, and make herself look like a saint—Oh, I do apologize. I speak too freely."

"You know you are among friends here. And we all agree that Athena—well, how can we help but pity her? How can we but humor her projects, no matter how inconvenient?"

"You can say that, Marie, but you have not been called upon five times in the past month for some new scheme or other. I have had to miss a luncheon and two receptions because of her. And having to look at her, in that chair—"

"Poor thing. *She* will never be married."

"But she will never be one of us—how can she? If she hadn't been gallivanting about like a street urchin when she was younger, instead of learning proper behavior and decorum like the rest of us, she would not have been crippled. But her father spoiled her and let her run wild. Now she has nothing to do but make herself superior to everyone else."

"That is true, Suzanne. Those expensive French gowns are wasted on her. How can she display them properly when she cannot stand, let alone dance? And she is so *good*. I feel a positive ogre in her presence."

"She must try even harder to be perfect when she has such a very great . . . defect."

One of the women lowered her voice to a whisper. "Let us not forget the rumor that her mother . . ."

"Millicent! Remember where you are."

"Let us also not forget that her brother is a very important and eligible man in our city," said the first woman in a droll voice. "It would not be wise to snub his sister." She paused to sip at her drink. "We must face facts, my dears. Athena is *our* charity case, and we must accept that burden."

There was a murmur of agreement, and the discussion turned to the menu. Morgan stared at his hands, clenched on the table.

So these were Athena's friends. These were the ones who had seemed so deferential and filled with praise when they were with her, the companions Athena looked upon with obvious trust. They spoke of her as if she were an object of disdain, not admiration.

Morgan tried, and failed, to understand his seething emotions. Athena Munroe was not even present, and yet she created a storm in his belly and heart that would not let him rest. The pity he had felt the first time he saw her returned, triple what it had been before.

Why? Why should one brief meeting have done this to him? What power did she hold, she who lacked even the honest respect of her own packmates? All he knew of Athena was what he had observed and what her critics had said of her—and what he knew of people like her. This was not his world, nor these his kind. What they did among themselves was meaningless to him.

But over the past few months he had remembered what it was to have friends, to not be alone. He recognized a fellow outcast, no matter how different from him. And Athena did not know she was an outcast.

Every negative characteristic he had expected to find in Athena lay exposed in these women: arrogance, derision, the shallow desire for comfort and ease. Yet Athena was helping the unfortunate, whatever her motives, and these fine "ladies" mocked her efforts. If she was not one of them, what was she?

He got up and, remembering the steak, threw several coins onto the table. He did not go to find Ulysses. He walked past the officious man and out the door, across the lobby and into the afternoon sunshine. He had begun to see that it was pointless to question the impulse that drove him; it was instinct, to be obeyed as human reason could not.

Instinct had led him to the circus. It had given him friends when he had not wanted them. Now instinct pulled him back to the lot.

To Athena Munroe.

As undignified as it might seem, Athena could scarcely contain her excitement as Harry French welcomed her once more to French's Fantastic Family Circus.

He had taken charge of her chair right at the carriage, chattering all the while as he took her across the lot and pointed out the various features of the circus: the midway, with its sideshow and concessions, the cookhouse, the tent and wagon quarters of the crew and roustabouts who made the circus possible—and, of course, the "big top," bright and new. Every portion of the lot was filled with activity, as if the troupers expected a huge crowd of paying customers rather than an audience of orphans.

It was just as well that no other guests would be present at today's rehearsal to witness Athena's childish enthusiasm. Although she had invited her friends and fellow supporters of the orphanage, every one of them had offered some excuse or apology. Ordinarily Athena might have been troubled by so many refusals, but she was too flustered to dwell on them for long.

She had *not* intended to look for Morgan Holt. He had been undeniably rude during their one previous meeting; some might have said that he behaved in a positively unnerving manner, with his hard stares and utter lack of propriety. He, like the woman Tamar, had been the only circus trouper she had met who did not offer a genuine welcome.

But Athena had not been afraid—not of him. That was the strange part; if anything, she had sensed a need in him that spoke to her innermost heart.

What could such a man need, especially of her? He was neither an indigent, a drunkard, or an orphan. He seemed to resent the very idea that he or his friends might require the assistance of a patron, no matter how well-intentioned or what the cause. He had gone out of his way to show himself immune to human frailties.

Yes, that was it—he had needed to *prove* something. But why to her? Morgan Holt could not know very much about her, except by hearsay.

She recalled everything about *him*, in perfect detail: his eyes, the thick mane of black hair, the lean muscle and natural grace with which he moved. The warmth of his strong, bare hand, hot enough to set her gloves afire. The way he had stayed with her and pushed her chair, as if they had known each other for years rather than minutes.

And the way in which he had defended her against the snake charmer. Tamar was one of his own kind, yet he had warned her away with grim resolve. For just that moment, he had seemed as gallant as any gentleman protecting his lady.

What had put that thought into her head? She was not his lady. The mere notion was ridiculous.

She and Morgan Holt had nothing in common. Yet in spite of the

huge differences that separated her from the circus folk, she liked
Caitlin, Ulysses, and Harry French. Yes, she liked them very much.

"Here we are," Harry said, pausing at the entrance to the big top. It
was the size of a very large doorway, wide enough to admit several people abreast. "This is what we call the front door, Miss Athena. The performers usually come in the back door—that is the entrance from the
backyard, where our troupers prepare for their acts."

Athena smiled up at him. "All these interesting terms. I believe you
could hold entire conversations amongst yourselves, and no one outside
the circus would understand a word!"

Harry chuckled. "That is the idea." He drew himself up in sham
pomposity. "You are greatly favored, my lady, to be privy to our secret
language."

"Indeed," Athena said, surprising herself. "I feel most privileged."

Harry flushed, cleared his throat, and guided her into the tent. Immediately Athena felt the space all around her, smelled the sawdust and
horses, heard the clipped words of performers calling to each other
from high above. She followed the sounds to the tops of the platforms
near the roof of the tent, where a man in tights executed a graceful
somersault in midair and was caught by a second man.

"Two of our aerialists," Harry said. "They are nearly finished, but
the clown and Caitlin's act come next. I have a place for you where
you'll be able to observe everything closely."

He guided the chair down an aisle between rows of wooden risers
that framed the front door, beneath a rope barrier, and to the very edge
of the low-walled ring that encircled the inside of the tent. He pulled
up a chair beside her.

"The Giovanni Brothers are newcomers to our little group," he
told her, pointing his chin at the men high above. "They joined our
wire-walker, Regina. We were able to add their act when our fortunes
took a turn for the better a few months ago. Thanks to you and your
brother, Miss Athena, we will be able to keep them."

Athena pulled her gaze from the aerialists and glanced at the old
gentleman. "Forgive me if I am too forward, but my brother did mention a fire that destroyed your original tent. Had you suffered many
misfortunes?"

"Alas, such adversities can plague a small show like ours. So much
depends on elements like the weather, other troupes in the vicinity, the
prosperity of the towns we visit, and the health of our animals." He
shrugged. "The large shows have begun to use locomotives to move

from city to city, and think the less of wagon shows like ours. Perhaps we are not as competitive as we might be. But I would not have it any other way."

"Because you are like a family," Athena murmured.

He looked at her in surprise. "Just so, my dear. A family. And like any family, we will do everything within our power to help each other and stay together."

Athena felt a twinge of envy and quickly smothered it. All that was left of her own family was her brother, and he had so little time to spare for anything but business. Yet he had brought the circus.

"That is why we are here on this earth—to help each other," she said.

"And it was our good fortune that your brother came when he did." He smiled, as if at a private memory. "Just as fortunate as Morgan's coming."

"Morgan Holt?" She spoke before she realized how quickly the name had come to her lips. "He has . . . he has not been with you long?"

"Only a bit longer than our flying friends. It was because of him that we were able to hold our band together through the summer."

Harry spoke with such warmth that Athena wondered what Morgan had done to earn it. Harry was one of those rare men who liked and trusted everyone, yet Athena recognized a deeper affection, almost fatherly. She had not forgotten a father's love.

"I don't believe that you ever told us what he does, Mr. French."

"What he does? Why . . ." He hesitated, floundering for words. "He is currently—ah—creating a new act."

"I see." She glanced at him, wondering why he had been so ready to speak of Morgan a moment ago and then became so evasive. "Perhaps his act involves some special trade secrets?"

"Ah. Yes, exactly so." He patted her hand. "You are very kind in indulging an old man. We must keep our unique attractions from . . . from those who might try to duplicate them."

"I quite understand. I can see that whatever you choose to present, it will be wonderful."

Just as she finished speaking, the promised clowns arrived in the ring, accompanied by several dogs, a large ball, and objects as diverse as a trumpet and parasol. The leading clown, dressed in mismatched and exaggerated garments, had very white skin and hair that did not appear to be painted. He led the others in a series of tricks and pratfalls that had Athena laughing with far more abandon than she would have shown if her friends had been beside her.

The clowns bowed in Athena's direction when their performance was finished, and after a pause, several handsome gray horses were led into the ring. Running lightly after them was Caitlin, with her mop of red hair. She held no whip, yet as soon as she entered the ring the horses fell into order and watched her every move with pricked ears.

"Caitlin is our equestrienne—our Lady Principal—but she has more than one skill," Harry commented, beaming with pride. "She trains liberty horses and performs bareback riding. You will see an exhibition of her riding skills later. Such versatile performers are a great asset to a small troupe such as ours."

Athena nodded, but her attention was on Caitlin. The girl was grace itself. Her feet barely seemed to touch the ground as she stood at the center of the ring and gave brief commands to the caparisoned horses, which reared and danced and turned in an equine ballet.

Of all the things Athena might see in a circus, this was hardest. Once she had been as light on her feet as Caitlin. Once she had ridden like the wind—and run faster. She felt her legs twitch, a moment of rare sensation, as they reacted in sympathy to the red-haired girl's fluid motions.

Athena rested her hands in her lap and clasped them tightly. It was good that she should remind herself of what she could not have again. Years ago she had abandoned unrealistic hope, but every so often the old longing returned. As it had done, however briefly, in Morgan Holt's company.

"She is truly amazing, Mr. French," she said. "I compliment you on . . ." She lost the thread of her thoughts. A familiar, imposing figure had appeared across the ring, staring in her direction.

Morgan. Her heart soared to the top of the tent, and she knew if she were not very careful it would likely plummet to the ground most painfully.

Harry saw Morgan as well. He shifted in his seat and glanced at Athena. "Please continue to enjoy the show, Miss Athena," he said. "If you will excuse me. . . ." He heaved up from his chair and set out along the sawdust path that skirted the outside of the ring.

Athena tried to concentrate on Caitlin's act, but her gaze sought Morgan across the ring as if some invisible wire connected them. She was hardly aware that one of Caitlin's horses had begun to buck and plunge, surging away from the others.

Someone screamed. Athena turned her head just as the animal leaped the ring and charged straight at her.

Seconds passed as if they were minutes. Athena grasped the wheels of her chair and tried to make them move. She was not afraid. She looked calmly across the ring to where Morgan had been standing.

He was not there. He was already running into the ring, leaving a trail of discarded clothing in his wake. In midstride his body was lost in a dark blur, and when he hit the ground again he was no longer a man. Four large paws threw up sawdust as a great black wolf dashed after the panicky horse.

Athena had the fascinating sensation of floating, as if she had become an aerialist herself. The wolf put on a burst of incredible speed, overtook the horse just a few feet from Athena's chair, and shouldered it aside. She could feel the rush of air as the wolf passed, hear its panting and the squeal of the horse.

Then she began to tremble. Raised voices faded in and out of her hearing. Only her vision remained sharp. With perfect clarity she saw Caitlin grab for the errant horse and take it in hand, watched the wolf skid to a stop and shake its dark coat. The unearthly mist surrounded it again, and when it cleared Morgan Holt stood in the wolf's place.

He was quite, quite naked. Magnificent. Athena bit down hard on her lower lip, struggling to escape the dreamlike unreality that had taken her mind captive. All her senses were working again, but her thoughts spun around and around in helpless circles.

She knew what she had seen. She *knew*.

Morgan took a step in Athena's direction. A trouper came up behind him and slung a heavy cape over his shoulders. Morgan fastened it and strode toward Athena, looking neither to the right nor left. Her view of him was blocked by the small crowd of circus folk who gathered about her. They seemed afraid to speak. Her own tongue was frozen.

"Miss Athena! Are you well?" Harry French's voice shook as he crouched beside her. "I have no words to express our—"

"Later, Harry." The crowd parted for Morgan, and he came to stand before her chair. His eyes—wolf's eyes—held hers. "Can't you see she needs quiet?"

Harry backed away. "Of course. Of course. Let her lie down somewhere. I—"

Without waiting for Harry to finish, Morgan swooped like a striking eagle and gathered Athena into his arms. She felt the thumping of his heart against her side, and his breath in her hair. His steps were so swift that she seemed to fly through the air on invisible wings.

No one had touched her this way except her brother, Romero, or Brinkley when they carried her to or from the carriage or from one chair to another. Those occasions had been impersonal, a matter of necessity. This was very different.

Morgan Holt *held* her. He could as easily have pushed her in the chair. She was not on the edge of death, no matter how shaken she was. But he carried her straight across the ring and through the rear entrance—the "back door," she incongruously recalled—to an antechamber furnished with chairs, a table, and a cot.

He laid her on the cot and settled her comfortably, smoothing her skirt without touching any higher than her knees. Lightning raced up and down her body, spiking below her waist. Phantom sensation—but oh, how wondrous!

Drunk. She felt as the inebriated must feel, though she had not touched a drop. Morgan produced a thin wool blanket and draped it over her. He dragged a chair beside the cot and sat down, wrapping the voluminous cape about him. She could not seem to forget that he was completely naked underneath it. His face was just a foot from hers, and she could see every detail of his features, so much more than she had remembered.

"Miss Munroe," he said. His voice was rough as gravel and filled with concern. Yes, concern, from Morgan Holt. "You are not hurt?"

"No." She smiled like a mooncalf. "I am quite all right."

He got up and stepped behind a blanket hung across one corner of the tent. He emerged a minute later in shirt and trousers, pausing to fill a mug with water from the pitcher on the small table. "Drink this," he said, pressing the edge of the mug to her lips.

The very mundane act of drinking restored her sense of reality. "I saw . . . what you did," she murmured. "I saw everything."

A muscle in his jaw tensed and relaxed. No denial came. He simply waited, staring into her eyes with all the grim patience of a natural predator. He looked ferocious enough to tear her limb from limb, but she was not afraid. Oh, nothing nearly so uncomplicated as fear.

It was not she who needed reassurance now.

She reached from under the blanket and touched his hand. He clenched it into a fist under hers.

"I understand why Harry would not tell me what you do in the circus," she said, gathering her words with care. "I am not shocked, or horrified. I know I am not mad." The shaking started again, a delayed reaction like the prickling that came to fingers warmed by the fireside after long exposure to bitter mountain winds. "I will not give your secret away. You see, I have one of my own." She took a long, deep breath. "I am like you. I am a werewolf."

Chapter 7

Cecily Hockensmith gave her name to the secretary in Niall's reception room and waited to be announced, gazing with appreciation at the tasteful appointments and the original Bierstadt on the immaculate wall of the office.

Niall had not designed the place, of course. He knew better than to entrust such matters to his own abilities, when his talents lay in other directions. But his had been the money behind everything she saw here, and in the house on Fourteenth Street. He owned the very building in which she stood, and many more in Denver besides. For all its rustic beginnings, this city might make an acceptable home for a lady who had been a leading light of New York's elite.

As long as that lady had the right husband, and all his considerable resources at her command. She had decided when she and her father had arrived, short on cash but long in ambition, that she would aim for the best. If she could not be comfortable in New York, she would be fabulously wealthy in Denver.

There was only one thing standing in her path.

She unrolled the poster halfway and looked in distaste at the words and pictures. Her feelings in this matter were quite genuine, insofar as the circus people were concerned, and Niall would be as grateful for her efforts on Athena's behalf as he had been in the past. He was beginning to recognize that Athena needed something other than what he could provide. Something that might be found far away from Denver.

As long as Athena was the focus of Niall's life, neither one of them could be happy. Nor could Cecily Ethelinda Hockensmith.

The bronze Dore clock on the marble mantelpiece chimed the hour. Cecily knew where most of Athena's circle was at the moment— enjoying luncheon in the Windsor's dining room as they did every

Thursday. Athena never joined them, and Cecily had not yet been invited into the sanctum of Denver's young female society.

That would come soon enough. Athena had welcomed her into her philanthropic sisterhood and to her home, but the unfortunate girl had less social influence than she believed. Cecily had eavesdropped on conversations not intended for her ears, or Athena's. She suspected that those haughty young ladies, who professed to be Athena's friends, needed only a nudge to look away from Miss Munroe and toward a more mature woman of greater sophistication.

"Miss Hockensmith? Mr. Munroe will see you now."

She nodded at the respectful secretary and followed him into Niall's office. It was not the first time she had been in the room, but it never failed to take her breath away. No similar office in New York was more impressive. Or more opulent.

She had learned that Niall did not keep such luxury for himself. He knew the value of impressing those who came to him seeking financial backing, or potential investors in his own enterprises. Money begat money. Niall Munroe had Midas's touch and utter indifference to his own personal comfort.

He rose from behind his leather-topped mahogany desk and bowed slightly. "Miss Hockensmith. Charmed to see you." He gestured to one of the matched chairs across from the desk and remained standing where he was. "How may I be of service?"

Cecily took her seat, suppressing a frown. After months of acquaintance, he was still formal with her. She might even say aloof, but that was insupportable. She could be patient. And most devoted to her cause.

"I hope I have not inconvenienced you, Mr. Munroe," she said in her most melodious voice. "I would not have come if I hadn't felt a certain urgency in my errand. Indeed, I . . . considered carefully before coming to see you."

His gray gaze settled on her and slid past. "Please speak freely, Miss Hockensmith. I am happy to assist you in any way I can."

He was obviously impatient with her. She got in the way of his business. She knew how to trouble those still waters and make him take notice. She knew how to take a small, unimportant thing and make it seem of great consequence.

"Thank you, Mr. Munroe. If you will allow me . . ." She rose, taking care that her skirts fell just right, and moved with conscious grace to his desk. "I will be as brief as possible. A few days ago, while we were visiting Athena at the circus—you may recall?"

"Yes, Miss Hockensmith. It was kind of you to share Athena's enjoyment."

"It was my pleasure, of course. But while we were there, we received these posters from the proprietor—Mr. French, I believe? I confess that I had not thought to look at mine until some time had passed. I am not at all familiar with circuses and the people who inhabit them, so I had not thought it of importance."

Niall glanced at the rolled paper she had placed on the desk. "Ah, yes. I remember."

"You can imagine my distress when I saw the nature of the performance these circus people intended to give our orphans." She unrolled the poster and used a pair of weights on Niall's desk to hold down the ends, turning it toward him.

He barely glanced at it. "Miss Hockensmith, I understand the nature of the performance. I see nothing harmful in a circus."

Cecily held on to her temper. Men in general could be obtuse, but Niall Munroe was worst than most. He needed a little more encouragement. "Please read it, Mr. Munroe." She placed a gloved fingertip near the top of the sheet. "Only look at what they consider their greatest attraction!"

He looked. He frowned, and his brows drew down in a way that more than appeased Cecily's disquiet.

"The Wolf-Man," he murmured. Cecily watched his face as he examined the garish picture of a creature half-man and half-beast, fanged and slavering, its long nails raking at the bars of a flimsy-looking cage. " 'The only true beast-man in existence, certified by the experts in the greatest Halls of Science, acclaimed throughout the nation. Stand within inches of its ferocious claws. Hear its terrifying growls. See it with your own eyes . . .' " He looked up at Cecily. "I saw nothing of this when I was on the lot.

"I have always heard it said that these people excel at deception. This 'Wolf-Man' is not the only hideous attraction of which they boast. There is the snake woman and her poisonous serpents, and any number of freakish creatures unfit to be seen by young children who have no parents to guide them."

Niall continued to stare at her, the thoughts running swift behind his eyes. Cecily pressed her advantage.

"That is not my sole concern," she went on. "I realize that Athena hired these people without being fully aware of their natures. She has made the best of things and her desire to entertain the children is laudable, but Athena is much too warmhearted to judge with the cool reason we must sometimes employ to protect what we hold dear. I must say that I do not feel that circus people are appropriate company for either Athena or the children."

Niall locked his hand behind his back and half turned, gazing at the velvet curtains drawn over the window. "They were to give only one performance."

"But what damage might be done while they are here? Athena is this very day observing a rehearsal." She leaned over the desk. "You must see, Mr. Munroe, that I speak only out of deepest regard for your sister. I have been in Denver a short while, but in that time I have observed that Athena's heart has complete control over her head. I fear for her."

Niall's shoulders hunched. She had scored a point in his most vulnerable region. "I had not known about this Wolf-Man—but the others . . ." His voice was as stiff as his posture. "I would not allow my sister to be in the company of anyone who might harm her. Of that you may be sure, Miss Hockensmith."

Ah. Of course he would be defensive. She must not let him think she found fault with his care of his beloved sister.

"Naturally you could not be aware of all this. You must concede, Mr. Munroe, that we women do understand each other better than even a brother could. You cannot be everywhere at once, nor think of every possibility. That is why I have taken it upon myself to help in any way I can."

At last he turned back to her. At last she had his full attention, even his appreciation. "I have not been unaware of your efforts, Miss Hockensmith. I have not disregarded your previous observations, and I realize that . . . even I cannot give Athena everything she may require."

"You are as fine a brother as any lady could wish. But Athena has no mother, no older sister to guide her. And though everyone in Denver society loves and admires your sister, Mr. Munroe, her very goodness may leave her defenseless against those who would take advantage of her. The uneducated and destitute, of any sort, are notorious for just such behavior."

He stared at the poster. "You once suggested that I send Athena away—to New York, perhaps. I did not see any benefit in it before. But we do have a second cousin there, in good society, who might provide companionship for her."

"And I know many in New York who would love her as much as we do." She clasped her hands eloquently. "It is only here that she is . . .

bound by her past. She feels such a need to prove herself, and I see no evidence that she intends to moderate her activities."

"I have spoken to her on that subject."

"But has she listened? Some time away, in the company of well-bred and older advisers, would allow her to find a new perspective and realize how much more there is in the world to enjoy."

Niall subjected her to the same intense, piercing gaze that he had given the poster. "I am not yet convinced that she would be better off away from the only family she has. You do not know her as well as I, Miss Hockensmith."

Quickly she changed strategies and smiled gently. "Naturally not. You understand better than anyone how to care for Athena."

Her retreat softened his stance. "Nevertheless, you have valid points, Miss Hockensmith. I will consider them. As for the circus . . . there is no business here that cannot wait." He removed the weights and let the poster curl up. "I will see Athena at once. Would you be so kind as to accompany me?"

Her heart leaped. "Of course."

He smiled, a more genuine expression this time. "You are a lady of great generosity yourself, Miss Hockensmith. As generous as your father is astute. I believe he and I shall soon be sealing our partnership."

Elated, Cecily showed him only humble satisfaction. "That is wonderful news, Mr. Munroe."

"Athena and I will hope to see you and your father at dinner in the coming week," he said. "But for the moment—" He stepped around the desk, took his hat from the mahogany stand, and offered his arm to Cecily. "Shall we go, Miss Hockensmith?"

She took his elbow and walked with him to the door. Let those overweening young ladies at the Windsor observe her now, and reconsider her worth. They had much to learn. Niall Munroe might be particularly unschooled where women were concerned, but he was still a man. And she was very much a woman.

Woman enough to rule all of Denver society.

"I am a werewolf."

Morgan had never been one to question his senses. He had relied on their accuracy all his life, and he was not prepared to doubt them now. He had not misunderstood Athena Munroe's startling announcement.

Her gaze held his, steady and sane, though she shivered under the blanket and was not so well as she claimed. He would swear that she wasn't crazy. She'd have no cause to make up such a story, when most people would run screaming in terror after what she had witnessed.

But he would have known. Surely he would have *known*. Yet he had returned to the lot because of her, and just in time to save her from serious injury, if not death. Now they were connected more surely than by any tenuous sympathy. Now it was so much worse.

Fool.

"Have you . . . nothing to say?" she asked, a catch in her voice. "Perhaps you need proof of some kind. Unfortunately, I do not know how to give it."

She looked so small, so fragile without the armor of her chair, her legs like a rag doll's beneath her skirts. She had been a feather in his arms—no, not a feather, for a feather had no substance. She was altogether real, and warm, and female.

A female of his blood. He did not want it to be true. Oh, no. He wanted to prove her a liar.

"If you are what you claim," he said, "there are ways of showing it." He glanced around the tent. "Tell me what is in that chest."

She looked at the painted wooden trunk. "I don't—"

"Tell me what you smell."

Her eyes widened with comprehension. Not shock, or fear, or amazement, but recognition.

"A test," she murmured. "Very well." She closed her eyes again and breathed in deeply. Her brow puckered in a frown.

"There are a number of items in the chest," she said slowly. "Something . . . made of flowers. Dried flowers, and straw. A hat. Caitlin's." She breathed in again. "Yes, it belongs to Caitlin. And there is also a piece of leather—very worn—that is also Caitlin's, but it has been used with horses. Metal . . . a buckle, perhaps. A bit of harness. And . . . yes, the smell of an old book, one that has been damp too many times. Like an old, musty library. I think it is Ulysses's. And something of Harry's. Wool. Some article of clothing." She opened her eyes. "I hope you do not expect me to identify the specific garment?"

Morgan stared at her face. He knew she could not have seen the contents of the chest, yet she had described them accurately and without hesitation.

She had a werewolf's senses. If he bade her listen to some distant sound, report a fragment of conversation from the big top, he was sure she would oblige him. But if he asked her to stalk a buck in the deep wood, or run tirelessly for hours on end, or strip herself naked . . .

He worked his fingers into fists. "Impressive," he said. "But there is a surer form of proof. Change."

He might as well have struck her. She paled, and then the color returned in a rush. "You mean change into a wolf, as you did?"

She spoke as if the very idea was unthinkable. "What is wrong, Miss Munroe? Have you never done it before? Or is it that those who live as you do are above such things?"

"As I do?" She tried to push up on her elbows, thought better of it, and lay down again. "I do not understand you."

"Here, in the city. Among those people."

She was too practiced at the games of her kind to reveal any hurt, but he sensed it in her nonetheless. "*Those* people?" she said with a brittle smile. "You mean my friends? My brother? Those with orderly lives and assets and connections?"

"If you were anything like me," he said, "you could not deny your blood. And if you did not deny it, you could not tolerate the pretty cage you live in." He leaned forward, holding her gaze. "You know what I am. You must know others. Why did you choose *this* time to admit your nature if you prefer your safe and easy life? Why tell me at all?"

She let the blanket fall to her waist and made a Herculean effort to prop herself up. Morgan moved to help her, but her eyes flashed such proud disdain that he fell back.

"I confess that I know little of . . . our kind," she said. "I have only known of one other like me—"

"Your brother?"

"My mother. She . . . went away when I was born."

A peculiar feeling came over him, a desire to ease the sorrow he heard in her voice, to protect her from future unhappiness. Insane, unaccountable emotions.

But it was instinct—deep, reliable instinct—that told him to believe her words. To accept her claims.

To trust her.

"And your father?" he asked, more gently.

"He was not like my mother, but he knew what she was. When I was old enough to understand, he gave me a letter she had written before she . . . went away. It explained a few things, but so much was left unsaid. I was not even sure if there were others like us, or how many. Until now—"

"What about your brother?"

"He has a different mother—" She paused, weighing her words. "He knows what I am, but he is like Papa."

Human. Human father, human brother, absent mother. Raised in sheltered privilege in the heart of a human city. Alone.

Was that why she had come to him—for the answers her mother had not given her?

"Is that why you can't Change?" he asked. "You had no one to teach you?"

"But I did. I taught myself." Even in her awkward position she managed to square her shoulders and maintain her dignity. "I could do what you did, once. When I was younger. Before—" She made a brief, dismissive gesture toward her legs.

Pain. For a moment it was stark in her eyes, along with memories too agonizing to bear. His mind formed an image of himself crippled as she was, and flinched away from the horror. What had seemed an inconvenience for a human was worse than death to a werewolf.

"Your pity is quite unnecessary," she said, lifting her chin. "I accepted it long ago." Her eyes gave the lie to her words, but the deceptively tranquil cadence had returned to her voice. She might have been addressing her lady friends at tea.

If he'd been wise, he would have accepted her denial, told her whatever she wished to know, and sent her on her way. She believed she had come to terms with her affliction; who was he to suggest otherwise? If she had made a tolerable life for herself in the human world, that was her own affair.

But he remembered the small-minded conversation of the women she called "friends." Human friends. They could not know what she was, and still they branded her an outsider, an object of the pity she rejected.

He had been drawn to her by senses more profound than mere intellect. Drawn to protect her. And now that she had given him the secret that made her even more an outsider than before . . .

In all his wanderings, he had never met another of the wolf blood—not in the saloons or on the dusty roads, in ramshackle towns or mining camps. Now he found his mirror in a woman of wealth, education, and the position humans so valued. But there was no wildness in Athena Munroe. Spirit, perhaps, and courage, but no desperate yearning for the freedom beyond human walls.

We are nothing alike. We cannot be.

"I have tried to devote my time and resources to the service of others," she said quietly. "I am quite content. I have put that other life aside. But when I saw you . . . change . . . I realized that there was still a small part of me that was not yet laid to rest."

With an unwelcome jolt of insight, Morgan recognized how great an admission she had made to him. Her physical disadvantages made her fight doubly hard to be competent and strong in every other part of her life. In one way they *were* alike; they both did everything possible to avoid needing. Athena helped others; they needed her, not the reverse.

There was little enough that *he* needed. But now Athena needed him, and he did not know the extent of that need. Did she expect him— him, of all people—to absolve her of her werewolf nature?

He jumped up from the chair and paced out a circle in the sawdust. "What do you want of me?"

Athena had managed to work her legs to the edge of the cot, as if she might put her weight on her feet and walk away. "If you would be so kind," she said, "I would like to sit up. I am fully recovered."

He was certainly not. But he went to her and lifted her again, carrying her to the chair. The contact was disturbing, and he was aware of her distinct female scent and the acceleration of her heartbeat. Once she was settled he released her quickly and stepped away.

"Please forgive me, Mr. Holt," she said. "I realize that you did not seek my confidences. I shall try not to impose too much. If you can tell me—" She bit her lower lip. "Did you ever meet a woman named Gwenyth Desbois?"

"Your mother?"

She nodded. Her eyes shone—with hope, perhaps. He hated himself for having to shatter it.

"No. I knew only one other of wolf blood—my own mother."

"I see." She gazed down at her hands. "I had thought that you, having traveled so widely, might have known more like us."

He shook his head, wishing he could lessen the sting. "I last saw my mother and sister when I was fourteen."

"So long ago? You were only a boy."

"I was not a boy for long."

"But you loved them. Something kept you apart from them. I know what it is to lose—" The corner of her mouth trembled. "I loved my father."

He did not pursue the path she offered. "They are gone," he said. "Life continues."

"Yes." After a time, she smiled. Always the smile, fore-bearing and generous, covering what she did not want the world to see. "I still have Niall, and my work."

Niall Munroe—arrogant, confident . . . and human. "Your brother knows what you are, and doesn't care?"

"As I said, he is my half brother. He has known since the first time I—for many years."

And he was undoubtedly glad that she kept her secret from anyone else. Few humans were so tolerant. "Your father was married twice?"

A faint blush came to her cheeks. "No."

So. Either she or her brother was what humans called a bastard—illegitimate, born to a mother without the status of a wife. Such things meant much in her world. When werewolves mated, it was for life . . . unless one of the pair was human.

"You have never tried to Change again?" he asked, eager to escape the subject.

"Not since the accident." Her smile was achingly brave and thoroughly fraudulent.

"Were you afraid?"

He had not meant the question to be so challenging. He did not expect an answer, but she gave it anyway. "I did not know what would happen if I tried to Change after I recovered from my injuries," she said. "It happened in the mountains, in wintertime. I was in wolf shape just before the accident happened, but I Changed back when my legs were hurt."

Then she *had* known what it was to run free. Once more he was forced to amend his assumptions about her. From his own experience, Morgan knew that an injury was not always the same in both shapes. It was risky to Change when severely wounded, for the great effort could lead to death. But a minor injury could be healed by the Change itself. What crippled the woman might not cripple the wolf.

But he couldn't be sure. If she tried to Change and became a wolf with two useless legs . . .

That was what she feared. That was why she tried to forget her dual nature—until he reminded her of it. Better to live half a life than become a mockery of nature.

But she had said some part of herself could not forget.

"The past is the past," he said. "I can't help you, Miss Munroe."

She dropped her gaze, seemed about ready to reply, and gave her head a small shake. "You have been most helpful, Mr. Holt. You saved my life, and answered my questions willingly. I can ask no more. Now, if you would be so kind as to bring my chair . . ."

The courteous wall was back in place, vulnerability banished behind the boundaries of propriety and status. "You owe me nothing. But I do ... ask ... that you not blame Caitlin or the troupers for what happened. It was an accident."

"You do care about them, don't you?" she said softly. Her eyes warmed, and for an unbearable moment she looked as though she might reach out to him. She regained her senses quickly enough. "Never fear. I intend to go ahead with the performance. I am sure Miss Hughes will make sure the horses are safe for the children. Please thank Mr. French for a most enjoyable visit, and reassure him of my goodwill."

Morgan recognized the dismissal. She had spilled out her heart to him, purged herself of doubts, and now she was ready to return to her life. He could banish any thought of a mysterious bond between them.

"One last piece of advice, Miss Munroe," he said. "Give your trust sparingly. Do not mistake enemies for allies."

He started for the exit before she could respond. Caitlin blocked the way just outside, pushing Athena's chair before her.

"Is she all right?" the girl asked, peering over his shoulder. "I was so worried, but I had to quiet the horses ... I can't believe that Pennyfarthing bolted like that. It is not like him, and he couldn't tell me what was wrong. Harry is beside himself, but he thought we ought to leave you two alone. She is all right, Morgan?"

"She isn't hurt."

"Was she terribly afraid of you?"

He wanted to laugh. "She accepted it quite ... well."

"Then she didn't think she was going mad? She won't tell anyone?"

"I doubt it."

Her eyes narrowed. "Something else is wrong, then. Is she angry at us? Will she withdraw her support?"

"She said she wouldn't."

"Did you quarrel?"

"Strangers seldom quarrel."

"Especially when one stranger has saved the other's life, and reveals his deepest secret."

He avoided her too-knowing gaze. "See for yourself. You can show her to Harry and take her back to her carriage."

"That is all?"

"What more do you want, Firefly? Her pledge of undying devotion?"

"Has it gone so far already, Morgan?"

"The lady is waiting."

"But not forever. Don't make that mistake, my friend."

He growled at her and bolted. Her low, taunting chuckle chased him halfway across the lot.

Chapter 8

Athena Munroe was very quiet when Caitlin went to fetch her. She smiled at Caitlin graciously enough, but it was the sort of automatic smile that meant her mind was elsewhere.

Caitlin knew the name of that "elsewhere." Something was definitely going on between Morgan and Athena, only Morgan would probably rather die than admit it. Caitlin had a good idea that she wouldn't be any more successful prying information out of Athena.

Yet Athena had seen what Morgan truly was. He said she accepted it, but no one used to her sort of life would be so calm when all her illusions of reality were turned upside down. Townies often accused troupers of double-dealing, but the townies were just as good at playing false. Maybe better.

A very delicate situation, indeed. But Caitlin had never been the least bit delicate.

"I'm sorry for what happened in the ring," she said cautiously. "Pennyfarthing has never done anything like that before. If I'd a notion he would bolt, I wouldn't have used him today."

Athena blinked and looked at Caitlin as if recognizing her for the first time. "Please do not give it another thought, Miss Hughes. I believe that Pennyfarthing was more frightened than I was. As you can see, I am quite well."

Are you, then? "I am glad. Do you like horses, Miss Munroe?"

Athena's smile wavered ever so slightly. "Yes."

That simple answer said so much more than a speech. What must it be like, to be able to ride and run and walk and then have all that taken away from you?

"Then we're still to give the performance for the children," Caitlin said.

"I am sure that such an incident won't be repeated."

"I'll make certain it does not." Caitlin moved behind Athena's chair. "You'll want to go home, Miss Munroe, after all the excitement. Harry is that upset over what happened. He wants to apologize personally, if you'll see him."

"Of course. I—" She stopped, and Caitlin could feel the storm gathering. "May I ask a frank question, Miss Hughes?" Athena did not turn her head, but her shoulders were as tense as Regina's high wire. "Have you always known what he is?"

No need to ask who "he" was . . . and no point in pretending not to understand. "Since he first came to us."

"Then he will always have a place with you here."

Now *that* was an interesting remark. "If he wants it. We take care of our own." She crouched eye to eye with Athena. "What you saw today—not many townies would accept it as well as you have."

"Townies. Is that what you call us?"

"Troupers have learned not to trust too easily."

"Morgan warned me not to trust. I could not live that way, never trusting anyone."

"Here, we trust each other. And now we must trust you. For Morgan's sake."

"You are very fond of him, Miss Hughes."

"He is like a brother to me. A difficult brother."

"A difficult man."

"But he *is* a man, Miss Munroe."

Athena looked away. "You need have no fear. I will not reveal his secret."

On impulse, Caitlin touched her hand. The kid-gloved fingers were rigid with unexpressed agitation. "You are a very brave lady," she said

"For a towny, Miss Hughes?"

"You'd better call me Caitlin from now on. In a way, you are part of our family now."

Athena's fingers relaxed and curled about Caitlin's. Her smile became something more than just another gesture of impersonal benevolence. "Thank you, Caitlin. My name is Athena." She slipped her hand free. "As you said, we have had more than enough excitement for one day."

"Yes." Caitlin got up and took the handles of the chair. "If you'll just say a word or two to Harry—he's in the cookhouse, probably fretting himself to death." She hesitated. "Do you wish me to send for Mr. Munroe?"

"That will not be necessary. I can do a number of things without my brother's help."

Ah, a sore spot. Caitlin well remembered how masterful Niall Munroe was, and it was no wonder that he'd have a protective streak where his sister was involved. In his world, men expected obedience from their women—and Athena was less free than most. Did she chafe under her brother's rule?

There were some things even great wealth didn't buy—not freedom, not loyalty, and not love. Ulysses knew that only too well. And Caitlin was more grateful than ever that what she had didn't depend on the crutch of money.

As long as the troupe survived.

Caitlin wheeled the chair around and pushed it out into the backyard. "I think," she said softly, "that you can do anything you set your mind to."

Athena did not reply. Caitlin respected her silence. It was the beginning of a friendship that surprised her, and likely surprised Athena even more. Caitlin had a feeling that it was not the last wonder to come of today's events.

They were halfway to the cookhouse when her feeling was proven correct. A tall figure came striding across the lot with fell purpose in every step.

Niall Munroe. Caitlin pulled the chair to a stop and listened to her heart thunder like her horses' hooves. "I think your brother has come for you, Athena," she said.

Mr. Munroe was not a man to waste time on formalities. He looked at Caitlin—once, again—and then turned to his sister.

"Are you finished with your visit, Athena?" he asked.

"Quite finished. You did not have to fetch me. I was—"

"I would prefer you to go straight home. Miss Hockensmith is waiting at the carriage, and she will go with you."

"What is this about, Niall? Why—"

"It need not concern you. I will take you to the carriage."

Athena's mouth set in an obstinate line, so unlike its usual gentle curve. Caitlin looked from sister to brother. Oh, yes, there was rebellion here. "You didn't have to worry about your sister, Mr. Munroe," she said. "She has been quite safe with us."

His face reddened, a most unexpected sight on one so exalted. "I wish to speak to you, Miss Hughes. If you will kindly remain here until I return."

"Of course. I have nothing better to do."

He ignored her mockery and stepped into her place behind the chair. As he pushed his sister away, Athena glanced back at Caitlin. It was a look of hidden anger and an appeal Caitlin did not know how to answer.

She set her jaw and waited. She was under no man's orders, least of all Niall Munroe's, but he was paying the bills. And she was determined to find out more about the kind of man who acted as if he owned the world and everyone in it.

At the edge of the lot, Athena and Munroe met another woman— Miss Hockensmith, whom Caitlin remembered from Athena's first visit—and Niall lifted Athena into the waiting carriage which had been joined by a second, smaller vehicle. He and Miss Hockensmith held a brief conversation, and then he turned on his heel and started toward Caitlin. Miss Hockensmith stared after him.

Caitlin met him with a provoking smile. "Do you always treat your sister as if she were a servant, Mr. Munroe?"

"That is none of your affair, Miss Hughes."

"Then why do you want to speak with me? Surely I am too lowly for a fine gentleman to dally with."

That intriguing flush returned, playing up the sharp lines of his face. He pulled a rolled paper from his coat and held it out to her.

"I have only one question, Miss Hughes. What is this 'Wolf-Man'?"

She took a second look at the paper and realized that it was one of the posters that Harry had given to the visitors. She knew the design well, and what it advertised. Was it possible, even remotely possible, that Athena had broken her word and told her brother what she had seen today?

No. But if not, why should Munroe be so disturbed? "It is only one of our sideshow acts."

"And just what sort of act is it?"

"Every troupe has its secrets. The Wolf-Man is one of our special attractions. People come to be frightened and thrilled, and we try not to disappoint them."

The rolled paper began to buckle in his grip. "I saw no such person when I came to Colorado Springs. Does he hide from public view, Miss Hughes? Is he some sort of monster unfit for respectable society? What does he do—change into a wolf before the audience's eyes?"

She laughed. "Surely you do not believe in such things, Mr. Munroe. Not a smart, educated gentleman such as yourself."

He actually flinched. "I have a right to know what I have employed."

"You are a rather big man to be afraid of fairy tales. Your sister was not so alarmed."

All at once his hand shot out to grip her wrist. "Did she meet this . . . this 'fairy tale'?"

She stared at his hand. "Harry introduced her to everyone. Don't you think your sister would have told you if we presented a danger to her orphans . . . or to you?"

He let her go just as suddenly as he had grabbed her. "Miss Hockensmith was right," he said. "You are not fit company—"

"So you do let at least one woman rule you," she said sweetly. She waved to the vigilant figure standing beside the carriage, and watched with fascination as Munroe's formerly cool demeanor vanished in a cloud of wrath.

"I wish to see this man, Miss Munroe. At once."

"What are you so afraid of? Anyone who is not exactly like you?"

"I will not have . . . freaks on display for my sister or her dependents."

"In that case," she said, reaching up to her hair, "you should know exactly what you have bought." With swift, efficient motions she pulled the unruly mass behind her ears.

"My God," he said. "What happened to your ears?"

"I was born with them," she said, "just as you were born with your money and your pride. I am one of the freaks you so despise, Mr. Munroe. You may insult me as much as you wish, but not my friends. Any one of them is twice the man you will ever be."

He took a step back, still staring at the neat points on the tips of her ears. "Where is Mr. French?" he asked in a strangled voice.

She turned her back and marched across the lot, not waiting to see if he followed. With every step she cursed herself for her utter lack of sense.

Thanks to her outburst, the troupe might lose the patronage of the Munroes. And if they lost that, they lost the money they so desperately needed to keep the family together.

She'd be damned if she'd let Munroe see her regret. She led him to the cookhouse, where Harry was nursing a glass of precious whiskey at one of the long plank tables, and stood aside. Harry scrambled to his feet with a nervous smile.

"Ah, Mr. Munroe! How delightful to see you. Your sister is most charming, most—"

"I must speak to you, Mr. French. Alone." He looked pointedly at Caitlin.

Harry threw her a glance full of alarm. There was nothing she could do to comfort him—nothing but find a way to hear what passed between him and Munroe. Her hearing was keener than most, but not keen enough to catch the conversation without blatant eavesdropping.

Morgan. She turned and went in search of him, hoping he had not gone running as he often did when he was troubled. But luck was with her; she found him watching the troupe's jugglers with tightly folded arms and a dark expression.

She grabbed his arm and pulled him away. It felt as if she were dragging an angry tiger at the end of a silken leash. "I need your help, Morgan. Niall Munroe is talking to Harry, and I must know what they are saying."

One good thing to be said about Morgan was that he never wasted time on useless questions. He went with her to the cookhouse entrance and they stopped behind a sheltering tent pole. Harry and Niall were still talking—or at least Niall was.

Morgan tilted his head. His eyes narrowed to slits, and the corner of his mouth twitched.

"Munroe is trying to buy Harry off," he said. "He is paying him to leave Denver at once, before the performance."

"How much is he offering?"

"Half of what he promised for the show." He lowered his head, and she thought she could see the hair lift along his skull. "What is this about, Firefly?"

"He thinks he is protecting his sister," she said. "From the freaks, like us."

"He knew what he was getting when he hired the troupe." Gooseflesh rose on Caitlin's skin when he looked at her. "Or is it something else?"

She touched his arm. "He saw one of the posters. He didn't know about the Wolf-Man before, Morgan. I don't think he could guess the real truth even if he tried. But he—" She shook her head. "He is afraid of anyone who doesn't fit in his world."

"How do you know this?"

Morgan's voice had grown soft and dangerous. She shivered. "It was my fault. I said things I shouldn't. But he had already made up his mind before he came here. He has ordered Athena to leave. If it were up to her—"

"You like Athena."

"I believe she can be trusted. So do you."

He didn't deny it. "Munroe has no right—"

"He thinks he has every right."

He returned to Niall's conversation. "Harry is not giving an answer. He says that he doesn't want to disappoint Miss Athena. He is asking Munroe for a little time to talk to the troupers, and to prove that the circus is safe."

Bless him. Caitlin risked a peep into the cookhouse. She did not need Morgan's translation to see how Munroe reacted to Harry's evasion. He made a brief, final statement—loud enough for Caitlin to hear—and turned, his face thunderous.

"He said," Morgan finished, "that it would not be wise for Harry to remain in town—that it would be an unfortunate mistake." His lips lifted, baring his teeth. "Harry has one day to decide."

It was so much worse than Caitlin had expected. She ducked out of the entrance as Munroe charged toward it, prepared to pull Morgan aside with physical force if necessary. But Morgan behaved himself. He retreated—"faded" was more the proper word—and Munroe shot out the door without seeing him.

"Do not waste your time on him, Firefly," Morgan said.

"What do you suggest? Will *you* talk to him? You're no better a diplomat than I am."

She set off after Munroe, running to match his long strides. She would apologize. She would beg, on her knees if necessary, for him to let the troupers remain long enough for the performance. Not only because of the money, but for Athena's sake.

Yes, for Athena. And maybe . . . just maybe for Morgan as well.

"Why the hurry, little fly? Do you have a new lover?"

Tamar could appear and disappear with the same disconcerting ease as Morgan. Caitlin slowed to a walk. "Not now, Tamar," she said. "I have important business."

"With him?" Tamar arched her long, elegant neck in the direction Niall had gone. "This should be most interesting."

Exasperated, Caitlin hurried on, hoping that Tamar would not interfere. She caught up with Niall just as he reached the waiting carriages.

"Mr. Munroe," she whispered, touching his arm. "I must talk to you."

His muscles were rigid under the fine wool of his coat. "I have nothing to say, Miss Hughes. My sister must return home."

"You are making a mistake," she said, pressing more firmly into his sleeve. "Please—"

He turned. Their gazes met, and locked. An incredible spark of . . . something . . . sizzled between them, forming a current that began at the eyes and rushed through Caitlin's body to the place where her hand touched his arm.

She could only guess what her own face must reveal, but Niall Munroe's might as well have served as a billboard. He leaned toward her—slightly, oh, so slightly—and his lips parted. A glazed look came into his eyes. Caitlin sucked in her breath.

"Mr. Munroe. We really must be on our way!"

Miss Hockensmith's voice from the carriage window broke the current. Niall jerked back his hand. Without another word to Caitlin, he gave a terse command to the coachman and climbed into the driver's seat of the smaller carriage.

One glimpse of Athena's distressed face was all Caitlin saw before the carriages rattled into motion, rolling and bumping across the pot-holed ground.

"So sad," Tamar said behind her. "It was such a promising romance, was it not? But you will always lose to such a rich and beauteous lady." She blinked half-lidded eyes and stroked the head of one of her ever-present serpents. "Unless, of course, you make a gift of the one thing no man will refuse. Do you wish me to teach you how it is done, little fly?"

"Keep out of this, Tamar. It has nothing to do with you."

"Oh, no?" Tamar lifted her black, painted brows.

Caitlin strode past her and returned to the cookhouse, dreading what she would find.

Harry was still there, every bit as miserable as when she had left him. Morgan was with him, and Ulysses had arrived along with a dozen of the other troupers. They were talking amongst themselves, trying to decide what had happened.

Caitlin shook her head as she approached, and Harry sighed. "Ladies and gentleman," he said, "it seems that we have an important and unpleasant decision to make. Gather the others, and we shall meet in the big top within the next half hour."

Efficient as always in a time of crisis, the troupers were assembled and waiting in the big top well before the half hour was up. Ulysses and Morgan kept their places close to Harry, like grotesquely mismatched royal guards. Caitlin was grateful once more that Morgan had not gone after Niall Munroe. She half feared he might have devoured Athena's brother for supper.

"My friends, my children," Harry said in his most carrying voice, "circumstances have compelled me to call this meeting so that we may discuss our future."

A general murmur followed his words, but he raised his plump hands to quiet it. "As you know, in only a few days we were to give a charitable performance for the children of the orphanage patronized by Miss Athena Munroe and her brother. We were to be paid a most handsome sum for this privilege." He lowered his head. "Alas, complications have arisen."

In far less words than he usually employed, Harry explained what Niall had told him. There were cries of disgust, a handful of curses, and much shaking of heads.

"Never trust townies," someone shouted. "They'll always break their word."

"Why?" another man demanded. "What is all this about, Harry?"

Harry wrung his hands. "Well, you see . . . when he hired us, he did not know about our main sideshow attraction, our own Morgan. I confess that I do not quite understand his reasoning, but he has taken it into his head that our Wolf-Man may be dangerous to the children and his sister. It is entirely ridiculous, but . . ."

The troupers fell silent. As one they looked at Morgan. He bore their stares with cold indifference, a curiosity among curiosities.

"Munroe is afraid of freaks," Caitlin said loudly, stepping forward. "Any sort of freak. But his sister is not like him." She swept the crowd with her stare. "She is a good woman. She saw what Morgan is, and wasn't afraid. She wants to help us."

"Does she hold the purse strings?" Florizel the clown cried out.

"You said Munroe made a threat if we didn't get out of town," said one of the Flying Grassotti Brothers. "We have heard that he's a powerful man in this city. He has offered us money to leave—it's not worth the risk to stay and make him angry."

How could she counter that argument? Circus folk never stood up well against townies, let alone prominent ones. They knew the wisdom of strategic retreat when townies became hostile. She glanced at Harry, at Morgan, and last at Ulysses.

Ulysses moved only a little, but every eye focused on him when he did. "Harry formed this troupe," he said quietly. "Many of us had no homes, no employment, nothing at all before he took us in. His hearth has always been open to anyone in need—anyone who is different, regardless of the nature of that difference." He looked directly at Florizel. "Once you aspired to be a great thespian of the legitimate stage. But no one would employ you because of your appearance. Your talent meant nothing. You were lost in the throes of dipsomania when we found you, and Harry gave you a chance to play to the crowds."

He turned to Regina, whose tall, impossibly thin body towered over everyone else. "Your brother cast you out when you refused to marry a man who would not touch you if not for your family wealth. You would not easily have found a partner outside, but here . . ."

He didn't finish his sentence. Regina clasped her long, spidery fingers around the thick ones of her husband, Tor the strongman.

"There are countless other stories like these," Ulysses said. "It is clear to me—"

"Harry asked for our opinions," Giovanni said. "You don't want us to stay, do you, Harry?"

"It . . . well, it is true that Mr. Munroe wishes us to leave and will pay us half the promised sum if we do so. But Miss Munroe—she is so very set on our performance. She even wishes to keep us on for a second one."

"I still don't see how it's worth turning a man like Munroe against us," Giovanni said. "If we have enough to see us through winter—"

"Only if nothing else happens," Caitlin said. "If we have another fire, or any bad luck at all—"

"We'll get along. Let's pull out, Harry. We don't need to borrow more trouble."

"I also vote that we leave," Tamar said, slipping up to the front of the gathering. "What do we owe to this . . . Athena Munroe? To any of their kind?"

"That's right."

"Tamar speaks truth. As long as he pays, he doesn't matter what his sister—"

A deep, reverberating growl sliced through the strident words. Morgan fixed his potent stare on each of the speakers in turn. Every one of them stepped back into the safety of the crowd.

"Cowards," he said. He didn't have to raise his voice; every word rang like the clash of cymbals. "You pride yourselves on being different and better than townies. You say you are a family. Now one comes to you who needs what you can give, and you turn your back on her."

A chorus of protests. "You are not making any sense, Morgan," Giovanni said. "Athena Munroe is rich as Croesus. How can she need our help?"

"She is not like us," Florizel said, daring to step forward again. "In what manner is she a freak, as Caitlin so kindly refers to us? She is a cripple, that is all."

Morgan snarled. Florizel's face lost what little color it had.

"A cripple," Morgan said. "An outsider among her own kind, who helps strangers without asking anything in return. She saw me Change today, and she was not afraid. And she did not change her mind about us."

Caitlin stood at Morgan's shoulder. "What Morgan says is true. She may be a towny, but she knows what it's like to suffer."

"We gave our word to perform for her orphans," Morgan said. "I will go to Munroe. I'll tell him that I will leave Denver if he allows the performance."

"You'll do that just for this lady and her orphans?" Florizel asked. "Have you been enjoying the lady's favors—what favors she has to bestow—and that is why her brother wants us gone?"

Caitlin had seldom seen Morgan make the actual Change into the "Wolf-Man," the creature he became in the sideshow. Now he began to transform, his body half-wreathed in black mist, fine dark hair flowing over his hands and feet and at the neckline of his shirt. His face remained almost untouched, but it was undeniably lupine. And deadly.

Harry intervened. "Morgan's honor and his word have been good from the first moment we met him," he said. "I trust his instincts, and Caitlin's. I think . . . I think they are right." He mopped at his face with a handkerchief. "I believe we should stay for the performance, and then leave."

"And what if Munroe refuses to pay anything?"

"Miss Munroe will see that you get your money," Morgan said. Between one heartbeat and the next, he was human again. "You decide whether or not you let a towny tell you where you can go and how you can live."

Harry coughed behind his hand. "I believe it is time for a vote. Will those who wish to leave say 'aye'?"

The few ayes were restrained and almost inaudible. When Harry asked for the nays, they rang out with conviction. Caitlin grinned at Morgan and Ulysses.

"This course does entail some risk," Ulysses said as the troupers began to disperse. "Munroe is a powerful man."

"I think you are underestimating Athena's strength of character," Caitlin said. "She wants us to stay, and I know she can stand up to her brother if she has to."

Harry blotted his face again. "I hope you are right, Caitlin. I do so wish to please the poor child. I confess that I have developed a certain . . . fondness for her."

"Calculated risks are occasionally necessary," Ulysses said, scrutinizing Morgan with interest, "if for no other reason than to preserve one's honor and keep one's word."

"Honor," Caitlin snorted. "When did honor ever get you anything, Uly? This is simply the right thing to do."

"Your reaction seems somewhat personal, Firefly."

"What's done is done," Harry said. "We've only to go ahead as best we can."

"And someone must explain to Athena what has happened," Caitlin added. "We will have to find an excuse to get her back to the lot. I'm certain her brother did not plan to tell her until we had left Denver."

"Maybe she won't defy him," Morgan said. "Her life depends on her brother's money. If he chooses, he could take away what freedom she has."

Caitlin stared at him in surprise. "It is true that he tries to protect her too much. I don't know what Niall Munroe is so afraid of, but he is not a—" She flushed and hurried on. "You spoke up for staying, Morgan. You want to help Athena—you even called her brave, yet you have no faith in her ability to fight for what she wants?"

She could see him withdrawing into himself again, denying the feelings that had prompted him to speak up for Athena with such uncharacteristic passion.

"What did you and Athena speak about in the backyard, Morgan?" Caitlin asked. "Are you testing her? Do you want her to fail, so that you'll have no reason to care?"

His head gave an almost imperceptible jerk. "Munroe thinks he can buy anything or anyone," he said through his teeth. "We are not his lapdogs."

"Neither is his sister. But if you're right, and Athena is willing to let us go—what then?"

"We must abide by her wishes, of course," Harry answered. "It is days like these when I wish I had retired years ago."

"Oh, Harry—" Caitlin paused when she realized that Morgan was halfway to the front door. "Where are you going?"

"To tell Miss Munroe," he said without breaking stride. "To find out what she wants."

Caitlin thought quickly. Who was better suited to deliver a clandestine message? *And who is more unpredictable when his heart is involved?* "You can't just walk into her house. You do not even know where she lives."

"I'll find out."

"If Niall sees you—"

"He will not see me." As if to prove his point, he seemed to vanish even before he reached the door.

There's no turning back now, Caitlin thought, haunted by that sense of destiny that had first come with Morgan Holt and returned with Niall Munroe.

"This is a hazardous game, Firefly," Ulysses said, stepping up beside her. "Morgan is not one to be made a pawn of fate."

"I thought you didn't believe in fate."

"Only when it trifles with those I consider my friends."

She rested her hand on his shoulder. "Then, my friend, let me keep the faith for all of us."

Chapter 9

Athena had never longed quite so much for the ability to pace. Her body was racked with shivers born of conflicting emotions that sought to pull her one way and then the other. The walls of her peaceful, silent room seemed about to crush her like some medieval implement of torture.

If she had faced only a single quandary this evening, she might have dealt with it easily enough. But the incidents had come as thick and fast as snowflakes in a mountain blizzard—first the near escape in the big top, then Morgan's incredible exhibition . . . the disconcerting conversation that followed . . . and finally Niall's sudden appearance and irrational behavior.

She was still angry with Niall. It was easier to nurse anger than face the other feelings that pummeled her from every direction. But even the anger frightened her, for only in recent weeks had she allowed herself to become angry for any personal reason.

Anger on behalf of the downtrodden was useful, and justified; anger due to hurt pride, or resentment, was the worst sort of selfishness. Athena knew it, and yet the knowledge did not seem to help.

She rolled her chair to the window. Niall had escorted Miss Hockensmith home, but he had not yet returned.

The passage of hours had not helped Athena's mood. She continued to relive the moment when Niall had come for her at the lot—how he had barely looked at her, dismissed her like a child, and ordered her away. How he had spoken to Caitlin, with less courtesy than to a servant. And when they had reached the privacy of home, he had refused to give any explanation for his behavior.

She had felt humiliated, treated so by her own brother in front of a friend. For Caitlin had become a friend, despite all the differences between them.

In a strange way, Caitlin reminded Athena of herself when she was younger—rash, passionate, refusing any concession to femininity or propriety—quick to give her loyalty, and her heart. What must she think after the way Niall had acted? She would believe that Athena was under her brother's thumb.

Athena had done nothing to dispel that impression. She had let Niall bully her back to the carriage, endured Cecily Hockensmith's sympathetic looks, and tormented herself with speculation upon Niall's business with the troupe.

What had gotten into him?

She picked up a bit of needlework she had left on a side table and set it back down again a moment later. Surely Niall couldn't have guessed what Morgan really was. *She* had been the only one privileged with that secret. That amazing, wonderful secret.

I am not alone.

That single, foolish thought came to her again and again, beating out a rhythm as constant and indisputable as a heartbeat. *I am not alone.*

It was not that Morgan had welcomed her with open arms as a fellow werewolf. But she had seen his eyes widen and his guard drop for just an instant when she had told him what she was.

The man she had glimpsed behind the mask . . . oh, that unveiling was fully as powerful as learning his secret. He had claimed she could not be of his blood because she lived in a city and enjoyed a comfortable life. Yet when she had spoken of her mother, there was such understanding in his eyes, such compassion, that she could have wept.

That unexpected sympathy was the reason that she let self-pity slip its tight rein. She had said little of the accident, but it was so much more than she had ever told to anyone except Papa, just before he died. She had even admitted that her mother and father had not been married.

Thank heaven she had recovered before she could wallow in events long past and irreversible. She had been able to accept Morgan's final rebuff—and his touch on her body—without flinching. And she had seen that all the tough ferocity he exhibited covered a great vulnerability and the sorrow of profound loss.

Loss so similar to her own. And he was loyal to his fellow troupers, protective of them as any elder brother might be. Yet his last words to her held a cryptic warning: *"Do not mistake enemies for allies."*

What had he meant? Surely Morgan was not her enemy. She would have liked—even been grateful for—his friendship.

Friendship? Did you hope that he could share some great mystery that you never discovered? What kind of relationship can exist when you will likely never see him again once the circus has gone?

Had she not restored the boundaries between them—the high walls of money, temperament, and belief? Did those walls not reach far higher than even the strongest wolf, whole of limb, could leap?

And why should she think *he* would ever wish to scale such barriers? He wanted no part of them.

Yet . . . *You are not alone,* her heart insisted. *And neither is he.*

She rapped her hand on the arm of her chair and turned hard away from the window. Sleep was what she required. A good night's rest cured so many ills, purged a multitude of unproductive thoughts. Most especially thoughts of what she should not want and could never have.

She bit her lip and frowned at the bed. Ordinarily she would call for Fran to assist her in moving from chair to bedstead, but it was pure selfishness to drag Fran out of her own cot at such an hour. Was it such an insurmountable gap, those few inches between her chair and the bed? Her arms were strong enough. The tiny ember of rebellion that had disturbed her of late, nursed along by the day's events, sparked into a flame.

Setting her jaw, she wheeled the chair as close to the bed as she could, aligning them side by side. She took a firm grip on the iron railing that ran the length of the bed, designed to keep her from falling out.

Perspiration broke out on her forehead, though the room was cool. The muscles in her arms already ached with the effort to come.

You can do this. You are strong enough. Alternately pushing and pulling, she began to transfer her weight from the chair to the bed rails. Her arms screamed in protest. She clenched her teeth and dragged herself up and over to the gap in the rail.

The chair rolled a few inches away. The space between it and the bed grew accordingly, widening into a chasm. The hem of her dressing gown caught on the arm of her chair. A stab of very real pain shot down her spine and lodged at its root.

She did not cry out. She would win, or they could find her on the floor in the morning. She made another laborious effort, and her dressing grown ripped and then slid from her shoulders.

For a moment she hung suspended between bed and chair, her upper half almost . . . almost . . . flat on the coverlet. Then some movement of her body shoved the chair another precious inch away. The dead weight of her lower half pulled her down, down, like grasping hands reaching from perdition.

She tumbled. Her elbow struck the bed railing as she fell, shooting pain into arm and shoulder. Far, far worse was the slow, ignominious slide to the floor.

She lay on the carpet, her nightdress bunched up about her useless knees and her elbow numb from the blow. Tears squeezed from the corners of her eyes. She let them fall. No one would see them tonight. But in the morning . . .

Rolling onto her stomach, she pushed up on her arms. It might take hours, but she could make it back to the chair or the bed. If one was not possible, the other must be. God forbid that Niall should find her like this.

A faint noise came from the direction of the stairs: footsteps ascending, so soft that she had to strain to hear them.

Morgan Holt had made her more aware of the keen senses she had always taken for granted. She knew the step of every member of the household, from Fran's light patter to Niall's purposeful thump. But this was not a tread she recognized.

Her skin began to prickle. Instinctively she reached for the hem of her nightdress and tried to tug it down over her knees. The movement set her off balance, and she fell back on her sore elbow just as the footsteps came to a halt outside her door.

It swung open. A familiar, disturbingly fascinating scent blew in with biting October air. The doorway filled with a lean and powerful figure.

Morgan Holt had come to return her call.

Morgan knew, when he opened the door, that Athena Munroe's alluring scent had led him to the right room. But she was not where he expected her to be.

She lay on the floor beside the fancy four-poster, her awkwardly bent legs half-covered by her nightdress, her face pinched with a mighty effort to conceal shock and pain. He knew at once what she had been trying to do.

He closed the door behind him and knelt beside her. Her shudder did not make him hesitate; he set his arms under her shoulders and knees and lifted her onto the bed. She brushed frantically at her gown, intent upon hiding her legs from his sight.

With an effort at detachment that should have come easily, he pulled the hem down to her ankles and drew the crumpled blankets to her waist. His fingertips brushed her calf; he snatched his hands away, but not before he felt the warmth of her damp skin and suffered a jolt of breathtaking arousal.

She flushed. "What are you doing here?"

His physical response to her left him so shaken that he could find no answer. Her emotions cascaded over him like a flash flood in the desert, and not a single one of his most impregnable defenses could hold them back.

Chagrin. Anger. Shame. All her self-contained pride was lost, for he had witnessed her failure. She recoiled from him, but it was not only because a man of her kind did not touch a woman so intimately unless he was her mate. She was ashamed because she was vulnerable, exposed—a wingless bird to be ridiculed, a rabbit to be devoured. She, who should have been strong and free.

His mind formed a picture of her rising stiffly from her chair, grimly bent on reaching her bed—her brave efforts to persevere even when her body betrayed her—her humiliating tumble to the floor. He knew what it was to regard a simple movement from chair to bed as if it were a leap across a hundred-foot chasm.

And how much courage it took to live with that insurmountable obstacle every day of her life.

Her gaze met his. He was the one, now, who recoiled at the assault upon his senses and his heart. It was as raw as an open wound, this terrible sharing. His skin seemed to take heat from hers, though they did not touch; he looked away only to discover the gentle swell of her breasts beneath the fine lawn of her nightdress, and the teasing disarray of her loose brown hair.

He crouched beside the bed, as much to protect himself as to become less threatening in her eyes. He was the invader here. This was her place, her territory; she could order him to leave. He would be smart to obey and run before . . . before . . .

"How did you get in?" she demanded. Her voice had grown more sure, though it cracked in midsentence. "The servants—"

"Did not hear me. But you did."

"Yes." She sat up against a bolster of pillows, drawing the blanket with her. "That does not explain why you come in the middle of the night, break into our house, and walk right into my . . . my room as if you had a right . . ."

"No right, but a reason," he said quietly, balancing his arms across his knees. "I came to bring you a message. Your brother—"

"If my brother were here—"

"But he is not."

"Do you make a habit of trespassing like a thief, Mr. Holt, when there is no man to stop you?"

He could not help but admire the increasing steadiness of her voice and the directness of her gaze. Nor could he be angry with her after what he had witnessed. Here was not the nice, formally polite, and benevolent lady who had descended from on high to view her brother's surprise gift. This was the woman he had glimpsed briefly in the tent after the near-accident—the she-wolf reawakened—and he liked her the better for her honest annoyance.

Yes, he *liked* her. Even the word felt strange as he rolled it around in his mind, tasting and exploring it as if he were a cub with an intriguing bit of bone.

"I come and go where I wish," he said, "but not to do you harm."

"I do not suppose that your upbringing, whatever it was, taught you that it does considerable harm to enter a lady's room uninvited and un-chaperoned. It is not only impolite—" She swallowed and gripped the edge of her blanket. "Among . . . townies, reputation is something of value. If anyone were to see you here, mine would be compromised."

"I know about your rules." He shifted, and her eyes flew to track his motion. "You and your friends waste too much time worrying about what isn't important."

"What do you mean by that?" She scooted higher on the pillows, forgetting to adjust her blanket upward. "What do you know of my friends, or any of the niceties of life?"

He dropped his chin onto his folded arms. Now was as good a time as any. He could tell her what he had overheard in the Windsor's restaurant. It might be a kindness to set her free from her illusions.

But he looked at her face and knew that the truth would destroy her. She was not strong enough. Perhaps she would never be. And when the circus left Denver—tomorrow, in a week, in a month—none of it would matter to him.

It shouldn't matter now. It shouldn't matter that her brother had her on a short leash and she chose not to see, or that she'd given up half of herself out of fear of losing what little she had.

What little she had. She would laugh at him if he said that, surrounded as she was with luxury and everything money could buy. All the things his family had done without, that his father had been so hungry for.

"You were right about my upbringing, Miss Munroe," he said. "We didn't have much. We lived in a small cabin in the mountains. One bed and a cot. Only the fire and candles for light. My parents—my ma hunted, and we fished and sold furs in town. We had books, but no schooling." Memories thick with the dust of years emerged from their hidden places, raising a fog in his mind. "We didn't need anything else, until Pa—"

Stop. He drove the memories back into oblivion and got to his feet. Where in hell had that come from? Why here, with her? She was no part of his past, or his future. And his future stretched no further than the next moment.

"Your parents," Athena said, her voice suddenly gentle. "You said that you hadn't seen your family since you were a boy. To lose them at so young an age . . . I am sorry that I spoke as I did."

He forced himself to look at her. Her face had resumed that gracious, almost saintly expression, raising in him a desire to snap and snarl until she lost it again. Deliberately he raked his gaze from her eyes to her chin and lower, where the high collar of her nightdress hugged the graceful arc of her neck.

Despite the lace and frills, the sheer fabric of the garment left little to the imagination. The pink tones of her skin gave the white lawn a rosy tint, and where her breasts lifted the cloth he could see the brown circles of her nipples. Each one formed a small, intriguing peak that grew more pronounced as she noticed his stare.

Humans—or werewolves in human form—were much like animals. Their bodies responded to instinct and desires that had nothing to do with intellect. Morgan's body was very much aware of Athena's.

He had not been oblivious to her during their previous encounters. He had been conscious of her sex and tolerated a certain attraction, even before he learned of her true nature. But the attraction had been only that, and easily set aside.

No longer. Something had changed. It wasn't only his respect for her courage in challenging the limitations of her body and spirit, or that he had unwillingly shared her emotions. It wasn't that he stood in her bedchamber, a room humans regarded as the proper place for sex. Nor was it that she wore a diaphanous nightdress instead of the armor of corsets and layered skirts. He had seen many women clothed in less, and regarded them as merely the means to ease his body's needs.

Athena was not like those women. He understood the difference between females raised as she had been, and the worldly inhabitants of the circus or saloon. She had no experience, of that he was certain, and no skill. Her allure was completely unintentional.

She regarded mating as a wanton beast that could tear her precious reputation to shreds, or worse—an enemy capable of making her remember what she had lost.

No matter how carefully she and her proper society friends tried to pretend otherwise, she knew why he looked at her and why she wanted to conceal herself from his gaze. Her skin flushed, color rising from under her collar and sweeping up to the roots of her hair. Her breathing quickened. He could hear the throb of her pulse under the soft flesh of her neck. Her scent had begun a subtle change as her body prepared itself for mating, and his nostrils flared to take in the fragrance of arousal.

She *wanted* him. And he wanted her. This girl, this haughty, naive woman in her cage of a chair—he wanted her as he had never wanted any woman in his life.

His feet moved of their own accord, carrying him toward her. His hands reached out to touch her, hold her, claim her.

Mine, the wolf howled. *Mine*.

"Stop," she whispered. "Morgan. Please."

He thought he had imagined the plea, but her hands fumbled at her blankets and her eyes begged for mercy. He stopped. Air flooded into his lungs. He shook his head to snap the spider-silk filaments of lust that bound him to Athena, and they released their tenacious grip.

But not entirely. His body still ached and cried out, refusing to be silenced. All he need do was breathe in her scent, and he was caught again. But he had come with a purpose, and he had yet to carry it out.

Niall Munroe had brought him here. He had betrayed Athena—his own, his family, his pack. And Athena was as ignorant of her brother's deception as she was of the hypocrisy of her society friends.

Morgan had intended to give Athena a chance to fight for herself.

Until now, he hadn't questioned his motives. Physical attraction, the drive to help one of his own kind, dislike of Niall Munroe, pity . . . it all led to this room and this moment. This undeniable need.

He let out a long breath. "It is time I told you why I came—"

"Just go." Athena's blanket was up to her chin, framing her pale face. "If you don't leave at once, I will be forced to call my maid. It would be better if I did not, for both our sakes."

He gave his body a final shake and seized the chance for a safer kind of skirmish. "Call your maid, Athena—but I hope that she is a very brave woman. I would not want to frighten her."

"You enjoy that, don't you?" The defiant spark returned to her eyes. "You like to intimidate people just because you can. The feelings of others mean nothing to you. I would remove you myself if I were not . . ." She lifted her chin. "You are no gentleman, Mr. Holt, preying on unprotected women. If you thought—if you *ever* thought—that I had any interest in you beyond your part in the circus, you were sadly mistaken."

She had come too close to the truth. Morgan smiled. "Why do you think I am interested? Do you have so many men panting after you, Athena? Do you fight your suitors off with the edge of your tongue, or does your brother do it for you?"

He regretted his cruelty instantly. Her pupils constricted as if he had reached out and shaken her. Then the fierce light in her eyes went out, and she stared down at her hands upon the blanket.

"I have no suitors," she said. "You can see why I do not. I spoke . . . out of pride. You have a remarkable ability to turn me into a shrew. I forget my manners . . . I behave quite abominably unlike myself. But you saved my life, and I will not forget that."

Morgan felt about as tall as Ulysses, and much less honorable. "Athen—"

"No matter why you came, Morgan, it must be obvious that you and I are too different even to speak to each other in a calm and reasonable manner. Let us call a truce, and pretend this misunderstanding never happened."

Misunderstanding? He would have laughed if he hadn't become so keenly sensible of her fragility. A single tear would drive him to his knees.

"Morgan," he said.

She blinked. "I beg your pardon?"

"You called me Morgan."

"I am sorry. I did not mean—"

"No one calls me Mr. Holt," he said. "That is for gentlemen."

"I apologized for my rudeness—"

"Morgan."

She hesitated a long moment, worrying the blanket between her fingers. "Morgan."

"Good." He sank down where he was, not trusting himself to go closer to her. "I am not your enemy, Athena. I came here to warn you that your brother is working against you."

"Niall? I do not understand."

"He brought us—the troupe—to Denver to play for your orphans. Now he wants to buy us off before the performance, and I don't think he intends to tell you until we're gone."

"Buy you off?"

"I saw him offering Harry money if we would leave. The troupe wanted you to know, so you could decide."

"That is ridiculous. My brother brought you all the way to Denver. Why would he send you away now?"

"Do you want the truth?"

A door shut behind her eyes. "Of course. I still do not understand—"

"He found out about the Wolf-Man act. That was why he was so upset when he came to get you on the lot, and why he wanted you out of the way."

She paled. "He didn't know you were in the show? But you have been with the circus all along—"

"He didn't see me when he hired the troupe, and I don't think he knows that I am the Wolf-Man. It is the idea he hates. He told Caitlin he did not want the children to see something unfit for them, but she thinks he's afraid and hides it by claiming he's protecting you. He would have kept the troupe if it wasn't for me."

"Why should Niall be afraid?" The soft curve of her lips took a stubborn set. "If your act is too frightening for the children, we can leave it out. What you say of my brother—you must have misunderstood him."

He could have stopped there, told her what the troupe had decided, and left it in her hands. That would be the easiest way. Once he started saying what was in his mind, he'd only dig himself in deeper with her.

But wasn't he halfway to hell already?

"I did not misunderstand, Athena. If your brother were an ordinary human, he wouldn't believe my act was anything but a trick. He must suspect that the Wolf-Man is like you . . . and soon he may realize who and what I am."

"But I have told you that he understands—"

"Why does he fear it so much if he accepts what you are? Why does he want us gone before you see us again?"

Her mouth opened on a sharp intake of breath. "I know my own brother. There must be some other reason for his . . . acting so strangely."

For all the vehemence of her words, Morgan knew she was lying. Oh, not on purpose, and not to him, but to herself. There was something in this she didn't want to face.

"You said your brother always knew what you were. His mother was human, but your mother was one of us."

"Yes." Her face was pinched, as if she anticipated some terrible pain. "My father loved my mother. He accepted her completely."

"But did your brother? You ran as a wolf before the accident. Maybe he envied you."

"No," she said. "You are wrong." She looked quickly from side to side, like a cornered animal seeking escape. "Were both your parents werewolves?"

"My . . . father was human."

"And did he envy your mother?"

"I don't know." His throat thickened up, and he had to swallow twice to clear it. "She loved him. He never raised a hand to her or said a harsh word, until he . . ."

She stared at him, waiting for him to finish. He couldn't. "We're talking about your brother, and why he is afraid," he said harshly. "Maybe he doesn't want you around another of your kind."

What is he protecting you from, Athena? Does he secretly hate what you are—what we are—the way humans hate what they don't understand? Or does he want you to forget what you were before your accident?

"My brother—" Athena began, struggling with her thoughts as he had with his. "You think he guesses, or will guess, what you are, and wants me away from you. But he has no reason to think you would harm me."

"I could never harm you, Athena."

He felt her reaction like a punch in the belly. "I know you would not," she said in a whisper. "Yet if Niall knew what you did tonight—"

"He doesn't know." He rose, stretching his spine until it cracked.

"But you do not want him to find me here. I came to tell you that the troupe will stand by you. If you want us to stay, we will, no matter what your brother says."

Too much had shocked her, too much had been said to dismiss, but she gamely wrestled her bewilderment into submission and fought her way back to firmer ground. "Why would you defy Niall when he offered to pay you?"

"Maybe we don't like being ordered about by townies."

"That is not a good reason. Niall has much influence—"

"Harry knows what the performance means to you. He likes you. So does Caitlin."

"That is kind of them. And . . . and you?"

"I don't like your brother."

She gave a startled laugh. "You are very blunt."

"I don't like what he does to you."

"To me?"

"Controlling you. Making sure you stay the way you are."

Her eyes widened. "He doesn't try to keep me here . . . this way. It cannot be helped." She shook her head, denying whatever unpleasant thoughts he had put in her mind. "Niall enables me to do what I can for the destitute and disadvantaged. He wants only what is best for me, to make me happy. He is a good man."

"He is human. You are not."

She was quiet for a long time. "You are a strange man, Morgan Holt. You hardly know me. Neither does Harry, or Caitlin. Yet you would do this for me."

"You help people you don't know. Why should the troupers be different? Or aren't we saintly enough?"

"I am not a saint," she said softly. "What do you want me to do?"

"It is not my choice."

"Yet you came here, when you could have sent a message tomorrow."

"Are you afraid to stand up to your brother?" he demanded. "Caitlin said you wouldn't be. She said you had a will of your own. Do you, Athena? Is it easier to go along and pretend you agree with your brother so that you can forget what you gave up?"

She stared at him, stricken. Caitlin's words came back to Morgan as vividly as if she stood in the room beside him. *"Are you testing her, Morgan? Do you want her to fail, so that you will have no reason to care?"*

And he realized that he stood on the edge of a precipice, half longing for her to send them away, half hoping that she had the courage to be what her blood made her. Not this cripple in a chair, but a woman of spirit and strength. She was a prisoner who did not recognize her prison or the jailers she trusted. Her independence and social influence were illusions, her good works false consolation, her pride and acceptance of her fate only brittle paper masks that would crumple at a touch.

Yet if she decided to fight, if she dared to face the realities she so willfully ignored, then he was bound to her course. To *her*. For somewhere, sometime since their first meeting, he had taken Athena Munroe into his pack just as he had the troupers—reluctantly, hating himself for his weakness, but bound just as surely.

He had not wanted this responsibility for another person. He had meant to spend his life alone, unattached, unfeeling.

But the circus had changed him—Caitlin, Harry, Ulysses. He had begun to forget what it was like to live in chains, and what had put him there.

Athena's low sigh called him back from the past. "You asked for my decision," she said, meeting his gaze. "I want you to stay. The children are expecting a special treat, and I will not disappoint them. I will find a way to convince my brother, no matter what it takes."

Chapter 10

Athena waited to see how Morgan would respond, profoundly grateful that she had managed to keep her composure intact—just barely—during this harrowing visit.

The facts that had been brought to light during their conversation still rattled about in her mind, making it difficult to concentrate on any one disquieting revelation. She was unable to decide which was worse: Morgan's untimely intrusion, his witnessing her helplessness, or what he had told her about Niall.

She believed Morgan, as painful as it was. Since that argument months ago when Niall had accused her of doing too much, a part of her had been preparing for just such a battle. She simply had not believed it would come so soon, or in such unexpected form.

She had lied to Morgan when she told him that Niall accepted her inhuman nature; in her heart she knew that he did not, not completely. It was a matter they had never discussed. But if Niall thought she might be reminded of her mother's heritage, and how it had brought her to this life of confinement . . .

How could she admit how much it hurt that Niall had schemed behind her back, all in the name of protecting her from herself?

Her reputation had become the least of her worries. Yet she could not ignore the effect Morgan had upon her, here in her own most private sanctuary. He was the wolf who spoke to the sleeping beast within her. The man who stared at her as if she were a desirable woman. Heaven help her, she had felt that stare like a touch whispering up and down her flesh, stirring sensations she had just begun to experience before the accident.

Why, oh why had Morgan come to waken them again? Why did he make her *feel* more than any man alive, more than any person had a right to?

And why was he so determined to protect her?

She held her head high and watched him weigh her answer as ruthlessly as he had judged her life. At last he cocked his head, and a smile tilted one corner of his mouth.

"Caitlin was right," he said. "You are brave enough."

"Thank you. And now you must leave. If my brother finds you here, nothing in the world will convince him to let the circus remain in Denver."

He inclined his head. "I will go."

Athena allowed herself to relax just a little, knowing there would be no further chance at sleep tonight. She would spend the wee hours concocting a way to broach the subject with Niall . . . while not revealing her source of information.

"Please convey my gratitude to Harry and the others," she said. "Ask them to wait until they hear from me. I will see that you get a message when I have spoken to Niall." Having a definite plan was comforting, however tenuous it was. "Regardless of Niall's response, I will make certain that the troupe receives the full payment they were promised."

"Even if you lose the fight?"

She shuddered inwardly at his insistence on using such violent terms. Perhaps he knew no other way.

If she pursued that line of thought, she would let herself be drawn to him, into his life, with the hope that somehow she might unravel the mystery of Morgan Holt. She wanted very badly to understand him, even though she knew such a course was dangerous beyond her wildest speculation.

The questions she might ask Morgan Holt would satisfy her curiosity, nothing more. The answers could not change what was.

"If I lose the battle," she said, "*you* will have lost nothing."

"And your brother will rule you for the rest of your life."

"You seem just as determined to 'rule' me as he is. Are all men as thoroughly vexing as the two of you?"

"Are all females as foolish as you and Caitlin?"

"You do not know—you, a man of the world? Have you not left a trail of broken hearts behind you?"

He twitched as if he would snap at her, and then his eyes kindled like golden lanterns. "Not yet. Should I begin now?"

Never in her life had Athena been so grateful for a distraction as she was when she heard the unmistakable sound of a slamming door downstairs.

"Niall is home," she whispered. "You must leave at once!"

He gave her a most wolfish smile. "What would happen if I didn't?"

"If you are quick, you can leave by the window. I am sure that climbing down from a second-story window is child's play for a man of your talents."

Stairs creaked below the landing. Athena gestured Morgan toward the window. He started in the right direction obediently enough, but at the last minute he turned and glided to her bedside.

Athena supposed that, somewhere deep inside, she was almost expecting what happened next. Morgan crouched beside her, his hands on the bed, and leaned very close. His heat washed over her like the summer sun. His thick, black, unfashionably long hair brushed the sheets, her pillow, her breasts.

And he kissed her. His mouth came down on hers, hard for only an instant before it gentled and began to caress. His weight pressed her back into the pillows. She might have felt smothered, terrified, but her senses had become so heightened that waves of pleasure pulsed all the way to her toes. One of her arms moved of its own accord to wrap about his shoulders. Firm muscle clenched under her palm.

"Athena," he murmured.

She caught her breath. Her lips throbbed. Her body throbbed. *"Morgan."*

A loose floorboard on the landing just outside her door groaned in warning. Morgan sprang back. He leaped for the window, threw it open and was gone. Cold air spilled through the curtains, making a vain attempt to cool Athena's heated skin. Hastily she rearranged her nightdress and scooted down under the blanket. There was no use in pretending that she hadn't been awake, not with the lamp still burning and the window wide open.

The door swung in. Niall entered the room and glanced about. His expression was, thank heaven, no more than slightly perplexed. He lacked the senses to know that someone else had been in the room.

"I saw the light on," he said. "Why aren't you asleep?" Before he could answer he noticed the billowing curtains and strode to the window to shut it. "You'll catch your death, Athena. Why is the window open?"

"I felt rather warm," she said meekly. "I could not sleep."

He frowned at her and stood by the bedside. "Are you feverish? Should I send for a doctor?"

"No. I am quite well . . . merely thinking."

He sat between the bars on the edge of the bed. "About what?"

Athena tried to remember how long it had been since she and Niall had had a heart-to-heart conversation that did not revolve around common courtesies or, more recently, arguments over her activities. "The circus," she answered honestly. "The performance for the children. It is only a few days away."

He had the grace to look uncomfortable. His fingers plucked at a bit of her blanket. "Would you be very disappointed . . . if the performance had to be cancelled?"

So he did feel obligated to say something, after all. She faced a clear choice: either pretend she knew nothing, using her supposed ignorance to undermine Niall's resolve, or confront him directly. She knew what she would have chosen yesterday.

Many things had been different yesterday. She would not have believed the time would come when she would be compelled to defy her brother. But then, she would not have believed the time would come when she was kissed in her own bed by a near stranger . . . least of all one like Morgan Holt.

"You plan to send the circus away," she said.

He looked at her sharply. "How did you know?"

"Something . . . something Cecily said today on the lot," she improvised. Cecily Hockensmith had acted rather strangely while she and Athena waited in the carriage for Niall's return, but Athena had been more concerned with her brother at the time. "I knew something was wrong by the way you behaved. It was not like you."

She drew a breath of relief when she saw that she had guessed correctly. "I discussed the matter briefly with Miss Hockensmith," Niall said, "and asked her to come with me when I went to the lot—"

"To ask the circus to leave Denver," she finished. "Why, Niall? They were a gift to me, to the children. Cecily said something about a bad influence, but surely—"

"I had hoped this would not come up until they were gone," Niall said, rising. "But since you have guessed, I see no reason to deny the truth." He strode across the room and addressed the wall, his hands clasped behind his back. "I made a mistake when I brought the circus to Denver. It is not a suitable entertainment for the children, nor are the performers fit company for you and the other young ladies."

"I see. And you discussed this with Cecily?"

"Miss Hockensmith agreed with me."

Athena bit her lip. It was difficult not to be a little upset with Cecily for taking her brother's side, but she knew that the other woman's motives were good even if her attitude was too severe. "What led you to make this decision, Niall?"

There. Either he would tell her the truth, or he would work his way around it as if it were a ticklish business deal.

He chose a middle path. "I received some new information that suggested it would be better if they did not remain. I offered them a substantial gratuity in compensation. They were happy enough to take it."

Now he was lying. "Were they? It's not really the children you wish to protect, is it, Niall? You are afraid for me."

He turned around and stared at her. "And if I am? You spend too much time with beggars and riffraff as it is. We discussed this before—"

"They are human beings, are they not? They are far more apt to be harmed than do harm themselves. The troupers are constantly on the verge of disaster, yet they are generous and warmhearted."

"You see? You already think of them as friends."

"We formed a contract with them, and you have always said that contracts must be honorably fulfilled. Even if you don't consider such a contract sacred, I do." She gathered her courage. "That is why you must agree to let them stay to complete the performance."

"I must? Did I hear you correctly, Athena?"

"Yes. I have asked very little of you in the past several years, except that you allow me to use my portion of the inheritance as I wish. Now I am asking for this."

He glowered and paced from one end of the room to the other. "I have already asked them to leave."

"Send a message and tell them that you have changed your mind. You need not give any explanation."

Now was the crucial moment. Either he must come up with a better argument than he had so far, or he would be forced to tell her his real reason for wanting the troupe—and most especially the "Wolf-Man"—out of her reach.

"If you do this, Niall," she said, "I'll stay away from the lot until the day of the performance."

"That is not enough. If I allow the circus to remain, you must promise to curtail some of your more intemperate activities."

Athena closed her eyes. She knew that he was using this as a means to do the very thing Morgan had accused him of—control her. "You ask a great deal," she said.

"So do you." The mattress creaked as he sat down again. "I am willing to compromise, but only if you will do the same."

Compromise? she thought with unaccustomed bitterness. *Negotiate is too nice a word. Manipulate is more accurate. You have all the advantages.*

"Very well," she said. "Will you send a message tomorrow morning?"

"Yes." He patted her hand. "It's for the best, my dear. The performance is to be on Sunday. I foresee no trouble as long as you remain at home until then."

Athena was very tempted to argue. She did not enjoy arguing, and she'd had her fill of it tonight with Morgan. But a kernel of anger lay hard and cold in her heart, threatening to grow into something larger and much more intractable. Something with claws and fangs and the tenacity to drive every obstacle from its path by any means.

Exactly like Morgan Holt.

She tucked her hand under the covers. "I am tired now. I think I would like to sleep."

"Good." He got up and went to turn off the lamp. "I'm sure that you will have plenty to do until Sunday. I'll ask Miss Hockensmith to visit and bring your friends."

She didn't answer. After a while the light went out, and the door closed softly. Niall's footsteps retreated down the hall to his own room. Another door closed. All was silent save for the tapping of cottonwood branches on her window.

Athena lay cold and stiff under the blankets, fighting to control her unreasonable passions. Her stomach clenched and roiled as if she had digested every last shred of the contentment she had cultivated since the accident.

You lied to me, Niall. You treat me like a child, and I ceased being a child when you carried me out of that snowdrift.

A child. To Niall, she would always be that, dependent and unable to guide her own destiny.

Morgan Holt did not see her that way. She shivered, remembering the kiss, and the icy kernel in her heart was all but consumed in a blaze of sheer physical yearning.

Morgan Holt believed she was brave and capable. He saw her as a woman grown. He didn't give her pretty words. He was barely courteous. Yet his actions spoke more eloquently than the most cultured speech.

And he had kissed her.

She touched her lips. It was just as well that she must stay away until the performance. If she met him again in private, she didn't know what she would say or do. What *he* would say or do, when there was no future to be shared between them.

In dreams, she could walk, and run, and even Change again. In dreams, all the barriers between her and Morgan Holt dissolved like snow in a teakettle, and she forgot that her life was laid out now as it would always be.

She closed her eyes and willed the dreams to come.

Niall ushered Athena, Miss Hockensmith, and the few friends who had chosen to attend the performance to the special seats set aside for them at the very edge of the ring. Workers were busy making final adjustments to the props to be used by the performers—the high wire, the trampoline, the various balls and banners and hoops. Scaffolding for the aerialists hung overhead. An off-key trumpet sounded outside the trouper's entrance at the opposite side of the ring, and teachers from the orphanage herded the last of their charges in the common seating area, which the circus people called the "blues."

Children's voices rang and echoed under the artificial cave of the tent. Sounds of innocent, uncomplicated joy. Niall glanced at the happy, upturned faces, and was glad he had not begrudged the orphans this small pleasure. Athena had invited the residents of Denver's other orphanages in addition to her own; nearly a hundred youngsters filled the blues.

Athena had been true to her word. She'd kept quietly at home until this afternoon. If there had been a slight strain between him and his sister, Niall had dismissed it as minor pique on his sister's part. She would get over it—she always did. No one in the world was less apt to hold a grudge than Athena.

Niall knew that better than anyone.

As confirmation of his judgment, Athena beamed impartially at him and at anyone else who came in sight, including Harry French. The old man had personally attended them and arranged for refreshments to be provided, bobbing up and down the while with ingratiating humility. Fortunately, he had not found the temerity to ask Niall why he had changed his mind about allowing the performance, though Niall had made certain that the "Wolf-Man" stayed away. There was little risk that Athena would be reminded of things best left buried.

Cecily Hockensmith touched his arm. "Oh, Mr. Munroe, I am so glad that you found a way to permit the show in spite of our concerns," she said. "Athena looks so happy. You were very clever to find a solution that pleases everyone."

"I do not like making my sister unhappy," he said, sparing her a glance. "There is no reason why such matters cannot be settled in an equitable manner."

"Indeed. My father has often said how much he admires your skills of negotiation."

He murmured some rote courtesy and gazed about the ring. If not for Athena and her friends, he would have preferred to remain in the office at work, Sunday or not. But this was a moment of triumph for Athena, and he would not ruin her pleasure in it.

He didn't know why he continued to scan the tent while Cecily Hockensmith chattered away beside him. When Harry French, replete in bright coat and vest, entered the ring to announce the start of the show, he listened for a while and then let his mind wander to the latest reports from his mining investments and banking interests.

The performance began with the inevitable clowns. They gamboled about the ring, playing out skits and teasing children in the audience with their absurd antics. Niall watched the first act, decided that it was competent and quite harmless, and returned to his calculations of profit and loss. The laughter and cries of children, punctuated by the occasional gasp or comment from Miss Hockensmith, hardly disturbed his ruminations.

A blast of music from the small band marked the change to the next act, a motley pack of trained dogs. It flew by like the first. Niall made a few changes to a contract written in his mind. Another performance, by a trio of acrobats, followed the second, and he composed a letter to the manager of his smelting operation in Argo.

It was only when the fourth act began that he finally took notice, though he could not have said at first why he did so. A line of caparisoned gray horses trotted into the ring, necks arched and plumes waving proudly. Behind them, light as a fairy, bounded a girl in tights and short skirt, her red hair burning like a halo about her piquant face.

That was when he knew what he had been watching for. Facts and figures vanished from his mind like chalk erased from a slate. Caitlin Hughes danced gracefully to the center of the ring, an ornamental whip in hand, and called out to her horses. They reared up in perfect formation, much to the delight of the children.

"I believe I recognize that girl," Miss Hockensmith said. "A tiny thing, is she not? I cannot imagine what sort of upbringing she must have had."

Niall barely heard her. He was remembering his last conversation—argument—with Miss Hughes, and how she had pulled back that remarkable hair to reveal her delicately pointed ears.

Ears like . . . like an elf out of legend. And she had been so defiant. Her eyes had flashed like the sapphire earrings Niall had given Athena two Christmases ago.

The girl was too far across the tent to see him now. His gaze followed her every motion as if she had cast a spell upon him. Once or twice Miss Hockensmith spoke, but he heard only her voice and not the words.

How remarkable Miss Hughes was. Niall tried to remember her coarse ways, her rudeness, and her physical oddity, but it grew increasingly difficult to do so. She handled the horses as if she spoke their language; they reared and bowed and frolicked at her slightest invitation.

All too quickly an assistant came to retrieve the horses, leaving one in the ring with her. She leaped up upon the animal's bare back and balanced there while her helpers positioned themselves at various points on the ring, suspending banners in the path she and her mount would follow around its circumference.

The horse began to trot and then broke into a canter. Caitlin might as well have been flying. As her mount approached a banner and ran underneath, she sprang straight up and over the stretched fabric, performing a double somersault and landing precisely on the animal's back. The ladies gasped and applauded.

Miss Hockensmith tugged at his sleeve. "Mr. Munroe—"

He pulled his arm away. Caitlin did a series of jumps and acrobatic feats, each more perilous than the last. A second horse was brought out, and she leaped from one back to another as they ran, sometimes somersaulting between. Niall forgot to breathe. Caitlin followed the curve of the ring toward the seats and looked directly at him.

It was impossible, but he could have sworn that their eyes met and locked across that distance. Something snatched annoyingly at his sleeve. He disregarded it and held his breath as Caitlin smiled.

Canvas cracked loudly overhead, tossed by the wind. Caitlin's mount approached the next banner and plunged sharply to the left, its hoof striking the wooden ring. Caitlin lost her balance—only for a moment, but just long enough to leave her unprepared for the next banner.

Niall shot to his feet. Caitlin struck the banner at an awkward angle and flew in the opposite direction to her shying mount. She hit the ground hard.

"My God!" Athena cried. "Niall!"

He needed no further encouragement. Hopping over the low barrier between the seats and the ring, he dashed to Caitlin's sprawled form. If she had been hurt . . . if she were—

She opened her eyes. "Oh. It's you," she said, slurring her words. "I cannot understand it. Pennyfarthing has always been my best gelding."

"Don't try to speak," he commanded. He stripped off his coat and spread it across her. Others had come, forming a worried wall about them. Harry French pushed his way through.

"Firefly! Are you hurt?"

Caitlin grinned weakly. "I have been better."

Niall glanced up at Harry. "The children should not see this. Please ask the teachers to take them out, and be so good as to distract them in some way until . . . until this is resolved."

"Naturally, naturally, just as you say," Harry said, looking very near tears. "But we must get a doctor—"

"Of course. Niall, you should send for Dr. Brenner at once."

Athena. Niall cleared his mind enough to look for her, and found her reclining in the arms of the man he recognized as Morgan Holt. He stared into Niall's eyes with unmistakable challenge.

Holt. Niall remembered how the ruffian had remained close to Athena during her first visit, but now he began to wonder what interest

Holt had in her. Who was he?

"Please, Niall," Athena said, all brisk purpose and unconcern for her compromising position. "We do not know how badly Caitlin is hurt."

She was right, and he had no time to worry about Morgan Holt at the moment. He turned back to Caitlin and tucked his coat more snugly under her chin. Her face was creased with pain.

"Lie quietly," he told her. "The rest of you, make sure she is kept warm and still. Her injuries may not be obvious to the eye."

The dwarf, Ulysses, stepped forward. "You need not worry, Mr. Munroe. We will take care of her until the doctor arrives."

Niall nodded. "I'll be back within the hour. Athena—"

"I will stay here, with Caitlin," she said. Her quiet conviction promised a lengthy argument if he protested.

"Mr. French, please get my sister her chair," he said. Belatedly he remembered Cecily Hockensmith and the other ladies. Miss Hockensmith stood safely beyond the ring of circus folk, her face set in a frown. The expression quickly transformed to one of worry when she caught his glance.

"Miss Hockensmith," he said, getting to his feet, "will you stay with Athena? I would be much obliged."

"Of course." She smiled tentatively as he made his way through the crowd. "I will do whatever I can."

"Thank you." He pressed her hand in passing and strode toward the tent's wide entrance. Once there he paused, half afraid that Caitlin would not be where he had left her.

But the crowd had dispersed enough to reveal her figure, covered now by a blanket as well as his coat. Harry French brought Athena's chair, and Holt settled her into it. Ulysses knelt beside Caitlin, speaking in his soft, pleasant Southern drawl.

Niall turned on his heel and headed for the carriage. The doctor would see to Caitlin. Now that the performance was effectively ended, time and distance would take care of Morgan Holt, whatever his interest in Athena, and dispose of the very unwelcome complication the circus had caused the Munroes.

He couldn't wait for life to return to normal again.

Chapter 11

Cecily stood with her hand resting on the back of Athena's chair and cursed Niall Munroe for the hundredth time.

Damn him. Damn him for giving in to his sister and her whims, damn him for making eyes at this crude snip of a girl, and damn him for leaving her here with these horrible people and their nauseating sentiments.

"Thank you for remaining," Athena said. "I know that this is not a pleasant situation, but I am grateful."

Cecily smiled. "You know that I would do anything for you and your brother, my dear," she said. She looked with distaste upon the red-haired devil's imp, whose flat chest seemed even less substantial when she lay on her back. What in heaven's name did Niall see in such a creature?

For he had seen something, of that she was sure. Her senses were remarkably keen where her own interests were concerned. She had noted how he ignored *her* while he watched the girl perform. He had failed to respond to several of her comments. He had left her sitting on the hard chair without a word of explanation and gone running off to be with his new flirt just because she had taken a little fall.

"There, now," the fat old man, Harry French, said to the girl. "It will be all right."

"Of course it will," Athena said. "Niall will get our own doctor. He is the best Denver has to offer."

Caitlin made much effort to return the smile, doubtless basking in the attention. "It is . . . very kind of you, Athena."

Athena. Cecily shuddered. How could Niall's sister allow the whore to call her by her Christian name? Cecily scowled and felt a prickle sweep up her spine.

Morgan Holt was watching her. He stood too close to Athena, on the other side of the chair, like some black-haired watchdog. It was if he could see right through Cecily and into her thoughts. She had disliked him instantly, but his low status made it possible to dismiss him. That was not so easy when he was a few feet away.

This was what came of Niall's permissiveness. She had thought that battle all but won. Now she must regroup, and consider new strategies to pave the way for Athena's departure from Denver.

She met Morgan Holt's stare and smiled with sure knowledge of her own superiority. So he found Athena attractive, did he? Niall must have observed the way he clung to Athena, and Cecily could easily make Holt's stubborn and inexplicable dedication to the girl sound much more ominous than it actually was.

And as for Miss Caitlin Hughes . . .

"You should go," Morgan Holt said.

Cecily started. "I beg your pardon?"

"Athena is with us. We don't need you."

Her amazement at his brazen command held her silent for several beats. Athena, talking to Caitlin, hadn't heard. Cecily curled her hand around Athena's shoulder. "I will do no such thing."

Incredibly, he bared his teeth at her. She managed to keep herself from stumbling away to some illusory safety. "How dare you," she whispered.

He took a step toward her. She gasped and placed an equal distance between them.

All at once it seemed that every eye was upon her. The dwarf with his curling golden locks looked up as if he were her equal in height and every other way. One of the clowns leered, and the strong man in his animal skin tunic worked his fists. Hostile, alien gazes met hers everywhere she turned.

The walls of the tent threatened to collapse upon her if she remained another second inside it. She hurried toward the exit. Once outside she was able to breathe again. With safety came sense, and righteous anger.

Who did they think they were to send her scurrying away like a frightened rabbit? What must Athena be thinking at this moment . . . if she had even noticed?

Ignored. First Niall, and now Athena. It was insupportable. And yet, when she set her feet to return to the tent, she found them rooted to the ground.

Morgan Holt was a madman. There was no telling what he might do if provoked, and he had plainly taken as much dislike to her as she had him. It might be best to wait until Niall returned.

She looked about for a place to sit and, finding none, folded her arms and prepared to endure. After far too long, she glimpsed the welcome sight of Niall's carriage turning into the lot. The coachman drove it up the midway and stopped close to the big tent.

Niall jumped out of the carriage, followed more sedately by a bearded and white-haired gentleman. Cecily went to join the men at the fastest pace her dignity allowed.

"Oh, Mr. Munroe," she said. "I am so glad you have returned quickly."

"Why are you not inside with Athena?" Niall demanded, scarcely sparing her a glance. He urged the doctor along with a wave and headed at a blistering clip toward the tent.

Cecily could not keep up. She slowed and allowed the men to precede her. She would *not* be made a fool of or treated in such a way, not by the Munroes or anyone else. She ought to leave, now, without a backward glance.

And jeopardize your future here? All she need do was swallow her pride and the situation could yet be salvaged and turned to her advantage. Clenching her fists, she prepared to try once more.

"How sad a thing it is to lose a lover."

She spun about to face the one trouper she had not noticed among those hovering over Caitlin—the snake charmer, Tamar. Cecily recoiled. The woman had the usual snakes draped about her shoulders like some grotesque necklace, but it was not that which alarmed Cecily. There was something inhuman about her dark, slanted eyes.

"I . . . I do not know what you mean," Cecily stammered.

"Oh, but you do." The snake woman smiled. Her teeth were white and slightly pointed at the tips. "This man you want, this Niall Munroe, is slipping through your fingers."

"What do you know of me or Mr. Munroe?"

"I have eyes." Tamar tickled the underside of one serpent's satin jaw with a red-nailed fingertip. "I know that you want this Niall Munroe. I know that our Caitlin also wants him, though she does not admit it. And I have seen how he looks at her and does not look at you."

Hearing her own thoughts laid out so plainly was a considerable shock. This woman, a stranger, had seen the sordid attraction between Niall and the little slut. She might not be the only one.

"Why do you tell me this?" Cecily demanded. "What possible reason—"

"You wish to be rid of your rival, do you not?" Tamar blinked, and Cecily realized with a chill that she had not seen the woman do so since the conversation began. "Maybe there is something that I also wish. Maybe we can help each other."

"You must be joking." Cecily glanced with disgust at the snake charmer's patently false hair, the garish cosmetics, the gown that concealed so little of her generous figure. "How could *you* possibly help me?"

"You dislike me, no? Maybe you think I am too low for you, like my snakes?" She smiled. "Never mind. You will agree, because you want the circus gone, as I do. And if Athena Munroe gets her wish, the circus will not go away for a very long time."

"What do you mean? You are to leave Denver now that the performance is over."

"I think not. Because our Caitlin was hurt, your friend Athena has said that she will ask her brother if the troupe may stay at his ranch in the mountains until she is well again. And that may take all winter, no?"

"Preposterous. Niall would never agree."

"Would he not?" Tamar shrugged. "He looks at our Caitlin as if he has never seen a woman before. Do you think that he will let her go so easily?"

The swift and obvious answer died on Cecily's tongue. She became as cold as Tamar and her snakes, examining all the possibilities with calm rationality.

As repulsive as she found the circus folk, and this creature in particular, Cecily had no allies against Caitlin and her tawdry charms. Tamar had presented herself as a fellow conspirator, with keen powers of observation and a cool sense of purpose. She would make a daunting enemy. She doubtless had resources Cecily could not hope to duplicate . . . if she could be trusted. And if she did not demand too high a price for her services.

"You said you can help me," Cecily said. "What do you propose?"

Tamar licked her lips with a flicker of her tongue. "I know the circus as you cannot. I can hear what is said, and tell you as I have told you of Athena's plans. There are many ways that I can . . . make difficulties for your lover and our Caitlin when they wish to be together."

Cecily had little doubt of that. "And what do you want in return? You said you wish the circus gone. Why?"

"I, too, have a lover," Tamar said, her eyes growing as cloudy as those of a snake about to shed its skin. "There is one not of our troupe who casts a spell on him, as the girl bewitches your man."

Thinking quickly, Cecily cast through her memory for characters who might fit such a vague description. Who on earth would take such a creature as Tamar for a lover? Whom would she pursue?

Who but one equally as bizarre? Not the dwarf, surely. The albino clown, perhaps—

No. The answer was evident. Which trouper had taken such a strangely personal interest in Athena that first day on the lot? Who had been standing so close, so protectively, to Athena's chair as if he had some special right?

"Morgan Holt," she said. "It is him, isn't it?"

Tamar hissed. "He is my wolf. Mine alone. She will not have him."

Her wolf? *Of course. The Wolf-Man. Morgan Holt is the Wolf-Man!* And he had set his sights on Athena.

Cecily smiled. "Let me be sure that we understand one another. You will act on my behalf to keep the girl away from Mr. Munroe, and I will do what I can—within reason, of course—to do the same with Athena and Morgan Holt."

"Then we understand each other." Tamar glanced toward the tent. "Use what I have told you. You will tell me where to send messages when I learn that which is of interest to us both. And you will help me when the time is right."

"Unless, of course, I persuade Mr. Munroe to do as he originally intended, and send your circus away. Then we shall both have what we want with no further trouble."

Tamar inclined her head. "I shall be most curious to see if you succeed."

Cecily found a bit of paper and a pencil in her chatelaine bag and wrote out her address. A definite risk to trust this creature, but she was confident that she could control their partnership. If not, she might as well pack her bags and leave Denver tomorrow.

She passed the folded paper to Tamar and quickly withdrew her hand. "Send a message to me if you learn anything more of use, but be discreet. If you cause me embarrassment, I can assure you that it will become most unpleasant."

"Threats?" Tamar laughed, a husky rattle from deep in her throat, like scales against stone. "I, too, can make threats. But it is better not to be enemies, no? Go to your fine lover before it is too late."

She turned and, with a swing of her hips, left Cecily alone to consider the wisdom of pacts with the devil.

The white-haired doctor put his implements, bottles, and bandages away in his bag and shook his head. Morgan knew that no one else was meant to see the gesture; he glanced at Athena in the chair beside him. She had missed it. Caitlin had not.

"It is so bad then, Doctor?" the equestrienne said, grinning crookedly. "Must I start planning my funeral?"

The old man glanced at Niall Munroe, who crouched at Caitlin's other side. He had hovered over the girl ever since his return with the physician, as possessive as a puma with a fresh kill. Munroe probably didn't think anyone noticed that, either.

"Perhaps we should speak in private, Miss Hughes," the doctor said.

"These are my friends," Caitlin said, bravely ignoring her pain. "I am not afraid for them to hear."

The doctor sighed. "Very well. As I told you before, your leg is broken. I have done what I can to set and stabilize it with a plaster of Paris cast, but time must do the healing. It is my considered opinion that you must have several months of complete bed rest if you ever wish to walk again. If you do not, I fear that you will be permanently—" He hesitated, looking from Niall to Athena.

"Please speak frankly, Dr. Brenner," Athena said. "I am not afraid to hear the truth." She reached down and squeezed Caitlin's finger. "Dr. Brenner has been our physician for many years. I trust his judgment completely. That is why you must do exactly as he says and have rest in a quiet place where you can be properly cared for."

An expectant hush fell over the group. Morgan stared at Niall, bracing for his reaction when Athena proposed her scheme for Caitlin's recovery. He moved an inch or two closer to Athena, his hip against her chair. Not quite touching *her*, oh, no; if he were to touch her now, after what had happened in her bedroom, he didn't know what he might do.

Carry her off and ravish her? he mocked himself. *It was a kiss. That is all.* And Athena showed no signs of being either flustered or disturbed in his presence.

She had probably dismissed the kiss, just as he had—an impulsive act swiftly explained as a momentary madness. Better this way. Better that whatever lay between them begin and end with that kiss. Even so, he could not bring himself to leave her side.

"Niall," Athena began. Morgan could feel her body tense, hear the swift intake of her breath. He tightened his grip on the back of her chair.

"Niall, I have been thinking ... about how we might help Caitlin." She glanced, once, at Morgan's face, and he smiled at her in encouragement.

Smiled at her. The expression felt strange on his face. But she seemed to take courage from it and faced her brother again.

"The doctor has said that Caitlin must have complete rest. It is obvious that she cannot travel far under these conditions, and a tent is not adequate accommodation for an invalid."

Niall stood up and brushed off his trousers. "Of course not. Miss Hughes may remain in the hotel until she is—"

"Not the hotel, either." Having dared to interrupt her brother, Athena forged ahead. "There is a much better place where she can be cared for and remain with her friends. Very little goes on at Long Park this time of year—why can we not allow the circus to winter there, while Caitlin recovers?"

"The ranch?"

"Yes. Of course there will be snow and cold temperatures, but Long Park is sheltered from the worst weather, and there is plenty of room. The second barn hasn't been used in years. It could hold the circus live-stock, and between the bunkhouse and the main house, surely there would be enough beds or cots for everyone. I have already discussed this with Mr. French, and he has agreed that in return for winter quar-ters he and the troupe will give two charity performances in the spring—"

Niall held up his hand, silencing her. Morgan stiffened.

"If you will excuse us," he said brusquely to the doctor, "I must speak to my sister." He stepped around Caitlin, shouldered Morgan aside, and took the handles of Athena's chair.

"It's all right," Athena said in a whisper meant only for Morgan. He stepped back, and Niall took her away from the group and to a place of relative privacy across the tent.

The conversation that followed was both quiet and vehement. Morgan ignored the murmurs of the troupers and watched Athena and Niall, listening to the debate progress. Keeping her calm, Athena pre-sented her argument. Her brother, as expected, was furious, though he made some effort to hide his anger from the unwelcome witnesses. She had put him in an awkward position by asking his cooperation in public.

But Athena did not back down. Her voice remained firm and full of conviction, even when Niall loomed over her and looked as if he would have liked to give her a good spanking.

God help him if he did.

"Morgan?"

He glanced down at Caitlin. She was white about the mouth and her eyes revealed great pain, in spite of the doctor's efforts.

"You should be moved to a bed, Miss Hughes," Dr. Brenner said. He followed her gaze up to Morgan. "Can you carry her?"

Caitlin gave a husky laugh. "I think . . . Morgan is up to the task. I will be all right. Thank you, Doctor."

He nodded and packed up his bag. "Mr. French, if I may have a few words?" With a wary glance toward the Munroes, he walked off with Harry.

"What are they saying—Athena and Niall?" Caitlin asked.

Morgan crouched beside her. "Athena is telling him what she told us. Munroe is against it."

Caitlin wrinkled her nose. "I could guess that. What else?"

"Munroe says that they have no responsibility for what happened, and he and Athena had agreed that the circus would leave right after the performance. He isn't saying it, but he does not want her around us."

"I know that, too." Caitlin sighed. "I tried to tell Athena that it was not a good idea."

"But she isn't giving in to him. She is telling him that whether or not they have responsibility for what happened to you, providing you with a place to recover is the right thing to do. It is . . . 'common decency.'"

"To her it would be. But Niall—"

"He says it would be too expensive to keep the troupe fed for the whole winter. She says that the cost is nothing to the Munroe fortune, and the charity performances in spring will more than make up for it."

"Go on."

"He tells her that she had no right to make such promises without consulting him, and she asks him what he's so afraid of."

"*That* will make him angry."

"Yes. But she . . ." He lost his train of thought as he watched Athena, the proud lift of her head and the set of her shoulders. Niall ranted and bullied, but she did not buckle.

"You're proud of her, aren't you?" Caitlin asked.

Proud? He began to deny it, but the word rang true. Yes, he was proud. She had stood up to her brother not once, but twice—both times for the sake of people she hardly knew.

Would she do the same for herself alone?

"She says," he continued, "that if he cares anything about you being able to walk or ride again—" He met Caitlin's eyes. "She asks how much he is willing to do to make sure that what happened to her does not happen to you."

Caitlin closed her eyes. "I never asked Athena what made her—"

"An accident. That is all I know." He looked at Niall's face. "Munroe is wavering."

"Because she compared herself to me. I wonder . . . He is so protective. Maybe it's more than just the duty of looking after a crippled sister."

Her statement caught Morgan's interest. Was there more to it? Was Niall's vigilance driven by something other than brotherly devotion? When the opportunity arose, he would ask Athena . . .

No. He didn't want more details of her life, poignant little facts that would work their way deeper into his heart. "Do you want to go to their ranch, Firefly?"

Caitlin shifted her body and winced. "I dread the thought of staying in bed for months."

"It is not likely to be months, is it?" Morgan had learned soon after he joined the circus that Caitlin had an ability to heal almost as strong as his own.

"Niall doesn't have to know how quickly I can be on my feet again." She smiled slyly. "What about you?"

Morgan had deliberately avoided imagining what it would be like to stay at a snowbound ranch through a long winter, idle and restless, with Athena in reach. Had she thought of that? Had she even considered what would happen if she and Morgan were thrown together time and time again?

"If you go to the ranch," he said, "I may not stay."

"Because of Athena?"

"You will not need me anymore."

"You are avoiding the obvious, Morgan. It's Athena you are afraid of."

"As you are 'afraid' of Munroe, Firefly?"

"Maybe I am."

They fell silent. Morgan saw that the troupers, satisfied with Caitlin's care, had dispersed. The doctor had left the tent; Ulysses and Harry stood talking a few feet away. The Munroes had finished their debate and Niall was pushing his sister's chair in Harry's direction. Nothing in either face suggested who had won the skirmish.

Miss Hockensmith chose that moment to return. She minced her way up to Munroe's side and bent an apologetic smile upon Athena. Words were exchanged, with a certain coldness on Munroe's part and a plaintive question by Miss Hockensmith.

"Please do go speak to Miss Hockensmith, Niall," Athena said. "I would like to say good-bye to Mr. French."

Niall's expression was as stormy as an August sky. "Very well. I will come back for you in a few minutes." He glanced at Caitlin and allowed Miss Hockensmith to lead him out of the tent.

Athena was already wheeling herself toward Caitlin and Morgan. Harry and Ulysses joined them—Harry, as usual, torn between worry and apology.

"Mr. French," Athena said, holding out her hands to him as if the past hour had been perfectly pleasant and unremarkable. "I must go now. The children have had a rather exciting day, and I wish to make sure that they return to the orphanage in good order."

"I quite understand, Miss Athena. Quite. We are all most grateful for your kind care of our Caitlin."

"It is nothing." She paused and looked at each of them turn. "As for that other matter . . . Niall has agreed."

Harry grinned. "Wonderful. Most wonderful. Yet another debt we owe you, my dear."

"I will not be seeing . . . a great deal of you over the winter. I promised my brother that I would remain in Denver while the troupe is at Long Park. I know you can be comfortable there. I will make sure of it, even if I cannot be present."

So that was how she'd sealed the bargain—with a promise to stay apart from the people her brother did not trust. It was no more than Morgan had expected.

Why, then, did he feel like tearing the tent apart with his bare fingers?

"It was the only way," she said, meeting his stare. "Caitlin will have plenty of rest among her friends, and she will be as good as new by spring."

"He'll let you come to see us later," Caitlin said. "I know he will."

"Perhaps." Athena continued to gaze at Morgan. Her lips parted, full and moist. His body remembered, vividly, how they had tasted. How they had responded.

Harry cleared his throat. "Perhaps you had better take Caitlin to my tent, Morgan, until we can get her to the hotel."

"I will arrange transportation," Athena said. Her tongue darted out to wet her lower lip. "Everything will be made ready at Long Park, and you'll have a guide through the pass. There may be some snow, but the weather should not be too severe."

Morgan broke the almost painful connection between them and knelt to gather Caitlin in his arms. She sucked in her breath at the motion, but her gaze darted from Athena to Morgan with avid attention. Athena noticed and turned quickly to Harry.

"Good-bye, Mr. French. Mr. Wakefield, Caitlin . . . Morgan."

"Good-bye for the time being," Harry said. "Thank you, my dear."

Morgan didn't remain for the end of the scene. He carried Caitlin out the back door and to Harry's tent.

"It's that bad, is it?" Caitlin murmured.

He grunted and laid her on Harry's cot. "Worry about your leg, not me."

"I worry about you denying what anyone can see."

The cold, relentless stare that Morgan frequently used to great effect did not work with Caitlin. "And what is that?"

For once her expression was perfectly sober, and not just because of the pain.

"Why, my friend," she said, "only that you're in love with Athena Munroe."

Chapter 12

Morgan seldom laughed. He did so now, a bark that sounded half cough and half growl. He could not have confirmed Caitlin's diagnosis more completely.

She had seen it coming, of course. At first the sparks between him and Athena had seemed mere attraction, the kind of curiosity a person might have about someone the very opposite of oneself. *Like me and Niall Munroe.*

But somewhere along the way curiosity and attraction had turned into something far more serious. Serious enough to frighten both of them. Badly.

As it frightened Niall.

"You are making this much more difficult than it needs to be," she said, trying to settle her aching leg more comfortably. "For once in your life you had better be willing to take advice. I understand Athena as you cannot. I am a woman too, you know."

"So Munroe has observed." He glared at her. "Are you in love with him?"

"That is foolish," she said lightly. "And even if I were, he'd have nothing to do with me."

"No? The way he stayed close to you, when you were hurt. . . ."

"Means nothing." She shrugged. "And we are talking about you, so don't try to change the subject."

"You are wasting your breath. Athena will not be coming to the ranch."

Caitlin chuckled, though the motion jarred her leg. "I have a feeling that she'll find a way."

Morgan muttered under his breath and paced up and down the short length of the tent. "You are her friend," he said. "If you speak to her again, tell her not to come."

"Why? She likes the troupe, and we like her. I have no right to even suggest it—unless you have a very good reason for me to give her."

He paused in midstride and fisted his hands behind his back. "It would be better if we never met again."

"Better for her, or for you?" She tried to sit up, but the pain was too intense. Damn the inconvenience of being so . . . so helpless, even if it was only for a little while. "I do not believe that you think less of her because of her affliction. I know you don't care for townies. You two are very different in many ways. But that isn't why you want her to stay in Denver." She took a deep breath. "You want to protect her from yourself. You don't think you're good enough for her, and it has nothing to do with money or position or any of those things. What happened to you that made you so sure she's better off without you?"

She had pushed too far and too fast. He swung to face her, head lowered and teeth bared.

"Enough," he said. "Do not speak of this again, Firefly."

"I'm not afraid of you, Morgan. I know you too well. You bluster and bully, but you wouldn't hurt me. Or her."

Never had a man looked more like an affronted and very hungry beast. But Morgan closed his mouth and backed toward the door, prepared to retreat where he could not win.

"I'm sorry," she said. "I have no right to judge you. But whatever you did in your past—whoever you were before you came to us—I know you are a good man. You've proved that to all of us. And as for Athena—"

A tall shadow loomed against the outer tent wall. Niall Munroe ducked his head into the tent and nearly bumped into Morgan. He scowled, caught sight of Caitlin, and quickly smoothed his expression.

"Miss Hughes" he said. "I beg your pardon. I would like to have a word with Mr. Holt."

Morgan bristled. "You'd better leave, Munroe."

"Not until you hear what I have to say. Privately."

Without a word, Morgan shoved past Niall and left the tent. Niall followed.

If her leg had hurt only a little less, Caitlin would have hobbled her way to the door and listened for all she was worth. As it was, she heard only the rumble of deep voices, rising in pitch and hostility as the minutes ticked by. Niall did most of the talking—or ordering, for Caitlin had a very good idea what he said. Morgan's replies were brief and edged like a knife thrower's blades. When it was over, only one man returned to the tent.

Niall Munroe paused momentarily at the entrance and then came inside, bending his long body awkwardly.

"Where is Morgan?" Caitlin demanded. "What did you say to him?"

Perhaps he had expected a kinder welcome. He straightened and removed his hat. His brown hair was mussed underneath, though the recent duel had been made with words and not fists.

"That need be no concern of yours, Miss Hughes," he said stiffly.

"Morgan is my friend," she said. "What concerns my friends also concerns me."

"Very well." He set his hat down on a stool beside the cot and folded his hands behind his back. "I asked him to stay away from my sister."

Gritting her teeth against the discomfort, she rose up on her elbows. "Did you, then? Why, pray tell?"

He held her gaze without apology. "It has been brought to my attention that he is showing a certain . . . interest in her, and that she has not been entirely indifferent."

Brought to his attention. Then it was not he who had observed the attraction, but someone else. And Caitlin had a very good notion of who that someone might be—the officious, pinch-faced, and resentful Cecily Hockensmith.

"I can assure you that nothing improper has gone on between Morgan and Athena," Caitlin said. "Harry wouldn't allow it, and neither would I."

"What you consider proper—" He thought better of what he'd been about to say and began again. "I was not mistaken, then, in believing that my sister is keeping company with Holt."

How much to admit, when his mind was already so set against Morgan? "They like each other," she said. "Why is that so terrible?"

"Because Athena is still very much a child in many ways, and has no experience with men. She is far too open-hearted, and Holt is—" He paused again, setting his jaw. "My sister is dependent upon me, and upon my judgment. Your 'Wolf-Man' is not fit company for a lady."

So Munroe had discovered the nature of Morgan's circus act. Doubtless that was also Miss Hockensmith's doing.

"I am surprised you deigned to visit me," Caitlin said, "for surely I'm no better company for so fine a gentleman as yourself. Will you tell your sister to avoid what you will not?"

He could have left then, and escaped her insulting questions entirely. But he lingered, staring about the tent as if it were filled with valuable and fascinating treasures rather than the flotsam and jetsam of circus life.

"I know the world as Athena does not," he said. "She is the one thing in my life with which I will take no risks and no chances."

"I see. And what did Morgan say to your kind request?"

His gaze jerked back to her. "He denies any interest in my sister."

Liar. Either you or Morgan is a liar of the worst sort, because you're lying to yourself. "Then you have nothing to worry about. I understand that Athena has promised to stay away from the ranch while we are there. You have arranged everything just as you want it." She eased back on to the cot. "You had better not waste any more of your valuable time, Mr. Munroe."

He swept his hat off the stool and sat down, straddling it with legs spread wide. "Is it not enough that we are giving you a place to stay for the winter, Miss Hughes? Have we not demonstrated our goodwill?"

"Troupers are not fond of unwilling charity."

"It's not unwilling, damn it—I beg your pardon." He swiped his hand across his brow, further ruffling his hair. "You must understand that—"

"That charity is all right from such as you to the likes of us, but not friendship?"

He blew out a sigh. "Miss Hughes—Caitlin—"

"Only friends should call each other by their Christian names, Mr. Munroe."

"What proof of friendship do you wish of me?" he roared.

She stared at him. He subsided into something like meekness. "I apologize. It is just that I—" His curse was not quite low enough to escape her notice. "I consider myself your friend . . . Caitlin. And I hope you will consider yourself mine."

Well, well, well. "Indeed? That *is* generous of you . . . Niall."

He didn't balk at the familiarity, so she was compelled to grant his sincerity. Still, he was far too high-and-mighty for his own good.

"Since we have become such bosom friends," she said, "you must explain to me why Athena and Morgan cannot be friends as well."

"It is different—"

"Just how is it different? I have little education myself, no name or money. I'm no better than Morgan."

He frowned. He brooded. He turned about on the stool so that he faced away from her, lost in his own thoughts. At last he seemed to reach a decision and met her gaze.

"My sister . . ." he began, "Athena is not like you. She has lost the kind of freedom you enjoy, and the ability to protect herself. She is vulnerable in body and in spirit. And she is that way because of me."

"What do you mean, because of you?"

"She was in an accident." He lowered his eyes, scuffing at the straw with the heels of his boots. "It happened in the mountains, during winter. We were at Long Park, and I—In those days, I had a tendency to be foolish. Reckless." He sighed. "I got myself into trouble. Athena believed she could save me. She was caught in an avalanche that did severe damage to her legs. The doctor told us she would never walk again."

Caitlin bit her lip. This man who spoke with such regret and shame was not the same whose arrogance had annoyed her and infuriated Morgan. She could scarcely believe that he had confided so much to her, of all people. Or was it *because* she was so different, so far outside the boundaries of his rarified circle, that she was a safe recipient for such a confession?

Guilt could drive a man to horrible acts. It certainly gave Niall reason to regard his sister as a fragile China doll, an heirloom kept high on a shelf, admired but never touched.

And perhaps it even explained why he had been moved to agree to Athena's scheme, and came to see Caitlin now. Her injury reminded him too much of his sister's, but this time he had a chance to make it come out right.

Caitlin had a very strong desire to reach out and touch him. She knew it would be a mistake. Pity, even sympathy, he would tolerate no better than Morgan. Were they so much alike, after all?

What sort of guilt made Morgan doubt his own worth, and drove him away from Athena?

"I am sorry," she said, meaning it. "But Athena is stronger than you know. She does not blame you, I am certain of it."

"Her heart is generous by nature. And that is why she is in that chair." Niall snatched up his hat and got to his feet. "Now you understand why Morgan Holt must stay away from her."

No, I do not understand, she thought. *There is something you are leaving out, my friend. Something more you will not admit.*

"I think you're wrong," she said. "I know you are."

He pushed his hat onto his head with unnecessary force. "The decision has been made. You and the circus will go to Long Park, and Athena will remain here. She has plenty to keep her busy all winter."

"And you?"

He glanced back at her from the tent door. "I will see that you have everything you require. Good-bye, Miss Hughes."

Caitlin closed her eyes and listened to him stride away. Well, now it was in the open. Her feelings had proven correct once again—about Morgan, and Athena, and Niall Munroe.

The only opinion she had not yet heard was Athena's. And that wouldn't be easy, if Niall resolved to keep his sister in Denver.

If there was one thing Caitlin loved dearly, it was a challenge. Niall was the biggest challenge she had ever faced. Doubtless he was rich because he was ruthless, and seldom failed to get his way. He was the kind of man who wouldn't hesitate to crush a rival.

But he was only human. He had weaknesses. And Caitlin Hughes, once her mind was made up, could be a very formidable opponent.

I give you fair warning, my stubborn friend. This is a game I intend to win.

The next five weeks were the longest of Athena's life.

It should have been a busy time, far too busy to allow for loneliness or daydreaming. The Winter Ball was drawing closer, and she was bound and determined that this second annual ball would be the finest and most well-attended of any in Denver that year.

Athena had frequently seen Cecily Hockensmith, but a good deal less of her own brother. Niall was constantly off on some business or other; currently he was in Chicago and had telegraphed to say that he expected to remain there through the end of the month. Caitlin's prediction that he would relent and allow Athena to visit the ranch did not come true.

Nevertheless, she took advantage of his absence by throwing herself with even more energy into the work he had disapproved: visiting the slums and tenements with clothing and coal, personally speaking to the forgotten girls with their fatherless babes, purchasing beds and school supplies for the orphans, and devising new charitable schemes that would reach far into the future. She drove the other ladies of her several philanthropic organizations almost as ruthlessly as she did herself.

It was never quite enough. Any stray, quiet moment, and her thoughts fled across the Front Range and to the ranch where she had spent every summer as a girl. Before she fell asleep each night, the image of a certain face seemed to shimmer in the air above her: thick black hair, golden eyes that sang to her of wild dashes by moonlight, a sensuous mouth promising more forbidden kisses.

At such times, she felt strange, phantom sensations below her waist, just as she had when Morgan visited her room. But she always managed to banish such fantasies, and remind herself that she missed all of the troupers: Harry, Caitlin, Ulysses, even those men and women she hardly knew. Morgan had no solitary claim on her affection.

Yet Morgan had smiled at her. That dreadful day of the performance, when everything had fallen apart, he had granted her courage with that simple expression and the unexpected warmth of his gaze.

Now he was thirty miles to the west, behind a wall of hills and mountains. Those mountains were already coated with snow, and soon the pass to Long Park would be all but impenetrable for the winter.

Ensconced in her sitting room late on a late November evening, wrapped in a woolen shawl against a chill that even the bountiful fire could not dispel, Athena eagerly unfolded the letter she had saved to read at the end of the day. It, like the others that came faithfully twice a week, was from Harry French.

Harry had made himself chief chronicler of all the events at Long Park, of Caitlin's condition, and of the doings of the troupers. Each time Athena opened one of his missives, she forced herself to read through slowly, refusing to jump ahead. She did the same tonight.

My Dear Miss Athena, the letter began,

You will be delighted to know that because of your brother's munificence and your own great kindness, we are all prospering at Long Park. As I wrote previously, the animals are well settled in the barn, which your brother had prepared for us; the rooms in the main house, and the accommodations in the bunkhouse, are indeed most praiseworthy. We could not ask for better.

Our small performance for the ranch workers met with great approval by your men, who at first seemed somewhat suspicious of us; they have since gone out of their ways to make us feel welcome. The victuals are plentiful, the fires blazing, and the mood merry. We lack only one thing—your own dear presence.

Caitlin asks after you constantly. She is very brave and does not admit any pain, but I must be frank and confess that I fear for her; there are times when the look in her eye does not bode well for her future. I wonder if she has not already given up hope of resuming her former activities. They have always been so important to her.

Athena dropped the letter in her lap. This was not good news. Not good at all. Harry had only hinted at a certain resignation in Caitlin's aspect, but until now had not said that the equestrienne might be abandoning hope.

Heaven forbid that should happen. Caitlin could not, *must* not lose what Athena had lost.

However, I beg you not to worry, dear Patroness. We will stand by her as we have always done, and refuse to grant her surrender. Either I, Ulysses, or Morgan—

Morgan. Athena swallowed and paused to catch her breath before resuming.

or Morgan are with her at every hour and keep her mind from such unproductive musings. We follow the doctor's instructions precisely. We have taken advantage of your kindness and read to her from books in your library, and Morgan brings her small gifts from outdoors: withered leaves and evergreen boughs or colored stones from the stream. Caitlin seems to enjoy them, and they lift her melancholy for a short while.

Gifts from Morgan. Athena smiled, recognizing in such simple gestures his reluctant generosity. Morgan cared for Caitlin as he would for a sister. He guarded her from every harm. How much more would he do for a woman he chose as his . . .

Quiet, she commanded her heart. *Be quiet.*

Morgan spends a great deal of time roaming the park, even in the most inclement weather. You know, of course, that such small inconveniences as bitter temperatures have little effect upon him. He is careful to conceal his dual nature from the ranch hands, but when he is not with Caitlin his restlessness is almost alarming. We have on occasion feared that he might leave and not return. He has repaid any debt he ever owed us, but we have continued to hope that he will choose to remain as one of our family.

As if the piercing mountain winds had reached across the miles and into her home. Athena pulled her shawl closer and rang the bell on the small table beside her. Brinkley appeared, and at her request he sent for a chambermaid to add more coal to the fire in the grate. Even after the flames leaped up with renewed vigor, Athena took no comfort in them.

Harry would not speak of Morgan leaving unless he felt it was a very real possibility. Surely Morgan would stay until Caitlin was on her feet again; surely he would inform Athena of such an intention, if only to say good-bye.

It was too much to hope that he would write as Harry did. Too much to ask that he send some personal message to her, when there was nothing tangible between them save for a shared secret and a stolen kiss.

Athena scanned the rest of the letter, barely registering the words, and tucked the folded paper inside her shawl. For a while she laid her head back against the chair and let the emotions rush through her, tumbling like a spring-swollen creek that carried rock and branch and earth inexorably before it.

When the deluge was over, only one consideration remained in her heart. Whatever Morgan might do, however he chose to regard her, he was not her principal concern. Caitlin was. Caitlin, on the brink of surrendering to the despair that had once nearly claimed Athena's spirit.

If there was a single action Athena could take to prevent that from happening, she must attempt it. Even if it meant breaking her word, defying Niall, and leaving last-minute particulars of the Winter Ball undone for several days. No one else could understand Caitlin's situation better than she. No one else could advise, coax, and bully with greater authority.

Cecily Hockensmith had been unstinting with her company and assistance with the ball. She could be entrusted with any details that must be addressed during Athena's absence.

Once the idea coalesced in Athena's mind, the practical impediments presented themselves in swift succession. As much as she liked and trusted Brinkley, Fran, Romero, and the others, she did not wish to involve the servants in her insubordination; she must make preparations and arrange transportation to Long Park without alerting them beforehand. Fortunately, her dealings with the charities gave her ideas about where she might discreetly employ a sturdy wagon and skilled driver.

However, she would require Fran's help with dressing and getting downstairs. Athena had not been forbidden to leave the house, and Fran wouldn't question her if she pretended to be going on another clandestine excursion to the tenements. If she lied to Fran, the maid would have an excuse for unwittingly assisting in her escape.

Athena was forced to admit that she was a little bit afraid of where this open defiance might lead. Niall had made his position very clear. But she had succeeded in winning him over before, and could do so again.

Cecily might help her in that as well. With the deed a fait accompli and Cecily taking Athena's part, Niall could not be entirely unreasonable.

This is for Caitlin. Niall's anger is a small price to pay for her recovery. And Morgan Holt had absolutely nothing to do with it.

She consulted her watch and saw that it was not yet too late to send a message to Cecily, asking her to come first thing in the morning. Just as she rang for Brinkley, he stepped into the room poised to make an announcement.

"Miss Hockensmith has called, Miss Munroe," he said. "I told her I would inquire if you were at home."

"Yes. Yes indeed, please show her in directly."

He bowed and went to do her bidding. Regretting the rather shabby nature of the old shawl, Athena pushed it farther down her shoulders and assumed a welcoming smile. Cecily glided into the room, brushing a bit of snow from her coat, and came to take Athena's hand.

"Ah, Athena. What miserable weather! I fear that winter has come." She allowed Brinkley to remove her coat. "I realize that it is late, but I so regretted not being able to see you today. You know how very dull Mrs. Coghill's dinners are, but I could not refuse her invitation."

"Of course not," Athena said. "Will you not sit down? Some tea, perhaps?"

"I do not believe that I could swallow another drop," Cecily said, sinking gracefully into a chair. "And how are you today, my dear girl? You have not worked too hard. I hope?"

Athena was in no mood for small talk when her mind was thrumming with plans. She dismissed Brinkley and waited until he had shut the sitting room door behind him. "Cecily . . . I have a great favor to ask of you."

"Indeed?" Cecily leaned forward. "Pray, tell me."

"I have decided to take a short excursion to the mountains. While I am gone, I would be most honored if you would assume final preparations for the Winter Ball."

"An excursion?" A faint shadow marred Cecily's alabaster brow. "Why would you wish to visit the mountains at such a—" Her expression cleared. "Athena, you cannot mean to go to the ranch."

"Yes. I have received correspondence from Harry French which suggests that Miss Hughes is not recovering as swiftly as we might wish. I feel that I must offer my friendship and every encouragement at this crucial time, which I cannot do here." She met Cecily's stare without apology. "I am aware that Niall does not wish me to go, but Miss Hughes's condition outweighs such personal considerations. I am sure you understand."

Cecily tugged at the fingertips of her white kid gloves. "I am afraid that I must advise against it, my dear. Not only is it likely to upset your brother, but this is hardly the time of year for such travel. And how would you go? You cannot drive yourself."

"I don't intend to. I can arrange everything, if you will agree not to speak of this to my brother until I am back in Denver."

"Isn't Mr. Munroe in Chicago?"

"Yes, and he is not to return until the day of the ball. I will be safely home in good time." Athena clenched her hands in her lap. "I know that you are very fond of my brother, Cecily. It is possible that you may hear from him. That is why I request that you say nothing of this beforehand. No harm will be done by it."

Cecily sighed and took on a pensive air. "You know that I am your friend, dear Athena, but I do not feel quite comfortable in deceiving your brother. And I must be concerned for you, as well. Even if you take your maid—"

"I will be going alone. I do not wish to involve the servants, though of course they will know where I am."

"I see."

It was obviously time to bargain. Athena had some familiarity with the method, for she had used persuasion many times when soliciting the sometimes reluctant contributions of the lions—and lionesses—of Denver society. She was sorry for the need to manipulate Cecily, but what she intended to say was not very far from the truth.

"It is a great deal to ask," she admitted, "and I abhor deception just as much as you do. But in many ways I have come to think of you as a sister. I consider it an excellent sign that my brother is not so much alone as he has been in the past."

Her gentle hint did not go unnoticed. Cecily straightened, and her eyes took on a certain gleam.

"I am flattered that you think so, Athena." She lowered her gaze. "I . . . I fear I have not been particularly successful in concealing my affection for Mr. Munroe."

Athena relaxed. "My brother can be quite stubborn, but he is blessed with many fine qualities. I will keep your assistance in this matter between the two of us, and Niall will know only of your tireless work for charity and the constancy of your friendship."

Cecily was quiet for several minutes, and Athena wondered if perhaps she had gone too far in suggesting the bribe of her influence with Niall. He had shown more attention to Cecily than he did most women, and a good word or two on Athena's part might make the difference.

Athena wondered why she had not more actively encouraged Niall to consider Cecily as a wife. She had recognized the possibility of it from the beginning of her acquaintance with the older woman—she had seen Cecily's strong interest in Niall—yet she hadn't pursued the scheme in spite of the advantages.

Niall could not be driven, in any case, and heaven help the woman who tried. The girl he chose to love must be far stronger than his sister was.

"Are you quite sure that you feel comfortable leaving the ball in my hands?"

Cecily's voice startled Athena back to attention. "I have no doubts whatsoever. Your taste and experience are impeccable."

"But if there are sudden changes—if alterations must be made—"

"Then I know that you will do just the right thing." Athena glanced at the clock on the mantel, impatient to have this over and done with so that she could begin planning for the trip.

"When did you intend to depart?" Cecily asked.

"The day after tomorrow, at dawn," she said, making a quick decision. "Will you help me, Cecily?"

"I will do all that I can." Cecily rose and shook out her skirts. "My carriage is waiting. I must be getting home."

"Of course." Athena released a quiet breath. "Is there anything you need to know about the ball? I will inform the necessary parties that you have complete authority, and additional expenses can be deferred until my return, but if there is anything else . . ."

The older woman smiled. "I have observed your work carefully for the past few months, my dear. I believe I can act as your deputy with all due efficiency." She paused at the door. "Take great care. I would never forgive myself if anything were to happen to you."

"You are a true friend, Cecily."

"And I hope one day to be much more—to you, and to Mr. Munroe. Good-night, Athena."

"Good-night."

Athena listened for Brinkley's steps and the sound of the front door closing on a gust of wind. She tugged the shawl back over her shoulders and wheeled her chair to the secretary. She chewed on the tip of her pen, considering the letters to be written, and began the first of them while sleet rattled against the windowpanes.

Tomorrow she would see the letters delivered. And in a few days, she'd be at Caitlin's bedside, among the people who had come to mean as much to her as any of her Denver friends.

Perhaps Morgan would smile at her again. She did not expect it, let alone anything more. If she could see Caitlin through her most difficult time, it was enough.

It would have to be.

Chapter 13

The necessities of business had never seemed so interminable or the conversation so dull as they had been for the past five weeks. Niall leaned his head against the seat of the Pullman Palace car on the railroad heading west from Kansas City, profoundly grateful to be going home.

Or was he? When he walked in the door of the house on Fourteenth Street, he would have to face Athena—and he knew the awkwardness that had grown between them would not have vanished so quickly.

It wasn't that he expected Athena to defy him. In matters of importance, she had always deferred to him no matter how stubborn she might appear. That was how it ought to be. And Miss Hockensmith—Cecily—was looking after her. In fact, he had felt relieved at the prospect of getting away, allowing Athena a chance to reconsider her foolishness and return to her normal routine.

But the niggling little worry remained: Athena was infatuated with the circus—worse, with Morgan Holt—and those people were a mere thirty miles away in the mountains. God only knew what they were doing at the ranch. And the girl—

He loosened his collar and tried to relax, though he had neither slept nor eaten well since he had left Denver. That girl—Caitlin—he had thought of her far too many times in Chicago, in the loneliness of his hotel room with the empty commotion going on in the street below. He had remembered her smile, the halo of red hair, her courage in the face of a serious injury.

The doctor had said she would recover with proper rest. That was the only reason she and the others were at Long Park. Apart from his providing them winter quarters, he was not responsible for what happened to Caitlin Hughes.

Yet he thought of her. He imagined her like Athena, confined to a chair, her vibrant spirit stilled forever. And the sickness of guilt welled up in his chest, reminding him that he was as much a cripple as his sister.

Athena had used their shared memories against him—he was too skilled a negotiator not to recognize that. Without directly calling upon the great debt he owed her, she had forced him to acknowledge the necessity of keeping Caitlin from the fate she had suffered.

It will not *happen to Caitlin.* He had made sure of that. He had behaved correctly, honorably. Athena was grateful.

But none of these truths comforted him. The closer the train drew to Denver, the more certain he was that he must see for himself how matters went at the ranch. He could speak to Mr. Durant and the foreman, make certain that the circus people were not taking too much advantage of their free accommodations. And while he was there, he would look in on Caitlin and carry a report back to his sister.

Yes. I will go to Long Park. Only a brief stop in Denver, and then I will be on my way.

The moment he made the decision, the tightness in his chest eased and his mind was clear again. He closed his eyes. The train's rocking became a soothing motion, and he no longer noticed the smoke or the discomfort of the long journey. For the first time in a month, he slept through the night.

For three whole days, Cecily kept her fingers crossed and prayed for just a little bit of luck. Athena had left Denver early yesterday morning; a mere day and a half later, Cecily had achieved more than she had any right to expect.

At first she had resented the position Athena had put her in. After all, the last thing she wanted to do was lie to Niall should he ask how his sister was faring—though, thank goodness, he had done so only once during his sojourn to Chicago. But Cecily had found it impossible to turn down the opportunity Athena unwittingly offered: that of making the Winter Ball her own.

True, there were relatively few details left to attend in the week and a half remaining before the event, but those could be made quite important with the right emphasis. The usual guests had already been invited, and the catering arranged, but Cecily had been doing her own investigating while she helped Athena. She knew that the grand ballroom at the Windsor was available the night of the ball. And she had decided, immediately upon Athena's departure, to change the venue from the Munroes' private ballroom to the public setting.

That, of course, meant more decorations, more hothouse flowers, and many other alterations. Cecily knew that Athena preferred intimacy and the same familiar circle of acquaintances to crowds and public display. With a complete lack of imagination, she chose guests who were generous with donations, not those who made fascinating company or offered new social or business opportunities.

Cecily had no interest in charity beyond what it could do for her social progress. She knew of several dignitaries and businessmen from other states or cities, and even outside the country—including a prince of some small European nation and at least one English earl—who were currently in town; she sent invitations to them and a number of other useful personages who had been left off the guest list for want of space.

After that, it was necessary to order additional foodstuffs, suitable for such elegant attendees. By the time the day of the ball arrived, the affair would bear little resemblance to the one Athena had planned.

And Athena, bless her naïveté, would remember that she had given Cecily carte blanche to do as she saw fit. She would seem both foolish and selfish if she protested the changes. Indeed, if the girl were gone only the few days she had proposed, Cecily would be most surprised. By the time she came back, it would be too late to return to the previous arrangements.

Cecily sighed with airy regret and stepped down from her carriage, glad to be home after a long day of shopping. The price of this deception might very well be the loss of Athena's trust and friendship. But Cecily had grown more and more confident of Niall's attachment to her; in fact, she had prepared several stories to explain Athena's absence should he return to Denver before his sister. Every one of them would reflect badly on Athena and leave Cecily the injured party.

That was a risk, too, of course. Niall might decide to believe his sister instead, if she chose to brand Cecily a liar. But whom would Niall trust when his sister had so blatantly broken her word?

The door to the Hockensmith house on Welton swung open as she reached it. The new butler, one of several servants recently employed thanks to Mr. Hockensmith's profitable partnership with Niall Munroe, bowed and took her coat.

"Miss Hockensmith," he said with just the right note of deference, "there is a gentleman waiting to see you."

"A gentleman?" She was both intrigued and annoyed; the man should know better than to admit a visitor when she was absent. "Who might that be?"

"Mr. Munroe. He arrived only a moment ago, and is waiting in the parlor."

Fear and excitement swallowed up Cecily's irritation. Niall had returned early, and might already know that Athena was gone—but Cecily was prepared for that very contingency.

"Very well, Parton. Please inform him that I will be with him directly." She hastened up the stairs to her room and made the necessary adjustments to hair and clothing, rehearsing her story as she did so.

She was quite clear-headed when she entered the parlor. Niall was on his feet, but he did not look particularly upset. Cecily released her breath and put on a look of grave concern.

"Mr. Munroe! I am so glad you have returned."

He swung about to face her, and his neutral expression changed into a frown. "Miss Hockensmith? What is the matter?"

So. He could not have been home, or he would know. The servants would have told him at once. "Have you come directly from the station?" she asked, urging him to sit.

"Yes. I will not be in Denver long. I came only to ask—" His frown deepened. "Why? Is it Athena?"

"Oh, dear. I had so hoped to reach your hotel before you left Chicago, but the telegraph must not have been delivered. Naturally, as soon as I learned—"

"Learned what? Where is Athena?"

"She has gone to the ranch." There. If he admired directness, he would appreciate hers more than ever now. "It is all my fault. Things had been going so well—Athena seemed quite settled and I was helping her with the ball. Then, three days ago, she made some remark about wishing to visit her friends from the circus, in spite of your instructions to the contrary."

"She has gone to the ranch?" Niall repeated, as if he did not quite believe it. "How?"

Cecily composed her face into a mask of contrition and embarrassment. "I . . . I fear that she has hired some conveyance to take her there. She did not notify me or the servants—I only learned of this yesterday when your butler sent a message to inform me of her absence and the note she had left." That, at least, was very close to the truth. She had played ignorant with the servants as well.

"I was so very sure I had talked her out of such an intemperate scheme," she continued. "I used every method of persuasion, you can be sure. It simply did not occur to me that I should mistrust her when she said she felt overtired and preferred to spend the next few days in seclusion. She seems so fragile, and she has been working so hard that I feared for her health. I even offered to send the doctor, but she refused. Apparently she lied to her maid about where she was going." She lifted her gaze in earnest appeal. "Oh, Mr. Munroe. I pray you can forgive me my terrible mistake."

Her gamble paid off. If Niall had been prepared to blame her for dereliction, her stream of explanations and apologies had taken the first edge off his anger.

"No," he said. "It is not your fault, Miss Hockensmith. I should not have expected you to succeed where I have failed." He strode to the window and twitched back the curtains. "I should have anticipated this all along. My sister has changed greatly in the past few months, and I have refused to see it. She has become adept at deceit and manipulation."

"But surely you are being too harsh—"

"There is no need for you to lessen the blow," he said. He turned back to her, all traces of anger hidden by a mask as expert as hers. "We were both taken in by her apparent innocence."

Cecily rose. It was time to give him a few pushes in the right direction, and let him think the solution was his all along. "Perhaps she has simply gone to look after the injured girl."

"You know that is not the reason. I may have been blind to the attraction before, but you were right. She has developed an inappropriate liking for Holt, and that is the true reason she has disobeyed me."

Cecily dared to touch his arm in sympathy. "Whatever you may fear, Mr. Munroe, I am certain that Athena is not lost to all common sense. She may be driven by feelings she does not understand—so many young girls are—and her judgment is flawed. She has lived too sheltered a life in Denver, and at the same time she has a child's confidence in her own invulnerability. When you bring her back, you will have a chance to set things right again."

"Set things right." A muscle in his jaw flexed. "I have not always listened to your advice in the past, Miss Hockensmith, but now I see that I must take direct action. Athena has grown to consider her position in Denver as unassailable. Her chair makes her safe from all censure. She does not believe that anything can change her world, even a flirtation with a scoundrel like Holt, and that is a conceit she cannot afford." He bent his head. "I have let her have her own way too often, and yet I have tried to protect her by keeping her close. Sending her away may be precisely what she requires."

Cecily gave a silent crow of triumph. "Indeed. I cannot disagree with you, Mr. Munroe." She hesitated for a calculated moment. "You did say that you have cousins in New York. If I may be so bold—perhaps it might be best if you send her directly there rather than bring her back to Denver. Any rumors will be extinguished quickly, and she will be well out of reach of temptation. I will be able to complete preparations for the ball, so Athena's efforts need not be undermined. I realize that it is very sudden—"

"No. Not at all." He met her gaze with grim approval. "I will leave for Long Park as soon as possible—if the weather holds, on a good horse I can reach it by tomorrow morning. I will begin making arrangements immediately for Athena's departure for New York." He took her hand. "I know that I may continue to count on your help, Miss Hockensmith."

"Always." She poured her heart into her eyes. "I will make inquiries of my own and be ready when you call upon me."

He lifted her hand as if he might kiss it. "You have been invaluable . . . Cecily. I will not forget."

His use of her name was the crowning touch on her victory. "We understand each other so well . . . Niall."

He smiled, but his thoughts were clearly focused on his imminent journey. "I will take my leave of you, for the time being." He strode into the hall and took his hat and coat from the butler. "Good afternoon, Miss Hockensmith. I will send word when I have Athena in my care."

After he was gone, Cecily sank onto a chair and caught her breath. Her good fortune had not only held, but doubled. Niall had already been prepared to think the worst of Athena. No matter what his sister might say now, he wasn't likely to believe her.

And Athena wouldn't be coming back to Denver. One major obstacle removed with little effort on Cecily's part—and the remaining impediments in her climb to the top of society would fall, one by one, when the Winter Ball proved a grand success. All the snobbish, insular doyennes of Denver would flock to her door once they realized just what Cecily was capable of.

Especially after she became Mrs. Niall Munroe.

Cecily stretched out her legs, licked her lips, and began to count her wedding presents.

It had been a day like this one—crisp, cold, and ready with a gentle gift of new snow—when Morgan had gone to the wolves and left the bitterness of his old life behind.

Once more he stood on such a threshold. Once more he considered casting off his previous existence just as he shook the snowflakes from his fur. But this change was not so easy.

This change was terrifying.

He crossed the open meadow at a fast lope, paws striking the ground noiselessly as he pursued the hare. Sharp air pierced the insides of his nostrils and whistled past his ears. Scents were always more acute at this time of year, and he knew, as he passed, where the bear had chosen her den, the bobcat had made his most recent kill, and the squirrel had stored her winter provisions.

Windswept leaves and moist earth, the dry stalks of tender plants, and brittle twigs brushed his pads and the short fur that fringed his feet. Most of the last week's snow had melted, for the days were not yet cold enough to maintain it. *But soon*, the wind promised. *Soon*, the pines whispered. *Soon it will be winter again, and you must choose.*

The hare dodged abruptly to the left, hoping to evade its deadly pursuer. But Morgan was more than wolf, just as he was more than man. He spun in midair and cut directly across the hare's path. It skidded to a stop no more than a foot from his lowered head. He could hear its stuttering heartbeat as it flattened to the ground and waited in silent, terrified resignation.

Morgan touched the trembling body with the tips of his toes. Years ago, he would not have paused as he did now. A wolf did not contemplate the feelings of his victims. He thought of his empty belly and the hard winter ahead.

Sentimental fool. Morgan backed away, shaking his head in disgust. The hare remained still. Morgan bared his teeth and snapped at the air. The hare leaped straight up and was off before the mist of Morgan's breath ebbed away.

Was this inexplicable urge for mercy not proof? Proof that, even if he wished, he could not go back to the wolves?

He heard them often, singing in the mountains. They stayed away from the ranch, but they were there. A new pack, one that would accept his presence just like the first. Until, one by one, they were killed by men or driven deeper into the wilderness.

Driven. Instinct and need drove the wolf. The thing that drove Morgan was a far more brutal master. It collared him with new memories and hopes, yanked and tugged him again and again toward those who had claimed his loyalty. Toward the ranch, and to the east and the city where Athena Munroe lived out her life of rules, rank, and restrictions.

She would not come here. She would be a fool to do so, and Athena was no fool. Yet each time Morgan ranged a little farther to the edge of the long park, gazed up at the hills and dreamed of escape, he turned and went back.

Just as he did today.

The slow-witted cattle that browsed on the brittle grass blinked at him as he gave them wide berth. Munroe's ranch hands, who answered to the foreman and seldom saw their employer, were not even aware that a wolf roamed the park. Morgan was careful to choose paths that concealed his tracks. The last thing he wanted was a pack of men up in arms over the presence of a lone wolf among their precious livestock.

The afternoon sky had taken on the flat gray patina of imminent snowfall, darkened with vertical drifts of smoke from the ranch's many chimneys. Morgan circled the outbuildings and the two bunkhouses, one reserved for the ranch hands and one for the troupers. He trotted out to the barn where the troupe's horses were stabled, nudged open the door, and jumped up into the hayloft where he kept his clothing.

He dressed and walked among the horses, making note of their condition. They were growing lazy and complacent here, just as he was.

Still, he walked a little faster as he approached the main house with its imposing stone exterior and sprawling, baronial magnificence. Long Park might run cattle, but at its center was a mansion a foreign prince might envy. Niall Munroe was not one to accept less than the best for himself or his sister. Athena would be as comfortable here as in her own home on Fourteenth Street.

And there was always the chance, however small, that she had come.

He entered the house by a side door reserved for the servants and followed the narrow hall to the ground floor guest rooms that had been reserved for Harry, Caitlin, Ulysses, and a few of the others. Since Morgan slept in the barn, Harry and Ulysses shared a room, while Caitlin had one to herself.

The door to Harry's room was open, releasing the smell of pipe smoke into the hall. Caitlin's door also stood ajar.

". . . can think of no reason why Harry writes so incessantly unless he hopes to effect a particular response from Miss Munroe," Ulysses's voice said. "I know he is fond of the young lady, but he has never been an admirable correspondent. I am bound to conclude that you have had some influence upon him, Caitlin."

"Me? What a suspicious mind you have, Uly. Naturally Harry wants to keep her informed of—"

"The gravity of your condition? His deep concern about your state of mind and indefinite prospects for recovery?"

"Can I help it if Harry exaggerates?"

"He knows as well as I that your injury is almost healed."

"But Athena heard the doctor say it was serious. She had no reason to believe I would recover so quickly."

Morgan folded his arms and leaned against the wall just outside the room. Ulysses coughed discreetly.

"Miss Munroe is of a naturally altruistic and accommodating nature and is apt to consider the welfare of others before her own. She made certain promises to her brother as a condition of our remaining here for the winter. Have you weighed the practical consequence of fomenting domestic rebellion?"

"If you mean that Niall Munroe might not get his own way for once—"

"You may grant, Firefly, that my preference for reason over passion has given me reliable powers of observation. It is my judgement that Mr. Munroe may only be pushed so far before he pushes back."

"And it is mine that Niall is not nearly as heartless as he thinks he is."

"Your heart tells you this because you believe that you are in love with him."

Caitlin burst out laughing. "Your almighty powers of observation, Uly? When were you ever in love?"

Ulysses was silent just a beat too long. "A man of my nature—and stature—is wisest to avoid the tender emotions and the complications that result therefrom. But I am human. I can recognize infatuation when I see it."

Morgan waited for Caitlin to deny it. When she did not, he let his hands fall to his sides and took an involuntary step toward the open door.

"I don't know," Caitlin whispered. "He and I—we have nothing in common. I'm no innocent, Uly. I am much older than I look. I know that Niall Munroe is a man—only a man—and I will not let him destroy the lives of the people I care about."

"Athena and Morgan."

"And you, and Harry, and the others. All we need do is get through this winter, and our luck will change for good. I know it."

Ulysses sighed, and his feet rapped on the floor as he hopped from his seat. "I have no right to tell you what you should or should not do," he said. "It is even possible that your faith and loyalty will prove more formidable than the untrammeled wealth and power of a man like Munroe. But be careful. Devotion exacts a heavy price."

Morgan stepped aside as Ulysses walked through the door. The dwarf paused, looked up at Morgan, and gently closed the door behind him.

"I will not ask if you overheard our discussion," he said.

"What is this about letters to Athena?" Morgan demanded.

"That you must ask Caitlin. I see that you have decided to remain with us another day."

"What makes you think I was planning to leave?"

"It has never been a question of if you would go, but when. It is not loyalty to the troupe that keeps you here."

"You shouldn't listen to Caitlin's wild fancies."

"Are they so improbable?" Ulysses glanced toward the closed door. "Miss Munroe did not seem, at first glance, to match Caitlin's strength of will. It has been brought to my attention that first impressions are deceiving." He turned toward the room he shared with Harry. "Do not be too severe upon the girl. If you find yourself with a desire for rational conversation, you know where to find me."

Unmollified, Morgan strode into Caitlin's room. She looked unsurprised to see him. Her lids fell halfway over her eyes.

"Hello, Morgan," she said weakly. "How was your run?"

"Are you in love with Munroe?"

"We've had this conversation before. I could ask the same—"

"I do *not* love Athena Munroe!"

His roar bounced about the room. The corners of Caitlin's lips curled up in satisfaction.

"Then why don't you leave?" she asked. "Athena may arrive any time."

"She is not coming here."

"Are you so sure?"

"What have you and Harry been doing?"

Caitlin examined her nails. "Oh, nothing. Athena has been worried about me, so we've been—"

"Lying. Telling her you're worse than you are. Caitlin—"

"You had better not growl at Athena the way you do at me. She's likely to growl back."

Morgan froze. "What do you mean by that?"

"Women in love can be very fierce creatures."

"She is not—"

"I know, I know. She is not in love with you." She rolled her eyes.

"And you haven't been stomping about the place like a bilious bull because Athena is out of your reach."

Morgan stepped back from the bed. "Do you think she binds me here, Firefly? Do you think I couldn't leave now and never look back?"

"I think you could try. But I hope you will not, my friend."

As she had done many times before—as only she and Athena, had the power to do—she left him silent. Caitlin was like the hare that he had neatly caught and released out of maudlin sentimentality. Like a lesser wolf in the pack whom he had failed to teach its place. She and Athena could twist him round and round their fingers, spinning him this way and that until he didn't know east from west or sky from earth.

Athena. When she looked into his eyes with that slight lift of her chin and that warmth in her hazel eyes, he almost forgot why he wanted to run.

"After all these months," Caitlin said softly, "I still don't know where you come from, or why you were hiding as a wolf in the wilderness. I know you were hiding—we all are, one way or another."

"You are wrong. I was free. The only kind of freedom worth having."

"Free from ties to other people. That is it, isn't it? It's what you've always been most afraid of. Owing us for saving your life. Making friends even when you didn't want to. Athena increases your dilemma a thousandfold."

"I choose my own path."

"I wonder if any of us do." She frowned at the bare toes that protruded from the cast on her leg. "Something happened to you, Morgan. Something bad enough that you never wanted to risk it happening again. People you cared about—they got hurt, or they hurt you. Ulysses's own family drove him out because he couldn't possibly be a true Wakefield looking the way he does. But he still writes to them, hoping to be reconciled." She looked up. "I know it's difficult to keep hoping when you don't want to. Love is the worst of all, because it's like a lantern shining on everything you don't want to see. Or remember."

Morgan clenched his fist around the top of the bedpost. "I don't like you as a philosopher, Firefly."

"I don't think I do, either." She laughed. "That's what happens when you are stuck in a bed listening to Ulysses read from musty old books written by dead Greeks and Romans."

The room around Morgan changed, its cheerful yellow walls closing in to become a gray, crumbling cell. "The dead should be forgotten."

"No one should be forgotten."

"You live in a dream, Firefly."

"And you, Morgan? Have you forgotten what it is to dream?"

Morgan released his aching fingers from the bedpost. "Men dream. Wolves do not. I know which is better off."

"We fool ourselves," she said. "I pretend just as much as you do that nothing really matters. At least I know I'm pretending."

"Then you know that Niall Munroe cares nothing for you," Morgan said cruelly. "He may take your body if you offer it, as he would from any whore."

"Perhaps I'll choose to give it to him. Have you forgotten the pleasures of the body, Morgan? Oh, no—I do remember you have enjoyed Tamar's company from time to time. She must be very skilled, and she knows exactly what she wants. Athena is only half a woman, isn't she?"

Her words slashed at Morgan from heart to belly. "Athena—" he began, choking, "Athena is . . . more than a woman. More than you can—" He broke off, breathing hard. Caitlin stared at him, her freckles as lurid as wagon paint.

A light tap came on the door. Harry stepped in, oblivious, filling the room with his voluble and sunny presence.

"Ah, Morgan, my boy. Ulysses said I would find you here. Caitlin, how are you on this very fine afternoon?"

"Isn't it snowing outside?" Caitlin asked, craning her head toward the lace-curtained window.

"So it is, so it is. But that should not dampen our pleasure in a most unexpected visit. One of the ranch hands just came to report a wagon coming up the lane. Some hired conveyance and driver, no doubt, for these mountain passes." He rubbed his hands. "Is it not wonderful news, Morgan? Our very own Miss Athena has come at last."

Chapter 14

Morgan stood toe to toe with Harry, looking down a full foot at the older man. "You brought her here," he accused. "You and Caitlin."

Harry's brows arched toward the ceiling. "Why, my boy, this is her property, after all!"

Morgan growled and walked around him. His heart sent jolts of lightning up and down his body with every beat. Had he not been waiting every day for this? Had he not sensed, deep in his soul, that she could not stay away any more than he could stop thinking about her?

But Harry and Caitlin had arranged this between them, played with his life and Athena's as if they were ivory pieces on Harry's chessboard. Morgan wouldn't have been astonished if Caitlin had planned her own injury, just to push him and Athena together.

But he could refuse to play by the rules they had set.

A cool, supple body blocked his path. If he had not been so preoccupied, he would have smelled Tamar a mile away, and avoided her.

"My wolf," she said. "What makes you frown so? Have the hunters set one too many traps for your liking?" She smiled, and he was driven back to the memory of kissing those lips, holding that willing body against him in the night.

He could have had her a thousand times since, if he had so much as looked at her. But he had kissed Athena. One kiss, lacking even the most basic intimacies of the flesh, and he was ruined for the taste of another mouth.

Tamar could have taken any number of lovers in the troupe, for all her strangeness. Instead, she chose to pursue him. She had schemed her way into one of the rooms in the main house, and had become impossible to avoid completely. Morgan had finally realized that she believed she had some claim on him because of their brief liaison.

Why, he did not understand. He had offered her nothing. Whatever ambition lay behind her calculating eyes, he could not fulfill it. Her beauty was like a jungle flower he had heard of, intoxicating to look at but thick with the smell of rotten meat.

"Yes," he said. "Too many traps." He tried to pass, but she held out an arm to stop him. She had great strength for a woman, coiled and always lying in wait.

"You will never have her," she said. The very calmness of her voice set his hair on end. "She would spit on you, my wolf, like all *gadje*."

"Do not speak of her, Tamar."

"Ah, the fierce growl." She laughed softly. "Why should I not speak of her? The others do. They all *love* her, the little helpless one." She drew her long nail down his cheek. "Do you love her, too? Do you dream of her useless legs coming to life and wrapping around you in the night? Do you imagine living in her big house in the city, with a fine lady's golden collar about your neck, or do you think she will follow you to rut in the woods like a beast?"

He grasped her wrist and pulled it away. "No."

"Men are children," she said in that same calm, passionless voice. "They want only what they cannot have or what will make them sick in the belly. She will make you sick. And when you have need of the cure, come to me."

She left him, gliding away without a single seductive glance. And a strange sensation washed through him, startling in its truth.

He was sorry for Tamar. He pitied her and her inexplicable obsession with him. He wondered what had made her what she was, and why she saw in him, of all men, a cure for her private pain.

Was this what humans called compassion? Had Athena taught him its meaning?

He wanted no part of it. He began to walk again, hardly knowing which direction he was headed. Tamar was just like the others, aiming to bend him to her desires.

He found himself at the end of the hall, where it opened up into the great parlor. The place echoed with emptiness, not quite as grand as the public rooms of Athena's Denver home, but large enough to hold a pair of average cabins or an ordinary farmhouse within its high walls. The wooden floor and rustic embellishments did little to make it seem less palatial. Padded and polished furniture was grouped around sumptuous woven carpets and a thick bearskin rug. The hearth was immense, its perpetual blaze constantly fed with the trunks of small trees.

The parlor's door stood open to the entrance hall. Snow blew in from the outer doors. Athena wheeled in, one of the ranch hands behind her with a pair of carpetbags.

Athena loosened the collar of her thick wool coat. "Please set the bags down anywhere, Sterling," she said to the hand. "I would appreciate it if you will make sure that my driver is given a meal and a bed for the night."

"I'll do my best, Miss Athena," Sterling said, dropping the bags onto the floor, "but it's mighty crowded here what with the circus folk and all. The foreman ain't none too happy with the tight quarters at the bunkhouse and them trick horses in the barn, and I hear Mr. Durant is thinking of quitting—begging your pardon, ma'am."

Athena smiled, tugging at her gloves. "Poor Mr. Durant. For many years all he has done is keep the house in readiness for guests that seldom arrive. I will be certain to tell him and the foreman that they will be very well compensa—"

She saw Morgan and stopped. Morgan was vaguely aware that

Sterling had vacated the room, leaving them alone. Athena continued to stare, her lips slightly parted, and Morgan felt as if he had been shot, skinned, and hung on the wall for a trophy.

He had told Caitlin that he could leave any time and never look back. He had lied. He could not make himself move a single step away from the woman across the room.

"Morgan," she whispered.

Absence makes the heart grow fonder, the old saw proclaimed. Now Athena understood exactly what it meant. One look at Morgan, standing so still by the hall, and she knew her coming had been inevitable. One breath of the air he breathed, and she wondered how her heart had continued to beat in the cold void of their separation.

A thrill of almost painful sensation shot up her legs from heel to hip. Morgan's eyes burned, compelling her. Commanding.

Come. Come to me.

It was as if he had been calling every moment of the past five weeks, and only now did she truly hear him. Her fingers clutched at the arms of her chair. The muscles in her legs, so long dormant, began to quiver and twitch.

Come. He smiled, lifting the burden of her fear. He held out his hand. *Come.*

Athena pressed all of her weight onto her arms and pushed up. Her feet touched the floor. Her knees quivered, but only for a moment. Then they locked, steadying her, and she rose. Slowly, carefully she stood up, the chair at her back, and swayed from the dizzying height of her own five and a half feet.

She had no time to contemplate the miracle. Morgan summoned her, his eyes ever more demanding, his fingers curled to beckon. She slid one foot along the smooth wooden floor. The second followed the first.

One step taken. Another. A third. She dared to look up from the ground again. Morgan's eyes flashed triumph and pride—for her. But he waited—waited until she had taken all the steps between them and only one more led directly into his arms.

She made it. She reached up and wrapped her arms about his shoulders—not for support, not out of need, but because she wanted him. With her own strength she drew his face to hers. She opened her mouth and inhaled the warmth of his breath.

And she kissed him. She kissed *him,* free to make that choice as she was free to stand and walk and feel again.

Morgan's mouth opened over hers, seizing what she offered. Some great mystery waited to be revealed in his embrace, a tale only he could illustrate with his lips and his tongue. She felt its erotic promise all the way down to her toes.

Let it not end too quickly. Let it never end. . . .

"Athena."

Something was wrong with Morgan's voice. She opened her eyes, and the shock of reality flung her back into her chair.

The chair she had never left. She was not on her feet, not in Morgan's arms. She remained exactly where Sterling had left her, and Morgan still waited by the hall.

All a dream. All a cruel, treacherous fantasy concocted by her addled mind. She could have wept, but many years of practice had taught her how to swallow the tears.

You forgot why you are here. You saw Morgan, and everything else disappeared, even Caitlin. This is your rightful punishment for such base selfishness.

Punishment, and a stark reminder that Morgan was not what her childish dreams made of him.

"Athena," he said. His eyes were not welcoming, but wary. "Are you ill?"

"No." She managed a smile. "I am quite well. How is Caitlin? I have come to make sure she is recovering as she should."

"You came here without your brother's permission?"

She couldn't tell if it was censure or admiration she heard in his voice. Hadn't he encouraged her to defy her brother in the past? "Niall is away on business." She lifted her chin. "Will you show me to Caitlin's room?"

He took half a step toward her, stopped, and made a strange, almost helpless gesture. "Athena. You should not have—" He shook his head, grim about the mouth. "I will take you to her."

"Miss Athena!"

Harry swept out of the hall, barely pausing to step around Morgan, and greeted Athena with a warm smile. "Welcome, welcome! Of course I have no right whatsoever to welcome you to your own home, but we are all so glad you have come. Caitlin will be pleased—"

"How is she?"

The sparkle in his eyes dimmed. "I have been worried about her, as you know, but—" He cast a wary glance back at Morgan. "Now you are here, she will surely make progress. Morgan, would you be so good as to take Miss Athena's bags to her room? Mr. Durant was quite plain that he was saving your chamber for you, my dear, as well as Mr. Munroe's, in case you should come—just as he ought, of course. Not that any of us would dream of appropriating it!" He took the handles of Athena's chair. "I confess that I feel some pity for Mr. Durant's situation. He was not at all prepared for us, even with the addition of the extra staff your good brother hired. I understand that Mr. Durant has been caretaker here for years . . . but even though most of the troupers are in the bunkhouse, the poor fellow has clearly not had to deal with so many guests. In spite of our efforts to help he seems . . . quite annoyed."

Athena remembered Mr. Durant as a nervous, efficient, but generally kind older man who had competently handled the large parties her father had given when she was a child. Prominent men and women had come from Denver to talk business or simply relax away from the city's summer heat, but that had been many years ago. Evidently Mr. Durant was out of practice.

"Don't worry, Harry. I will speak to him myself this evening."

"I am sure that he will be quite upset to have missed you—I believe he is consulting with the foreman about a shortage of provisions." Harry pushed her chair away from the door, and Athena was very much aware of Morgan gathering up the baggage and trailing along behind.

"You did not bring your maid, my dear?" Harry went on. "I know there are several young women here to clean and cook and whatnot. Perhaps one of them might attend you—"

"That will not be necessary," Athena said, wishing that she had eyes in the back of her head. "I should be staying for just a few days, and I will need only occasional assistance."

"Quite so, quite so. Nevertheless, I will see if I can locate a girl for you so that you may refresh yourself. Caitlin is sleeping at the moment, but when she wakes—" He paused halfway across the room and gazed at the great oak staircase in dismay. "Oh dear. How extraordinarily foolish of me. Your rooms are on the second floor, are they not?"

"I haven't been to Long Park many times in the past several years. Niall had meant to have an elevator installed, but it seemed unnecessary . . ." *And he always carried me. But he isn't here. Mr. Durant isn't strong enough, and neither is Harry. That leaves—*

"Morgan, if I may impose upon you once again," Harry said.

Athena held her breath. Morgan stalked up beside them, bent over Athena, and lifted her into his arms. It was not the first time he had held her so, but since the kiss—since her fantasy of walking—the act was charged with almost unbearable excitement.

And shame for her pitiful expectations.

Morgan mounted the stairs, unspeaking, while Harry puffed along at a much slower pace. "To the right," she whispered when they reached the landing. Morgan carried her to the room she indicated, balanced her weight on one arm, and used his free hand to open the door.

The room's furnishings and decorations were the frothy, unsophisticated selections of a young girl, unchanged since before the accident. Morgan hesitated when he saw the white, lace-canopied bed, and then gently set her down upon it.

She stared up at him. He stared back. The room grew very warm despite the empty fireplace. Huffing like a bellows, Harry appeared in the doorway.

"Morgan," he said between breaths. "The bags—"

Morgan backed away and fled the room. Athena pressed her hands to her face, wishing for a handful of snow to cool her flush.

"There, there, my dear girl. What is the matter?"

She tried to gather herself into a more dignified position on the bed and smiled at Harry, inviting him to sit in the delicate wicker chair at her dressing table. He closed the door, gave the chair a dubious glance and sat down cautiously. The chair creaked, but held.

"I suppose I am tired, that is all," she said. "The driver I hired was quite competent, but the wagon was not comfortable, I fear."

"Your brother does not know you have come."

"No. He's away, and I made the decision on my own." Best not to elaborate on that point; sharing such worries with Harry did neither of them any good. And there was something else that she could no longer keep to herself. "Harry . . . is Morgan . . . is he upset that I have come?"

Harry leaned forward, eliciting a groan from the chair, and clasped his hands between his knees. "My dear child," he said with uncharacteristic gravity, "How can you ask such a question?"

"He . . . I . . ." She turned her face aside. "I have never spoken of this to anyone. It feels very strange . . . wrong—"

"No, no. Never say so." Harry placed his hand over his heart. "I am honored beyond words that you choose to speak to me as you would to your own father. You see, I have regarded you as something of my daughter from the day we met. And Morgan is like the son I never had."

Casting discretion to the snow-laden wind, Athena met his gaze. "I loved my father very much," she said. "I still miss him dreadfully. But if I could have a second one, I would choose you."

"Thank you, my dear. Thank you." He reached into his pocket for a handkerchief. "I have seen much in my time. Very little surprises me. Nothing you may say will disturb me, I assure you."

Athena swallowed. "I hardly know how to begin. Ever since I met you . . . the circus . . . I have felt as if you are a second family."

"As we have felt of you."

"And . . . and—" Oh, why did all eloquence desert her at times like this? Yet how often had she spoken with real intimacy to anyone, discussed anything but charitable work, social affairs, fashion, or household management? Among all the women she considered her friends, why would she never dream of confiding in them as she did this garrulous and good-hearted old man?

Because she trusted him—trusted Harry, and Caitlin, even Morgan more than she did her own kind, the very people whom she regarded as her peers.

And she was not ashamed.

"Tell me what you know of Morgan," she said in a rush. "Where he comes from, who his people were. Please, Harry. I must know."

"I have been waiting for you to ask that for quite some time, my dear. I will tell you what I know, though in many ways Morgan is as much an enigma to me as to you."

Athena hugged herself. "I know what he is. It doesn't shock me—"

"And that is why I find it so easy to love you."

The lump in Athena's throat had doubled in size. She tried, and failed, to remember when she had heard such tender words from anyone since Papa's death. "It is as if he doesn't wish to speak of his past— not his family or what he wants from life. Why, Harry? What happened to him?"

"No one knows. He came to us as a wolf pursued by hunters, and changed into a man before our eyes. Our troupe has always been a home for those who have no place in the outside world, so naturally we took him in. He felt he owed us a debt, and though he did so reluctantly, he repaid us by becoming our 'Wolf-Man' act. He was so successful in drawing audiences that he was almost entirely responsible for saving us from certain ruin. He could have left us many times, and seemed to wish to—and yet he has remained."

"He cares about you."

"Yes, though he will not willingly admit it."

"How did he live before he came to you?"

"That I know. He spent many years as a wolf, among the beasts—deliberately avoiding the haunts of men. But his reasons I cannot tell you. There is great bitterness in him, a desire to see only the worst in mankind."

"And you always see the best."

"I try." He studied his plump, interlaced fingers. "He will not speak of his family, except to say that he lost his parents and sister before he fled to the woods. I suspect some dark tragedy, and that he blames himself. They say there is a boy in every man, and the boy that Morgan was came to manhood in sorrow." He gave her a sad smile. "Yet there is something in him that allows one to forgive his rough nature. At heart, he is deeply generous and protects those he considers friends, even though he would deny he has any friends at all."

"And you want to help him," Athena murmured. "You want to find out why he suffers, and mend it somehow. . . ."

"I am certain that there is only one person in the world who can bring about such healing," Harry said quietly. "The one he does not believe exists."

Athena was afraid to decipher his words. "He has never tried to talk to you, as I do now?"

"Never. But in my heart of hearts, I dare to think that he sees me, just a little, as his foster-father."

"Thank you, Harry." Despite the brevity of their conversation, Athena felt both drained and exhilarated. Harry loved Morgan. So did Caitlin. What *she* felt could not be so unthinkable.

But what did she feel?

"You must rest now, my dear," Harry said, rising to his feet. "I will find a maid to attend you, and inform you as soon as Caitlin is awake." He cupped the side of her face. "Sleep well, my child. And have faith."

She covered his hand with hers. "Thank you, Harry."

He opened the door and nearly tripped over the bags Morgan had left just outside. With a brief shake of his head, he lifted them one by one and set them in the room.

The ache in Athena's chest continued long after he was gone. A maid arrived within the hour to bring water for washing and help her unpack the bags. Mr. Durant, too, found time to come to her, apologetic for having neglected her but clearly overwhelmed by his additional responsibilities.

She absolved him of any need to personally look after her and arranged to have the hired girl within calling distance. She remained on the bed rather than ask Durant or some stranger to lift her in and out of her chair. Harry failed to return, and Morgan stayed away. At last she grew too sleepy to wait. The maid helped her into her nightdress, and she buried herself beneath the quilted coverlet.

Exhaustion overcame worry, and she closed her eyes. Out of the mist of half-sleep, she woke to an intense pain in her legs, so sharp and sudden that she cried aloud.

Pain in her legs. She reached down to touch them, certain she must still be dreaming. She closed her eyes again, willing herself back to sleep—but instead, she plunged into another dream, this one even more fantastic.

For she was running. Running, not on two legs, but four—running as a wolf, jaws wide to catch the falling snow. And at her side . . .

At her side was Morgan. Morgan as a magnificent black wolf, dwarfing her with his size and power. Yet for all his strength, she matched his blistering pace; her paws were like snowshoes, skimming over the soft quilt of fresh snow. The cold did not reach through the lush density of her coat, and her nostrils were filled with smells as rich and subtle as the colors on an artist's canvas.

They raced the wind itself, she and Morgan. And he looked sideways at her, yellow eyes brilliant with pain, and laughed. With a burst of speed, he lunged ahead of her.

She faltered. For an instant, she knew that this could not be happening, that she had no hope of catching up to him.

But Harry's gentle voice was there, inside her: *"I am certain that there is only one person in the world who can bring about such healing."* And she understood that she must help Morgan, though she did not know how or why; she must heal him, and heal herself as well.

Heal myself? The sheer incongruity of the thought hurled her forward, and at the same time she could feel the snowy world dissolving around her, replaced with hard-edged shadows and woven carpet.

Carpet firm and warm beneath her feet. Two feet. She could see her toes in the darkness, very white at the end of a long column of fabric. They wiggled at her.

Another cruel, intolerable jest at her expense. She looked for her bed, determined to end it.

The bed was several feet away. She would have to walk to reach it. Walking meant standing.

She was standing. Her legs hurt, oh, they hurt most terribly, the way her hands felt when they had been exposed to the cold and then held before a fire.

This was no dream.

She put her hands to her cheeks. Not a dream. Not the pain, and not the fact that her muscles were far too weak to hold her up much longer.

Impossible, her heart told her as she turned carefully toward the bed. *Impossible,* echoed her mind as she measured out the distance she must cover—the same distance she had traveled unconsciously only moments ago.

She began to tremble. Not only her legs, overtaxed as they were, but her entire body. It was joy. She gulped on laughter and tasted saltiness on her lips.

I can stand. I can walk. I am free.

It seemed only natural that Morgan should come then, to share her triumph. Completely right that he should walk up to her—his feet bare, trousers half-buttoned and shirt open at the neck—and kiss her.

This time . . . oh, yes. This time it was real.

Morgan had carried the memory of their one previous kiss for weeks, obsessed with an impulsive act he should have dismissed a moment after it was done.

Now he knew why he had been unable to forget it. Her mouth opened under his so sweetly, with such trust, that he knew she had been thinking of it, too. Wanting it as much as he did.

But it hadn't been mere desire that had driven him that final step. He had been running . . . running as he always did when the company of others became unbearable. Especially the company of this woman. He had found little peace in the outing, for he had not been alone.

Somehow *she* had followed him. He had become aware of her presence as the first hint of false dawn seared the edge of the sky, outlining the jagged, snow-topped profiles of the mountains. The silence had been absolute. One minute he ran alone, and the next he felt her by his side, a ghost-wolf, racing him as he raced his own fears.

He had known it was impossible. She was not really there. But her spirit had come to him, as the Indians said sometimes happened in the night. She had challenged him on his own ground, unafraid. And he had sensed that there was more to this vision than a dream they both shared.

As the stars faded overhead, he doubled back on his tracks and loped to the ranch, not knowing what he might find. No one stirred on the grounds or in the house when he entered it. Up the stairs he had run, soundless, to the door of Athena's room.

And there she stood—*stood*, in the center of the carpet, on her two legs. Her face bore the look of a startled deer. Then she began to shake, and Morgan felt the mingled fear and triumph as if it were his own.

Triumph, and pride. Pride in her, in the achievement she had made against all the odds. Deep and unexpected joy that she could be whole, and free.

He did not question. He went to her, took her in his arms, and kissed her.

This was a kiss as the other had not been—lingering, ardent, and shared with equal fervor. In it Morgan poured all the desire he had kept so tightly sealed away, unfettered by Athena's new strength.

She could do more than stand. Her arms were strong and sure about his neck. The she-wolf who had run beside him was present in full measure, and her teeth locked on his lower lip with a ferocity for which he was unprepared.

The wolf in him cried out for conquest. He explored the velvet interior of her mouth with flickers of his tongue, and then deeper thrusts. She seemed ready to devour him. If she had never kissed a man before that night in her bed-chamber, she learned very quickly.

It was as much the werewolf blood that sang in her heart as it did in his own. Powerful, undeniable attraction. The wolf she could not be while bound to her chair had awakened to all the possibilities of liberation.

He gathered her thick, loose hair in his fists and pulled her head back, kissing and nipping her bared neck. She hissed with pleasure. A distant part of him wondered at so vast a change in her, and cast the thought aside.

Take her, the wolf demanded. *She wants you. You want her. Nothing else matters.*

No one would see. No one need know. A single frenzied coupling, and he would be gone again with none the wiser.

Gone? Did he think he could run from such a binding? Once it was done . . .

As if they were truly of one mind, they drew apart at the same moment. Athena was panting and flushed, her lips slightly swollen, her eyes vivid, more golden than green or brown. She swayed. He caught her again and carried her to the bed.

She lay back without protest. He could see how her legs trembled, pushed to the very edge of their strength. It was remarkable that they had supported her so long. Surely they would not have done so had she been of pure human blood.

"Morgan," she whispered. "I did it. I . . . stood up."

Already the kiss was relegated to the back of her thoughts. He could not blame her. He should be relieved, though his body ached and cursed him for his cowardice.

"Yes," he said. He considered the edge of the bed and chose to crouch beside it instead. "How did it happen?"

"I don't know. One moment I was dreaming, and the next—" She ran her tongue over her lower lip. Morgan winced. "I dreamed that I was running as a wolf. With you."

"I felt it," he said. "I saw you, in my mind."

"You did?" She smiled, as if she had just discovered that there was a joy greater than recovering the use of her legs. "It wasn't only a dream?"

He began to understand. She had dreamed of running, of her wolf blood carrying her to freedom, and her body had acted. It had defied the doctors and naysayers who had declared that she would never walk again . . . including herself. He should have sensed from the beginning that her paralysis was made up of denials and assumptions, not of a ruined body. That was why he had kissed her the first time, goaded her to defy her brother, allowed himself to get so close. . . .

When did you become so wise?

"If you can walk," he said, avoiding her question, "your injuries must be healed."

"Healed." She breathed the word, exhaled it, savoring a taste she had not expected to sample again. "Is it possible?"

"Your legs held you up. Your muscles must be weak and thin, but they work. Can you feel them?"

"Yes." Wonder in her eyes, she ran her hands down her body from waist to thigh. Her nightdress molded to the shape beneath, and Morgan clenched his teeth. "I *can*. It hurts."

The pain must be great, but she bore it without complaint. Pride swelled his heart to uncomfortable proportions. "I only know a little about such injuries, but I have seen men who have not used arms or legs for many months, and they can get well if they do not give up. It will continue to hurt, after so long. The wolf will help. It was the wolf that healed you."

She met his gaze. "But I . . . I haven't Changed in years."

"Your body doesn't forget. Just as your muscles don't forget how to stand. They will learn to walk and then run again." He stared into her eyes. "You are brave enough to do it, Athena. You always have been."

She pulled herself up to lean on the pillows, carefully flexing her knees. "But if all it needed was courage, then why did it take me so many years to find it?"

Ask Ulysses, he wanted to tell her. *He is the philosopher—he and Caitlin.* "What were you afraid of?" he asked.

"I—" She closed her eyes, and he could feel her traveling back over the years, to that snowy mountainside long ago. "I don't know. I believed the doctors. I believed Niall."

Niall. Morgan bit back a snarl. "He kept you in that chair."

"No! No." She shook her head, refusing to hear anything against her brother. "Nothing is that simple. He did everything for me."

"He did not understand the wolf," Morgan said. "Neither did you."

The confusion in her eyes cleared, and a new energy coursed through her. Morgan could see it, radiating from her body. "I believed the wolf was gone forever. I made myself believe it." She looked at him in such a way that his throat closed up and he couldn't have spoken had he wished to.

"It wasn't only the wolf inside me that made this happen," she said softly. "It wasn't a miracle. It was you. Your inspiration, your belief in me . . . even your bullying. You were an example I had never found anywhere else."

He jumped to his feet. "You give me too much credit."

"I don't think I do. You are so much more than you know, Morgan."

"And you know *nothing* of me."

"Then tell me." She leaned forward, deliberately working the muscles of her legs. "If you have suffered . . . I want to help you as you have helped me. I owe you so much. Let me repay at least a little."

He started for the door, and stopped. Every nerve burned with conflicting urges. *Run. Stay. Avoid her at all costs. Take her. Possess her. Make her yours forever.*

"There are many who care about you, Morgan," she said behind him. "You do not want to owe anyone . . . and you don't want anyone owing you. Do you think I have not seen that time and again in my work?"

"Among your charity cases?" he snapped. "Those who are too weak to survive on their own, and too proud to admit it?"

"The circus needed your help, and you gave it. You could have left, but you stayed. You had no reason to encourage me, yet you did. I cannot understand you, Morgan . . . and yet, somehow, I do."

"You are a child."

"I had a father who loved me, and a brother who protects me even when he is too diligent. Perhaps I let myself be protected. But who protected you?"

"I don't need protection."

She paused, and he thought he had driven her from the subject. But she was not finished.

"You lost your family when you were young," she said. "But you have a new family now. Caitlin, and Ulysses, everyone in the circus. They are all your friends. And Harry regards you as a son."

He couldn't bear it. The bit of conversation he had heard between her and Harry, when he had left the bags by the door—that had been more than he wanted to know. And yet he had envied their easy intimacy, the affection between parent and child. His last conversation with Aaron Holt had been . . . best forgotten.

"What was your father like?" she asked.

He turned on her. "He was a dreamer, a wastrel, a man who could not care for his family." He closed his eyes, seeing the haggard, agonized, pleading face that bore so little resemblance to the man he had known in boyhood. "He left my mother . . ."

Too hard. Too much. "I went looking for him," he said. "To bring him home."

"Did you find him?"

She seemed to sense the enormity of what she asked, for her voice had grown very small. He smiled brutally. "I found him."

"You hated him," she whispered. "Oh, Morgan—"

Was that pity in her eyes, her voice? Was she reaching out, her fingers poised to stroke his cheek, pat his hair as if he were a disconsolate child—one of her precious, pitiful orphans?

He moved faster than human eyes could see and grasped her about the wrist.

"Don't pity me," he growled. "Don't you dare pity me."

He crouched over her, his legs to either side of her hips, pinning her arms to the bed. Athena understood, oh, yes, she knew—but she was calm, unafraid.

He did not want her fear. He wanted . . . he wanted . . .

"Morgan—"

He silenced her once more with his lips.

Chapter 15

Athena knew better than to show fear. The wolf was in Morgan's eyes, in his need, and she knew she had pressed too quickly.

But she needed, too. She needed to understand him, and now—as he kissed her with a harshness that swiftly transformed into a hungry caress—she realized she needed something far more physical.

The very physical desires she had denied herself, knowing that no man would be able to satisfy them even should he wish to bother with a cripple. The entirely selfish fulfillment that benefitted no one but herself.

Now she had begun to *want*—not dream, not wish, but actively seek what had not been within her grasp until this moment.

That frightened her as Morgan himself could not. Her legs had begun to waken from their long sleep, but she hadn't reckoned how every other part of her would so brilliantly come alive at his touch.

It had happened before, with him, but not like this. His fingers tangled in her loosened hair, fiercely holding her still as he kissed her with all the thoroughness she had imagined in her waking dream downstairs.

But his anger, his seeming ferocity, was as much a facade as his ordinary human shape. Even now his hold on her was tender as that of a she-wolf carrying her pup in jaws that could crush bone.

His mouth formed her name against her lips, and he released her arms. She left them where they were, though she felt far from passive. Her instinct was to reach for him and pull him down, down, into herself.

But *he* must feel in control. She sensed that the way she sensed the crushing sorrows of young, unwed mothers or the anger of men who could not find work to feed their families. In such cases she knew how to respond—how to give, heal, mend—but now she must find her way like one blind.

One blind who had just begun to see.

Morgan nuzzled her ear, hot breath sizzling against the cool flesh at her hairline, and did something indescribable with his tongue. She gave a brief cry of surprise. He kissed her again, first on the lips and then on her forehead, her eyelids, her nose, her chin. Each kiss was little more than a breath, yet charged with such potency that she could not mistake it for anything like a brotherly salute.

No sooner had she recognized the utterly erotic nature of the caresses than he surprised her again. His tongue swept down the angle of her jaw, from earlobe to chin. It was as if he were sampling her before beginning his feast, a promise of more to come.

More than what had transpired in her bedroom, or even in her dream. It could go so much further, if she dared let it. All she need do to stop it was tell him "no."

He pressed his mouth to the underside of her jaw, where the pulse beat very fast, where she was most defenseless. She bent her head back and closed her eyes. He nipped her here, there . . . love-bites that she vaguely thought must be common among his kind. *Their* kind.

Then he began to unbutton the top of her nightdress. She held her breath. One button undone: he peeled back the two seams and kissed the space between. One more: another kiss. The third button lay nestled in a valley of flesh. The last ended just where her breasts pushed up so shamelessly against the sheer linen.

Needles of sensation prickled in her belly and nipples. When he got below the buttons, he wouldn't be doing what an importunate suitor might have done, if she had suitors. She had no illusions about his intention.

Why? her much-abused common sense cried. *Why here, now?*

Why not? Did you expect avowals of love, a slow and formal courtship that any normal woman might prefer? Are you normal? Is he?

Might this not be your only chance to know what it is to be loved?

He laced his fingers through hers and pulled her arms above her head. He did not hold her there. Instead, he let his hand slide down her body, grazing shoulder and breast and hip without lingering, coming at last to rest on the juncture of her legs.

Her legs, which were no longer dead weights but strange appendages not yet sure how they belonged to the rest of her. They would not yet obey her, but they could *feel.*

She *felt* the heat of his palm through the lawn of her gown. She *felt* him begin to slide the fabric up her thighs, inch by inch, from the middle of her calf and higher. She *felt* the draft of cool air lick at her bared skin as his tongue had licked at her ear and chin.

Then his hand was on her, nothing between.

He brought his face close to hers. His lungs worked like those of a man who had been running many miles without rest. Her nostrils drew in scents that belonged only to him, unique and intoxicating, wolf and human. Damp, heavy locks of his hair curled under her jaw and into the cleft between her breasts.

"You feel so much for others," he whispered hoarsely in her ear. "But do you feel for yourself, Athena?"

He moved his hand under the bunched cloth of her nightdress. His fingertip just barely—or so she thought—brushed the small, tight curls at the tops of her thighs.

She had read of electric shocks and had imagined what they must be like. But that was scarcely an adequate comparison when he touched the most private place beneath that downy shield.

He had asked if she felt for herself. No answer was necessary. Pleasure like pain danced and burned with each small rotation of his finger, wringing gasps from deep in her chest. Standing on her own feet, walking, running again . . . all that was nothing compared to the ecstasy that reached into the very center of all she was or could ever be.

Was this it, the thing women spoke of in veiled allusions and whispers when men were safely out of hearing? The thing that made sharing a man's bed more than a duty and a way of making children?

Morgan. He touched her again, and her voice lost its way somewhere between throat and tongue.

To feel . . . to feel so gloriously was worth any price. To feel *this* at Morgan's hands, with his body stretched out above her was a miracle she did not deserve.

But what did Morgan get for himself? He had started this to silence her—to prove something to her, to himself, that he was master of his own fate and hardened against any sentiment she could offer. Yet his attempt at mastery had become a giving—of pleasure, of new feelings and wonder such as Athena had never known.

Did he realize what he did to her? Was it part of his game? Or was it as real and sincere as the renewed wholeness of her body?

He was no fool, and neither was she. The exact nature of the physical consummation between man and woman was but a vague idea in Athena's mind, but it must be connected to the way he touched her, the way her body responded and grew moist and warm and wanting. She could understand, now, how women bore children outside the bonds of marriage.

But Morgan's skilled fingers were not the organs capable of planting new life in a woman's body. Children—good heavens, children—she had dismissed that future as completely as she had one that freed her from the chair.

Children, marriage, physical love. Suddenly all three had become solid and tangible, vivid landscapes she could see through an open window instead of hazy specters glimpsed in a fog of resignation.

Morgan had made them all possible. He alone. He gave and gave, without knowing how much, and now he gave again. She knew in her heart that he wouldn't force himself upon her, risk getting her with child. God forbid that he should create such an unbreakable tie between them.

But if he thought of her—of her reputation, which he had seemed to ignore in Denver—and of the future he would alter forever if he continued—then how could she accuse him of such a sensible selfishness?

No. If he had meant to prove his independence, his indifference to human tenderness, he had chosen the wrong way. He gave unstintingly, denying himself the kind of fulfillment men must derive from such a joining. And she could not bear the thought that he had nothing but the dubious comfort of knowing he could make her *feel*.

That was when she realized she had fallen in love with him.

The notion was so blindingly obvious that she was briefly numb to sensation. Everything froze—lungs, heart, even her ability to hear and see.

She *loved* Morgan Holt. It wasn't mere attraction for one like herself, one who could understand. It wasn't some sort of rebellion against the life she thought she had chosen after the accident. It wasn't even this, this marvelous thing he did with his lips and his hands.

And it was not at all what she expected love to be. She had thought it beyond her reach, an emotion connected with gallant, handsome, courteous men who had wealth and presence and would never look twice at a woman in a invalid's chair. Men like her brother and his associates, the husbands and fathers of her society friends.

Morgan was not gallant, or courteous, or even handsome in the way of those men. He was bad-tempered, gruff, impolite, indifferent to propriety, and far too plain-spoken. It was rare that he considered the feelings of others as he ought . . . as she tried to do.

But his was a breadth of soul, a tormented devotion, a passionate loyalty that could not be bought but, once given, was eternal. He had decided soon after their first meeting that she belonged to his small circle of family and friends. She knew he would never let harm come to her, and that he would fight to the death on her behalf.

All *that* he gave, having nothing but himself. But he felt. He felt as deeply as anyone she had ever known.

How could she make sense of this emotion, this knowledge of what he meant to her? She saw how much she had taken from him, and was ashamed. She did not take without giving back.

She must *give* to Morgan—help, and succor, and healing, if she could. Even love, if there was any chance in the world that he might accept it. But there was a more immediate gift within her power to bestow. A small, temporary gift that mattered less to her than to her society, but might begin to repay the debt she owed him.

If she had the courage.

Morgan stroked her with gentle pulses, and she momentarily lost the power to consider such abstracts as courage and selfishness. Lightheaded, she arched up, up, her spine curving as if to bring every inch of her body into contact with his. Higher, higher, unfurling wings to carry them both into the heavens.

It was coming, the moment of perfect freedom. No more chair, no more waiting, no bondage even to the earth. Just one more stroke, one more caress, and she would prove . . . prove to herself, and everyone . . .

Morgan stopped. Athena opened her eyes with a wordless protest, but the look on his face kept her silent. She heard the thump of footfalls running up the stairs a second after he did.

Niall. She barely had time to pull her nightdress over her knees before he burst through the door.

"My God," he said hoarsely. "Athena." His gaze fixed on Morgan. "You damned bastard—"

"Niall!"

Athena's cry might as well have been a whisper. It did not penetrate Niall's rage. He could see nothing but the man who had despoiled his sister.

Morgan Holt. The cur crouched over her on the bed—*her* bed—an ugly snarl on his face as if he would defend her against her own brother. *Defend* her, by God, when he had stolen what little of value she had left.

Niall clenched his fist and dove at his enemy. Morgan sprang up and met him in midstride. Niall felt his fist connect with flesh and bone, heard the satisfying grunt of pain as Morgan staggered and fell to his knees with the force of the blow.

But he did not remain down. He stood again, shaking blood from his split lip, and braced his legs apart. Niall obliged him with a second strike directly to the jaw. Morgan's head snapped to one side.

"Niall, stop it!"

He was aware of the motion at the edge of his sight, a figure in pale linen lurching toward him with an awkward gait. Confusion stopped him from hitting again, though Morgan remained stubbornly on his feet. If one of the whoreson's circus friends had come to help him . . .

A hand caught at his arm. Athena's face swam into focus.

"Niall!"

Athena. He blinked. She could not be here. She was on the bed. But the bed was empty, coverlet and sheets rumpled but unstained. The hand that gripped his arm with such frantic strength was slender and feminine.

She was standing—leaning her weight against him, but on her own two feet. Shock reverberated through Niall. He had come into the room expecting the worst, and finding it . . . but he had not been prepared for this. Not Athena able to stand, to walk, to participate willingly in her own ruination.

He met her gaze, a strange, cold calm muting his rage to a dull throb behind his eyes. "How long?" he asked in a soft, reasonable voice. "How long have you been lying to me, Athena?"

A vise made of five steel fingers caught him about the throat. He clawed at an arm roped with muscle, implacable in its grip. Vision narrowed to a pair of slitted amber eyes and a mouth full of bared white teeth.

Then the grip relaxed, and he caught himself as he fell, scrambling out of reach while he labored to fill his lungs with precious air. His back hit the wall, and he let it hold him up until he could see clearly again.

They stood together, not touching but close, the bastard and Niall's shameless, half-human sister. Athena's hair was half loose about her shoulders like that of a cheap Cherry Creek slut, her lips bruised with kissing. Morgan . . .

Morgan stood in front of her, head lowered, shoulders hunched like a bear ready to charge. Coarse black hair fell in his eyes, giving him the look of a madman. His lip and nose bled where Niall had struck true, but he hardly seemed aware of the injuries. An almost inaudible growl rumbled from his throat.

He was an animal. Worse than an animal. Niall thought of the rifle downstairs—his father's, hung on the wall when Walter Munroe first took up with Gwenyth Desbois, and never used again. Father had abandoned hunting for pleasure because of that woman. But the rifle was still there.

The door was close. All he had to do was avoid provoking an attack. He took a step backward.

"Niall," Athena said. She moved one of her feet, sliding it across the floor. "It isn't what you think. Please, listen to me!"

He looked at her in such a way that she faltered, folding her arms across her chest as if she could ward off the contempt in his gaze.

"I am no more blind than you are lame," he said. "You are a whore, just like your mother."

He wasn't quite sure what happened then, or how it started. Morgan's teeth were the first to change. They began to lengthen, became more pointed, the incisors graced with a cutting edge like miniature daggers. Then the face . . . subtly, slowly, so gradually that Niall could not have said exactly how the transformation progressed. His stomach roiled with horror at the sight of something that God and Nature had never intended.

Skin stubbled with a day's growth of beard darkened further, taking on the rough texture of short fur. Nose blended into upper lip. Ears shifted, lengthened. The body took on proportions that mocked the human shape, pushing and pulling at the seams of Morgan's clothing.

And through it all, the eyes barely changed. They focused on Niall with all the single-minded purpose of a starving predator in sight of an easy meal.

The face of Morgan Holt was no longer that of a man. Nor was it a beast, though it most closely resembled a wolf. A wolf . . . the Wolf-Man. A legend made to frighten children and entertain jaded audiences. A creature like Athena's mother. Like Athena.

Morgan Holt's circus act was no act at all. And Niall understood everything.

In such moments—as if he were in the middle of a crucial business negotiation—Niall's mind became as sharp as the Wolf-Man's fangs. He knew that Morgan had the strength to tear him apart with little effort, and that for some reason he had not done so. He saw that Athena was moving, hobbling, setting herself between the two men as if her slight body could hold them apart.

"I will not let you hurt each other," she cried. Her voice trembled, but it did not fail. "Now you know what Morgan is. I broke my word by coming here, but I did not lie to you. I couldn't risk telling you the full truth."

"Because I would stop you from seeing him again? From going to your . . . what is he? Your mate?" Niall laughed. "Have you been waiting for another like you to come along and take you away? Will you be the bitch to his dog, Athena?"

Morgan lunged. Athena interposed herself, almost falling, and Morgan stopped to catch her. Niall noted with icy curiosity that each of Morgan's fingers was tipped by a curved black nail, and wondered if he could speak in a human tongue.

"She has done nothing," Morgan said in a rasping voice, answering his question. "If you do not leave her alone, I will—"

"Now isn't it just like men to grunt and squabble like pigs over slops."

The voice was a little breathless, but Niall would have recognized it in a shout or a whisper. He spun toward the door. Caitlin stood at the entrance, with Harry French supporting her on one side and Ulysses Wakefield on the other. Lines of strain framed her eyes, but she was perfectly capable of impaling Niall with a look of utter scorn.

"The gallant white knight, charging up to save a lady's honor," she said, looking past him at Morgan without batting an eyelash at his grotesque appearance. "You're no better, Morgan Holt." Her eyes lit with pleasure as they found Athena. "And you. Look at you!"

"Caitlin!" Athena exclaimed. "You should not be out of bed. I . . . I am quite well. Everything is all right."

Everything was clearly not all right, but Niall knew the most dangerous moment had passed. "This is none of your business," he said, addressing French. "Get out."

Athena pulled halfway from Morgan's grip. "Harry, take her back—"

"And miss all the fun?" Caitlin leaned forward, almost dragging the two men with her. "I think this should become one of our regular acts, don't you, Harry?"

The old man glanced in an agony of worry from one face to another. "Oh, dear. I did not know . . . I did not realize that Mr. Munroe had arrived until we heard the shouting, and Caitlin insisted—"

"It was very kind of you to come visit us," Caitlin said to Niall, smiling sweetly. "I am sorry you are so put out, Mr. Munroe, but if you insist on entering private rooms unannounced, you are bound to see things you don't like."

Niall opened his mouth to answer and was held mute by the sparkle in Caitlin's blue eyes. Dammit, how could he be thinking of her eyes at a time like this? She had always approved of Athena's attraction to Holt. Good God, *she* had probably urged Athena to abandon her principles and humanity for a night of passion in this monster's arms.

"You . . . you defend my sister giving herself to this . . ." He waved toward Morgan, sick in his gut. "You knew what he was, you and your circus freaks. And you let Athena get near him—"

"I think you'll find she has a mind of her own. Athena has known what he is since he saved her life from a runaway horse in the big top." Caitlin cocked her head. "You didn't want her near Morgan because of his act. But you couldn't have known it wasn't an act at all. You don't look like a man who's shocked by something he's never seen before."

"He isn't," Athena said quietly. She stepped away from Morgan's support and stood free on unsteady legs. "He isn't shocked because Morgan and I share the same nature. My mother . . . she was a werewolf, too."

Caitlin's eyes widened. "Of course. It explains so much—why you reacted so calmly when you saw Morgan change, and why you have been drawn to each other." She looked at Niall. "But that means that you must also be—"

"I am not," he snapped. "My mother was a normal woman. She was Walter Munroe's *wife*."

"Ah. I see." Caitlin's stare was so bleak that Niall had difficulty in meeting it. "Athena's mother was his mistress, then."

Her frankness should not have surprised him at this late date. "It doesn't matter. She is my sister, and I promised to protect her from harm."

"And a fine job you make of it."

Seldom had Niall felt such anger. It was as if his skull were an overheated boiler, blackening his vision with scalding steam. When he looked at Caitlin, he dared not loose his rage. But Athena, and Morgan, were another matter entirely.

"I thought she needed protecting," he said, turning on his sister. "Look at her! She has been deceiving everyone, pretending helplessness to win sympathy and support for her charities . . . and for herself." He ignored Athena's horrified protest. "Did you think you could make me dance to your tune by playing the cripple, Athena? Has that been your game all along, just like . . . just like pretending you aren't exactly the same as your mother?"

Morgan snarled. Caitlin hopped forward on one leg. "And who do you take after, Niall Munroe?" she demanded. "You've never been driven by fear for your sister, have you? It's hatred—hatred of anyone different, hatred and guilt, eating you up inside because you helped put Athena in that chair. Controlling her and calling it protection is the only way to salve your guilt and cage what you don't understand!"

Her words echoed in the total silence that followed. Niall heard the accusation over and over, hating Caitlin for revealing his shame, sickened by the truth.

And she knew only half of it.

He had to get out, before he disgraced himself further. But he'd be damned if he'd leave Athena in the hands of these people, no matter what Caitlin claimed as his motive. He had never retreated from a fight without some plan for ultimate victory.

Caitlin provided the distraction he needed. As if she had used up all her strength in castigating him, she gave a soft moan and stumbled sideways. Niall stepped in and caught her before anyone else moved, steadied her, and handed her over to Holt. Morgan took her reflexively, leaving Niall free to grab Athena.

She felt almost boneless as he lifted her, and he was certain when he held her in his arms that her legs were not those of a healthy woman. They were too thin, lacking the full development of muscle. She might be able to stand, even hobble, but she was by no means recovered. Perhaps her deception hadn't been quite as heinous as he had believed.

Niall shouldered his way past Harry and the dwarf and paused in the doorway, Athena rigid in his hold. Caitlin's presence prevented Holt from following. His yellow eyes tracked Niall with an unspoken vow that the battle was far from over. The world narrowed down to the two of them, a long, red tunnel of hatred that connected them as surely as Athena bore her mother's bestial blood.

"Listen well, Morgan Holt," Niall said. "I make you a solemn promise. If you ever touch my sister again, I will kill you."

Almost tenderly, Morgan passed the half-conscious Caitlin to Harry French and started toward Niall. Athena pushed against Niall's chest, and her eyes locked with Holt's.

Niall had no explanation for what followed. Woman and beast-man gazed at each other, and it was as if yet another tunnel linked them, excluding everyone else—a tunnel made of light instead of hate. Athena smiled. She held out her hand, stopping Holt with a gesture as graceful as a dancer's.

"Please stay, Morgan," she said. "Look after Caitlin. She needs you now."

Holt blinked slowly, and the bizarre transformation that had taken him before began to reverse itself. When it was done he was human again, though the shadows under his cheekbones seemed more pronounced and pain pinched the corners of his mouth. Niall hoped that the Change had been excruciating.

He turned his back on Holt, on all of them, and carried his sister out of the jaws of hell.

Chapter 16

At times like these, Athena thought, it would have made perfect sense to weep. But her eyes remained stubbornly dry, though the twisting pain in her legs was a constant reminder that the worst was yet to come.

Niall all but ran down the stairs, charging blindly away from the terrible danger that existed in his mind. At the foot of the stairs he paused, irresolute, and carried her down the hall to the door of Walter Munroe's study.

The room had been closed up ever since Papa had died. It was dark inside, and smelled of mildew and old books. Athena's throat ached with the memories stacked on the shelves and in every corner.

Niall deposited her on the dusty leather-padded chair behind Papa's desk and stood back as if she might somehow corrupt him if he touched her any longer than necessary. That hurt, too, but all the hurts had blended together so that it was difficult to tell one from another.

If she had been able, she would have stood up and marched right back up the stairs to Morgan. But her legs had been pressed beyond their limits, the atrophied muscles seized with spasms, and they would not have carried her as far as the door.

"Are you happy now?" Niall demanded.

He looked drained, ill—not the vital, confident man she knew, but a stranger more terrifying than Morgan in his half-wolf shape. He had threatened to kill Morgan, and Athena believed him. He would try, at the risk of his own life, if Morgan came near her again.

Unless she could make him understand.

"I didn't lie to you about my legs, Niall," she began, gathering the words slowly. "I only just learned that I was able to stand. I didn't think it was possible. I believed the doctors, just as you did."

He flung back his head and gave a harsh laugh. "A miracle, is that it? A miracle that just happens to come when you lie with Morgan Holt?"

She let the cutting remark pass. "I know that you have felt responsible all these years. I didn't want you to. That was why I tried to make a life for myself, as much as I could, and a place in society that wasn't dependent upon you. I succeeded, Niall. But you never saw it as success."

"Is this success, Athena?" he asked. "Choosing these . . . people over the life our father worked to build for the family? Animal instinct instead of the civilized behavior my mother tried to teach you? Instinct to follow after your own kind?"

"It's what you were afraid of, wasn't it? When you learned of Morgan's act—"

"I didn't guess what he was. I only thought he would remind you of what you should forget. I hoped and prayed that your confinement and your social activities would make you give up any idea of ever . . . changing again."

"Then Caitlin was right," she said. "It was fear that made you try to protect me from the world. Fear, and guilt." She swallowed. "Did you ever love me, Niall? Or have you always hated?"

"I hated what you were. I hated Gwenyth Desbois, because of what she did to Mother."

Athena closed her eyes. "I always suspected, but . . . I tried not to believe it."

He leaned over the desk. "Do you know what life was like before that whore seduced Father . . . before she convinced him that rutting with an animal was better than staying faithful to his wife?"

"My mother . . . Morgan is not an animal," she whispered.

"I hoped you would be different. I did my best to make it so." His face was the color of chalk, or the gently falling snow beyond the windows. "I was glad when you were hurt. Glad, Athena. I could have not asked for a better way to . . . keep you from turning into something like her. But I wasn't careful enough."

She stared at him, filled with such anger and pity that no answer would come. He pushed away from the desk and walked about the study, aimlessly touching the spine of one book and then another without seeing the titles.

"You can't fight what you are," he said in a dull voice. "There is too much of that animal in you, Athena. And it's because I love you that I can't let you give in to it."

"Because you love me, or hated my mother? I know your mother was hurt, Niall. I am sorry for that. But she never loved me, either. I always sensed her resentment, even though she didn't let our father see how she felt. If Papa hadn't insisted that you and I be treated the same, I don't know what—"

"Our father." He snorted. "He doted on you. You were always special. After the whore was gone, you reminded him of her. He would have given you anything."

Athena fell back, remembering something Morgan had said not so long ago. "Did you envy me, Niall? Were you jealous that Papa could love me? Or was it because I could do things that no ordinary person could? Did you want to be like me?"

He laughed. "The very idea disgusts me. I could never understand how our father could touch that woman. But I thought you should be considered innocent of her stain, because you didn't choose to be born. Now you have to choose." He faced her again, haggard and wan. "You boasted of the life you've made, all the people you have helped. Everyone in society respects you. That life must be important to you, Athena. Now you will have to decide how important it is."

A dreadful foreboding spilled like acid into Athena's stomach. Cramps seized her thighs, and she fought down a cry. She could not be weak, not now.

"You pride yourself on being unselfish, don't you?" he said, taunting her like the cruel stranger he had become. "Athena Munroe never thinks of herself. She is the most generous, the most noble lady in Denver. So noble that she will sacrifice what she wants for the sake of others." He sat on the edge of the desk, one leg swinging as if they were having a friendly chat. "I have a proposition for you, dear sister. I could send the circus away, as soon as the weather clears—pay them for the one performance and nothing more. Your Caitlin seems able to walk, so there's no further need to pamper her."

"Caitlin—"

"Be quiet, unless you wish me to throw them all out in the snow right now." He studied his manicured fingers. "I can make them leave, and I can tell the sheriff that they've abused our hospitality and stolen property from Long Park—you can be sure I'd be believed where people like them are concerned. Just as decent folk will believe that you were seduced by the confidence games of Harry French and his followers."

"You would lie—"

"I'd do more than lie. I learned many tricks running our father's businesses. It would be easy to make sure the circus can never return to Colorado. They might have to travel some distance to find winter quarters, with the weather getting bad."

Athena shook her head, but he went on relentlessly. "That's not all, Athena. I still have control of your bank accounts. Our father left it to my judgment when I should let you have charge of them. I don't think you'll ever be ready to manage your own inheritance . . . unless you prove to me that you can live the quiet, reasonable life of any decent woman."

Athena saw where he was leading. "Niall, you can't punish innocent people because of what I—"

"So many depend on your charities," he went on, ignoring her. "All those young mothers. The orphans. The unemployed men. What would they do if your contributions were suddenly cut off? Oh, you've talked plenty of others into giving, but a word in the ears of husbands and fathers would stop up that source as well. You know the women, but I know the men. They'd be glad not to have the burden of philanthropic obligations." He sighed. "And then there's your famous Winter Ball. Less than two weeks away now, isn't it? Everyone will be there, ready to compliment you on your fine work. It would be a shame if you were unable to continue with it, and someone else took the credit."

The ball, which Athena had left in Cecily's hands, expecting to return well before the date. The ball that she had schemed and struggled to make the finest charity event of the year, the pinnacle of all her efforts, the defining element of her place in Denver society.

And Niall meant to take it from her. She did not doubt that he could. Cecily was enamored of him; if it came down to it, wouldn't Cecily choose obedience to his will over friendship for Athena?

A small, cold hand gripped her heart. How had Niall known to come here? It was no accident. Athena had trusted Cecily to keep her secret, but she had expected to return to Denver before Niall did. If Niall had discovered his sister's absence and confronted Cecily, how would it benefit her to defy the man she wanted? And she had not *promised* to help. She had said she would "do all I can."

Niall knew exactly how to strike at his sister. All these years Athena had thought him oblivious to her work, but now she saw her error. Either he or someone else had been watching very carefully.

"Miss Hockensmith—Cecily—warned me months ago that you were taking on too much," Niall said. "It is perfectly natural that you should be relieved of your burdens and given a chance to . . . recuperate in another city, perhaps with our cousins in New York. As for Holt—I meant what I said. If he comes near you again, I will kill him. Even creatures like him can be killed, one way or another."

The full weight of Niall's threats pushed Athena deep into the chair, paralyzing her will as the accident had stilled her legs. She could see no way out. If she defied Niall, she would lose everything—all she had worked for, the funding for her charities, the ball, her place in Denver . . . and Morgan's life as well.

"You think you would be happy with Holt," Niall said. "You must decide whether you'll be happier with him, living as a vagabond and an animal, or among civilized people in your family home, surrounded by your friends and equals and able to help the less fortunate to your heart's content."

He was silent after that. Athena could hear the ticking of a clock somewhere in the house, the creak of footfalls upstairs, whispered voices in the hall, but Morgan's voice was not among them.

She let out a shuddering breath. "I need time . . . time to think about what you have said," she whispered. "Niall, if you would only listen—"

"I've done enough of that. You lied to me, Athena, when you promised to remain in Denver if the circus came to the ranch. I can't trust you again. If you expect to keep anything of the life you made in Denver—if you have your friends' welfare at heart—you will have to submit yourself to me and do exactly as I tell you. Any deviation—" He shrugged. "I can impose punishment at any time."

Which meant that she would live with an impediment more sure than the one that had immobilized her legs for so many years. He could command her life completely, and she had no means of stopping him. Even if she found the courage to Change again, it would be at too great a cost.

"Now you can play the martyr with true sincerity." he said, driving the nails deeper. "Your wicked half brother will keep you prisoner in the dark castle. But you will still have everything you always did, Athena—and you'll be safe."

She had enough determination left to sit up straight and look him in the eye. "Let me be sure that we understand one another. In exchange for my . . . cooperation . . . you will allow the circus to remain for the winter, unmolested only to depart when the passes clear in spring. You will not interfere, in any way, with my charities, and will continue to provide the funds I require to properly maintain them. You will leave Morgan alone."

"If you never contact him, and he stays away."

Why was it that Niall's betrayal struck most piercingly in that personal case, instead of in the matter of the charities and the circus quarters? Was she truly as selfish as he implied, to consider her happiness . . . this fragile new happiness she had hardly dared to imagine . . . over the welfare of others?

But she had presumed too much without consulting Morgan. Perhaps he would not regard this as a sacrifice at all. She had decided, in a moment of passion, that she loved Morgan Holt. But he, and his deepest desires, remained a mystery.

Niall assumed she wanted a life with Morgan. A *life*. What did that mean? What would Morgan say if she were to propose such a thing, out of the blue, without a single sensible plan? Would the future she envisioned have anything to do with the one he saw for himself?

Would you ever be brave enough to ask him? Would he ever ask you?

"I agree," she said, letting the words tear out of her in a rush before she could consider the damage they did. "I accept your conditions."

"I knew you had not lost all your sense, Athena, or your pride." Niall hesitated. "Did Holt . . . did he—"

"He did not ruin me, Niall. But it wouldn't matter if he did, because I will not be saving myself for anyone else, will I?"

He had no answer for her bitterness. Now that he had won, he almost seemed ashamed. But the moment passed. He got up from the desk.

"I'll have one of the maids see to your things. You will sleep in my room tonight, and I'll stay in the parlor. We will return to Denver as soon as possible." He left the room for a moment, doubtless to make sure the way was clear, and returned to lift her up again. She lay passively in his arms while he carried her back upstairs and left her on the plain, masculine bed in his room, locking the door behind him.

The day dragged by. A muffling snow fell outside, creating a womb of white that cast unreality on everything that had happened. Athena tried not to hear the sounds around the house, or listen for Morgan's voice. No one came to see her save a maid, with her bags and fresh linens and water. The maid helped her dress—a belated attempt to restore her dignity—and then Athena sat in the plain oak chair in a corner and let her mind go blank.

Night fell. The maid brought her dinner on a tray, and she ignored it. After ten, she heard the unmistakable wail of a wolf's howl within the ranch boundaries. Her heart clenched.

Morgan. Was he trying to speak to her? Thank heaven he hadn't come to her. Maybe she had been right. Maybe he was relieved at the separation, or the others had wisely talked him out of further confrontation.

She wished she had the ability to howl back with the eloquence of his powerful voice.

Stay away, Morgan. Please, stay away.

She drifted into a half sleep. Her chin bounced on her chest, and she woke with a start. Someone was outside the window. Her senses told her that it was after midnight. Knowing what she would find, she gritted her teeth and planted her feet on the floor. Pain spiked from heel to knee. She hobbled to the window and pushed back the curtains.

A black wolf stood hock-deep in snow, gazing up at the window. Frosted breath rose in a cloud from his muzzle. She had seen him as a wolf twice before . . . when he had saved her, and in her dream . . . but now she realized the full measure of his magnificence. No ordinary wolf had ever been so big, so thick of coat, so brilliant of eye. Love became a knot in her chest, struggling to untwine.

He loped toward the wall. Athena lifted the sash on the window. She lost her balance, grabbed at the nearest furniture, and made her way to the chair. Even if her legs had been whole and strong, they would not have held her now.

Morgan made no sound as he scaled the wall. A silhouette darkened the gray square of moonlight. Athena felt a chill of memory, as if she were reliving the past a second time—the night that Morgan had come to her room in the Denver mansion. Once more he had found his way to her in spite of all obstacles.

And she had nothing to give him.

The window creaked as it opened wider, just big enough to admit a man. Morgan's dark, human head appeared in the room, framed by his mane of damp hair. He balanced on the sill and leaped to the floor.

It took her an instant to realize that he was naked. He straightened. She stared. She wished she had drunk some of the water the maid had brought, for her mouth was dry as cotton.

She had seen him naked before, in the big top, but not so close. Every proportion, every line of his body was perfect—not too large or muscle-bound, not too slight, but ideally suited for a life of running and hunting, jumping and adapting to the wild in all its harshness and beauty. Comparing him to a statue was far too inadequate. His chest was lightly dusted with dark hair that ran in an arrow to the base of his stomach. She dared not look there. Yet.

"How . . . how is Caitlin?" she asked.

"Resting." He shook his head, as if to cast off all outside distractions. "Did Niall hurt you?"

In his voice was a promise of what he would do if she answered in the affirmative. "He is my brother," she whispered. "He does . . . what he thinks is best for me."

"Do you still believe that?"

The clean, snow-kissed, masculine scent of him displaced all the air in the room. She could hear the sound of his pulse, just below the skin at the base of his neck where it met his broad shoulders. And below . . . all the way past the slender firmness of his waist and hips . . . he was vibrantly alive. Alive and wanting her.

"Niall is human," she said, listening to the sound of her voice as if it belonged to another woman. "How can he understand?"

"Understand what? That you cannot be collared like a dog? That he does not own you?"

His contempt might as well have been aimed at her. He expected her to spurn the world she had always known, pretend it didn't matter. In that she had failed. Failed his expectation, failed herself, and failed him.

She would have preferred any other way, any other time and place, to tell him. But there was no escaping it. He would stand there, naked to her eyes, his body fluent as his tongue was not, and hear her make her choice.

Feel nothing. Cut off your senses. Pretend you have no need, no wanting, no heart.

"Morgan," she said, "I am going with Niall, back to Denver. I will never see you again."

Morgan heard the words. They were clear, precise, dispassionate, as if Athena were reciting a lesson from the *McGuffey's Reader* Morgan remembered from childhood.

He heard the words, but they made no sense. The only thing that did was the clamoring of his body, the hot yearning for Athena, the need to finish what he had begun in her room. Finish it completely, and to hell with Niall Munroe and all the scruples of human society.

She sat there, so prim in her gown buttoned up to the neck, hands clasped in her lap. He might have been a supplicant before a queen, as he had once thought of the society women who fluttered about her chair.

But she had not been a queen when he had caressed her. She had been helpless with need, prepared to surrender everything . . . yes, even the maidenhood her kind valued so highly. If he had chosen to take it. But he had been undecided, torn between his desire and freedom, between the life he thought he wanted and the bonds her surrender would wind about his neck.

If he listened to his body now, the decision was simple. If Athena made a single welcoming gesture, gave him one sweet look of yearning . . .

"*I am going with Niall,*" she had said. "*I will never see you again.*"

Stupid words. Meaningless, born of habitual fear of her brother, the habit of obedience. And fear, too, of him and what he made her become.

Very well. *He* would decide, here and now. Every instant they had spent together, every memory of her when they were apart, led to this.

He held out his hand. "Come," he said. "We will leave now. Tonight. Your brother will never find us."

She stared at his hand. "What?"

"Put away your fear." He took a step toward her. "You are not a human. You will heal quickly, now that you know your injuries are in your mind and not your body. Soon you will be able to run. And before that—now—you can Change."

Stark terror crossed her face. "Change . . . I . . . No, Morgan. It's been too long—"

"Stop." He stared down at her, willing her all the courage he knew she had. "Stop believing what you can't do. Believe in what you are. Take off your clothes and come with me."

As quickly as it had come, her fear was gone. "Come where, Morgan?"

Her question sent ice trickling down the length of his spine. He had asked her to come with him. To become—yes, to become his mate, to remain with him until death. He had offered to another person the thing he had thought long dead in himself. And she asked "where."

"With me," he said. "Into the woods. The mountains. We'll run, you and I, as we did in dreams. We will hunt and breathe clean air and drink water that has never tasted the metal of man. You will be free, Athena."

"Free?" She dropped her head, and her shoulders rose and fell in a shudder. "What is freedom?"

He heard the tears in her voice and closed the space between them, reached for her, clasped her shoulder and felt it tense in his gentle grip.

"You created your own cage, and let your brother make the bars too strong to break," he said. "But I can break them. I will teach you everything you need to know. I will protect you until you can protect yourself. I will never leave your side."

He lifted her chin. Tears hung like stars on her cheeks. He bent and kissed them, one side and then the other, tasting the salt and Athena. Then he crouched, took her face between his hands, and kissed her lips.

She responded as she had in her room, passionately, with a new edge of violence that excited and almost frightened him. It was the she-wolf in her, coming alive at his touch, waiting for a final word to burst forth and make her all she was meant to be. Her fingers caught in his hair, pulled and wound about, crushing him against her.

Then she pushed him away and let her arms fall limp. "I cannot come with you."

He heard her this time, but he refused to believe. "Athena—"

"I can't, Morgan. I can't live in the way you want, in the wild, apart from people and society." There were no tears now, no passion. "I am not like you. I have become . . . used to my life. I have responsibilities. I try to help people, and if I were to vanish . . . who would help them in my place?"

He stepped back, searching her eyes. The she-wolf had disappeared. This was the haughty, closed-in woman he had first met on the circus lot, the one who had been so scrupulously fair and polite to her inferiors. To him.

"You think they need you," he said, cruel in his anger. "They need your money. How many others in your city have money to give?"

"You don't understand. Not everyone is generous—"

"As fine and generous as you?"

"No." She warded him away, turning her face. "But I have the time and the inclination to work. I have . . . a place, a role that others accept. Others who might not give if I were not there to ask."

"Even though you are no longer a cripple?"

"I am the same, inside. The things that mattered to me . . . before . . . they still matter now. My friends are still my friends."

"And Caitlin? Harry, Ulysses? They are not?"

She stared fixedly at the far wall. "I care for them. For . . . But they are part of a different world, as I am a part of mine. And yours is different from both. Too different, Morgan. Can't you see that . . . we are simply . . . too different?"

"That is not the reason," he said. He grasped the top of the chair and pulled it around, forcing her to look at him. "It's still your fear. You do not want to give up the fancy house and the fine clothes and the people who lick your jaw like hungry pups, because that is all you know how to be. You like the power of giving people what they need when they have nothing. Making them beg—"

"*No.* I have never made anyone beg, for anything."

"Haven't you? What do those poor folk see when they look at you with your fine ways, and know that you can give or take what they need? Do they hate you while they pretend to offer their throats? All those fine ladies who follow you—what do you give them, Athena? A reason to think they are fine and noble people because they help the poor crippled girl help the ones they never see?"

The stark pain in her eyes stopped him cold. He knew he had hurt her, that he had come very close to a truth he hardly fathomed himself.

"Athena," he groaned. "I do not want to . . . Damn you, listen to me. You have a chance to be strong, not to need anyone." He fumbled to put his confused feelings into words. "When you don't need, you can give freely. When you don't care what those others think of you, you can make your own place. Your real place. Don't you understand?"

She stared at him, and he thought he saw the beginnings of comprehension before she shut him out again.

"Do you know your own place, Morgan?" she said. "Do you know what you want out of life? Have you ever thought beyond the next hour?" She smiled with weary resignation. "You can cast off all your ties. I can't. I can't. But—" She closed her eyes. "You . . . you could come with me."

He held very still. "With you?"

"To Denver. Not right away. After . . . after I've had time to make Niall understand, when he has overcome his anger."

She did not elaborate. She didn't have to. He saw what she meant in those few words, and terror clawed its way up from his belly to fill his mouth and his brain.

"Come with you?" he said in a mocking echo. "Join you in your cage? Live in your fine house and wear your fine clothes and become a lapdog for your ladies?"

"Isn't it what you asked me to do . . . give up everything?" She didn't look at him. He was cold, bitterly cold, though the winter wind should not have affected him at all. Athena was sucking all the heat from his body, all the tenuous hopes from his heart, all the foolish dreams from the future he had never considered.

Just like before. Just as it always was and would ever be.

He backed toward the window. "I ask you for nothing," he said. "I want nothing from you, or anyone."

She made no attempt to stop him as he reached the window and gathered his muscles to jump. The eagerness of his body had drowned in sorrow and rage and bewilderment; he could look at her and see a stranger, an enemy, and not the woman he had asked to become the mate of his life.

Let her look at him, one last time. Let her know what she had rejected. Let her feel what he felt.

"Go," he said. "Go with your brother. Cripple yourself again, and pray that all your fine things will make you forget what you have thrown away."

Her eyes met his, moist and expressionless. He leaped up and back, balanced on the sill, and let himself fall from the window.

Snow cushioned his landing, but he welcomed the jarring blow that rattled his bones and shook the despair loose from his head. Barely pausing, he Changed and began to run as hard and as fast as he could, away from the room and the ranch and Athena.

It was a strange thing, that he returned. He dragged himself back to the barn to dress just before dawn, aware that the snow had started again and boded a storm for the day ahead. A storm that might trap anyone—any human—who desired to leave the mountains.

A wolf could leave any time. That was what kept Morgan circling the house like a whipped cur, until Harry stepped out one of the side doors shortly after sunrise and blew a puff of pipe smoke into the expectant air.

Harry was looking for something. Someone. Morgan knew what he hoped to see, and what the others must think. He would make sure they knew how wrong they were.

Morgan Changed in the barn, pulled on his clothes and stalked up to the porch. Harry started slightly when he saw Morgan, and then his shoulders fell.

"It looks like snow," he remarked as Morgan joined him. "Bad weather. I feel it in my bones."

"A storm." Morgan willed the hair to lie flat against his neck. "You don't have to worry. You are safe here."

"Are we staying?"

"Athena would not let Munroe drive you out," he said bitterly. "She cares too much about . . . helping."

Harry glanced at him. "Morgan, I am sorry. I wish I could have done something to intervene. We all do. We've known. . . . almost from the beginning how the girl felt about you, and you her." He coughed behind his hand. "I'm a meddling old fool. I made her come here, with my letters, when I should have stayed out of your business. But all we want . . . all *I* want, is your happiness. Yours and Athena's."

He blinked several times. "I know you well enough—I presume to know—that what you want to do now is run off. Permanently. But—"

He took a long breath and faced Morgan. "I ask you to trust me, Morgan. Trust me, as you would your own kin. You're like a son to me, even though . . . though I'm a poor excuse for a father. Even so, as a father I advise you to wait. Be patient. Stay a little longer. Whatever obstacles may stand before you now, they can be overcome."

Morgan swallowed and looked toward the mountains. Harry reached out a hand, hesitated, and let it come to rest on Morgan's shoulder. It felt curious, that touch, after Athena's. Too close, too intimate, like that of kin. Family.

A father's touch.

"You do not want to be my father," he said, holding absolutely still, afraid of his own terror. "Do you know what happened to my real father, Harry?" He lifted his hands. "I killed him. I killed him with these two hands."

Chapter 17

"I don't believe it," Caitlin said. "Not for a moment."

Ulysses looked at her gravely and met Harry's gaze. They sat, the three of them, in Caitlin's room while the storm raged through its third day outside the sturdy walls of the ranch house. The wind howled no more fiercely than Morgan had done every night since Niall's arrival. No one had seen Morgan since Harry's brief conversation with him, but he had not gone. The howls proved as much.

Caitlin knew that Harry had waited to tell her and Ulysses Morgan's terrible revelation, working himself into a dither over how much to share. In the end, he had been unable to keep it to himself. It was not in his nature to suffer alone, or let others suffer likewise. His heart was too big to hide in a corner.

All the troupers had been hiding, in one way or another, while Niall remained at Long Park. He avoided them, and Athena kept to her room—Niall's room, given to her after the incident with Morgan—but the atmosphere felt as poisonous as the smoke belching from one of those horrid Denver smelters. Ulysses had learned, from listening to maids who hardly noticed his existence, that Athena was to return to Denver with Niall as soon as the weather permitted. She was not to see Morgan again, and she was to keep apart from the circus folk.

A devil's bargain, Caitlin thought. Niall had demanded her obedience in exchange for the safety of the circus—and perhaps of the man she loved. That she loved Morgan, Caitlin had no doubt. Just as she knew Morgan could not live without her.

"No," she repeated firmly. "Morgan could not have killed his own father. Didn't he say anything else, Harry?"

The old man's face sagged as if he had lost several pounds in as many days. "No. He left me with that, and walked away. As if he . . . wanted me to think the worst."

"He lives under the weight of an intolerable burden," Ulysses said quietly. "Intolerable enough to make him avoid the company of other people—as you observed yourself many times, Firefly. He punishes himself."

"For murder?" Caitlin snorted. "No. There must be much more to the story. Did he talk to you, Uly? You must tell us."

Ulysses only looked away, avoiding the question. Caitlin longed to shake him. "You're hiding something, I know it. But I also know Morgan is not a killer. I would feel it if he were."

"There are times when feelings are inadequate."

"And sometimes they are all we have," Harry said. "If he had something to do with his father's death, there must have been a very good reason."

"I agree," Uly said. "But I am at a loss as to how to assist him."

"The help he needs most is with Athena—and Niall." Caitlin said.

"Interference now might make matters worse," Uly said. "Morgan must recognize the danger of confronting Munroe directly."

"And what of you, Firefly?" Harry asked gently.

She knew what he was asking but chose to pretend otherwise. "I know there must be a way of thwarting Niall," she said. "He needs to be distracted until Athena finds a means of outwitting him. With a little encouragement . . ."

"I don't like the look on your face, Firefly," Harry said.

"Niall is as dangerous as Morgan," Ulysses cautioned. "You have seen that for yourself."

"And you've repeatedly warned me to take care, like an old grandmother," Caitlin said with a laugh. "Did you think I really swooned up in Athena's room?"

Ulysses and Morgan exchanged glances. Harry assumed a stern expression ill-suited to his jolly St. Nicholas features.

"We are here on Munroe's sufferance," he said. "Athena would never allow any harm to come to us, but if she chooses to defy her brother, he may eject us forthwith." He met Caitlin's eyes. "I won't see us cast out, Firefly, as long as we are capable of leaving of our own free will. Nor will I allow you to place yourself in jeopardy, of body or of soul. I will give orders for the troupers to prepare to depart as soon as the storm passes."

"You don't mean it, Harry. It's almost winter. We can't travel now—and you want to see Athena and Morgan together just as much as I do."

"Yes. But I have witnessed the consequences of our meddling, and I feel—" He blinked, giving the impression of a slightly befuddled owl. "I feel in my bones that we must go."

"Is this because of what Morgan said?"

"I fear what he will do if he is driven too far," Harry admitted. "I'll try to persuade him to come with us. Then, when everything is calm again, he may return."

Caitlin studied Harry with growing trepidation. She had never seen him look so grave, or so determined. Did he truly believe that she would get herself, or the troupe, into a predicament she couldn't climb out of?

"You're wrong, Harry," she said. "No good will come of running away now."

"I have made my decision." He got to his feet and started toward the door. "I shall tell the others to begin preparations, and we will leave at the first sign of clear weather."

When Harry was gone, Caitlin looked at Ulysses. "You agree with him, don't you?"

"I would make any personal sacrifice on Morgan's behalf," he said. "I would assist Miss Munroe if I were able. But it is my considered judgment that the welfare of the troupe must take precedence over that of Athena and Morgan. They must make their own choices." He paused. "I am sorry, Caitlin."

She saw that arguing with him was as futile as it would have been with Harry. Men could be so stubborn once they had an idea in their heads, no matter how wrong it was. She'd thought that Harry followed his heart more than most, but even he fell prey to the idea that money meant power, and women had to be protected from their own foolish notions.

She lay in bed, fuming silently, for a good hour after Ulysses left. The troupe must not leave until the business with Athena and Morgan was resolved. She had taken great pains to throw them together, and she'd be damned if she'd let Niall Munroe ruin her plans.

The storm might pass at any moment, but it would take several days for the troupe to prepare to move. Even in fair weather, the snow would impede progress and make the pass difficult to negotiate. That gave her a little more time.

If Harry and Ulysses feared some rash action on her part . . . well, she would make very certain not to disappoint them.

"A letter has just arrived, Miss Hockensmith," Parton said, presenting the paper on a silver tray with a little bow. "It was marked urgent."

Cecily paused to accept the envelope, listening to make sure that the ladies assembled in her parlor were still engaged in conversation. When Parton had gone to retrieve more refreshments for her influential guests, she examined the return address with an eager smile.

It was marked from Yankee Gulch, the only substantial town nearest Niall's ranch. Her hope that the letter might be from Niall was all too quickly dashed. The spidery writing was definitely not his, nor did it belong to Athena.

Niall had been gone several days, doubtless due to the bad weather blanketing the mountains. She had been glad for the respite. With the Winter Ball only days away, nothing could interfere with the social coup she was about to achieve.

She frowned at the envelope and turned it over in her hands. If it was not from Niall or Athena . . .

She began to read, wrinkling her nose at the highly spiced scent of the paper, and nearly dropped it.

You promised to help me, it began without salutation, *if I aided you in keeping Munroe and our Caitlin apart. I gave you information that you were to use to control the girl and influence your lover. But now you must know that he is here, with Caitlin, as Athena is with my wolf.*

Cecily held the letter by her fingertips, wishing she could burn it immediately. She did not have to read the scrawled name at the bottom of the letter to know who had sent it.

Tamar. Tamar, that horrid snake-woman with her veiled threats and promises, whom Cecily had hoped she would never hear from again. She had not even guessed the gypsy could read, let alone write.

Your brother intends to make Athena return to Denver, the letter went on, *but Morgan remains under her spell. She is now able to stand and walk, which removes an obstacle between them. Morgan may attempt to follow. I have spoken to Harry French and convinced him that our Caitlin will put herself in danger by pursuing your brother and trying to meddle in Athena's affairs. He has agreed that we must leave this place. We will be departing when weather permits. But if Morgan does not come with us, you must make sure that Athena is made to wish never to see him again.*

I know that Morgan was sent to prison for the crime of killing his own father. You must learn the truth of these matters swiftly, so that when Athena returns you may tell her what breed of man her lover is. When she turns against him, he will come to me. Do not fail.

Cecily crumpled the paper in her fist, her mind racing with the information Tamar had imparted. So Niall had seen Caitlin, had he? And the girl was still pursuing him, in spite of her supposed injury?

And Morgan Holt was a convict. A patricide. Cecily smiled with satisfaction. She was not surprised, for it fully justified her complete dislike of the man and his cohorts. A crime of that kind could not easily be forgiven. Even Athena would quail and shudder at such knowledge, especially when she had so adored her own father.

And she was able to walk! Cecily's smile soured. It had occurred to her, once or twice, that Athena's lameness might be a ploy to win the sympathy of society and support for her causes. Certainly many of the ladies would not have been so generous had she not been a cripple, and thus worthy of pity herself.

Had "love" transformed Athena, or had she decided she wanted something more than what had contented her in the past? Niall would not be so cursed protective if his sister could walk. But the girl might prove much more troublesome and difficult to influence. She might even fight for the position Cecily was stealing from her.

Cecily shoved the letter into a fold of her skirt and walked slowly toward the parlor. Tamar claimed that Cecily owed her, but Cecily recognized no such debt. Indeed, if she chose she could simply ignore the information about Morgan and allow matters to take whatever course fate decreed. If the foolish child fell into the hands of a convicted murderer and ran off with him, why that was of no consequence as long as Cecily had Niall's devotion and he did not suspect her of any personal involvement. Why should he? Athena would be out of the way once and for all, ruined in society.

On the other hand, if Cecily were to confirm Tamar's information and report it to Niall, he would have even more reason to be grateful to her for alerting him.

Yes. Cecily paused at the doorway to the parlor, listening to Mrs. Merriwether's lavish expressions of anticipation for the ball to come. She would take great personal delight in exposing Morgan Holt to Niall, Athena, and the world. That would put an end to his contemptuous looks and loutish disrespect for his betters. All she need do was make a few discreet inquiries—her father certainly knew the right people, now that he was in partnership with Niall—and she could learn everything necessary to shatter Athena's puerile hopes of romance.

Smoothing her skirts, Cecily sailed into the parlor and graciously accepted the homage of her new and most devoted courtiers.

Four days after Niall's disastrous arrival, the snow stopped falling. That same morning, just after dawn, he bundled Athena into the ranch's heavy drag and ordered the driver to take them to Denver.

Athena had nothing to say to Niall, and he maintained the same grim silence. She stared out the window and looked for Morgan, tormenting herself with the thought that she would never see him again. Once, near the edge of the park, she heard a wolf howl. That was all.

She had known that Morgan would refuse her invitation to return with her. She had known that she risked nothing in asking him, that there was no question of breaking her bargain with Niall.

She could have told him all her reasons for declining his offer to take her with him. But when he had made his accusations, pride had left her mute. Let him believe such things of her. Let him go back to his wild life and freedom.

She did not let Niall see her weep.

Passage through the mountains was difficult because of the depth of the snow, and they stopped to change horses and stay overnight in a hotel in Golden. By the time they reached Denver on the evening of the second day, Athena had made herself numb to all feeling.

Cecily was at the house to greet them as if she had known exactly when they would arrive, and instructed Brinkley to see to their comfort with presumptuous confidence. Once they were settled in the sitting room, she fawned over Niall—elegantly, of course—and acknowledged Athena with a brief nod. She did not mention the ball, though it was only four days away.

Athena hadn't the heart to ask. For the first time she saw something in the older woman she neither liked nor understood. She had assumed that Cecily was her friend and confidante, but Niall had said she'd warned him about Athena "taking on too much" some time before. How long had Cecily been talking behind her back? Did she see Athena as a hindrance to her social ambitions—the crippled sister who would only be in the way?

Athena had misjudged so many people. Could she have been so wrong about Cecily's friendship? And if she had been wrong about that, how much else had she also misjudged? How would her society friends respond to her ability to walk again? Would they be happy for her? Would they welcome her as an active, mobile member of their elite circle?

She had always been safe in the assumption that she was one of them, regardless of her inability to shop or take luncheon at the Windsor or waltz at a dance. Not merely one of them, but a leader, an impeccable hostess able to persuade the wealthiest Denverites to attend her gatherings, join her charitable societies, and donate liberally to her causes.

She should have been eager to resume her work and her place as founder of one the grandest balls of the year. Yet all the things that had once seemed so important had become more duty than pleasure, responsibilities that must be seen to no matter how much she wished she could crawl into a cave and hibernate until the heartache had passed.

Morgan had become a part of her. It was more than love, more than any longing she had ever suffered. She could almost feel him across the miles, sense his anger and confusion and pain, as if their very emotions had merged into one. One heart, one being, one soul. A soul denied any hope of solace.

Niall's raised voice drew her out of the pit into which she had fallen. He was still speaking to Cecily, and his expression told Athena that he had heard some news he did not like. He looked up and stared at her as if she were Morgan himself.

"Niall? What is it?"

He jerked his head aside and gave Cecily a terse command. She nodded, glanced at Athena with a too-blank expression, and left the room.

"I am returning to Long Park at once," he said, as soon as they were alone. "You will remain here in Cecily's care. I have asked her to make certain that you are confined to the house this time, and will instruct the servants accordingly. Remember that if you break your promise—"

"Returning?" She gripped the armrests of her chair so hard that her fingers ached. "Why? I have done what you asked—"

"You do not need to know my reasons. Do as Miss Hockensmith tells you—she has the wisdom and experience you so obviously lack—and I may explain when I come back to Denver."

"No." She tensed the muscles in her legs, preparing to face him on her feet. "That is not good enough, Niall. Your reasons may have bearing on our agreement, and that gives me the right to know."

Never before had he looked so ready to strike her. She refused to retreat. After a moment he drew back, fists balled at his sides.

"I will leave it to Miss Hockensmith to explain," he said. "Perhaps you will hear from her what you would not accept from me."

Before she could protest, he turned on his heel and strode into the hall. Brinkley appeared with a tray of hot tea, set it down on the table beside her, and gave her a glance of such sympathy that she wondered what he knew. But he, too, fled just as she gathered the words to ask. She was forced to wait, needles of pain stabbing into her legs, while Niall made preparations to leave and Cecily spoke to him in the hall.

An hour before midnight, just as the long-case clock struck like a portent of doom, Niall put on his coat and left the house. Only something terrible would drive him out at such an hour, when the darkness would impede travel into the mountains. What could be so urgent?

Cecily knew. She had been harbinger of the mysterious bad tidings. She had broken Athena's confidence. She was to be Athena's official jailer, at Niall's behest. Athena meant to get an explanation, even if it meant assuming that Cecily was her adversary . . . or her enemy.

Gritting her teeth against the discomfort, Athena pushed herself up and focused her attention on getting to the sitting room door, one shuffling step at a time. Once there, she caught her breath, renewed her courage, and compelled her trembling legs to bear her just a little farther.

Brinkley caught sight of her at the end of the hall, stopped in amazement, and rushed up to support her. She leaned on his arm with some gratitude. If it was not her imagination, her legs were getting stronger . . . but they were not yet strong enough for the tasks she might have to ask of them.

"Thank you, Brinkley," she said. "Please take me to Miss Hockensmith."

His usually stolid face showed a flicker of emotion, and she knew she had not misinterpreted it. "You don't like Miss Hockensmith, Brinkley?"

"I beg your pardon, Miss Munroe. It isn't my place to like or dislike the lady."

"But you do have an opinion."

He assumed a carefully neutral expression and guided her down the hall toward the library. "Miss Hockensmith seems very free about the house, Miss Munroe. I think—" He hesitated.

"Go on." She pulled him to a stop. "I need to know what I am up against, and you may be able to tell me."

His mouth tightened. "I believe Miss Hockensmith sees herself as mistress here, very soon."

Well, that was certainly no surprise. Athena started to move again, anger lending new energy to her muscles. "Thank you for being frank, Brinkley. Will you speak honestly to me if I ask again?"

He looked down at her gravely. "Miss Munroe—we—the staff hope the best for you. Now that you can walk . . . perhaps things will be different."

Different. How had the servants perceived life in the Munroe house? Had they considered it a burden to wait upon her? She had tried to be fair in her running of the household, but Niall was, at best, brusque with the staff and treated them rather like machines. Brinkley's admission made clear that he did not want Cecily Hockensmith as mistress of the house.

But she would be that, if she married Niall. And suddenly Athena recognized what she had so avoided acknowledging until now—that the life she had returned to would be forever changed if Cecily became Mrs. Munroe. Cecily would arrange the house as she saw fit, give the orders, and take her place above Athena in the scheme of home life.

A great chasm seemed to open under Athena's unsteady feet. Of course she should have known that everything must alter when Niall married. She had wanted him to concentrate on someone other than herself. She wanted him to be happy. But his happiness meant that she must either live as a dependent in the house she had managed, or strike out on her own.

That had ceased to be impossible. She could walk. She was getting stronger. But this was the home she had loved, had made the perfect refuge from the world outside. Every detail had been refined to her specifications. It was her sanctuary, and she had seldom felt any desire to leave it.

Yet, when she had gone to Long Park, it had been a break with the past she had not recognized for the profound event it had become. She had ventured far, not only in miles but in spirit. She had not returned unchanged.

The Athena-that-was and the Athena of today were sisters, but they were no longer identical. One had been content in a life of service, of holding a secure place in society, even if that place was one of confinement and few surprises. She had believed that correcting social injustice was the only worthy undertaking for one such as herself. One who had nothing else to contribute.

The new Athena had lost that contentment and sense of purpose. She didn't know who she was, or what she was capable of. But the wolf could not go back in her cage.

Heaven help her. It was the wolf who hated Niall and suspected Cecily of the basest duplicity. It was the wolf who made her question all the truths she had lived by, who spurned the sacrifices she had made, who tore her apart inside with claws of steel.

And it was the wolf who howled that she would always be alone.

Alone. It is Morgan or nothing. There will be no other.

"Miss Munroe? Are you ill?"

She opened her eyes at Brinkley's voice and saw that they had somehow reached the end of the hall. "I am sorry, Brinkley. Is Miss Hockensmith in the library?"

"Yes. Do you wish me to remain nearby, Miss Munroe?"

"I'll be all right. Thank you, Brinkley."

He escorted her to the library door, and she released his arm to demonstrate that she could negotiate the short remaining distance on her own. He lingered until she had stepped into the room, and quietly shut the door behind her.

Cecily was seated in Niall's substantial leather chair behind his mahogany desk, leaning back in a most unladylike pose as if she had a perfect right to claim anything that was his.

"It is time you told me why Niall left so quickly after you spoke to him," Athena said.

Cecily bolted upright in the chair and looked genuinely astonished, as if she had expected Athena to remain meekly in the sitting room until the servants escorted her upstairs to bed. Had Niall not told her she could walk?

"Athena!" she said, putting a hand to her throat. "You startled me. I had thought you would be much too tired to stay up late after your long journey." Her gaze swept the length of Athena's body. "My dear, how very wonderful! How long have you been able to walk?"

Athena had no intention of allowing Cecily to escape the question. All of her senses boiled with anger and distrust. She chose, against the habit of many years, to listen to what they told her.

"Niall is returning to the ranch," she said. "He made clear that you were to be my caretaker in his absence, and prevent me from leaving the house without your chaperonage. I presume that is why you are still here."

Cecily's expression changed from one of feigned pleasure to a much more honest wariness. "Your brother is concerned for your welfare, as I am. It is unfortunate—"

"Yes. Something is most unfortunate if he felt the need to leave almost as soon as we arrived . . . but it was also unfortunate that you told him where I had gone when I trusted you to keep my secret."

"Why, my dear . . ." Cecily rose and walked around the desk, brushing her fingertips along the burnished wood. "I had no choice but to tell him where you had gone when he asked me. I did not wish to break your confidence, but your brother is not easily denied."

"No, he is not. But because you prefer his regard to my friendship, I find myself a prisoner in my own home. And you have not suffered by it, have you?"

Cecily's eyes sparked with affront. "I beg your pardon. I have always wanted only what is best for you. I have the experience that you do not, and that is why Mr. Munroe trusts me to look after you while he is gone."

"And why has he gone, Cecily? You haven't answered my question." She took a step forward, careful not to grab for the doorframe. "Kindly tell me the truth."

The pleasant curve of Cecily's lips grew thin and hard. "Is it the truth you really want, my dear? The truth of what I think of you, and of your lover?"

Athena braced herself against the blows to come. "Yes."

"Very well." Cecily smiled, a look as cold and calculating as it was triumphant. "But first you must sit down, dear child, or you may fall down. I do not believe you are quite steady on your feet."

"I prefer to stand."

Cecily leaned against the desk and folded her arms across her chest. "Yes, I informed your brother of your location when he arrived earlier than you had estimated. He would have discovered your absence soon enough." She sighed and shook her head. "You will recall that I made you no promises—quite deliberately. I prefer not to break my word if it can be helped."

"What else did you tell him?" Athena demanded when she fell silent.

"Why, merely that you judgment was not sound, and that you should perhaps live elsewhere for a time to gain much-needed experience and become detached from your various . . . obsessions. I am happy to say that your brother agreed with my judgment."

"Obsessions?"

"Your charitable causes, of course, which drive you to such excess. And also your infatuation with Holt—for is he not the real reason you went to the ranch? To be with your wild-man lover?"

A week ago she could have answered in the negative with complete sincerity. Then she had told herself that Caitlin's welfare was her sole reason for the unprecedented journey. That willful naïveté was dead.

"Morgan is not my lover," she said calmly. "But I love him. He has an honesty you would never understand."

Cecily laughed. "Indeed. Is he the knight in shining armor come to rescue you from life as a cripple?"

"It is because of him that I can walk," she said. "He gave me the courage to challenge the things I had always believed without question . . . about the world, and myself."

"And now you see the truth?" She continued to chuckle unpleasantly. "How amusing. Since you are so devoted to complete honesty, you will be most unhappy to learn that your Morgan Holt is less than the noble savage you believe."

"What do you mean?"

"Why, have you never asked him about his past? Have you so little interest in the honor and good name of your brother and the respect of your friends?"

Cecily knew nothing of Morgan's true nature, or of Athena's. Her insinuations bore on some other secret, one that Cecily plainly considered most detestable. And she was right . . . what did Athena know of his past, except that he had suffered?

"I know that Morgan is a good man," she said. "What he did before—"

"Is far worse than your imagination can conceive. You take such pride in helping the destitute and ignorant, the great and needy unwashed, and yet you remain so sadly callow." She put on an air of mock regret. "My dear Athena, it is indeed time that you knew the truth. Your lover is far worse than an uncouth boor who should not be allowed among civilized people. He is a murderer—a convict who spent years in prison. And you, child, are simply another one of his victims."

Chapter 18

Athena was hardly aware that she was moving until her back struck the wall. For a moment her thoughts were in chaos, and then she knew exactly how to respond.

"You are a liar," she said. "You would say anything to further your own cause . . . whatever that may be. If you think that you can win my brother by tricks and stratagems such as this, you are the one who is sadly mistaken. Once I tell him how far you will go to become his wife—"

"Do you think that is all I want?" Cecily's lids dropped over her eyes, as lazily vicious as a panther's. "Oh, yes, I do intend to marry your brother. And I do want you out of the way . . . which will be so much easier now that you must no longer be carried to and fro like a spoiled princess." She laughed again. "No, not a princess. A goddess. The goddess Athena, always ready to condescend to the unfortunate of any rank, and bestow her vast wisdom and generosity upon an unenlightened world. Yet all the time you perched so high upon your throne, you have had no idea how society regards you."

"But you will tell me, won't you, Cecily?"

"As your friend, I have no choice." Cecily toyed with the cuff of her sleeve. "You fancy yourself a leader of Denver society, and I suppose you are—if only because your brother is one of the most important, influential, and wealthiest men in the West. No one wishes to offend him by offending you. But when the ladies come to your house for meetings and bully their husbands and brothers and fathers into making donations . . . do you think they do it out of sheer admiration and devotion? Oh, no. They pity you, Athena . . . and they have come to resent what you force them to do with your 'gentle' persuasion. You make them suffer guilt for not feeling as you do. And so they allow you to rule them in small ways—and go about the rest of their lives without you quite happily."

All the breath squeezed from Athena's lungs. "You are new to Denver society. You cannot know—"

"I am not such a newcomer anymore, dear girl. You have helped with introductions, and your brother's partnership with my father has done wonders for my position here. The crowning touch was in giving me control of the Winter Ball which I have perfected in ways your dull sensibilities would fail to grasp. It will be a triumph, I will take the credit, and Denver will have a new princess to adore."

Athena's legs had gone beyond the point of mere pain and felt like blocks of ice. "I do have friends in Denver. They will come to realize what you are, and so will my brother."

"Will they?" She clucked sadly. "Your brother is already convinced that I have been right all along in my warnings about you. He has had the evidence that you cannot be trusted to run your own life, especially not in Denver among so many unprofitable memories. I always knew that having a cripple underfoot would be annoying, but you have a will strong enough to oppose mine. Soon you will be gone to New York, and Niall will ask me to marry him. And as for your lover . . . I doubt that you need be troubled by him ever again."

The doorframe bit into Athena's palm. "Why did Niall return to Long Park?"

"It should be obvious. Once I told him what Holt is, he knew he must personally see to it that such a foul criminal—a man who killed his own father—is driven from Colorado. Permanently."

Athena allowed her weight to sag against the wall. Morgan had killed his own father? It was unthinkable, inconceivable. One might as well accuse Niall of killing his beloved mother.

And yet Morgan was a werewolf. He was impelled by urges an ordinary man could not understand. Was it so impossible that a man with a wolf's nature might kill more easily than one fully human, could lose control to the beast within him?

She shook her head violently, sickened by her doubts. Morgan was no murderer . . . and even to consider that he had committed patricide was absurd. Ludicrous.

Niall had gone after Morgan, believing such stories, already driven by rage. It would not be a simple matter of protecting Athena or society from a supposed murderer. Oh, no. This would be personal. How much of an excuse would he need for his hatred to become lethal? And how much would it take for Morgan to strike back with the same fell purpose?

"Do you know what you have done?" Athena whispered. "You've not only endangered Morgan but my brother as well."

"Come, now. Do you have so little faith in your brother?"

Think, Athena. "Who told you? Who passed on these lies about Morgan?"

"They are not lies, I assure you. I have had the information from very reliable sources. As for who alerted me to the grave danger Holt presents . . . you remember that horrid snake-woman from the circus? It seems she has no more love for you than I have for that red-haired hussy who set her cap for Niall. We found ways to be useful to one another."

Red-haired hussy. Who could she mean but Caitlin? Athena thought back on the times she had seen her brother and Caitlin together. If there had been an attraction there, she had been too caught up in her own problems to see it. But Cecily had not been so oblivious.

Niall and Caitlin. It was almost as mad a notion as branding Morgan a killer. And Tamar . . . she had always seemed to resent Athena, but why would she betray Morgan? What did she know about his hidden past?

Cecily was right about one thing: Athena could not trust her own judgment, which had been so horribly flawed from the beginning. She had put her faith in false friends, underestimated her brother's guilt and resentment, and complacently believed herself to be a respected and useful member of society. Cecily might exaggerate the opinions of the women of Denver, but there was a grain of truth in that particular claim that Athena couldn't ignore.

I wanted to see, in myself and everyone else, only what made me feel important and needed.

She met Cecily's eyes. "You have taught me a valuable lesson, Cecily. From this moment on, I will not unquestioningly accept what others tell me. I will discover the truth for myself, with my eyes open. Morgan will give me the truth, and Niall will listen to what I have to say."

"Even if he would—which I strongly doubt—you will not have the opportunity to speak to him, my dear. You are to remain here, safe and sound. Remember?"

Cecily's smile filled Athena with such rage that she hardly perceived the emotion for what it was. "How do you intend to stop me?"

The older woman's mouth dropped open, as if she had seen a wolf rise up on its hind legs and speak.

"Do I shock you?" Athena asked. "Perhaps you do not know me as well as you think you do."

Cecily's mouth closed with a snap. "You will remain here as your brother ordered, or . . ."

"Or you will . . . what will you do, Cecily? Are you prepared to restrain me yourself?"

"The servants. Niall left strict orders—"

"You assume that all the servants will obey without question."

Cecily took a step back, her gaze flashing to the door behind Athena and then to the bellpull in the corner of the room. She rushed around the desk to yank the cord.

Brinkley stepped into the room so quickly that Athena knew he must have been waiting very nearby. "Miss Munroe," he said, "how may I be of assistance?"

"*I* called you here," Cecily said sharply. "Mr. Munroe left clear instructions that Miss Munroe is not to leave the house unchaperoned. Miss Munroe may not be inclined to cooperate. Please escort her to her room, and lock the door."

"Do I understand that you wish me to imprison Miss Munroe?"

"Do not presume to question my instructions, or those of your employer! If you do not feel capable of controlling one half-lame girl—"

"It is all right, Brinkley," Athena said. "I don't expect you to defy my brother."

The butler raised a well-shaped brow. "Why, Miss Munroe, I do not recall any such orders."

"You—you heard him as clearly as I did!" Cecily cried. "I warn you, my man, if you continue in this way—"

"I have been considering a return to England," Brinkley said to Athena. "Perhaps this would be a convenient time to give my notice."

Athena could have hugged him. "You can go if you wish, Brinkley, but I am sure you can find excellent employment here in Denver if you must leave us."

"Perhaps. I fear that the other staff may also wish to give notice, if"—he looked down his nose at Cecily—"they are compelled to take instruction from Miss Hockensmith."

"How dare you!" Cecily started toward him, stopped, and glared at Athena. "You will not get away with this, either of you."

"Don't worry, Cecily. You can tell Niall that I forced you to let me go."

"You . . . you can't! You can barely walk. How do you intend to—"

"I did it before, remember? And this time I can drive myself. If I leave at dawn, I should be able to reach Long Park not too long after Niall."

"You are mad! If you drive into the mountains alone you will surely meet with disaster!"

"It is kind of you to be so concerned, Cecily, but I have resources you know nothing of."

Cecily's face hardened. "I will not let you go, servants or no servants." She gestured to Brinkley. "Get out."

The butler looked at Athena. She nodded. "This is between Miss Hockensmith and me. I will not be requiring your services tonight. You may tell Fran that she may also retire."

"You need only call, Miss Munroe." He left without a backward glance at Cecily.

The moment the door was closed, Cecily advanced on Athena. Her fists were clenched, and for all her fine garments and meticulous coiffure, she looked like nothing so much as a fishwife.

"Make no mistake," she hissed, "I will stop you." She reached for Athena's arm. Athena batted her hand away Cecily gasped and fell back a step.

"Good Lord," she said. "You are brazen! I will advise your brother to send you to a madhouse!"

"In that case, let me give you a good reason for the recommendation." Athena smiled, and the wolf crouched on its haunches and prepared to spring. Cecily struck again, bent upon knocking her off balance. Athena twisted to the side, allowing Cecily to strike the wall, and pulled the older woman's arm behind her back.

Cecily shrieked. Athena kept her grip with surprising ease, reaching deep within for the strength of the wolf, the strength she had known and embraced before the accident.

"You might as well give up," she said. "You cannot hurt me, but I might hurt you if you struggle."

All the fight went out of Cecily, and Athena began to relax. She saw the flash of light on metal an instant before the hairpin plunged toward her shoulder.

Deftly she spun Cecily about and dodged the makeshift weapon. The silver hairpin scraped across the door and fell to the carpet. Athena growled.

She growled, just as Morgan did, teeth bared. Cecily forgot to cry out in pain and shrank away from her in horror.

"I warned you," Athena said. "You had better leave this house at once." She released Cecily, who stumbled away, clutching her wrist.

"What are you?" she whispered.

"You may pray that you never find out." She stepped aside, leaving the doorway clear. Cecily did not need further encouragement. She rushed past Athena and scurried into the hall, her dark hair falling loose about her shoulders.

The front door slammed. Athena leaned against the door and felt her body's reaction to what she had done. Her legs no longer cramped and trembled, but they would not hold her up much longer. She was living on energy borrowed from the very wolf she had only begun to acknowledge.

She knew she had to act before that energy gave out. There was no leisure to contemplate how dramatically she had changed, or how close she had come to real violence. No time for regrets or second thoughts. By the time the sun rose, she would be well on her way toward the mountains. And Morgan.

Bracing herself against any surface within reach, she made her way out of the library, into the hall, and back to the sitting room. Brinkley came to her before she had the chance to call.

"Miss Hockensmith has left us," she said, finding a seat on the nearest chair. "I don't believe she will be back. I would appreciate your help, if you still feel able to give it."

"I do, Miss Munroe. And so do the others. Your maid is prepared to resign with the rest of us, if necessary."

Athena closed her eyes and leaned her head against the back of the chair. "Thank you, but I think I am capable of doing this alone."

"Shall I ask Romero to prepare a carriage, Miss Munroe?"

Would Brinkley be so cooperative if he knew she intended to ride rather than take a carriage? "I will speak to him later. For the moment, I would like to go up to my room."

Brinkley offered his assistance, and she permitted herself the luxury of riding up in the elevator rather than taking the stairs. Once in her room, she shut the door and leaned against it, well aware that her plans were pitifully tenuous.

The boy's trousers and oversized flannel shirt were still in the chest where she had packed them away years ago. The trousers were too large, but with the help of a pair of her brother's suspenders they fit well enough. She had Brinkley retrieve her shearling jacket from the storage closet and asked Monsieur Savard to pack a meal to carry with her on the road.

At dawn she crept out of the house and to the stable without alerting Brinkley, dodged Romero, who had fallen asleep in the carriage house waiting for her, and selected the sturdiest riding horse. Her legs had received enough rest that they held her up with relatively little pain as she saddled and bridled her mount. After several tries, she made it into the saddle.

It felt strange to hold the reins again, to feel the power of a horse at her command. Her legs were by no means back to normal, but they seemed more capable with every passing hour, and she had little fear that they would betray her when she needed them most.

They, like the servants, like the circus folk, could be trusted. As she knew she could trust her own heart.

Before sunrise she left the house and all her doubts behind. For the first time in her life, she wondered if she would ever return.

I am coming, Morgan. You will not face my brother alone. And when we meet again, the whole truth will finally be spoken.

Niall pushed his exhausted horse a few more paces and then reined it in, looking down on tree and meadow from the rocky escarpment that bordered the southern end of the park.

The weather had been clear all during his journey into the mountains. Driven by rage and little else, he had made it halfway to the ranch before he realized that he and his mount needed a few hours of rest and sleep.

Even so, it had taken him only a few hours longer than usual to cover the distance from Denver, and it was just midday. His anger had been muted by weariness, but the sight of the ranch sprawled out below, and the numerous figures scurrying among the buildings, rekindled his determination.

Before the sun set, he'd have it out with Morgan Holt once and for all.

He clucked to the horse and guided it down the steep pack trail into the valley, a much more difficult and direct route than the road through the pass. Oddly enough, it was not thoughts of Morgan that accompanied him. The face he saw in his mind's eye belonged to someone else entirely—mocking and impish and topped by a tangle of curling red hair.

Caitlin. She was down there, as unsuspecting as the rest that he was on his way. What would she think if she knew he was coming? Would she mock him and spit in his eye the way she had done when she'd defended Morgan and Athena? Or would she . . . might she possibly . . .

His mouth curled in disgust. She had deceived him just as much as the others. She'd led him to think that she risked permanent crippling if she didn't have proper rest and quiet.

The doctor said as much, he reminded himself. *You had no reason not to believe him.*

Yet that same doctor had predicted that Athena would never walk again. So much for the opinions of doctors. Caitlin was strong enough to stand between him and something he wanted. His sister had turned from an obedient, well-bred, and quiet young lady to a willful, defiant hussy. It was no coincidence that she had become so only after close association with the circus.

And with the former convict Morgan Holt.

Niall gritted his teeth and felt the horse let out a great breath as it reached level ground. Little eddies of snow whirled about its hooves. No one else had come this way in some time . . . nothing human, at any rate. The air was brisk and cold, with a stillness that suggested bad weather to come.

Sensing food and refuge very near, the horse picked up its pace and set off across the park at a trot. Niall didn't mind the jarring. Physical discomfort drove the image of Caitlin from his mind. A man couldn't think of a woman when his legs ached and his fingers were numb.

Unless he began to picture a fire, a tumbler of whiskey, and a warm bed already occupied by a supple, naked, and very female body . . .

The horse snorted as he jerked on the reins. *Damn it.* He'd see the witch soon enough, and the reality would abolish these ridiculous fancies. Lust for one such as Caitlin Hughes? It embarrassed him. Yet when he tried to imagine Cecily Hockensmith sharing his bed, he shuddered with something far worse than embarrassment.

He kicked his horse into a brief but satisfying canter that carried him to the farthest outbuilding. Smoke rose in dark plumes from several chimneys, and he noted that there was considerably more activity among the circus people than he had seen before. People and animals moved to and fro. Wagons stood in the half shelter of buildings, and men were loading the vehicles in preparation for a journey.

Niall could not mistake what he saw. The circus was getting ready to leave the ranch, livestock, tents, and all. Was Harry French mad, or simply an idiot?

Or had he guessed that the troupers wouldn't be welcome at Long Park after the display in Athena's bedroom? In that, at least, he wasn't wrong. Niall had been too angry at Cecily's revelation to consider what he would tell French when he arrived. He might have decided to let the circus stay—except for Morgan Holt.

But if they had already chosen to run, well . . .

His horse attempted to head for the barn, and Niall pulled it about toward the main house. He dismounted at the steps to the wide, snow-blanketed veranda. A ranch hand conveniently appeared to take the animal to a stall, and Niall ran up the stairs and through the front door with hardly a pause to kick the snow from his boots.

After the noise and bustle outside, the house was very quiet. Niall paused in the parlor to consider his course of action. Morgan might be here, or he might already be gone. Harry French wasn't likely to reveal the truth either way.

Nor was Caitlin. Yet his feet inevitably carried him down the hall as if she had lifted her voice in a siren's call, summoning him to destruction.

He opened the door to her room as silently as he could. She was there, in her bed. He had half expected to find her on her feet, no longer compelled to keep up the pretense of serious injury. But she was quite alone, plucking at the edge of her blanket with nimble, nervous fingers. *Worried*, he thought. *Worried about my sister—and Holt.*

He slammed the door shut. Caitlin jerked and turned to stare at him, and he noticed for the thousandth time the way her freckles only added to her allure instead of decreasing it. The way her hair seemed to blaze in any kind of light, as if illuminated from within. The way her eyes . . .

"What are you doing here?" she demanded. "Where is Athena?"

He laughed. It was no better a welcome than he had expected.

"Athena is safely at home," he said, walking toward the bed. "Where she will remain. I am . . . grateful to see you looking so well, Miss Hughes."

"*You* do not look well at all," she said, studying him with a frown. "You must have left Denver almost as soon as you got back. Did you ride all night?"

Was that worry in her voice? "Aren't you interested in the reason I returned so quickly?"

She settled back on her mounded pillows with a false air of non-chalance. "I do not even try to guess what may be passing through your mind, Niall Munroe."

"And you are a liar." He found a chair and pulled it alongside the bed. "But I'll tell you anyway. Where is Morgan Holt?"

She showed no surprise at his question, and he wondered how much she really knew. "I have no idea. We haven't seen him since you left. You should be glad that he's gone—" She narrowed her eyes. "Or aren't you?"

"It depends upon whether or not I wish to see a killer run loose."

That caught her attention. She straightened, holding his gaze with eyes as frank and fearless as a child's. But this was no child . . . far, far from it. "Are you calling Morgan a killer, even though he had the chance to hurt you and didn't?"

"I'm calling him what he is," Niall snapped. "I'm surprised you are so sanguine about having such a creature in your midst, you and French . . . and yet you defended him. Encouraged him—"

"Even though he is not quite human?" She smiled, and her eyes crinkled at the edges. "I sometimes think he is more human than anyone I know."

"And how well do you know him, Caitlin? Did you know that he was in prison for years after murdering his own father?"

"In prison?"

She hadn't known. It was a small but important point in her favor. "I only just discovered it myself. But it explains a great deal about Holt and his behavior . . . his dishonorable treatment of my sister, and his propensity for violence. That is why I have returned, Caitlin—to make sure he can't harm anyone else."

She considered his statement in silence. He sensed that his revelation hadn't been a complete shock to her, any more than Cecily's had been to him.

"Well?" he demanded. "Do you still consider Holt your friend? Would you defend him now?"

"Even if what you claim is true . . . and I'm not saying it is . . . what do you think you can do about it?"

Niall had played out several scenarios in his mind during the ride from Denver, and every one of them had ended with Holt in a whimpering, bloody puddle at his feet. Beyond that . . .

"Do you truly believe," Caitlin said, "that you can simply walk up to him and . . . what? Make him turn himself in to the authorities?"

"I do not fear him."

"Then you are a fool. A wise man would be afraid. But you have no right to do anything to him. He has not hurt anyone in all the time I've known him. You cannot ruin his life, and Athena's, simply because you hate what you cannot understand."

"If I hated everything I did not understand," he said, "I would hate you."

She caught her lower lip between her teeth. "You might as well hate me if you intend harm to my friends."

He smiled bitterly. "I'm only interested in finding Morgan Holt. The rest of you . . . You are leaving, are you not?"

"Within the hour. Harry decided that it would be the right thing to do. It was obvious that you would want us gone. You need not worry that we'll cause you any more trouble, Mr. Munroe."

"It's too late to worry about that, Miss Hughes."

"You have had your way. Isn't that enough?"

He jumped to his feet. "No. It's far from enough." He crossed to the bed in two strides, gripped Caitlin's shoulders, and kissed her.

She did not even bother to resist. The temporary stiffness came from shock, but an instant later she was pliable and willing in his arms. Her mouth opened to his with all the enthusiastic skill of an experienced whore.

Oh, yes, she wanted him, just as he wanted her. No sentimentality or inconvenient expectations, not even the benefit of love or even real liking—simply raw, unbridled lust. And Caitlin was not ashamed. No, not in the least.

He ended the kiss and pushed her away. She leaned back, neither offended nor outraged by his liberties. Her freckles were very prominent.

"What was that for?" she said, catching her breath.

"You know." He turned his back on her so that he wouldn't see her lips and the frank desire in her eyes. "You've known since the day we met."

"That you want me? That I want you?" She laughed softly. "What a relief it is to say it aloud and stop pretending. I was never very good at pretending."

"No." He folded his arms across his chest and stared at the wall. "Ordinarily I am very good at it. One must be, in my type of work. But I seem to have lost my abilities where you are concerned."

"And that troubles you?"

"Why should it trouble me, that I am infatuated with a girl of no parentage, dubious morals, and interests that directly conflict with my own?"

"And what sweet, loverlike words they are," Caitlin said as if to herself. "No woman could wish for a more devoted suitor."

Niall turned on her. "How many have you had, Caitlin? Scores, I should think. Hundreds. Am I just another conquest, or am I a particular prize?"

"What arrogance. You think the worst of me for having taken other lovers, but I'm sure you feel no qualms about the women you've had. Oh, no. All your remorse is for wanting me."

He was torn between the desire to strike her and kiss her again until she was incapable of speech. "I allowed the circus to stay on the ranch for your sake, and yours alone. You've repaid me by taking Athena's part against her own brother, and against what is best for her.

Holt is a convict, a murderer, and I will not allow him to remain where he has any chance of contacting my sister again."

The change of subject steered the conversation back where he wanted it, but he could not concentrate. Caitlin's eyes continued to laugh at him, though he could have sworn he saw hurt under the humor. Could a woman like Caitlin be hurt, truly hurt, by a man?

"I see," she said at last. "Well, I cannot help you. I do not know where Morgan is, and I wouldn't tell you if I did. I may want you, Niall Munroe, but not at any price."

"Not even the price of wealth beyond your imagining?"

"I will not betray my friends for money—"

"I do not speak of betrayal." He took a step toward her and stopped, unable to think of what to do with his hands. "I speak of . . . you and me, Caitlin. Of what we might have together."

"Can I believe what I just heard?" She closed her eyes. "Are you offering me—"

"Everything." He perched on the edge of the chair, fighting the absurd urge to go down on his knees. "Security, fine clothing, carriages, jewelry, all the things you have never had. A real home to live in, Caitlin, not a tent. No need to endanger your life ever again."

"You wish me to leave the circus? To abandon all my friends, the life I have always known, to become your . . ." Slowly her mouth relaxed, and she met his gaze. "To become your mistress. That is what you are offering, isn't it?"

Heat rose in his face. Damn her, the woman could make him feel like a little boy who had just been caught with his fingers in the pie. How could he let her have such power over him?

"Yes," he said coldly. "That is exactly what I am offering. But the mistress of Niall Munroe would lack nothing, I assure you." He looked toward the window, feeling a cold rush of air against his cheek even though the sash was closed. "I have never taken a mistress. I have never believed I wanted one, until now. I want you, Caitlin. I admit it. And I am willing to pay whatever you ask."

The look on her face was so gentle that he could have wept. "There is only one problem, my friend. I'm used to freedom. I come and go and behave exactly as I wish, and no man tells me what I must or must not do. Your society would never allow that, not even in a great man's mistress. And I don't care to be owned. Not even by you."

He stared at her blankly until he realized exactly what she had said. She'd turned him down. Turned *him* down, whom very few ever refused without profound regret. She, who had nothing, who lived from day to day with no guarantee of the next night's dinner, shunned by all decent folk, refused a life of ease and luxury. And him.

"I have seldom in my life asked anything twice," he said. "I am accustomed to getting what I want. But I will offer once more. Come to Denver with me. Live in a fine house that you may call your own, where you may do whatever you please within its walls. I do not expect you to move in society or become like other women. I do not ask that you change yourself. I demand only that you and I enjoy each other as we wish, in all the freedom you desire."

"But don't you see? I would change myself if I did what you ask. The woman you want now would cease to exist, and you would grow to despise what you admire in me. As I would grow to despise you." She sighed. "I'm sorry, Niall. There is only one reason that would compel me to accept, and that is if you give up this persecution of Morgan and Athena." She held out her hand. "Let them live their own lives, Niall, and I will share yours."

He backed away from the bed, averting his eyes from her appeal. So she could be bought, after all . . . at a price he refused to pay.

Damn her.

"Very well," he said. "You have made your position clear. But understand me, Caitlin—my offer has no bearing on my intentions toward Morgan or my desire to protect my sister. I will do whatever is necessary, with or without your help." He bowed stiffly. "If you will forgive me, I have a murderer to find."

Caitlin's hand hovered in midair, fingers curled in supplication, even as he shut the door on impossible dreams.

Chapter 19

It is too risky. We ought to delay departure for at least another day," Ulysses said, studying the sky as if it were a dangerous and unpredictable beast.

Which, Caitlin thought, was precisely the truth. And she would rather face that dangerous beast than spend a single night under the same roof as Niall Munroe.

There was no sign of the noonday sun behind the flat gray canopy of clouds. She, Harry, and Ulysses stood near the barn, where the entire circus caravan was assembled and ready to make the journey east through the pass—a dozen wagons, fifty horses and ponies including Caitlin's, and the much-prized calliope. Niall, thank heaven, had not emerged from the house.

Caitlin balanced her weight on a pair of makeshift crutches, aware of the stiffness in her leg but no longer in pain. If her injury couldn't stop her from leaving the place, no human being was going to do so. Not even a well-meaning friend.

"You are as unlike your namesake as any man could be, Ulysses Wakefield," she chided. "Where is your sense of adventure? Your trouper's spirit? Or, for that matter, your pride?"

"I have never been one for suicidal acts," Ulysses said. "Nor do I wish to see the troupe caught in a snowstorm. My desire to leave does not seem quite as urgent as yours, Firefly."

Caitlin had told no one about Niall's offer. Despite Uly's misgivings, Harry was obviously as eager to leave as she was. It was difficult to say whether he worried more for her or Morgan—who was still in the vicinity, to judge by the wolf tracks that appeared every night near the house. He could not quite break his final ties to the troupe. Or to Athena, though he hadn't gone after her.

How can men be such fools?

"We are ready to go," Harry said, tugging his worn scarf more snugly about his neck. "Everything is in order, and I do not relish the prospect of remaining here with Munroe hovering over us like a starving buzzard."

"I have spoken with many of the others, and they all agree," Caitlin added. "We will have to get through the pass while the weather is clear. If we don't do it now, we may not get another chance before winter's end." With an unreadable glance at Caitlin, Harry hurried off to consult with the boss hostler. Horses stamped, dogs barked, and troupers waited impatiently for the order to move.

The order came at last, and the caravan lurched into motion with much cracking of whips, groaning of harness, and hails passed down the line of wagons. Billows of vapor rose from the horses' mouths. The hazy light could not dim the bright colors of wagons and props, or the resplendent patchwork of apparel worn by the troupers. But there was no fanfare, and the circus folks were subdued as they trampled a path through the snow past the outbuildings and into the park. The ranch hands paused in their work to see them off, a few tipping their hats, and

Mr. Durant came out onto the veranda, undoubtedly glad to see the last of his unwanted guests.

Caitlin sat beside Harry in the office wagon, her injured leg propped out straight before her, and refused to look back. Niall had no reason to pursue them. He, like Durant, would be happy to see them gone. His only remaining interest in the troupers lay in what they knew of Morgan, and no one had answers that satisfied him.

Inching along the half-covered dirt road all too slowly, the caravan passed through the gate that marked the boundary of the inner pastures. Before them stretched a blanket of white punctuated by the bare limbs of leafless shrubs, and the deeper green of fir and spruce. Ruts and furrows marked where ranch hands and their cattle had passed. Soon even those signs disappeared, replaced by the subtler tracks of fox, rabbit, and deer.

When the last wagon had crossed the point halfway to the pass, a light snow began to fall. Caitlin sneezed and readjusted her blankets. A little snow couldn't hurt them, surely.

But soon even she wasn't able to pretend that all was well. The drizzle of snowflakes transformed into dense clumps that settled on every surface not warm enough to melt it. Soon the snow fell so thickly that Caitlin could not see any farther back than the next two wagons in line, and the trees beside the meadow became unidentifiable shadows. The mountains had entirely vanished.

"Oh, dear," Harry murmured, his gloved hands very tight on the ribbons. "This does not look good. Not good at all." He clucked to the horses, but they were already struggling to break a trail through the ever-deepening snow. Their ears lay flat against their heads in eloquent protest.

Caitlin closed her eyes and whispered an almost-forgotten prayer. "Ulysses was right," she said. "We must go back."

"I agree. The road has disappeared. I cannot see how to find the pass, even if we could cross it. But there is a small difficulty. I am not sure how to get back to the ranch."

"But surely we can retrace our steps—"

"We can but try." Only his worried eyes were visible between hat and scarf as he turned the ponderous wagon about. The horses heaved and plunged sideways through the unbroken snow. The wagon's wheels caught on some buried obstruction, but with many pleas and promises, Harry got the horses to pull them free.

Gradually the other wagons followed Harry's example, each driver taking his cue from the one ahead of him. Visibility had declined to the length of a single wagon. Harry drove back the way they had come, using the caravan itself as his guide. Disembodied voices cried out questions and instructions. Caitlin caught a glimpse of Ulysses, but he was soon lost in the blizzard.

It seemed hours before Harry reached the end of the line of wagons. Then there was nothing ahead but a wall of white, blending earth and sky together in a featureless void. Even the tracks left by the caravan were rapidly filling, as if Nature resented the blemish the intruders had made on her chaste perfection.

"I do not know where to go," Harry said, his voice sunk to a whisper. "Every direction looks the same."

"The boss hostler has a compass," Caitlin said. "Go find him, Harry, and I'll wait here."

He sighed and passed the ribbons to her. With a grunt he eased himself down from the high, narrow driver's seat, landing awkwardly in the knee-deep snow. He trudged back toward the nearest wagon, no more than a smudge in the distance. His breath trailed skyward in steam-train puffs with every step.

As long as he keeps close to the wagons, he can't lose his way, Caitlin reminded herself as the minutes passed. The wagon behind was invisible now, and no others had come nearer. It was difficult to believe anyone else existed in this bizarre world of nothingness. Even sound had become muffled, and she doubted that she could have heard a shout from a few feet away.

After an hour, she began to be afraid. If Harry had gotten himself lost, she would have to find him. The crutches were useless in snow. Unhitching one of the horses and riding it bareback was hardly a better option. But if she did not try, some roving cowhand looking for stray cattle after the storm would find them frozen to death only a few miles from safety.

Niall, she thought, grasping at the name as if it were a magical incantation. *If you ever cared for me, even a little, come and find us. Help us.*

But it was not Niall who answered her silent call. At first she thought the dark shape emerging from the haze was Harry, safe and sound, and she laughed in relief. But the figure was too low to the ground to be human.

Morgan. She sat up, ignoring the gale that tore at her clothing, and squinted against the snow. "Morgan!"

He glided toward her like a dark angel borne on imperceptible wings, his coat repelling the snow as if it were the gentlest of spring showers. He stopped well distant from the nervous horses and made a low, questioning sound between a bark and a growl.

"Thank God you're here," she shouted into the wind. "We're lost! Harry is back there somewhere, and I'm afraid—you must find him!"

Morgan lowered his muzzle in a wolfish nod and turned gracefully on his hind legs, bounding off with ears pricked toward sounds only he could hear. Caitlin slumped on the seat and dared to breathe again. Strange how she had prayed for Niall when Morgan was by far the better choice to save them. Niall, after all, was only a man.

Yet she continued to imagine, with absurd persistence, that Niall was even now on his way. When Harry and Morgan returned to the wagon, the old gentleman clutching Morgan's fur and stumbling along in the path he had made, she cursed herself for wishing Niall out in this nightmare.

Perhaps Niall was lost as Harry had been. Perhaps he would die proving false all the terrible judgments she had made of him out of anger and hurt.

At the end of his strength, Harry climbed onto the wagon's seat, and Caitlin covered him with her own blanket. He tried to speak, teeth chattering each time he opened his mouth. His ice-rimed moustache was stiff as a board.

"Don't try to talk," she said. "Morgan?"

The wolf appeared beside her, his immense paws resting on the side of the wagon. His slanted eyes met hers, and he Changed.

As remarkable as it was to see a naked man standing thigh-deep in snow and unaffected by the cold, Caitlin was in no mood to marvel. "We have to get back to the ranch," she said. "Can you lead us?"

"Yes." He glanced the way he and Harry had come. "I'll take word to the rest of the caravan and gather the wagons." He paused, frowning at Harry. "He will be all right, Firefly. Keep him warm. I'll be back as soon as I can."

"Morgan . . . Did you . . . did you by any chance see Niall on your way to us?"

His eyes were hard as topaz. "No. No one could follow you in this, even if he wished." He turned and leaped into the snow, moving twice as fast as any human. Caitlin inured herself to another wait, warming Harry with the heat of her body and their shared blankets.

A horse's urgent whinny was the first indication that Morgan had succeeded in reaching the others. Soon another wagon pulled alongside Harry's, Ulysses at the reins. He nodded to her calmly, but his eyes told a different tale.

"Is everyone all right?" Caitlin called.

"Well enough. It is fortunate that Morgan arrived when he did." He gestured behind him, and Caitlin saw the shadows of other wagons drawing near. Morgan ran among them, human and then, in a heartbeat, wolf again.

It was as a wolf that he took the lead and guided the troupers to shelter. The going was difficult, far more so than it had been in the other direction, but Morgan was endlessly patient and resourceful in keeping the caravan together, providing encouragement to the weary horses, and pulling wagons out of snowdrifts.

Riders met them when they reached the outskirts of the ranch. Morgan scrambled into the back of the wagon while Caitlin pulled up at the ranch hand's signal.

"Miss Hughes?" the leader said, his face obscured under layers of scarves and bandannas. "We thought you wouldn't make it back. We were just headed out to look for you."

"We are all right," she said, glancing at Harry. "Please tell . . . tell everyone that we're safe."

The rider shook his head. "Mr. Munroe set out after you when the storm began. Some of the men went with him, but they got separated. They came back, but he hasn't. Did you see him, miss?"

Her heart plummeted to the heels of her boots. "He . . . Mr. Munroe went looking for us?"

"Yes, miss. As soon as the snow lets up, we'll be going ourselves. Mr. Munroe ain't used to this kind of weather."

The men saluted and rode off. Morgan jumped down from the rear of the wagon and ran alongside, keeping the vehicle between himself and the riders.

Sick to her stomach, Caitlin guided the wagon toward the barn, only half-aware of the other wagons rolling up behind. Several hands were there to help her and Harry to the bunkhouse. Shivering, miserable teamsters unharnessed the horses and secured them in the barn.

Caitlin did not see Morgan again. She sat on the edge of a cot, rocking back and forth while constant noise and movement swirled around her. Someone threw another blanket over her shoulders, and Harry came by, much improved, to ask her a question she didn't quite hear.

She looked up. Harry and Ulysses stood side by side, stout old man and handsome dwarf, gazing at her as if they had grim news to impart. Caitlin prepared herself for pain.

"You're worried about Munroe, aren't you?" Harry asked softly. "You needn't worry any longer."

Hope seeped into the shriveled husk of her heart. "Is he here?"

"He is still missing," Ulysses said. "But we came to tell you that Morgan has volunteered to search for him. If any man—any creature upon this earth—has the skill to locate him, it is he."

"Morgan . . . volunteered?" Morgan, who hated Niall and was hated in return? Why should he wish to save his enemy from almost certain death?

Because, like it or not, he had an unbreakable tie to Niall Munroe. Caitlin didn't imagine that Morgan did it for her sake. Niall was Athena's sister, and she knew that Morgan would risk anything to spare her the sorrow of losing the last member of her family.

So much for indifference. So much for freedom and breaking all bonds of love or friendship.

Now all she had to do was pray—pray, not only that Morgan found Niall, but that they didn't kill each other when he did.

"You'd be crazy to go on in this storm, miss," the innkeeper said, shaking his finger at Athena. "They say it'll be the worst of the season. Can't figure how you made it this far."

Athena stood in the doorway of the livery stable and gazed out at the blowing snow. Even after a long stop in Golden, it did indeed seem something of a miracle that she'd come all the way from Denver in increasingly bad weather. Though she scarcely felt the cold, the journey had been far from pleasant. Her legs had gone well past the point of pain, numb appendages useful only for gripping the belly of her horse.

The gelding had shown great spirit in carrying her so far into the mountains, to this small mining town with its narrow street of saloons, shops, and the single hotel and stable. Dandy certainly deserved a warm stall, an ample portion of oats, and a good night's sleep.

But Yankee Gulch was still miles away from where she wanted to go. Where she *must* go.

"I can't let you take one of my horses out tonight," the innkeeper said fretfully. "There's only another hour of daylight. It'd be the same as murder—you and the horse, both."

He was right about the horse, and hers certainly could not go any farther. She faced the unpalatable choice of staying the night, knowing that Niall must already be at Long Park, or risking the life of some innocent beast.

That she could not do. But the third alternative filled her with such terror that she felt a coldness far more savage than anything nature could provide.

She sighed and turned to the innkeeper. "You said that you have a room," she said. "I will take it for the night, and leave in the morning."

The grizzled man relaxed and scratched under the brim of his stained hat. "Good. Now let's get out of this cold, and I'll make sure your horse is well taken care of tonight. The rooms ain't fancy, but on a night like this—" He shrugged and gestured toward the door of the adjoining hotel.

The room was every bit as plain as the innkeeper had warned, and only marginally clean. It stank of a previous tenant's stale sweat and cigar smoke, fouling each breath she took.

Athena swallowed her distaste and set her small pack on the uneven floor. The sheets on the bed, while much mended, appeared reasonably tidy. Not that she expected to get much sleep.

She pulled the single, rickety wooden chair up to the window and watched the snow cover the street, the cheaply constructed buildings and the handful of wagons tied up in front of the general store. The few pedestrians moved hastily, anonymous figures with lowered heads and white-caked boots. Denver, and the comforts of home, seemed a million miles away.

Going back was another possibility she did not consider. The tightness in her stomach told her that her instincts were correct. She must get to the ranch. The two men she loved most in the world were in horrible danger.

In spite of her conviction that sleep was out of the question, her chin began to nod on her chest. She tried to eat a little of the bread Monsieur Savard had packed for the journey, but it was as dry and tasteless as sand. The small room felt like a cage—the kind of cage Morgan had described when he had spoken of her life—and the unthinkable idea she had rejected began to seem inviting. Only that final, lingering fear held her back.

She dozed fitfully in the chair. Out of the maelstrom of her imagination, a picture formed in stark black and white. At first all she could see was snow: snow on the ground, among the trees, in the sky, painting everything one sullen, lifeless hue.

Then she saw the black shape, lying in the snow—black fur, black tail, black muzzle. The eyes were open, but they did not see. The body lay perfectly still. No breath plumed from the open jaws. But there was one other color present in this ashen world . . . one vivid shade that wept in the snow beside the great wolf's head.

Scarlet. The color of fresh, bright blood.

Athena sat up in the chair, choking on a scream.

Only a dream, she told herself. But that was a lie. She had "dreamed" of running with Morgan as a wolf, sharing what he felt as he ran alone. Part of it had been real. What if this apparition, too, were real . . . or soon to be?

All her choices were gone. Morgan needed her, now, and there was but one way she could face the storm and make it through alive.

Shaking with reaction, she kicked her bag under the bed and pulled a wad of banknotes from her pocket, leaving them where they would be found by the innkeeper. The sun had gone down; few if any people would be on the street to see her leave or try to stop her.

She crept down the stairs, willing the other guests to remain in their rooms. The smell of greasy cooking hung in her nostrils, but the innkeeper was busy elsewhere, and she passed through the lobby unseen.

The snow continued to fall as heavily as before. Athena ran to the stable and made sure that Dandy had his blanket and oats. She had only one more favor to ask of him.

Hiding behind his sturdy bulk, she quickly stripped out of her clothing. First came the coat, and then the two layers of shirts, and then the cinched trousers. Icy wind whistled through chinks in the stable walls, curling around her bare flesh. But the cold was unimportant, as easily shrugged off as the shirts and trousers and boots.

She stood naked at Dandy's head, stroking his muzzle as much to comfort herself as him. He could rest at his ease, his care assured by the generous payment she'd left in her room. But *she* had a long way to go.

And that journey must begin with an act of courage she was not sure she possessed. Nor could she take that first step among the horses. Making a quick search of the stable, she discovered a small loft where she concealed her bundled clothing—no need to give the poor innkeeper more concern than he would already face when he found her gone.

Straw crackled under her bare feet as she crept to the stable door. She had no need to worry for the sake of modesty, or of being dragged away to an asylum for the insane. The street was empty of man or beast. Even the most recent wagon tracks had been erased. Yankee Gulch was dark save for one or two lights shining in windows, but her wolfish night vision made it seem almost as bright as day.

Wading through the snow, she circled the stable to the alley beside it. It was as good a place as any to attempt the impossible.

Not impossible. You did it once, easily. When you were hardly more than a girl, you couldn't imagine a life without it. Or a life without the use of your legs.

Now you have your legs again. Claim the rest of yourself, Athena. For Morgan's sake.

She closed her eyes and *willed*.

Nothing happened. She stood on two weak legs, her loosened hair lashing about her face. It would be so easy to give up and admit defeat.

I cannot. It has been too long. My body does not know how.

She sat down in the alley, burying her face in her hands. Better to just lie here and let the snow cover her up. How could she help Morgan—she, who had lived a soft and easy life, believed herself so important, and yet had no real courage to face a true challenge when it came?

Who was she, to think she had the power to save him?

She flung her head up and stared at the falling snow. That same snow fell on him now, in a place where he might lie dying and alone.

She clenched her fists and pushed to her feet. She remembered what it had been like when Changing required no more than a thought. She remembered racing through the forest up at the ranch, borne to ecstasy on a hundred smells and sounds even her superior human senses could not detect.

Above all, she remembered running beside Morgan, wolf with wolf, utterly free.

A peculiar frisson swept through her body. It was as if every muscle, every bone, every nerve twisted inside out, yet there was no pain. A mist rose about her like a silken veil, untroubled by the wind.

She threw up her arms and gave herself to the Change. Life flowed and shifted. Her sight altered, taking in the world from a vantage much closer to earth. Scents and sounds burst in upon her senses like a tidal wave.

For a moment all she could do was breathe, struggling to manage the overwhelming assault. Gradually what seemed so alien became familiar, as natural as walking had been before the accident. She took a step on four wide paws. Her hind legs trembled, the lingering remnant of her lameness, but they carried her out of the alley, first at a walk and then a trot and a gallop.

She ran down the deserted street and to the shacks at the outskirts of town, past the mine and the tailings and waste of man's grubbing in the earth. The forest called to her, and the mountains, with songs only one of her blood could hear.

Instinct pointed the way to Long Park when no trail remained for a human being to follow. Instinct, and a very human emotion called love.

Athena howled defiance into the blizzard and ran as she had never run before.

Niall had come this way. Morgan sniffed at the ground, detecting the odors buried under a layer of newfallen snow. Any tracks Munroe had made were long gone; if he were not dead already, no human born could find him.

But a werewolf could. And Morgan planned to do so, setting aside his hatred of the man he hunted. For Athena's sake.

He almost felt Athena beside him, bounding over frozen creeks and through thickets of serviceberry shrubs. But she was in Denver now, safe and warm where she ought to be.

He sat on his haunches and chocked on a howl. The last words he had spoken to her had been filled with cruelty and bitterness. That was her final memory of him—angry, hating, blaming her for being what she was instead of what he wished her to be.

She had not made the same mistake. She had understood that he wouldn't go with her. Perhaps that was why she had asked.

Damn you, Athena Munroe. I will find your precious brother. And then you must let me go. Let me go, do you hear?

His growls flew away in the wind. Tensing his muscles, he leaped up and over a snowbank and followed the trail of scent. No other animals were foolish enough to be abroad; the forest and park looked as they must have done before the first intruding human had walked in these mountains. Peaceful. Still as death, or forgetfulness. A sweet offer of ending he could not accept.

A few hours before dawn, he found his quarry. Niall crouched in the partial shelter of a fallen tree, his coat drawn up over his head. There was no sign of his mount. Morgan smelled the ash where he had tried to start a fire, but no flame could survive this gale.

Morgan stalked closer, ears flat to his head. He heard the ragged sound of Niall's breathing, felt the warmth of body heat—alive, then. He shook off savage regret and drew closer.

Niall's head jerked up. His brows were frosted with rime, his skin nearly blue. He tried to move, feeling in his pocket.

Morgan dashed in and seized Niall's wrist between his teeth, tasting leather and sheepskin. Munroe's smell was rank with fear and exhaustion. He met Morgan's gaze, and the last spark of fight went out of him.

He had one more shock to face. Morgan released him and backed way, shaking the foul scents from his coat. It was almost a relief to Change and find his senses dulled, as they always were in human shape.

Munroe exhaled a great cloud of steam and tried to sit up. "You," he said hoarsely.

"Yes." Morgan crouched on his heels. "I've come to take you back to the ranch."

Munroe laughed. "You have come to . . . save me?"

"I would just as soon let you die here. But there are two who care for you, and it is for their sakes that I came tonight."

"Two?" He shivered and tried to adjust his collar with frozen fingers.

"Your sister, and Caitlin."

"Caitlin." He shifted again and fell back. "Is she all right?"

"She and the others are safe."

Niall closed his eyes. "You found them?"

"Yes. Your men said that you went out to look for them after the storm began. That earns you the right to live."

"The right to live," he echoed. "And what gives you the right to judge me, Holt? You, who murdered your own father?"

Morgan felt no surprise. He'd lived too long among men to keep such secrets indefinitely, and no one had better motive to uncover those secrets than Niall Munroe.

But Munroe's accusation did not touch him. It was as if Athena's brother spoke of another man, summoned memories of another life.

"You do not deny it," Munroe said. He sat up, emboldened by Morgan's silence. "Not that it would do you any good. I blame myself for not having discovered it long ago. The only thing I don't understand is why you were not hanged."

"Then there is something about me you don't know."

"That you claim justification for patricide?" He laughed again, teeth chattering. "A man capable of that could do anything. But you are not a man, are you? You're a beast that thinks nothing of killing."

"A beast like your sister."

"No!" Munroe scrambled to his feet and leaned on the fallen tree. "My sister cannot help what she is. I will not let her give in to the monstrous heritage her mother imposed upon her." His eyes glazed. "I knew she was evil the first time I saw her in my father's bed."

Morgan became aware of his body again. "She?"

"Gwenyth Desbois. The bitch who seduced my father and stole his love for my mother." Munroe's teeth flashed white in the rigid oval of his face. "I saw her Change long before Athena learned how to twist her body into an animal's. And my father knew. He *knew* what she was, and wanted her anyway. He forced my mother to raise Athena as her own—"

"And you hate Athena for that. You've hated her since she was born."

"Shut up! You know nothing about it, what it was like to know what she was. I would have kept it from her, let her live an ordinary life. But our father told her everything when he thought she was old enough to understand. He ruined her." He slammed his fist against the tree, shaking snow from the dead branches. "And you—you will destroy her completely. That's why I must stop you just as I stopped her mother."

Morgan cocked his head. "What happened to Athena's mother?" he asked softly.

"I was eight when I first saw them together. My mother didn't know. She didn't find out for years. And I was too young to do anything then. But when I was twelve, I got rid of the bitch, and Father never knew."

Twelve. Two years younger than Morgan had been when he'd left home forever, vowing to find his own father and bring him back to California. He had abandoned his childhood by the time he was fifteen.

At eight years of age, Munroe had seen his father in bed with his mistress. Four years later, he had gotten rid of her. The ugly pictures that formed in Morgan's mind came from the darkest of places within himself: images of a boy with a revolver, a woman begging for mercy, the terrible finality of a gunshot.

A gun, a knife, poison—it didn't matter. Niall was too clever to implicate himself in Gwenyth Desbois's death. It wasn't easy to kill a werewolf, but it could be achieved by someone with knowledge, resolve, and sufficient hatred.

"I had to do it," Niall said. "I had to set my father free and restore my mother's honor. It was the only way."

Hatred was a ruthless master. It could make a boy, or a man, believe that whatever he did was justified. It could convince him that his reasons were pure and good and unselfish.

The boy had stood there with the gun and listened to the pleas. He had seen the upraised hands, the hollow eyes, the quiver of the lips. He had aimed, so carefully. One shot was all it took.

"You see why I must stop you," Niall said, his voice very far away. "There is just enough human left in Athena to be worth saving."

Morgan saw the gun in Niall's hand. He knew what it meant, and what it would take to stop his enemy. A gathering of muscle and sinew, a leap, a single blow, a clean snapping of the bones in a human neck.

Another murder.

Niall fired. The bullet seared Morgan's side, a startling instant of pain that seemed less real than the calm indifference of his thoughts. He staggered. A second bullet grazed Morgan's temple.

For Athena.

He fell. Blood steamed in the snow. Morgan felt his body laboring to heal the wounds, but he let the blood flow and the pain wash over him. He willed his heartbeat to slow, his lungs to cease their struggle for air. He closed his eyes.

Niall's presence was a faint warmth above him. He waited for a third shot, but it didn't come. His body absorbed Niall's kick without reacting. Cold metal pressed into his jaw. He stopped his heart just as Niall's fingers sought the pulse at the base of his neck.

"So easy," Niall murmured. "You didn't even fight, you bastard. Why?" He lurched up and away, his movements receding with Morgan's awareness. "Damn you. Damn you to hell."

Chapter 20

Athena knew the way. As a woman she might have become lost, but the wolf could not be confused or misled by distorted senses. She ran without pause through the storm, and at the coming of dawn she knew she had reached Munroe land.

She could not have said what made her stop so close to her goal, with the scents of woodsmoke and horses and humanity thick in her nostrils. The place was very much like any other in the park, where evergreens grew thick at the edge of a meadow. No animal or bird broke the silence. But she stopped, her fur bristling and her ears tilted to catch the sound of a voice.

Morgan's voice. And she realized what it was that had halted her. The wind had gone still; the cacophony of a thousand scents, tangled by the storm, had settled back into a gentler song. And one subtle note rang sweet and beloved among all the others.

Morgan. She turned her muzzle toward the scent, all her weariness dropping away. Morgan was here, very close, perhaps behind the next stand of firs.

She raced across the meadow, leaving a deep gully in the snow behind her. Halfway across she slowed, and her hind legs began to cramp and seize up with pain that shouted in her body like a warning of doom.

Wrong. Morgan's scent was wrong. What had seemed a pure, sweet melody was tainted. Mingled with Morgan's scent was another she knew as well as her own, and a third she recognized and feared above all others.

Niall had been here, or very close. And either he, or Morgan, had shed blood.

Not even the pain in her legs could slow her now. She forced her muscles to obey and leaped up, broke the surface of snow in her descent and leaped again. The edge of the meadow loomed ahead. She clawed her way onto a jutting boulder and entered the cover of the trees.

The smell of blood grew thicker, Morgan's scent stronger as Niall's faded. Athena's paws hardly touched the ground. In a small clearing, protected from the worst of the storm, she found him.

He lay on his back in snow melted by his own blood, limbs twisted and dark hair thick across his face. The ground all around him had been trampled by booted feet. Niall's boots.

Niall had been here. The sharp tang of metal and gunpowder played counterpoint to the stench of blood. No mist of breath rose from Morgan's parted lips.

Athena covered the remaining distance in a single jump. She lost her balance, fell to her side, and scrambled the last few feet on shaking legs.

Morgan lay unmoving. Athena nudged his chin with her muzzle and snarled in his face. His skin was cold. She clawed at him frantically, heedless of the scratches she left on his bare skin. His chest didn't move. She grabbed his arm between her teeth and tugged him this way and that with small, despairing whimpers.

Only then, when every attempt had failed, did she sit back on her haunches and howl. Wolves could not weep. But she was also human, and humans possessed a strange and foolish quality called hope.

Hope gave her the strength to Change. Hope kept her heart beating as she lay atop him, spreading her arms and legs over him like a living blanket. Hope warmed her breath as she kissed his unyielding lips.

"Be alive," she whispered. "Damn you, Morgan, be alive." She pushed her fingers into his hair and lifted his head as if he could see the determination in her eyes. "Are you going to give up, after fighting the world with every breath? Is this how it ends? Well, you've underestimated me for the last time, Morgan Holt."

She kissed him again, bruisingly, biting into his lower lip until she tasted blood. Hating him, and loving him more than life itself.

He gasped. His chest arched up as if pulled by invisible cords, and he sucked in a lungful of air. Bright, fresh blood welled from the wounds in his side and temple.

"Morgan!" she cried, searching for something to stanch the flow. But he didn't hear her. His eyes remained closed. Dark mist formed over his body, the telltale sign of impending Change.

She slid away from him just as the transformation began. It was neither swift nor smooth; midway through the Change, he hovered between wolf and man just as he had in her bedroom at Long Park. Only this time it was not by choice. His body could not complete the Change in its weakened state, so near to death. Blood continued to stain the snow.

Athena caught at his fur-mantled shoulders and shook him. "Decide, Morgan!" she shouted. "Live or die. Wolf or man. But if you choose death, I'll know you were a coward!"

His eyelids fluttered, revealing the alien yellow of a wolf's eyes. He shuddered violently, and the mist became like a choking cloud. The shape under Athena's hands finished its transition. The black wolf lay on its side, barely breathing.

She buried her hands in Morgan's fur, feeling for the wounds. Her fingers came away dry. No more blood. Bone and muscle felt firm and whole. His heart beat strongly under his ribs.

Without questioning the miracle, Athena let herself go limp and rested her head on his flank. She knew she had slept when she felt hands—human hands—in her hair, stroking it away from her face.

She blinked and sat up. Morgan lay beside her, his bare skin unmarked and his eyes free of pain. He let his hand fall and gazed up at her, waiting for her questions.

"I'm not dreaming?" she whispered.

"No." He smiled—that faint, almost imperceptible smile she had finally learned to recognize. "And neither am I."

She reached out, touching any part of him that she could reach. It was not her imagination. The wounds that had bled so freely were gone as if they had never existed. At first she thought even the blood-stained snow had vanished, but then she saw the dark blotch several feet away and realized that Morgan had moved both of them to clean ground.

It was daylight now, and the storm had passed, but the temperature remained below freezing. Athena felt as warm as if she and Morgan lay wrapped in blankets before a crackling fire.

"You healed yourself," she said in wonder. "How?"

"It is a dangerous thing," he said. "A great risk to take when there is no other choice. One of us who is injured badly—if we Change, we either die or heal ourselves."

"I thought you were dead." Her eyes welled with belated tears. "You weren't breathing."

"But I heard you." He caught a tendril of her hair and tucked it behind her ear. "You called me a coward."

Her fist bunched with the savage desire to strike the gentle mockery from his face. "Did you find that amusing? Did you enjoy making me think you were dead?"

"No. I had to convince Niall that I was."

Niall. Athena closed her eyes, and the tears spilled over. "He thought he'd killed you," she said. "When he said he was returning to Long Park, I knew something was wrong. I left Denver as soon as I guessed what he intended."

"You risked everything," he said. "You Changed, Athena. You brought me back."

Somehow that victory seemed hollow. Whatever Morgan said, she had not saved him. The admiration in his eyes, the pride in his voice made the coming trial that much more unbearable.

"Yes." she said. "I Changed."

"Because you feared for me. But you must have known it was Niall who was in danger."

She met his gaze, and she knew. She knew that Morgan understood the reason Niall had come back to kill him. Cecily's accusations hung between them, unspoken but impossible to ignore. Even now, after his miraculous reprieve from death.

Especially now.

"I will believe you, Morgan," she said. "Whatever you tell me, I will believe."

He looked away. "My great secret," he said. "It would not have mattered if I had remained among the wolves. But Harry and his people drew me back to men, where the past is never forgotten. Not even by the ones who lived it."

Then it was true. The horrible things she had refused to accept . . . some part of them must be true. But the question she knew she must ask froze on her tongue.

"I was in prison," he said, his voice without expression. "Niall discovered it. That was why he came back. To protect you."

Athena sat very still, afraid that if she moved her entire body might shatter like a figure sculpted of ice. "Cecily told me," she said. "She was the one who told Niall."

"About me. About what I am." He made a harsh sound under his breath. "It is true." At last he looked at her. "You didn't believe it until now. You had *faith* in me."

How bitterly he mocked himself. She recognized the contempt, the unrelenting self-judgment. Whatever he had done, his punishment had never stopped. He carried it with him always.

He would tell her everything if she asked. Every ugly detail of his crime and imprisonment, anything she might possibly wish to know. And he would hope, as he told her, that she would turn from him in disgust and horror.

"You should not have come back, Athena," he said. "Your brother would have been safe."

He spoke with such reluctance, as if he were revealing a great weakness—as if sparing a life were more shameful than taking one. In spite of what he had said earlier, he assumed she'd escaped Denver to protect Niall. And hadn't she? Hadn't she been equally afraid for both men, knowing that Niall didn't have a chance against a werewolf?

But she knew her brother. His ruthlessness, and his tenacity. He would have been prepared to face a werewolf . . . or a murderer.

"A man who killed his own father." Those had been Cecily's words. And Morgan admitted it. But he had not hurt Niall. Her heart filled with the conviction that he had deliberately allowed Niall to attack and leave him for dead, so that he would not be compelled to kill her brother.

She could think of only one reason he would risk his own life to spare Niall's.

"If you are a murderer," she said, "it would be easy to kill a man you hate."

He stared at her, stubbornly mute. He would force her to draw her own conclusions rather than do anything to clear his name, or his worth in her eyes.

So it was up to her. She must decide: whether to believe Cecily and Niall and Morgan himself, or look beyond the cold facts to the man behind them. The man whose goodness shone like the biblical light under a bushel. The man she loved.

Words were inadequate. Here, in the wilderness, the two of them sat in the snow unaware of the cold or the nakedness that would have killed a normal man or woman.

Here, human language had no power to express the feelings that crowded her chest and seared her throat.

But there was another kind of communication far more eloquent. Suddenly and most acutely she was aware of her nakedness in a new and tantalizing way—hers, and Morgan's.

Morgan seemed to read her thoughts. He tensed his muscles and tried to stand, but his knee buckled. He caught himself against a fir and leaned there, breathing hard. Athena bit back a cry of alarm.

"We are both weary," she said. "We need rest before . . . before anything else."

"Are you ill? Your legs . . ."

Naturally he would worry about her and not himself. "I am tired. My legs hurt, and we need time to recover." *And to decide what to do.* She left those words unspoken, but he heard them.

"I'll take you to the ranch."

So that Niall has another chance to kill you? So you can run away for the last time?

"No. Not yet." She kept her voice tranquil, her expression calm. "I just need to rest. Somewhere quiet. Please, Morgan."

The muscles in his jaw flexed. "There is a cave not far from here. It isn't much better—"

"It will do." She started to rise and Morgan rushed in to support her. She felt the vibration of muscles under his skin as he tried to lift her. "I can walk," she insisted. "Take me to the cave, Morgan."

He withdrew instantly, and she realized he believed that she didn't want him to touch her. The thought sickened her, but she swallowed her protest and let him move ahead, forging through the snow at a pace too rapid for a weakened man to sustain. Even so, he glanced back at her every few steps to make sure she followed.

They hadn't far to go. His path led through the trees and to a granite escarpment that formed a stairstep of ledges up the hill, ending in an overhang crusted with icicles. Beneath was the dark mouth of a cave. Morgan entered, moved around inside, and emerged a few minutes later.

"It's safe," he said, addressing the air over her head, refusing to look at her body or into her eyes. "A bear denned here once, but not for a long time."

She nodded and stepped over the lip of the entrance. Morgan pressed himself against a rock so that she would not touch him by accident. Her feet shuffled among dried leaves and pine needles, redolent of several former inhabitants. It was a soft, warm, and comforting scent, like that of a well-worn nursery blanket. The roof of the cave just cleared the top of her head.

This would be the place. Here Athena Sophia Munroe would do something her former self could not have dreamed of, just as she had never dreamed of, walking again.

She knelt on the mat of leaves and watched Morgan come in, hesitate, and settle against the curved stone wall near the entrance. "I can make a fire," he offered.

I'm not cold, she almost said, and realized her mistake. She needed to draw him close, but he was staying as far away as he could.

Was his self-contempt so powerful? Was it that he didn't trust himself with her? Did he no longer want her?

No. Not unless his body acted independently of his mind. She knew what she saw, what he tried to hide. *He thinks you don't want him. Maybe he hasn't enough strength. Maybe this is wrong.*

Wrong, yes, by the rules that governed people like Cecily Hockensmith. But not wrong for them. This was not only right, but necessary.

All the questions were silenced. She stood and walked toward him, each step taken with great care. He looked up and flinched as if she confronted him with a loaded rifle and death in her eyes.

She dropped to her knees before he could move. "Morgan," she said, and touched his arm. "I don't hate you. I could never hate you."

He didn't respond. She brushed his face with her fingertips. Every muscle in his body tightened.

"Whatever you may have done, Morgan . . . whoever you were in the past . . . it is not who you are now. I *know* you. Did you think I would stand as your judge, like Niall, and condemn you?"

His laugh was barbed like the new wire fences being strung across the prairie. "The saintly Miss Munroe, always so generous to the wretched."

The insult had no power to wound. She understood its source.

"Would a saint do this?" she whispered. She took his face between her hands and kissed him. His lips, firm and set, resisted for the space of a second. Then he groaned deep in his chest and pulled her into his arms.

Victory was sweet, but Athena knew at once that the savoring must come later. Morgan's kiss was urgent, almost ferocious, brimming with needs she could not expect him to control. Didn't wish him to. Not when she had the power to ease his pain for this little while.

She allowed her body to melt into his. He raised up onto his knees, taking her with him, so that their bodies touched along nearly every point: breast to breast, hip to hip, thigh to thigh. He was burning as if with fever. She felt the stiff fullness of him pressed to her belly and went hot and cold by turns.

Not fear. There was no room for fear. But this was the next great Change, the one that followed the transformation of her heart and her human body. This was the threshold from which she could not return to what she had been.

Morgan must not sense any hesitation or doubt. This was for him. Just for him. He'd have no cause to rue what they did together now, no matter how many other things in his past he regretted. This was their chance to make one perfect memory to last a lifetime.

Athena was prepared to accept Morgan into her body even without the sweet persuasion of kisses and caresses. She almost wished him to pull her down and consummate the hunger they shared.

But he anointed the corner of her mouth with a whispered kiss, his tongue darting out to touch the rim of her lips. Its very delicacy was arousing. She opened her mouth, needing to feel some part of him inside her. He ignored the invitation and gently closed his teeth over her lower lip.

The sensation of his suckling was exquisite, tugging at nerves that reached deep into her belly. She closed her eyes and stopped resisting. When he had carefully explored every line and curve of her mouth, he bent his head to her shoulder and grazed his teeth across the sensitive skin at the juncture of her neck. There was no pain, only delight, but he soothed each nip with his tongue. His breath sizzled in her ear.

"Morgan," she sighed. "It is—"

He pressed his finger to her mouth and shook his head. She understood. There were to be no words, nothing of the human world to invade this oasis in the snow. Morgan lifted her against him and pulled her down again, warm skin on skin. Her breasts came to rest in the hollow of his shoulders. Effortlessly he positioned her, hands about her waist, until her nipples brushed his chin and then his lips.

Once before he had touched her there. What he had done in her room at the ranch was nothing compared to this. The very tip of his tongue teased her nipples to throbbing peaks, and then he took her into his mouth.

Athena had learned, long ago, that women's breasts were made to feed and nurture infants. Now she discovered that they held secrets of pleasure only a man could unlock. Morgan suckled her, kneading her flesh between his hands. He drew tiny circles with his tongue and drew his teeth to the very tip before filling his mouth with her. Athena let her head fall back, revelling in the body Morgan so adored.

This body, this woman's body so perfectly designed to fit his. And Morgan was determined to make himself acquainted with every part of it. Athena was not sure she could stand the wait.

He gave her no choice. His was a gentle tyranny of pleasure. When he had finished with one breast he moved to the other and gave it equal attention, drinking in her moans with quick kisses.

Then he slid her down, her thighs parted to either side of his hips. She did not quite dare to look between them. The sleek hardness of his erection pushed against her, the hot tip very near to the place that had become so wet and swollen. Already her body knew what it would feel like, how the delicious agony would be soothed only when he filled the hollow ache inside.

But his fingers found her instead, skimming between her legs until they found the hidden nub. His thumb stroked in a rhythmic motion while his other arm supported her even when her legs could no longer hold her up.

A little more, just a little more, and she would find her way to paradise. But it was too soon. This time, when it happened, she wanted him with her in every way. Blindly she reached for any part of him that she could touch and found the warm, ridged plane of his belly.

He caught her wrist and pressed her hand to his chest. He bent her back, and her newly supple body arched to lift her hips over Morgan's thighs, her knees to either side of his, her hair spread across the cave floor.

She was utterly exposed. Helpless, yes, but not in the way she had been in her chair. This was willing surrender, excitement, anticipation of inconceivable joys ahead.

It was not long in coming. Something slipped inside her, past the yielding gateway so open to Morgan's touch. She gasped in surprise.

He leaned over her and kissed her brow. "I am making you ready," he said. And she knew it was fingers that had found their way inside, preparing her, making her mad for a bolder penetration.

"You're so wet," he whispered, brushing her ear with his lips. "So eager to take me inside you."

The human words he had foresworn held an unbearable magic. Yes, she was wet, and ready, and eager with wanting him. But her mouth would not form the sounds to make him obey. She closed her eyes and endured with mingled pain and pleasure, and when the heat of his mouth replaced his fingers, she knew how naive she truly was.

His tongue followed the same burning path as his hands had done, teasing and suckling her, lapping up her wetness, thrusting deep only to withdraw again. Her body climbed to the precipice, leaving her mind still bound to the dull earth.

"No," she gasped. "Morgan, I want . . . both of us. Together."

The heat of his breath left her, and for a moment she was cold and bereft. Then his strong hands were parting her thighs, lifting her bottom, drawing her onto him. Poised, at last, to finish what he had begun.

"When I go inside you," he whispered, "there is no turning back."

She lifted her hand to cover his mouth as he had done hers, silencing him, feeling her wetness on his lips. Then he was inside her, as she had imagined, only a thousand times better. There was no pain, only the fullness of him stretching, filling, completing.

Morgan had known, the moment he had held Athena naked in his arms, the moment he had tasted her, that their joining would be unlike any he had felt before. It wasn't only the many years of enforced celibacy. It wasn't that his one time with Tamar had been so cold and bereft of emotion. No, it was so much more than that, more even than the desire he had felt for Athena almost from the day they had met.

Athena was his. He would be the first to possess her, to take the virginity she willingly conceded to him. She gave herself without reluctance or false modesty. The scent of wanting wreathed the cave, and the intoxicating flavor of his desire still lingered on his tongue.

He knew that this act of love was a gift of the moment. After it was over, the questions would still be there—the questions and the doubts and the fears. And he didn't care. For now there was only one reality, and both wolf and man cried out to seize it for the first and last time. For a while he and Athena would grasp salvation in both hands.

Yet when he entered her, holding himself back and desperate not to hurt her, he knew how pitiful had been his greatest expectations.

She was slick, hot, and tight around him, and as he moved deeper she pushed her fingers into the carpet of leaves under her back and moaned sweetly. The small barrier gave easily, and still he held back until she reached up and grasped his shoulders in urgent demand.

With a groan of relief he thrust hard and true. It was like coming back to a home long lost. She arched into him, lifting her hips, drawing him deeper still. He cupped her firm buttocks in his hands to hold her steady as he withdrew and thrust again more swiftly. Her gasps came in time to his movements, the very beat of life itself.

But she was too far away. He drew her up so that she straddled his lap and her nipples pressed into his ribs. Her eyes were closed, her skin flushed, her lips parted in an expression of ecstasy.

He wanted to see her eyes, watch them looking into his as he rocked her again and again.

"Look at me," he demanded. "Look at me, Athena."

She did as he commanded. Her lashes fluttered open, revealing changeable eyes almost swallowed up by the black of her pupils. Her gaze held his as if they could join minds as well as bodies, and he remembered the time in Denver when he had felt her all the way to her soul.

She gave her soul to him now, holding his gaze as he carried her to completion. Her little gasps became a long sigh of wonder. He had a moment to savor his triumph, and then he was borne away to that same perfect place.

Athena fell against him, panting, and he held her trembling body close. They were still as one in every way. But separation would come, as inevitable as sunrise, and all he would have was the memory of her silken heat and the rapture in her eyes.

Silence claimed the cave, but it was not the peaceful quiet of rest after vigorous loving. Morgan had no hope for such a reward, and he felt, in Athena's stubborn grip on his body, that she had not found it either. The one thing he could give her had lasted but a few, mindless moments.

Yet when she finally withdrew, it was all he could do to keep from pulling her back and beginning again. His body should not be capable of wanting her, but it did. *He* did. He leaned his head back on the cool stone wall and closed his eyes.

Go, he wished her. *For your sake, Athena. Go.*

He cursed when he felt her breath on his cheek, but even curses deserted him as her hands moved to cup him below. So slight a touch made him full and firm as if he hadn't just taken her.

"This is so new to me," she murmured. Her fingers traced up and down his length, lingering at the velvet tip. "You don't mind?"

He groaned. "Mind? Athena—"

"What you did . . . was so wonderful. I want to do the same for you."

The same? He had never imagined she might touch him, explore him the way he had done with her. She was a sheltered lady, ignorant of the ways of the flesh until he had taught her. But her hands moved again, and he was compelled to admit that she had learned very quickly indeed.

But that was not the final surprise. Just as he had resigned himself to suffering the exquisite torture of her caresses, her hands left him, and her mouth continued the work they had begun. He held on to sanity with fraying resolve. She wanted to give, unselfishly as always, but he would not be in her debt. Not even in this.

With implacable gentleness he grasped her shoulders and pulled her up. Her eyes reflected puzzlement, even hurt. He kissed her mouth and lay back on the blanket of leaves, stretching her out across the length of his body. He eased her legs on either side of his hips to straddle him.

She looked down at him and understood. He gave her control, mastery over what they did together—*together*, sharing pleasure and fulfillment. Morgan became her willing prisoner, and she did not fail to accept his invitation.

Tiny movements of her thighs and hips teased and tormented him as she found just the right position. She eased down, down, taking him in, and then finished with a heady plunge. It was she who controlled the rhythm, who smiled with amazed satisfaction as he became helpless in her power. Her hair swept across his chest in time to her motions. Her small, even teeth nipped at his shoulders.

Neither of them could control the inevitable finish. Morgan was as inept as a boy with his first woman. And yet, by some marvel of the magic they made together, they found the heavens in flawless harmony.

Athena lay with her head tucked beneath his chin, her heartbeat slowing with his. Morgan closed his eyes. If she remained here long enough, her flesh would become his flesh, her bones his bones, her very being an inseparable part of him. But he held her there until she slept and the sun's steep angle cast the cave into twilight.

Darkness let him conceal the thing he could admit in his heart but would never speak.

I love you, he whispered into the fragrance of her hair. *I love you. But love is never enough.*

Chapter 21

The sun was a copper ball in a clear blue sky when Niall reached the ranch. He saw the circus wagons massed at the side of the second barn, half buried in snow that glistened like bright new trappings.

Morgan had told the truth. Caitlin was safe.

Niall dragged his feet the last few steps to the house, up the stairs and onto the veranda. He had long since ceased to notice his weariness. His heart had dissolved a little more with each step away from the murder, melting like an ice block to pool in his legs and freeze anew.

Many other feet had trod this way in the past few hours. Caitlin would be with the others. Her friends, her family, the people she trusted. They would all hear what he had to say. It didn't matter what they thought of him. No one else's judgment could affect him now.

He didn't bother to wipe his boots as he entered the hall. A blast of warmth buffeted his face, sending rivulets of water from his hat and his snow-crusted clothing.

The hearth in the parlor blazed with an immense fire, hungrily consuming the heavy branches upon which it fed. To one side stood a table laid out with the remains of a meal and several steaming pots of coffee. The space in front of the fire was crowded with people, among them many faces Niall had come to know well: Harry French, the dwarf Ulysses, Tamar the snake charmer . . . and Caitlin. Caitlin, who looked up as he paused on the threshold.

"Niall!" she cried. She started toward him. Her gaze fastened on the closed door at his back and returned to his face. Her footsteps slowed and stopped.

"Morgan went out to find you," she said. "Where is he?"

So that was to be his greeting. Did she know he had been the first to go after her and her companions? Did she care that he had returned unharmed?

If she did not, it was no more than he deserved.

All of them were staring at him now. Their faces told him what they expected to hear.

He pulled off his gloves and let them fall to the floor. "I heard that you tried to leave in the storm. I am . . . glad that you returned safely." Taking his time, he went to the table and poured himself a mug of coffee. It was still hot, and very bitter.

"Where is Morgan?" That was Ulysses, the dwarf, behaving as if he were three times his height. Niall saw something of the old Southern aristocracy in his face, the indomitable stubborn will that could not be entirely broken by any misfortune.

Harry French gripped the back of an armchair and gazed at him through watery blue eyes. The snake charmer glared. The other circus folk, the ones he had never bothered to identify, held an unnatural silence.

Niall set down the mug. "Morgan Holt is dead. I killed him."

The long-case clock at the other end of the room tripped out its steady, imperturbable beat. No one spoke. Ulysses clenched his fists and started toward Niall. Harry held him back.

Caitlin only stared.

Niall turned to French. "You may remain at Long Park as long as necessary—all winter, if you choose." He flexed his fingers. They were coming back to life, as his heart was not. "I will not be here to disturb you."

Harry shook his head. A tear tracked its way down one seamed cheek. Ulysses rested his small hand on the old man's arm.

There was no warning of the attack when it came. Tamar burst out from among the other troupers and charged at Niall, her mouth open on a wordless scream. He put up his hands to stop her, but she carried him back with the weight of her body and sent them both tumbling to the floor.

Niall felt her nails score her cheek and her poisonous breath in his face. His own body was paralyzed. Disembodied voices cried alarm, and hands reached down to restrain his assailant. She struggled, not like a wild cat with tooth and claw, but like a serpent, hissing and darting her head from side to side.

"Murderer," she whispered as troupers pulled her away from him. "I curse you!"

Two brawny men carried Tamar away. The others fled the room as if they could not bear to breathe the same air as the cursed Niall Munroe. Even Harry French left, and Ulysses.

Only Caitlin remained. She had not spoken another word.

This was to be his just punishment.

"It is true, Caitlin," he said. "I killed him."

She swayed, and he had to lock the muscles in his legs to prevent them from carrying him to her side.

"Are you going to tell me . . . that you had no choice?" she whispered. "When he went to save you?"

"No." He stared into the black, round pit of coffee in the mug on the table, imagining it the gateway to hell. "I did it to save my sister." With an effort he met her gaze. "It's not the first time I have done something like this. You should know the whole truth."

"You have—" She choked, swallowed. "Murdered before?"

He picked up the mug and drained the lukewarm coffee. "When I was twelve years old, I drove Athena's mother away. She stole my father from my mother and made Athena what she is. A beast, like Holt. She never came back. She chose her own life over her daughter and the man she claimed to love." He held the mug to his lips long after it was empty. "I did it for my family. I don't regret it."

They said that confession was good for the soul, but his felt no less black. "I don't ask you to understand. As I said, I will not be troubling you further. I'm returning to Athena immediately. She will be leaving for New York as soon as I can arrange it."

"So that she can forget?"

Niall set down the mug so sharply that it cracked, and a last drop of dark liquid leaked onto the table. "Yes."

"And what if Morgan isn't dead?"

Her words cut through his calm facade. "What?"

"He is not an ordinary man. Did you make quite sure that you'd killed him?"

The thought struck him hard between the eyes. "He was dead. I shot him twice."

"He once told me that his kind heal very fast. Didn't you ever notice that about your sister? The way she was able to walk so quickly after she began to try again?"

He had noticed. But he had chosen to ignore what Athena's rapid progress might mean. If Caitlin was correct . . .

Tears flooded his eyes. It was a shameful thing for a man to weep, worse still when he did not comprehend the reasons: anger and frustration that he might not have succeeded. Relief that he had not become a murderer himself. And fear—that worst of all.

He prayed that Caitlin hadn't seen his weakness. "You should not have suggested that possibility," he said harshly. "Now I will have to find him and make certain."

"You're crazy!" She limped forward, forcing him to avert his face. "I refuse to believe that you would hunt him down again, when you have a chance to atone for your mistake!"

"By giving my sister to him? You have no right to ask that of me. No right."

"But I do." Her silence compelled him to look up. She had stopped a few feet away, skin flushed and eyes very bright. "You gave me that right. Damn you, Niall Munroe, is it that you cannot see what love is?" She lifted one small, graceful hand. "Or can it be that you don't believe yourself worthy of love and forgiveness?"

"I ask no forgiveness."

"But you want it, just the same." She came closer, lips parted. "Maybe my forgiveness doesn't matter much, but I forgive you, Niall. You have not lost all your chances. You can choose to let Athena make her own life. You can change yours."

He laughed bitterly. "For the sake of love?"

"I have faith in you. You wanted me once, as your mistress. If you still do . . . it is not too late for us."

His legs had become paralyzed with more than cold and weariness. They kept him still as she put her roughened fingertips to his face, holding him prisoner with eyes incapable of deception.

"I will go with you, Niall—wherever and however you wish." She lifted her face to his and kissed him.

Need surged within him, scattering every other thought. He lifted her supple weight in his arms and returned the kiss with interest, devouring that full, tender mouth with all the violence of unrequited lust. She did not recoil. In her little body was a whirlwind of passion every bit a match for his. She leaned into him, small breasts tucked into the hollow of his shoulders. Her warmth dissipated the last of the cold, a source of heat more effective than any fire could have been.

Heat, and desire. His body hungered for her the way a man near death hungered for life. She *was* life. If he took what she offered, he would choose a path he had never considered before, one that led to beginnings and not endings. He would not be weak, but strong—everything a man was meant to be.

A few steps up the stairs and they'd be at his bedchamber. Already the wiry muscles in her thighs clasped him about the hips, inviting him inside. He knew he could take her again and again and never be satisfied. She'd buck and writhe beneath him, astride him, in every imaginable way a woman could accept a man. Her eyes told him that no pleasure, no erotic wish, was to be denied.

Breathing hard, he clasped her to him and carried her to his bed. Already she was undoing the hooks and buttons of her bodice, baring the light chemise that was her only concession to modesty. He could not shed the layers of his clothing swiftly enough. In frenzied impatience she helped him, tearing at fastenings and pulling sleeves.

She was the first to be naked, her petite form unmarred save for a few small bruises. Her cast had been removed, and her leg seemed whole and sound save for her slight limp. *She* was not like Athena, and yet . . .

Before he could complete the thought, her hands were upon his trousers, tugging and caressing at the same time. The torment was almost intolerable. Somehow she came to be astride him, her clever fingers teasing him free of all restraint. A whisper touch danced over his hot, aching flesh.

"Ah," she whispered. "What a grand mount it is. Let me ride, my stallion. Let me ride as I've never ridden before."

Niall stood at the center of one last moment of sanity, one final chance to take control. *Must get back to Denver,* the cold part of his brain muttered. *If Morgan isn't dead . . . if Athena . . .*

Then rational thought ceased, because he was being enveloped in heat and warmth, and Caitlin's mouth was on his. She rode just as she had promised, fulfilling the wildest fantasies he had ever entertained as boy or man. He thrust hard, and she fell upon him with cries and groans, her head flung back and her hair aglow as if from a thousand tiny sparks.

He came as quickly as an untried boy. Caitlin collapsed across his chest, refusing to set him free. And he found, much to his amazement, that his body was not finished with her. Not nearly finished.

She gave a little cry as he rolled her beneath him. He held himself above her, gazing into her heavy-lidded eyes.

"Do you think you've won?" he asked softly. "Do you think you've had the better of me, Caitlin?" He cupped her cheek in his palm, the first gentle caress he had given her since their joining. "No woman masters me. Not even you."

She squirmed, the motions of her body arousing him all over again. "Niall, it isn't what you—"

He thrust his tongue into her mouth, absorbing her protest. In a heartbeat her arms were linked behind his neck. He reached back and caught her wrists, pulled them one by one to the pillow above her head.

"Now it is my turn," he said, and held her hands trapped with one of his while his other slid between her thighs. He sought and found the moist, sensitive part of her that had clasped him so boldly and stroked with a fingertip. She released a low, satisfying moan.

He took his time with her, as he never had with the easy women he'd known in the past—teasing, caressing, watching her face as it altered from surprise to pleasure to mindless ecstasy. So she didn't think he could be a lover, to give as well as take?

Let her realize just how wrong she was. Keeping his own lust in check, he kissed her from forehead to the tips of her toes, lingering at her breasts, finely formed and winsome—those he'd once considered so small—and the intimate place he had made ready with his touch. She tasted of sunshine and exotic spices, simple and complex all at once.

Caitlin Hughes was no virgin. She was a sorceress of ancient carnal rites made to entrap a man—innocent and wanton, sweet and sinful, naive and wise beyond her years. Yet now she was his, and he possessed her as fully as she had seduced him. Her thighs were already parted for his entrance. As he thrust inside her, he began to understand why reasonable men would risk everything, give up the world itself, for the sake of a woman.

"Caitlin," he whispered. "Damn you, Caitlin."

She only locked her ankles behind his waist and pulled him deeper. This time she was the one who reached the peak first, shuddering with rhythmic pulses of abandoned joy. He followed a moment later and felt his seed pour into her body.

He should have slept then, or left the room without a backward glance as he had done with the other nameless women who had given themselves for something far more concrete than love. But Caitlin looked up at him with gentle wisdom, inviting him into a place that went beyond mere bodies and brushed the soul with velvet wings.

She had opened the gates too wide, and through them he saw terrible visions of all he had been and done. The sheets upon which Caitlin lay were stained with blood. Morgan's blood. And beside the bed, look-ing on with mocking eyes, was Gwenyth Desbois.

You will never be free of us, she whispered. *Never.*

Niall pushed away from Caitlin and jumped to the floor. Morgan and Desbois vanished. Caitlin sat up, reaching after him. Beckoning him to return to the bed he had made for himself.

"Niall?"

He snatched up his shirt and trousers. "I must go to Denver."

He expected her to make some claim upon him, subtle feminine blackmail for the privilege of enjoying her favors, or a storm of tears to awaken his guilt. He should have known better. She swung her legs over the bed and stood before him, hands on hips as if they had never shared a lovers' bed.

"Don't be a fool," she said. "There are things more powerful than all your wealth and influence. This is a battle you cannot win."

He turned his back on her and buttoned his shirt with shaking fin-gers. "You should not stand against me, Caitlin. I would very much re-gret it should any harm come to you."

She laughed. "Is that your fine declaration of love, Niall Munroe?"

"Love?" He faced her again, ignoring the blatant lure of her body. "Is that what you thought we shared? I am sorry to disappoint you, but I trust you will accept reimbursement for your time, even if it is only in the paltry form of money."

She caught her breath. He saw how well he had struck, and hated himself for it. Hated her more for having made him feel guilt, and ten-derness, and shame. For having made him *feel*.

"Damn you," he said. "Damn you and all your kind—"

An explosion of pain ended his curse. Fireworks burst in his head, and then he was falling, falling endlessly into the pit reserved especially for men destroyed by love.

"What have you done?"

Caitlin snatched the branch from Tamar and tossed it aside. It thudded against the wall and came to lie at the foot of the bed that she and Niall had so recently shared.

She dropped to her knees beside Niall and touched his forehead. Her fingers came away bloody. She pressed her ear to his chest, numb with terror, and heard the muted beat of his heart. His breaths were shallow but steady.

Still alive. Thank the gods, still alive.

Working quickly, she snatched a pillow from the bed and gently rested Niall's head upon it. She dipped a towel in water from the wash-basin and dabbed at the wound. It was not a large cut, though the swelling had already begun. She devised a makeshift bandage of pieces torn from the bedsheet and wrapped it about Niall's head. Knowing she hadn't the strength to lift him, she covered him with a blanket and tucked it close.

Only then, when her ministrations were complete, did she turn on the snake charmer with all the fury at her command.

"Why?" she demanded. "Why, Tamar?"

"You ask why?" Tamar showed her small, slightly pointed teeth in an unrepentant smile. "He killed my Morgan. He deserves to die."

Caitlin closed her eyes and prayed for fortitude. "You are an idiot, Tamar."

"And you are a traitor and a whore to lie with him who murdered my love!"

Caitlin became aware of her nakedness and draped herself in the torn sheet. "Morgan was never your love," she said, forcing herself to calm. "And he is not dead. I was making sure that he had a chance to re-cover and get away before Niall realized that fact."

Tamar's vicious mask crumbled into bewilderment. "How is he not dead? Tell me!"

"I think that is something we would all like to know."

Harry and Ulysses walked into the room, eyes carefully avoiding the disheveled bed and Caitlin's state of undress. Ulysses crouched be-side Niall, and Harry took Tamar's arm in a firm grip.

"Munroe said he had shot Morgan," Ulysses said, inspecting Caitlin's bandage. "Do you believe that he was lying?"

"No." Caitlin shivered and sat on the edge of the bed, watching Niall's quiet face. It was the first time she had ever seen him at peace, even for a moment. "Will Niall be all right?"

Ulysses sighed and sat back on his heels. "A man who remains un-conscious too long may not recover. You must hope that he wakes soon."

How coldly he spoke, as if Niall's life or death didn't matter. But he still regarded Niall as the man who had murdered his friend.

"Morgan is not dead," she said, putting her conviction into every word. "Think, Uly. He could have killed Niall if he chose. But other things are important to him now. He must have known that his best chance of keeping himself and Niall alive would be to use Niall's igno-rance and feign death."

"You assume a great deal, Firefly."

"I don't assume. I believe. Morgan has a reason to want to live. If he has any strength at all, he is on his way to Denver at this very moment."

Ulysses and Harry exchanged glances. Harry fished in his pocket for a handkerchief. After a moment he composed himself and straightened, casting Tamar a stark glance that failed to cover his relief.

"Caitlin is right," he said. "Morgan does have a reason to live. And if he is alive, he will go to Athena."

"As Niall would have, once he realized there was a chance that Morgan survived." She took Ulysses's place beside Niall, stroking bloodstained hair away from his pale forehead. "I could have let him go on believing that Morgan was dead, but he had already begun to torment himself over what he had done. He is not an evil man. I had to give him a little hope of redemption. But I also had to stop him from going after Morgan again."

Ulysses's glance at the bed was evidence enough that he understood. Harry blushed. Tamar took advantage of the moment and pulled free.

"If my wolf is alive, I must go to him at once," she said.

Caitlin jumped to her feet. "*You* are not going anywhere. You've brought only pain to everything you touch."

"And who are you to stop me?"

Tamar's hateful face blurred in Caitlin's vision. She knew then that she was prepared to do anything, even kill, to protect Morgan and Athena. And Niall, who needed everything she had to give. "If he dies—"

"I fear that Caitlin is correct, Tamar," Ulysses said, stepping between them. In his hand was a tiny pearl-handled derringer. "We cannot let you leave."

Tamar stared down at him with unconcealed contempt. "Will you shoot me, little man?"

"If I must. But I think that you also wish to live."

She spat at him. Ulysses stood unwavering, his gaze fixed to Tamar's face. "Morgan cannot love you, Tamar. His heart is bestowed upon another, and his kind mate for life."

Her eyes widened. "And do you think I would turn to you if I cannot have him?"

Caitlin watched with growing bafflement. For Ulysses to threaten violence was unthinkable. But something in his face, the stoic pain of a man pushed beyond his endurance, told a tale that shocked her more than the pistol in his hand.

"No," Ulysses said quietly. "I do not believe that. But you have done enough mischief, and it must stop."

"You cannot get to Denver alone," Harry added, making a last attempt to reason with her. "Ulysses and I will leave immediately and make sure that Morgan is all right. It is better this way, Tamar."

She answered by turning quickly toward the door. Ulysses raised the derringer and fired. The bullet pierced the doorjamb a few inches to the left of Tamar's shoulder.

Caitlin had never seen Tamar blanch, but she did so now, staggering back into Harry's arms. Harry forced her hands behind her back, hardly less pale than she.

Ulysses lowered the pistol. His hand was shaking. Caitlin knew that he had not missed due to lack of skill, or even nerves. In his face she read the conviction that he could never hurt Tamar, no matter what the provocation.

"I know there is one thing you truly love, Tamar," he said. "Since I knew you were apt to cause further difficulties, I took the liberty of commandeering your serpents and securing them in a safe but hidden location where you are unlikely to find them. They require warmth, and they will continue to receive it as long as you comport yourself reasonably. I trust I have made myself understood."

Tamar's mouth fell open. Ulysses had, indeed, found the one weak spot in the snake charmer's arsenal.

"I will have my vengeance," she hissed.

Ulysses shrugged and glanced at Harry. "Lock her in one of the rooms," he said. "She will not try to escape as long as her snakes are in custody."

Shaking his head sadly, Harry hustled Tamar out of Niall's room. Caitlin checked to make sure that Niall was still breathing steadily and touched Ulysses's shoulder.

"You and Harry must go right away," she said. "Morgan and Athena will need all the help they can get if he's made it back to Denver."

"And you?"

She ached for the sadness in his eyes. "I must remain here with Niall until he wakes up."

"Yes." Ulysses frowned at Niall. "You may not have to wait too long. I believe he is stirring. I would definitely prefer to be well gone before he regains full consciousness."

Caitlin gazed at Niall's face and saw the faint twitch of his lips, the flutter of an eyelid. Thank the ancient ones.

Harry appeared at the door. "It's done," he said. "I think you were right about the snakes, Uly. But how shall we get to Denver? The wagons are far too slow."

"There are several more practical conveyances in the carriage house. Mr. Munroe is in no position to object if we borrow one, and the horses to draw it. We will enlist our fellow troupers to create a distraction in the event that any of the ranch laborers attempt to interfere."

Harry nodded. Caitlin left Niall's side long enough to hug the old man and plant a kiss on the top of Ulysses's golden curls.

"Good luck," she said. "Do everything you can to help Morgan and Athena. They were meant to be together."

"We will find a way," Harry said. He nodded at Niall. "Firefly, are you sure?"

"Yes." She smiled wryly. "But the mad are always certain."

Ulysses took her hand and placed the pistol in it. "Keep this, just in case."

She wanted nothing more than to fling it across the room, but she placed it on the bed instead. "You had better go."

With a final, worried look, Harry followed Ulysses from the room.

Caitlin took up her vigil at Niall's side, noting each sign of returning consciousness. They came with increasing frequency, and at last he opened his eyes, blinked, and tried to focus on her face.

"What?" he murmured. His hand flailed toward his head and the large lump that had formed there. "Caitlin?"

"It's all right." She checked the bandage and stroked his cheek. "You must rest."

"Something is—" He tried to sit up, gasped, and subsided back to the floor. Caitlin tucked the blankets about him, prepared to sit on top of him if necessary.

Fortunately, his body seemed to realize what his will did not. He closed his eyes again and fell into what Caitlin prayed was an ordinary, healing sleep. An hour passed, and then another. He woke and asked for water; she poured from the pitcher and held the glass to his lips. Day became night; he slept fitfully, waking often with vague questions and requests for water. By the time dawn came with its false promise of peace, she knew he would not remain still much longer.

His features frozen in concentration, Niall rose onto his elbows. He felt the lump on his head and met Caitlin's gaze.

"How?" he asked hoarsely. "Someone . . . hit me."

"Yes." There was no point in lying. "Tamar struck you from behind."

"Tamar." He tried to gather his feet under his body and reached out for Caitlin's support. She helped him rise and cross to the bed, remembering at the last instant to cover the pistol with a corner of the coverlet.

"She was very angry, but she can't hurt anyone now," Caitlin said, easing him down. "It was a bad blow. You must be careful, Niall."

"Holt . . . might still be alive. I must get to Denver."

The blow had obviously not dulled his memory in the slightest. "I wish Tamar had managed to knock some sense into that thick skull of yours," she said. "If you try to ride now, you will suffer for it. I doubt you can even drive a wagon."

He pushed her away. "I warned you before, Caitlin. Don't . . . try to stop me."

She thought of the pistol at the end of the bed, and of how far she'd be willing to go to protect him and the others she loved. Uly hadn't been able to shoot Tamar. Could she so much as threaten Niall? Would he believe such a threat?

Simple persuasion, even of the sexual variety, would not work on him now. And that left but one option.

"If I don't try to stop you," she said, "then I am coming with you."

"No." The word was instant, sharp, and lucid. "I don't want you involved in what I must do."

"But I am involved. And there is nothing you can do to change that." She gripped his arm, compelling him to look at her. "You have suffered a blow to the head. What if you fall unconscious again? What if you cannot drive or ride? You would be foolish to go alone." She smiled grimly. "And even if you keep me from accompanying you, I will follow."

He stared at her, weighing her words. Would he dismiss her, as he would most anyone who made a similar promise . . . or would he realize she meant exactly what she said?

"You damned, stubborn wench. You would get yourself killed." He gathered his weight onto his feet and tried to stand. His body tilted dangerously. "I can't stop you . . . now. But you will do as I say and not interfere. Do you hear me?" He grabbed her shoulders, pressing a little too heavily. "Do you, Caitlin Hughes?"

"I hear you." *But do not ask me to promise anything. Do not ask me to choose between you and my dearest friends.*

"Then—" He gritted his teeth. "Help me dress. We must go."

How he hated asking for her help. Meekly she collected his clothing and assisted him with the lightest touch possible, as if she were a servant and not a lover who had seen his every vulnerability. When they were both bundled up and Niall had collected two saddlebags' worth of provisions, he led her out to the barn and met one of the ranch hands walking hurriedly toward the house.

"Mr. Munroe," the man said, taken aback. He shot a glance at Caitlin. "I was just comin' to find you. Them circus folk—they stole one of the buggies. Chuck says they must a' left a few hours before sunset last night."

Niall swore. "No one stopped them?"

"Some of their friends played a trick to get us away. Said they'd seen a wolf after the cattle, so we all went out . . ." He ducked his head. "I'm sorry, Mr. Munroe."

Niall swung on Caitlin. "Did you know about this?"

"Yes. Harry and Ulysses were worried about Morgan, as I was."

"The old man and the midget? Even with the night's travel, they can't be that far ahead." Niall turned back to the ranch hand. "Saddle two of the fastest horses, and do it quickly."

The man hastened to obey. Soon he was leading out two horses, both fine mounts to Caitlin's experienced eye. Before Niall or the hand could offer help, she leaped onto the smaller horse's back and caught up the reins. Niall followed, gingerly, wincing at the pain in his skull.

He would not want her solicitude now. All she could hope was that she had some small influence upon him when the time came to face the battle that lay ahead.

Chapter 22

Dawn crept into the cave on velvet feet, so soft that neither human eyes nor ears could detect it.

Athena heard. She kept her eyes squeezed shut and begged the light to retreat, to let night come again. Endless night, untroubled by future or past. A night made only for loving and being loved.

Morgan's chest rose and fell beneath her cheek, and his arm held its protective curve about her waist, loose but undeniably possessive.

As merciless as the passing of time, the light teased its way beneath her lids. She opened them slowly. Her first sight was of Morgan's broad chest, the fine, dark mantle of hair, the slope of his hard belly. She checked herself before her gazed strayed lower.

There was no going back to last night's joyful interlude. She clung desperately to the last threads of it, as she'd once done when she woke from a dream of running on crippled legs. But like all dreams, this too must come to an end.

Moving by the tiniest increments, she leaned back to study Morgan's face. It had not yet taken on the harsh lines and wariness it usually wore by daylight, nor did his features reflect the surrender and abandon of their lovemaking. Jaw, lips, eyes, forehead, all were relaxed. Waiting. Holding fast to the peace he so seldom allowed himself.

She ached to touch him. But if he still slept, she couldn't rob him of these moments. She wished she could sleep again and find herself in a new dream, one in which she and Morgan were together with no thought of the vast gulf that lay between them.

A raven croaked harshly among the pines outside. Morgan opened one eye and muttered an inaudible curse. His arm tightened about her as if he expected her to flee.

"Good morning," she whispered. She kissed his cheek, challenging him to reject that homely intimacy. His jaw flexed and released. "Did you sleep well?"

He might have thought her mad for indulging in such banal civilities, as if they were an ordinary newlywed couple the first morning after their marriage—a little shy, a little awkward, still aglow with sensual discoveries and looking forward to many more such adventures to come.

But he turned his head to look at her, and all the tenderness he found so difficult to show lay raw and exposed in his eyes. "Did you?"

"Very well." She tucked her head on his shoulder and laced her fingers through his. "I only wish . . ."

He stiffened. "What do you wish?"

She threw caution to the winds. "I wish that you and I could make this moment last forever."

He sat up, taking care to let her down gently as he changed position. Athena swallowed the sudden thickness of tears and drew her knees to her chest. *You have ruined it. Words . . . words only frighten him away.*

Morgan sat with his back to the sloping cave wall just as he had last night before the loving, as unapproachable as a heathen idol carved of stone. She knew the nature of the heart that beat within his broad chest, the gentleness of which he was capable, the stubborn loyalty that belied his judgment of himself. But he wanted to pretend she did not understand.

"It's no use, Morgan," she said. "We cannot go back."

He stared fiercely at the opposite wall. A gust of cold air blew in the cave mouth, lifting long black strands of hair across his face and shoulders. He made no attempt to brush them away.

"No," he said. "You cannot go back to what you were."

It was not what she had meant. "An invalid? Living in denial of half of myself? You're right, Morgan. I can only go forward, as you must."

He said nothing. She wanted to scream and jump up and down, if only to make him look at her. The closeness of their joining had been as fragile as a snowflake, evaporated in an instant of heat and passion. How could everything they had built last night have vanished so completely?

With an effort she composed herself. Violent emotion would only drive him further away. The wrong words might frighten him, but they were all she had.

"We never finished our discussion," she said. "There is still time for you to tell me everything, Morgan. I said I would listen, and not judge. I meant it. And whether you like it or not, you can't shut me out so easily. You see . . . I love you."

The cave reverberated with her calm declaration. Her heart tripped out a frantic tattoo. Morgan blinked, once, the only sign that he had heard and understood.

"There," she said with false lightness. "I have given you my greatest secret. I doubt that yours is any more terrifying."

Slowly he looked at her, expressionless to any eyes but hers. "What do you want of me?"

No tears, she commanded. *It is his way. It is always his way to hide when he feels too much.* "I want to know what you want. I want to understand why you think you must protect me from yourself when we have given each other so much."

He took in a long, deep breath and let it out again, wreathing his face in mist. "Will you come with me, now?"

"What?"

"I asked you once before," he said. "Will you come with me—away from Denver, from Colorado, taking nothing, giving up everything you've known? Will you, Athena?"

Yes, her heart cried. *Yes, yes, and yes.* But there was something wrong with his question and her own response to it. She hesitated, and in that hesitation lay the cold, hard seed of doubt.

So much had altered since the first time he had asked her to abandon her life. She had remembered how to Change, and healed herself. She had begun to discover that what seemed important was only window dressing and false pride. She had learned to love, not with charitable dispassion, but with her entire soul.

She was not the person she had been a few months ago. But Morgan demanded her complete surrender without offering his trust in return. He had tried to drive her away even as he claimed her for his own. He asked her to run, not toward a real life together, but away from what he feared in himself.

"You want me to go with you," she said. "But you expect me to do so in ignorance. You want me to trust you, when you will not trust me with the things that have hurt you and made you what you are. You refuse to believe that I'm strong enough to accept whatever you tell me." She held out her hand, cupping her palm as if she could touch his face. "All I ask is that you confide in me, Morgan. Confide in the woman who loves you. If you do that now, for me, I will go with you to the ends of the earth."

Dry leaves rustled across the cavern floor. Athena's heart beat five, ten, twenty times before Morgan moved. He smiled, only with his mouth, and she knew that she had lost her gamble.

"Your love is not enough," he said, almost gently. "The answers you want are only the beginning. You would find no contentment, no peace. You would always expect what I can't give you."

"You mean that you could not love me."

"Love breaks like thin ice on a lake just when you think it is sound to cross." He lowered his head so that the dark mass of his hair concealed his face. "It's a hard lesson, but it will make you stronger in the end."

"Strong . . . as you are? Is this your example, Morgan?" She uncurled and stood to face him. "Is it strength to pretend that none of this ever happened? Should I let my past determine my future, crawl back into my chair and play at being helpless so that I will be safe until the day I die?"

"You will not be safe in Denver."

Such irrational anger stirred in Athena that it was as if the wolf had taken her mind without Changing her body.

"Oh?" she choked out. "What danger will I face, once you are gone?

My heart will be cast in iron, but I'll still be able to help those who can find some use in hope. If I'm careful, I can concoct an explanation for my recent behavior that may convince society to accept me back into its midst."

His eyes burned through the veil of his hair. "You will not be safe as long as your brother is alive."

"I know . . . I know that he tried to kill you, but he is not an evil man. I will talk to him. I'll make him understand, and he'll regret what he did—"

"No." Morgan stood, moving as if every bone and muscle in his body had been torn apart. "Niall told me the truth about your mother, Athena. He hid it from you all these years. He wanted you to remain dependent and weak, so that he wouldn't have to remember the woman who stole your father's love."

"What truth?" she whispered.

Morgan hesitated, staring toward the mouth of the cave.

"What truth?" She strode toward him and stood so close that he had no choice but to meet her gaze. "Tell me!"

He lifted his hand and let it fall. "He told me that he got rid of your mother."

Her knees locked, keeping her on her feet. "I don't understand."

"He hated her. He hated what she was, and that your father loved her more than he did his own mother. He was still a boy when he—"

"*No.*" She pressed her hands over her ears. "I don't believe it."

"He had no reason to lie to me." The gentleness of Morgan's voice pierced her shock as no shout could. "Listen to me. You must be on guard against him. He knows what you are, and he hates you for it, just as he hated your mother. You betrayed him when you came to me. He will not forgive you, Athena. If he killed once, he can kill again."

"Like you?" She backed toward the entrance. "Do you presume to understand what Niall is because you have committed murder?"

The words were out of her mouth before she could stop them. She had sworn not to judge him, not to use his past against him, and she had failed in her promise. "Morgan—"

His eyes were frosted glass. "I should have killed him."

In that moment she believed that he had done what Cecily claimed, that he could kill a man without compunction or regret. She stood on the lip of the cave, half in light and half in shadow, riven just as surely between woman and wolf, trust and betrayal, love and hate.

There was no certainty, no peace. The two men she loved most had become deadly strangers. Doubt ate at her like a cancer. Her familiar world had done more than change; it had shattered. She had only the smallest hope of putting it back together again. And she must do it alone. For Morgan's sake, for Niall's . . . and because she had no right to happiness she had not earned.

"I am going," she said. "I'm going to find my brother and make him tell me the truth." She stepped into harsh noon light, and Morgan tensed to follow. "*No.* Don't come after me. You owe me nothing." She closed her eyes to the sight of his beloved face. "You are free."

He laughed wretchedly. "Don't trust him, Athena—"

She Changed and was ready when he followed. She turned on him, snapping and snarling, until he had to retreat or defend himself. But he did not Change. He knelt in the snow, hands on his thighs, and watched her go.

Phantom tears gathered behind her wolf's eyes. *It must be this way. Niall is still my brother. You would destroy us both if you killed for my sake. And I am not strong enough, my love. Not strong enough to believe in you.*

Athena lost herself in the wolf and ran, with all her strength, until she knew nothing but the flex of muscle and the rush of wind through her fur. When she reached the ranch she traced a wide circle around the buildings and approached from the rear of the house, a shadow all but invisible to human eyes. At the door she Changed, slipped into the house, and dashed up the stairs to her room. There she hastily donned a calico skirt and shirtwaist, barely enough to cover her nakedness.

Voices echoed downstairs, but none of them was Niall's. She took the stairs two at a time and confronted a pair of startled troupers, men she recognized as Harry's star aerialists.

"Where is Mr. Munroe?" she demanded.

They exchanged glances. "Miss Athena?" one of them said. "He left with Caitlin, just after dawn."

She had no time to consider the implications of Caitlin's involvement. "Where did they go?"

"I heard it was to look for you in Denver," the other man said. "Harry and Ulysses left last night. They said you might be in trouble." He paused. "Can we help, Miss Athena?"

She shook her head and tried to clear her mind. Did Harry and Ulysses know that Niall had tried to kill Morgan? Was that why they had gone to Denver? Why had Niall taken Caitlin, when surely he must believe that Morgan was dead and he was returning to face his sister's anguish? Caitlin would hate him just as much for what he had done.

Without another word to the troupers, Athena ran back upstairs and threw open the wardrobe. On one of the shelves she found a pair of trousers and a flannel shirt. She pulled out a pair of old boots and quickly made a bundle of the clothing, cinching it with a braided leather cord. She carried the bundle outside, dropped it in the snow, stripped, and Changed.

Wolf's jaws closed around the cord. She could reach Denver much more quickly in wolf shape, but there was no telling when she might catch up with Niall. If she found him in the city, she would need the clothing.

She would need every tiny advantage she could get.

Human voices shouted, severing her thoughts. She had been seen, and no rancher would balk at shooting a wolf. She burst from a standstill into a dead run. Rifle shot cracked in her wake. Pellets of snow brushed her fur, and a second bullet exploded in the ground where she had been an instant before. Then she was beyond human reach, headed unerringly toward Denver.

It was when she had reached the foothills, just as the sun was sinking behind the Front Range, that she remembered the significance of this night, the detail she had so completely put from her mind. It was the night of the Winter Ball.

She barked a wolf's laugh around the leather between her teeth. The ball. The very pinnacle of her social life, the event of which she had been so inordinately proud. What had once seemed worth a year's painstaking effort had become just another self-indulgent folly, a consolation prize to a woman who had misplaced the true meaning of life.

Cecily would be at the ball, lording it over everyone. Nothing would stop her, not even Athena's escape and its possible consequences to her designs upon Niall. Niall would expect Athena to be there under Cecily's vigilant eye. But he would not find his sister. Not before she found him.

Tonight's Winter Ball would indeed be one to remember.

I am sorry, Mr. Munroe," the unfamiliar servant said with a diffident shake of his head, "but Miss Hockensmith has gone to the ball."

The Winter Ball. Dammit, he had entirely forgotten about that bit of foolishness. Cecily had mentioned that she'd changed the venue to the Windsor, but he'd forgotten that as well.

Nothing tonight was what it should be. There had been no groom lodged in the rooms over the stable to take his and Caitlin's weary mounts. Romero was gone. The house was noticeably devoid of servants. Niall stood in the hall of his own home, staring into the face of a man he did not know. Caitlin waited behind him, her gaze taking in the vastness of the high ceiling and the gilt and marble embellishments. She was no more lost than he.

"Who the devil are you?" he demanded, tossing the servant his gloves. "Where is Brinkley?"

"I regret to say that Mr. Brinkley has tendered his resignation," the man said with an air of false regret. "Miss Hockensmith felt it necessary to replace him and the other servants who have since departed."

Good God. Had the entire world fallen apart in the short time he had been gone? "The other servants?"

The man cleared his throat. "There have been a number of changes in the staff during the past several days, sir. You may wish to consult Miss Hockensmith for the details. Would you and the young lady care to rest in the parlor while I send for tea?"

"Miss Munroe has accompanied Miss Hockensmith to the ball?"

This time the butler was not so quick with an answer. "I . . . am not informed as to Miss Munroe's whereabouts, sir."

"What do you mean?" Niall seized the man's collar. "Where is my sister?"

"Sir . . . I . . . ah—" He choked and went very pale. "She has not been in residence since my arrival. Miss Hockensmith said that . . . that she had run mad, threatening to . . . to kill Miss Hockensmith if she attempted to restrain Miss Munroe. That is . . . all I know!"

Niall let him fall to the ground. Athena, run mad? Escaped? And Cecily had traipsed off to the ball as if all was well, knowing where Athena must have gone. The sudden resignation and hiring of servants was nothing compared to this.

"She went to warn Morgan," Caitlin said behind him. "She must have, knowing how much you hated him. Lord, if she made it to the mountains—"

"She could be anywhere. Lost . . ." *Or with* him. Niall stumbled toward the door.

"You can't go back to the mountains now," Caitlin said, grasping his arm. He tried to shake her off, but her grip was sure and fearless. "You're exhausted, and you would not know where to look. She will find Morgan if he hasn't found her first."

"If you are right, and he is alive." Niall stopped at the door, leaning his head against the paneled wood. "He may have her now."

"Then you have a chance to do right, Niall. Let them go. Let them live the life they were meant to have."

Niall ignored her, icy panic racing through his veins. "Cecily," he said, biting off the name. He snatched his coat from the stand where the new butler had hung it and threw it around his shoulders. He didn't bother to question the servant further, but strode down the hall and to the rear door facing the carriage house. Caitlin's footsteps drummed at his heels.

He harnessed one of the horses to the fastest buggy and swung into the seat. Caitlin climbed up beside him. With a grunt he lashed the chestnut out of the carriage house, down the lane and into the street.

In a matter of minutes he had reached Eighteenth and Larimer. The carriages of ballgoers made the streets almost as congested as they were during the business day, and as he neared the Windsor every available space was occupied by a conveyance. He drew the buggy as close to the Windsor as possible and tied the horse to a lamppost.

"You have no part in this," he told Caitlin. "Stay here."

She shook her head, jaw set. He jumped down from the seat and started for the Windsor at a furious pace, not looking behind to see if she followed.

Only two hours into the ball, Cecily reflected, and everything was utterly perfect.

She gracefully deflected a compliment from one of Denver's leading dowagers and waved her fan with an elegant tilt of her wrist. The Windsor ballroom was crowded from end to end with Denver's elite and visiting dignitaries, many of them people that bitch Athena would never have thought to invite. The orchestra played sparkling melodies to delight every ear, and the refreshments in the adjoining room had been created by some of the city's most skilled chefs. This was Cecily's triumph, and hers alone.

As long as Athena and her brother did not spoil it. Cecily glanced about the mirrored chamber for the hundredth time. It was sheer foolishness to think that the bitch would return after her escape four days ago. Doubtless she had either perished in the mountains or found her lover and run off with him—if she had miraculously managed to reach him before Niall.

Nevertheless, Cecily had circulated sly rumors about the reasons for Athena's sudden disappearance. When she had told a few choice gossips that Athena was able to walk—that she had doubtless been deceiving society for years—she had spiced the narrative with the hushed, embarrassed account of how the girl had run mad and attacked her like a wild beast, threatening her very life.

How ready were the bored matrons and misses of Denver to believe such a lurid tale, especially when Cecily encouraged speculation that Athena had manipulated them into making excessive contributions for pity's sake. Cecily showed them the substantial bruise on her arm where Athena had grabbed her. She expressed compassion for the young woman who had fallen prey to bad elements and her own weak nature. A little truth here, a bit of exaggeration there, and she had laid the groundwork to explain Athena's violent deterioration.

Cecily had alerted the police, of course, and told them that Miss Munroe had declared her intent to travel into the mountains alone. If they had found the girl, Cecily would be seen as having done her duty, and Niall could not fault her. Any accusations Athena might make could be explained as resulting from her lunacy; Cecily had every confidence of victory in a contest of wits. But the police had not found Athena, nor had anyone been able to contact her brother because of the bitter storm. It was a tragedy indeed.

But the ball must go on. Everyone agreed, most solemnly, that Cecily was holding up very well. She had done everything she could, but Munroe had expected too much in asking her to care for a madwoman. Poor, demented Athena had done so much to create the ball, even if she had turned her back on society as well as sanity. It would be the height of irresponsibility to cancel the affair and deprive the blameless unfortunates who would benefit from the money collected.

So Cecily had forged ahead, swallowing her unease. She well knew she had Niall to face, assuming he returned from his confrontation with Holt. Perhaps he would not. Cecily felt only a lingering regret at the prospect. If Athena was mad—and clearly she was—*he* might be unstable as well. She could no longer bring herself to believe that marriage to Niall Munroe brought advantages enough to outweigh the disadvantages—particularly when she had begun to make some very promising acquaintances among Denver's wealthy bachelors.

Cecily issued a brave smile for the benefit of her peers and declined a dance offer from one such gentleman. Best to appear a little reserved, a little sorrowful over the recent events than seem too quick to dismiss them. There would be ample time for celebration after the ball, when her new social position was firmly established and she had dealt with Niall. If he survived.

She was speaking to Mrs. Gottschalk, her back to the ballroom doors, when the murmur of many voices swelled to the buzzing of a disturbed hive of bees. The music lurched to a halt. Cecily paused in her solemn speech and turned around.

Niall Munroe stood in the doorway, mud-splattered and dressed as if he had arrived straight from the wilderness, which very likely he had. At his shoulder stood the red-haired creature Caitlin, as bedraggled as he.

Cecily shrank in on herself as if she could hide from the gaze that raked the crowd. Voices lifted in question, but no one approached Niall. He exuded violence like a rabid dog.

"Does he know?" someone whispered behind her.

"Why would he be here if he did not? Look at his face!"

"The poor man . . ."

"He must have known she was mad."

Oh, he knew; of that Cecily was certain. He had concealed Athena's lunacy behind a mask of propriety and dependence. And he also knew that she was missing. He had surely been to the house and spoken to the servants.

Cecily tried to breathe and felt her corset tighten about her chest. She should be well prepared for this moment. She knew what she ought to do. She would appear all the more heroic if she placed herself at Niall's disposal before he came in search of her.

But her feet would not carry her. Niall scanned each corner of the room, and at last his gaze fell upon her.

He moved like a man bent upon murder. Cecily braced for attack.

"You let her go," he snarled, oblivious of several hundred pairs of eyes. "Where is she?"

Cecily drew upon her dignity and clasped her hands in an attitude of deep concern. "Mr. Munroe. I understand why you are upset. I am sure this has been quite a shock. If only I had been able to reach you." She would not ask him to find a more private place to talk. She wanted the safety of witnesses.

"I trusted you to watch her!" he shouted. "You let her go . . . you always wanted her out of the way, didn't you?"

A woman exclaimed in frightened tones. "He is as mad as she!" another cried.

"Mr. Munroe," Mr. Osborn said, moving to Cecily's defense. "Please lower your voice. There are ladies present, and this is not the time or place to—"

Niall struck out and sent the man staggering back. Caitlin caught his arm and hung on as fiercely as a bulldog. A wave of motion rippled outward from the disturbance as ladies and gentlemen scurried away.

"It is not . . . it is not what you think," Cecily said. "She attacked me. She threatened me with serious harm. The servants took her part against me. I had no choice but to allow her to leave. Of course I contacted the police immediately, but . . . your sister is not well, Mr. Munroe. You must believe I would never have willingly let her go."

"She attacked you? Athena?" He laughed. "You're lying."

She flushed. "You are distraught. You know she is able to walk. Her strength is greater than it appears. She was determined to go after her lover—the murderer Morgan Holt."

A fresh swell of exclamations followed, but Niall's wild glance imposed silence once more. He loomed over Cecily. "He has not come here?"

"Here?" Cecily shuddered. "But I thought you—" She bit her lip. "I warned you about him. You said that you would deal with him yourself!"

He seized her upper arms and shook her. "If anything has happened to my sister—"

"But nothing has, Niall," a hoarse voice said from across the room. "Not in the way you mean."

Chapter 23

Cecily felt her knees begin to buckle. A figure draped in oversized trousers and shirt walked down the open path the crowd had made for Niall's entrance. Athena's approach was not nearly so violent, but every eye turned to her and the silence became even more profound.

Athena's face was white, her hair a rat's nest, her breathing ragged. But she stood before her brother as if she were the taller and more powerful, capable of felling him with a single blow.

"Athena!" Caitlin exclaimed.

"Athena," Niall stammered. "You are . . . Where have you been?"

His attempt to regain control of the situation failed miserably. Athena stared up at him, unblinking.

"Did you kill my mother?"

Niall's mouth fell open. She showed him no mercy. "I know you were responsible for her disappearance just after I was born. Did you kill her?"

Cecily had never seen Niall turn white as he did now. "Athena, what are you doing?"

"I am seeking the truth." She smiled, a look that sent a chill down Cecily's spine. "It's too late to worry about my reputation now, isn't it? I am sure that Cecily has told everyone what they didn't already know." The smile vanished. "Tell me."

"Athena . . . you don't understand." He looked about as if for support and found only one gaze that would meet his. Caitlin Hughes stepped up beside him. It was a measure of how far he had fallen that he seemed to take comfort in her presence.

"I did not kill her," he said in a firmer voice. "I drove her away. I had to. She was ruining our father's life, and she would have ruined yours. I tried to save you."

"To save me," she whispered, "or yourself? Are you that afraid of me?"

Niall's face darkened in fury. "Who told you about your mother?" he demanded. He swung on Caitlin. "Was it you?"

"No." Athena glanced at Caitlin with a remote gentleness in her eyes. "Morgan told me. You thought he was dead, didn't you? You believed you'd killed him. But you didn't succeed, Niall. He deceived you. And I found him."

The expression on Niall's face transformed from consternation to contempt in a handful of seconds. "You . . . you have been with him, haven't you? Turning against your own family, your own kind . . . Lying with him like any whore, just like your mother—"

A blur of motion was all Cecily saw before Niall crashed onto his back on the ballroom floor. The blur resolved into another man, barefoot and wearing only a calf-length greatcoat. He stood over his fallen victim with teeth bared and eyes ablaze.

Morgan Holt. Morgan Holt had come. Those terrible eyes turned from Niall, rested briefly on Athena, and fixed unerringly upon Cecily.

With a mindless shriek, Cecily turned and fled.

Athena watched her go, feeling nothing, just as she suffered no regret or embarrassment under the horrified and titillated stares of those she had once called friends. All the emotions that had driven her for the past hours—rage, confusion, terror—had deserted her; it was as if she

stood at the eye of a tornado, hearing it howl about her while she remained untouched.

It was a way of protecting herself from hurt, just as she had made a
fortress of her lameness and the chair that restricted her freedom.
From the chair she had watched the world go by, seeking to affect it
while remaining unaffected, a serene goddess of mercy and charity who
had forgotten what it was to be human.

She had run to Denver to demand the truth of Niall, and all the
while she had been running away from the truth of her heart. The truth
she was still afraid to feel. Because of her weakness Niall lay sprawled
on the polished floor, waiting for a mortal blow. As Morgan waited to
give it.

Morgan had followed her. She should have known he would. She
should have known he'd endanger himself to protect her from her
brother . . . and take his revenge.

He had looked at Athena but once since she had entered the
room—met her gaze like a stranger, as emotionless as she. The man she
had loved was gone, replaced by a cold-blooded killer. And only she
could stop him.

She, and Caitlin. The equestrienne knelt beside Niall at the same
instant Athena placed herself between Morgan and her brother.

"You cannot hurt him, Morgan," Athena said. "You know you
can't."

The stranger's merciless eyes hardly touched upon hers. "He will
destroy you, as he destroyed your mother."

"He did not kill my mother," she said. "He drove her away, but he
says he didn't kill her. I believe him."

Though she had not lifted her voice, Morgan flinched as if she had
struck him. The frightening, alien mask dropped away, replaced by
naked pain. Pain that cut through her own detachment and left her raw
and defenseless.

"You believe him," Morgan said. He looked down at Niall and took
a step back, his muscles loosening from their posture of threat. "You
still trust him."

"Yes, Athena. You must trust me." Niall got to his knees, his attention on Morgan. "I know the truth about this man. He is a convict and
a murderer." He raised his voice to reach the farthest corners of the
ballroom. "Morgan Holt killed his own father."

A collective gasp rose from the onlookers. Several women appeared on the verge of swooning, and no few of the men looked about for possible weapons. Athena ignored them all. Morgan's anguished eyes had become her world.

"It is true," he said, speaking only to her. "I killed my father. I served nine years in prison. And I would have murdered your brother to protect you." He held up his hands and turned them palm up, flexing his fingers into fists. "Maybe he speaks the truth. I am a killer at heart. You were right to leave me."

Like a dam bursting under the weight of a raging spring flood, her heart gave way. Everything she had been holding inside, every doubt, every unbearable image was dislodged by the deluge until she was scoured clean and bright and new.

"No," she said. "I was wrong. I said I would listen, and trust you, but I was deceiving myself." She glanced at Niall with profound sorrow. "I came after my brother because I couldn't face the one who mattered most. Niall was an enemy I could conquer. My feelings for you were not. I was afraid that Niall was right, and that I had loved a murderer. I would rather have lost you forever than find such a crippling flaw within myself."

Morgan shook his head. "The only flaw is in me."

Athena held out her hand. Morgan gazed at it, unmoving. She kept her hand in place, fingers extended, offering him the forgiveness he refused to permit himself.

"I will tell you what I believe," she said. "I believe that whatever crime you committed was done only because you had no other choice. I believe that you paid in full for your mistakes. I believe that there is great good in you, Morgan Holt, and someone must make you see it."

"You're the only one who can," Caitlin said, restraining Niall with a hand on his shoulder. She gave him an apologetic glance and lifted her voice to address the crowd. "Morgan has had two chances to kill Mr. Munroe, and he could easily have escaped. But it was Niall who left Morgan for dead in the mountains. Morgan chose to feign death rather than be forced to kill his enemy."

"As he was forced to kill his father."

Athena turned toward the cultured tenor voice, recognizing it at once. Very little had the power to shock her now, and all she felt was gratitude and heartfelt joy as Ulysses Marcus Aurelius Wakefield and Harry French walked into the ballroom.

A distant part of her mind acknowledged how out of place they

570 CALL OF THE WOLF

seemed in this glittering company—Harry in his loud waistcoat and red jacket, Ulysses a golden-haired mannequin of a Southern gentleman. But they were her family as these wealthy, distinguished people could never be. They were showmen, professional charlatans, and yet they were the most honest of all. She loved them only a little less than she loved Morgan. And they were here to save him.

Ulysses paused in the center of the room, standing as tall as his stature permitted. He did not wear the protective robes and anonymity of the Little Professor. He was entirely exposed to the fascinated distaste of those who should have been his peers, and Athena knew how difficult it must have been for the gentle man who had been cast out of his own elite world.

"Ladies and gentlemen," he said. "I see that Mr. French and I have arrived at a most propitious moment. We are members of French's Fantastic Family Circus, who have recently been in the employ of Miss Athena Munroe." He executed a bow in her direction. "I am Ulysses Marcus Aurelius Wakefield, and the gentleman beside me is Harold B. French. We have observed the events that have recently occurred involving Miss Munroe, Mr. Munroe, and Mr. Holt. It is now necessary to clarify statements that the latter two gentlemen have made with regard to Mr. Holt's more distant past."

Morgan took a sharp step toward Ulysses. "No."

Ulysses lowered his gaze. "I regret breaking a confidence, my dear friend, but it must be done."

Turning her back on Niall, Athena went to stand beside Morgan. She took his hand in hers. The tendons below his knuckles stood out like steel cords. She held him all the more tightly.

"It is true," Ulysses said, "that Morgan Holt committed patricide, a most heinous crime among civilized peoples. Mr. Holt was tried and convicted and spent many years in prison. If it had not been for a single witness in his favor, he would have been sentenced to death. He neither defended himself nor attempted to escape, though he had many opportunities to do so during his incarceration." He met Morgan's gaze again. "I made it my business to learn all I could of the circumstances of this affair. I know the truth behind the tragedy."

The ballroom might as well have been empty in its absolute silence. Heads topped by gleaming tiaras and meticulously pomaded hair turned from Ulysses to Morgan.

He stared at the floor and closed his eyes. His protest was so soft that Athena felt rather than heard it.

"Ladies and gentlemen," Ulysses said, "Morgan Holt's father left his

wife, son, and daughter in California to seek a fortune in mining when
Morgan was but a lad of thirteen. He promised to return but did not.
His family was compelled to fend for itself with no source of income,
until Morgan determined to go after his father and bring him home.

"He was fourteen when he left his mother and sister. I will not relate all the tribulations that he was forced to overcome in his journey, or
how his childhood was lost before he attained the age of fifteen years.
But when he reached Colorado Territory and found his father at last, he
had learned how to hate."

"Morgan," Athena murmured, resting her forehead on his shoulder. "Oh, my love."

"The claim his father had staked in the mountains was poor,"
Ulysses went on, "but Aaron Holt would not give it up. He refused to
return to his family, no matter how his son tried to persuade him. His
lust for wealth was greater than his love. And so he and his son quar-
reled bitterly, and Morgan departed with many harsh words and an
even greater despair.

"Many months later he returned and found his father again. But
Aaron Holt had changed. He had fallen prey to men who make their
living from cheating and theft, and they had left him—" Ulysses
paused. "I beg your pardon, ladies, but what I am about to relate is not
for delicate ears. You may wish to leave the room before I continue."

No one stirred. Morgan heard the faint shuffle of slippered feet,
the rush of breath from a hundred throats, the creaking of corsets as
women shifted for a better view of him. He heard the steady beat of
Athena's heart and felt her warmth along his side. But Ulysses's voice
had become a drone, a meaningless jumble of words that had no power
to describe what had happened on that terrible day in the Colorado
mountains.

It had been sunny, an unusually warm late spring afternoon. But
Morgan scarcely felt the sun and balmy breezes, nor noticed the riot of
wildflowers growing fat and lush on the hillsides and in the meadows.

All he could see was Aaron Holt—not the hearty, stubborn man he had
left in such anger, but a wasted, hollow-eyed invalid who was more of a
stranger to Morgan now than he had ever been. He lay against a boulder at
the heart of his claim, stinking in soiled clothes and lying in his own waste.

Morgan knew that he was dying.

"They tried to jump my claim," Aaron Holt said, his voice like a
rusty hinge. "The thieving bastards. I fought 'em. Didn't . . ." He
coughed, and the motion jarred his gangrenous leg.

It was a miracle that he could speak at all. Morgan could smell the poison, the swift rotting of flesh. The smell of death—lingering, painful death.

"They were scared enough not to come back," Aaron whispered. "But . . . they left me with a memento." He gestured at his seeping left leg, deep bronze and purple with infection, no longer recognizable as living tissue. The original wound had been lost in the swelling.

Aaron was skeletal from lack of food, half-delirious with fever. The first thing Morgan had done was bring him water and try to make him eat the jerky and day-old bread he'd brought, but his father had pushed it aside untouched.

"I'll find a doctor," Morgan said, half-afraid that Aaron Holt would not be alive when he returned. But his father laughed, a sound more dreadful than weeping, until tears ran down his cheeks.

"I'm dying," he said. "Can't eat, can't sleep. My leg is rotting. No doctor can save me now." He shook his head at Morgan's mute denial. "I wouldn't go to town . . . when there was some chance for me. Now all I can do is—" He stopped, and he looked at Morgan with such desperation that Morgan's eyes filled with tears. "I know I haven't . . . been much of a father to you, boy. I know you hate me. I reckon you don't owe me any favors. But now I've got to ask you one." He drew in a deep breath and let it out again with a rattling wheeze. "I hurt, boy. Can't take it no more. Don't have the strength to end it myself. You got to do it for me."

Morgan heard the words, but it took him several minutes to understand. *End it.* His father wanted him to end his misery, and there was only one way to do that.

"I've . . . got a gun, hidden under those rocks," Aaron said. "All it takes . . . is one bullet, boy."

"No." Morgan stepped back, stumbled on a stone, caught his balance again. "I won't do it."

"You got to. You got to, boy. I'll be dying another week, and I can't . . ." He coughed again and sank back against the boulder. "I'm beggin' you. Please—"

After that Aaron Holt was quiet for a time, exhausted by his efforts to talk. Morgan tried to make him drink, but his father refused every attempt to help. That evening, Morgan made a fire and covered his father with all the blankets he could find. During the long night, Aaron dreamed. He wept and shouted and screamed in agony, and Morgan could smell the rot spread, inch by inch, eating Aaron's body from within.

By dawn, Aaron could barely move. It was as if he had used up all the life left within him . . . all but the pain. Every breath he took was a struggle. He screamed when Morgan touched his leg to adjust it under the blankets.

There was no hope for Aaron Holt. Morgan knew it. He had become familiar with death in the past several years of searching. He had seen it take many forms, but none so horrible as this.

"You . . . want revenge," his father panted, opening one red-rimmed eye. "You want to see me die slow, don't you?"

Morgan hung his head, the emotion so choked up inside him that he thought he would strangle on it. "I don't hate you, Pa."

"Then help me!" Aaron moaned. "Have mercy. Mercy."

The sun rose higher, promising another warm day. It traced all the tendons and veins standing out in Aaron Holt's neck and hands. Nothing in its caress could comfort Morgan's father, now or ever.

Morgan got up. He walked to the pile of rocks where Aaron had concealed his revolver, and shoved the stones aside. The gun felt heavy and awkward in his hand. He had never carried one; he didn't need it, being what he was.

But Aaron Holt was human.

"Bless you, boy," he whispered. "God . . . bless you."

With the gun loose at his side, Morgan stood over his father and stared up the hillside where rows of evergreens marched upward to the sky. "Is there anything you want me to tell Mother and Cassidy?"

His father only closed his eyes. "The head," he croaked. "That's the fastest way. I won't . . . feel it. No more pain. Blessed . . . peace."

Morgan hated him then, more than he had ever done. He lifted the gun and thought of all the times he had dreamed of facing Aaron Holt and making him wish he were dead.

Aaron Holt wished he was dead. That was all. He had nothing to give, no amends to make, no regrets. Only one last demand from the son he had abandoned.

"Please," he whispered. "Damn you. Damn you."

The sun wheeled madly overhead. Morgan's hand began to tremble. He made a fist. The trembling stopped.

"Now. Do it . . . *now*."

Morgan raised the revolver and took aim with exquisite care.

"Thank . . . God," Aaron whispered.

Morgan fired once. Between one moment and the next, Aaron Holt's pain was over. The echo rang across the hills, and crows rose up from a nearby pine with raucous cries.

An old miner and his mule emerged from the underbrush. Morgan was distantly aware of the man's frightened face and the way he glanced from Morgan to the body and back again.

"You kilt him," the old man said.

"He was my father," Morgan said. There were no tears. No feeling at all.

The old miner gripped his mule's halter as if for dear life. "We was comin' to check up on 'im. Hadn't heard in a week. Now he's dead." He narrowed his eyes. "You were his son?"

Two other men came up behind the miner, both in rough garb and weathered with years in the mountains. "Hank! You all right?" one of them said. He stared at Morgan. "We heard the shot. What the hell?"

"Aaron's dead," Hank said. "His own son shot him."

The newcomers started for Morgan and stopped at the sight of the gun. Morgan let it fall from his fingers. One of the men circled him cautiously and darted in to snatch the gun.

"He's dead, all right," the second man said grimly, bending over the body. "You saw him do it, Hank?"

"Well, I . . ." The old man chewed the frayed ends of his moustache. "I heard them quarrel afore, back in March during the thaw. Didn't know the boy was Aaron's son. But . . ."

"We got to take you to town, boy," the man with the gun said, aiming it at Morgan's chest.

"I did hear Aaron tell him to do it," the old miner stammered. "He looks in a bad way. Maybe it was a mercy."

"That's for the law to decide." The first man nodded to the second. "Get some rope, Bill. Can't take no chances with a man who'd murder his own pa."

Hank opened his mouth as if to speak, but quickly closed it again. Morgan waited quietly while Bill tied his hands behind his back. He welcomed the discomfort when the men dragged him back to their claim a mile away and talked of how they would get him to town and hand him over to the law. He could have escaped them easily, but he did not.

He didn't defend himself when he went to trial. Old Hank spoke of what he had heard, how Aaron Holt seemed to beg to be killed, and the local doctor testified that Aaron had been in the grip of fatal gangrene poisoning and must have been suffering unbearable pain.

In the end, that was what had spared Morgan death. What they gave him was worse. They locked him up in a place that would have driven him mad at any other time. They caged him for nine years, and when they judged his silence as rebellion they beat him. He let them. He always healed. After a while they left him alone. Alone with his own thoughts and memories.

That was the true punishment, the one he could never escape. Only the wolf gave him peace. And then that, too, was taken away.

"Why didn't you tell me?"

Morgan climbed out of the pit of memory, reaching toward the light of the voice.

Athena's voice. She held him, and her hazel eyes glittered with tears.

"I would have understood," she whispered. "It wouldn't have changed anything between us."

Ulysses's voice rang in dramatic conclusion. "And so Morgan Holt paid for his crime. A crime of mercy, a reluctant easing of inconceivable torment. He has served his sentence. He has been punished enough, and must be punished no more."

People in the crowd began to murmur, a tide of sound suddenly released by the end of Ulysses's tale. Morgan found his mind remarkably clear. He eased his arm from Athena's grip and turned slowly to Niall, who had scrambled to his feet, Caitlin solemn and pale at his side. Niall's gaze slid away from his.

"I offer a bargain," Morgan said. "Let Athena go. She is not what you are. Give her what is hers, and I will leave and not return."

"No, Morgan," Athena said. "It's not your bargain to make." She swung on her brother, head lifted, and compelled him to meet her eyes.

"I loved you, Niall," she said. "I trusted you. I refused to believe ill of you, even when I should have seen the truth. You cared for me all these years. I will never forget that. But now I understand what made you so careful with me. It was guilt—not only about the accident, but because of my mother." She did not lower her voice, though she must have known how her words would be taken by the avid audience. "You robbed me of her and lied to me all my life. You were afraid that I would become just like her if I had my freedom." She gave a heartrending smile. "You were glad when I was hurt, weren't you? I was safe in my chair, with my domestic and charitable work. I let you convince me that it was all I could aspire to. Your mistake was trying to take even that away. And my great good fortune—" She reached for Morgan's hand. "My great joy is that someone came along to teach me about courage and daring to hope. Someone who has suffered more than you or I can imagine."

"Athena," Niall said, swallowing heavily. "You must understand—"

"But I do, Niall. And I pity you." She looked at Caitlin. "If anyone can help him, you can."

Caitlin bent her head. "Thank you."

Niall looked at Caitlin as if she had grown horns and a tail. "You," he whispered. He stared at Morgan and Athena in turn. It was no longer merely fear in his eyes, but something more complex made up of equal parts bewilderment and desperation. Morgan recognized the kind of madness that came to a man when everything he had believed, every foundation of his world, disintegrated beneath his feet.

As Cecily had done before him, he turned hard on his heel and fled the room at a run. Caitlin hesitated, anguish in her eyes, and ran after him. A hum of excited comment rose and fell about the ballroom.

Athena clenched her fists at her sides and did not follow. Morgan wanted to hold her, comfort her with all the loving words he had never been able to say. He remained still.

Ulysses and Harry came to join them. Ulysses nodded to Morgan, eloquent in his silence. Harry's eyes were moist.

"My boy," he said. He reached out as if to pat Morgan's shoulder and tucked his hand into his waistcoat instead. "My dear boy." He cleared his throat. "I know . . . I know that your father loved you, and you loved him in spite of everything. What lies between a parent and child is not easily torn asunder."

"He's right," Athena said. She was not afraid to touch him, no matter how little he responded. "You have lived with this for too many years. Let it go. Walk away from it, just as I learned to walk away from my chair and everything that held me prisoner." She placed her hand on his chest, fingers spread, as if she could reach inside his ribs and replace what was missing. "Forgive your father, Morgan. Forgive yourself."

"Listen to her." Harry blinked, and a tear leaked from the corner of his eye. "Morgan . . . I am as proud of you as if you were my own son. That is why I must insist that you do not throw away the one thing that can give you peace." He took Morgan's hand and then Athena's. Gently he placed her fingers in his. "Love one another. That is all that matters."

Morgan could not have spoken if he wished. The obstruction in his throat had grown and grown to fill all the hollow places in his body, pressing on his eyelids and the casing of ice around his heart.

He looked into Athena's eyes. They were clear, sane, bright with love. For him.

"I cannot stay here, among men," he said, so that only she could hear.

"I know."

"I won't let you give up all this for me."

"All this?" She glanced around the room, her gaze sweeping over the sea of faces as if they were so many antique paintings on a wall. "Do you think I want this now? They would not have me again even if I did. And I wouldn't have them." She cupped his hand between hers. "I decided even before I returned to Denver that my old life was over. I should have known before, but a part of me was still bound to that chair. The one you made me recognize for what it was. *You*, Morgan."

"You knew I had killed."

"And I doubted, for a while. But love—" She glanced at Harry with a warm smile. "Love is stronger than doubt."

Still he refused to let himself believe. "The people you help . . . you cannot abandon them."

"For all the mistakes he made, my brother was right in one way," she said. "He accused me of trying to do everything myself, as if I could save all of Denver single-handedly." She dropped her gaze. "I was arrogant. I wanted to make myself indispensable—to Niall, to society, to the needy, because I had nothing else then." Her eyes found his. "There are many good people in my employ who can do what I did. All they need is money. After what has happened, I think I can convince Niall to release my fortune so that I can give the charities whatever they require to go on without me. And—" She turned his hand over in hers and kissed his palm. "There are people who need help everywhere. It doesn't matter where we go or what we do. I choose a life with you, Morgan Holt. I love you."

Morgan's chest rose in a great, heaving breath. The frigid sheath behind his ribs cracked in one painful, miraculous spasm. Melting droplets rushed up his throat and into his eyes. He heard the hoarse sound of sobbing and realized the tears were his own.

"Athena," he said. He took her face between his hands. "My love." He kissed her, tasting salt on his lips and hers, daring the entire world to judge. All the anger, the self-contempt, the grief that had consumed him flowed out with that kiss, passed into Athena and came back to him cleansed and purified.

"I love you," he said. "Will you have me, Athena?"

"Yes. Oh, yes." She kissed him boldly, passionately, spitting in the collective eye of shocked society matrons. "But only if it is forever."

Morgan responded as ardently as Athena could have wished. She rejoiced in his tears, for she knew they came as a release—release from the prison in which he had bound himself since his father's death. She felt no shame for her own silent weeping. Only three people in this grand ballroom mattered to her now.

"Athena," Morgan murmured into her hair. "Will you dance with me?"

She drew back in amazement. "You know how to dance?"

"Ulysses showed me once. I have never practiced."

"And I," she said, "have almost forgotten how."

With solemn deliberation, Morgan placed one hand on her waist and took her other in his. There was no music. Athena didn't need it. It sang out in her heart, a melody too perfect to be rendered by human hands.

Morgan took an awkward step, and then another. It was the first time Athena had ever seen him less than graceful. She loved him all the more for his imperfection, and the courage he showed in a place so alien to his nature. She followed him, gazing into his eyes, as he grew more sure and his steps took on a smooth, three-quarter rhythm.

Then they were flying about the ballroom and Athena was laughing, glorying in the dance and the man who held her. Morgan smiled. He waltzed her with wild abandon to the ballroom doors and carried her with him down the stairs. The same flabbergasted hotel staff and patrons who had seen them enter singly watched them leave together, hand in hand.

They dashed into the street, past the waiting carriages and out of the business district to the very edge of town. Morgan shed his clothing, eyes alight with challenge. Athena never hesitated. She flung her clothes aside and took Morgan's hand. He bent back his head and howled loudly enough to wake the dead. Naked man dissolved into great black wolf.

In seconds Athena was beside him. He licked her muzzle tenderly, and she could hear the words he did not speak, the words that had set them both free.

I love you.

• • •

Ulysses gazed at the open doors, vaguely surprised at the tightness in his chest. It was not his way to become sentimental, particularly when matters had resolved themselves so fortuitously.

Harry's broad hand came to rest on his shoulder. He didn't speak; no words were adequate to the occasion. Unlike Ulysses, Harry felt no compunction about his tears. He sniffled, dug about in his pocket for a handkerchief, and blew his nose.

The din in the ballroom had reached a high pitch, men and women competing with each other to exclaim most volubly upon the appalling events that had just taken place. Ulysses glanced up at Harry. Harry nodded, and a smile spread across his round, florid face.

Together they turned to face their audience. Harry raised his hands dramatically. The roar of voices faded to a murmur, and them into silence. Harry bowed and came up with a broad grin that lifted his moustache nearly to his eyebrows.

"Ladies and gentlemen," he said. "The performance is finished. Good night."

Epilogue

Denver looked very small from the top of the hill, and very far away.

Athena adjusted her knapsack and leaned against Morgan. He would have no regrets about leaving the city far behind. What surprised her most was that she had so few.

The only matters she had left undone since the ball had found their own sort of resolution. Niall had fled Denver that very night, and so had Caitlin. When Athena had returned to Fourteenth Street the following evening, she had found a message from the family banker informing her that she had been given full control of her inheritance, as well as a substantial portion of the Munroe fortune.

Niall, wherever he had gone, had made that one last act of atonement. The money was more than enough to keep Athena's charities going indefinitely, under the care of trusted employees. As she had told Morgan, her direct supervision was hardly necessary. And whatever the Denver society ladies thought of her now, they would not entirely stop their own contributions. Athena had them too well trained.

Cecily Hockensmith had certainly believed she had all of Denver at her feet. Athena could not guess what she was thinking now. Since the ball, she had remained locked up in her house and had issued no invitations or ventured out to a single luncheon. Once it might have mattered to Athena whether or not the harpy received her just punishment and became persona non grata among the very people she wished to impress. Now her fate was unimportant. No matter how she schemed and simpered, she would never be happy.

And as for French's Fantastic Family Circus . . .

"Where do you suppose Harry will take the troupers after the winter is over?" she asked Morgan.

He reached for her hand and squeezed it gently. "I don't know. He will need to find replacements for Caitlin and Ulysses—and Tamar." His lips wrinkled on that last name. Tamar and her serpents had been gone when Harry and Ulysses returned to Long Park, and no one had bothered with inquiries as to her whereabouts.

Only Ulysses, Harry had told her, seemed troubled. A few days later he had announced his intent to return to the Wakefield mansion in Tennessee, there to face his family for the first time in many years.

"It took great courage for Ulysses to stand before Denver society as he did," Athena said. "I think that was what made him decide to go back home."

"He has always hurt because of their treatment of him," Morgan said. "It will not be easy."

"But it is worth it." She laced her fingers through his. "It's worth it to know what you are truly meant to be, without fear. And yet—" She sighed. "I worry about Caitlin. If she went after Niall, she cannot expect happiness. He will have to change a great deal before he can accept love."

"As I did?" Morgan gave her a twisted smile. "I didn't think I needed anyone. You proved me wrong." He kissed her fingers. "Do not be concerned for Caitlin. She can take care of herself. You didn't think she was an ordinary woman?"

She peered up at him. "Are you saying . . . She is not . . . not—"

"No, not like us. She was traveling this country alone before you and I were born."

Athena was well past the point of amazement at such revelations. "I see. And yet she chose Niall."

They were silent for a while, watching light and shadow roll across the prairie beyond the city's edge. Snow settled lightly on Athena's hair. A new, increasingly familiar restlessness came over her, and she knew that the time of farewells was over. She tugged at Morgan's hand.

He held back, scanning the horizon once more. "Are you sure, Athena?"

She knew what he asked. Quickly she stepped up behind him and wrapped her arms around his waist. "I'm sure, Morgan. As sure as I am standing here with the man I love."

He twisted around and looked into her eyes. "Then let's go," he said. "The whole world is waiting."

Susan Krinard graduated from the California College of Arts and Crafts with a BFA and worked as an artist and freelance illustrator before turning to writing. An admirer of both romance and fantasy, Susan enjoys combining these elements in her books. Her first novel, *Prince of Wolves*, garnered praise and broke new ground in the genre of paranormal romance. She has won the *Romantic Times* Award for Best Contemporary Fantasy and Best Historical Fantasy, the PRISM Award for Best Dark Paranormal Fantasy, and has been a finalist for the prestigious RITA Award.

Susan loves to hear from her readers. Write to her at:

Susan Krinard
P.O. Box 51924
Albuquerque, NM 87181
(For a reply, please send a self-addressed stamped envelope.)

Or e-mail her at: sue@susankrinard.com

Her website, www.susankrinard.com, contains information on all her books and a link to receive her monthly and quarterly newsletters.